Ian Jacob Rose

First Ship: 5/
USS Gridley (DD

2017
I
017

First Home Base 5/18
Everett Washington

SWO.....
Grad: April 6 2018
Class 09-18D

A SEA STORY

BOOK ONE

All characters appearing in this work are fictitious. Any resemblance to real persons, living or dead, is purely coincidental.

N.W.S., 1977 – L.F.
A Sea Story / Book One
ISBN 978-0-9853554-1-8
A Sea Story.
2013
PUBLISHED IN THE U.S.A.

TO THE MEN AND WOMEN OF THE NAVY

BOOK 1

Indoctrination. Code of Conduct training shall be initiated without delay upon entry of members into the Navy and shall continue throughout their military careers, providing periodicand progressive training appropriate to risk of capture or exploitation.

Wartime application. Code of Conduct training for wartime will be conducted as outlined in enclosure (2) to enclosure (1). The articles of the Code of Conduct addressed there examine situations and decision areas likely to be encountered by all prisoners of war (POWs). The degree of knowledge required by Navy personnel is dictated by the member's susceptibility to capture, sensitive information possessed by the captive and captor's assessment of the captive's usefulness and value.

Peacetime application. Code of conduct training for peacetime will be conducted as outlined in enclosure (3) to enclosure (1). The term peacetime means that armed conflict does not exist or where armed conflict does exist, the United States is not involved directly. Personnel captured or detained by hostile foreign governments or terrorists are usually exploited for purposes designed to assist the captors, ransoms for captive, false confessions or information and propaganda efforts are examples of captor's methods designed to make either the captives or their governments appear weak or discredited. Personnel detained or held captive can be assured that the U.S. Government will make every good faith effort to obtain their earliest release. The degree of knowledge required by Navy personnel in peacetime depends upon their risk of detention or capture by a hostile government or terrorists.

INTRODUCTION

The Yellow Cab drops me off at the fore of the cement walkway. White trellises join columns along the upper and lower verandas of a two-story red brick building. Twin lanterns guard the short rise of blue stairs up to a wood-paneled entranceway.

Through these doors walks the future of the Navy.

My orders say only to report to Building 626 not later than 11 o'clock on the 21st of August 1999. A man in basic camouflage stands in the shade of a tree near the corner of the lot. I cut across the grass in his direction.

"Good morning, Sir."

"Round-the-side with the others."

"Right away."

"Now."

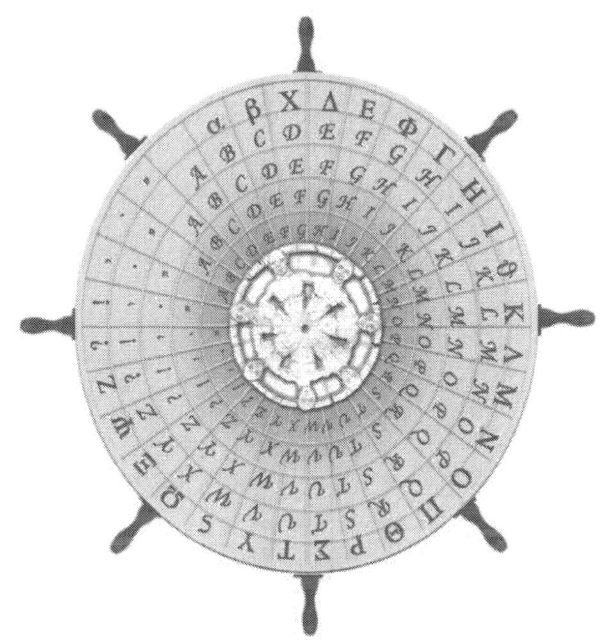

CHAPTER I

WEEK 1

"Line it up. Repeat after me. Say it loud. *Yes, Sir.*"

"Yes, Sir!"

"*No, Sir.*"

"No, Sir!"

"*Aye aye, Sir.*"

"Aye aye, Sir!"

"*No excuse, Sir.*"

"No excuse, Sir!"

"*This Indoctrination Candidate does not know but will find out, Sir.*"

"This Indoctrination Candidate does not know but will find out, Sir!"
"Altogether now and much louder. *Yes, Sir.*"
"Yes, Sir!!"
"*No, Sir.*"
"No, Sir!!"
"*Aye aye, Sir.*"
"Aye aye, Sir!!"
"*No excuse, Sir.*"
"No excuse, Sir!!"
"*This Indoctrination Candidate does not know but will find out, Sir.*"
"This Indoctrination Candidate does not know but will find out, Sir!!"
"You must get louder."
"He said *louder*!"
"On your own. Begin."
"Yes, Sir!!"
"No, Sir!!"
"Aye aye, Sir!!"
"No excuse, Sir!!"
"This Indoctrination Candidate does not know but will find out, Sir!!"
"Yes, Sir!!"
"No, Sir!!"
"Aye aye, Sir!!"
"No excuse, Sir!!"
"This Indoctrination Candidate does not know but will find out, Sir!!"
"Yes, Sir!!"
"No, Sir!!"
"Aye aye, Sir!!"
"No excuse, Sir!!"
"This Indoctrination Candidate does not know but will find out, Sir!!"
"Yes, Sir!!"
"No, Sir!!"
"Aye aye, Sir!!"
"No excuse, Sir!!"
"This Indoctrination Candidate does not know but will find out, Sir!!"
"Louder."
"He said *louder*!"
"Yes, Sir!!"
"No, Sir!!"
"Aye aye, Sir!!"
"No excuse, Sir!!"
"This Indoctrination Candidate does not know but will find out, Sir!!"

"Yes, Sir!!"

"No, Sir!!"

"Aye aye, Sir!!"

"No excuse, Sir!!"

"This Indoctrination Candidate does not know but will find out, Sir!!"

"Yes, Sir!!"

"No, Sir!!"

"Aye aye, Sir!!"

"No excuse, Sir!!"

"This Indoctrination Candidate does not know but will find out, Sir!!"

"Yes, Sir!!"

"No, Sir!!"

"Aye aye, Sir!!"

"No excuse, Sir!!"

"This Indoctrination Candidate does not know but will find out, Sir!!"

"Yes, Sir!!"

"No, Sir!!"

"Aye aye, Sir!!"

"No excuse, Sir!!"

"This Indoctrination Candidate does not know but will find out, Sir!!"

"Yes, Sir!!"

"No, Sir!!"

"Aye aye, Sir!!"

"No excuse, Sir!!"

"This Indoctrination Candidate does not know but will find out, Sir!!"

"Yes, Sir!!"

"No, Sir!!"

"Aye aye, Sir!!"

"No excuse, Sir!!"

"This Indoctrination Candidate does not know but will find out, Sir!!"

"Very well. As you were. These are your five basic responses here at Officer Candidate School. In the rare instance you feel compelled to say anything else, anything at all, do so with a Sir-exclamation-point attached to the end of it."

"That's a response!"

"Yes, Sir!!"

"Improper response!"

"Improper response, Indoctrination Candidates. *Yes, Sir* responds to a question. *Aye aye, Sir* responds to an order. Mine was an order. Try it again."

"That's a response!"

"Aye aye, Sir!!"

"Good. You will respond always at the position of attention."

"That's a response!"

"Aye aye, Sir!!"

"Holding a thousand yard stare at all times."

"That's a response!"

"Aye aye, Sir!!"

"And always, yes always, in the ballistic."

"Aye aye, Sir!!"

"Louder!"

"Aye aye, Sir!!"

"Louder!"

"Aye aye, Sir!!"

"In the ballistic!"

"Aye aye, Sir!!"

"We are your Candidate Officers. You will address Candidate Officers at all times as *Sir* and *Gentlemen* or, in the appropriate case, *Ma'am* and *Ladies*."

"That's a response!"

"Aye aye, Sir!!"

"Louder!"

"Aye aye, Sir!!"

"Rank applies. The greater the numbers of bars on the collar insignia, the higher the rank of the Candidate Officer. One bar is a Candidate Ensign. Two bars is a Candidate Lieutenant Junior Grade. Three bars is a Candidate Lieutenant. Four bars is a Candidate Lieutenant Commander. Five bars is a Candidate Commander. Six bars is a Candidate Captain. You will respect rank with a call to attention followed by the greeting of the day each time a senior-ranking Candidate Officer assumes command of the deck."

"That's a response!"

"Aye aye, Sir!!"

"Louder!"

"Aye aye, Sir!!"

"Louder!"

"Aye aye, Sir!!"

"You are Indoctrination Candidates. Your time here, no matter how brief, is a great many things. What it is not is an all-expenses-paid, fun-packed, coking-and-joking cruise ride courtesy of the United States Navy. Is that clear?

"That's a response!"

"Yes, Sir!!"

"That said, rest assured that your safety, as well as the safety of your peers, is our number-one priority. Most accidents are preventable. Accidents result from actions performed incorrectly, either knowingly or unknowingly, by people who fail to exercise the sufficient foresight, lack the requisite training, knowledge, or

motivation, or who fail to recognize and report hazards. Safety starts with you. You will avoid accidents by complying with approved procedures, warnings, cautions, and safety regulations."

"That's a response!"

"Aye aye, Sir!!"

"Should you find yourself, or observe another candidate, in any form of physical or mental jeopardy due to extreme stress, exhaustion or an otherwise abnormal situation, you will call out *Training Time Out* in the ballistic, or *T.T.O.*"

"That's a response!"

"Aye aye, Sir!!"

"Candidate Officer Jefferies."

"Yes, Indoctrination Commander?"

"Ever called a T.T.O.?"

"Negative."

"Ears."

"That's a response!"

"Aye aye, Sir!!"

"Improper response! Improper response!"

"Improper response, Indoctrination Candidates. *Open, Sir* is the appropriate response to the call for *ears*. Ears!"

"Open, Sir!!"

"Louder!"

"Open, Sir!!"

"Do not mistake a T.T.O. for a stress card or a physical training pass. Think *immediate medical attention.*"

"That's a response!"

"Aye aye, Sir!!"

"If you would rather quit, depart Pensacola at any time, you may in the alternative choose to *D.O.R.* Candidate Officer Jefferies, what's the navspeak for D.O.R.?"

"Dead-on-request."

"Dead-on-request. A student in a voluntary, high-risk training course who desires to quit needs only make such intentions clear. Statements such as *D.O.R.* or even *I quit* will do just fine. Such students will be immediately and expeditiously removed from the training area. Have a nice day. A written summary of action taken will be entered in the student's service record and Command's permanent records. The appropriate division will then take appropriate administrative action. You are here of your own free will. Do any among you now present wish to D.O.R.?"

"No, Sir!!"

"How do you know? How do you know?"

"How do you know, Indoctrination Candidates? The appropriate response was no response at all. Do any among you now present wish to D.O.R.? Better. You will find military life fundamentally different from your life as a civilian. The military has its own laws, rules, customs, and traditions, including numerous restrictions on personal behavior that would not be acceptable in civilian society. That life is behind you. You now represent the military establishment. This special status brings with it the responsibility to uphold and maintain the dignity and high standards of the U.S. Navy at all times and in all places. As such, you will uphold the highest standards of morale, good order and discipline, and cohesion during your time here at O.C.S."

"That's a response!"

"Aye aye, Sir!!"

"You will abide by all military laws, rules, customs, and traditions."

"Aye aye, Sir!!"

"Should you engage in unacceptable conduct, fail to abide by military laws and regulations, this may be grounds for involuntary separation before the end of your term of service. Is that perfectly clear?"

"Yes, Sir!!"

"This includes conduct of any nature that would bring discredit on the Navy in the view of the civilian community. Patterns of disciplinary infractions, causing dissent or disruption to unit readiness, discreditable involvement with civil or military authorities will not be tolerated. You will not be asked whether you are a heterosexual, or a homosexual, or a bisexual. However, you should be aware that homosexual acts, statements that demonstrate a propensity or intent to engage in homosexual acts, and homosexual marriages or attempted marriages are grounds for discharge from the Armed Forces. Is that clear?"

"Yes, Sir!!"

"Louder!"

"Yes, Sir!!"

"Let me be equally clear. The Navy will not tolerate harassment or violence against any Service Member, for any reason."

"That's a response!"

"Aye aye, Sir!!"

"For any reason."

"Aye aye, Sir!!"

"Louder!"

"Aye aye, Sir!!"

"Finally, here is some gouge for the descent. Everything you do here, you do so for a reason. Pay attention. Keep your head on a swivel. You'll be just fine."

"That's a response!"

"Aye aye, Sir!!"

"And never give up. Especially when you meet the D.I."

"That's an *aye aye, Sir*!"

"Aye aye, Sir!!"

"Ears!"

"Open, Sir!!"

"Indoctrination Candidates! Upon receiving the command of execution *move*! You will! Proceed to your starboard side, line up in single file in front of the outside hatch and stand-by for further orders! Is that clear?"

"Yes, Sir!!"

"Is that clear?"

"Yes, Sir!!"

"Ready! Move!"

"Aye aye, Sir!!"

••

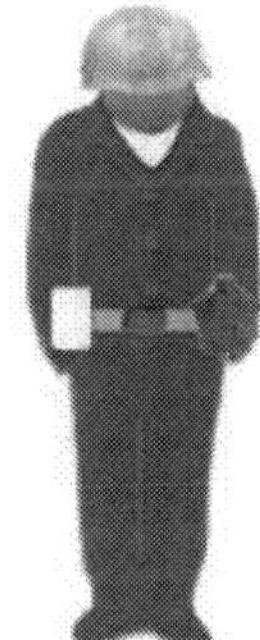

Indoctrination Candidate

Indoctrination Candidates will commence a regiment of daily physical training during the first week of indoctrination and must be able to perform aerobic activity, muscular strength exercises and endurance exercises. Aerobic activity includes running approximately three miles three or four times per week, primarily on track or road surfaces.

••

Two Candidate Officers sit behind a metal desk. Others circle in the peripheral. An old phone booth stands off to the side. Calls rain down from the second floor of the stairwell.

"Welcome, Poopies! Oh Poopies!"

"Poopies! Poopies! Poopies!"

"Can we keep them, Ma? Can we keep them, please?"

"We've been waiting for you, Poopies! You have no idea the time we've been waiting! We've been waiting such a long, long time!"

"Poopies! Poopies! Oh Poopies!"

"Give them up here, Ma! Give them up here!"

"Which one you think is the wetter?"

"That one there."

"I see him. Affirmative. Written all over him."

"What about that one?"

"Close call. Aren't they all?"

"Hey Poopie! You there! Don't be scared! Why you scared?"

"Don't wet those civvies, Poopie! Not them civvies! Not yet!"

"Least not until we get you hydrated!"

"Stand-by, Poopies! Stand-by!"

"We want them Poopies, Ma! We need them Poopies! Give us them Poopies! Up here, Ma! Give them up here! Give them up here!"

"Be cool, Johnny Cash! Keep it together! We just want a quick chat!"

"Yeah, Johnny! Start freaking out now, you won't last the a.m.!"

"Just who do you think you're eyeballing, Poopie? Yeah, that's right! I saw you, Gorgeous!"

"We see you, Johnny Cash! Oh, yeah! We see you too Poopie! We see you too!"

"Nasty freaking Poopie!"

"Eyeballing us with those pretty eyeballs! You won't look so pretty without that pretty suit! You won't look so pretty without all that pretty hair!"

"Stand-by, Johnny Cash! We don't like your attitude!"

"Poopie there must be hard of hearing! Eyeballs near about popping out of his head! Like he got no lids!"

"Looks like a pet project to me!"

"We're gonna have some fun, Poopie! You hear that? We're gonna have some kind of fun! Isn't that right, Poopie?"

"I don't believe it. You smell that, Gentlemen?"

"Yes, Sir."

"Nasty scared civilian."

"Nasty scared civilian."

"Hey Poopie! Do you know what time it is?"

"You guessed it, Poopie! It's no turning back time!"

"Hey! Wanna know why we call you Poopies? Zero-three guesses?"

"But the first two don't count!"

"How scared are you, Poopie? How scared?"

"Not scared?"

"Not yet."

"Stand-by, Poopie! You stand by! You'll get there! Wait until you get up here! Don't you worry your pretty little head about it!"

"We're not coking-and-joking, Poopie! Not one bit! You hear me? Not one bit!"

"Ask yourself if this was really such a good idea? If you really want to be here?"

"It's okay. You didn't know. Recruiters are all puppies and rainbows, lollipops and bunny slippers. Funny thing about quotas. One minute you're walking in the door, next thing you know it's *serve and protect.*"

"No big deal, Poopie! People make mistakes!"

"Poopie phone home! Poopie phone home! Poopie phone home!"

"This doesn't have to be you, Poopie."

"Turn back now, Poopie."

"Mom and Dad will understand. Mom will be thrilled. Dad might not brag about it at poker night, but trust me, he'll be happy too. Take a minute."

"Think about it, Poopie. Poopie phone home."

"Next four! Over here."

"That's a response! *Aye aye, Sir.*"

"Aye aye, Sir!!"

"Louder!"

"Aye aye, Sir!!"

"Behind the line."

"Line it up! That's a response!"

"Aye aye, Sir!!"

"Position of attention. Heels touching. Chest out. Shoulders square. Fingers curled. Thumbs along your trouser seams."

"That's a response!"

"Aye aye, Sir!!"

"Thousand yard stare at all times."

"Aye aye, Sir!!"

"From the left. Name."

"Christopher Jackson, Sir!"

"Improper response, Indoctrination Candidate. Repeat after me."

"That's an *aye aye, Sir*!"

"Aye aye, Sir!"

"*This Indoctrination Candidate's name is Indoctrination Candidate Jackson, Officer Candidate School, Indoctrination Class Zero-Four-Zero-Zero, United States Navy.*"

"This Indoctrination Candidate's name is Indoctrination Candidate Jackson! Officer Candidate School! Indoctrination Class Zero-Four-Zero-Zero! United States Navy! Sir!"

"Social Security number."

"Five! Two! Zero! --."

"Improper response! Improper response!"

"As you were. *This Indoctrination Candidate's Social Security number is*. Waiting on you."

"This Indoctrination Candidate's Social Security number is! Five! Two! Zero! One! Five! Seven! Two! Six! Five! Sir!"

"Date of birth."

"This Indoctrination Candidate's date of birth is! Three! December! Nineteen-Seventy-One! Sir!"

"You a prior?"

"Yes, Sir!"

"Numbers run from zero-one to one-zero-zero around here. Think fast."

"That's a response! That's a response!"

"Aye aye, Sir!"

"Your date of birth, Indoctrination Candidate."

"Aye aye, Sir! This Indoctrination Candidate's date of birth is! Zero! Three! December! One! Nine! Seven! Four! Sir!"

"No such thing as the number nine. You meant *niner*. Read it back to me."

"Aye aye, Sir! This Indoctrination Candidate's birthday is! Zero! Three! December! One! Niner! Seven! Four! Sir!"

"Very well. Religion."

"This Indoctrination Candidate's religion is Baptist, Sir!"

"Blood type."

"This Indoctrination Candidate's blood type is O negative, Sir!"

"Your designator is *one-one-niner-five*. Go on, say it."

"Aye aye, Sir! This Indoctrination Candidate's designator is! One! One! Niner! Five! Sir!"

"Want to call home?"

"No, Sir!"

"Are you sure? Got your quarter right here."

"Yes, Sir!"

"Very well. Stand-by."

"Aye aye, Sir!"

"Name."

"This Indoctrination Candidate's name is Indoctrination Candidate Zurich! Officer Candidate School! Indoctrination Class Zero-Four-Zero-Zero! United States Navy! Sir!"

"Social Security number."

"This Indoctrination Candidate's Social Security number is! Two! One! Five! Six! Niner! Six! Niner! Two! Two! Sir!"

"Looks like we have a Poopie paying attention. That's good, Poopie. Good job. Date of birth."

"This Indoctrination Candidate's date of birth is! Zero! One! September! One! Niner! Seven! Six! Sir!"

"Would you look at that? Johnny Cash here does catch on quick."

"Beauty and brains. Total Poopie package."

"Religion."

"This Indoctrination Candidate's religion is Protestant, Sir!"

"Any particular denomination?"

"No, Sir!"

"Blood type."

"This Indoctrination Candidate's blood type is O positive, Sir!"

"Your designator is *one-six-three-five*. Let's hear it."

"Aye aye, Sir! This Indoctrination Candidate's designator is! One! Six! Three! Five! Sir!"

"You must be feeling pretty good about yourself, Poopie?"

"That's a response!"

"This Indoctrination Candidate does not know but will find out, Sir!"

"Nominated for understatement of the year. Want to call home?"

"No, Sir!"

"You sure?"

"Yes, Sir!"

"We got a quarter right here. Last best chance with a voice?"

"No, Sir!"

"Very well. Stand by."

"Aye aye, Sir!"

"Name."

"This Indoctrination Candidate's name is Indoctrination Candidate Potts, Sir!"

"Are you gaffing us off, Poopie?"

"No, Sir!"

"Are you sure?"

"Yes, Sir!"

"Repeat after me."

"That's a response!"

"Aye aye, Sir!"

"*This Indoctrination Candidate's name is Indoctrination Candidate Potts, Officer Candidate School, Indoctrination Class Zero-Four-Zero-Zero, United States Navy.*"

"This Indoctrination Candidate's name is Indoctrination Candidate Potts! Officer Candidate School! Indoctrination Class Zero-Four-Zero-Zero! United States Navy!"

"*Sir.*"

"Sir!"

"Failure to communicate! Failure to communicate!"

"Not the sharpest tool in the shed. Altogether now, Poopie."

"That's an *aye aye, Sir*!"

"We got your prescription upstairs! We got some Extra Military Instruction for your mental fitness! Don't you worry, Poopie!"

"Careful about making a name for yourself, Potts. It's early in the game and you're already behind. You start cutting corners now, Indoctrination Candidate, you're entering a world of hurt. You cut corners, people die. Attention to detail saves lives. We are entitled to a full and proper response. Do you understand me?"

"Sir! Yes, Sir!"

"Hold the Sir Sandwich, Indoctrination Candidate."

"That's a response!"

"Aye aye, Sir!"

"Thousand yard stare at all times."

"That's a response!"

"Aye aye, Sir!"

"Your name, Indoctrination Candidate."

"This Indoctrination Candidate's name is Indoctrination Candidate Potts! Officer Candidate School! Indoctrination Class Zero-Four-Zero-Zero! United States Navy! Sir!"

"Better. Social Security number."

"This Indoctrination Candidate's Social Security number is! Two! Three! Two! Seven! Four! Eight! Seven! Six! Five! Sir!"

"Your date of birth."

"This Indoctrination Candidate's date of birth is! Zero! Five! July! One! Niner! Seven! Three! Sir!"

"Religion."

"This Indoctrination Candidate's religion is Presbyterian, Sir!"

"Blood type."

"This Indoctrination Candidate's blood type is O positive, Sir!"

"Alright, Potts. Your designator is *one-three-niner-five*. What are you waiting on?"

"Aye aye, Sir! This Indoctrination Candidate's designator is! One! Three! Niner! Five! Sir!"

"Want to call home?"

"No, Sir!"

"Got your quarter right here. Let them know you're off to a great start?"

"No, Sir!"

"Stand by."

"Aye aye, Sir!"

"Name."

"This Indoctrination Candidate's name is Indoctrination Candidate Fortunato! Officer Candidate School! Indoctrination Class Zero-Four-Zero-Zero! United States Navy! Sir!"

"Are you now. Social?"

"This Indoctrination Candidate's Social Security number is! Two! Three! Five! Six! Zero! Zero! Seven! Eight! Two! Sir!"

"Date of birth."

"This Indoctrination Candidate's date of birth is! One! Niner! April! One! Niner! Seven! Seven! Sir!"

"Religion."

"This Indoctrination Candidate's religion is Roman Catholic, Sir!"

"Blood type."

"This Indoctrination Candidate's blood type is O positive, Sir!"

"Your designator is *one-one-six-five*. Let's hear it."

"This Indoctrination Candidate's designator is! One! One! Six! Five! Sir!"

"Phone call?"

"No, Sir!"

"You sure?"

"Yes, Sir!"

"One-zero-zero percent sure?"

"Yes, Sir!"

"As you wish. You four. Drop your gear in the stairwell."

"That's an *aye aye, Sir!*"

"Aye aye, Sir!!"

"Upstairs. Proceed. Off you go."

"Aye aye, Sir!!"

"Zero-four inches from the bulkhead at all times! *Aye aye, Sir!*"

"Aye aye, Sir!!"

"Repeat after me! *Left-right-left-right!*"

"That's an *aye aye, Sir!*"

"Aye aye, Sir!! Left-right!! Left-

right!! Left-right!!"

"Ready! Halt!"

"He said *freeze*, Poopies! That's a response!"

"Aye aye, Sir!!"

"Position of attention! Position of attention!"

"That's a response!"

"Aye aye, Sir!!"

"Up against the bulkhead! Zero-four inches! Zero-four inches at all times!"

"That's a response! That's a response!"

"Aye aye, Sir!!"

"Thousand yard stare at all times, Poopies! At all times!"

"That's a response!"

"Aye aye, Sir!!"

"You just stepped onto my deck! Where's my greeting of the day?"

"A Two-bar just asked you a question, Poopie! You going to gaff him off just like that?"

"No, Sir!"

"Then just where is his greeting of the day? Where is it?"

"This Indoctrination Candidate does not know but will find out, Sir!"

"Oh my. This one here is learning."

"Could be a Poopie Einstein sighting. Think we should call it in?"

"No such thing. Poopies dumb as bricks."

"Never know. Might be wired different. Let's ask him. Hey Poopie, are you Poopie Einstein?"

"No, Sir!"

"Are you wired different?"

"No, Sir!"

"See?"

"Only he might not tell us, being Poopie Einstein and all."

"Good point. You wouldn't tell us if you were, would you, Poopie?"

"This Indoctrination Candidate does not know but will find out, Sir!"

"Too smart for that."

"No, Sir!"

"Too clever."

"No, Sir!"

"Too crafty."

"No, Sir!"

"Ears."

"Open, Sir!"

"You will give the *greeting of the day* each time you cross through a hatch or onto a deck. You will call *attention on deck, stand-by* followed by the greeting of the day each time a person of senior rank comes on deck. The greeting of the day is *good morning, Sir* before Twelve Hundred, *good afternoon, Sir* after Twelve Hundred and *good evening, Sir* after colors. Got it?"

"Yes, Sir!"

"Your three Poopie compadres here got it too?"

"Yes, Sir!"

"How do you know? How do you know?"

"This Indoctrination Candidate does not know but will find out, Sir!"

"Hello? Hello? I think a Three-bar just stepped on deck! Where's his call to attention? Where's his greeting of the day?"

"Attention on deck, stand-by! Good morning, Sir!"

"What about you three? You don't feel like sounding off? You want to curl up on the couch, watch a movie together?"

"That's a response!"

"No, Sir!!"

"You want to have a cookie baking contest?"

"Well? Well? That's a response!"

"No, Sir!!"

"Greeting of the day! Greeting of the day! Sound off!"

"Good morning, Sir!!"

"Are you eyeballing me, Poopie? Who do you think you are?"

"No excuse, Sir!"

"Who do you think you are?"

"No excuse, Sir!"

"General Quarters! General Quarters! Battle stations! Battle stations! We got laces inboard over outboard!"

"Outboard over inboard! Outboard over inboard! Fix yourselves!"

"That's a response!"

"Aye aye, Sir!!"

"Now! Now!"

"That's an *aye aye, Sir*!"

"Aye aye, Sir!!"

"Louder!"

"Aye aye, Sir!!"

"Faster! Faster! Battlestations! Waiting on you!"

"Waiting on you! Waiting on you!"

"General Quarters! General Quarters! Waiting on you! Laces outboard over inboard! Outboard over inboard! Outboard over inboard!"

"That's a response! That's a response!"

"Aye aye, Sir!!"

"Position of attention when you sound off to a Candidate Officer! Position of attention!"

"That's an *aye aye, Sir*!"

"Aye aye, Sir!!"

"Louder!"

"Aye aye, Sir!!"

"Stop whispering!"

"Aye aye, Sir!!"

"Outboard over inboard! Outboard over inboard!"

"Aye aye, Sir!!"

"No! No! No bridges! No bridges! Start over!"

"Aye aye, Sir!!"

"Faster! Faster! Faster! Faster!"

"That's an *aye aye, Sir*!"

"Aye aye, Sir!!"

"Outboard over inboard! Outboard over inboard!"

"Aye aye, Sir!!"

"This should not be taking you so long, Indoctrination Candidates!"

"What's going on here?"

"Hello? Hello? A Four-bar just stepped on deck! A Four-bar just stepped on deck! Where's his call to attention? His greeting of the day?"

"Attention on deck, stand-by!! Good morning, Sir!!"

"As you were."

"That's an *aye aye, Sir*!"

"Aye aye, Sir!!"

"A single person calls attention on deck, Indoctrination Candidates. Figure it out."

"That's an *aye aye, Sir*!"

"Aye aye, Sir!!"

"Well?"

"Attention on deck, stand-by!!"

"As you were. What did we just say?"

"What's the excuse? What's the excuse?"

"No excuse, Sir!!"

"We're waiting."

"Attention on deck, stand-by!"

"Good morning, Sir!!"

"Outboard over inboard! Outboard over inboard!"

"This shouldn't be taking so long, Indoctrination Candidates."

"You heard the Four-bar! This should not be taking so long!"

"Slow motion, Poopies! Slow motion! Someone push fast forward! Push it now!"

"That's a response!"

"Aye aye, Sir!!"

"What's the matter with you? What's the matter? I think a Four-bar just stepped off deck!"

"Hello? Hello?"

"Attention on deck, Stand-by!"

"Good morning, Sir!!"

"Outboard over inboard! Outboard over inboard!"

"Bridges? Bridges? Start over!"

"Aye aye, Sir!"

"Faster, Poopies, faster! Faster! Faster! Faster!"

"What is taking so long, Indoctrination Candidates?"

"That's a response! That's a response!"

"No excuse, Sir!"

"Everyone! Together!"

"No excuse, Sir!!"

"Faster! Smarter! Better!"

"Are you done, yet? Are you done, yet?"

"That's a response!"

"No, Sir!!"

"You have no time, Indoctrination Candidates! You have no time!"

"Attention on deck, stand-by!"

"Good morning, Sir!!"

"Poopie Einstein strikes again. Going to have to keep an eye on this one."

"Faster, Poopie! Faster!"

"That's a response!"

"Aye aye, Sir!"

"Hello? Hello?"

"Attention on deck, Stand-by!"

"Good morning, Sir!!"

"Waiting on you, Johnny Cash! Waiting on you! Waiting on your fancy shoes! What's your excuse?"

"No excuse, Sir!"

"Come on, Poopie! Waiting on you!"

"No excuse, Sir!"

"Coking-and-joking! Coking-and-joking!"

"No excuse, Sir!"

"Position of attention when you sound off to a Candidate Officer! Position of attention!"

"Aye aye, Sir!"

"Outboard over inboard! Outboard over inboard!"

"Aye aye, Sir!"

"Waiting on you! Waiting on you!"

"Aye aye, Sir!"

"Waiting on you!"

"Aye aye, Sir!"

"Now tuck the laces outboard."

"That's an *aye aye, Sir*!"

"Aye aye, Sir!!"

"Louder!"

"Aye aye, Sir!!"

"Go. Next station."

••

Code of Conduct

I am an American, fighting in the forces which guard my country and our way of life. I am prepared to give my life in their defense.

I will never surrender of my own free will. If in command, I will never surrender the members of my command while they still have the means to resist.

If I am captured, I will continue to resist by all means available. I will make every effort to escape and aid others to escape. I will accept neither parole nor special favors from the enemy.

If I become a prisoner of war (POW), I will keep faith with my fellow prisoners. I will give no information nor take part in any action which might be harmful to my comrades. If I am senior, I will take command. If not, I will obey the lawful orders of those appointed over me and will back them up in every way.

When questioned, should I become a prisoner of war, I am required to give name, rank, service number and date of birth. I will evade answering further questions to the utmost of my ability. I will make no oral or written statements disloyal to my country and its allies or harmful to their cause.

I will never forget that I am an American, fighting for freedom, responsible for my actions, and dedicated to the principles which made my country free. I will trust in my God and in the United States of America.

••

"Poopies need Poopie suits. Upon receiving the command of execution *go*, you will march up to this hatch here, take a thirty-inch step, halt, and then face. Is that perfectly clear?"

"Yes, Sir!!"

"You will raise your right arm and rap, loudly now, zero-three times on the frame and wait until you are called into the space. Is that clear?"

"Yes, Sir!!"

"Upon receiving permission to enter, you will step onto the deck, giving the greeting of the day, and square yourself one-two to one-eight inches from the desk. Got it?"

"Yes, Sir!!"

"How do you know? You will identify yourself, *reporting for duty as ordered*."

"That's a response!"

"Aye aye, Sir!!"

"One at a time. Go."

"You! Get in that hole!"

"Aye aye, Sir!"

"Enter."

"Good morning, Sir!"

"What? You think that means the rest of you can chill? Relax? Coking-and-joking? Coking-and-joking? Well? That's a response!"

"No, Sir!!"

"Coking-and-joking! Coking-and-joking!"

"Hello? Hello? I think a Candidate Lieutenant Commander just stepped on deck! Where's his greeting of the day?"

"Attention on deck, Stand-by!"

"Good morning, Sir!!"

"I think a Candidate Lieutenant Commander just stepped off deck!"

"Attention on deck, Stand-by!"

"Good morning, Sir!!"

"I think a Candidate Lieutenant Commander just stepped on deck! Where's his greeting of the day?"

"Attention on deck, Stand-by!"

"Good morning, Sir!!"

"I think a Candidate Lieutenant Commander just stepped off deck!"

"Attention on deck, Stand-by!"

"Good morning, Sir!!"

"Louder!"

"Aye aye, Sir!!"

"Attention on deck, Stand-by!"

"Good morning, Sir!!"

"Attention on deck, Stand-by!"

"Good morning, Sir!!"

"Attention on deck, Stand-by!"

"Good morning, Sir!!"

"Attention on deck, Stand-by!"

"Good morning, Sir!!"

"Attention on deck, Stand-by!"

"Good morning, Sir!!"

"Next!"

"Poopie, you're up. Halt. And face. Three times hard."

"Aye aye, Sir!"

"Enter."

"Indoctrination Candidate Zurich! Officer Candidate School! Indoctrination Class Zero-Four-Zero-Zero! United States Navy! Reporting for duty as ordered! Sir!"

"Very well. Let's get you measured. Lose the go-fasters. Up on the scale."

"Aye aye, Sir!"

"Chin up."

"Aye aye, Sir!"

"Back straight."

"Aye aye, Sir!"

"Seven-five inches. What does that read?"

"One! Seven! Five! Pounds! Sir!"

"Waistline?"

"Three! Four! Inches! Sir!"

"Seven-five at one-seven-four. Issued zero-one pair of large Poopie trousers. Zero-one Poopie blouse, large. Zero-one Poopie belt with brass buckle. Arms out."

"Aye aye, Sir!"

"Here you go. Go stand next to your Shipmate over there."

"Aye aye, Sir!"

"Next!"

"Enter."

"Indoctrination Candidate Potts! Officer Candidate School! Indoctrination Class Zero-Four-Zero-Zero! United States Navy! Reporting for duty as ordered, Sir!"

"Very well. Up you go. That's a response."

"Aye aye, Sir!"

"Without the go-fasters."

"Aye aye, Sir!"

"What does that read?"

"One! Six! Eight! Sir!"

"Shoulders back. One-six-eight at seven-zero. Waist?"

"Three! Four! Inches! Sir!"

"Issued. Zero-one pair Poopie trousers, medium. Zero-one Poopie blouse, medium. Zero-one Poopie belt and brass buckle. Arms out."

"That's a response, Indoctrination Candidate. I do believe he's earned it."

"Aye aye, Sir!"

"Go stand over there with your Shipmates."

"Aye aye, Sir!"

"Next!"

"Enter."

"Indoctrination Candidate Fortunato! Officer Candidate School! Indoctrination Class Zero-Four-Zero-Zero! United States Navy! Reporting for duty as ordered, Sir!"

"Alright then, Fortunato. Lose those go-fasters, hop up on the scale and tell me what it reads."

"Aye aye, Sir! One! Eight! Five! Sir!"

"Chin up. Seven-three inches. Waist?"

"Three! Five! Inches! Sir!"

"Fortunato. One-eight-five at seven-three. Issued zero-one pairs of Poopie trousers, large. Zero-one Poopie blouse, large. Zero-one Poopie belt and brass buckle. How does that sound?"

"This Indoctrination Candidate does not know but will find out, Sir!"

"Belay my last, Poopie. Nobody cares. Arms out."

"Aye aye, Sir!"

"All of you. Dismissed."

"Aye aye, Sir!!"

"Good morning, Sir!"

"Good morning, Sir!"

"Good morning, Sir!"

"Good morning, Sir!"

"Negative, Indoctrination Candidates. First and last only sound off with the greeting of the day."

"First and last only! First and last only! Get back in that hole!"

"Aye aye, Sir!!"

"Good morning, Sir!"

"Good morning, Sir!"

"What are you doing back here? Who authorized you to enter this space?"

"Scram, Poopies!"

"Aye aye, Sir!!"

"Out of the hole! Out of the hole!"

"Good morning, Sir!"

"Good morning, Sir!"

"Negative, Poopies. Middle men say *step*."

"Middle men say step! Get back in that hole!"

"Aye aye, Sir!!"

"Enter."

"Good morning, Sir!"

"Step!"

"Step!"

"Good morning, Sir!"

"Scram!"

"Aye aye, Sir!!"

"Good morning, Sir!"

"Step!"

"Step!"

"Good morning, Sir!"

"Zero-four inches from the bulkhead! Zero-four inches! Line it up!"

"That's a response!"

"Aye aye, Sir!!"

"Right face!"

"That's a response!"

"Aye aye, Sir!!"

"Ready! March!"

"Aye aye, Sir!!"

"*Left-right-left-right*! Sound off!"

"Aye aye, Sir!! Left-right!! Left-right!! Left-right!! Left-right!! Left-right!! Left-right!! Left-right!! Left-right!! Left-right!! Left-right!!"

"Arms! Six to the front, three to the rear!"

"That's an *aye aye, Sir*!"

"Aye aye, Sir!!"

"Arms! *Six to the front*! *Three to the rear*!"

"Six to the front!! Three to the rear!!"

"Louder!"

"Six to the front!! Three to the rear!!"

"*Left-right-left-right*!"

"Left-right!! Left-right!!"

"Go! Go! Go! Go!"

"Aye aye, Sir!!"

"You have no time, Indoctrination Candidates!"

"Aye aye, Sir!!"

"*Left-right-left-right*!"

"Left-right!! Left-right!!"

"Keep it moving! Keep it moving!"

"That's a response!"

"Aye aye, Sir!! Left-right!!"

"You have no time, Indoctrination Candidates! You have no time!"

"That's an *aye aye, Sir*!"

"Aye aye, Sir!!"

"Go! Go! Into the hole! Into the hole!"

"That's a response!"

"Aye aye, Sir!!"

"Good morning, Sir!"

"Step!"

"Step!"

"Good morning, Sir!"

Gray wall lockers stand next to low racks topped by thin mattresses. The intersection of four brown desks serves as an island in the center of the space. A small tin trash can sits off to the side. I spot my suitcase at the foot of the rack on the far left-hand side.

"Keep it moving, Poopies! Keep it moving! Around the table! Go! Go! Go!"

"That's a response!"

"Aye aye, Sir!!"

"*Left-right-left-right!*"

"Left-right!! Left-right!!"

"Sharp right turns, Poopies! Sharp right turns!"

"That's a response!"

"Aye aye, Sir!!"

"Go! Go! Go!"

"Aye aye, Sir!! Left-right!! Left-right!! Left-right!! Left-right!! Left-right!! Left-right!!"

"And step! And step! And step! Sharp turns, Indoctrination Candidates! Sharp turns!"

"Aye aye, Sir!! Left-right!!"

"Ready! Halt!"

"Aye aye, Sir!!"

"Into your Poopie suits."

"That's an *aye aye, Sir!*"

"Aye aye, Sir!!"

"You have zero-three minutes."

"Aye aye, Sir!!"

"Go! Go! Go!"

"Aye aye, Sir!!"

"Well, what are you waiting for? What are you waiting for?"

"No excuse, Sir!!"

"Attention on deck, stand-by!"

"Good morning, Sir!!"

I strip down to my boxer shorts. Faded green trousers fit loosely around the waist. Worn buttons of the matching blouse slide easily into mesh holes. The frayed end of the web belt pushes through the folding metal clasp of a dirty brass buckle.

"Attention on deck, stand-by!"

"Good morning, Sir!!"

"Empty all gear! Empty all trash! Let's go, Poopies! Let's go!"

"Aye aye, Sir!!"

"No! No! On top of the rack! On top of the rack! Where do you think you are, Poopie? Where do you think you are?"

"No excuse, Sir!"

A Candidate Officer combs through my belongings.

"What in the world? What in the world? Eyeballs!"

"Snap, Sir!"

"What's this contraband doing in here?"

"No excuse, Sir!"

"Louder!"

"No excuse, Sir!"

"Aspirin? Do you have a prescription for this?"

"No, Sir!!"

"Contraband!"

"No excuse, Sir!"

"Oh this is fancy! This is fancy! This is a sweet little thing! What are you some kind of businessman?"

"No, Sir!"

"Going to do some deals after Taps?"

"No, Sir!"

"Thinking of calling home?"

"No, Sir!"

"Are you a special individual?"

"No, Sir!"

"Are you sure? We can itemize your calls for you? Alphabetical order or time of call? Well? That's a response!"

"No excuse, Sir!"

"Round-the-table! Go!"

"Aye aye, Sir!"

"All of you! Round-the-table! Go! Go! Go!"

“That’s a response!”

“Aye aye, Sir!!”

“*Left-right-left-right!*”

“Left-right!! Left-right!!”

“Hello? Hello? Pretty sure a Five-bar just stepped on deck! What are you waiting on? What are you waiting on?”

“Attention on deck, stand-by!”

“Good morning, Sir!!”

“Good morning. I trust you find the accommodations to your liking. This is your new home. Like every good home, there are some rules. You will notice the blue book at the intersection of the desks. This book contains the Officer Candidate Regulations, the O.C.R., your Bible for every duty and action here at O.C.S. Is that clear?”

“Yes, Sir!!”

“Louder!”

“Yes, Sir!!”

“Louder!”

“Yes, Sir!!”

“You will also notice the accessories. Warbelts and chrome domes. Your wargear. Rule number-one. Unless otherwise instructed, you will not leave this space without your wargear.”

“That’s a response!”

“Aye aye, Sir!!”

“Next to your wargear, you will find a canteen. The canteen is filled with water. Rule number-two. Your canteen will remain at least half full at all times. Is that clear?”

“Yes, Sir!!”

“Unless otherwise instructed, you will not exit this space without your canteen. You will carry your canteen at all times in your port hand, fingers joined tightly over the cap, body of the canteen resting squarely along the forearm, elbows locked, at a ninety degree angle. Grounded at all times. Is that clear?”

“Yes, Sir!!”

“Let’s see it.”

“Aye aye, Sir!!”

"Forearms parallel to the deck! Forearms parallel to the deck! That's a response!"

"Aye aye, Sir!!"

"Elbows in!"

"Aye aye, Sir!!"

"I see daylight! I see daylight!"

"No excuse, Sir!!"

"You will remain fully hydrated at all times. Your hydration is of the utmost importance."

"That's a response! That's a response!"

"Aye aye, Sir!!"

"You will also find a combination lock. The combination to your combination lock is the three-digit sequence taped to the back. The dialing sequence is zero-two full rotations past the first number to the left, zero-one full rotations past the second number to the right and a final turn back to the left until you reach the third and final number. This leads me to rule number-three. You will not leave this space without securing all gear inside your wall locker. Failure to secure your wall locker is a serious offense that is met with serious consequences here at Officer Candidate School. Any questions?"

"No, Sir!!"

"How do you know, Indoctrination Candidates?"

"How do you know? How do you know?"

"This Indoctrination Candidate does not know but will find out, Sir!!"

"Secure your gear."

"That's a response! That's a response!"

"Aye aye, Sir!!"

"Let's go, Poopies! Let's go! You have no time!"

"Aye aye, Sir!!"

"This should not be taking so long, Poopies! Secure your trash!"

"Zero-two rotations! Zero-two rotations!"

"Aye aye, Sir!"

"Try it again! Try it again!"

"Aye aye, Sir!"

"This should not be taking so long, Poopies!"

"That's an *aye aye, Sir*!"

"Aye, Sir!!"

"You're done. Position of attention."

"You're done! You're done! Position of attention! That's a response!"

"Aye aye, Sir!!"

"Rule number-four. This floor will continue to shine at all times. The space underneath your racks will remain free from dust and grime at all times. The

upright surfaces of your wall lockers, your desks, your window blinds will remain free of dust and grime at all times. The trash receptacle will be lined with a clean bag at all times."

"That's a response!"

"Aye aye, Sir!!"

"Rule number-five. You are entitled to three square meals a day and a rack to sleep on between the hours of Twenty-Two Hundred and Zero-Five Hundred. Racks are made and maintained according to strict regulations between the hours of Zero-Five Hundred and Twenty-Two Hundred."

"That's a response!"

"Aye aye, Sir!!"

"My colleague, Candidate Officer Skeer here, will demonstrate."

"Eyeballs!"

"That's a *snap, Sir*!"

"Snap, Sir!!"

"Louder!"

"Snap, Sir!!"

"The mattress is tied at the foot. You have zero-two sheets. You pull the bottom sheet even with the foot of the mattress and tuck under at the head. You leave one-six inches at the head of the rack."

"That's an *aye aye, Sir*!"

"Aye aye, Sir!!"

"You make a hospital corner. You place one finger on top of the corner, lifting the sheet up with your other hand. You tuck the lower drape under the mattress. At an angle of forty-five degrees. Hold the corner in place while you bring the sheet over. Tuck the rest. Straight edge, nice and crisp. Repeat for all four corners."

"That's a response!"

"Aye aye, Sir!!"

"Next step. Place the top sheet over the bottom sheet. Wide seam at the head. Even with the top of the mattress and tucked under at the foot. You lay the blanket on top of the sheets, leaving zero-six inches between the top edge of the blanket and sheet. And tuck. Pull the blanket to the inner edge of the seam, then fold both the top sheet and blanket to zero-four inches. Got it? You fold it again, one-eight inches from the fold to the head of the mattress. This leaves a zero-eight inch fold. Zero-four inches from pillow to fold. Then you fold the corners same as the sheet. You make it tight."

"That's a response! That's a response!"

"Aye aye, Sir!!"

"Louder!"

"Aye aye, Sir!!"

"Thank you, Candidate Officer Skeer. We'll be looking to bounce this here quarter off the final product. You have zero-five minutes."

"That's a response!"

"Aye aye, Sir!!"

"And pray God there's no more contraband in here when we get back. We will find it."

"That's an *aye aye, Sir*!"

"Aye aye, Sir!!"

"Louder!"

"Aye aye, Sir!!"

"Go! Go! Go! You're already behind!"

"Aye aye, Sir!!"

"Attention on deck, stand-by!"

"Good morning, Sir!!"

••

General Orders of a Sentry

To take charge of this post and all government property in view.

To walk my post in a military manner, keeping always on the alert, and observing everything that takes place within sight or hearing.

To report all violations of orders I am instructed to enforce.

To repeat all calls from posts more distant from the guardhouse than my own.

To quit my post only when properly relieved.

To receive, obey and pass on to the sentry who relieves me, all orders from the Commanding Officer, Command Duty Officer, Officer of the Deck, and Officers and Petty Officers of the Watch only.

To talk to no one except in the line of duty.

To give the alarm in case of fire or disorder.

To call the Officer of the Deck in any case not covered by instructions.

To salute all Officers and all colors and standards not cased.

To be especially watchful at night, and, during the time for challenging, to challenge all persons on or near my post and to allow no one to pass without proper authority.

••

"Indoctrination Class Zero-Four-Zero-Zero. Ears."

"Open, Sir!!"

"Ears!"

"Open, Sir!!"

"You will be marching into chow. Wargear is not permitted inside the chow hall. You will ground your warbelts and chrome domes in an expeditious but orderly fashion. Chrome domes grounded first. Canteens grounded to chrome domes. Warbelts grounded around your chrome domes and canteens. Is that clear?"

"Yes, Sir!!"

"Louder!"

"Yes, Sir!!"

"Remember your place in formation. Maintain cohesion at all times, aligned to the starboard side. Is that clear?"

"Yes, Sir!!"

"Louder!"

"Yes, Sir!!"

"Indoctrination Class Zero-Four-Zero-Zero! Upon receiving the command of execution *ground your wargear*! You will! Ground your warbelts, chrome domes and canteens to the starboard side! Is that clear?"

"Yes, Sir!!"

"Ready! Ground your wargear!"

"Aye aye, Sir!!"

"Where is your place, Poopie? Find your place!"

"This Indoctrination Candidate does not know but will find out, Sir!"

"Find your place!"

"Aye aye, Sir!"

"Chrome domes first! Chrome domes first!"

"That's an *aye aye, Sir*!"

"Aye aye, Sir!!"

"You have no time, Indoctrination Candidates."

"That's an *aye aye, Sir*!"

"Aye aye, Sir!!"

"Louder!"

"Aye aye, Sir!!"

"Fall in!"

"That's a response!"

"Aye aye, Sir!!"

"What do you think you're doing, Poopie? Where are you going? Back in formation! Back in formation!"

"No excuse, Sir!"

"You have no time, Indoctrination Candidates."

"*Aye aye, Sir!*"

"Aye aye, Sir!!"

"You are falling behind, Indoctrination Class Zero-Four-Zero-Zero. You have no time."

"*Aye aye, Sir!*"

"Aye aye, Sir!!"

"Indoctrination Class Zero-Four-Zero-Zero! Upon receiving the command of execution *half-step, march*! You will! Follow the guidon, half-step up this ladderwell, perform an immediate column left and reform at the door! Are we clear?"

"Yes, Sir!!"

"Ready! Half-step! March!"

"Aye aye, Sir!!"

"Left-right! Left-right! Left-right! Left-right! Left-right! Column left! March!"

"Aye aye, Sir!!"

"And step! And step! And step! And step! And step! And step! Left-right! Ready! Halt!"

"Aye aye, Sir!!"

"He said *halt*, Poopie!"

"No excuse, Sir!"

"What? Sound off!"

"No excuse, Sir!"

"You have no time, Indoctrination Candidates."

"That's an *aye aye, Sir!*"

"Aye aye, Sir!!"

"Indoctrination Class Zero-Four-Zero-Zero! Upon receiving the command of *column of files from the right*! You will! Proceed into the chow hall in single file, right column first, column-by-column! Am I clear?"

"Yes, Sir!!"

"Louder!"

"Yes, Sir!!"

"First and last through the hole will sound off with the greeting of the day! Those in between will count off *zero-two, zero-three, zero-four*! Whatever your sequence in formation! Clear?"

"Yes, Sir!!"

"Upon entering the chow hall, you will make an immediate right turn and follow the guidance of the Candidate Officers to your place setting! You will remain at the position of attention with your gougebook fully extended in your port hand at a ninety degree angle until your entire class is ready to be seated! Crystal clear?"

"Yes, Sir!!"

"Good. How about a volunteer?"

"You heard him, Poopie! Front and center!"

"Aye aye, Sir!"

"Congratulations, Indoctrination Candidate. You are our Doorbody."

"Aye aye, Sir!"

"Doorbody, is the chow hall deck all clear?"

"This Indoctrination Candidate does not know but will find out, Sir!"

"Take a peek inside through the window and tell me if you see a line."

"Aye aye, Sir!"

"Well?"

"No, Sir!"

"*Chow hall deck all clear.*"

"Chow hall deck all clear, Sir!"

"Louder!"

"Chow hall deck all clear, Sir!"

"Everyone!"

"Chow hall deck all clear, Sir!!"

"Then crack that door, Doorbody, stick your head in there and repeat after me. *Indoctrination Class Zero-Four-Zero-Zero, marching into chow.*"

"Aye aye, Sir! Indoctrination Class Zero-Four-Zero-Zero! Marching into chow!"

"As you were. When you cross that threshold, you are at war. You will sound off with your warface on."

"Aye aye, Sir!"

"Warface on! Warface on!"

"Aye aye, Sir! Indoctrination Class Zero-Four-Zero-Zero! Marching into chow!"

"Better. Altogether now!"

"Indoctrination Class Zero-Four-Zero-Zero!! Marching into chow!!"

"Louder!"

"Indoctrination Class Zero-Four-Zero-Zero!! Marching into chow!!"

"Louder!"

"Indoctrination Class Zero-Four-Zero-Zero!! Marching into chow!!"

"Very well. Indoctrination Class Zero-Four-Zero-Zero! Column of files! From the right! Ready! March!"

"Aye aye, Sir!!"

"Good afternoon, Sir!"

"Zero-two!"

"Zero-three!"

"Zero-four!"

"Zero-five!"

"Zero-six!"

"Zero-seven!"

"Zero-eight!"

"Zero-niner!"

"One-zero!"

"One-one!"

"One-two!"

"One-three!"

"One-four!"

"One-five!"

"One-six!"

"One-seven!"

"One-eight!"

"One-niner!"

"Two-zero!"

"Two-one!"

"Two-two!"

"Two-three!"

"Two-four!"

"Two-five!"

"Two-six!"

"Two-seven!"

"Two-eight!"

"Two-niner!"

"Three-zero!"

"Three-one!"

"Three-two!"

"Three-three!"

"Three-four!"

"Three-five!"
"Three-six!"
"Three-seven!"
"Three-eight!"
"Three-niner!"
"Four-zero!"
"Four-one!"
"Four-two!"
"Four-three!"
"Four-four!"
"Four-five!"
"Four-six!"
"Four-seven!"
"Four-eight!"
"Four-niner!"
"Five-zero!"
"Five-one!"
"Five-two!"
"Five-three!"
"Five-four!"
"Five-five!"
"Five-six!"
"Five-seven!"
"Five-eight!"
"Five-niner!"
"Six-zero!"
"Six-one!"
"Six-two!"
"Six-three!"
"Six-four!"
"Six-five!"
"Good afternoon, Sir!"
"Let's go! Let's go! Let's go!"
"Aye aye, Sir!!"
"Line it up in front of a tray, Indoctrination Candidates!"
"Aye aye, Sir!!"
"In front of a tray, Poopie!"
"Aye aye, Sir!"
"You! Other side!"
"Aye aye, Sir!"
"Position of attention!"

"Aye aye, Sir!"

"Gougebook out, Indoctrination Candidates! Port arms up, parallel to the deck!"

"Aye aye, Sir!!"

"Parallel to the deck, Indoctrination Candidates!"

"Aye aye, Sir!!"

"Thousand yard stare at all times, Indoctrination Candidates!"

"Aye aye, Sir!!"

"Port arms up! Parallel to the deck!"

"Aye aye, Sir!!"

"Reading your palms!"

"Aye aye, Sir!!"

"Louder!"

"Aye aye, Sir!!"

"Louder!"

"Aye aye, Sir!!"

"Put it away, Indoctrination Class Zero-Four-Zero-Zero!"

"Aye aye, Sir!!"

"Indoctrination Class Zero-Four-Zero-Zero! Upon the command of execution *seats*! You will! Crash hard into your seat! Ready! Seats!"

"Aye aye, Sir!!"

"Upon the command of *adjust*! You will bring your chest flush to the table! Is that clear?"

"Yes, Sir!!"

"Ready! Adjust!"

"Aye aye, Sir!!"

"Pray at will! Head bowed!"

"Aye aye, Sir!!"

"As you were, Indoctrination Candidates. When you pray, you pray in silence."

"That's an *aye aye, Sir*!"

"Aye aye, Sir!!"

"Pray at will!"

"Eat!"

"That's an *aye aye, Sir*!"

"Aye aye, Sir!!"

"As you were! Utensils down!"

"Aye aye, Sir!!"

"Indoctrination Class Zero-Four-Zero-Zero, this is your two-zero minute warning!"

"That's an *aye aye, Sir*!"

"Aye aye, Sir!!"

"You have two-zero minutes to eat and hydrate. Is that clear?"

"Yes, Sir!!"

"Ears!"

"Open, Sir!!"

"Feeding is an eight-count exercise. First count. Snap your head down so that your chin touches your chest. Second count. Using your port hand, I repeat, port hand, reach across your tray and pick up your warspoon. Third count. Scoop your food and hold. Zero-two inches above and centered over your plate. Fourth count. Warspoon in mouth. Hold there. Fifth count. Return warspoon to the proper position on the right side of the tray. Sixth count. Snap your head up. Seventh count. Chew. Eighth count. Swallow. Your tray will remain grounded to the edge of the table at all times. Your plate and spoon will remain grounded to the bottom rim of your tray at all times. Your cups will remain grounded to the top rim of your tray at all times. Is that clear?"

"Yes, Sir!!"

"Eat. Zero-one. Head snap. Zero-two. Warspoon. Zero-three. Scoop. Two inches. Zero-four. Eat. Zero-five. Spoon grounded. Zero-six. Head up. No chewing. Zero-seven. Chew. Zero-eight. Swallow. Together now."

"That's an *aye aye, Sir*!"

"Aye aye, Sir!!"

"Eat. Zero-one. Zero-two. As you were. Zero-two. Zero-three. As you were. Zero-three. Zero-four. As you were. Zero-four. Zero-five. As you were. Zero-five. Zero-six. As you were. Zero-six. Zero-seven. As you were. Zero-seven. Zero-eight."

"You will finish chewing, Indoctrination Candidates!"

"Aye aye, Sir!!"

"You will not sound off with your holes full!"

"Aye aye, Sir!!"

"Hydration is a twelve count exercise. Eyeballs."

"Snap, Sir!!"

"First count. Right hand out, fingers joined. Second count. Twist hand, prepare to grab the cup. Third count. Bring your hand down to the table in a swift motion. Fourth count. Grab cup, fingers joined. Fifth count. Lift cup. Sixth count. Bring cup to mouth. Seventh count. Hydrate. Eighth count. Bring cup back out. Ninth count. Cup down and grounded to the tray. Tenth count. Hand out. Eleventh count. Twist back. Twelfth count. Return hand to lap. Is that clear?"

"Yes, Sir!!"

"Is that clear?"

"Yes, Sir!!"

"Hydrate. Zero-one. Zero-two. Zero-three. Zero-four. Zero-five. Zero-six. As you were. Zero-six. Zero-seven. Zero-eight. Zero-niner. One-zero. One-one. One-two."

"Thousand yard stare at all times, Indoctrination Candidates!"

"Aye aye, Sir!!"

"Again. Zero-one. Zero-two. Zero-three. As you were. Zero-three. As you were. Zero-three. Zero-four. Zero-five. Zero-six. Zero-seven. As you were. Zero-seven. Zero-eight. As you were. Zero-eight. Zero-niner. One-zero. One-one. One-two."

"Indoctrination Class Zero-Four-Zero-Zero! This is your one-five minute warning!"

"That's an *aye aye, Sir!*"

"Aye aye, Sir!!"

"Hydrate. Zero-one. As you were. Zero-one. Zero-two. Zero-three. Zero-four. Zero-five. Zero-six. As you were. Zero-six. Zero-seven. Zero-eight. Zero-niner. One-zero. One-one. One-two."

"You must remain fully hydrated at all times, Indoctrination Candidates! Your utmost hydration is of the utmost importance!"

"That's an *aye aye, Sir!*"

"Aye aye, Sir!!"

"Louder!"

"Aye aye, Sir!!"

"Louder!"

"Aye aye, Sir!!"

"Hydrate. Zero-one. Zero-two. Zero-three. Zero-four. Zero-five. Zero-six. Zero-seven. As you were. Zero-seven. As you were. Zero-eight. As you were. Zero-eight. As you were. Zero-eight. Zero-niner. One-zero. One-one. One-two."

"Now your pie holes."

"That's an *aye aye, Sir!*"

"Aye aye, Sir!!"

"Eat. Zero-one. Zero-two. Zero-three. Zero-four. Zero-five. Zero-six. Zero-seven. Zero-eight. Again. Zero-one. Zero-two. Zero-three. Zero-four. As you were. Zero-four. Zero-five. Zero-six. Zero-seven. Zero-eight."

"Clean plates, Indoctrination Candidates! Empty cups!"

"That's an *aye aye, Sir!*"

"Aye aye, Sir!!"

"Hydrate. Zero-one. Zero-two. Fingers grounded."

"That's an *aye aye, Sir!*"

"Aye aye, Sir!!"

"Zero-three. Zero-four. Zero-five. As you were. Zero-five. Zero-six. Zero-seven. As you were. Zero-seven. As you were. Together now. Zero-seven. Zero-

eight. Zero-niner. One-zero. One-one. One-two. Again. Zero-one. Zero-two. Zero-three. Zero-four. Zero-five. Zero-six. Zero-seven. Zero-eight. Zero-niner. As you were. Zero-niner. One-zero. One-one. One-two. Eat. Zero-one. Zero-two. As you were. Zero-two. Zero-three. Zero-four. Zero-five. As you were. Zero-five. Zero-six. Zero-seven. Zero-eight. Again. Zero-one. Zero-two. Zero-three. Zero-four. As you were. Zero-four. As you were. Zero-four. As you were. Zero-four. Zero-five. Zero-six. Zero-seven. Zero-eight."

"Thousand yard stare at all times, Indoctrination Candidates!"

"Aye aye, Sir!!"

"Eat. Zero-one. Zero-two. Zero-three. Zero-four. Zero-five. Zero-six. Zero-seven. Zero-eight. Better."

"Indoctrination Class Zero-Four-Zero-Zero! This is your one-zero minute warning!"

"Aye aye, Sir!!"

"Hydrate. Zero-one. Zero-two. As you were. Zero-two. Zero-three. Zero-four. Zero-five. Zero-six. Zero-seven. Zero-eight. Zero-niner. One-zero. One-one. One-two. Eat. Zero-one. Zero-two. Zero-three. Zero-four. Zero-five. Zero-six. Zero-seven. As you were. Zero-seven. Zero-eight. Hydrate. Zero-one. Zero-two. Zero-three. Zero-four. Zero-five. Zero-six. Zero-seven. As you were. Zero-seven. As you were. Zero-seven. Zero-eight. Zero-niner. One-zero. One-one. One-two."

"If you have finished a cup, raise the cup above your head! A Candidate Officer will refill it for you!"

"That's an *aye aye, Sir*!"

"Aye aye, Sir!!"

"You must hydrate, Indoctrination Candidates! Hydration is of the utmost importance!"

"Aye aye, Sir!!"

"Thousand yard stare at all times, Indoctrination Candidates!"

"Aye aye, Sir!!"

"Eat. Zero-one. Zero-two. Zero-three. As you were. Zero-three. As you were. Zero-three. As you were. Zero-three. Zero-four. Zero-five. Zero-six. Zero-seven. Zero-eight. Hydrate. Zero-one. Zero-two. Zero-three. Zero-four. Zero-five. Zero-six. Zero-seven. Zero-eight. Zero-niner. One-zero. One-one. One-two. Eat. Zero-one. Zero-two. Zero-three. Zero-four. Zero-five. As you were. Zero-five. Zero-six. Zero-seven. Zero-eight. Hydrate. Zero-one. Zero-two. As you were. Zero-two. Zero-three. Zero-four. Zero-five. Zero-six. Zero-seven. Zero-eight. Zero-niner. One-zero. One-one. One-two. Eat. Zero-one. Zero-two. Zero-three. Zero-four. Zero-five. Zero-six. Zero-seven. Zero-eight. Hydrate. Zero-one. Zero-two. Zero-three. Zero-four. Zero-five. Zero-six. Zero-seven. Zero-eight. Zero-niner. One-zero. One-one. One-two."

"Thousand yard stare at all times, Indoctrination Candidates!"

"Aye aye, Sir!!"

"Louder!"

"Aye aye, Sir!!"

"Eat. Zero-one. Zero-two. Zero-three. Zero-four. Zero-five. As you were. Zero-five. Zero-six. Zero-seven. Zero-eight. Again. Zero-one. Zero-two. Zero-three. Zero-four. Zero-five. Zero-six. As you were. Zero-six. Zero-seven. Zero-eight. Again. Zero-one. Zero-two. Zero-three. Zero-four. Zero-five. Zero-six. Zero-seven. Zero-eight. As you were. Zero-eight."

"Indoctrination Class Zero-Four-Zero-Zero, this is your zero-five minute warning!"

"That's an *aye aye, Sir*!"

"Aye aye, Sir!!"

"Zero-five minutes, Indoctrination Candidates! You will clean the plates in front of you!"

"That's an *aye aye, Sir*!"

"Aye aye, Sir!!"

"You will finish those cups, Indoctrination Candidates!"

"Aye aye, Sir!!"

"Hydration is of the utmost importance."

"That's an *aye aye, Sir*!"

"Aye aye, Sir!!"

"Eat. Zero-one. Zero-two. Zero-three. Zero-four. As you were. Zero-four. Zero-five. Zero-six. Zero-seven. Zero-eight. Hydrate. Zero-one. Zero-two. Zero-three. Zero-four. Zero-five. Zero-six. Zero-seven. Zero-eight. Zero-niner. One-zero. One-one. One-two. Eat. Zero-one. Zero-two. Zero-three. Zero-four. Zero-five. As you were. Zero-five. Zero-six. Zero-seven. Zero-eight. Hydrate. Zero-one. Zero-two. Zero-three. Zero-four. Zero-five. Zero-six. Zero-seven. As you were. Zero-seven. As you were. Zero-seven. Zero-eight. Zero-niner. One-zero. One-one. One-two."

"Cups grounded! Utensils grounded!"

"That's an *aye aye, Sir*!"

"Aye aye, Sir!!"

"Louder!"

"Aye aye, Sir!!"

"Eat. Zero-one. As you were. Zero-one. Zero-two. Zero-three. Zero-four. Zero-five. Zero-six. Zero-seven. Zero-eight. Hydrate. Zero-one. Zero-two. Zero-three. Zero-four. Zero-five. Zero-six. Zero-seven. Zero-eight. Zero-niner. One-zero. One-one. One-two."

"Your hydration is of the utmost importance, Indoctrination Candidates! You will remain fully hydrated at all times!"

"That's an *aye aye, Sir*!"

"Aye aye, Sir!!"

"Louder!"

"Aye aye, Sir!!"

"Cups touching! Utensils grounded!"

"Aye aye, Sir!!"

"Louder!"

"Aye aye, Sir!!"

"We still can't hear you!"

"Aye aye, Sir!!"

"Louder!"

"Aye aye, Sir!!"

"Eat. Zero-one. Zero-two. Zero-three. Zero-four. Zero-five. Zero-six. Zero-seven. Zero-eight. As you were. Zero-eight. Hydrate. Zero-one. Zero-two. Zero-three. Zero-four. Zero-five. Zero-six. Zero-seven. Zero-eight. Zero-niner. One-zero. One-one. One-two. Again. Zero-one. Zero-two. Zero-three. Zero-four. Zero-five. Zero-six. Zero-seven. Zero-eight. Zero-niner. One-zero. One-one. One-two."

"Indoctrination Class Zero-Four-Zero-Zero! This is your zero-one minute warning!"

"Aye aye, Sir!!"

"You will finish your plates, Indoctrination Candidates."

"That's an *aye aye, Sir*!"

"Aye aye, Sir!!"

"Louder!"

"Aye aye, Sir!!"

"Those cups will be empty."

"Aye aye, Sir!!"

"Hydrate. Zero-one. Zero-two. Zero-three. Zero-four. Zero-five. Zero-six. Zero-seven. Zero-eight. Zero-niner. One-zero. One-one. One-two. Eat. Zero-one. Zero-two. Zero-three. Zero-four. Zero-five. Zero-six. Zero-seven. Zero-eight. Hydrate. Zero-one. Zero-two. Zero-three. Zero-four. Zero-five. Zero-six. Zero-seven. Zero-eight. Zero-niner. One-zero. One-one. One-two. Eat. Zero-one. Zero-two. Zero-three. Zero-four. Zero-five. Zero-six. Zero-seven. Zero-eight. Hydrate. Zero-one. Zero-two. Zero-three. Zero-four. Zero-five. Zero-six. Zero-seven. Zero-eight. Zero-niner. One-zero. One-one. One-two."

"Indoctrination Class Zero-Four-Zero-Zero, this is your immediate warning!

"Time is up, Indoctrination Candidates. On your feet. Attenhut!"

"Aye aye, Sir!!"

•••

The Chain of Command

Section Leader
Class Chief Petty Officer/Class Drill Instructor
Class Officer
Assistant Operations Officer
Operations Officer
Executive Officer, Officer Training Command
Commanding Officer, Officer Training Command
Commander, Naval Aviation Schools Command
Commander, Naval Education and Training Command
Chief of Naval Operations
Secretary of the Navy
Secretary of Defense
Vice-President of the United States
President of the United States.

••

"Take your seats, Indoctrination Candidates, wargear grounded underneath your desks. Simply because we are not in the ballistic, does not relieve you of the duty of an appropriate response."

"Aye aye, Sir."

"Candidate Lieutenant Michaels is distributing work forms for reimbursement of travel, pay information and your service records. You have no time, Indoctrination Candidates. You will follow the instructions given to a T, filling out each form deliberately, intelligently, and without the slightest error. Is that clear?"

"Yes, Sir."

"Very well. Starting off with the main event. Pay. You will be compensated at the E-Five pay grade via direct deposit. You should have within your possession a personal check. Raise your hand if you are already behind and do

not have a personal check. Good. Void it. Draw a line through the check and write the word *void* in capital letters. This voided check will be attached to the green and white direct deposit form in front of you. We will fill it out together. Is that clear?"

"Yes, Sir."

"In Block Alpha, enter your full name. Last, first, and middle initial. Your address, city, state and zip code. Your telephone number. Be sure that your name is written exactly as it appears on the check, along with your current address, or at least the one on record with your banking institution. Bravo. Name the person entitled to payment. This should be you, or, if you have a spouse, potentially your spouse. Charlie should not apply. Delta is the type of depositor account, either checking or savings. Pick one. Echo. Echo is your depositor account number. This is an eight-digit number, typically the second number on the bottom of your check. You cannot be paid with an incorrect depositor account number. Foxtrot. Check military active duty. Double check your information is without error. Your bank account number. Your routing number. Is this clear?"

"Yes, Sir."

"Next. You reported to Pensacola on orders. As such, you are entitled to certain compensation for reasonable travel expenses. You will find a blank travel voucher located behind the routing forms in your packets. Is anyone unable to locate that voucher?"

"No, Sir."

"How do you know, Indoctrination Candidate?"

"This Indoctrination Candidate does not know but will find out sir."

"Is anyone unable to locate that voucher? Good. Box one. Check electronic funds transfer. Box two. Check P.C.S. Skip box three. Box four. Your name. Last, first and middle initial. Box five. Write your pay grade, which everyone should know now as E-Five. Box six. Your nine-digit, belay my last, niner-digit Social Security number. Box seven. Your O.C.S. address. Prepare to copy."

"Aye aye, Sir."

"Your current address is *Naval Aviation Schools Command, one-eight-one Chambers Avenue, Pensacola, Florida.* Area code *three-two-five-zero-eight dash five-two-two-one.* Telephone number *eight-five-zero four-five-two three-one-eight-one.* Is there anyone that needs this repeated?"

"Yes, Sir."

"Very well. Naval Aviation Schools Command, one-eight-one Chambers Avenue, Pensacola, Florida. Area code three-two-five-zero-eight dash five-two-two-one. Telephone number eight-five-zero four-five-two three-one-eight-one. Skip boxes eight through ten. Box eleven. Your organization. Your organization is *Naval Air Station Training Command Pensacola, Florida.* Draw a diagonal line through boxes twelve, thirteen, and fourteen. Is anyone not still with me? A

mistake now will make life more difficult later. Yours and ours. Good. Pay attention. Listen carefully to my directions prior to completing the follow-on section."

"Aye aye, Sir."

"Box fifteen relates to the means by which you travelled between your residence and Officer Candidate School. For fifteen Alpha you will all put down *niner-niner.*"

"Aye aye, Sir."

"Underneath niner-niner, you will write the date that you departed from your residence or prior duty station in the form of a three letter abbreviation for the month of August. A.U.G. Alpha. Uniform. Golf. For example, if you departed from your home on August eighteenth, write *Alpha Uniform Golf one-eight.* Everyone got it?"

"Yes, Sir."

"How do you know? Is anyone not clear on this? Good. Fifteen Bravo. The local time of departure as a function of the Twenty-Four Hundred clock. For example, if you departed your residence at eight a.m., write *Zero-Eight Hundred.* If you departed at two p.m., write *Fourteen Hundred.* Write *residence* for place, listing your city and state. Ears."

"Open, Sir."

"Next step. For fifteen Delta, means or mode of travel, there are two modes of travel. Commercial or personal. Starting with commercial travelers, the commercial travelers only, those among you who did not come here by personal vehicle, who traveled to Pensacola on an airplane, by bus, or by train. You likely took a taxi cab to the airport, bus station or train station. If you did, write *C.A.*, Charlie Alpha. If you did not, if you were dropped off at the airport by family or friends, boyfriend or girlfriend, write *P.A.*, Papa Alpha. Returning to the date column, enter the date you arrived at the airport, bus station or train station. This should match the date you departed from your residence. Write the time you arrived. If you traveled by commercial air, write *airport* and the city you departed from. If you took a bus, write *bus station* and the city you departed from. If you took a train, write *train station* and the city you departed from. Any questions? Very well. Moving over to block Echo, reason for stop, write *A.T.*, Alpha Tango. In the diagonal, one block down, returning to means or mode of travel, for commercial air, write *C.P.*, Charlie Papa. For commercial bus, write *C.B.*, Charlie Bravo. For commercial rail, write *C.R.*, Charlie Romeo. Now, to complete the row, write the time you departed. Is anyone confused or lost? Yes."

"Sir, Indoctrination Candidate Orton, Officer Candidate School, Indoctrination Class Zero-Four-Zero-Zero, United States Navy, requests permission to speak to Class Indoctrination Commander, Candidate Commander Monroe, United States Navy."

"Granted."

"Sir, what was block Echo again?"

"Alpha Tango. Anyone else? Very well. Now move back to the date column and write the date you arrived in Pensacola, identical as above. The same rules apply. Write the time. Write *airport, bus station* or *train station, Pensacola, Florida.* For block Echo, once again, write *A.T.*, Alpha Tango. Write the local time you departed from the airport or station. If you took a taxi, for means or mode of travel, write *C.A.*, Charlie Alpha. If a friend or family member picked you up, write *P.A.*, Papa Alpha. Everyone still follow? Very well. For your last step, moving back to the date column, copy the date of travel from the row above. Write the hour you reported to the quarterdeck and got your orders stamped. List *Naval Aviation Schools Command Pensacola* for the place. And *M.C.*, Mike Charlie, in block Echo. Mission complete. Ears."

"Open, Sir."

"Break. Break. Now, for the second group, those of you who drove to Pensacola, who traveled by privately owned conveyance, your turn. Ready? Good. In the first row of section fifteen, under means or mode of travel, write *P.A.*, Papa Alpha. Or, maybe, for those of you Poopie Rockstars, if any, who showed up on a motorcycle, write *P.M.*, Papa Mike. Row-two now. For those of you who arrived at N.A.S. Pensacola the day of departure, write that date, the local time and *Naval Aviation Schools Command Pensacola* for the place. And in block Echo, write *M.C.*, Mike Charlie. For those of you who were authorized to overnight en route, write the date and local time of arrival, the city and state where you overnighted. Reason for stop is *A.D.*, Alpha Delta. Means of travel is again Papa Alpha or Papa Mike as appropriate. Next line. Repeat as necessary. For the last leg of your trip, when you arrived in Pensacola, put the date, local time, *Naval Aviation Schools Command Pensacola* as the final destination, and give it the Mike Charlie. Does anyone have any questions?"

"Sir, Indoctrination Candidate Thurman, Officer Candidate School, Indoctrination Class Zero-Four-Zero-Zero, United States Navy, requests permission to speak to Class Indoctrination Commander, Candidate Commander Monroe, United States Navy."

"Granted."

"This Indoctrination Candidate requests permission to go to the Head."

"Raise your hand if you need to use the Head. Very well. Groups of five. Candidate Officer Jefferies will show you the way."

"*Aye aye, Sir.*"

"Aye aye, Sir."

"Courtesy extends to the civilian staff. Is that clear?"

"Yes, Sir."

"We'll restart the problem and clock in zero-five minutes. I'll field questions in the meantime. Remember to spread the gouge."

"Aye aye, Sir."

"Yes."

"Sir, Indoctrination Candidate Siegel, Officer Candidate School, Indoctrination Class Zero-Four-Zero-Zero, United States Navy, requests permission to speak to Class Indoctrination Commander, Candidate Commander Monroe, United States Navy."

"Granted."

"Sir, base security said we would need a permit for long-term parking."

"That is correct. P.O.V. passes will be distributed on Tuesday, if you make it that far, with proof of insurance and P.O.V. registration. Your P.O.Vs are secure. Yes."

"Sir, Indoctrination Candidate Jackson, Officer Candidate School, Indoctrination Class Zero-Four-Zero-Zero, United States Navy, requests permission to speak to Class Indoctrination Commander, Candidate Commander Monroe, United States Navy."

"Granted."

"Sir, will confiscated personal items be returned?"

"Yes, all contraband items have been bagged and tagged. They will be returned to you at the completion of training. Think getting out of prison. Yes."

"Sir, Indoctrination Candidate Tronstein, Officer Candidate School, Indoctrination Class Zero-Four-Zero-Zero, United States Navy, requests permission to speak to Class Indoctrination Commander, Candidate Commander Monroe, United States Navy."

"Granted."

"Sir, when will we be permitted to make phone calls?"

"You received an opportunity to make a zero-five minute phone call on arrival. You will be notified of follow-on opportunities as appropriate. Yes."

"Indoctrination Candidate Sumarian, Officer Candidate School, Indoctrination Class Zero-Four-Zero-Zero, United States Navy, requests permission to speak to Class Indoctrination Commander, Candidate Commander Monroe, United States Navy."

"Permission granted."

"Sir, may we send and receive letters?"

"You may. You have a letter you want to send?"

"No, Sir."

"Any and all mail received at Officer Candidate School during Indoctrination is sorted, secured and held pending your first mail call. You will be issued official stationary for any correspondence you may wish to send. Your duly elected

Mailbody will handle collection and distribution duties when appropriate. Was anyone here not given notice of the O.C.S. mailing address prior to travel?"

"Yes, Sir."

"Very well. Prepare to copy."

"That's an *aye aye, Sir.*"

"Aye aye, Sir."

"Copy. *Oscar Charlie your name, Officer Candidate School, Class Zero-Four-Zero-Zero, Officer Training Command Pensacola, one-five-zero Chambers Avenue, Suite Charlie, N.A.S. Pensacola, Florida three-two-five-zero-eight dash five-two-six-seven.* In case of emergency, family or next of kin may also reach out by calling *eight-five-zero four-five-two three-four-one-six* or *eight-five-zero four-five-two two-six-eight-zero.* In the event of a death or medical emergency, D.O.D. regulations also require that notice be given through a local chapter of the Red Cross. Does that answer your question?"

"Yes, Sir."

"In the back."

"Indoctrination Candidate Chu, Officer Candidate School, Indoctrination Class Zero-Four-Zero-Zero, United States Navy, requests permission to speak to Class Indoctrination Commander, Candidate Commander Monroe, United States Navy."

"Granted."

"Sir, this Indoctrination Candidate was told that it would be possible to fill prescriptions at Officer Candidate School."

"That is correct. You will have an opportunity to fill prescriptions during your medical screening. If you have not done so already, declare all prescriptions. All other medications are considered contraband and will be treated as such. Possession of contraband is grounds for rolling out of your class or worse. Am I clear?"

"Yes, Sir."

"Which reminds me of safety. If you are sick, let us know. I repeat. Let us know. Given the heat index, you will likely be operating under Black Flag conditions. If you feel at risk, do not hesitate to call a Training Time Out. If you are med down, be it from a cold or shin splints, you require medical attention. The sooner you receive medical attention, the sooner you will return to med-up status and resume training. Every effort will be made to return you to your Class. Just be sure to remember the difference between a Commando who heads to sick bay and a Sick Bay Commando. You entered as a member of Class Zero-Four-Zero-Zero. Graduating as a member of Class Zero-Four-Zero-Zero is in your interest. Won't mean a thing for your military career, but you may, however, be reminded of the decisions you make now when reminiscing about the great times at O.C.S. at the O Club down the road. Additional questions? Very well. Candidate Officer Jefferies, how are we looking on bodies?"

"All present, all accounted for, Indoctrination Commander."

"Very well. Ears."

"Open, Sir."

"Lock it up."

"Aye aye, Sir."

"A Field Service Record is maintained for each Officer of the Navy. Your *F.S.R.* This record will follow you throughout your naval careers, from admin office to admin office, available to assist your Commanding Officer in making personnel decisions. You have a duty to ensure that your documents are duly maintained and properly organized at all times. You will create, maintain, use and dispose of this record with the proper care. Is that clear?"

"Yes, Sir."

"Rest assured that the inviolability of naval personnel records and the information contained therein has long been recognized by the Navy in view of the confidential nature of such records. The release of information is sharply restricted and rigidly controlled, except that information that each Officer has specifically approved for release for publicity purposes as part the Officer Biography Sheet in your packets. S.F.R. information may not be otherwise divulged, nor may access to the record be granted, except to the persons properly and directly concerned. Is that clear?"

"Yes, Sir."

"In the same spirit, adverse information cannot be filed in your F.S.R. unless you have an opportunity to review that material and submit a statement concerning it. You can decline the opportunity to make a statement, but that declination will have to be signed and dated and entered into the F.S.R. Is that clear?"

"Yes, Sir."

"Take it from a former P.N., come ten years time, when up for review, this record will reflect directly on your military service as an Officer. An incomplete or poorly executed service record is a sorry way to sink a career. Is that clear?"

"Yes, Sir."

"With that understanding, we will proceed page by page and block by block. If you do not find a particular form in your record, raise your hand and a Candidate Officer will assist you. If you make an error and the error is small, simply cross out the error and initial. If the error is large, and it starts to get ugly, raise your hand. Is that clear?"

"Yes, Sir."

"Do it right. Do it once. Let's begin. On the right side of your F.S.R. you will find Administrative Remarks in reference to your military orders. No action is required. Behind your Administrative Remarks will find a history of your military assignments. You will see your current assignment, *N.A.S. Pensacola Officer*

Candidate School, completed for you. For you Priors out there, whether you reported directly or decided it wasn't so bad after all, list your previous commands. Next you will find your Officer Data Card, reflecting your current status as a member active duty of the U.S. Navy. The O.D.C. provides up to date information to be considered for detailing and selection boards. If the name of your undergraduate institution and course of study are not listed, list them now."

"Aye aye, Sir."

"Is anyone not finished up with the O.D.Cs? Very well. Your Officer Qualifications form. If you have prior military experience, list it now. For civilians, list any skills or experience you think might be of interest to the Navy. Languages. Training. Specializations. E.S.P. Upon receiving your commission, should you receive your commission, these qualifications will be forwarded to BUPERS. Now is the time to brag. Is everyone complete with this section?"

"No, Sir."

"Impressive. How about now?"

"Yes, Sir."

"Next. Your Dependency Status Action. For those of you with dependents, please review these forms for accuracy. If you have claimed a spouse, child, step-child or parent at your naval recruiting station, please ensure that the information accurately reflects your current domestic situation. Anyone unclear as to what a dependent is? Very well. Moving on, you will find your Serviceman's Group Life Insurance election, S.G.L.I., and certification. Participation is highly encouraged. This is one of the better benefits in the Service. And something you want to take full advantage in this line of work. At the top left-hand corner of the form, you have three choices. *Name, change or update your beneficiary. Reduce the amount of your insurance.* Or *decline insurance coverage.* If you wish to take advantage of this excellent military benefit, check name, change or update your beneficiary. Write your last name, first name and middle name in the designated block. Your rank, title or grade. Which is?"

"E-Five, Sir."

"Your Social Security number. Your branch of service, do not abbreviate, is the *United States Navy*. Your current duty location. *N.A.S. Pensacola Officer Candidate Schoo*l. If you name more than one principal beneficiary and one or more predecease you, the shares will be divided equally among the remaining principal beneficiaries. If there are no surviving principal beneficiaries, the proceeds will be divided among the contingent beneficiaries. Select your beneficiaries now. List the complete name, first, middle and last and address of each beneficiary. The Social Security number, if known, or each beneficiary, relationship to you and share to each beneficiary. You also have a payment option as a lump sum or thirty-six equal monthly payments. Choose one. If you wish to insure yourself for less, please state that amount in a numeral of ten

thousand dollars. Your contribution will be prorated to that amount. If you do not wish to take advantage of S.G.L.I., do not want any insurance, check decline insurance coverage and write *I do not want insurance at this time.* You'll have another shot to sign up before graduation if you want to think about it. Is that clear?"

"Yes, Sir."

"Good. Next form. Should you die in the line of duty, you will want to have an accurate Record of Emergency Data, known as your Page Two. Complete your Page Twos without error or omission."

"Aye aye, Sir."

"Part one serves as an application for dependent allowances and is used to capture military spouse data. Part two provides an immediately accessible, up to date Record of Emergency Data and is the official document used to determine the person or persons to be notified in case of emergency or death, the person or persons to receive the death gratuity when no spouse or child exists, the person or persons to receive unpaid pay and allowances including money accrued during missing or captured status, unused leave, travel, per diem, transportation of family members, transportation of household goods and savings deposits found due from the Department of the Navy, dependents to receive allotment of pay if you are missing or unable to transmit funds, commercial insurance companies to be notified in case of death, and as a screen for your S.G.L.I. designation. Begin filling out your Page Twos now."

"Aye aye, Sir."

"In box one, for Unit I.D., enter the O.C.S. P.S.D. five-digit Unit Identification Code. *Three-zero-five-zero-zero.* Your UIC. For block two, ship or station, enter *Naval Aviation Schools Command Pensacola, Florida.* Leave three and four blank. For five, enter the name, if any, of your spouse. If you do not have a spouse, leave the box blank. Enter your spouse's date of birth in the following format. Day. First three letters of the birth month. And last two digits of the year. For example, if your spouse was born on October twelfth, Nineteen-Seventy-Four, you will write one-two, O.C.T., Oscar Charlie Tango, seven-four. You will follow this format for the remainder of your naval careers. Avoids confusion. Am I clear?"

"Yes, Sir."

"Your relationship to your spouse is either husband or wife. Box eight. Enter the place of marriage, city and state. Box niner. Date of marriage. Day. Month. Year. Citizenship of your spouse. If carrying dual citizenship, include both. And current address. If in transition, list your permanent address. Boxes thirteen through sixteen. Information about dependents. If you have a child, if you have a step-child, if you claim a person other than yourself on your tax form, you have a dependent. Enter the name of your dependent, date of birth, relationship. For

box seventeen, answer yes or no. Repeat as necessary. Take your time. This is important. Get it right."

"Aye aye, Sir."

"Everyone squared away? Great. Box thirty-three. The name of the father. If you are the father, write your name. If you are not the father, write the father's name. Write the address of the father. If you do not know the address of the father, write your own address, and be sure to update your Page Two at your follow-on command. Write the name and address of the mother. Box thirty-niner. Were you previously married? Yes or no. How did that marriage end? Death. Annulment. Divorce. When did it end? Where did it end? Was that spouse previously married? How did that marriage end? When did that marriage end? Where did that marriage end? Navy wants to know. Box forty-seven. Other. In case of. Your next of kin. Your sister. Your brother. Your aunt or uncle. Your mother. Your best friend growing up. Other. Just in case. The next of kin of your spouse, other than any child. Their address. The relationship to your spouse. Box fifty-three. Beneficiary or beneficiaries for unpaid pay and allowances. Address. Relationship. Percent. Select accordingly. Box fifty-seven. Person to receive your allotment if in a missing in action status. Box sixty. Beneficiary or beneficiaries for gratuity pay. Box sixty-four. If you have other life insurance policies outside S.G.L.I. Box sixty-seven. Your religion. Sixty-eight to seventy-seven. Associated special considerations the Navy should be aware of in case of death. Your rank. Which is?"

"E-Five, Sir."

"Name of designator. You. Your Social. Location of your will or other valuable papers in case of emergency. Be specific. And finally, any remarks, special requests or considerations. Sign and date. Does anyone have any questions? Take your time on this one."

"Aye aye, Sir."

••

The Sailor's Creed

I am a United States Sailor. I will support and defend the Constitution of the United States of America and I will obey the orders of those appointed over me. I represent the fighting spirit of the Navy and those who have gone before me to defend freedom and democracy around the world. I proudly serve my country's Navy combat team with honor, courage and commitment. I am committed to excellence and the fair treatment of all.

••

"Indoctrination Class Zero-Four-Zero-Zero! Upon receiving the command of execution *march*! You will! Make an immediate right face, march down this passageway, down the inside ladderwell, and line up against the bulkhead, single file in the passageway below! Is that clear?"

"Yes, Sir!!"

"Sound off!"

"Yes, Sir!!"

"We want to feel these bulkheads, Indoctrination Candidates!"

"Aye aye, Sir!!"

"We want to see them move!'

"Aye aye, Sir!!"

"Louder!"

"Aye aye, Sir!!"

"Better. Class Zero-Four-Zero-Zero! Ready! March!"

"Aye aye, Sir!! Left-right!!"

"Good morning, Sir!"

"Left-right!! Left-right!!"

"Good morning, Sir!"

"Let's go! Let's go! Let's go! You have no time, Indoctrination Candidates!"

"Aye aye, Sir!!"

"Use the handrails, Indoctrination Candidates! Your safety is the number-one priority!"

"Aye aye, Sir!!"

"Let's go! Let's go! Let's go!"

"Aye aye, Sir!! Left-right!! Left-right!! Left-right!! Left-right!! Left-right!! Left-right!! Left-right!! Left-right!! Left-right!! Left-right!! Left-right!! Left-right!! Left-right!! Left-right!! Left-right!! Left-right!! Left-right!! Left-right!!"

"Good morning, Sir!"

"Left-right!! Left-right!!"

"Good morning, Sir!"

"You have no time, Indoctrination Candidates!"

"Aye aye, Sir!!"

"Line it up, Poopies! Line it up!"

"That's a response!"

"Aye aye, Sir!!"

"What the heck do you think you're doing?"

"No excuse, Sir!"

"Line it up! Line it up!"

"Aye aye, Sir!!"

"Zero-four inches from the bulkhead!"

"Aye aye, Sir!!"

"You have no time, Indoctrination Candidates!"

"That's an *aye aye, Sir*!"

"Aye aye, Sir!! Left-right!! Left-right!! Left-right!! Left-right!! Left-right!! Left-right!! Left-right!! Left-right!! Left-right!! Left-right!!"

"Cadence, Indoctrination Class Zero-Four-Zero-Zero!"

"Aye aye, Sir!!"

"Louder!"

"Aye aye, Sir!! Left-right!!"

"Freeze!"

"Aye aye, Sir!!"

"Ears!"

"Open, Sir!!"

"Indoctrination Class Zero-Four-Zero-Zero! Upon receiving the command of execution *go*! You will! Proceed in groups of four down the passageway, starboard side, and reform at the first hatch! Am I clear?"

"Yes, Sir!!"

"You will take a thirty-inch step, halt, and face! You will raise your right arm and rap zero-three times on the frame! You will stand-by until you are called onto the deck! You will enter directly, give the greeting of the day, and square yourself twelve to eighteen inches from the armory window! You will give your name and *report for rifle issue* as *ordered*! Is that clear?"

"Yes, Sir!!"

"Ready! Groups of four! Starboard side! Go!"

"Aye aye, Sir!!"

"Let's see that brass!"

"Aye aye, Sir!!"

"Heat and friction! Heat and friction!"

"That's an *aye aye, Sir*!"

"Aye aye, Sir!!"

"Where's my Gougebody?"

"Gougebody, aye aye, Sir!"

"Very well. Gouge the class!"

"Aye aye, Sir! Indoctrination Class Zero-Four-Zero-Zero! The first article of the Code of Conduct is! *I am an American*! *fighting in the forces which guard my country and our way of life*! *I am prepared to give my life in their defense*!"

"As you were, Gougebody. From the top, now in manageable lengths."

"Aye aye, Sir! Indoctrination Class Zero-Four-Zero-Zero! *The first article of the Code of Conduct is*! *I am an American*! *Fighting in the forces which guard my country and our way of life*!"

"Aye aye, Gougebody!! The first article of the Code of Conduct is!! I am an American!! Fighting in the forces which guard my country and our way of life!!"

"*I am prepared to give my life in their defense*!"

"I am prepared to give my life in their defense!!"

"Indoctrination Class Zero-Four-Zero-Zero! The second article of the Code of Conduct is! *I will never surrender of my own free will*!"

"Aye aye, Gougebody!! The second article of the Code of Conduct is!! I will never surrender of my own free will!!"

"*If in command*! *I will never surrender the members of my command while they still have the means to resist*!"

"If in command!! I will never surrender the members of my command while they still have the means to resist!!"

"Heat and friction, Indoctrination Candidates! Heat and friction!"

"Aye aye, Sir!!"

"Indoctrination Class Zero-Four-Zero-Zero! The third article of the Code of Conduct is! *If I am captured! I will continue to resist by all means available!*"

"Aye aye, Gougebody!! The third article of the Code of Conduct is!! If I am captured!! I will continue to resist by all means available!!"

"*I will make every effort to escape and aid others to escape!*"

"I will make every effort to escape and aid others to escape!!"

"*I will accept neither parole nor special favors from the enemy!*"

"I will accept neither parole nor special favors from the enemy!!"

"Indoctrination Class Zero-Four-Zero-Zero! The fourth article of the Code of Conduct is! *If I become a prisoner of war! I will keep faith with my fellow prisoners!*"

"Aye aye, Gougebody!! The fourth article of the Code of Conduct is!! If I become a prisoner of war!! I will keep faith with my fellow prisoners!!"

"*I will give no information nor take part in any action which might be harmful to my comrades!*"

"I will give no information nor take part in any action which might be harmful to my comrades!!"

"*If I am senior! I will take command! If not! I will obey the lawful orders of those appointed over me! And will back them up in every way!*"

"If I am senior!! I will take command!! If not!! I will obey the lawful orders of those appointed over me!! And will back them up in every way!!"

"Louder!"

"Aye aye, Sir!!"

"Heat and friction!"

"Aye aye, Sir!!"

"We want to see that shine!"

"Aye aye, Sir!!"

"If you don't see shine, you are behind!"

"Aye aye, Sir!!"

"Indoctrination Class Zero-Four-Zero-Zero! The fifth article of the Code of Conduct is! *When questioned! Should I become a prisoner of war! I am required to give name! Rank! Service number and date of birth!*"

"Aye aye, Gougebody!! The fifth article of the Code of Conduct is!! When questioned!! Should I become a prisoner of war!! I am required to give name!! Rank!! Service number and date of birth!!"

"*I will evade answering further questions to the utmost of my ability!*"

"I will evade answering further questions to the utmost of my ability!!"

"*I will make no oral or written statements disloyal to my country and its allies or harmful to their cause!*"

"I will make no oral or written statements disloyal to my country and its allies or harmful to their cause!!"

"Indoctrination Class Zero-Four-Zero-Zero! The sixth article of the Code of Conduct is! *I will never forget that I am an American*! *Fighting for freedom*! *Responsible for my actions*! *And dedicated to the principles which made my country free*!"

"Aye aye, Gougebody!! The sixth article of the Code of Conduct is!! I will never forget that I am an American!! Fighting for freedom!! Responsible for my actions!! And dedicated to the principles which made my country free!!"

"*I will trust in my God and in the United States of America*!"

"I will trust in my God and in the United States of America!!"

"General Orders of a Sentry, Gougebody!"

"Aye aye, Sir! Indoctrination Class Zero-Four-Zero-Zero! The first General Order of a Sentry is! *To take charge of this post and all government property in view*!"

"Aye aye, Gougebody!! The first General Order of a Sentry is!! To take charge of this post and all government property in view!!"

"Indoctrination Class Zero-Four-Zero-Zero! The second General Order of a Sentry is! *To walk my post in a military manner*! *Keeping always on the alert*! *And observing everything that takes place within sight or hearing*!"

"Aye aye, Gougebody!! The second General Order of a Sentry is!! To walk my post in a military manner!! Keeping always on the alert!! And observing everything that takes place within sight or hearing!!"

"Heat and friction, Indoctrination Candidates! Heat and friction!"

"Aye aye, Sir!!"

"Indoctrination Class Zero-Four-Zero-Zero! The third General Order of a Sentry is! *To report all violations of orders I am instructed to enforce*!"

"Aye aye, Gougebody!! The third General Order of a Sentry is!! To report all violations of orders I am instructed to enforce!!"

"Indoctrination Class Zero-Four-Zero-Zero! The fourth General Order of a Sentry is! *To repeat all calls from posts more distant from the guardhouse than my own*!"

"Aye aye, Gougebody!! The fourth General Order of a Sentry is!! To repeat all calls from posts more distant from the guardhouse than my own!!"

"Knowledge is verbatim, Indoctrination Candidates! *Aye aye, Sir*!"

"Aye aye, Sir!!"

"Louder!"

"Aye aye, Sir!!"

"Heat and friction!"

"Aye aye, Sir!!"

"Indoctrination Class Zero-Four-Zero-Zero! The fifth General Order of a Sentry is! *To quit my post only when properly relieved*!"

"Aye aye, Gougebody!! The fifth General Order of a Sentry is!! To quit my post only when properly relieved!!"

"Indoctrination Class Zero-Four-Zero-Zero! The sixth General Order of a Sentry is! *To receive*! *Obey*! *And pass on to the sentry who relieves me*!"

"Aye aye, Gougebody!! The sixth General Order of a Sentry is!! To receive!! Obey!! And pass on to the sentry who relieves me!!"

"*All orders from the Commanding Officer! Command Duty Officer! Officer of the Deck! And Officers and Petty Officers of the Watch only!*"

"All orders from the Commanding Officer!! Command Duty Officer!! Officer of the Deck!! And Officers and Petty Officers of the Watch only!!"

"Indoctrination Class Zero-Four-Zero-Zero! The seventh General Order of a Sentry is! *To talk to no one except in the line of duty!*"

"Aye aye, Gougebody!! The seventh General Order of a Sentry is!! To talk to no one except in the line of duty!!"

"Heat and friction!"

"Aye aye, Sir!!"

"Louder!"

"Aye aye, Sir!!"

"Indoctrination Class Zero-Four-Zero-Zero! The eighth General Order of a Sentry is! *To give the alarm in case of fire or disorder!*"

"Aye aye, Gougebody!! The eighth General Order of a Sentry is!! To give the alarm in case of fire or disorder!!"

"Indoctrination Class Zero-Four-Zero-Zero! The ninth General Order of a Sentry is! *To call the Officer of the Deck in any case not covered by instructions!*"

"Aye aye, Gougebody!! The ninth General Order of a Sentry is!! To call the Officer of the Deck in any case not covered by instructions!!"

"You must get louder, Indoctrination Class Zero-Four-Zero-Zero!"

"Aye aye, Sir!!"

"We want to feel these bulkheads!"

"Aye aye, Sir!!"

"We want to see that shine!"

"Aye aye, Sir!!"

"Indoctrination Class Zero-Four-Zero-Zero! The tenth General Order of a Sentry is! *To salute all Officers and all colors and standards not cased!*"

"Sir!! The tenth General Order of a Sentry is!! To salute all Officers and all colors and standards not cased!!"

"Indoctrination Class Zero-Four-Zero-Zero! The eleventh General Order of a Sentry is! *To be especially watchful at night!*"

"Aye aye, Gougebody!! The eleventh General Order of a Sentry is!! To be especially watchful at night!!"

"*And during the time for challenging! To challenge all persons on or near my post! And to allow no one to pass without proper authority!*"

"And during the time for challenging!! To challenge all persons on or near my post!! And to allow no one to pass without proper authority!!"

"You four."

"Aye aye, Sir!!"

"*Left-right-left-right*!"

"Left-right!! Left-right!!"

"Stand-by."

"Aye aye, Sir!!"

"Again!"

"Aye aye, Sir! Indoctrination Class Zero-Four-Zero-Zero! The first General Order of a Sentry is! *To take charge of this post and all government property in view*!"

"Aye aye, Gougebody!! The first General Order of a Sentry is!! To take charge of this post and all government property in view!!"

"Indoctrination Class Zero-Four-Zero-Zero! The second General Order of a Sentry is! *To walk my post in a military manner*! *Keeping always on the alert*! *And observing everything that takes place within sight or hearing*!"

"Aye aye, Gougebody!! The second General Order of a Sentry is!! To walk my post in a military manner!! Keeping always on the alert!! And observing everything that takes place within sight or hearing!!"

"Heat and friction, Indoctrination Candidates! Heat and friction!"

"Aye aye, Sir!!"

"Louder!"

"Aye aye, Sir!!"

"Indoctrination Class Zero-Four-Zero-Zero! The third General Order of a Sentry is! *To report all violations of orders I am instructed to enforce*!"

"Next!"

"Into the hole, Poopie! Into the hole!"

"Aye aye, Sir!"

"Enter."

"Good afternoon, Sir! Indoctrination Candidate Zurich! Officer Candidate School! Indoctrination Class Zero-Four-Zero-Zero! United States Navy! Reporting for rifle issue as ordered, Sir!"

"Louder."

"Aye aye, Sir! Good afternoon, Sir! Indoctrination Candidate Zurich! Officer Candidate School! Indoctrination Class Zero-Four-Zero-Zero! United States Navy! Reporting for rifle issue as ordered, Sir!"

"Step up to the window, Poopie."

"Aye aye, Sir!"

"Thousand yard stare at all times."

"Aye aye, Sir!"

"What's that? I couldn't quite hear you."

"Aye aye, Sir!"

"Well, now. That's more like it. Gentlemen, I think we may have found ourselves a candidate for Adjutant. Ears."

"Open, Sir!"

"Upon receiving the command of execution *go*, you will locate and confirm the seven-digit serial number of your rifle. Ready. Go."

"Aye aye, Sir!"

"We're waiting, Poopie. Ready to copy."

"Aye aye, Sir! This Indoctrination Candidate's --."

"As you were. The serial number will do."

"Aye aye, Sir! Six! Five! Three! Niner! Six! Three! Five! Sir!"

"Again."

"Six! Five! Three! Niner! Six! Three! Five! Sir!"

"Now without looking."

"Aye aye, Sir! Six! Five! Three! Niner! Six! Three! Five! Sir!"

"Put it on repeat."

"Aye aye, Sir! Six! Five! Three! Niner! Six! Three! Five! Six! Five! Three! Niner! Six! Three! Five! Sir! Six! Five! Three! Niner! Six! Three! Five! Three! Niner! Six! Three! Five! Three! Niner! Six! Three! Five! Three! Niner! Six! Three! Five!"

"Very well. As you were. Failure to account for or secure your weapon at all times carries with it serious penalties at Officer Candidate School. Do you understand the words that are coming out of my mouth, Poopie?"

"Yes, Sir!"

"At all times."

"Aye aye, Sir!"

"Louder."

"Aye aye, Sir!"

"You will remember that serial number."

"Aye aye, Sir!"

"Dismissed. About face. Off you go."

"Aye aye, Sir! Good afternoon, Sir!"

"End of the line! Go!"

"Aye aye, Sir! Left-right! "

"Aye aye, Gougebody!! The ninth General Order of a Sentry is!! To call the Officer of the Deck in any case not covered by instructions!!"

"Indoctrination Class Zero-Four-Zero-Zero! The tenth General Order of a Sentry is! *To salute all Officers and all colors and standards not cased*!"

"Aye aye, Gougebody!! The tenth General Order of a Sentry is!! To salute all Officers and all colors and standards not cased!!"

"Indoctrination Class Zero-Four-Zero-Zero! The eleventh General Order of a Sentry is! *To be especially watchful at night*!"

"Aye aye, Gougebody!! The eleventh General Order of a Sentry is!! To be especially watchful at night!!"

"*And during the time for challenging*! *To challenge all persons on or near my post*! *And to allow no one to pass without proper authority*!"

"And during the time for challenging!! To challenge all persons on or near my post!! And to allow no one to pass without proper authority!!"

"Heat and friction, Indoctrination Candidates! Heat and friction!"

"Aye aye, Sir!"

"Again!"

••

Dog Tags

Identification tags are Monel or other adopted metal approximately two inch long by one and one-eighth inch wide and about point-zero-two-five inch thick, finished with rounded corners and smooth edges. A necklace consisting of a twenty-five inch of non-corrosive, nontoxic, and heat-resistant material with a two-point-five inch extension of the same material shall be issued with the tags.

Completed tags shall be made up with one tag suspended by passing the necklace through the hole in the tag and the second tag suspended by passing the necklace extension through the hole in the tag and securing the extension to the necklace. Each tag has a capacity for five lines of type, eighteen spaces to the line, and shall be embossed by a machine provided for that purpose. The following are the contents of each line.

First line. Record the name of the member with last name, first name, and middle initial (e.g., Doe, John R.). When the space in the first line is insufficient, the first line shall contain the last name only. Second line. The first and middle initial is placed on the second line. Third line. Record the military personnel identification number (Social Security number). Fourth line. Record the blood type and R.H. factor. Fifth line. Record the religious preference of the member. Show any religion or faith group designated by the member. If possible, spell out the preference.

••

"Let's go Zero-Four! You have no time! We want to hear those go-slowers coming and going!"

"Coming and going, Indoctrination Candidates! Coming and going!"

"Hey, Poopies. What are you four still doing coking-and-joking in the hole? What's the hold up?"

"No excuse, Sir!!"

"Your class is waiting."

"Aye aye, Sir!!"

"Don't make us come in there. You have no time. Let's go."

"Aye aye, Sir!!"

"Lock check."

"Check."

"Check."

"Hold on. Almost there."

"Attention on deck, Stand-by!"

"Good evening, Sir!!"

"Let me spell it out for you! You have no time! You have no time! Line it up! Get-out-of-the-hole! Out-of-the-hole! Go! Go! Go! Go!"

"Aye aye, Sir!!"

"Go! Go! Go! Go!"

"Good evening, Sir!"

"Step!"

"Step!"

"Go! Go! Go!"

"Aye aye, Sir!! Left-right!! Left-right!! Left-right!! Left-right!! Left-right!! Left-right!! Left-right!! Left-right!! Left-right!! Left-right!! Left-right!! Left-right!!"

"You three! Halt! Stop right there! Get back here! About face! Let's go!"

"Chop-chop. Line it up. Position of attention. Up against the bulkhead."

"Up against the bulkhead! That's an *aye aye, Sir*!"

"Aye aye, Sir!!"

"Zero-four inches! Zero-four inches!"

"Aye aye, Sir!!"

"What's wrong with this picture, Poopie? Well?"

"That's a response! That's a response!"

"This Indoctrination Candidate does not know but will find out, Sir!"

"How many Shipmates do you count?"

"This Indoctrination Candidate does not know but will find out, Sir!"

"Eyeballs, Poopie."

"Snap, Sir!"

"Count them off."

"Aye aye, Sir! Zero-one! Zero-two! Sir!"

"Seems to me you're missing a Shipmate. You're the last in line, where did your buddy go? Huh?"

"Good evening, Sir!"

"Oh. Lost and found? Not so fast, Poopie. Freeze."

"Aye aye, Sir!"

"Back in your hole. You're burning."

"Back in your hole! Back in your hole!"

"Aye aye, Sir! Good evening, Sir!"

"Start screaming, Poopie! You're burning in the hole!"

"That's a response!"

"Aye aye, Sir!"

"Scream!"

"Aye aye, Sir!"

"Burn!"

"Aye aye, Sir!"

"Scream!"

"Aye aye, Sir!"

"Burn!"

"Aye aye, Sir!"

"Louder!"

"Aye aye, Sir!"

"Hello? Hello? I do believe a Four-bar just stepped on deck! Where is his call to attention? His greeting of the day?"

"Attention on deck, Stand-by!"

"Good evening, Sir!!"

"What happened here?"

"Poopie here deep-sixed a Shipmate. Left him burning in the hole. We're investigating how this could have happened."

"Any excuse?"

"Well? Well? A Four-bar is waiting on his response!"

"No excuse, Sir!"

"That simply won't answer the mail under the circumstances, Indoctrination Candidate. You left your Shipmate to die in a hole."

"Tits up! Burning in the hole!"

"Burning in the hole! Burning in the hole!"

"Have to wonder why he wouldn't check on his buddy before leaving the hole."

"Who doesn't check on his buddy, right?"

"Certainly suspicious, Gentlemen. You know, he might be one of those Poopies who spells team with an *I*."

"One of those."

"Let's ask him."

"Hey Poopie. Do you spell team with an *I*?"

"No, Sir!"

"Are you sure?"

"Yes, Sir!"

"Hard to believe."

"Only two teams we know spelled with an *I*. You know who those teams are, Poopie?"

"No, Sir!"

"Team Iran and Team Iraq."

"Those teams ring a bell, Indoctrination Candidate?"

"Yes, Sir!"

"*I* get the feeling you're a Team Iran guy. Am *I* right?"

"That's a response! That's a response!"

"No, Sir!"

"Louder, Indoctrination Candidate."

"Freaking *Aya*tollah! That's a response!"

"No, Sir!"

"Louder!"

"No, Sir!"

"What's the matter with your voice? We can't hear you!"

"No, Sir!"

"Are you sure, now?"

"Yes, Sir!"

"Are you perfectly sure?"

"Yes, Sir!"

"Seems we have ourselves a Saddam junior on our hands, Candidate Lieutenant Commander. Game is up, Indoctrination Candidate. Are you a Uday or a Qusay? Well?"

"That's a response! That's a response!"

"No, Sir!"

"Improper response."

"This Indoctrination Candidate does not know but will find out, Sir!"

"Well now. A Saddam junior. That is bad news."

"There's just no telling sometimes."

"Hello? Hello? A Five-bar just stepped on the deck! Why are you gaffing off your Indoctrination Commander, Poopies?"

"Attention on deck, stand-by!"

"Good evening, Sir!!"

"Louder!"

"Good evening, Sir!!"

"What's going on here, Gentlemen?"

"We've found ourselves a bona fide individual, Indoctrination Commander. A regular Poopie Rockstar."

"A Haley's freaking Comet individual."

"Once every seven-six years."

"What a shame."

"Plays for Team Iraq. Says he's a Saddam Junior. We're still not sure if he's an Uday or a Qusay."

"What's your name, Indoctrination Candidate?"

"This Indoctrination Candidate's name is Indoctrination Candidate Zurich! Officer Candidate School! Indoctrination Class Zero-Four-Zero-Zero! United States Navy! Sir!"

"And what did you do as an individual?"

"This Indoctrination Candidate left Indoctrination Candidate Potts! Officer Candidate School! Indoctrination Class Zero-Four-Zero-Zero! United States Navy! Burning in the hole, Sir!"

"Why would you leave your buddy burning in the hole?"

"No excuse, Sir!"

"A little late for excuses. Listen to him. He's burning in the hole."

"Hello? Hello? I think a Six-bar just stepped on deck!"

"Attention on deck, Stand-by!"

"Good evening, Sir!!"

"Gentlemen, what's this? A Poopie was left burning in the hole?"

"You heard right, Regimental Commander. Burning in the hole."

"Who is responsible for this?"

"This one here. Left him burning in the hole."

"Burning in the hole."

"Indoctrination Candidate, why did you leave your buddy burning in the hole?"

"No excuse, Sir!"

"Your buddy is burning. He's dying in there. Do you understand me?"

"Yes, Sir!"

"Follow me."

"Aye aye, Sir!"

"See him in there?"

"Yes, Sir!"

"You hear him?"

"Yes, Sir!"

"You killed him, Zurich. You killed him. Tell your Shipmate that you killed him."

"Aye aye, Sir! This Indoctrination Candidate killed you!"

"Louder!"

"This Indoctrination Candidate killed you!"

"*Killed you. Left you burning in the hole.*"

"This Indoctrination Candidate killed you! Left you burning in the hole!"

"Louder."

"This Indoctrination Candidate killed you! Left you burning in the hole!"

"Louder!"

"This Indoctrination Candidate killed you! Left you burning in the hole!"

"Hey Crispy! Who told you to stop screaming? You're still dead and you're still burning in the hole!"

"That's a response!"

"Aye aye, Sir!"

"Tell your Shipmate here that you're burning."

"Aye aye, Sir! This Indoctrination Candidate is burning!"

"*Burning. Burning in the hole.*"

"This Indoctrination Candidate is burning! Burning in the hole!"

"Louder."

"This Indoctrination Candidate is burning! Burning in the hole!"

"Louder!"

"This Indoctrination Candidate is burning! Burning in the hole!"

"Now you. Say *bang-bang-bang, you're dead.*"

"Aye aye, Sir! Bang-bang-bang, you're dead!"

"No, point your finger at him."

"Aye aye, Sir!"

"Negative, Indoctrination Candidate. Like a gun."

"Aye aye, Sir!"

"*Bang-bang-bang, you're dead.*"

"Bang-bang-bang, you're dead!"

"*Bang-bang-bang, you're dead.*"

"Bang-bang-bang, you're dead!"

"*Bang-bang-bang, you're dead.*"

"Bang-bang-bang, you're dead!"

"Louder!"

"Bang-bang-bang, you're dead!"

"Keep it going. Now you."

"Aye aye, Sir! This Indoctrination Candidate is burning! Burning in the hole!"

"Bang-bang-bang, you're dead!"

"What about you two? You leave one Shipmate to burn in the hole while another jumps on the grenade?"

"No excuse, Sir!!"

"Pathetic. Jump in anytime."

"Aye aye, Sir!! Bang-bang-bang, you're dead!!"

"This Indoctrination Candidate is burning! Burning in the hole!"

"Bang-bang-bang, you're dead!!"

"This Indoctrination Candidate is burning! Burning in the hole!"

"Bang-bang-bang, you're dead!!"

"This Indoctrination Candidate is burning! Burning in the hole!"

"Bang-bang-bang, you're dead!!"

"This Indoctrination Candidate is burning! Burning in the hole!"

"Bang-bang-bang, you're dead!!"

"This Indoctrination Candidate is burning! Burning in the hole!"

"Bang-bang-bang, you're dead!!"

"As you were."

"Aye aye, Sir!!"

"You don't ever leave a Shipmate behind. Got it?"

"Yes, Sir!!"

"Go back in and get him. Now move. Together."

"Aye aye, Sir!!"

"You heard him! Let's go! Let's go! Let's go!"

"Good evening, Sir!"

"Step!"

"Good evening, Sir!"

"Let's go! Your class is waiting, Indoctrination Candidates!"

"Aye aye, Sir!!"

"Let's go! Let's go! Let's go!"

"Good evening, Sir!"

"Step!"

"Step!"

"Good evening, Sir!"

"*Left-right-left-right!*"

"Left-right!! Left-right!!"

"Your class is waiting, Indoctrination Candidates! Waiting on you!"

"That's a response!"

"Aye aye, Sir!! Left-right!!"

"You have wasted your time and ours, Indoctrination Candidates! You have no time!"

"That's an *aye aye, Sir!*"

"Aye aye, Sir!! Left-right!!"

We rejoin the class at the trail end of the line.

"Indoctrination Class Zero-Four-Zero-Zero! Upon receiving the command of execution *count off*! You will! Count off zero-one to six-two! And give me your super-motivational slogan! Ready! Count off!"

"Aye aye, Sir!!"

"Zero-one!"

"Zero-two!"

"Zero-three!"

"Zero-four!"

"Zero-five!"

"Zero-six!"

"Zero-seven!"

"Zero-eight!"

"Zero-nine."

"One-zero!"

"As you were!"

"That's a response!"

"Aye aye, Sir!!"

"Try it again."

"Aye aye, Sir!!"

"Count off!"

"Aye aye, Sir!!"

"Zero-one!"

"Zero-two!"

"Zero-three!"

"Zero-four!"

"Zero-five!"

"Zero-six!"

"Zero-seven!"

"Zero-eight!"

"Zero-niner."

"One-zero!"

"One-one!"

"One-two!"

"One-three!"

"One-four!"

"One-five!"

"One-six!"

"One-seven!"

"One-eight!"

"One-niner!"

"Two-zero!"

"Two-one!"
"Two-two!"
"Two-three!"
"Two-four!"
"Two-five!"
"Two-six!"
"Two-seven!"
"Two-eight!"
"Two-niner!"
"Three-zero!"
"Three-one!"
"Three-two!"
"Three-three!"
"Three-four!"
"Three-five!"
"Three-six!"
"Three-seven!"
"Three-eight!"
"Three-niner!"
"Four-zero!"
"Four-one!"
"Four-two!"
"Four-three!"
"Four-four!"
"Four-five!"
"Four-six!"
"Four-seven!"
"Four-eight!"
"Four-niner!"
"Five-zero!"
"Five-one!"
"Five-two!"
"Five-three!"
"Five-four!"
"Five-five!"
"Five-six!"
"Five-seven!"
"Five-eight!"
"Five-niner!"
"Six-zero!"
"Six-one!"

"Six-two!"

"Highly motivated!! Truly dedicated!! Indoctrination Candidates, Sir!!"

"Ears!"

"Open, Sir!!"

"He said *ears*!"

"Open, Sir!!"

"Time is a wasting, Indoctrination Candidates! You are too slow! Far-too-slow! Lights-out is approaching! You will not put this class in violation of the O.C.R.!"

"That's a response!"

"Aye aye, Sir!!"

"Louder!"

"Aye aye, Sir!!"

"Louder!"

"Aye aye, Sir!!"

"Louder!"

"Aye aye, Sir!!"

"Indoctrination Class Zero-Four-Zero-Zero! Upon receiving the command of execution *march*! You will! Perform an immediate right face and proceed in single file into the Rainlocker! You will crap! Shave! And shower! You will do so in silence! Is that clear?"

"Yes, Sir!!"

"We want to feel these bulkheads! We want to see them move! Is that clear?"

"Yes, Sir!!"

"Is that clear?"

"Yes, Sir!!"

"Ready! March!"

"Aye aye, Sir!! Left-right!!"

"Good evening, Sir!"

"Left-right!! Left-

right!! Left-right!! Left-right!! Left-right!! Left-right!! Left-right!! Left-right!! Left-right!! Left-right!!"

"Good evening, Sir!"

White undershirts lie atop blue shorts along the wall. Bodies push against each other underneath weak showerheads.

"Christ, never thought I'd be a Ricky again."

"I hear you, Ricky."

"Was betting on a little less Ricky, a little more knife and fork."

"Let me get in there a second, Ricky."

"Sure thing."

"Thanks, man."

"Stand-by for the Rainmaker."

"Not tonight."

"When do you think?"

"Soon enough."

"You won't find any Rainmakers here. This is Devil Dog country."

"I bet they're not so tough."

"Stand-by."

"Why do we hear voices in there, Indoctrination Candidates? You have no time!"

"Lock it up, Rickies. This ain't Basic."

"Roger that, R-POC."

Candidates take turns shaving along rows of sinks. One holds a stack of bloody paper towels to his chin.

"Let's go, Indoctrinations Candidates! You have no time!"

"Time's up! Time's up!"

"You have no more time! Let's go! Let's go! Let's go! Everyone out! Up against the bulkhead!"

"Good evening, Sir!"

"All the way around, Indoctrination Candidates! All the way around!"

"Aye aye, Sir!!"

"You do not cut corners here at Officer Candidate School!"

"That's an *aye aye, Sir*!"

"Aye aye, Sir!!"

"*Left-right-left-right*!"

"Left-right!! Left-

right!! Left-right!! Left-right!! Left-right!! Left-right!! Left-right!! Left-right!! Left-right!! Left-right!!"

"Good evening, Sir!"

"Line it up!"

"That's an *aye aye, Sir*!"

"Aye aye, Sir!!"

"*Left-right-left-right*!"

"Left-right!! Left-right!!"

"Let's go Zero-Four-Zero-Zero! What is taking you so long, Indoctrination Candidates? Line it up!"

"Aye aye, Sir!! Left-right!!"

"Zero-four inches from the bulk-head! Four inches!"

"Aye aye, Sir!! Left-right!!"

"Freeze!"

"Aye aye, Sir!!"

"Indoctrination Class Zero-Four-Zero-Zero! Upon receiving the command of execution *count off*! You will! Count off zero-one to six-two! And give me your super-motivational slogan! Ready! Count off!"

"Aye aye, Sir!!"

"Zero-one!"

"Zero-two!"

"Zero-three!"

"Zero-four!"

"Zero-five!"

"Zero-six!"
"Zero-seven!"
"Zero-eight!"
"Zero-niner!"
"One-zero!"
"One-one!"
"One-two!"
"One-three!"
"One-four!"
"One-five!"
"One-six!"
"One-seven!"
"One-eight!"
"One-niner!"
"Two-zero!"
"Two-one!"
"Two-two!"
"Two-three!"
"Two-four!"
"Two-five!"
"Two-six!"
"Two-seven!"
"Two-eight!"
"Two-niner!"
"Three-zero!"
"Three-one!"
"Three-two!"
"Three-three!"
"Three-four!"
"Three-five!"
"Three-six!"
"Three-seven!"
"Three-eight!"
"Three-niner!"
"Four-zero!"
"Four-one!"
"Four-two!"
"Four-three!"
"Four-four!"
"Four-five!"
"Four-six!"

"Four-seven!"
"Four-eight!"
"Four-niner!"
"Five-zero!"
"Five-one!"
"Five-two!"
"Five-three!"
"Five-four!"
"Five-five!"
"Five-six!"
"Five-seven!"
"Five-eight!"
"Five-niner!"
"Six-zero!"
"Six-one!"
"Six-two!"
"Highly motivated!! Truly dedicated!! Indoctrination Candidates, Sir!!"

"Indoctrination Class Zero-Four-Zero-Zero! Upon receiving the command of execution *move*! You will return to your spaces! Secure all gear! And stand-by for Taps! Is that clear?"

"Yes, Sir!!"

"Louder!"

"Yes, Sir!!"

"Ready! Move!"

"Aye aye, Sir!! Left-right!! Left-right!! Left-right!! Left-right!! Left-right!! Left-right!! Left-right!! Left-right!! Left-right!! Left-right!! Left-right!! Left-right!! Left-right!! Left-right!!"

"Good evening, Sir!"

"Step!"

"Step!"

"Good evening, Sir!"

"Left-right!! Left-right!!"

"Good evening, Sir!"

"Step!"

"Step!"

"Good evening, Sir!"

"Left-right!! Left-right!!"

"Good evening, Sir!"

"Step!"

"Step!"

"Good evening, Sir!"

"Left-right!! Left-right!!"

"Good evening, Sir!"

"Step!"

"Step!"

"Good evening, Sir!"

"Taps! Taps! Lights out! All hands turn in your bunks! Maintain silence about the decks! The smoking lamp is out in all berthing spaces! Taps!"

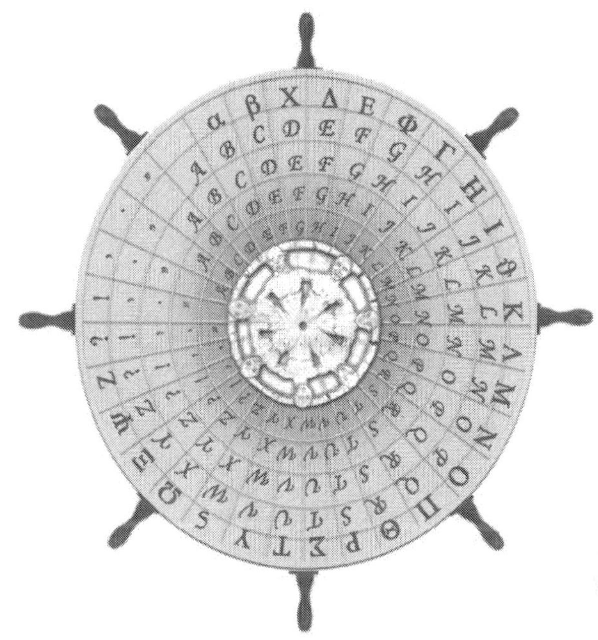

CHAPTER II

WEEK 2

Wood mallets beat hard against aluminum trash can covers.

"Wake up, Indocs! Rise and shine!"

"Wakee-Wakee!"

"Wakee! Wakee!"

"Into your Poopie suits! Into your Poopie suits!"

"Up and at em, Zero-Four-Zero-Zero! Big day today! Big day!"

"Wakee-Wakee!"

"Let's go Indoctrination Class, Zero-Four-Zero-Zero! Let's go! Let's go! Let's go!"

"You need to *go-faster*!

The call comes over the one-M.C.

"Reveille! Reveille! Reveille! All hands heave up and thrice out! Now reveille! The smoking lamp is lighted in all authorized spaces! The Uniform of the Day is as follows! Navy wash khaki uniform wear for all Officer Candidates! With wash khaki cover! Navy working khaki uniform for E-Seven and above! With C.N.T. cover! Carry guidons! Carry flags! Close all outboard windows! Daily exercise will be held on the parade ground! Weather forecast is! Sunny! With a daily low of seven-five degrees Fahrenheit! Daily high of niner-eight degrees Fahrenheit! Visibility of one-zero miles! Niner-zero percent humidity! Wind conditions light! Zero-three miles variable! Arising from the southeast! Black flag conditions are forecasted in the course of the day! Again reveille! Again reveille! Reveille! Reveille! Reveille! All hands heave up and thrice out! Now reveille! The smoking lamp is lighted in all authorized spaces! The Uniform of the Day is as follows! Navy wash khaki uniform wear for all Officer Candidates! With wash khaki cover! Navy working khaki uniform for E-Seven and above! With C.N.T. cover! Carry guidons! Carry flags! Close all outboard windows! Daily exercise will be held on the parade ground! Weather forecast is! Sunny! With a daily low of seven-five degrees Fahrenheit! Daily high of niner-eight degrees Fahrenheit! Visibility of one-zero miles! Niner-zero percent humidity! Wind conditions light! Zero-three miles variable! Arising from the southeast! Black flag conditions are forecasted in the course of the day! Now reveille!"

"Attention on deck! Stand-by!"

"Good morning, Sir!!"

"You have zero-two minutes to strip those racks in accordance with the O.C.R.!"

"Aye aye, Sir!!"

"Attention on deck! Stand-by!"

"Good morning, Sir!!"

"Let's go, Zero-Four-Zero-Zero! You have no time!"

"Strip them down, Poopies! Strip them down!"

"Let's go! Let's go! Let's go!"

"Attention on deck! Stand-by!"

"Good morning, Sir!!"

"You have zero-five minutes to make up these racks in accordance with the O.C.R.!"

"Aye aye, Sir!!"

"Attention on deck! Stand-by!"

"Good morning, Sir!!"

"Should have seen that one coming."

"Yours first this time."

"Works for me."

"You get that side."

"Other way."

"Sure?"

"Moderately."

"No, you're right."

"Yours now."

"Out of your holes! Out of your holes! Zero-Four-Zero-Zero!"

"Let's go, Zero-Four-Zero-Zero! Let's go!"

"Up and at them! Another great Navy day!"

"You have no time, Indoctrination Candidates! You have no time!"

"You need to go-faster!"

"Go-faster, Indoctrination Candidates! Go-faster!"

"You have no time, Indoctrination Candidates! You have no time!"

"Everyone ready?"

"Not there yet."

"Come on, Potts. They're going to rip it up anyway."

"One second. Almost there."

"Let's go, Zero-Four-Zero-Zero! You do not want to be late to the party! Not today!"

"Potts."

"Okay."

"Lock check."

"Check."

"Check."

"Check."

"Clear."

"Here we go. First and last."

"Good morning, Sir!"

"Step!"

"Step!"

"Good morning, Sir!"

"Left-right!! Left-right!!"

Candidates pour into the P-way.

"Good morning, Sir!"

"Step!"

"Step!"

"Good morning, Sir!"

"Left-right!! Left-right!!"

"We can't hear you!"

"Aye aye, Sir!! Left-right!! Left-right!! Left-right!! Left-right!! Left-right!! Left-right!! Left-right!! Left-right!! Left-right!! Left-right!!"

"Good morning, Sir!"

"Step!"

"Step!"

"Good morning, Sir!"

"Left-right!! Left-right!!"

"Good morning, Sir!"

"Step!"

"Step!"

"Good morning, Sir!"

"Left-right!! Left-right!! Left-right!! Left-right!! Left-right!! Left-right!! Left-right!! Left-right!! Left-right!! Left-right!! Left-right!!"

"Line it up, Poopies!"

"Aye aye, Sir!!"

"We can't hear you!"

"Aye aye, Sir!!"

"You have no time, Indoctrination Candidates!"

"Aye aye, Sir!!"

"*Left-right-left-right!*"

"Left-right!! Left-right!! Left-right!! Left-right!! Left-right!! Left-right!! Left-right!! Left-right!! Left-right!! Left-right!! Left-right!! Left-right!! Left-right!! Left-right!! Left-right!! Left-right!! Left-right!!"

"Good morning, Sir!"

"Step!"

"Step!"

"Good morning, Sir!"

"Let's go Zero-Four-Zero-Zero! What's taking you so long, Indoctrination Candidates? Line it up! You have no time!"

"Aye aye, Sir!!"

"Go! Go! Go!"

"Aye aye, Sir!!"

"Faster! Faster! You have no time, Indoctrination Candidates!"

"Aye aye, Sir!! Left-right!!"

"Line-it-up! Up against the bulkhead now! Zero-four inches!"

"Aye aye, Sir!!"

"Thousand yard stare at all times, Indoctrination Candidates! Thumbs aligned to trouser seams!"

"Aye aye, Sir!!"

"Let's go! Let's go! Let's go! What's taking so long, Indoctrination Candidates? You have no time! Line it up!"

"Aye aye, Sir!! Left-right!! Left-right!! Left-right!! Left-right!! Left-right!! Left-right!! Left-right!! Left-right!! Left-right!! Left-right!! Left-right!! Left-right!! Left-right!!"

"Zero-four inches, Indoctrination Candidates!"

"Aye aye, Sir!! Left-right!!"

"Freeze!"

"Aye aye, Sir!!"

"Indoctrination Class Zero-Four-Zero-Zero! Upon receiving the command of execution *count off!* You will! Count off! And give us your super-motivated slogan! Ready! Count off!"

"Aye aye, Sir!!"

"Zero-one!"

"Zero-two!"

"Zero-three!"

"Zero-four!"

"Zero-five!"

"Zero-six!"

"Zero-seven!"

"Zero-eight!"
"Zero-niner!"
"One-zero!"
"One-one!"
"One-two!"
"One-three!"
"One-four!"
"One-five!"
"One-six!"
"One-seven!"
"One-eight!"
"One-niner!"
"Two-zero!"
"Two-one!"
"Two-two!"
"Two-three!"
"Two-four!"
"Two-five!"
"Two-six!"
"Two-seven!"
"Two-eight!"
"Two-niner!"
"Three-zero!"
"Three-one!"
"Three-two!"
"Three-three!"
"Three-four!"
"Three-five!"
"Three-six!"
"Three-seven!"
"Three-eight!"
"Three-niner!"
"Four-zero!"
"Four-one!"
"Four-two!"
"Four-three!"
"Four-four!"
"Four-five!"
"Four-six!"
"Four-seven!"
"Four-eight!"

"Four-niner!"

"Five-zero!"

"Five-one!"

"Five-two!"

"Five-three!"

"Five-four!"

"Five-five!"

"Five-six!"

"Five-seven!"

"Five-eight!"

"Highly motivated!! Truly dedicated!! Indoctrination Candidates, Sir!!"

The Candidate Officers melt away.

"On your faces! On your faces! Get down! On your faces, you Nasty Pigs! Push! *Aye aye, Sir!*"

"Aye aye, Sir!!"

"Push-ups is a two-count exercise! Starting position is the freaking front leaning rest position! Palms directly beneath the shoulders! Feet together on floor! Back, buttocks and legs straight from head to heels! Am I clear? *Yes, Sir.*"

"Yes, Sir!!"

"Do it now!"

"Aye aye, Sir!!"

"I will count the cadence! You will count the repetitions! That's an *aye aye, Sir*, you Nasty-freaking-Pigs!"

"Aye aye, Sir!!"

"Get your freaking Pig Backs straight! That's a response!"

"Aye aye, Sir!!"

"Stop whispering, Pigs!"

"Aye aye, Sir!!"

"Down! *Aye aye, Sir!*"

"Aye aye, Sir!!"

"I am Officer Candidate Class Zero-Four-Zero-Zero Drill Instructor! Staff Sergeant Willett! United States Marine Corp! You will address me as Officer Candidate Class Zero-Four-Zero-Zero Drill Instructor! Staff Sergeant Willett! United States Marine Corp! Am I clear? *Yes, Sir.*"

"Yes, Sir!!"

"Up! *Zero-one.* Sound off!"

"Zero-one!!"

"I! Along with your Class Chief Petty Officer, Senior Chief Petty Officer Jones! Identified by the red cord over his left shoulder! And your Class Officer! Lieutenant Bryant! Represent your Class Team! Down! *Aye aye, Sir!*"

"Aye aye, Sir!"

"Get your freaking heads up! That's a response!"

"Aye aye, Sir!!"

"My mission is to turn you! Nasty! Pathetic! Lethargic! Indoctrination Candidates! Into United States Naval Officers! Am I clear?"

"Yes, Sir!!"

"Up!"

"Zero-two!!"

"You are entrusted to my care! I will train you to the best of my ability! I will develop you into smartly disciplined! Physically fit! Basic trained Officers! Thoroughly indoctrinated in love of service and country! I will demand of you and demonstrate by my own example! The highest standards of personal conduct! Morality! And professional skill! Am I clear?"

"Yes, Sir!!"

"A commissioned Naval Officer carries himself at all times! With the highest of military virtues! Honor! Courage! Commitment! Respects the Chain of Command! Accepts nothing but the very best! From themselves! And from others! These are the hallmarks of a Military Officer! Am I clear?"

"Yes, Sir!!"

"Louder!"

"Yes, Sir!!"

"Down!"

"Aye aye, Sir!!"

"The discipline and respect-for-authority that you learn here is vital! To respecting! And honoring! Over two hundred years of military tradition! Every person here! Fat! Skinny! Slow! Fast! Can become a Military Officer! Up!"

"Zero-three!!"

"You can expect disciplined military training! Firmness! Fairness! Dignity! And compassion! The same courtesy that we extend to our fellow Marines and Shipmates! Am I clear?"

"Yes, Sir!!"

"Am I clear?"

"Yes, Sir!!"

"Down!"

"Aye aye, Sir!!"

"I have just told you what you can expect of us! This is what we expect of you! You will do everything that you are told to do! Obey orders quickly and willingly! You are expected to give one hundred percent of your person at all times! We have earned our posts as leaders! And will accept nothing less from you! Up!"

"Zero-four!!"

"Down!"

"Aye aye, Sir!!"

"You will honor the uniform that you wear! Conduct yourself with the utmost honesty in everything you do! An Officer never lies! Cheats! Or compromises! You will respect the rights and property of others! An Officer never steals! Is that clear?"

"Yes, Sir!!"

"Up!"

"Zero-five!!"

"Everything here has a meaning! You must remember every lesson! Procedure! And custom you learn here! But above else! You must never quit! Give-up! Some among you will experience fear and wish to D.O.R.! Some will conquer that fear! Others will walk away shamed! Unable to meet the high bar necessary to protect and defend our country! The right to become United States Naval Officers! Down!"

"Aye aye, Sir!!"

"Up!"

"Zero-six!!"

"Your education begins now! The first movement that I will explain and demonstrate is the position of attention! The position of attention is the basic military position from which most other movements are executed! The commands for this movement are the commands of execution *attention* and *fall in*! You will be at the position of attention at all times unless given another command! Am I clear?"

"Yes, Sir!!"

"Down!"

"Aye aye, Sir!!"

"At the position of attention! Your feet are flat on deck! Heels touching! Spread evenly at an angle of forty-five degrees! Your weight distributed evenly between your left and right! Your legs straight but not locked! Hips squared to the front! Midsection in! Chest out! Shoulders square! Am I clear?"

"Yes, Sir!!"

"Up!

"Zero-seven!!"

"Your fingers are extended and joined! Tightly curled! Tight! Am I clear?"

"Yes, Sir!!"

"Am I clear?"

"Yes, Sir!!"

"Down!"

"Aye aye, Sir!!"

"Your thumbs are locked! Cocked! Placed along the seam of the trouser! If wearing a uniform without a trouser seam! There's a freaking imaginary trouser seam that runs down the center of your thigh! You got that?"

"Yes, Sir!!"

"Your nasty palms do not dangle outboard! Your nasty palms are locked! Inboard into your thighs! Your forward knuckles pressed into the thigh! Is that clear?"

"Yes, Sir!!"

"Your chin is lifted! Head and eyes straight to the front! Down!"

"Aye aye, Sir!!"

"Ears! *Open Sir.*"

"Open, Sir!!"

"This is freaking imperative! Your nasty! Disgusting! Mouths are shut! Shut! Do you hear me?"

"Yes, Sir!!"

"If you cannot breathe! You will find some other orifice to breathe through! Your mouths will open only to sound off! Or to sing the cadence at P.T.! Am I perfectly clear?"

"Yes, Sir!!"

"If I see any nasty freaking teeth or nasty freaking little red tongues! Your nasty freaking holes will eat grass! Am I clear?"

"Yes, Sir!!"

"Goddamn-it, am I clear?"

"Yes, Sir!!"

"Up!"

"Zero-eight!!"

"When I give the command of execution *get up on your Nasty Pig Feet!* You will get up on your Nasty Pig Feet! And assume the position of attention! Am I clear?"

"Yes, Sir!!"

"Get up on your Nasty Pig Feet!"

"Aye aye, Sir!!"

"Ground your goddamn thumbs, you! Freaking Moron! Freaking Weirdo!"

"No excuse, Sir!"

"Goddamn right no excuse, Pinhead! Freaking Slime! On your backs! On your backs! All of you! Leg-lifts! *Aye aye, Sir.*"

"Aye aye, Sir!!"

"Leg-lifts is a four-count exercise! Starting position is hands under hips! Legs extended! Feet together six inches above the deck! Six inches! *Aye aye, Sir.*"

"Aye aye, Sir!!"

"First count! Lift both legs together! Second count! Lower legs to starting position! Third count! Bring legs back up! Fourth count! Return legs to starting position! Am I freaking clear?"

"Yes, Sir!!"

"I will count the cadence! You will count the repetitions! Begin! *Aye aye, Sir!*"

"Aye aye, Sir!!"

"One-two-three!"

"Zero-one!!"

"One-two-three!"

"Zero-two!!"

"One-two-three!"

"Zero-three!!"

"One-two-three!"

"Zero-four!!"

"One-two-three!"

"Zero-five!!"

"Legs straight!"

"Aye aye, Sir!!"

"Angle of forty-five degrees!"

"Aye aye, Sir!!"

"Six inches above the deck!"

"Aye aye, Sir!!"

"Sound off!"

"Aye aye, Sir!!"

"One-two-three!"

"Zero-six!!"

"One-two-three!"

"Zero-seven!!"

"One-two-three!"

"Zero-eight!!"

"One-two-three!"

"Zero-niner!!"

"One-two-three!"

"One-zero!!"

"One-two-three!"

"One-one!!"

"One-two-three!"

"One-two!!"

"One-two-three!"

"One-three!!"

"One-two-three!"

"One-four!!"

"One-two-three!"

"One-five!!"

"On your feet! Position of attention! *Aye aye, Sir.*"

"Aye aye, Sir!!"

"On your faces. *Aye aye, Sir*!"

"Aye aye, Sir!!"

"On your feet!"

"Aye aye, Sir!!"

"On your backs!"

"Aye aye, Sir!!"

"On your feet!"

"Aye aye, Sir!!"

"On your faces!"

"Aye aye, Sir!!"

"On your feet!"

"Aye aye, Sir!!"

"On your backs!"

"Aye aye, Sir!!"

"On your feet!"

"Aye aye, Sir!!"

"On your faces!"

"Aye aye, Sir!!"

"On your backs!"

"Aye aye, Sir!!"

"On your feet!"

"Aye aye, Sir!!"

"On your faces!"

"Aye aye, Sir!!"

"On your feet!"

"Aye aye, Sir!!"

"On your backs!"

"Aye aye, Sir!!"

"On your feet!"

"Aye aye, Sir!!"

"On your faces!"

"Aye aye, Sir!!"

"On your backs! On your backs! *Aye aye, Sir*!"

"Aye aye, Sir!!"

"Flutter-kicks! Flutter-kicks is a four-count exercise! Starting position on your Nasty Pig Backs! Hands under hips! Legs extended! Feet together, six inches above the deck! Starting positions! Move! *Aye aye, Sir.*"

"Aye aye, Sir!!"

"Stop whispering to me!"

"Aye aye, Sir!!"

"Six inches! *Aye aye, Sir!*"

"Aye aye, Sir!!"

"Count one! Lift your freaking right leg one and a half feet up from the deck! Count-two! Lift your freaking left leg to same position returning your freaking right leg to the starting position! Count-three! Right freaking leg back up! Left freaking leg down! Count-four! Use your freaking imagination! Clear?"

"Yes, Sir!!"

"You will count the cadence! You will count the repetitions! Begin!"

"Aye aye, Sir!! One-two-three!! Zero-one!! One-two-three!! Zero-two!! One-two-three!! Zero-three!! One-two-three!! Zero-four!! One-two-three!! Zero-five!! One-two-three!! Zero-six!! One-two-three!! Zero-seven!! One-two-three!! Zero-eight!! One-two-three!! Zero-niner!!"

"Legs straight!"

"Aye aye, Sir!! One-two-three!! One-zero!! One-two-three!! One-one!! One-two-three!! One-two!! One-two-three!! One-three!! One-two-three!! One-four!! One-two-three!! One-five!!"

"Donkey kicks! On your faces, you Nasty Things! Move! *Aye aye, Sir!*"

"Aye aye, Sir!"

"Donkey Kicks is a four-count exercise! Starting position is a crouch position! Then you kick like a freaking donkey! Freaking *aye aye, Sir.*"

"Aye aye, Sir!!"

"You will count the cadence! You will count the repetitions! *Aye aye, Sir.*"

"Aye aye, Sir!!"

"Begin!"

"Aye aye, Sir!! One-two-three!! Zero-one!! One-two-three!! Zero-two!! One-two-three!! Zero-three!! One-two-three!! Zero-four!! One-two-three!! Zero-five!! One-two-three!! Zero-six!! One-two-three!! Zero-seven!! One-two-three!! Zero-eight!! One-two-three!! Zero-niner!! One-two-three!! One-zero!! One-two-three!! One-one!! One-two-three!! One-two!! One-two-three!! One-three!! One-two-three!! One-four!! One-two-three!! One-five!!"

"Leg-lifts! Start counting!"

"Aye aye, Sir!! One-two-three!! Zero-one!! One-two-three!! Zero-two!! One-two-three!! Zero-three!! One-two-three!! Zero-four!! One-two-three!! Zero-five!! One-two-three!! Zero-six!! One-two-three!! Zero-seven!! One-two-three!! Zero-eight!! One-two-three!! Zero-niner!! One-two-three!! One-zero!! One-two-three!!

One-one!! One-two-three!! One-two!! One-two-three!! One-three!! One-two-three!! One-four!! One-two-three!! One-five!! One-two-three!! One-six!! One-two-three!! One-seven!! One-two-three!! One-eight!! One-two-three!! One-niner!! One-two-three!! Two-zero!!"

"Up! Up against the bulkhead, Pigs! Up!"

"Aye aye, Sir!!"

"Count off! That's a freaking response!"

"Aye aye, Sir!!"

"Zero-one!"

"Zero-two!"

"Zero-three!"

"Zero-four!"

"Zero-five!"

"Zero-six!"

"Zero-seven!"

"Zero-eight!"

"Zero-niner!"

"One-zero!"

"One-one!"

"One-two!"

"One-three!"

"One-four!"

"One-five!"

"One-six!"

"One-seven!"

"One-eight!"

"One-nine!"

"I don't think so! On your faces! *Aye aye, Sir.*"

"Aye aye, Sir!!"

"I don't think so! On your feet! *Aye aye, Sir.*"

"Aye aye, Sir!!"

"On your faces!"

"Aye aye, Sir!!"

"I don't think so! On your freaking feet!"

"Aye aye, Sir!!"

"On your faces!"

"Aye aye, Sir!!"

"On your feet!"

"Aye aye, Sir!!"

"Count off!"

"Aye aye, Sir!!"

"Zero-one!"
"Zero-two!"
"Zero-three!"
"Zero-four!"
"Zero-five!"
"Zero-six!"
"Zero-seven!"
"Zero-eight!"
"Zero-niner!"
"One-zero!"
"One-one!"
"One-two!"
"One-three!"
"One-four!"
"One-five!"
"One-six!"
"One-seven!"
"One-eight!"
"One-niner!"
"Two-zero!"
"Two-one!"
"Two-two!"
"Two-three!"
"Two-four!"
"Two-five!"
"Two-six!"
"Two-seven!"
"Two-eight!"
"Two-niner!"
"Three-zero!"
"Three-one!"
"Three-two!"
"Three-three!"
"Three-four!"
"Three-five!"
"Three-six!"
"Three-seven!"
"Three-eight!"
"Three-niner!"
"Four-zero!"
"Four-one!"

"Four-two!"
"Four-three!"
"Four-four!"
"Four-five!"
"Four-six!"
"Four-seven!"
"Four-eight!"
"Four-niner!"
"Five-zero!"
"Five-one!"
"Five-two!"
"Five-three!"
"Five-four!"
"Five-five!"
"Five-six!"
"Five-six!"
"Five-seven!"
"Five-eight!"
"Highly motivated!! Truly dedicated!! Indoctrination Candidates, Sir!!"

••

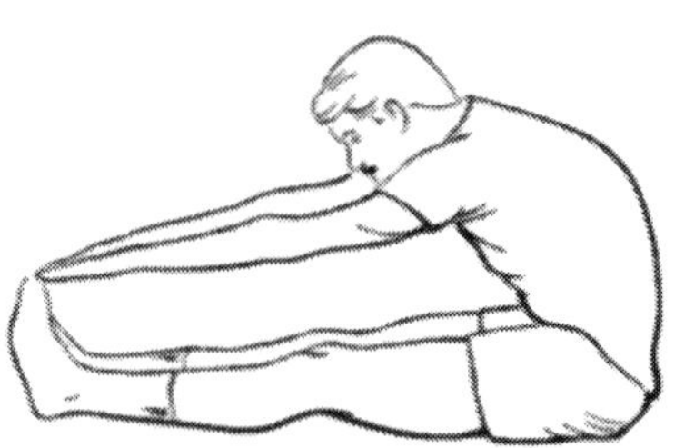

Sit and Reach

Sit on deck, legs extended, knees very slightly flexed. Feet together and toes pointed up. Shoes are optional. Reach slowly forward and touch toes with fingertips of both hands simultaneously. Hold reach for one second. Do not bounce or lunge.

••

"Good morning, Gentlemen. If I may ask you to gather around please. Take a knee up in the front, if you would? There we are. Thank you. Now how's everybody doing this morning?"

"Outstanding, Ma'am."

"I'm sure. Delightful as always. My name is Cynthia Kronke. Please call me Cindy. I am the executive director of your Navy Exchange, the N.E.X., here at N.A.S. Pensacola. Today you will be receiving your basic uniform issue. On Saturday you will receive your tailored wash khaki, Johnny Cash and working white uniforms. Everything you will need to survive your training tests and reviews. Everything. Least if you don't rush in like a bull in a china shop with all that stenciling. Now I want to make one brief comment before we get this show on the road. I need your full attention, okay?"

"Yes, Ma'am."

"I get you all at the beginning. The beginning. I get to stand up here and give the same speech every time. Every time. I talk about the N.E.X., about the quality of our uniforms and how you can find our shops worldwide, on just about every Navy facility. That we are part of a federal non-appropriated funded instrumentality and, as such, a self-supporting command with profits reinvested in your Navy Morale, Welfare and Recreation programs. That we give back seventy percent of the profits generated within the Exchange System. That the remaining thirty percent that we retain goes into maintenance and building new stores. Upkeep. So when you buy N.E.X. products, you support the Navy community. Your community. I say this every time. Ya'll understand?"

"Yes, Ma'am."

"Now in six weeks time, once they shrink you down, you will be measured again for your full uniform sets. And that's when you will also meet some Gentlemen from Abbotts. These Gentlemen will come in with uniform sets, uniforms to touch and feel, talk about the thread count of their polywool khakis, silky service dress blues and gold buttons. Gold buttons. How they have been outfitting the finest Naval Officers for the past fifty years. How they travel up to the Academy to dress the Cadets too. How they keep your measurements on record. How they ship worldwide. How you want to feel first rate. And so on. So forth. As future Navy Officers, you deserve the finest. Really. The Gentlemen from Abbotts have every right. But I can also assure you that the Navy Exchange offers you the finest, most durable uniforms khakis, dress whites and dress blues, that the Navy, your Navy, has to offer. I say this every time. Without question. You choose how you please. So that is that. Don't say I didn't warn you. Okay?"

"Yes, Ma'am."

"Good. Now there are four stations. One with Mister Roberts. One with Mister James. One with Miss Wilson. One with Mister Benoit. Please organize yourself in lines of equal length, rotating clockwise between stations. Pick a spot.

Start building a pile. Once you have collected all your gear, please see me on how to pack your Sea Bags. That's the hard part. Thank you, everyone. Off you go."

"Over here, Gentlemen. Line up to the right please. Thank you. First up. Name."

"Morris, Sir."

"Morris, Franklin. Here we are. Alright, let's get her started. Two sea bags. To add. Nail scissors. One pair. Black pens, two packs. Memo pad. Watch cap. Ball cap. Ear muffs. Six pack athletic socks. Wash clothes. One. Two. Shower towels. One. Two. Men's black gloves. One pair. P.T. shorts. One, two and three. Sweatpants. Two pairs. One pair shower shoes. P.T. shirts, large. Three pairs. Sweatshirts. Two. Undershirts. Twin packs. Skivvies. Two packs. O.C.S. kit. Shirt stays white, black. Garrison devices. Two. And your soft shoulder boards. There you are. Take a look and please sign or initial on the dotted line. Thank you. Next. Name."

"Jackson, Sir."

"Jackson, Christopher. How you doing today, Mister Jackson?"

"Good, Sir. How about yourself?"

"Just fine, son. Alright, let's see. Two sea bags. And for the goodies. One pair nail scissors. Black pens. Two packs. Memo pad. Watch cap. Ball cap. Ear muffs. Six pack of athletic socks. Wash cloth. One. Two. Towels. One and two. Men's black gloves. One pair. P.T. shorts. Three pairs. Sweatpants. Two pairs. Shower shoes. P.T. shirts. Large. Three pairs. Sweatshirts. Two. Undershirts and skivvies. Two packs each. One O.C.S. kit. Shirt stays white, black. Two garrison devices. Soft shoulder boards. That should do her. Sign or initial. Dotted line."

"Thanks, Sir."

"Next. Name."

"Nastor Potts, Sir."

"Potts, Nastor. Here we are. Ready?"

"Yes, Sir."

"Two sea bags. Nail scissors. Black pens. Two packs. Memo pad. One. Watch cap. One. Ball cap. One. Ear muffs. Six pack of athletic socks. Two wash clothes. Two shower towels. One pair gloves. Black. Three pairs P.T. shorts. Sweatpants. Two pairs. Shower shoes. P.T. shirts. Two pairs. Let's see, we'll go large to be safe. Right? Two sweatshirts. Two packs undershirts. And two packs skivvies. One O.C.S. kit. Shirt stays white. Black. Two garrison devices. Soft shoulder boards. You good with that, son?"

"Yes, Sir."

"Sign or initial here. Next. Name?"

"Francisco Fortunato, Sir."

"Francisco Fortunato. Quite a name there, son, but you'll get the same as the others. Two sea bags. Nail scissors. Black pens. Two packs. Memo pad. Watch

cap. Ball cap. Ear muffs. Athletic socks. Wash clothes. Shower towels. Two. Men's black gloves. P.T. shorts. Three pairs. Two pairs sweatpants. One pair shower shoes. P.T. shirts. Two large. Two sweatshirts. Also large. And undershirts. Two packs. Two packs skivvies. One O.C.S. kit. Shirt stays white and black. Two garrison devices. Soft shoulder boards. Sign or initial."

"Yes, Sir."

"Next. Name."

"Michael Zurich, Sir."

"Z. Well that should make it easy, won't it? Right here. Zurich. Don't get all that many Zs. Heck, got to be my first Zurich. Doesn't happen every day. Well, Mister Zurich, away we go. Two sea bags. And for the goodies we got your nail scissors. Twin packs of pens. Black. Memo pad. Watch cap. Navy ball cap. Ear muffs. Athletic socks. Wash clothes. One. Two. Towels. One. Two. Men's black gloves. One pair. Three pairs of P.T. shorts. Sweatpants. Two pairs. One pair shower shoes. Two P.T. shirts. Large. Sweatshirts. Two. And two packs undershirts. Skivvies. One O.C.S. kit. Shirt stays white. Shirt stays blacks. Two garrison devices. And soft shoulder boards. We square?"

"Yes, Sir."

"Great. Sign right there next to your name. Next."

"--utility kit. Cotton swabs. Dental floss. Soap dish. Toenail clippers. Toothbrush. Toothbrush holder. Shaving cream. Mouthwash. Shampoo. Toothpaste. Combination locks. Ditty bag. Deodorant. Foot powder. Shoe polish kit. Stationary kit. And soap. Sign here. Next. Name."

"Jackson, Ma'am."

"Thank you. Compass drafting pivot. Check. Laundry bag, marking kit, notebook and pen. Six pack of handkerchiefs. Parallel plotter. Mechanical pencils. Scotch tape. Sewing kit. Ruler. Highlighter. Utility kit. Cotton swabs. Dental floss. Soap dish. Toenail clipper. Toothbrush. Toothbrush holder. Shaving cream. Mouthwash. Shampoo. Toothpaste. Combination locks. Two. Ditty bag. Deodorant. Foot powder. Shoe polish kit. Stationary kit. Soap. One. Two. Three packs. You agree? Sign here."

"Yes, Ma'am."

"Next."

"Good afternoon, Ma'am."

"Good afternoon to you. Name?"

"Potts, Ma'am."

"Mister Potts. Compass drafting pivot. Laundry bag. Marking kit. Notebook. And pen. Six pack of handkerchiefs. Parallel plotter. Mechanical pencils. Scotch tape. Sewing kit. Ruler. Highlighter. Utility kit. Cotton swabs. Dental floss. Soap dish. Toenail clipper. Toothbrush. Toothbrush holder. Shaving cream. Mouthwash. Shampoo. Toothpaste. Combination locks. Two. Ditty bag.

Deodorant. Foot powder. Shoe polish kit. Stationary kit. Three bars of soap. Sign or initial."

"Thank you, Ma'am."

"Off you go. Next."

"Fortunato, Ma'am."

"Gotcha. Here we go. Compass drafting pivot. Laundry bag. Marking kit. Notebook. And pen. Six pack of handkerchiefs. Parallel plotter. Mechanical pencils. Scotch tape. Sewing kit. Ruler. Highlighter. Utility kit. Cotton swabs. Dental floss. Soap dish. Toenail clipper. Toothbrush. Toothbrush holder. Shaving cream. Mouthwash. Shampoo. Toothpaste. Combination locks. Two. Ditty bag. Deodorant. Foot powder. Shoe polish kit. Stationary kit. Three bars of soap. Yes? Sign here. Good job. Next."

"Good afternoon, Ma'am. Zurich, Ma'am."

"Well, hello there. How's it going?"

"Hanging in there. Miss Wilson."

"Glad to hear it, Handsome. Here we go. Compass drafting pivot. Laundry bag. Marking kit. Notebook. And pen. Six pack of handkerchiefs. Parallel plotter. Mechanical pencils. Scotch tape. Sewing kit. Ruler. Highlighter. Utility kit. Cotton swabs. Dental floss. Soap dish. Toenail clippers. Toothbrush. Toothbrush holder. Shaving cream. Mouthwash. Shampoo. Toothpaste. Combination locks. Two. Ditty bag. Deodorant. Foot powder. Shoe polish kit. Stationary kit. Soap. One. Two. Three. Sign or initial. Next."

"--tie. Black. Four pairs socks. Black. One pair socks. White. One vinyl pancake. Khaki. One C.N.T. pancake. White. One garrison khaki P.C. cover. Check. Head size?"

"Not sure, Sir."

"Let's see. Hard to tell, big fella. Lean down here for a second. Seven and three-quarters."

"Thanks, Sir."

"One L.C.D.R. frame. Seven and three-quarters. You agree with what I just said, initial here. Don't forget your cover now."

"Thank you, Sir."

"Next."

"Potts."

"Nastor Potts, huh?"

"Yes, Sir."

"Nastor Potts. Issued. One khaki P.W. belt. One white C.N.T. belt. One black P.W. belt. Four brass tips. Three buckles. One tie. Black. Check. Four pairs socks. Black. Check. One pair socks. White. Check. One vinyl pancake. Khaki. Check. One C.N.T. pancake. White. Check. One garrison khaki P.C. cover. Check. Head size?"

"I don't know, Sir."

"How does this here fit?"

"Loose."

"That is loose. Try a seven and a quarter."

"That fits."

"Alright, then. One L.C.D.R. frame, seven and a quarter. And garrison cover. Initial here. Next."

"Good afternoon, Sir. Francisco Fortunato."

"Fortunato, Francisco. Here you are. Issued. One khaki P.W. belt. One white C.N.T. belt. One black P.W. belt. Four brass tips. Three buckles. One tie. Black. Check. Four pairs socks. Black. Check. One pair socks. White. Check. One vinyl pancake. Khaki. Check. One C.N.T. pancake. White. Check. One garrison khaki P.C. cover. Check. Head size?"

"I'm not sure, Sir."

"Let's see. I'd rate you a seven-five. How's this here feel?"

"Good."

"Seven and a half. L.C.D.R. frame. And garrison cover, khaki polycotton. That should do it. Agreed? Initial here. Next. Name?"

"Zurich, Michael, Sir."

"Good afternoon, there, Mister Zurich. How are you doing today?"

"Fine, Sir. How about yourself?"

"No complaints, Michael. Things are alright."

"That's good."

"Ready?"

"Sure."

"One khaki P.W. belt. One white C.N.T. belt. One black P.W. belt. Four brass tips. Three buckles. One tie. Black. Check. Four pairs socks. Black. Check. One pair socks. White. Check. One vinyl pancake. Khaki. Check. One C.N.T. pancake. White. Check. One garrison khaki P.C. cover. Check. Know your head size?"

"Around seven and a half on a ball cap."

"Try this on for size. How's it feel?"

"A little loose."

"How loose?"

"Loose."

"How's this?"

"Tighter. Still loose. But ballpark."

"Loose is good. You want it a little loose. Shrinks when you sweat."

"Seven and a half, Sir."

"Seven and a half it is. One L.C.D.R. frame. And cover. All check. You agree with what I've just said, initial here."

"Thank you, Sir."

"You're quite welcome, son. Take care of yourself, you hear?"

"Thank you, Sir."

"--white C.N.T. short-sleeve. Working black long-sleeve. Johnny Cash. Khaki polycotton trousers. Four pairs. White C.N.T. trousers. One pair. Black working trousers. One pair. One O.C.S. kit. Shirt stays white. Shirt stays black. Two garrison devices. Soft shoulder boards. And black gloves. For Saturday. One khaki polywool short-sleeve shirt. One white polycotton long-sleeve shirt. One pair khaki polywool trousers. One pair service dress blue trousers. One service dress white jacket. One service dress blue jacket. One bow tie. One Ensign kit. One single ribbon holder. One Officer large cap device. One Officer chin strap. And hard shoulder boards. Sign here. Next. Name?"

"McKenzie, Sir."

"Thank you. Alright. Mister McKenzie. Up on the box, please. Arms out. Good. Steady. Chest. Forty-two. Neck. Sixteen. Sleeve. Thirty-four. Shoulders. Nineteen. Call you a forty-two regular. Trunk. Twenty-nine, say thirty. Waist. Thirty-four. Inseam. Thirty-two. Issued. Black relaxed jacket. One. All weather coat. One. Still owed. Khaki polycotton long-sleeve. Large. Three times. Khaki polycotton short-sleeve. Three. White C.N.T. short-sleeve. One. Working black long-sleeve. Johnny Cash. Khaki polycotton trousers. Four pairs. White C.N.T. trousers. One pair. Black working trousers. One pair. Working black long-sleeve. Four pairs of khaki polycotton trousers. One O.C.S. kit. Shirt stays white. Shirt stays black. Two garrison devices. Soft shoulder boards. And black gloves. And black gloves. For Saturday. One khaki polywool short-sleeve shirt. One white polycotton long-sleeve shirt. One pair khaki polywool trousers. One pair service dress blue trousers. One service dress white jacket. One service dress blue jacket. One bow tie. One Ensign kit. One single ribbon holder. One Officer large cap device. One Officer chin strap. And hard shoulder boards. Sign here, Mister McKenzie. Next."

"Rooney, Sir."

"Alright, then. Step on up, please. Chin up. There you go. Chest. Forty-four. Neck. Seventeen plus. Arms out. Sleeve. Thirty-six. Shoulders. Twenty-two. Forty-four long if I've ever seen one. Trunk. Thirty-one and a half. Larges for blouses to match. Let's see about the waist. Thirty-seven. A good thirty-seven. Now that's gonna shrink by the looks of you, but we'll cross that bridge when you get there, alright? Alright. Inseam. Thirty-four. Issued. Black relaxed jacket. One. All weather coat. Stand-by for three pairs khaki polycotton long-sleeve. Larges. Three khaki polycotton short-sleeve. One white C.N.T. short-sleeve. One Johnny Cash long-sleeve. Four pairs of khaki polycotton trousers. One pair of white C.N.T. trousers. And one pair black working trousers. One O.C.S. kit. Shirt stays white. Shirt stays black. Two garrison devices. Soft shoulder boards. And

black gloves. For Saturday. One khaki polywool short-sleeve shirt. One white polycotton long-sleeve shirt. One pair khaki polywool trousers. One pair service dress blue trousers. One service dress white jacket. One service dress blue jacket. One bow tie. One Ensign kit. One single ribbon holder. One Officer large cap device plus chin strap. And hard shoulder boards. Be sure to check the list on Saturday. Sign here. Thank you, son. Next!"

"Morris, Sir."

"Alright, Mister Morris. Thank you. Up on the box with you. Arms out. Chest. Forty-two. Neck. Sixteen. Sleeve. Thirty-four. Shoulders. Nineteen. Call you a forty-two regular. Trunk. Twenty-nine and a half. Waist. Thirty-four. Inseam. Thirty-two. Issued. Black relaxed jacket. One. All weather coat. Stand-by for three pairs khaki polycotton long-sleeve. Larges. Three khaki polycotton short-sleeve. One white C.N.T. short-sleeve. One Johnny Cash long-sleeve. Four pairs khaki polycotton trousers, one pair of white C.N.T. trousers. And one pair black working trousers. One O.C.S. kit. Shirt stays white. Two garrison devices. Soft shoulder boards. And black gloves. For Saturday. One khaki polywool short-sleeve shirt. One white polycotton long-sleeve shirt. One pair khaki polywool trousers. One pair service dress blue trousers. One service dress white jacket. One service dress blue jacket. Bow tie and white gloves. Next."

"Jackson, Sir."

"Thank you, Mister Jackson. Step on up. Chest. Forty-one. Neck. Sixteen and a quarter. Sleeve. Thirty-three. Shoulders. Eighteen. Call you a forty-two regular. Trunk. Thirty. Waist. Thirty-three. Inseam. Thirty-two. Issued. Black relaxed jacket. One. All weather coat. One. Stand-by for three pairs khaki polycotton long-sleeve. Larges. Three khaki polycotton short-sleeve. One white C.N.T. short-sleeve. One Johnny Cash long-sleeve. Four pairs of khaki polycotton trousers. One pair of white C.N.T. trousers. One pair black working trousers. O.C.S. kit. Shirt stays white. Shirt stays black. Two garrison devices. Soft shoulder boards. And black gloves. One pair. For Saturday. One khaki polywool short-sleeve shirt. One white polycotton long-sleeve shirt. One pair khaki polywool trousers. One pair service dress blue trousers. One service dress white jacket. One service dress blue jacket. Bow tie and white gloves. One Ensign kit. One single ribbon holder. One Officer large cap device. One Officer chin strap. And hard shoulder boards. Sign here. Off you go. Next!"

"Potts, Sir."

"Nastor Potts. I got you. Up on the box, Potts. Arms out. Chest. Forty-two. Neck. Sixteen and three-quarters. Sleeve. Thirty-three. Shoulders. Eighteen. Call you a forty-two regular, with some give. Trunk. Thirty sharp. Waist. Thirty-five. Larges for blouses. Inseam. Stand-up straight now. Thirty-one. Issued. Black relaxed jacket and all weather coat. Three pairs khaki polycotton long-sleeve. Larges. Three khaki polycotton short-sleeve. One white C.N.T. short-sleeve. One

Johnny Cash long-sleeve. Four pairs of khaki polycotton trousers. One pair of white C.N.T. trousers. One pair black working trousers. One O.C.S. kit. Shirt stays white. Shirt stays black. Two garrison devices. Soft shoulder boards.Black gloves. For Saturday. One khaki polywool short-sleeve shirt. One white polycotton long-sleeve shirt. One pair khaki polywool trousers. One pair service dress blue trousers. One service dress white jacket. One service dress blue jacket. Bow tie and white gloves. One Ensign kit. One single ribbon holder. One Officer large cap device. One Officer chin strap. And hard shoulder boards. Sign here. Next."

"Francisco Fortunato, Sir."

"Well, now. Oh my. That come with sides? Step on up on the box, my man. Watch yourself now. Neck. Sixteen and a half. Arms out. Sleeve. Thirty-five and some change. We'll go forty-four long with an extra-large blouse. Trunk. Thirty-one. Waist. Thirty-four. Too tight? Thirty-five. Inseam. Thirty-four. And a half. Issued. Black relaxed jacket. All weather coat. Here we go. Three pairs khaki polycotton long-sleeve. Larges. Three khaki polycotton short-sleeve. One white C.N.T. short-sleeve. One Johnny Cash long-sleeve. Four pairs of khaki polycotton trousers. One pair of white C.N.T. trousers. One pair black working trousers. You'll need alterations down the line. See you in week-seven. One O.C.S. kit. Shirt stays white. Shirt stays black. Two garrison devices. Soft shoulder boards. Oh, and one pair black gloves."

"Yes, Sir."

"For Saturday. One khaki polywool short-sleeve shirt. One white polycotton long-sleeve shirt. One pair khaki polywool trousers. One pair service dress blue trousers. One service dress white jacket. One service dress blue jacket. Bow tie and white gloves. One Ensign kit. One single ribbon holder. One Officer large cap device. One Officer chin strap. And hard shoulder boards. Sign here."

"Zurich, Sir."

"Like the capital?"

"Yes, Sir."

"Why I'll be. Up you go. Arms out. Chest. Forty-three. Neck. Sixteen and a quarter. Sleeve. Thirty-three and a half. Shoulders. Eighteen and a half. Call you just about a forty-three long. Waist. Thirty-two. Inseam. Thirty-one, thirty-two. Issued. Black relaxed jacket and all weather coat. Issued. Four pairs khaki polycotton long-sleeve. Larges. Four khaki polycotton short-sleeve. One white C.N.T. short-sleeve. One Johnny Cash long-sleeve. Four pairs of khaki polycotton trousers. One pair of white C.N.T. trousers. One pair black working trousers. One O.C.S. kit. Shirt stays white. Shirt stays black. Two garrison devices. Soft shoulder boards. And black gloves. For Saturday. One khaki polywool short-sleeve shirt. One white polycotton long-sleeve shirt. One pair khaki polywool trousers. One pair service dress blue trousers. One service dress

white jacket. One service dress blue jacket. Bow tie and white gloves. One Ensign kit. One single ribbon holder. One Officer large cap device. One Officer chin strap. And hard shoulder boards. Sign here. Remember to check the list. Sign here."

"Thank you, Sir."

"You're quite welcome, Son. Next!"

"--black and white. Sign here. Next."

"Potts, Sir."

"Good morning, Potts. Take off your shoes, please. Step right here. All the way back. That's it. Ten. Let's see. We have a run on size ten. Here we go. Oxfords. One pair black. One pair white. Please sign here. Thank you. Next."

"Fortunato, Sir."

"Step right up. Perfect. Size eleven. Let's see. Oxfords black. Size eleven. Here we are. And Oxfords white. Sign here. Thank you. Next."

"Zurich, Sir."

"Step right into the brannock there. Perfect. Ten and a half. Almost eleven. What do you usually wear?"

"Eleven, Sir."

"Try this one for size. How does that feel?"

"A little loose, Sir."

"A little loose. Let's see. Wiggle your toes for me. Close. Up to you. Ten and a half will be tight."

"Should be fine, Sir."

"Eleven it is. You'll be wearing sport socks underneath if you're smart, anyway. That's a tip. Didn't hear it from me."

"Yes, Sir."

"Start packing it up, Indoctrination Candidates. You have no time."

••

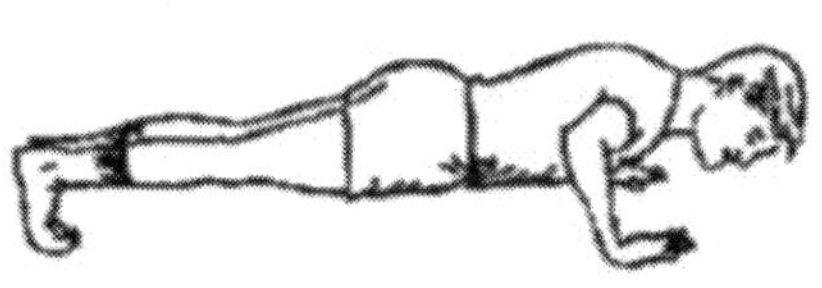

Push-ups

Push-ups shall be performed on a firm or a suitably padded level surface. Participant shall begin in front leaning rest position. Palms of hands placed on floor directly beneath or slightly wider than shoulders. Both feet together on floor. Back, buttocks and legs shall be straight from head to heels and must remain so throughout test. Toes and palms of hands shall remain in contact with floor. Feet shall not contact a wall or other vertical support surface. Participants shall lower entire body as a single unit, by bending elbows until upper arms, shoulders and lower back are aligned and parallel to deck. Participants shall return to starting position by extending elbows, raising body as a single unit until arms are straight. Participants may only rest in the up position while maintaining arms, back, buttocks and legs in straight position.

Push-ups are repeated correctly as many times as possible in two minutes. Event is ended if participant touches deck with any part of body except hands and feet, raises one or both feet or hands off deck or ground, fails to maintain back, buttocks or legs straight from head to heels.

••

"When I say *go*! You will move straight ahead! Aligning yourselves behind the platoon of Candidate Officers! Four columns! One arm's length from the Pig in front of you! Aligned to the freaking starboard side! Am I clear?"

"Yes, Sir!!"

"When we go, you will maintain this alignment! Am I clear?"

"Yes, Sir!!"

"I don't think so! Stop whispering to me you freaking Pigs!"

"Aye aye, Sir!"

"Freaking all of you! *Aye aye, Sir*!"

"Aye aye, Sir!!"

"When you open your goddamn pie holes, you freaking sound off! When you open your goddamn pie holes to sound off, I want to see blood and lung tissue splatter on the Pig in front of you! Am I clear?"

"Yes, Sir!!"

"Let me hear it now!"

"Yes, Sir!!"

"You! Stop whispering!"

"Aye aye, Sir!"

"Louder, Freak!"

"Aye aye, Sir!"

"Go!"

"Aye aye, Sir!!"

"What the hell are you waiting for? Go! Go!"

"Aye aye, Sir!!"

"Ten-nine-eight-seven-six-four-two-one! Aligned starboard! *Aye aye, Sir!*"

"Aye aye, Sir!!"

"Louder!"

"Aye aye, Sir!!"

"Blood and guts! Sound off!"

"Aye aye, Sir!!"

"Adjust!"

"Aye aye, Sir!!"

"Ready! March!"

"Aye aye, Sir!!"

"Arms! Six inches to the front! And three to the rear! Is that clear?"

"Yes, Sir!!"

"*Six to the front! Three to the rear!*"

"Six to the front!! Three to the rear!!"

"*Six to the front! Three to the rear!*"

"Six to the front!! Three to the rear!!"

"Keep it going, Maggots! *Aye aye, Sir!*"

"Aye aye, Sir!! Six to the front!! Three to the rear!! Six to the front!! Three to the rear!! Six to the front!! Three to the rear!! Six to the front!! Three to the rear!! Six to the front!! Three to the rear!! Six to the front!! Three to the rear!!"

"Right turn! March!"

"Aye aye, Sir!!"

"*Six to the front! Three to the rear!*"

"Six to the front!! Three to the rear!! Six to the front!! Three to the rear!! Six to the front!! Three to the rear!!"

"Thirty-inch steps, Pigs!"

"Aye aye, Sir!!"

"One hundred and twenty steps per minute!"

"Aye aye, Sir!!"

"One arm's length, Freak!"

"No excuse, Sir!"

"Thirty-inch step, Moron!"

"Aye aye, Sir!"

"Your left! Your left! Your left! Right! Left! Ho! Hai! Ho! Ho! Hai! Ho! Always on the left foot! The mighty-mighty left foot! Ho! Hai! Ho! Open your holes! *Aye aye, Sir!*"

"Aye aye, Sir!"

"*Left! Left! Lefty! Right! Layo!*"

"Left!! Left!! Lefty!! Right!! Layo!!"

"*Left! Left! Keep-it-in-step!*"

"Left!! Left!! Keep-it-in-step!!"

"*Left! Left! Lefty-right-a-left-right!*"

"Left!! Left!! Lefty-right-a-left-right!!"

"*Lefty-right-left-right!*"

"Lefty-right-left-right!!"

"*Lefty-right-a-lo!*"

"Lefty-right-a-lo!!"

"*Always on the left foot!*"

"Always on the left foot!!"

"*The mighty-mighty left foot!*"

"The mighty-mighty left foot!!"

"*Lefty-right-a-lo!*"

"Lefty-right-a-lo!!"

"*Six to the front! Three to the rear!*"

"Six to the front!! Three to the rear!!"

"*Six to the front! Three to the rear!*"

"Six to the front!! Three to the rear!!"

"Thirty-inch steps, Pigs!"

"Aye aye, Sir!!"

"One hundred and twenty steps per minute!"

"Aye aye, Sir!!"

"Right turn! March!"

"Aye aye, Sir!!"

"Your left! Your left! Your left-right-left! Your left! Your left! Your left-right-left! Ready! Halt!"

"Aye aye, Sir!!"

"Ears!"

"Open, Sir!!"

"Upon receiving the command of execution *do it now*! You will ground your warbelts and chrome domes and freaking canteens to the starboard side! *Aye aye, Sir!*"

"Aye aye, Sir!!"

"You will do so in an orderly fashion! Reflecting formation! Chrome domes grounded first! Warbelts grounded around your chrome domes! Your canteens secured between your Nasty Pig Hooves! Is that clear?"

"Yes, Sir!!"

"Is that clear?"

"Yes, Sir!!"

"Do it now!"

"Aye aye, Sir!!"

"Move! Go! Start moving! Faster! Ten-nine-eight-seven-six-five-four-three-two-one! No! No! Not like that! Pick-them-up! Freaking Nasties! Back in formation! *Aye aye, Sir*!"

"Aye aye, Sir!!"

"Faster! Faster! You Nasty Pigs! Ten-nine-eight-seven-six-five-four-three-two-one! Back in formation! Back in formation! You! What the hell do you think you're doing? What is your major malfunction, Maggot?"

"No excuse, Sir!"

"Where's your place?"

"No excuse, Sir!"

"Where is your freaking place, Dirt-for-brains?"

"No excuse, Sir!"

"Find two brain cells! Rub them together!"

"Aye aye, Sir!"

"I asked you a question!"

"This indoctrination candidate does not know but will find out, Sir!"

"Slime! You're goddamn right you'll find out. You Nasty freaking Pig Freak! Get! Get! Get!"

"Aye aye, Sir!"

"Ears!"

"Open, Sir!!"

"Let's try this again, Morons! *Aye aye, Sir*!"

"Aye aye, Sir!!"

"Upon receiving the command of execution *move*! You will ground your wargear and canteens to the starboard side! Is that clear?"

"Yes, Sir!!"

"Move!"

"Aye aye, Sir!!"

"Ten-nine-eight-seven-six-five-leave-it-moron-four-three-two-one! What? What? Why you taking your clothes off, Freak? Freaking Weirdo! Back-in-formation! Back-information! Ten-nine-eight-seven-six! Faster! Faster! What? What? Where's your wargear, Freak? Where's your wargear?"

"No excuse, Sir!"

"Three-two-one! Freeze Pigs!"

"Aye aye, Sir!!"

"Ground your wargear! Do it now!"

"Aye aye, Sir!!"

"Now!"

"Aye aye, Sir!!"

"Ten-nine-eight-seven-six-five-four-three-two-one! Freeze!"

"Aye aye, Sir!!"

"Minor freaking miracle. Back in formation! Back in formation! That's a freaking response!"

"Aye aye, Sir!!"

"Ten-nine-eight-seven-six-five-four-three-two-one! Freeze!"

"Aye aye, Sir!!"

"Cover!"

"Aye aye, Sir!!"

"Shut your faces! Cover!"

"Aye aye, Sir!"

"I said shut your freaking hole, Weirdo! Cover! Better. You! Freak! Get up here!"

"Aye aye, Sir!"

"About face!"

"Aye aye, Sir!"

"Repeat after me, Idiot!"

"Aye aye, Sir!"

"*Indoctrination Class Zero-Four-Zero-Zero, upon receiving the command of execution march, you will.*"

"Indoctrination Class Zero-Four-Zero-Zero! Upon receiving the command of execution march! You will!"

"*Half-step up this ladderwell.*"

"Half-step up this ladderwell!"

"*Perform an immediate column-left.*"

"Perform an immediate column-left!"

"*And reform at the door.*"

"And reform at the door!"

"That's an *aye aye, Section Leader*!"

"Aye aye, Section Leader!!"

"*Ready march*, Pig."

"Ready! March!"

"Aye aye, Section Leader!!"

"*Left-right-left-right*!"

"Left-right!! Left-right!! Left-right!! Left-right!! Left-right!! Left-right!!"

"Half-step, Freaks!"

"Aye aye, Sir!! Left-right!! Left-right!! Left-right!! Left-right!! Left-right!! Left-right!! Left-right!! Left-right!! Left-right!! Left-right!! Left-right!! Left-right!! Left-right!! Left-right!! Left-right!! Left-right!! Left-right!! Left-right!!"

"*Ready halt*, Pig."

"Ready! Halt!"

"Aye aye, Section Leader!!"

"*Ready adjust*, Pig."

"Ready! Adjust!"

"Aye aye, Section Leader!!"

"Repeat after me, Maggots! *Aye aye, Sir*!"

"Aye aye, Sir!!"

"*Discipline*!"

"Discipline!!"

"*D! I! S! C! I! P! L! I! N! E!*"

"D!! I!! S!! C!! I!! P!! L!! I!! N!! E!!"

"*Discipline*! *Is*! *The unconditional*! *Obedience-to-orders*! *Respect-for-authority*! *And self-reliance*!"

"Discipline!! Is!! The unconditional!! Obedience-to-orders!! Respect-for-authority!! And self-reliance!!"

"*Freeze-candidate-freeze*!"

"Freeze-candidate-freeze!!"

"Where's my freaking Doorbody?"

"Doorbody, aye aye, Sir!"

"Get up here!"

"Aye aye, Sir!"

"*Report status of chow hall deck*."

"Report status of chow hall deck!"

"Aye aye, Section Leader! Chow hall deck all clear, Section Leader!"

"Altogether now, Maggots!"

"Chow hall deck all clear, Section Leader!!"

"Crack the freaking door!"

"Aye aye, Sir!"

"When you march through this freaking hatch! The first person into the hole will snap his nasty face to the right and sound off with greeting of the day! The rest of you Maggots will follow with *zero-two*, *zero-three*, *zero-four*! And so on and so forth! Whatever your freaking number! Blood and guts! Am I clear?"

"Yes, Sir!!"

"You get inside! You line up in two columns! Am I clear?"

"Yes, Sir!!"

"*Class Zero-Four-Zero-Zero, marching into chow*."

"Class Zero-Four-Zero-Zero, marching into chow!"

"All of you!"

"Class Zero-Four-Zero-Zero, marching into chow!!"

"Stop whispering to me! Louder!"

"Class Zero-Four-Zero-Zero, marching into chow!!"

"You! Column of files from the right! Go!"

"Aye aye, Sir! Good morning, Sir!"

"Zero-two!"

"Zero-three!"

"Zero-two!"

"Zero-five!"

"Zero-six!"

"Zero-seven!"

"Zero-eight!"

"Zero-niner!"

"One-zero!"

"One-one!"

"One-two!"

"One-three!"

"One-four!"

"One-five!"

"One-six!"

"One-seven!"

"One-eight!"

"One-niner!"

"Two-zero!"

"Two-one!"

"Two-two!"

"Two-three!"

"Two-four!"

"Two-five!"

"Two-six!"

"Two-seven!"

"Two-eight!"

"Two-niner!"

"Three-zero!"

"Three-one!"

"Three-two!"

"Three-three!"

"Three-four!"

"Three-five!"

"Three-six!"

"Three-seven!"

"Three-eight!"

"Three-niner!"

"Four-zero!"

"Four-one!"

"Four-two!"

"Four-three!"

"Four-four!"

"Four-five!"

"Four-six!"

"Four-seven!"

"Good morning, Sir!"

Drill Instructors pace the length of the twin columns at intervals. Candidate Officers call out from the perimeter.

"Single step, Indoctrination Candidates!"

"Aye aye, Sir!!"

"Upon receiving the command of execution *forward march*, you will respond with *step freeze* and pass the word to *stand fast*!"

"Aye aye, Sir!!"

"Forward march!"

"Step freeze!!"

"Stand fast."

"Forward march!"

"Step freeze!!"

"Stand fast."

"I see that tongue again, I'm ripping it out of your freaking head, Pig!"

"No excuse, Sir!"

"You sound off to me!"

"Aye aye, Sir!"

"You sound off to me!"

"Aye aye, Sir!"

"Forward march!"

"Step freeze!!"

"Stand fast."

"Thousand yard stare at all times, Indoctrination Candidates!"

"Aye aye, Sir!!"

"Thumbs to trouser seams!"

"Aye aye, Sir!!"

"Forward march!"

"Step freeze!!"

"Stand fast."

"Forward march!"

"Step freeze!!"

"Stand fast."

"I see daylight! I see daylight! Thumbs to trouser seams! You!"

"Aye aye, Sir!"

"Why are you whispering to me?"

"No excuse, Sir!"

"Forward march!"
"Step freeze!!"
"Stand fast."
"Thousand yard stare at all times, Indoctrination Candidates!"
"Aye aye, Sir!!"
"Thumbs to trouser seams!"
"Aye aye, Sir!!"
"Forward march!"
"Step freeze!!"
"Stand fast."
"Forward march!"
"Step freeze!!"
"Stand fast."
"Thumbs to trouser seams!"
"Aye aye, Sir!"
"Forward march!"
"Step freeze!!"
"Stand fast."
"Thumbs to trouser seams!"
"Aye aye, Sir!"
"I see daylight! I see daylight!"
"Aye aye, Sir!"
"Freaking what?"
"Aye aye, Sir!"
"What?"
"No excuse, Sir!"
"Forward march!"
"Step freeze!!"
"Stand fast."
"Forward march!"
"Step freeze!!"
"Stand fast."
"Forward march!"
"Step freeze!!"
"Stand fast."
"Thousand yard stare at all times, Indoctrination Candidates!"
"Aye aye, Sir!!"
"What do you think you're looking at?"
"No excuse, Sir!"
"You enjoying the show, Moron?"
"No, Sir!"

"What?"

"No, Sir!"

"What?"

"No excuse, Sir!"

"I see those eyeballs again, I'm ripping them clean out of your sockets! Do you understand me?"

"Yes, Sir!"

"Freaking what?"

"Yes, Sir!"

"Forward march!"

"Step freeze!!"

"Stand fast."

"Forward march!"

"Step freeze!!"

"Stand fast."

"Forward march!"

"Step freeze!!"

"Stand fast."

"Close your suck hole! Close your suck hole!"

"Aye aye, Sir!"

"You close it now!"

"Aye aye, Sir!"

"You freaking keep it closed!"

"Aye aye, Sir!"

"Forward march!"

"Step freeze!!"

"Stand fast."

"Forward march!"

"Step freeze!!"

"Stand fast."

"Forward march!"

"Step freeze!!"

"Stand fast."

"Thousand yard stare at all times, Indoctrination Candidates!"

"Aye aye, Sir!!"

"Thumbs to trouser seams!"

"Aye aye, Sir!!"

"Forward march!"

"Step freeze!!"

"Stand fast."

"Forward march!"

"Step freeze!!"

"Stand fast."

"Forward march!"

"Step freeze!!"

"Stand fast."

"Thumbs to trouser seams, you little Freak!"

"Aye aye, Sir!"

"What?"

"No excuse, Sir!"

"Forward march!"

"Step freeze!!"

"Stand fast."

"Forward march!"

"Step freeze!!"

"Stand fast."

"Forward march!"

"Step freeze!!"

"Stand fast."

"You! Thumbs!"

"Aye aye, Sir!!"

"Get your nasty chin up! You Pig!"

"Aye aye, Sir!"

"You! I see your goddamn Pig Paws! Freaking Pig Hooves!"

"Aye aye, Sir!"

"Goddamn knuckles pressed tight into your thighs! All of you! *Aye aye, Sir*!"

"Aye aye, Sir!!"

"You! You! You! You! And You! I want five people in line at all times! Five people in line! Move!"

"Aye aye, Sir!!"

"Eyeballs!"

"Snap, Sir!!"

"You march! Up to the stand! And slap! You pick up the freaking tray! Flip the freaking tray one hundred and eighty degrees! And secure the freaking tray into your body! *Aye aye, Sir*!"

"Aye aye, Sir!!"

"Locked! Cocked! At all times! Your elbows are tight into your body! Your forearms are parallel to the deck! Is that clear?"

"Yes, Sir!!"

"Maintaining a thousand yard stare at all times! Am I clear?"

"Yes, Sir!!"

"You step up! With intensity! You reach out parallel! Then down! Then up! Just like this! Sharp! Swiftly! In control! Am I clear?"

"Yes, Sir!!"

"Your freaking spoon! Your freaking fork! Your freaking knife! Understood?"

"Yes, Sir!!"

"Spoon! Fork! Knife! All grounded to your tray! Clear?"

"Yes, Sir!!"

"You take your freaking tray! And you march up to the freaking chow line! You give the greeting of the day! *Good afternoon, Sir. Good afternoon, Ma'am.* With respect! Freaking *aye aye, Sir.*"

"Aye aye, Sir!!"

"You choose what you want! *Thank you, Sir. Thank you, Ma'am.*"

"Aye aye, Sir!!"

"You ground your freaking plate between your freaking silverware!"

"Aye aye, Sir!!"

"Move! What the hell are you waiting for, Pig? That's a freaking response!"

"No excuse, Sir!"

"Go! Go!"

"Aye aye, Sir! Good afternoon, Ma'am!"

"You! Freaking Weirdo! I said respectful! You don't freaking sound off to civilians, Freak Nasty! Try it again! That's a freaking response!"

"Aye aye, Sir! Good afternoon, Ma'am."

"Chicken or beef, Darling?"

"Chicken please, Ma'am."

"Sides?"

"Mash potatoes, please, Ma'am. And the broccoli, please, Ma'am."

"Here you are."

"Thank you, Ma'am."

"God bless."

"Thank you, Ma'am."

"Let's go Indoctrination Candidates! Line it up along both sides of the table! Go! Go! Go!"

"That's an *aye aye, Sir.*"

"Aye aye, Sir!!""

"You! Port side!"

"Aye aye, Sir!"

"Your other port!"

"Aye aye, Sir!"

"Thousand yard stare at all times, Indoctrination Candidates!"

"Aye aye, Sir!!"

"Gougebooks out, Indoctrination Candidates! Studying your gouge!"

"Aye aye, Sir!!"

"Angle of ninety degrees, Indoctrination Candidates! Ninety degrees!"

"Aye aye, Sir!!"

Willett takes a seat on the table.

"Put it away, Freaks!"

"Aye aye, Sir!!"

"Sit, Freaks!"

"Aye aye, Sir!!"

"Pray at will!"

"Aye aye, Sir!!"

"You shut your pie holes when you pray. Eat!"

"Aye aye, Sir!!"

"Stuffing your freaking holes is a ten count exercise. First count. Snap your freaking head down. Second count. Left hand picks up warspoon. Third count. Scoop. Fourth count. Shove that spoon and food all the way down your pie hole. Fifth count. Ground spoon on tray. Sixth count. Snap head up. Seventh Count. Chew. Eighth count. Swallow. This is your two-zero minute warning. *Aye aye, Sir.*"

"Aye aye, Sir!!"

"Eat!"

"Aye aye, Sir!!"

"Shut your faces. Like pigs in a trough. Eat. Zero-one. Zero-two. As you were. Zero-two. Zero-three. Zero-four. As you were. Zero-four. Zero-five. As you were. Zero-five. Zero-six. Zero-seven. Zero-eight. As you were. Zero-eight. All together, Freaks! *Aye aye, Sir.*"

"Aye aye, Sir!!"

"Hydration. Hydration is a twelve count exercise. First count. Right hand out, fingers joined. Second count. Twist hand, prepare to grab the cup. Third count. Hand down. Fourth count. Grab cup. Fifth count. Lift cup. Sixth count. Bring cup to mouth. Seventh count. Hydrate. Eighth count. Bring cup back out. Ninth count. Cup down and grounded to the tray. Tenth count. Hand out. Eleventh count. Twist back. Twelfth count. Return hand to lap. *Aye aye, Sir.*"

"Aye aye, Sir!!"

"Hydrate. Zero-one. As you were. Zero-one. As you were. Zero-one. Zero-two. As you were. Zero-two. Zero-three. Zero-four. As you were. Zero-four. As you were. Zero-four. As you were. Zero-four. Zero-five. Zero-six. As you were. Zero-six. Zero-seven. As you were. Zero-seven. Zero-eight. Zero-niner. As you were. Zero-niner. One-zero. One-one. One-two."

Drill instructors converge on the tables.

"Eat. Zero-one. Zero-two. Zero-three. As you were. Zero-three. Zero-four. As you were. Zero-four. Zero-five. As you were. Zero-five. Zero-six. As you were. Zero-six. As you were. Zero-six. Zero-seven. Zero-eight. As you were. Zero-eight. Again. Zero-one."

"Wrong nasty hand! That's a response!"

"No excuse, Sir!"

"You Nasty Thing! Position of attention! Position of attention when you sound off to me!"

"Aye aye, Sir!"

"Open your hole!"

"Aye aye, Sir!"

"Sit your nasty ass down!"

"Aye aye, Sir!"

"I see daylight! I see daylight! You nasty freaking Candidate!"

"Aye aye, Sir!"

"Improper response! Improper response!"

"No excuse, Sir!"

"What?"

"No excuse, Sir!"

"Sit!"

"Aye aye, Sir!"

"Eat. Zero-one. Zero-two. Zero-three. As you were. Zero-three. Zero-four. As you were. Zero-four. Zero-five. As you were. Zero-five. Zero-six. As you were. Zero-six. As you were. Zero-six. Zero-seven. Zero-eight. As you were. Zero-eight. Again. Zero-one. As you were. Zero-one. Zero-two. As you were. Zero-two. Zero-three. As you were. Zero-three. Zero-four. As you were. Zero-four. Zero-five. As you were. Zero-five. Zero-six. As you were. Zero-six. As you were. Zero-six. Zero-seven. As you were. Zero-seven. Zero-eight. As you were. Zero-eight."

"You finish freaking chewing before feeding your freaking face! You hear me?"

"Aye aye, Sir!"

"You hear me?"

"Yes, Sir!"

"Freaking what?"

"Yes, Sir!"

"I see daylight! I see freaking daylight! That's a freaking, response! You hear me?"

"No excuse, Sir!"

"On your freaking feet!"

"Aye aye, Sir!"

The felt brim of a Smokey Bear hat pushes into my forehead. A second Drill Instructor closes from behind.

"Why you touching me? Why you touching me? Get the hell away from me!"

"Aye aye, Sir!"

"Are we dating?"

"No, Sir!"

"Are we drinking buddies?"

"No, Sir!"

"Am I your teddy bear?"

"No, Sir!"

"Get the hell away from me!"

"Aye aye, Sir!"

"Why you touching me! Stop touching me! That's a freaking response!"

"Aye aye, Sir!"

"That's a response!"

"Aye aye, Sir!"

"Shut the hell up, freaking Candidate! Shut the hell up! That's an order! You shut the hell up!"

"That's a freaking response! That's a response!"

"Aye aye, Sir!"

"I thought I told you to shut your face!"

"Louder! Stop whispering!"

"Aye aye, Sir!"

"Shut your freaking hole! Shut your freaking face!"

"That's a response!"

"Aye aye, Sir!"

"Why are you still talking, freaking Candidate? You shut the hell up!"

"That's a response!"

"Aye aye, Sir!"

"Louder!"

"Aye aye, Sir!"

"Why you touching me? Why you touching me?"

"No excuse, Sir!"

"You get the hell away from me, Freak! That's a response!"

"Aye aye, Sir!"

"You shut your freaking mouth, Pig! You shut your freaking mouth!"

"That's a freaking response, Pig!"

"Aye aye, Sir!"

"Louder!"

"Aye aye, Sir!"

"Louder!"

"Aye aye, Sir!"

"Sit down!"

"Aye aye, Sir!"

"Sixteen ounces of water is required for minimum hydration, Indoctrination Candidates! A zero-two cup minimum! Three-two ounces of water is required for optimal hydration! If you require a refill, raise your cup, a Candidate Officer will come find you!"

"That's an *aye aye, Sir*!"

"Aye aye, Sir!!"

"Hydrate. Zero-one. Zero-two. As you were. Zero-two. Zero-three. Zero-four. As you were. Zero-four. As you were. Zero-four. Zero-five. As you were. Zero-five. Zero-six. As you were. Zero-six. Zero-seven. As you were. Zero-seven. Zero-eight. Zero-niner. As you were. Zero-niner. One-zero. One-one. As you were. One-one. One-two. Eat. Zero-one. As you were. Zero-one. Zero-two. As you were. Zero-two. Zero-three. As you were. Zero-three. Zero-four. Zero-five. As you were. Zero-five. Zero-six. As you were. Zero-six. Zero-seven. Zero-eight. As you were. Zero-eight."

"Spoon! You Nasty Thing you!"

"Aye aye, Sir!"

"What's wrong with this picture?"

"No excuse, Sir!"

"I can see nasty freaking food! That's a response!"

"Aye aye, Sir!"

"Improper response!"

"No excuse, Sir!"

"Why do I see food? Why do I see little freaking bits? Nasty freaking bits! Shut your freaking mouth you Nasty Thing!"

"That's a response! That's a response!"

"No excuse, Sir!"

"On your freaking feet when you sound off to me, Pig!"

"Aye aye, Sir!"

"I said shut your freaking mouth!"

"That's a freaking response!"

"No excuse, Sir!"

"Louder!"

"No excuse, Sir!"

"Stop freaking whispering to me!"

"That's a response! That's a freaking response!"

"No excuse, Sir!"

"Sit!"

"Aye aye, Sir!"

"You must finish your plates, Indoctrination Candidates! You must drain your cups! You have no time!"

"That's a response!"

"Aye aye, Sir!!"

"Louder!"

"Aye aye, Sir!!"

"This is your one-zero minute warning, Indoctrination Candidates!"

••

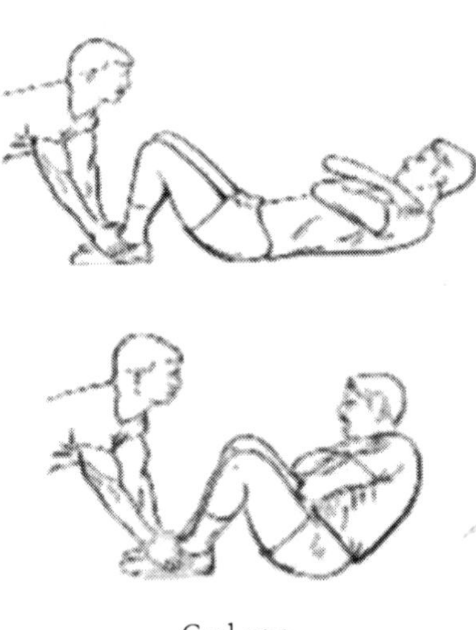

Curl-ups

Event shall be conducted with partner on a level surface, on a blanket, mat or other suitable padding. Shoes are optional. Curl-ups are conducted as follows. Participants shall start by lying flat on back with knees bent, heels about ten inches from buttocks. Arms shall be folded across and touching chest with hands touching upper chest or shoulders. Feet shall be held to floor only by partners' hands. Participants curl body up, touching elbows to thighs while keeping hands in contact with chest or shoulders. After touching elbows to thighs, participants lie back touching lower edge of shoulder blades to deck. Participants may rest in either up or down position.

Curl-ups are repeated correctly as many times as possible in two minutes. Incorrectly performed curl-ups shall not be counted. Results for event ended in less than two minutes shall be the number of curl-ups properly completed at time of termination. Event is ended in participant lowers legs, raises feet of ground or floor, lifts buttocks off of ground or floor, fails to keep arms across or touching chest, fails to keep hands in touch with chest or shoulders.

••

"Left! Left! Lefty! Right! Layo! Left! Left! Keep-it-in-step! Left! Left! Lefty-right-a-left-right! Lefty-right-left-right! Lefty-right-a-lo! Left! Left! Lefty! Right! Layo! Left! Left! Keep-it-in-step! Left! Left! Lefty-right-a-left-right! Lefty-right-left-right! Lefty-right-a-lo! Always on the left foot! The mighty-mighty left foot! Lefty-right-a-lo! Class Zero-Four-Zero-Zero, upon receiving the command of execution *column right, march*! You will! Take a single thirty-inch stride in cadence! A thirty-inch stride in preparation for a right turn pivot at an angle of nine-zero degrees! And follow the lead of the guidon!"

"That's an *aye aye, Sir*!"

"Aye aye, Sir!!"

"Louder!"

"Aye aye, Sir!!"

"Louder!"

"Aye aye, Sir!!"

"Louder!"

"Aye aye, Sir!!"

"Column right! March!"

"Aye aye, Sir!!"

"Step! Pivot! Step! Pivot! Step! Pivot! Step! Pivot! Step! Pivot! Step! Pivot! Step! Pivot! Step! Pivot! Step! Pivot! Step!"

"That's an *aye aye, Sir*!"

"Aye aye, Sir!!"

"Your left! Your left! Your left-right-left! Your left! Your left! Left-right-left! Lefty-right-a-left-right! Left-left! Keep-it-in-step! Left foot! Left foot! Left-right-left! Left-left! Left-right-left! Left-left! Left-right-left! Left-left! Keep-it-in-step! *Arms*!"

"Six to the front!! Three to the rear!!"

"Louder!"

"Six to the front!! Three to the rear!!"

"Thirty-inch steps, Indoctrination Candidates!"

"That's an *aye aye, Sir*!"

"Aye aye, Sir!!"

"One hundred and twenty steps per minute!"

"Aye aye, Sir!!"

"Louder!"

"Aye aye, Sir!!"

"Louder!"

"Aye aye, Sir!!"

"Left! Left! Lefty! Right! Layo! Left! Left! Keep-it-in-step! Left! Left! Lefty-right-a-left-right! Lefty-right-left-right! Lefty-right-a-lo! Left! Left! Lefty! Right! Layo! Left! Left! Keep-it-in-step! Left! Left! Lefty-right-a-left-right! Lefty-right-left-right! Lefty-right-a-lo! Your left! Your left! Your left-right-left! Your left! Your left! Keep-it-in-step! Indoctrination Class Zero-Four-Zero-Zero! Upon receiving the command of execution *halt*! You will! Take a single stride in cadence! After that single stride! You will come to a halt! Is that clear?"

"Yes, Sir!!"

"Ready! Halt!"

"Aye aye, Sir!!"

"Louder!"

"Aye aye, Sir!!"

"Louder!"

"Aye aye, Sir!!"

"Ready! March!"

"Aye aye, Sir!!"

"Thirty-inches!"

"*Aye aye, Sir*!"

"Aye aye, Sir!!"

"*Aye aye, Sir*!"

"Aye aye, Sir!!"

"*Arms*!"

"Six to the front!! Three to the rear!!"

"Louder!"

"Six to the front!! Three to the rear!!"

"Louder!"

"Six to the front!! Three to the rear!!"

"Fists closed! Fingers grounded!"

"*Aye aye, Sir*!"

"Aye aye, Sir!!"

"Thumbs to the outside!"

"Aye aye, Sir!!"

"Louder!"

"Aye aye, Sir!!"

"One arm's length from the Candidate in front of you!"

"That's an *aye aye, Sir*!"

"Aye aye, Sir!!"

"Louder!"

"Aye aye, Sir!!"

"*Aye aye, Sir*!"

"Aye aye, Sir!!"

"Aligned to the starboard side!"

"That's an *aye aye, Sir*!"

"Aye aye, Sir!!"

"Louder!"

"Aye aye, Sir!!"

"Right turn! March!"

"Aye aye, Sir!!"

"And step! And step! And step! And step! And step! And step! And step! And step! And step! And step!"

"That's an *aye aye, Sir*!"

"Aye aye, Sir!!"

"*Arms*!"

"Six to the front!! Three to the rear!!"

"Louder!"

"Six to the front!! Three to the rear!!"

"Aligned to the starboard side!"

"*Aye aye, Sir*!"

"Aye aye, Sir!!"

"Louder!"

"Aye aye, Sir!!"

"Everyone!"

"Aye aye, Sir!!"

"Your left! Your left! Your left-right-left! Your left! Your left! Keep-it-in-step! Lefty-right-a-lo-right! Lefty-right-a-left-right! Left! Left! Keep-it-in-step! Left foot! Left foot! Lefty-right-a-lo! *Arms*!"

"Six to the front!! Three to the rear!!"

"Louder!"

"Six to the front!! Three to the rear!!"

"Louder!"

"Six to the front!! Three to the rear!!"

"Maintain alignment!"

"That's an *aye aye, Sir*!"

"Aye aye, Sir!!"

"Thirty-inch steps, Indoctrination Candidates!"

"Aye aye, Sir!!"

"One hundred and twenty steps per minute!"

"Aye aye, Sir!!"

"Louder!"

"Aye aye, Sir!!"

"Ready! Halt!"

"Aye aye, Sir!!"

"Indoctrination Class Zero-Four-Zero-Zero! Upon receiving the command of execution *ground your canteens*! You will ground your canteens!"

"Aye aye, Sir!!"

"Ground your canteens!!"

"Aye aye, Sir!!"

"Upon receiving the command of execution *move*! Beginning with the rear of the platoon! And in orderly groups of four! You will! Proceed inside this hatch and follow the guidance of the civilians inside!"

"Aye aye, Sir!!"

"Louder!"

"Aye aye, Sir!!"

"Under no circumstances will you address the civilians in the ballistic. Is that clear?"

"Yes, Sir!!"

"You four. Move."

"Aye aye, Sir!!"

"You four. Stand-by in the ladderwell."

"Aye aye, Sir!!"

"Well? What are you waiting for? Let's see that brass!"

"Aye aye, Sir!!"

"Heat and friction! Heat and friction, Indoctrination Candidates!"

"That's an *aye aye, Sir*!"

"Aye aye, Sir!!"

"We want to see that shine!"

"Aye aye, Sir!!"

"Where's my Gougebody?"

"Gougebody, aye aye, Sir!"

"Gougebody! Gouge the class!"

"Aye aye, Sir! Indoctrination Class Zero-Four-Zero-Zero! The first article of the Code of Conduct is! *I am an American*! *Fighting in the forces which guard my country*! *And our way of life*! *I am prepared to give my life in their defense*!"

"Aye aye, Gougebody!! The first article of the Code of Conduct is!! I am an American!! Fighting in the forces which guard my country!! And our way of life!! I am prepared to give my life in their defense!!"

"Indoctrination Class Zero-Four-Zero-Zero! The second article of the Code of Conduct is! *I will never surrender of my own free will*! *If in command*! *I will never surrender the members of my command while they still have the means to resist*!"

"Aye aye, Gougebody!! The second article of the Code of Conduct is!! I will never surrender of my own free will! If in command!! I will never surrender the members of my command while they still have the means to resist!!"

"Knowledge is verbatim, Indoctrination Candidates! Attention to detail saves lives!"

"Aye aye, Sir!!"

"Those of you struggling to with the knowledge at this point are behind, Class Zero-Four-Zero-Zero. The D.Is will eat you alive. Everyone, now."

"That's an *aye aye, Sir*!"

"Aye aye, Sir!!"

"Indoctrination Class Zero-Four-Zero-Zero! The third article of the Code of Conduct is! *If I am captured*! *I will continue to resist by all means available*! *I will make every effort to escape*! *And aid others to escape*! *I will accept neither parole nor special favors from the enemy*!"

"Aye aye, Gougebody!! The third article of the Code of Conduct is!! If I am captured!! I will continue to resist by all means available!! I will make every effort to escape!! And aid others to escape!! I will accept neither parole nor special favors from the enemy!!"

"Heat and friction, Indoctrination Candidates! Heat and Friction!"

"Aye aye, Sir!!"

"Louder!"

"Aye aye, Sir!!"

"Indoctrination Class Zero-Four-Zero-Zero! The fourth article of the Code of Conduct is! *If I become a prisoner of war*! *I will keep faith with my fellow prisoners*! *I will give no information*! *Nor take part in any action which might be harmful to my comrades*! *If I am senior, I will take command*! *If not, I will obey the lawful orders of those appointed over me*! *And will back them up in every way*!"

"Aye aye, Gougebody!! The fourth article of the Code of Conduct is!! If I become a prisoner of war!! I will keep faith with my fellow prisoners!! I will give no information!! Nor take part in any action which might be harmful to my comrades!! If I am senior, I will take command!! If not, I will obey the lawful orders of those appointed over me!! And will back them up in every way!!"

"Indoctrination Class Zero-Four-Zero-Zero! The fifth article of the Code of Conduct is! *When questioned*! *Should I become a prisoner of war*! *I am required to give name, rank, service number and date of birth*! *I will evade answering further questions to the utmost of my ability*! *I will make no oral or written statements disloyal to my country and its allies*! *Or harmful to their cause*!"

"Aye aye, Gougebody!! The fifth article of the Code of Conduct is!! When questioned!! Should I become a prisoner of war!! I am required to give name, rank, service number and date of birth!! I will evade answering further questions to the utmost of my ability!! I will make no oral or written statements disloyal to my country and its allies!! Or harmful to their cause!!"

"Heat and friction, Indoctrination Candidates! Heat and friction!"

"That's an *aye aye, Sir*!"

"Aye aye, Sir!!"

"Indoctrination Class Zero-Four-Zero-Zero! The sixth article of the Code of Conduct is! *I will never forget that I am an American*! *Fighting for freedom*! *Responsible for my actions*! *And dedicated to the principles which made my country free*! *I will trust in my God*! *And in the United States of America*!"

"Aye aye, Gougebody!! The sixth article of the Code of Conduct is!! I will never forget that I am an American!! Fighting for freedom!! Responsible for my actions!! And dedicated to the principles which made my country free!! I will trust in my God!! And in the United States of America!!"

"Next four. Man the stairwell."

"Aye aye, Sir!!"

"Indoctrination Class Zero-Four-Zero-Zero! The first General Order of a Sentry is! *To take charge of this post*! *And all government property in view*!"

"Aye aye, Gougebody!! The first General Order of a Sentry is!! To take charge of this post!! And all government property in view!!"

"Heat and friction, Indoctrination Candidates!"

"Aye aye, Sir!!"

"Louder!"

"Aye aye, Sir!!"

"Indoctrination Class Zero-Four-Zero-Zero! The second General Order of a Sentry is! *To walk my post in a military manner*! *Keeping always on the alert*! *And observing everything that takes place within sight or hearing*!"

"Aye aye, Gougebody!! The second General Order of a Sentry is!! To walk my post in a military manner!! Keeping always on the alert!! And observing everything that takes place within sight or hearing!!"

"Indoctrination Class Zero-Four-Zero-Zero! The third General Order of a Sentry is! *To report all violations of orders I am instructed to enforce*!"

"Aye aye, Gougebody!! The third General Order of a Sentry is!! To report all violations of orders I am instructed to enforce!!"

"Indoctrination Class Zero-Four-Zero-Zero! *The fourth General Order of a Sentry is*! *To repeat all calls from posts more distant from the guard house than my own*!"

"Aye aye, Gougebody!! The fourth General Order of a Sentry is!! To repeat all calls from posts more distant from the guard house than my own!!"

"Heat and friction! Heat and friction!"

"Aye aye, Sir!!"

"Louder!"

"Aye aye, Sir!!"

"Indoctrination Class Zero-Four-Zero-Zero! The fifth General Order of a Sentry is! *To quit my post only when properly relieved*!"

"Aye aye, Gougebody!! The fifth General Order of a Sentry is to quit my post only when properly relieved!!"

"Heat and friction, Indoctrination Candidates!"

"Aye aye, Sir!!"

"Indoctrination Class Zero-Four-Zero-Zero! The sixth General Order of a Sentry is! *To receive! Obey! And pass on to the sentry who relieves me! All orders from the Commanding Officer! Command Duty Officer! Officer of the Deck! And Officers and Petty Officers of the Watch only!*"

"Aye aye, Gougebody!! The sixth General Order of a Sentry is!! To receive!! Obey!! And pass on to the sentry who relieves me!! All orders from the Commanding Officer!! Command Duty Officer!! Officer of the Deck!! And Officers and Petty Officers of the Watch only!!"

"As you were, Indoctrination Class Zero-Four-Zero-Zero! The sixth General Order of a Sentry is! *To receive! Obey! And pass on to the sentry who relieves me! All orders from the Commanding Officer! Command Duty Officer! Officer of the Deck! And Officers and Petty Officers of the Watch only!*"

"Aye aye, Sir!! Sir!! The sixth General Order of a Sentry is!! To receive!! Obey!! And pass on to the sentry who relieves me!! All orders from the Commanding Officer!! Command Duty Officer!! Officer of the Deck!! And Officers and Petty Officers of the Watch only!!"

"You four. On deck."

"Aye aye, Sir!!"

"Indoctrination Class Zero-Four-Zero-Zero! The seventh General Order of a Sentry is! *To talk to no one except in the line of duty!*"

"Aye aye, Gougebody!! The seventh General Order of a Sentry is!! To talk to no one except in the line of duty!!"

"Indoctrination Class Zero-Four-Zero-Zero! The eighth General Order of a Sentry is! *To give the alarm in case of fire or disorder!*"

"Aye aye, Gougebody!! The eighth General Order of a Sentry is!! To give the alarm in case of fire or disorder!!"

"Indoctrination Class Zero-Four-Zero-Zero! The ninth General Order of a Sentry is! *To call the Officer of the Deck in any case not covered by instructions!*"

"Aye aye, Gougebody!! The ninth General Order of a Sentry is!! To call the Officer of the Deck in any case not covered by instructions!!"

"Indoctrination Class Zero-Four-Zero-Zero! The tenth General Order of a Sentry is! *To salute all Officers! And all colors and standards not cased!*"

"Aye aye, Gougebody!! The tenth General Order of a Sentry is!! To salute all Officers!! And all colors and standards not cased!!"

"Next four! Get up there!"

"Aye aye, Sir!!"

"Indoctrination Class Zero-Four-Zero-Zero! The eleventh General Order of a Sentry is! *To be especially watchful at night! And, during the time for challenging! To challenge all persons on or near my post! And to allow no one to pass without proper authority!*"

"Aye aye, Gougebody!! The eleventh General Order of a Sentry is!! To be especially watchful at night!! And, during the time for challenging!! To challenge all persons on or near my post!! And to allow no one to pass without proper authority!!"

"Let's hear the Chain of Command, Gougebody."

"Chain of Command, aye aye, Sir! Indoctrination Class Zero-Four-Zero-Zero! The first person in your Chain of Command is! *Section Leader*! *Candidate Commander Monroe*!"

"Aye aye, Gougebody!! The first person in this Indoctrination Candidate's Chain of Command is!! Section Leader!! Candidate Commander Monroe!!"

"Indoctrination Class Zero-Four-Zero-Zero! The second person in your Chain of Command is! *Class Drill Instructor*! *Staff Sergeant Willett*! *United States Marine Corp*!"

"Aye aye, Gougebody!! The second person in this Indoctrination Candidate's Chain of Command is!! Class Drill Instructor!! Staff Sergeant Willett!! United States Marine Corp!!"

"Indoctrination Class Zero-Four-Zero-Zero! The third person in your Chain of Command is! *Class Officer*! *Lieutenant Bryant*! *United States Navy*!"

"Aye aye, Gougebody!! The third person in this Indoctrination Candidate's Chain of Command is!! Class Officer!! Lieutenant Bryant!! United States Navy!!"

"Indoctrination Class Zero-Four-Zero-Zero! The fourth person in your Chain of Command is! *Assistant Operations Officer*! *Lieutenant Commander Harris*! *United States Navy*!"

"Aye aye, Gougebody!! The fourth person in this Indoctrination Candidate's Chain of Command is!! Assistant Operations Officer!! Lieutenant Commander Harris!! United States Navy!!"

"Indoctrination Class Zero-Four-Zero-Zero! The fifth person in your Chain of Command is! *Operations Officer*! *Lieutenant Commander Roy*! *United States Navy*!"

"Aye aye, Gougebody!! The fifth person in this Indoctrination Candidate's Chain of Command is!! Operations Officer!! Lieutenant Commander Roy!! United States Navy!!"

"Next four. Into the hole."

"Aye aye, Sir!!"

"Good morning, Sir."

"Step."

"Step."

"Good morning, Sir."

Two sets of twin barber chairs face into the space. Hair litters the floor. I make out my reflection between wall-to-wall mirrors.

"Have a seat, honey."

"Thank you, Ma'am. Just a little off the top."

"I wish, Honey. Beautiful hair. Anyone ever told you that?"

"No, Ma'am."

"Now, that's not true. Real shame. Not to worry. Best thing about hair is it grows back."

"Yes, Ma'am."

"You can relax in here. They can't come in."

"It's only Candidate Officers, Ma'am."

"None of them. I told them as much. Told them I was going to slip with the razor one of these days on account of the screaming and hollering. Bad enough having all that racket outside. Head forward."

"Yes, Ma'am."

The razor works against my scalp. My hair rolls off the blade onto the floor.

"There we go. You boys take care of yourselves, you hear? You'll be just fine."

"Thank you, Ma'am. We'll tell them you said so."

"That's right, Honey. You tell them."

"Everyone ready? Let's line it up. Good afternoon, Sir!"

"Step!"

"Step!"

"Good afternoon, Sir!"

"Back in formation!"

"Aye aye, Sir!!"

"Your brass needs shine, Indoctrination Candidates! It needs that shine!"

"Aye aye, Sir!!"

"Heat and friction! Heat and Friction!"

"That's an *aye aye, Sir*!"

"Aye aye, Sir!!"

"Indoctrination Class Zero-Four-Zero-Zero! The eleventh person in your Chain of Command is! *The Secretary of the Navy*! *The Honorable Richard Danzig*!"

"Aye aye, Gougebody!! The eleventh person in this Indoctrination Candidate's Chain of Command is!! The Secretary of the Navy!! The Honorable Richard Danzig!!"

"Indoctrination Class Zero-Four-Zero-Zero! The twelfth person in your Chain of Command is! *The Secretary of Defense*! *The Honorable William Cohen*!"

"Aye aye, Gougebody!! The twelfth person in this Indoctrination Candidate's Chain of Command is!! The Secretary of Defense!! The Honorable William Cohen!!"

"Heat and friction, Indoctrination Candidates! Heat and friction!"

"Aye aye, Sir!!"

"Louder!"

"Aye aye, Sir!!"

"Indoctrination Class Zero-Four-Zero-Zero! The thirteenth person in your Chain of Command is! *The Vice-President of the United States*! *Vice President Albert Gore*!"

"Aye aye, Gougebody!! The thirteenth person in this Indoctrination Candidate's Chain of Command is!! The Vice-President of the United States!! Vice President Albert Gore!!"

"Indoctrination Class Zero-Four-Zero-Zero! The fourteenth person in your Chain of Command is! *The President of the United States*! *President William Clinton*!"

"Aye aye, Gougebody!! The fourteenth person in this Indoctrination Candidate's Chain of Command is!! The President of the United States!! President William Clinton!!"

"Next four!"

"Aye aye, Sir!!"

"Heat and friction, Indoctrination Candidates! Heat and friction!"

••

Side-Straddle Hops

A four-count exercise from a standing position with feet together and hands at sides. Count-one. Jump up while bringing hands together over the head and landing with feet shoulder width apart. Count-two. Jump back to starting position. Repeat for count-three and count-four.

••

"Thousand yard stare, Freakshow! I see your freaking eyeball again, I'm ripping it out and freaking eating it! You got that?"

"Yes, Sir!"

"You! You call that freaking aligned? Do you?"

"No, Sir!"

"You! Freak! I must be freaking dreaming! What program are you on?"

"No excuse, Sir!"

"Not this one, Freak! Where's your place?"

"No excuse, Sir!"

"Where's your freaking place?"

"No excuse, Sir!"

"Where's your freaking place?"

"This Officer Candidate does not know but will find out, Sir!"

"Find it!"

"Aye aye, Sir!"

"Imbecile. Ears!"

"Open, Sir!!"

"There are two types of commands! The first! The preparatory command! Such as *forward*! Indicates a movement is to be made! The second, the command of execution, such as *march*, causes the desired movement to be made! On some commands, such as *fall in*! *At ease*! And *rest*! The preparatory command and the command of execution are combined! Do I make myself clear?"

"Yes, Sir!!"

"The first movement that I will explain and demonstrate is the hand salute! The purpose for this movement is the form of courtesy used between members of the armed services! This movement has a single count! This movement is executed when at the position of attention or marching at quick time! Do you have any freaking questions about this movement?"

"No, Sir!!"

"How do you freaking know? On the command of execution *hand salute*! On the count of one! Smartly! And in the most direct manner! Raise your nasty paws until the tip of the right forefinger touches the lower portion of your headdress above and slightly to the right of the right eye! Fingers are extended and joined! The thumb is along the hand and the palm is down! Am I clear?"

"Yes, Sir!!"

"Louder!"

"Yes, Sir!!"

"You will remain in this position until given another freaking command!"

"Aye aye, Sir!!"

"I will now execute this movement in cadence! Hand salute! You got it?"

"Yes, Sir!!"

"Ready! Hand salute!"

"Aye aye, Sir!!"

"You should be able to see the entire palm when looking straight ahead! Wrist and forearm are straight! Straight! The forearm is inclined at an angle of

forty degrees! The upper arm is parallel to deck, with the elbow in line with the body! Got it?"

"Yes, Sir!!"

"I see freaking daylight, Pig!"

"No excuse, Sir!"

"You! Upper arm parallel to the deck!"

"Aye aye, Sir!"

"Parallel to the freaking deck!"

"Aye aye, Sir!"

"Wrist and forearm straight, Pig!"

"Aye aye, Sir!"

"You don't ground those fingers, I'll solder them shut! You got that?"

"Yes, Sir!"

"Freakshow! I can see your freaking thumb! That's a freaking response!"

"No excuse, Sir!"

"I can see your freaking teeth, Pig!"

"No excuse, Sir!"

"Shut your hole!"

"Aye aye, Sir!"

"Shut it!"

"Aye aye, Sir!"

"The command to terminate is *ready two*! On the command *two*! Smartly and in the most direct manner return the right hand to the right side and assume the position of attention! You will remain in this position until given another command! Do you have any freaking questions?"

"No, Sir!!"

"How do you freaking know? Ready! Two!"

"Aye aye, Sir!!"

"I don't think so! As you were!"

"Aye aye, Sir!!"

"Ready! Two!"

"Aye aye, Sir!!"

"This isn't dominos, Freaks! Get them back up! Angle of forty degrees! Wrist and forearms straight! I see any more freaking thumbs, I'm cutting them off! Am I clear?"

"Yes, Sir!!"

"Ready! Two!"

"Aye aye, Sir!!"

"Ears!"

"Open, Sir!!"

"The next movement that I will explain and demonstrate is the position of rest! The purpose for this movement is to give Nasty! Lethargic! Pathetic! Freaks! Like you! A rest from the position of attention! You will go to rest upon receiving the commands *parade rest*! *At ease*! Or *fall out*! Parade rest and at ease are one-count movements! Falling out is not a precision movement and has no freaking counts! These movements are executed, and executed only, when halted at attention! Freaking clear?"

"Yes, Sir!!"

"I will begin with parade rest! On the preparatory command shift the weight of your body to your right leg! But I don't want to freaking see it! Am I clear?"

"Yes, Sir!!"

"On the command of execution and for the count of one! Move your left foot smartly twelve inches to the left of your right foot! Twelve inches! Twelve inches from the inside of your right heel to the inside of your left heel! The heels remain on line! The legs remain straight without stiffness! The body weight rests equally on both legs! That's an *aye aye, Sir*!"

"Aye aye, Sir!!"

"At the same time! Clasp the hands behind the back! The left hand is placed just below the belt! The right hand is placed inside the left hand! The thumb of the right hand grasps the thumb of the left hand! The fingers are extended and joined and the palms are to the rear! Am I clear?"

"Yes, Sir!!"

"Stop whispering to me, you Nasty Pigs!"

"Aye aye, Sir!!"

"The elbows are in line with the body! The only command you may receive while at parade rest is back to the position of attention! Silence and immobility!"

"Aye aye, Sir!!"

"On the command of execution *atten-hut*, smartly bring your left heel against your right heel! At the same time drop the arms to the side and assume the position of attention! Am I clear?"

"Yes, Sir!!"

"Eyeballs!"

"Snap, Sir!!"

"I will now execute this movement in cadence! Parade rest! One-freaking-count! Atten-hut! One-freaking-count!"

"Aye aye, Sir!!"

"Your turn! Atten-hut!"

"Aye aye, Sir!!"

"Ready! Parade rest! As you were!"

"Aye aye, Sir!!"

"Shift at *parade*! Execution at *rest*! Let's try it again! All together this time, Maggots!"

"Aye aye, Sir!!"

"Parade rest!"

"Aye aye, Sir!!"

"Twelve inches, Freakshow! Correct yourself!"

"Aye aye, Sir!"

"Right hand inside the left! Right hand inside the left, Freak!"

"Aye aye, Sir!"

"Why you eyeballing me? Why you eyeballing me?"

"No excuse, Sir!"

"You! Ground your freaking thumb now!"

"Aye aye, Sir!"

"Atten-hut!"

"Aye aye, Sir!!"

"Parade rest!"

"Aye aye, Sir!!"

"Right inside the left, Freak! Correct yourself!"

"Aye aye, Sir!"

"Fingers grounded, Friendly Fire!"

"Aye aye, Sir!"

"Stop whispering to me!"

"Aye aye, Sir!"

"Atten-hut!"

"Aye aye, Sir!!"

"Ears!"

"Open, Sir!!"

"The next movement that I will explain and demonstrate is the position of ease! On the command *at ease*, the only requirement is that your right foot remains in place! You may move your left foot! You may place your hands in front of the body! You may move about and adjust equipment or uniform! In other words, you fix yourself! Place your feet shoulder width apart! And clasp your freaking hands in front of you! In freaking silence! Is that clear?"

"Yes, Sir!!"

"The only command you may receive while at ease is back to the position of attention! On the command of execution *atten-hut*, smartly bring your left heel against your right heel! And at the same time drop the arms to the sides and assume the position of attention! Am I clear?"

"Yes, Sir!!"

"Eyeballs!"

"Snap, Sir!!"

"I will now execute this movement in cadence! You got that?"

"Yes, Sir!!"

"Atten-hut! Did I say you could freaking look around, Pig?"

"No, Sir!"

"What?"

"No, Sir!"

"Freaking what?"

"No excuse, Sir!"

"As you were, Pigs!"

"Aye aye, Sir!!"

"Upon my command! Attenhut!"

"Aye aye, Sir!!"

"At ease!"

"Aye aye, Sir!!"

"Freaking individuals. Attenhut!"

"Aye aye, Sir!!"

"The next movement that I will explain and demonstrate is falling out! Upon the command of execution *fall out*, you will leave your position in ranks! You will go to a pre-designated area or remain in the immediate vicinity! Right now, you will go to my pre-designated grass and push! Am I clear?"

"Yes, Sir!!"

"Fall out, Pigs!"

"Aye aye, Sir!!"

"Ten-six-four-three-one. On your faces!"

"Aye aye, Sir!!"

"Down. *Aye aye, Sir*!"

"Aye aye, Sir!!"

"The only command you may receive from after falling out is to fall in! On the command *fall in*! You will assume your position in ranks at the position of attention! That's a freaking *aye aye, Sir*!"

"Aye aye, Sir!!"

"Up! *Zero-one*!"

"Zero-one!!"

"Down!"

"Aye aye, Sir!!"

"Up!"

"Zero-two!!"

"Down!"

"Aye aye, Sir!!"

"Up!"

"Zero-three!!"

"Down!"

"Aye aye, Sir!!"

"Up!"

"Zero-four!!"

"Down!"

"Aye aye, Sir!!"

"Up!"

"Zero-five!!"

"On your feet now! Run in place!"

"Aye aye, Sir!!"

"On your faces!"

"Aye aye, Sir!!"

"On your feet!"

"Aye aye, Sir!!"

"On your faces! *Aye aye, Sir!*"

"Aye aye, Sir!!"

"Fall in!"

"Aye aye, Sir!!"

"Ten-nine-eight-five-three-two-one! What the hell do you think you're doing, Slime?"

"No excuse, Sir!"

"Where's your place?"

"This Indoctrination Candidate does not know but will find out, Sir!"

"Back in my grass! Thank the idiot!"

"Aye aye, Sir!!"

"Ten-nine-eight-seven-six-five-two-one! On your faces!"

"Aye aye, Sir!!"

"On your feet now! Run in place!"

"Aye aye, Sir!!"

"On your faces!"

"Aye aye, Sir!!"

"Push! Down-up! Down-up!"

"Aye aye, Sir!! Zero-one!! Zero-two!!"

"On your feet!"

"Aye aye, Sir!!"

"On your faces!"

"Aye aye, Sir!!"

"Fall in!"

"Aye aye, Sir!!"

"Ten-nine-eight-seven-three-two-one! Freeze! Cover! The next movement that I will explain and demonstrate is facing right! Facings are executed in the

cadence of quick time! While facing, your arms will not swing out from you freaking sides! Your arms will remain freaking glued to your trouser seams as in the position of attention! *Aye aye, Sir.*"

"Aye aye, Sir!!"

"If I see any freaking limbs, I'm cutting them off. Am I clear?"

"Yes, Sir!!"

"Right face is a two-count movement! On the count of one! On the command of execution *face*, raise your left heel and right toe slightly! Slightly! Turn to the right heel and left toe! Keep your left leg straight but not stiff! Clear?"

"Yes, Sir!!"

"On the count of two! Place the left foot smartly beside the right, returning to the position of attention! Front and center, Pig!"

"Aye aye, Sir!"

"Eyeballs!"

"Snap, Sir!!"

"You will freaking demonstrate!"

"Aye aye, Sir!"

"Right freaking face!"

"Aye aye, Sir!"

"As you were! Tighter!"

"Aye aye, Sir!"

"Smarter!"

"Aye aye, Sir!"

"Left heel up! Right toe slightly!"

"Aye aye, Sir!"

"Right! Face!"

"Aye aye, Sir!"

"Find your place, Pig."

"Aye aye, Sir!"

"You will now execute this movement in cadence!"

"Aye aye, Sir!!"

"Ready! Right! Face!"

"Aye aye, Sir!!"

"Your other right, Freak!"

"Aye aye, Sir!"

"Your other freaking right!"

"No excuse, Sir!"

"Arms glued to the seams, Pig!"

"Aye aye, Sir!"

"Right! Face!"

"Aye aye, Sir!"

"Right! Face!"

"Aye aye, Sir!"

"Right! Face!"

"Aye aye, Sir!"

"Left face is executed in the same freaking manner! On the count of one! At the command *face*, raise your right heel and left toe slightly! Turn to the left heel and right toe! Keep your right leg straight but not stiff! Clear?"

"Yes, Sir!!"

"On the count of two! Place the right foot smartly beside the left! returning to the position of attention! Am I clear?"

"Yes, Sir!!"

"You will now execute this movement in cadence!"

"Aye aye, Sir!!"

"Ready! Left! Face!"

"Aye aye, Sir!!"

"Freaking Moron! Your other freaking left! Get in my grass!"

"Aye aye, Sir!"

"Freaking all you! Now! *Aye aye, Sir*!"

"Aye aye, Sir!!"

"Ten-nine-three-two-one! Push!"

"Aye aye, Sir!!"

"Fall in!"

"Aye aye, Sir!!"

"Ten-nine-six-five-four-three-two-one! Freeze!"

"Aye aye, Sir!!"

"Freaking lethargic! Grass!"

"Aye aye, Sir!!"

"Ten-nine-eight-three-two-one! Leg-lifts!"

"Aye aye, Sir!!"

"On your feet! Run in place!"

"Aye aye, Sir!!"

"On your faces!"

"Aye aye, Sir!!"

"On your backs!"

"Aye aye, Sir!!"

"On your feet!"

"Aye aye, Sir!!"

"Fall in!"

"Aye aye, Sir!!"

"Too slow. Back in my grass!"

"Aye aye, Sir!!"

"Fall in!"

"Aye aye, Sir!!"

"Too slow. Back in my grass!"

"Aye aye, Sir!!"

"Fall in!"

"Aye aye, Sir!!"

"Ten-nine-eight! Pathetic. Back in my grass! *Aye aye, Sir!*"

"Aye aye, Sir!!"

"On your faces!"

"Aye aye, Sir!!"

"On your feet!"

"Aye aye, Sir!!"

"Run in place now!"

"Aye aye, Sir!!"

"Get them up now!"

"Aye aye, Sir!!"

"Fall in!"

"Aye aye, Sir!!"

"Ten-nine-eight-seven-six-three-two-one! Freeze!"

"Aye aye, Sir!!"

"Stop whispering to me!"

"Aye aye, Sir!!"

"Cover! If you don't start freaking listening! We can do this all day! *Aye aye, Sir!*"

"Aye aye, Sir!!"

"The next movement that I will explain and demonstrate is the about face! About face is a two-count movement! On count-one! On the command of execution *face*! Place your right freaking toe half a foot length behind and slightly to the left of your heel! Do not change the position of your left foot! Remainder of your weight is on the left heel! Is that freaking clear?"

"Yes, Sir!"

"Do not! Do not change the position of your left foot! It's freaking stapled to the deck! Weight on the back heel! *Aye aye, Sir!*"

"Aye aye, Sir!!"

"On count-two! Turn smartly to the right until facing rear! One-eight-freaking-zero degrees! The turn is made on the left heel and ball of the right foot! Right foot! *Aye aye, Sir!*"

"Aye aye, Sir!!"

"You come back around at the position of attention! Position of attention! Thousand yard stare at all times!"

"Aye aye, Sir!!"

"Front and center, Pig!"

"Aye aye, Sir!"

"Eyeballs!"

"Snap, Sir!!"

"You will freaking demonstrate!"

"Aye aye, Sir!"

"About! Face!"

"Aye aye, Sir!!"

"You must be out of your damn mind! Freaking Moron! Back in my grass, Pigs! Thank the Moron! Ten-three-one! Push!"

••

Eight-count Body Builders

An eight-count exercise from a standing position. Count-one. Bend legs and place hands on deck. Count-two. Extend both legs backward supporting body weight with extended arms (starting position for a push-up). Count-three. Bend elbows, lowering chest toward deck (a push-up). Count-four. Extend arms. Count-five. Separate legs while keeping arms extended. Count-six. Bring legs back together as on count-four. Count-seven. Flex legs and bring them back to count-one position. Count-eight. Stand and return to starting position.

••

The call comes over the one-M.C.

"Indoctrination Class Zero-Four-Zero-Zero, this is your one-zero minute warning!"

"Indoctrination Class Zero-Four-Zero-Zero, this is your zero-five minute warning!"

"Indoctrination Class Zero-Four-Zero-Zero, this is your zero-one minute warning!"

"Indoctrination Class Zero-Four-Zero-Zero, this is your immediate warning!"

"Attention on deck, stand-by!"

"Good afternoon, Sir!!"

"As you were, Candidates. You do not to sound off to a Naval Officer."

"No excuse, Sir."

"That's a hit for the room."

"Aye aye, Sir."

One of the Officers squares up in front of me. She returns my salute. I pull back to attention.. .

"Good morning, Ma'am."

"Good morning, Candidate. That's one ugly salute. Try it again."

"Aye aye, Ma'am."

"I see your thumb. Pull it back."

"Aye aye, Ma'am."

"Straighten the wrist."

"Aye aye, Ma'am"

"Shoulder back."

"Aye aye, Ma'am."

"Straighten that wrist."

"Aye aye, Ma'am."

"That's a hit."

"Aye aye, Ma'am."

"Very well. Position of attention."

"Aye aye, Ma'am."

"Underwhelming gig line."

"Aye aye, Ma'am."

"Let's take a look at that brass."

I undo the clasp to my belt.

"You see the inside, there?"

"Yes, Ma'am."

"Did you shine it?"

"Yes, Ma'am."

"Are you satisfied with the result?"

"No, Ma'am."

"I don't even know what to say about this table display."

"No excuse, Ma'am."

"Unfit salute. Gig line. Dirty brass. Improper table display. And an improper response."

"Aye aye, Ma'am."

"Very well. What is the fifth article of the Code of Conduct?"

"Ma'am, the fifth article of the Code of Conduct is when questioned, should I become a prisoner of war, I am required to give name, rank, service number and date of birth. I will evade answering further questions to the utmost of my ability. I will make no statements disloyal to my country and its allies or harmful to their cause."

"Is that verbatim?"

"Yes, Ma'am."

"Are you positive?"

"Yes, Ma'am."

"Very well. Who is the eighth person in your Chain of Command?"

"Ma'am, the eighth person in this Officer Candidate's Chain of Command is Captain Johnson, Commander, Naval Aviation Schools Command."

"What is the sixth General Order of a Sentry?"

"Ma'am, the sixth General Order of a Sentry is to receive, obey and pass on to the sentry who relieves me, all orders from the Commanding Officer, Command Duty Officer, Officer of the Deck, and Officers and Petty Officers of the Watch only."

"You'll need that voice. Dig deeper."

"Aye aye, Ma'am."

Shouts echo down the passageway.

"Very well. I could hit you all day. You are behind, Zurich. We demand more in the Officer corp. Do you understand me?"

"Yes, Ma'am."

"At ease, Candidate."

"Aye aye, Ma'am."

"Attention on deck, stand-by."

"Good morning, Sir."

A blur of camouflage charges into the space.

"Attention on deck, stand-by!"

"Good morning, Sir!!"

"Push! Push! Push!"

"Aye aye, Sir!!"

"On your faces, Freaks! On your freaking faces!"

"Aye aye, Sir!!"

"Give me the Code of Conduct, Maggot!"

"Aye aye, Sir! Sir! The first article of the Code of Conduct is! I am an American! Fighting in the forces which guard my country! And our way of life!"

"Hit! Irish pennant! Freaking I.P.!"

"Aye aye, Sir! I am prepared to give my life in their defense! Sir! The second article of the Code of Conduct is! I will never surrender of my own free will!"

"Hit! Freaking I.P.! Hit! Freaking I.P.! Hit! Freaking I.P.! Disgusting! Lethargic! Pig!"

"Aye aye, Sir! If in command! I will never surrender the members of my command while they still have the means to resist!"

"Side-straddle hops! Start hopping!"

"Aye aye, Sir! Sir! The third article of the Code of Conduct is! If I am captured! I will continue to resist by all means available! I will make every effort to escape! And aid others to escape! I will accept neither parole nor special favors from the enemy!"

"Mother of all freaking I.Ps! That's a hit! Where's my freaking response?"

"No excuse, Sir! Sir! The fourth article of the Code of Conduct is! If I become a prisoner of war! I will keep faith with my fellow prisoners!"

"Hit! Does that look like twelve inches to you, Puke?"

"No, Sir!"

"What's your freaking excuse?"

"No excuse, Sir! I will give no information! Nor take part in any action which might be harmful to my comrades! If I am senior, I will take command!"

"On your face!"

"Aye aye, Sir! If not! I will obey the lawful orders of those appointed over me! And will back them up in every way! Sir! The fifth article of the Code of Conduct is! When --!"

"Sticker!"

"Aye aye, Sir!"

"Sticker!"

"Aye aye, Sir!"

"Sticker! You think this is a sticker party, Dirt-for-Brains?"

"No excuse, Sir!"

"Three freaking hits!"

"Aye aye, Sir! When questioned! Should I become a prisoner of war! I am required to give name! Rank! Service number! And date of birth! I will evade answering further questions to the utmost of my ability! I will make no oral or

written statements disloyal to my country! And its allies! Or harmful to their cause!"

"I don't think so! Get on the rack!"

"Aye aye, Sir!"

"No, Moron! On your freaking back!"

"Aye aye, Sir!"

"Leg-lifts!"

"Aye aye, Sir!"

"General Orders of a Sentry!"

"Aye aye, Sir!

"General Orders of a Sentry!"

"Aye aye, Sir!"

"Stop whispering to me!"

"Aye aye, Sir!"

"Louder!"

"Aye aye, Sir!"

"What are you waiting for?"

"No excuse, Sir!"

"Now!"

"Aye aye, Sir! Sir! The first General Order of a Sentry is to take charge of this post! And all government property in view! Sir! The second General Order of a Sentry is to walk my post in a military manner! Keeping always on the alert! And observing everything that takes place within sight or hearing!"

"Hit! Does this look like six inches to you? Does this look like six inches to you? Where's my freaking response? Where is it? Respond, Freak!"

"No excuse, Sir!"

"Does this look like six inches to you?"

"No, Sir!"

"Stop whispering to me!"

"Aye aye, Sir!"

"What?"

"Aye aye, Sir!"

"Scissor-kicks!"

"Aye aye, Sir! Sir! The third General Order of a Sentry is to report all violations of orders I am instructed to enforce! Sir! The fourth General Order of a Sentry is to repeat all calls from posts more distant from the guard house than my own! Sir! The fifth General Order of a Sentry is to quit my post only when properly relieved! Sir! The sixth General Order of a Sentry is to receive! Obey! And pass on to the sentry who relieves me! All orders from the Commanding Officer! Command Duty Officer! Officer of the Deck! And Officers! And Petty Officers! Of the Watch only!"

"Are you eyeballing me? Are you eyeballing me, Freak?"

"No, Sir!"

"Are we dating? You want to buy me a drink?"

"No, Sir!"

"Do you want to be here?"

"Yes, Sir!"

"Do you want to go home?"

"No, Sir!"

"Are you sure?"

"Yes, Sir!"

"Are you sure?"

"Yes, Sir!"

"Louder!"

"Yes, Sir!"

"Stop whispering to me!"

"Yes, Sir!"

"On your feet when you sound off to me Pig!"

"Aye aye, Sir!"

"Hop and pops! I want to hear you count!"

"Aye aye, Sir! One-two-three! Zero-one! One-two-three! Zero-two! One-two-three! Zero-three! One-two-three! Zero-four! One-two-three! Zero-five! One-two-three! Zero-six! One-two-three! Zero-seven! One-two-three! Zero-eight! One-two-three! Zero-niner! One-two-three! One-zero! One-two-three! One-one! One-two-three! One-two!"

"Pack it up, Pigs!"

"Aye aye, Sir!!"

"Attention on deck, Stand-by!"

"Good morning, Sir!!"

Gear canvasses the room.

"Christ."

"Let's get it together guys. Sounds like we're on the move."

"Let's go, Indoctrination Class Zero-Four-Zero-Zero! Pack up your gear! Pack it up!"

"You have no time, Indoctrination Candidates! You have no time! Leave nothing behind! Everything in your seabags! Time to hump!"

"No way. Impossible. It's impossible."

"Steady, Potts. Pack what you can. Secure the rest."

"What about rifles?"

"Secure it. Trust me."

"Let's go, Indoctrination Candidates! Let's go!"

"Attention on deck! Stand-by!"

"Good morning, Sir!!"

"What are you doing coking-and-joking in the hole? Secure your rifles! Pack your seabags! You're on the move!"

"Aye aye, Sir!!"

"To the brim."

"Aye aye, Sir!!"

"Well? Let's go! Let's go! Let's go!"

"Aye aye, Sir!!"

"Attention on deck! Stand-by!"

"Good morning, Sir!!"

"Everyone set?"

"Does it look like I'm set?"

"Trust me. We'll circle back later on. Think about it."

"I don't know."

"Listen. We got to go, brother. Fold it later."

"Alright. Alright."

"Lock check."

"Check."

"Check."

"Check."

"Clear."

"Good morning, Sir!"

"Step!"

"Step!"

"Good morning, Sir!"

"Left-right!! Left-right!!"

"Good morning, Sir!"

"Step!"

"Step!"

"Good morning, Sir!"

"Left-right!! Left-right!!"

"Good morning, Sir!"

"Step!"

"Step!"

"Good morning, Sir!"

"Left-right!! Left-right!!"

"Line it up!"

"Aye aye, Sir!!"

"You have no time, Indoctrination Candidates!"

"Aye aye, Sir!! Left-right!! Left-right!! Left-right!! Left-right!! Left-right!! Left-right!! Left-right!! Left-right!! Left-right!! Left-right!! Left-right!! Left-right!! Left-right!!"

"Good morning, Sir!"

"Step!"

"Step!"

"Good morning, Sir!"

"Left-right!! Left-right!!"

"Good morning, Sir!"

"Step!"

"Step!"

"Good morning, Sir!"

"Let's go, Indoctrination Class Zero-Four-Zero-Zero! You have no time!"

"Aye aye, Sir!!"

"Line it up!"

"Aye aye, Sir!! Left-right!!"

"Good morning, Sir!"

"Left-right!! Left-right!!Left-right!! Left-right!!"

"Good morning, Sir!"

“Left-right!! Left-right!!”

“Freeze!”

“Aye aye, Sir!!”

“Count off!”

“Aye aye, Sir!!”

“Zero-one!”

“Zero-two!”

“Zero-three!”

“Zero-four!”

“Zero-five!”

“Zero-six!”

“Zero-seven!”

“Zero-eight!”

“Zero-niner!”

“One-zero!”

“One-one!”

“One-two!”

“One-three!”

“One-four!”

“One-five!”

“One-six!”

“One-seven!”

“One-eight!”

“One-niner!”

“Two-zero!”

“Two-one!”

“Two-two!”

“Two-three!”

“Two-four!”

"Two-five!"
"Two-six!"
"Two-seven!"
"Two-eight!"
"Two-niner!"
"Three-zero!"
"Three-one!"
"Three-two!"
"Three-three!"
"Three-four!"
"Three-five!"
"Three-six!"
"Three-seven!"
"Three-eight!"
"Nine-niner!"
"Four-zero!"
"Four-one!"
"Four-two!"
"Four-three!"
"Four-four!"
"Four-five!"
"Highly motivated!! Truly dedicated!! Indoctrination Candidates, Sir!!"
"Seabags up, Indoctrination Candidates!"
"Aye aye, Sir!!"
"Arms parallel to the deck!"
"Aye aye, Sir!!"
"Fingers joined but not interlocking!"
"Aye aye, Sir!!"

"Indoctrination Class Zero-Four-Zero-Zero! Upon receiving the command of execution *march*! You will! Perform an immediate right face! March smartly to the exit! Descend the ladderwell in an orderly fashion! And regroup in platoon formation on the pavement below! Is that clear?"

"Yes, Sir!!"

"Ready! March!"

"Aye aye, Sir!! Left-right!! Left-

right!! Left-right!! Left-right!! Left-right!! Left-right!! Left-right!! Left-right!! Left-right!! Left-right!! Left-right!!”

“Good morning, Sir!”

“Left-right!! Left-right!!Left-right!! Left-right!!”

“Good morning, Sir!”

“Left-right!! Left-right!!”

“Safety first, Indoctrination Candidates!”

“Aye aye, Sir!! Left-right!! Left-right!! Left-right!! Left-right!! Left-right!! Left-right!! Left-right!! Left-right!! Left-right!! Left-right!! Left-right!! Left-right!! Left-right!! Left-right!! Left-right!! Left-right!! Left-right!! Left-right!!”

“At a deliberate pace!”

“Aye aye, Sir!! Left-right!!”

“Platoon formation!”

“Aye aye, Sir!! Left-right!! Left-right!! Left-right!! Left-right!! Left-right!! Left-right!! Left-right!! Left-right!! Left-right!! Left-right!! Left-right!! Left-right!! Left-right!! Left-right!! Left-right!! Left-right!!”

“Freeze!”

“Aye aye, Sir!!”

“Cover!”

“Seabags up, Indoctrination Candidates!”

“Aye aye, Sir!!”

“Arms parallel to the deck!”

“Aye aye, Sir!!”

"Fingers joined but not interlocking!"

"Aye aye, Sir!!"

"Class Zero-Four-Zero-Zero! Right face!"

"Aye aye, Sir!!"

"Forward march!"

"Aye aye, Sir!!"

"Your left! Your left! Your left-right-left! Your left! Your left! Keep-it-in-step! Your left! Your left! Your left-right-left! Your left! Your left! Keep-it-in-step!"

"Aligned to the starboard side!"

"Aye aye, Sir!!"

"Louder!"

"Aye aye, Sir!!"

"Get them up!"

"Aye aye, Sir!!"

"Up!"

"Aye aye, Sir!!"

"Your left! Your left! Your left-right-left! Your left! Your left! Keep-it-in-step!"

"Get them up!"

"Aye aye, Sir!!"

"Louder!"

"Aye aye, Sir!!"

"Your left! Your left! Your left-right-left! Your left! Your left! Keep-it-in-step!"

"Arms parallel to the deck, Indoctrination Candidates!"

"Aye aye, Sir!!"

"Left! Left! Keep-it-in-step! Your left-right-left! Your left! Your left! Your left-right-left!"

"Up!"

"Aye aye, Sir!!"

"Your left! Left! Left turn! Right turn! March!"

"Aye aye, Sir!!"

"And step! And step! And step! And step! Your left! Your left! Your left! Your left! Your left! Left! Your left! Your left! Your left-right-left! Your left-right-left! Your left! Your left! Your left-right-left!"

"Get them up!"

"Aye aye, Sir!!"

"Arms parallel to the deck!"

"Aye aye, Sir!!"

"Fingers joined but not interlocking!"

"Aye aye, Sir!!"

Stragglers fall behind. The formation dissolves into a trail.

"Pick it up, Poopies!"

"Aye aye, Sir!!"

"Maintain alignment!"

"Aye aye, Sir!!"

"Hold formation!"

"Aye aye, Sir!!"

"T.T.O., Sir!"

"What's that?"

"T.T.O., Sir!"

"Platoon! Halt!"

"Aye aye, Sir!!"

"Indoctrination Candidate Howell, fall out."

"Aye aye, Sir!"

"Why the time out?"

"Sir! Indoctrinate Candidate Howell! Indoctrination Class Zero-Four --!"

"As you were. Speak freely."

"This Indoctrination Candidate requests permission to go to the Head! Sir!"

"You're in luck, Howell. Heading in that direction. Sooner you get back in formation, sooner you get there."

"An emergency, Sir!"

"Oh, damn. Sorry about that, Howell. Listen, don't sweat it. It happens sometimes. More than you might think. Seriously. Sometimes worse."

"Aye aye, Sir!"

"Hold the ballistics. Go on and drop the seabag. Follow Hyde here. He'll get you where you need to go."

"Aye aye, Sir."

"Keep your head up. Don't sweat the gear. We'll make sure it gets back to you."

"Aye aye, Sir."

"Indoctrination Class Zero-Four-Zero-Zero! Forward march!"

••

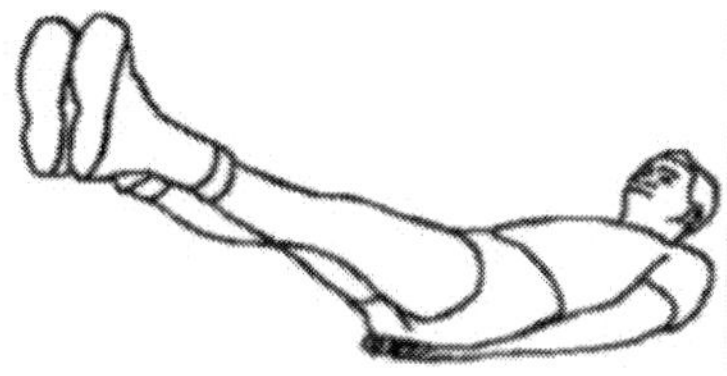

Leg-Lifts

A four-count exercise. Lie on back with hands under hips, legs extended, and feet together six inches above deck. Count-one. Lift both legs together one and one-half feet, keeping legs straight. Count-two. Lower legs to starting position. Count-three. Bring legs back up. Count-four. Return legs to starting position and repeat.

Hello-Dollies

A four-count exercise. Lie on back with palms on deck and hands under hips, legs extended, and feet together, six inches above deck. Count-one. Spread legs two to three feet apart. Count-two. Bring legs back together. Abdominals and hip flexors. Repeat for counts three and four.

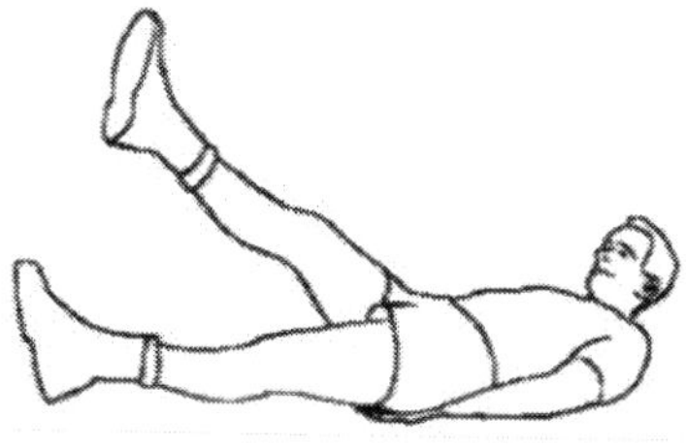

Flutter Kicks

A four-count exercise. Lie on back with hands under hips, legs extended, and feet together six inches above deck. Count-one. Lift right leg one and a half feet, keeping leg straight. Count-two. Lift left leg to same position while returning right leg to starting position. Count-three. Bring right leg back up and return left leg to starting position. Count-four. Repeat.

••

"Leg-lifts! Leg-lifts is a four-count exercise! You will count the cadence! You will count the repetitions! Begin!"

"Aye aye, Sir!! One-two-three!! Zero-one!! One-two-three!! Zero-two!! One-two-three!! Zero-three!! One-two-three!! Zero-four!! One-two-three!! Zero-five!! One-two-three!! Zero-six!! One-two-three!! Zero-seven!! One-two-three!! Zero-eight!! One-two-three!! Zero-niner!! One-two-three!! One-zero!! One-two-three!! One-one!! One-two-three!! One-two!! One-two-three!! One-three!! One-two-three!! One-four!! One-two-three!! One-five!! One-two-three!! One-six!! One-two-three!! One-seven!! One-two-three!! One-eight!! One-two-three! One-niner!! One-two-three!! Two-zero!! One-two-three!! Two-one!! One-two-three!! Two-two!! One-two-three!! Two-three!! One-two-three!! Two-four!! One-two-three!! Two-five!! One-two-three!! Two-six!! One-two-three!! Two-seven!! One-two-three!! Two-eight!! One-two-three!! Two-niner!! One-two-three!! Three-zero!!"

"On your feet! On your feet! *Aye aye, Sir!*"

"Aye aye, Sir!!"

"Run in place!"

"Aye aye, Sir!!"

"Push!"

"Aye aye, Sir!!"

"Down! Up!"

"Zero-one!!"

"Down! Up!"

"Zero-two!!"

"Down! Up!"

"Zero-three!!"

"Down! Up!"

"Zero-four!!"

"Down! Up!"

"Zero-five!!"

"Down! Up!"

"Zero-six!!"

"Down! Up!"

"Zero-seven!!"

"Down! Up!"

"Zero-eight!!"

"Backs straight!"

"Aye aye, Sir!!"

"Down! Up!"

"Zero-niner!!"

"Down! Up!"

"One-zero!!"

"Leg-lifts!"

"Aye aye, Sir!!"

"On your backs!!"

"Aye aye, Sir!!"

"Leg-lifts is a four-count exercise! You will count the cadence! You will count the repetitions! Begin!"

"Aye aye, Sir!! One-two-three!! Zero-one!! One-two-three!! Zero-two!! One-two-three!! Zero-three!! One-two-three!! Zero-four!! One-two-three!! Zero-five!! One-two-three!! Zero-six!!"

"Louder!"

"Aye aye, Sir!! One-two-three!! Zero-seven!! One-two-three!! Zero-eight!! One-two-three!! Zero-niner!! One-two-three!! One-zero!! One-two-three!! One-one!! One-two-three!! One-two!! One-two-three!! One-three!! One-two-three!! One-four!! One-two-three!! One-five!! One-two-three!! One-six!! One-two-three!! One-seven!! One-two-three!! One-eight!!"

"Legs straight! Angle of forty-five degrees! *Aye aye, Sir*!"

"Aye aye, Sir!! One-two-three!! One-niner!! One-two-three!! Two-zero!! One-two-three!! Two-one!! One-two-three!! Two-two!! One-two-three!! Two-three!! One-two-three!! Two-four!! One-two-three!! Two-five!! One-two-three!! Two-six!! One-two-three!! Two-seven!! One-two-three!! Two-eight!! One-two-three!! Two-niner!! One-two-three!! Three-zero!!"

"On your feet now!"

"Aye aye, Sir!!"

"On your backs now!"

"Aye aye, Sir!!"

"On your feet now!"

"Aye aye, Sir!!"

"On your backs now!"

"Aye aye, Sir!!"

"On your feet now!"

"Aye aye, Sir!!"

"On your backs now!"

"Aye aye, Sir!!"

"On your feet now!"
"Aye aye, Sir!!"
"On your backs now!"
"Aye aye, Sir!!"
"On your feet now!"
"Aye aye, Sir!!"
"Run in place now!"
"Aye aye, Sir!!"
"Run in place now!"
"Aye aye, Sir!!"
"Pick them up!"
"Aye aye, Sir!!"
"Open your pie holes now! *Aye aye, Sir!*"
"Aye aye, Sir!!"
"Louder!"
"Aye aye, Sir!!"
"Backs against the wall! *Aye aye, Sir!*"
"Aye aye, Sir!!"
"Seated position!"
"Aye aye, Sir!!"
"Canteens extended at a ninety degree angle!"
"Aye aye, Sir!!"
"Ninety degrees!"
"Aye aye, Sir!!"
"Fingers grounded!"
"Aye aye, Sir!!"
"Ninety degrees!"
"Aye aye, Sir!!"
"Get them up!"
"Aye aye, Sir!!"
"Up!"
"Aye aye, Sir!"
"You! Pig Nasty! Get up here!"
"Aye aye, Sir!"
"Now! Damnit!"
"Aye aye, Sir!"
"You will demonstrate the eight-count body builder!"
"Aye aye, Sir!"
"Freaking eyeballs!"
"Snap, Sir!!"

"The eight-count body builder is an eight-count exercise! You begin in the upright position! *Aye aye, Sir*!"

"Aye aye, Sir!!"

"You think I'm not watching? Get that freaking canteen up, Pig!"

"Aye aye, Sir!"

"You!"

"Aye aye, Sir!"

"All of you!"

"Aye aye, Sir!!"

"The first count puts you in a crouched position! Your palms on the deck! Shoulder width apart! Do it now!"

"Aye aye, Sir!"

"The second count puts you in the push-up position! Your legs kicked out with authority! Back straight! Your head up! Straight!"

"Aye aye, Sir!"

"The third count you push! Push, Freak!"

"Aye aye, Sir!"

"The fourth count is a scissor-like motion! Your legs shoulder width apart! The fifth count returns you to the push-up position! On the sixth count you push! Push, Freak!"

"Aye aye, Sir!"

"The seventh count brings your knees back to your chest! The eighth and final count returns you to the position of attention! Am I clear?"

"Yes, Sir!!"

"Find your place, Maggot."

"Aye aye, Sir!"

"Eight-count body builders, you Nasty Things! The eight-count body builder is an eight-count exercise! You will count the cadence! You will count the repetitions! *Aye aye, Sir* everyone!"

"Aye aye, Sir!!"

"Louder!"

"Aye aye, Sir!!"

"Begin!"

"Aye aye, Sir!! One!! Two!! Three!! Four!! Five!! Six!! Seven!! Zero-one!! One!! Two!! Three!! Four!! Five!! Six!! Seven!! Zero-two!! One!! Two!! Three!! Four!! Five!! Six!! Seven!! Zero-three!! One!! Two!! Three!! Four!! Five!! Six!! Seven!! Zero-four!! One!! Two!! Three!! Four!! Five!! Six!! Seven!! Zero-five!! One!! Two!! Three!! Four!! Five!! Six!! Seven!! Zero-six!! One!! Two!! Three!! Four!! Five!! Six!! Seven!! Zero-seven!! One!! Two!! Three!! Four!! Five!! Six!! Seven!! Zero-eight!! One!! Two!! Three!! Four!! Five!! Six!! Seven!! Zero-niner!! One!! Two!! Three!! Four!! Five!! Six!! Seven!! One-zero!! One!! Two!! Three!! Four!! Five!! Six!! Seven!!

One-one!! One!! Two!! Three!! Four!! Five!! Six!! Seven!! One-two!! One!! Two!! Three!! Four!! Five!! Six!! Seven!! One-three!! One!! Two!! Three!! Four!! Five!! Six!! Seven!! One-four!! One!! Two!! Three!! Four!! Five!! Six!! Seven!! One-five!! One!! Two!! Three!! Four!! Five!! Six!! Seven!! One-six!! One!! Two!! Three!! Four!! Five!! Six!! Seven!! One-seven!! One!! Two!! Three!! Four!! Five!! Six!! Seven!! One-eight!! One!! Two!! Three!! Four!! Five!! Six!! Seven!! One-niner!! One!! Two!! Three!! Four!! Five!! Six!! Seven!! Two-zero!!"

"On your feet now!"

"Aye aye, Sir!!"

"On your backs now!"

"Aye aye, Sir!!"

"On your feet now!"

"Aye aye, Sir!!"

"On your faces! Push!"

"Aye aye, Sir!!"

"On your feet!"

"Aye aye, Sir!!"

"On your faces!"

"Aye aye, Sir!!"

"On your backs!"

"Aye aye, Sir!!"

"On your feet!"

"Aye aye, Sir!!"

"On your backs!"

"Aye aye, Sir!!"

"On your feet!"

"Aye aye, Sir!!"

"On your backs!"

"Aye aye, Sir!!"

"On your faces!"

"Aye aye, Sir!!"

"On your faces!"

"Aye aye, Sir!!"

"On your feet!"

"Aye aye, Sir!!"

"On your faces!"

"Aye aye, Sir!!"

"On your feet! Side-straddle hops! Start counting!"

"Aye aye, Sir!! One-two-three!! Zero-one!! One-two-three!! Zero-two!! One-two-three!! Zero-three!! One-two-three!! Zero-four!! One-two-three!! Zero-five!! One-two-three!! Zero-six!! One-two-three!! Zero-seven!! One-two-three!! Zero-

eight!! One-two-three!! Zero-niner!! One-two-three!! One-zero!! One-two-three!! One-one!! One-two-three!! One-two!! One-two-three!! One-three!! One-two-three!! One-four!! One-two-three!! One-five!! One-two-three!! One-six!! One-two-three!! One-seven!! One-two-three!! One-eight!! One-two-three!! One-niner!! One-two-three!! Two-zero!! One-two-three!! Two-one!! One-two-three!! Two-two!! One-two-three!! Two-three!!"

"Louder!"

"Aye aye, Sir!! One-two-three!! Two-four!! One-two-three!! Two-five!! One-two-three!! Two-six!! One-two-three!! Two-seven!! One-two-three!! Two-eight!! One-two-three!! Two-niner!! One-two-three!! Three-zero!! One-two-three!! Three-one!! One-two-three!! Three-two!! One-two-three!! Three-three!! One-two-three!! Three-four!! One-two-three!! Three-five!! One-two-three!! Three-six!! One-two-three!! Three-seven!! One-two-three!! Three-eight!! One-two-three!! Three-niner!! One-two-three!! Four-zero!! One-two-three!! Four-one!! One-two-three!! Four-two!! One-two-three!! Four-three!! One-two-three!! Four-four!! One-two-three!! Four-five!!"

"Run in place! *Aye aye, Sir*!"

"Aye aye, Sir!!"

"Get your knees up!"

"Aye aye, Sir!!"

"Higher!"

"Aye aye, Sir!!"

"Louder!"

"Aye aye, Sir!!"

"Higher!"

"Aye aye, Sir!!"

"Atten-hut!"

"Aye aye, Sir!!"

"Ears!"

"Open, Sir!!"

"Stop whispering, Pukes!"

"Aye aye, Sir!!"

"Ears!"

"Open, Sir!!"

"Upon receiving the command of execution *scram*! You will! Double time to your Maggot holes, secure your canteens and retrieve your firearms! Am I clear?"

"Yes, Sir!!"

"You have thirty seconds! Scram!"

"Aye aye, Sir!!"

"Thirty! Twenty-nine! Twenty-eight! Twenty-seven! Twenty-six! Twenty-five! Twenty-four! Twenty-three!"

"Left-right!! Left-right!!"

"Good afternoon, Sir!"

"Step!"

"Step!"

"Good afternoon, Sir!"

"Left-right!! Left-right!!"

"Good afternoon, Sir!"

"Step!"

"Step!"

"Good afternoon, Sir!"

"Left-right!! Left-right!!"

"Twenty! Nineteen! Eighteen!"

"Left-right!! Left-right!!"

"Good afternoon, Sir!"

"Step!"

"Step!"

"Good afternoon, Sir!"

"Left-right!! Left-right!!"

"Good afternoon, Sir!"

"Step!"

"Step!"

"Good afternoon, Sir!"

"Left-right!! Left-right!!"

"Good afternoon, Sir!"

"Step!"

"Step!"

"Good afternoon, Sir!"

I fumble with the combination lock. Gear pours from the locker. My rifle leans canted in the back.

"You're done! You're freaking done! Out of your holes! Line it up! Line it up!"

"Everyone ready?"

"Ready."

"Ready."

"Stand-by."

"Come on, man."

"Ready."

"Lock check."

"Check."

"Check."

"Check."

"Clear."

"Good afternoon, Sir!"

"Step!"

"Step!"

"Good afternoon, Sir!"

"Left-right!! Left-right!!"

"Good afternoon, Sir!"

"Step!"

"Step!"

"Good afternoon, Sir!"

"Left-right!! Left-right!!"

"Good afternoon, Sir!"

"Step!"

"Step!"

"Good afternoon, Sir!"

"Left-right!! Left-right!!"

"Good afternoon, Sir!"

"Step!"

"Step!"

"Good afternoon, Sir!"

"Left-right!! Left-right!!"

"Nine! Eight! Seven! Six!"

"Left-right!! Left-right!! Left-right!! Left-right!! Left-right!! Left-right!! Left-right!! Left-right!! Left-right!! Left-right!! Left-right!! Left-right!! Left-right!! Left-right!! Left-right!!"

"Good afternoon, Sir!"

"Five! Four! Three! Two! One!"

"Left-right!! Left-right!! Left-right!! Left-right!! Left-right!! Left-right!! Left-right!! Left-right!! Left-right!! Left-right!! Left-right!! Left-right!! Left-right!!"

"Freeze Pigs!"

"Aye aye, Sir!!"

"Count off!"

"Aye aye, Sir!!"

"Zero-one!"

"Zero-two!"

"Zero-three!"

"Zero-four!"

"Zero-five!"

"Zero-six!"

"Zero-seven!"

"Zero-eight!"

"Zero-niner!"

"One-zero!"

"One-one!"

"One-two!"

"One-three!"

"One-four!"

"One-five!"
"One-six!"
"One-seven!"
"One-eight!"
"One-niner!"
"Two-zero!"
"Two-one!"
"Two-two!"
"Two-three!"
"Two-four!"
"Two-five!"
"Two-six!"
"Two-seven!"
"Two-eight!"
"Two-niner!"
"Three-zero!"
"Three-one!"
"Three-two!"
"Three-three!"
"Three-four!"
"Three-five!"
"Three-six!"
"Three-seven!"
"Three-eight!"
"Three-niner!"
"Four-zero!"
"Four-one!"
"Four-two!"
"Highly motivated!! Truly dedicated!! Indoctrination Candidates, Sir!!"
"Backs against the wall!"
"Aye aye, Sir!!"
"Seated positions!"
"Aye aye, Sir!!"
"Rifles up, parallel to the deck!"
"Aye aye, Sir!!"
"Angle of ninety degrees!"
"Aye aye, Sir!!"
"Louder!"
"Aye aye, Sir!!"
"Louder!"
"Aye aye, Sir!!"

"Louder!"

"Aye aye, Sir!!"

"Parallel to the deck!"

"Aye aye, Sir!!"

"Parallel to the deck, Pig!"

"Aye aye, Sir!"

"Stop whispering to me!"

"Aye aye, Sir!"

"Stop whispering, Freak!"

"Aye aye, Sir!"

"Down! *Aye aye, Sir!*"

"Aye aye, Sir!!"

"Up! *Aye aye, Sir!*"

"Aye aye, Sir!!"

"Louder! *Aye aye, Sir!*"

"Aye aye, Sir!!"

"Down!"

"Aye aye, Sir!!"

"Up!"

"Aye aye, Sir!!"

"Cheating are we, Nasty Pig?"

"No excuse, Sir!"

"You cut corners, people die! You got that, Friendly Fire?"

"Yes, Sir!"

"Stop whispering to me, you little Freak!"

"Aye aye, Sir!"

"I said stop whispering! Stop whispering! Stop whispering! Stop whispering! You freaking Puke!"

"Aye aye, Sir!"

"Sound off!"

"Aye aye, Sir!"

"Sound off!"

"Aye aye, Sir!"

"Freak!"

"Aye aye, Sir!"

"Puke! You want to give up?"

"No, Sir!"

"You push!"

"Aye aye, Sir!"

"Down-up! Down-up! Down-up! Start counting!"

"Aye aye, Sir! Zero-one! Zero-two! Zero-three! Zero-four! Zero-five! Zero-six! Zero-seven! Zero-eight! Zero-niner!"

"The rest of you! Keep them up!"

"Aye aye, Sir!!"

"Is that all you can do? You pathetic! Lethargic! Excuse for a Swine!"

"No, Sir!"

"What's the matter? Are you done, Pig? Is it quitting time?"

"No, Sir!"

"Are you too tired?"

"No, Sir!"

"You thinking Dead-on-Request?"

"No, Sir!"

"White flag?"

"No, Sir!"

"Tits up?"

"No, Sir!"

"Don't be shy, Pig! Your mother wasn't. Sound off!"

"No, Sir!"

"Louder!"

"No, Sir!"

"On your feet, Pig! Seated position!"

"Aye aye, Sir!"

"Get them up, Pigs!"

"Aye aye, Sir!!"

"Steady."

"Aye aye, Sir!!"

"Supermans!"

"Aye aye, Sir!!"

"I will count the cadence! You will count the repetitions!"

••

The Superman

A no count exercise. Either lie on stomach or on hands and knees. Opposite arm and leg (i.e., right arm, left leg) should be lifted and held for three to five seconds, then slowly lowered. Same movements should then be made with other arm and opposite leg. Superman can be made more difficult by adding weights to arms and legs. To avoid hyperextension of back, leg should not be raised higher than hip when in kneeling position.

••

Classes join in a semi-circle at the base of the outside stairwell. Flags fly atop guidons.

"Take this and pass it around."

"Thank you, Sir."

"Lose the *Sir*. We're all Officer Candidates here."

The cold water runs through my body. I lean back on the steps.

"Class Zero-Four-Zero-Zero, take a minute to catch your collective breath. You've been pushed to the limit, taken some good mashings the last couple of days. We know the feeling. You can stand down. You've survived Black Saturday. Hoorah."

"Hoorah!!"

"The folks you see around you are Officer Candidates, the full complement of zero-eight classes now in training at Officer Candidate School, Class Two-Five-Niner-Niner to Zero-Three-Zero-Zero. And now you. Today we congratulate you for completing your Indoctrination Week and welcome you to Battalion as Officer Candidate School Class Zero-Four-Zero-Zero. Hoorah."

"Hoorah!!"

"Of those sixty-two civilians who reported to Regiment, forty-two of you stand strong. This is the beginning of your training as Officer Candidates. To guide you in your training, we are pleased to present you with the Class Zero-Four-Zero-Zero guidon. Protect it. Over the next twelve weeks, working together, you will have the opportunity to earn and fly banners for Military Training Test, Drill, P.T., Academics and Personnel Inspection, all keys to leaving here as an Honor Class. Hoorah, Class Zero-Four-Zero-Zero."

"Hoorah!!"

"Hoorah."

"Hoorah!!"

"Oh, and you'll be able to ditch your Poopie gear for good. That's right. No more chrome domes and warbelts."

"Hoorah!!"

"But first, for your consideration, make way for Follies! Ladies and Gentlemen, Officer Candidate Class Two-Five-Niner-Niner! What do you have for us today?"

"Poopie Quick Change, Sir."

"Ladies and gents, Two-Five-Niner-Niner with Poopie Quick Change!"

"Hello? Hello? I think a Four-bar just stepped on deck!"

"Attention on deck, stand-by!"

"Good afternoon, Sir!!"

"When you sound off to me, you sound off like you have a pair, Poopies. Is that clear?"

"Yes, Sir!!"

"No! No! Put the Big Pair on!"

"Aye aye, Sir!!"

"I don't think so."

"We're talking massive! Huge! Monstrous!"

"Aye aye, Sir!!"

"Into your Poopie suits, Indoctrination Candidates."

"Aye aye, Sir!!"

"You heard him! Into your hole!"

"Aye aye, Sir!!"

"Good afternoon, Sir!"

"Step!"

"Step!"

"Good afternoon, Sir!"

"Let's go, Poopies! Let's go! You have no time! Waiting on you, Poopies! Waiting on you! Get back out here! Now! Now! Now!"

"Aye aye, Sir!!"

"Good afternoon, Sir!"

"Step!"

"Step!"

"Good afternoon, Sir!"

"What's this? You. Where is your chrome dome?"

"No excuse, Sir!"

"Where is it? Where is it? That's a response!"

"No excuse, Sir!"

"Get back in there and square yourselves away, Poopies."

"What are you waiting for? What are you waiting for? That's a response! That's a response!"

"Aye aye, Sir!!"

"Good afternoon, Sir!"

"Step!"

"Step!"

"Good afternoon, Sir!"

"Let's go, Poopies! Let's go! You have no time! Get out here!"

"Aye aye, Sir!!"

"Good afternoon, Sir!"

"Step!"

"Step!"

"Good afternoon, Sir!"

"What? What's this? You. What happened to your blouse?"

"That's a response! That's a response!"

"No excuse, Sir!"

"Well, get back in there and get it."

"Aye aye, Sir!!"

"Good afternoon, Sir!"

"Step!"

"Step!"

"Good afternoon, Sir!"

"Let's go! Let's go! Let's go! Waiting on you! Waiting on you! Get out here right now!"

"Aye aye, Sir!!"

"Good afternoon, Sir!"

"Step!"

"Step!"

"Good afternoon, Sir!"

"What? I must be dreaming. You. What happened to your go-fasters?"

"This Indoctrination Candidate does not know but will find out, Sir!"

"Unsatisfactory, I'm afraid. You know the drill, Poopies."

"Well? You heard the Eight-bar! What are you waiting for? Get back in there and get them! Now! You have no time!"

"Aye aye, Sir!!"

"Good afternoon, Sir!"

"Step!"

"Step!"

"Good afternoon, Sir!"

"Let's go! Let's go! Let's go! You have no time, Poopies! You have no time! Get out here! Get out here right now!"

"Aye aye, Sir!!"

"What is taking so long? Let's go!"

"Good afternoon, Sir!"

"Step!"

"Step!"

"Good afternoon, Sir!"

"What in God's name, Indoctrination Candidate? Where on earth are your trousers?"

"No excuse, Sir!"

"That will have to do. You are out of time. Off you go."

"March, Poopies, march!"

"Aye aye, Sir!! Left-right!!"

"Thank you, Class Two-Five-Niner-Niner. How about a round of applause for Poopie Quick Change! That was outstanding. Barrel of laughs, especially for Zero-Four, I imagine. Alright, next up, please give a warm welcome to Class Two-Six-Niner-Niner with?"

"Officer Candidate Class Two-Six-Niner-Niner presents the Gong Show, Sir!"

"The Gong Show. Alright, who's the first contestant?"

"That would be us, Sir. Hooker and the Jabbers. Just have to warm up the golden tonsils. Do! Re! Mi! Fa! So! La! Ti! Do! Mi! Mi! Mi! Mi!"

"Do!! Re!! Mi!! Fa!! So!! La!! Ti!! Do!!"

"Mi! Mi! Mi! Mi!"

"Mi!! Mi!! Mi!! Mi!!"

"Get on with it."

"Aye aye, Sir!"

"*Kum-ba-ya, my Lord, kum-ba-ya*!
Kum-ba-ya, my Lord, kum-ba-ya!!
Kum-ba-ya, my Lord, kum-ba-ya!!
O Lord, kum-ba-ya!!
Someone's crying, Lord, kum-ba-ya!
Someone's crying, Lord, kum-ba-ya!!
Someone's crying, Lord, kum-ba-ya!!"

"Stand-by. Here comes the hook."

"*Someone's praying, Lord, kum-ba* --!"

"Verdict is in, I'm afraid, Shipmates. Crowd has spoken. You've been gonged! Thank you. Next. I won't even ask."

"A favorite standard for your consideration, Sir."

"Let's hear it."

"*Doe a dear*! *A female dear*! *Ray*! *A drop of golden* --!"

"Gong!"

"*Sun*! *Miiiiiiiii*! *A name*! *I call* --!"

"You're done. Next."

"*Myself!*"

"Gong!"

"*Man! I really hate to run!*"

"Someone give him the hook for crying out loud. Thank you. Atrocious. Who do we have next?"

"Colonel Bogie, Sir."

"Very well, Colonel. Proceed."

"Start me off with the Colonel's March, boys."

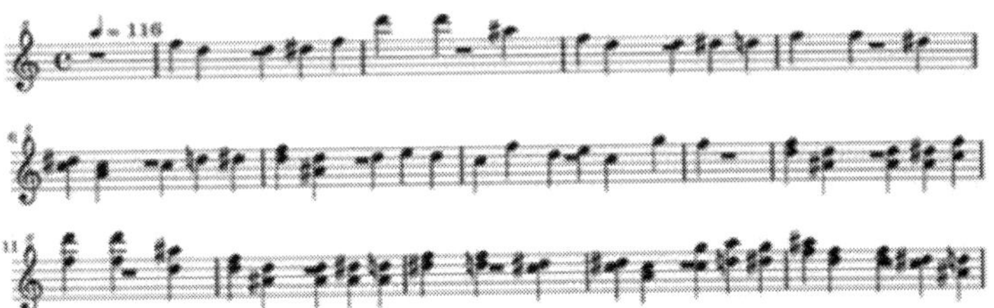

"*Land of soap and water*
Services having a bath
D.I.'s looking through the keyhole
Having a jolly good laugh beeeeecause
Marine Corp has got two big balls
Army has too but very small
Air Force is somewhat similar
Coast Guard no balls at all
Go Navy!! Biggest of all!!"

"A rousing rendition, boys. Any other contestants?"

"Right here, Sir!"

"Very well. Who might you be?"

"Ballistic Barbara, Sir!"

"Ballistic Barbara."

"Ballistic Barbara, Sir!"

"We heard you the first time, Barbara. Carry on."

"Aye aye, Sir! *Don't tell me not to live! Just ship and rudder!*
Don't tell me I gotta push! Cause I don't want to!
Hop and pops, yes! But not in summer!
Don't you rain on my drill parade!"

"Gong! Thank you, Barbara. A very original interpretation. Other contestants? No? Very well. Now to select the winner. Line it up. Alright. Let's hear it. Who liked Kumbaya the best? Not bad, not bad. No dice, Billups."

"What?"

"I'm not even asking."

"Come on!"

"Negative. What about Colonel Bogie? Very impressive, Colonel. Only thing standing in the way of you and your boys appears to be Ballistic Barbara. What's the verdict? My goodness, Barbara, you have fans. Go figure. I think we have ourselves a winner."

"You like me! You really like me!"

"Thank you Two-Six-Niner-Niner. Who's on deck for Two-Seven?"

"How dare you ask me a question? How dare you?"

"Whatever, Sir. Ladies and Gentlemen, it gives me great pleasure to welcome back a fan favorite. Put your hands together for the Mystery Drill Instructor."

"Attention on deck, Stand-by!"

"Good afternoon, Sir!!"

"Good afternoon, folks! I'm the Mystery Drill Instructor! How's everyone doing today?"

"Outstanding, Sir!!"

"You're goddamn right, you Nasty Pigs! Semper Fi! Kill them all! Burn the village! Eat the children! That's a response!"

"Aye aye, Sir!!"

"I got jokes! I got jokes! You want jokes, Pig Nasties? I got jokes!"

"Yes, Sir!!"

"Alright! Alright! Freaking jokes and cokes! Hey folks! I just flew in from the coast! Thank God it wasn't in an Osprey! Am I clear? Am I clear?"

"Yes, Sir!!"

"Semper Fi! Do or die! Semper Fi! Do or die! Nasty Freaks! Freaking Pukes! I tell you what! I get no respect! No respect at all! You know what happened? Do you?"

"No, Sir!!"

"When I asked my Poopies to *sound off*, they put me on mute! Stop freaking laughing Pigs! I get no respect! You know what else?"

"No, Sir!!"

"When Poopies see me pass in the chow hall! They ask for the check! I get no respect! You know what happened?"

"No, Sir!!"

"I went over to the Air Force and they told me to push! I get no respect! Freaks! Freaking freak! Freak! Freaks! No respect! You know what else?"

"No, Sir!!"

"Louder!"

"No, Sir!!"

"Nasty Pig candidate gaffed me off yesterday! When I asked him for my salute, he gave me the finger! No respect! Stop laughing! Stop freaking laughing! Repeat after me, Pigs!"

"Pigs, Sir!!"

"You think I'm funny? Am I your drinking bunny? What's so funny? Thank you! Thank you! I'm here for zero-five more weeks! Don't forget to tip your waitresses! Try the beef!"

"Let's hear it for the Mystery Drill Instructor, folks! My advice is to never, ever, take that bag off that head of yours. God speed. Alright, folks. For our main event today, please give a warm welcome to Class Zero-One-Zero-Zero with --. Wait, what's this? What happened?"

"You wouldn't believe it, Candidate Commander Monroe."

"What? What happened?"

"We were ambushed, Sir. Three against a hundred. Never saw it coming. They were all over us."

"Slow down. Just tell me what happened."

"Well, Sir. We were marching back from chow and these guys came out of nowhere. Hollering and a screaming. Straight out of hell. Warfaces like you wouldn't believe."

"Did you fight back?"

"Yes, Sir. I mean, of course, Sir. Fought them tooth and nail. But they just kept coming and coming. Barely got out of there, Sir. I tell you what, though, we put up a hell of a fight. You would have been proud, Sir. Clawing and biting all the way to the end."

"Are you okay? Do you need medical attention?"

"On our way, Sir."

"So who was it? Who were they?"

"Three of the toughest Coasties I ever saw, Sir."

"Coasties. Christ. Off you go."

"Aye aye, Sir!!"

"Any other submissions? Zero-Two? Zero-Three? Going once? Going twice? Disappointing, but at least you have your priorities in order. Alright, let's hear it for today's performers."

"Hoorah!!"

"Not a chance."

"Hoorah!!"

"One more time."

"Hoorah!!"

"Are you motivated? Round the horn!"

"Aye aye, Sir!!"

"Class Two-Five-Niner-Niner, bring it on!"

"Make us strong!!"

"Bring it on!"

"You won't live long!!"

"Bring it on!"

"Prove us wrong!!"
"Hoorah!!"
"Class Two-Six-Niner-Niner! Cocked and locked!"
"Ready to rock!!"
"Cocked and locked!"
"Ready to rock!!"
"Cocked and locked!"
"Ready to rock!!"
"Hoorah!!"
"Class Two-Seven-Niner-Niner!"
"What's in store?"
"Get some more!!"
"What's in store?"
"Get some more!!"
"What's in store?"
"Get some more!!"
"Hoorah!!"
"Class Zero-One-Zero-Zero, push all day!"
"Don't ever stop!!"
"Hop and pops!"
"Feel just fine!!"
"Blood and guts!"
"Now that's the stuff!!"
"Hoorah!!"
"Class Zero-Two-Zero-Zero, drag me to!"
"The gates of hell!!"
"What to do?"
"Just ring the bell!!"
"Hoorah!!"
"Class Zero-Three-Zero-Zero, get some!"
"Rise and shine!"
"Don't ask why!!"
"Rise and shine!"
"Quick kiss good-bye!!"
"Rise and shine!"
"Good day to die!!"
"Rise and shine!"
"No hug goodbye!!"
"Hoorah!!"
"Class Zero-Four-Zero-Zero, your turn!"
"Motivation is contagious!!"

"Hoorah!"
"Motivation is contagious!!"
"Hoorah!"
"Whatever works. Anchors Aweigh. Attenhut!"
"Aye aye, Sir!!"
"*Stand Navy out to sea,*
Fight our battle cry.
We'll never change our course
So vicious foes steer shy-y-y-y.
Roll out the T.N.T.,
Anchors Aweigh,
Sail on to victory and
Sink their bones to Davy Jones,
Hooray!
Anchors Aweigh my boys,
Anchors Aweigh.
Farewell to college joy,
We'll sail at break of day-ay-ay-ay.
Though our last night ashore
Drink to the foam.
Until we meet once more,
Here's wishing you a happy
Voyage home.
Blue of the Mighty Deep,
Gold of God's Sun,
Let these colors be
Till all of time by done, done, done.
On seven seas we learn navy's stern call.
Faith, courage, service true, with
Honor, over honor, over all."
"The Marine Corp Hymn!"
"*From the Halls of Montezuma*
To the shores of Tripoli
We fight our country's battles
In the air, on land and sea
First to fight for right and freedom
And to keep our honor clean,
We are proud to claim the title
Of United States Marine.
Our flag's unfurled to every breeze
From dawn to setting sun,

We have fought in every clime and place
Where we could take a gun.
In the snow of far-off Northern lands
And in sunny tropic scenes,
You will find us always on the job
The United States Marines.
Here's health to you and to our Corps
Which we are proud to serve,
In many a strife we've fought for life
And never lost our nerve.
If the Army and the Navy
Ever look on Heaven's scenes,
They will find the streets are guarded
By United States Marines."

"Class Zero-Four-Zero-Zero, welcome to Officer Candidate School. You control your own destiny from here on out. Your Section Leader has the conn. Oh by the way, phone calls tomorrow, for those of you with a voice. Section Leader, they're all yours. Take charge of your platoon and carry out the Plan of the Day."

"Aye aye, Sir! Class Zero-Four-Zero-Zero! Fall in!"

"Aye aye, Section Leader!!"

"Officer Candidate Class Zero-Four-Zero-Zero!"

"Hoorah!!"

"Upon receiving the command of execution *march*! You will! Proceed up the outside ladderwell in single file, column of files from the right, return to your spaces and change into your wash khaki uniforms!"

"Aye aye, Section Leader!!"

"Column of files! From the right! Ready! March!"

"Aye aye, Section Leader!!"

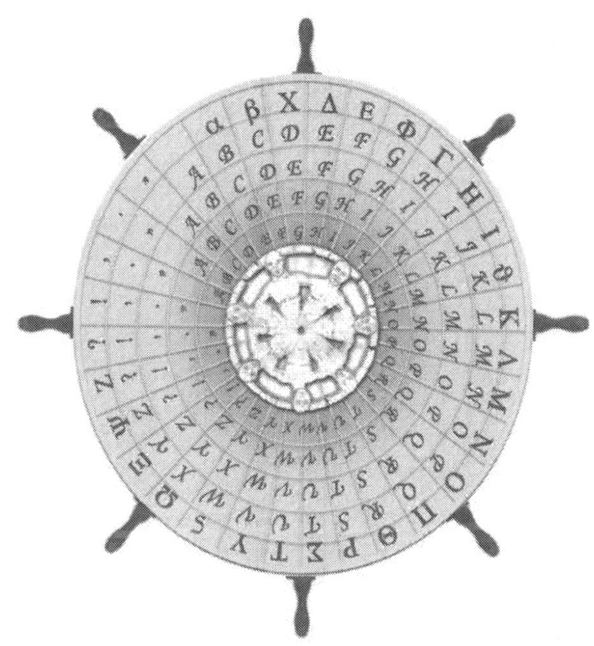

CHAPTER III

WEEK 3

"Reveille! Reveille! Reveille! All hands heave up and thrice out! Now reveille!

The smoking lamp is lighted in all authorized spaces! The Uniform of the Day is as follows! Navy wash khaki uniform wear for all Officer Candidates! With wash khaki cover! Navy working khaki uniform for E-Seven and above! With C.N.T. cover! Carry guidons! Carry flags! Close all outboard windows! Daily exercise will be held on the parade ground! Weather forecast is! Sunny! With a daily low of seven-seven degrees Fahrenheit! Daily high of one-zero-one degrees Fahrenheit! Visibility of zero-niner miles! Niner-one percent humidity! Wind conditions light! Zero-three miles variable! Arising from the southeast! Black flag conditions are forecasted in the course of the day! Again reveille! Again reveille! Reveille! Reveille! Reveille! All hands heave up and thrice out! Now reveille! The smoking lamp is lighted in all authorized spaces! The Uniform of the Day is as follows! Navy wash khaki uniform wear for all Officer Candidates! With wash khaki cover! Navy working khaki uniform for E-Seven and above! With C.N.T. cover! Carry guidons! Carry flags! Close all outboard windows! Daily exercise will be held on the parade ground! Weather forecast is! Sunny! With a daily low of seven-seven degrees Fahrenheit! Daily high of one-zero-one degrees Fahrenheit! Visibility of zero-niner miles! Niner-one percent humidity! Wind conditions light! Zero-three miles variable! Arising from the southeast! Black flag conditions are forecasted in the course of the day! Now reveille!"

"Let's go, Zero-Four! Let's go!"

"Lock check."

"Check."

"Check."

"Check."

"Let's go."

The class assembles in the passageway.

"Class Zero-Four-Zero-Zero! Are-you-ready? Count off!"

"Aye aye, Sir!!"

"Zero-one!"

"Zero-two!"

"Zero-three!"

"Zero-four!"

"Zero-five!"

"Zero-six!"

"Zero-seven!"

"Zero-eight!"

"Zero-niner!"

"One-zero!"

"One-one!"

"One-two!"

"One-three!"

"One-four!"

"One-five!"

"One-six!"

"One-seven!"

"One-eight!"

"One-niner!"

"Two-zero!"

"Two-one!"

"Two-two!"

"Two-three!"

"Two-four!"

"Two-five!"

"Two-six!"

"Two-seven!"

"Two-eight!"

"Two-niner!"

"Three-zero!"

"Three-one!"

"Three-two!"

"Three-three!"

"Three-four!"

"Three-five!"

"Three-six!"

"Three-seven!"

"Three-eight!"

"Three-niner!"

"Four-zero!"

"Four-one!"

"Four-two!"

"Class Zero-Four-Zero-Zero! Upon receiving the command of execution *move*! You will! Perform an immediate right face! Double time down the passageway to the outside ladderwell! Descend the ladderwell in an orderly fashion! And regroup in platoon formation in the assembly area below!"

"Aye aye, Section Leader!!"

"Ready! Move!"

We file down the outside ladderwell. Street lamps flood the asphalt in the pre-dawn light.

"Good morning, Sir!"

"Good morning, Sir!"

"Glad you could join us, Pigs. Atten-hut!"

"Aye aye, Sir!!"

"Right face!"

"Aye aye, Sir!!"

"Forward! Forward march!"

"Aye aye, Sir!!"

"Your left! Your left! Your left-right-left! Your lefty-right-a-lo-right! Left! Left! Lefty-right-a-lo! Left-left-lefty-right-a-lo-right! Left-left-keep-it-in-step-now! Left-left-lefty-right-a-lo! Ready! Double-time! March!"

"Aye aye, Sir!!"

"On your left! Your left! Your lefty-right-a-lo-right! Lefty-right-lefty-right-lefty-right-a-lo! Open your pie holes, Nasties!"

"Aye aye, Sir!!"

"*Left! Left! Lefty-right-a-lo-right!*"

"Left!! Left!! Lefty-right-a-lo-right!!"

"*Lefty-right-a-lo!*"

"Lefty-right-a-lo!!"

"*Lefty-right-a-left-right!*"

"Lefty-right-a-left-right!!"

"*Lefty-right-a-lo!*"

"Lefty-right-a-lo!!"

"*Lefty-right-a-lo-right!*"

"Lefty-right-a-lo-right!!"

"*Left! Left! Keep-it-in-step!*"

"Left!! Left!! Keep-it-in-step!!"

"*A whole lotta left!*"

"A whole lotta left!!"

"*A whole lotta left!*"

"A whole lotta left!!"

"*Keep-it-in-step!*"

"Keep-it-in-step!!"

"*Left! Left! Lefty! Right! Layo!*"

"Left!! Left!! Lefty!! Right!! Layo!!"

"*Left! Left! Keep-it-in-step!*"

"Left!! Left!! Keep-it-in-step!!"

"*Left! Left! Lefty-right-a-left-right!*"

"Left!! Left!! Lefty-right-a-left-right!!"

"*Lefty-right-left-right!*"

"Lefty-right-left-right!!"

"*Lefty-right-left-right!*"

"Lefty-right-left-right!!"

"*Lefty-right-a-lo!*"

"Lefty-right-a-lo!!"

"*Left! Left! Lefty! Right! Layo!*"

"Left!! Left!! Lefty!! Right!! Layo!!"

"*Left! Left! Lefty-right-a-left-right!*"

"Left!! Left!! Lefty-right-a-left-right!!"

"*Lefty-right-left-right!*"

"Lefty-right-left-right!!"

"*Lefty-right-a-lo!*"

"Lefty-right-a-lo!!"

"On your left! Your left! Your left! Your left! Ready! Halt!"

"Aye aye, Sir!!"

"At double interval! Ready! Fall in!"

"Aye aye, Sir!!"

A Drill Instructor leaps atop a thick wooden table in the center of the parade field.

"Attention on deck, stand-by!"

"Good morning, Sir!!"

"Open your freaking suck holes!"

"Good morning, Sir!!"

"Louder!"

"Good morning, Sir!!"

"Wake em up!"

"Good morning, Sir!!"

"You all better get louder this morning! You hear me?"

"Yes, Sir!!"

"Your first stretch will be the triceps stretch! Starting positions! Move!"

"Aye aye, Sir!!"

"And stretch!"

"Aye aye, Sir!! Zero-one!! Zero-two!! Zero-three!! Zero-four!! Zero-five!! Zero-six!! Zero-seven!! Zero-eight!! Zero-niner!! One-zero!!"

"Changeover!"

"Switch!! Zero-one!! Zero-two!! Zero-three!! Zero-four!! Zero-five!! Zero-six!! Zero-seven!! Zero-eight!! Zero-niner!! One-zero!!"

"Recover!"

"Aye aye, Sir!!"

"Your next stretch will be the I.T.B. stretch! Starting positions! Move!"

"Aye aye, Sir!!"

"And stretch!"

"Aye aye, Sir!! Zero-one!! Zero-two!! Zero-three!! Zero-four!! Zero-five!! Zero-six!! Zero-seven!! Zero-eight!! Zero-niner!! One-zero!!"

"Changeover!"

"Switch!! Zero-one!! Zero-two!! Zero-three!! Zero-four!! Zero-five!! Zero-

six!! Zero-seven!! Zero-eight!! Zero-niner!! One-zero!!"

"Recover!"

"Aye aye, Sir!!"

"Your next stretch will be the posterior shoulder stretch! Starting positions! Move!"

"Aye aye, Sir!!"

"And stretch!"

"Aye aye, Sir!! Zero-one!! Zero-two!! Zero-three!! Zero-four!! Zero-five!! Zero-six!! Zero-seven!! Zero-eight!! Zero-niner!! One-zero!!"

"Changeover!"

"Switch!! Zero-one!! Zero-two!! Zero-three!! Zero-four!! Zero-five!! Zero-six!! Zero-seven!! Zero-eight!! Zero-niner!! One-zero!!"

"Recover!"

"Aye aye, Sir!!"

"Your next stretch will be the chest stretch! Starting positions! Move!"

"Aye aye, Sir!!"

"And stretch!"

"Aye aye, Sir!! Zero-one!! Zero-two!! Zero-three!! Zero-four!! Zero-five!! Zero-six!! Zero-seven!! Zero-eight!! Zero-niner!! One-zero!!"

"Recover!"

"Aye aye, Sir!!"

"Your next stretch will be the inside hurdle stretch! Starting positions! Move!"

"Aye aye, Sir!!"

"And stretch!"

"Aye aye, Sir!! Zero-one!! Zero-two!! Zero-three!! Zero-four!! Zero-five!! Zero-six!! Zero-seven!! Zero-eight!! Zero-niner!! One-zero!!"

"Changeover!"

"Switch!! Zero-one!! Zero-two!! Zero-three!! Zero-four!! Zero-five!! Zero-six!! Zero-seven!! Zero-eight!! Zero-niner!! One-zero!!"

"Recover!"

"Aye aye, Sir!!"

"Your next stretch will be the groin stretch! Starting positions! Move!"

"Aye aye, Sir!!"

"And stretch!"

"Aye aye, Sir!! Zero-one!! Zero-two!! Zero-three!! Zero-four!! Zero-five!! Zero-six!! Zero-seven!! Zero-eight!! Zero-niner!! One-zero!!"

"Changeover!"

"Switch!! Zero-one!! Zero-two!! Zero-three!! Zero-four!! Zero-five!! Zero-six!! Zero-seven!! Zero-eight!! Zero-niner!! One-zero!!"

"Recover!"

"Aye aye, Sir!!"

"Your next stretch will be ankle rotations! Starting positions! Move!"

"Aye aye, Sir!!"

"And stretch!"

"Aye aye, Sir!! Zero-one!! Zero-two!! Zero-three!! Zero-four!! Zero-five!! Zero-six!! Zero-seven!! Zero-eight!! Zero-niner!! One-zero!!"

"Changeover!"

"Switch!! Zero-one!! Zero-two!! Zero-three!! Zero-four!! Zero-five!! Zero-six!! Zero-seven!! Zero-eight!! Zero-niner!! One-zero!!"

"Recover!"

"Aye aye, Sir!!"

"Your next stretch will be the lower back stretch! Starting positions! Move!"

"Aye aye, Sir!!"

"And stretch!"

"Aye aye, Sir!! Zero-one!! Zero-two!! Zero-three!! Zero-four!! Zero-five!! Zero-six!! Zero-seven!! Zero-eight!! Zero-niner!! One-zero!!"

"Recover!"

"Aye aye, Sir!!"

"Your next stretch will be the abdominal stretch! Starting positions! Move!"

"Aye aye, Sir!!"

"And stretch!"

"Aye aye, Sir!! Zero-one!! Zero-two!! Zero-three!! Zero-four!! Zero-five!! Zero-six!! Zero-seven!! Zero-eight!! Zero-niner!! One-zero!!"

"Recover!"

"Aye aye, Sir!!"

"Your next stretch will be the quadriceps stretch! Starting positions! Move!"

"Aye aye, Sir!!"

"And stretch!"

"Aye aye, Sir!! Zero-one!! Zero-two!! Zero-three!! Zero-four!! Zero-five!! Zero-six!! Zero-seven!! Zero-eight!! Zero-niner!! One-zero!!"

"Changeover!"

"Switch!! Zero-one!! Zero-two!! Zero-three!! Zero-four!! Zero-five!! Zero-six!! Zero-seven!! Zero-eight!! Zero-niner!! One-zero!!"

"Recover!"

"Aye aye, Sir!!"

"On your feet! *Aye aye, Sir!*"

"Aye aye, Sir!!"

"Exercises!"

"Aye aye, Sir!!"

"Your first exercise will be side-straddle hops! Side-straddle hops is a four-count exercise! I will count the cadence! You will count the repetitions! You will

do one-five of them! Starting positions! Move!"

"Aye aye, Sir!!"

"Exercise!"

"Aye aye, Sir!!"

"One-two-three!"

"Zero-one!!"

"One-two-three!"

"Zero-two!!"

"One-two-three!"

"Zero-three!!"

"One-two-three!"

"Zero-four!!"

"One-two-three!"

"Zero-five!!"

"One-two-three!"

"Zero-six!!"

"One-two-three!"

"Zero-seven!!"

"One-two-three!"

"Zero-eight!!"

"One-two-three!"

"Zero-niner!!"

"One-two-three!"

"One-zero!!"

"One-two-three!"

"One-one!!"

"One-two-three!"

"One-two!!"

"One-two-three!"

"One-three!!"

"One-two-three!"

"One-four!!"

"One-two-three!"

"One-five!!"

"Recover!"

"Aye aye, Sir!!"

"Your next exercise will be cherry-pickers! Cherry-pickers is a four-count exercise! I will count the cadence! You will count the repetitions! You will do one-five of them! Starting positions! Move!"

"Aye aye, Sir!!"

"Exercise!"

"Aye aye, Sir!!"
"One-two-three!"
"Huh!! Zero-one!!"
"One-two-three!"
"Huh!! Zero-two!!"
"One-two-three!"
"Huh!! Zero-three!!"
"One-two-three!"
"Huh!! Zero-four!!"
"One-two-three!"
"Huh!! Zero-five!!"
"One-two-three!"
"Huh!! Zero-six!!"
"One-two-three!"
"Huh!! Zero-seven!!"
"One-two-three!"
"Huh!! Zero-eight!!"
"One-two-three!"
"Huh!! Zero-niner!!"
"One-two-three!"
"Huh!! One-zero!!"
"One-two-three!"
"Huh!! One-one!!"
"One-two-three!"
"Huh!! One-two!!"
"One-two-three!"
"Huh!! One-three!!"
"One-two-three!"
"Huh!! One-four!!"
"One-two-three!"
"Huh!! One-five!!"
"Recover!"
"Aye aye, Sir!!"

"Your next exercise will be leg-lifts! Leg-lifts is a four-count exercise! You will count the cadence! You will count the repetitions! You will do one-five of them! Starting positions! Move!"

"Aye aye, Sir!!

"Zero-six inches! Exercise!"

"Aye aye, Sir!! One-two-three!! Zero-one!! One-two-three!! Zero-two!! One-two-three!! Zero-three!! One-two-three!! Zero-four!! One-two-three!! Zero-five!! One-two-three!! Zero-six!! One-two-three!! Zero-seven!! One-two-three!! Zero-

eight!! One-two-three!! Zero-niner!! One-two-three!! One-zero!! One-two-three!! One-one!! One-two-three!! One-two!! One-two-three!! One-three!! One-two-three!! One-four!! One-two-three!! One-five!!"

"Steady!"

"Aye aye, Sir!!"

"Zero-six inches!"

"Aye aye, Sir!!"

"Zero-six inches!"

"Aye aye, Sir!!"

"Your next exercise will be scissor-kicks! Scissor-kicks is a four-count exercise! You will count the cadence! You will count the repetitions! You will do one-five of them! *Aye aye, Sir!*"

"Aye aye, Sir!!"

"Exercise!"

"Aye aye, Sir!! One-two-three!! Zero-one!! One-two-three!! Zero-two!! One-two-three!! Zero-three!! One-two-three!! Zero-four!! One-two-three!! Zero-five!! One-two-three!! Zero-six!! One-two-three!! Zero-seven!! One-two-three!! Zero-eight!! One-two-three!! Zero-niner!! One-two-three!! One-zero!! One-two-three!! One-one!! One-two-three!! One-two!! One-two-three!! One-three!! One-two-three!! One-four!! One-two-three!! One-five!!"

"Keep them up!"

"Aye aye, Sir!!"

"Zero-six inches, Nasties!"

"Aye aye, Sir!!"

"Your next exercise will be hello-Dollies! Hello-Dollies is a four-count exercise! You will count the cadence! You will count the repetitions! You will do one-five of them! *Aye aye, Sir!*"

"Aye aye, Sir!!"

"Exercise!"

"Aye aye, Sir!! One-two-three!! Zero-one!! One-two-three!! Zero-two!! One-two-three!! Zero-three!! One-two-three!! Zero-four!! One-two-three!! Zero-five!! One-two-three!! Zero-six!! One-two-three!! Zero-seven!! One-two-three!! Zero-eight!! One-two-three!! Zero-niner!! One-two-three!! One-zero!! One-two-three!! One-one!! One-two-three!! One-two!! One-two-three!! One-three!! One-two-three!! One-four!! One-two-three!! One-five!!"

"Recover!"

"Aye aye, Sir!!"

"Your next exercise will be push-ups! Push-ups is a two-count exercise! I will count the cadence! You will count the repetitions! You will do as many as I tell you to do! Is that clear? Starting positions! Move!"

"Aye aye, Sir!!"

"I don't think so! On your feet!"
"Aye aye, Sir!!"
"On your faces!"
"Aye aye, Sir!!"
"I don't think so! On your feet!"
"Aye aye, Sir!!"
"On your faces!"
"Aye aye, Sir!!"
"I don't think so! On your feet!"
"Aye aye, Sir!!"
"On your faces!"
"Aye aye, Sir!!"
"Down! Up!"
"Zero-one!!"
"Down! Up!"
"Zero-two!!"
"Down! Up!"
"Zero-three!!"
"Down! Up!"
"Zero-four!!"
"Down! Up!"
"Zero-five!!"
"Down! Up!"
"Zero-six!!"
"Down! Up!"
"Zero-seven!!"
"Down! Up!"
"Zero-eight!!"
"Down! Up!"
"Zero-niner!!"
"Down! Up!"
"One-zero!!"
"Down! Up!"
"One-one!!"
"Down! Up!"
"One-two!!"
"Down! Up!"
"One-three!!"
"Down! Up!"
"One-four!!"
"Down! Up!"

"One-five!!"

"Down! Up!"

"One-six!!"

"Down! Up!"

"One-seven!!"

"Down! Up!"

"One-eight!!"

"Down! Up!"

"One-niner!!"

"Down! Up!"

"Two-zero!!"

"On your feet!"

"Aye aye, Sir!!"

"Too freaking slow! On your faces!"

"Aye aye, Sir!!"

"On your feet!"

"Aye aye, Sir!!"

"On your faces!"

"Aye aye, Sir!!"

"On your feet!"

"Aye aye, Sir!!"

"On your faces!"

"Aye aye, Sir!!"

"On your feet!"

"Aye aye, Sir!!"

"On your faces!"

"Aye aye, Sir!!"

"On your feet!"

"Aye aye, Sir!!"

"Ears!"

"Open, Sir!!"

"Nasties! Upon receiving the command of execution *fall out*! You will! Fall out and regroup in formation as columns of four for the run! Am I clear?"

"Yes, Sir!!"

"Ready! Fall out!"

"Aye aye, Sir!!"

••

An O-One in the United States Navy is an Ensign. His insignia is a one gold bar collar device, or one one-half inch gold stripe outboard of one gold five-pointed star on black shoulder boards, or one one-half inch gold stripe below one gold five-pointed star on service dress blue uniform sleeves.

An O-Two in the United States Navy is a Lieutenant Junior Grade. His insignia is a one silver bar collar device, or one one-half inch gold stripe outboard of one one-quarter inch gold stripe outboard of one gold five-pointed star on black shoulder boards, or one one-half inch gold stripe below one one-quarter inch gold stripe below one gold five-pointed star on service dress blue uniform sleeves.

An O-Three in the United States Navy is a Lieutenant. His insignia is a two silver bar collar device, or two one-half inch gold stripes outboard of one gold five-pointed star on black shoulder boards, or two one-half gold stripes below one gold five-pointed star on service dress blue uniform sleeves.

An O-Four in the United States Navy is a Lieutenant Commander. His insignia is a one gold oak leaf collar device, or one one-half inch gold stripe outboard of one one-quarter inch gold stripe outboard of one one-half inch gold stripe outboard of one gold five-pointed star on black shoulder boards, or one one-half inch gold stripe below one one-quarter inch gold stripe below one one-half inch gold stripe below one gold five-pointed star on service dress blue uniform sleeves.

An O-Five in the United States Navy is a Commander. His insignia is a one silver oak leaf collar device, or three one-half inch gold stripes outboard of one gold five-pointed star on black shoulder boards, or three one-half inch gold stripes below one gold five-pointed star on service dress blue uniform sleeves.

An O-Six in the United States Navy is a Captain. His insignia is a one silver eagle collar device, or four one-half inch gold stripes outboard of one gold five-pointed star on black shoulder boards, or four one-half inch gold stripes below one gold five-pointed star on service dress blue uniform sleeves.

An O-Seven in the United States Navy is a Rear Admiral (Lower half). His insignia is a one silver five-pointed star collar device, or one silver five-pointed star outboard of one silver fouled anchor on black shoulder boards, or one two-inch gold stripe below one gold five-pointed star on service dress blue uniform sleeves.

An O-Eight in the United States Navy is a Rear Admiral (Upper half). His insignia is a two silver five-pointed stars collar device, or two silver five-pointed stars outboard of one silver fouled anchor on black shoulder boards, or one two-inch gold stripe below one one-half inch gold stripe below one gold five-pointed star on service dress blue uniform sleeves.

An O-Nine in the United States Navy is a Vice-Admiral. His insignia is a three silver five-pointed stars collar device, or three silver five-pointed stars outboard of one silver fouled anchor on black shoulder boards, or one two-inch gold stripe below two one-half inch gold stripes below one gold five-pointed star on service dress blue uniform sleeves.

An O-Ten in the United States Navy is an Admiral. His insignia is a four silver five-pointed stars collar device, or four silver five-pointed stars outboard of one silver fouled anchor on black shoulder boards, or one two-inch gold stripe below three one-half inch gold stripes below one gold five-pointed star on service dress blue uniform sleeves.

"Get up here, Pig!"

"Aye aye, Sir!"

"Rifle."

"Aye aye, Sir!"

"Stand-by."

"Aye aye, Sir!"

"The next movement that I will explain and demonstrate is order arms! Order arms is the position of the individual at attention with the rifle! You will assume order arms on the command atten-hut from the rest! You will assume order arms on the command fall in or order arms! Do I make myself clear?"

"Yes, Sir!!"

"Properly executed, the butt of the rifle rests on the deck! The stock rests along the outer edge of the right shoe! The pistol grip is to the front and the barrel is in a near vertical position! The rifle is grasped by the right hand at the junction of the front sight assembly and the barrel! The barrel rests in the V formed by the thumb and forefinger! The fingers are extended and joined and placed on line with the barrel! Am I clear?"

"Yes, Sir!!"

"Louder!"

"Yes, Sir!!"

"Fetch."

"Aye aye, Sir!"

"Scram."

"Aye aye, Sir!"

"Your turn, Pigs! On my command! Order! Arms!"

"Aye aye, Sir!!"

"You! Get it vertical, Pig!"

"Aye aye, Sir!"

"You! Keep it freaking grounded!"

"Aye aye, Sir!"

"Fingers joined, Maggot!"

"Aye aye, Sir!"

"Fingers freaking joined!"

"Aye aye, Sir!"

"The next movement that I will explain and demonstrate is port arms from order arms! The purpose for this movement is as the key position assumed in drill from one position to another! This movement has two-counts! Port arms from order arms is executed from the position of attention! Port is the preparatory command! Arms is the command of execution! You, Pig! Get over here!"

"Aye aye, Sir!"

"Rifle."

"Aye aye, Sir!"

"Stand-by."

"Aye aye, Sir!"

"Eyeballs!"

"Snap, Sir!!"

"At the command of execution! And for the count of one! Slide the right hand up and grasp the barrel near the flash suppressor! Fingers are joined and wrapped around the barrel with the thumb wrapped around the inboard portion! Am I clear?"

"Yes, Sir!!"

"Without loss of motion! Raise and carry the rifle diagonally across the front of the body until the right hand is level with and slightly to the left of the face! The right wrist is on the outboard portion of the front sight assembly! The elbow is held down without strain and nearly touches the handguard! The barrel is up and bisecting the angle formed by the neck and left shoulder! The pistol grip is to the left! The butt is in front of the right hip! Am I clear?"

"Yes, Sir!!"

"Am I clear?"

"Yes, Sir!!"

"At the same time! Smartly! Grasp the handguard with your left hand just above the slipring! The sling is included in the grasp! The fingers are joined and grasping the rifle! The little finger is in line with the slipring with the thumb on the inboard side of the handguard! The left wrist and forearm are straight! The elbow is held in against the body! Sound off, Freaks!"

"Aye aye, Sir!!"

"On the second count! Count-freaking-two! Release the grasp of the right hand and smartly regrasp the small of the stock! The fingers are joined and wrapped around the small of the stock with the thumb wrapped around the inboard portion! The right wrist and forearm are straight and parallel to the deck! The elbow is held into the side and the upper arm is in line with the back! The rifle is zero-freaking-four! Zero-four inches from the body! I will demonstrate this movement in cadence! Port! Arms! One! Two! Order! Arms! Port! Arms! One! Two! Order! Arms! You got that, Freaks?"

"Yes, Sir!!"

"Scram."

"Aye aye, Sir!"

"By-the-numbers! On my command!"

"Aye aye, Sir!!"

"Port! Arms!"

"One!! Two!!"

"I don't think so! As you freaking were! First count and first count only!"

"Aye aye, Sir!!"

"Port! Arms!"

"One!!"

"Get your hand higher, Potts!"

"Aye aye, Sir!"

"Ground that freaking thumb, Elkind!"

"Aye aye, Sir!"

"Ready! Two!"

"Two!!"

"As you were! Not up! Not sideways! At the freaking diagonal!"

"Aye aye, Sir!!"

"Right forearms at the horizontal!"

"Aye aye, Sir!!"

"Second count! Ready! Two!"

"Two!!"

"Elbow down, Lin!"

"Aye aye, Sir!"

"Four inches, Tronstein!"

"Aye aye, Sir!"

"Get your freaking rifle up, Fortunato!"

"Aye aye, Sir!"

"What?"

"Aye aye, Sir!"

"You better stop whispering to me, Pig!"

"Aye aye, Sir!"

"I don't freaking think so! Fall out! Get in my grass!"

"Aye aye, Sir!!"

"Ten-nine-three-two-one! Side-straddle hops!"

"Aye aye, Sir!!"

"Rifles up! Start freaking counting! Aye aye, Sir!"

"Aye aye, Sir!! One-two-three!! Zero-one!! One-two-three!! Zero-two!! One-two-three!! Zero-three!! One-two-three!! Zero-four!! One-two-three!! Zero-five!! One-two-three!! Zero-six!! One-two-three!! Zero-seven!! One-two-three!! Zero-eight!! One-two-three!! Zero-niner!! One-two-three!! One-zero!! One-two-three!! One-one!! One-two-three!! One-two!! One-two-three!! One-three!! One-two-three!! One-four!! One-two-three!! One-five!! One-two-three!! One-six!! One-two-three!! One-seven!! One-two-three!! One-eight!! One-two-three!! One-niner!! One-two-three!! Two-zero!! One-two-three!! Two-one!! One-two-three!! Two-two!! One-two-three!! Two-three!! One-two-three!! Two-four!! One-two-three!! Two-five!! One-two-three!! Two-six!! One-two-three!! Two-seven!! One-two-three!! Two-eight!! One-two-three!! Two-niner!! One-two-three!! Three-zero!!"

"Eight-count body builders!"

"Aye aye, Sir!!"

"Start counting!"

"Aye aye, Sir!! One!! Two!! Three!! Four!! Five!! Six!! Seven!! Zero-one!! One!! Two!! Three!! Four!! Five!! Six!! Seven!! Zero-two!! One!! Two!! Three!! Four!! Five!! Six!! Seven!! Zero-three!! One!! Two!! Three!! Four!! Five!! Six!! Seven!! Zero-four!! One!! Two!! Three!! Four!! Five!! Six!! Seven!! Zero-five!! One!! Two!! Three!! Four!! Five!! Six!! Seven!! Zero-six!! One!! Two!! Three!! Four!! Five!! Six!! Seven!! Zero-seven!! One!! Two!! Three!! Four!! Five!! Six!! Seven!! Zero-eight!! One!! Two!! Three!! Four!! Five!! Six!! Seven!! Zero-niner!! One!! Two!! Three!! Four!! Five!! Six!! Seven!! One-zero!! One!! Two!! Three!! Four!! Five!! Six!! Seven!! One-one!! One!! Two!! Three!! Four!! Five!! Six!! Seven!! One-two!! One!! Two!! Three!! Four!! Five!! Six!! Seven!! One-three!! One!! Two!! Three!! Four!! Five!! Six!! Seven!! One-four!! One!! Two!! Three!! Four!! Five!! Six!! Seven!! One-five!! One!! Two!! Three!! Four!! Five!! Six!! Seven!! One-six!! One!! Two!! Three!! Four!! Five!! Six!! Seven!! One-seven!! One!! Two!! Three!! Four!! Five!! Six!! Seven!! One-eight!! One!! Two!! Three!! Four!! Five!! Six!! Seven!! One-niner!! One!! Two!!

Three!! Four!! Five!! Six!! Seven!! Two-zero!! One!! Two!! Three!! Four!! Five!! Six!! Seven!! Two-one!! One!! Two!! Three!! Four!! Five!! Six!! Seven!! Two-two!! One!! Two!! Three!! Four!! Five!! Six!! Seven!! Two-three!! One!! Two!! Three!! Four!! Five!! Six!! Seven!! Two-four!! One!! Two!! Three!! Four!! Five!! Six!! Seven!! Two-five!!"

"On your feet!"

"Aye aye, Sir!!"

"On your faces!"

"Aye aye, Sir!!"

"On your backs!"

"Aye aye, Sir!!"

"On your feet!"

"Aye aye, Sir!!"

"On your backs!"

"Aye aye, Sir!!"

"On your faces!"

"Aye aye, Sir!!"

"On your feet!"

"Aye aye, Sir!!"

"Side-straddle hops! Rifles up! Do it now!"

"Aye aye, Sir!! One-two-three!! Zero-one!! One-two-three!! Zero-two!! One-two-three!! Zero-three!! One-two-three!! Zero-four!! One-two-three!! Zero-five!! One-two-three!! Zero-six!! One-two-three!! Zero-seven!! One-two-three!! Zero-eight!! One-two-three!! Zero-niner!! One-two-three!! One-zero!! One-two-three!! One-one!! One-two-three!! One-two!! One-two-three!! One-three!!"

"Get them up!"

"Aye aye, Sir!!"

"Higher!"

"Aye aye, Sir!! One-two-three!! One-four!! One-two-three!! One-five!! One-two-three!! One-six!! One-two-three!! One-seven!! One-two-three!! One-eight!! One-two-three!! One-niner!! One-two-three!! Two-zero!! One-two-three!! Two-one!! One-two-three!! Two-two!! One-two-three!! Two-three!! One-two-three!! Two-four!! One-two-three!! Two-five!! One-two-three!! Two-six!! One-two-three!! Two-seven!! One-two-three!! Two-eight!! One-two-three!! Two-niner!! One-two-three!! Three-zero!!"

"Fall in!"

"Aye aye, Sir!!"

"Ten-nine-eight-seven-four-two-one! Adjust. Cover. Get back up here, Maggot!"

"Aye aye, Sir!"

"Rifle."

"Aye aye, Sir!"

"Stand-by."

"Aye aye, Sir!"

"Eyeballs!"

"Snap, Sir!!"

"The next movement that I will explain and demonstrate is port arms to order arms! Port arms to order arms is a three-count movement! On the first count, at the command order arms! The right hand is moved from the small of the stock back to the barrel! The palm of the right hand is to the rear! Fingers are joined and wrapped around the barrel! Thumb wrapped around the inboard portion! This puts your little finger just above the bayonet stud! The right wrist is on the outboard portion of the front sight assembly! The elbow is held down without strain and nearly touches the handguard! Clear?"

"Yes, Sir!!"

"On the second count! Lower the rifle initially with the left hand while changing the grasp of the right hand to the junction of the barrel and the front sight assembly! Without loss of motion! Release the grasp of the left hand from the handguard! With your right hand! Carry the weapon to your right side until the butt is three inches from the deck! The barrel is in a vertical position and the pistol grip is to the front! At the same time guide the weapon with the left hand until the right thumb is on the trouser seam! The fingers of the left hand are extended and joined and touch the rifle near the flash suppressor! The palm of the left hand is towards the rear! The left wrist and forearm are straight and the left elbow is in against the body! Am I freaking clear?"

"Yes, Sir!!"

"On the third count! Return the left hand to the left side as in the position of attention! At the same time, gently lower the rifle to the deck with the right! I will demonstrate this movement in cadence! Order! Arms! One! Two! Three! Got that, Pig Nasties?"

"Yes, Sir!!"

"Scram Pig."

"Aye aye, Sir!"

"By the numbers! Port! Arms!"

"One!!"

"Ready! Two!!"

"Two!!"

"Order! Arms!"

"One!!"

"As you were!"

"Aye aye, Sir!!"

"All together. Order! Arms!"

"One!!"

"Elkind, if I see that freaking thumb again, I'm cutting it off!"

"Aye aye, Sir!"

"Ready! Two!"

"Two!!"

"As you were! You carry the weapon, Freaks! Weapons control at all times! Guide with the left!"

"Aye aye, Sir!!"

"Altogether this time! Steady!"

"Aye aye, Sir!!"

"Ready! Two!"

"Two!!"

"Zero-three inches!"

"Aye aye, Sir!!"

"Get that rifle up, Reston!"

"Aye aye, Sir!"

"Steady!"

"Aye aye, Sir!!"

"Get that elbow in tight, Shaffer!"

"Aye aye, Sir!"

"Ready! Three!"

"Three!!"

"As you were!"

"Aye aye, Sir!!"

"You return the left hand to the left side at the position of attention! You lower the rifle to the deck with the right hand at the same freaking time! Am I clear?"

"Yes, Sir!!"

"Ready! Three!"

"Three!!"

"Stock to the right shoe, Siegel!"

"Aye aye, Sir!"

"Rifles vertical!"

"Aye aye, Sir!!"

"Ready! Port! Arms!"

"One!!"

"Ready! Two!"

"Two!!"

"Four inches from the waistline! Fix yourself!"

"Aye aye, Sir!"

"At the freaking diagonal, Pig!"

"Aye aye, Sir!!"
"You're too low, Kramer!"
"No excuse, Sir!"
"Order! Arms!"
"One!!"
"Ready! Two!"
"Two!!"
"Ready! Three!"
"Three!!"
"Ready! Port! Arms!"
"One!!"
"Adjust! Right little finger just above the bayonet stud, Freak!"
"Aye aye, Sir!"
"Elbow in and down, Pig!"
"Aye aye, Sir!"
"Little finger is in line with the slipring with the thumb on the inboard side of the handguard, Maggot!"
"Aye aye, Sir!"
"Left wrist and forearm are straight, Weirdo!"
"Aye aye, Sir!"
"The elbow is held in against the body, Clown!"
"Aye aye, Sir!"
"Tight!"
"Aye aye, Sir!"
"Ready! Two!"
"Two!!"
"Small of the stock, Freakshow!"
"Aye aye, Sir!"
"I see your freaking thumb, Pig!"
"No excuse, Sir!"
"Right forearm parallel to the deck, Friendly Fire!"
"Aye aye, Sir!"
"Parallel!"
"Aye aye, Sir!"
"Elbows grounded, Maggots!"
"Aye aye, Sir!!"
"Tighter!"
"Aye aye, Sir!!"
"By the numbers! Ready! Order! Arms!"
"One!!"
"Right palm to the rear!"

"Aye aye, Sir!!"

"Fingers joined and wrapped around the barrel!"

"Aye aye, Sir!!"

"Thumb wrapped around the inboard portion! Little finger just above the bayonet stud!"

"Aye aye, Sir!!"

"Right wrist outboard of the front sight assembly!"

"Aye aye, Sir!!"

"Elbows down!"

"Aye aye, Sir!!"

"Down!"

"Aye aye, Sir!!"

"Ready! Two!"

"Two!!"

"Slow it down!"

"Aye aye, Sir!!"

"The right moves to the junction of the barrel and the front sight assembly! Bring it up one inch, Freak!"

"Aye aye, Sir!"

"Release with the left! Pistol grip to the front! Smooth carry to the right! Fingers of the left return extended near the flash suppressor! Left elbow tight into the body! Right thumb to the trouser seam! Butt three inches from the deck!"

"Aye aye, Sir!!"

"Ready! Three!"

"Three!!"

"Returning the left to the position of attention while lowering the stock of the rifle to the deck!"

"Aye aye, Sir!!"

"Rifles vertical!"

"Aye aye, Sir!!"

"Ears!"

"Open, Sir!!"

"You freaking sound off, you hear me?"

"Yes, Sir!!"

"By-the-numbers! Port! Arms!"

"One!!"

"Ready! Two!"

"Two!!"

"Elkind, I swear to Christ."

"No excuse, Sir!"

"Order! Arms!"
"One!!"
"Ready! Two!"
"Two!!"
"Three inches from the deck!"
"Aye aye, Sir!!"
"Ready! Three!"
"Three!!"
"Elbows in!"
"Aye aye, Sir!!"
"Get them in!"
"Aye aye, Sir!!"
"Without-the-numbers! Port! Arms!"

••

An E-One in the United States Navy is a Seaman Recruit. He has no insignia.

An E-Two in the United States Navy is a Seaman Apprentice. His insignia is two parallel diagonal slashes.

An E-Three in the United States Navy is a Seaman. His insignia is three parallel diagonal slashes.

An E-Four in the United States Navy is a Petty Officer Third Class. His insignia is one chevron below one eagle.

An E-Five in the United States Navy is a Petty Officer Second Class. His insignia is two chevrons below one eagle.

An E-Six in the United States Navy is a Petty Officer First Class. His insignia is three chevrons below one eagle.

An E-Seven in the United States Navy is a Chief Petty Officer. His insignia is three chevrons below one rocker below one eagle. In khaki uniform his insignia will be a gold fouled anchor collar device with a silver U.S.N. centered across the anchor.

An E-Eight in the United States Navy is a Senior Chief Petty Officer. His insignia is three chevrons below one rocker below one eagle below one star centered about the eagle. In khaki uniform his insignia will be a gold fouled anchor collar device with a silver U.S.N. centered across the anchor below one silver star.

An E-Nine in the United States Navy is a Master Chief Petty Officer. His insignia is three chevrons below one rocker below one eagle below two stars centered about the eagle. In khaki uniform his insignia will be a gold fouled anchor collar device with a silver U.S.N. centered across the anchor below two silver stars.

The Master Chief Petty Officer of the Navy is an E-Nine. His insignia is three chevrons below one rocker below one eagle below three stars centered about the eagle. In khaki uniform his insignia will be a gold fouled anchor collar device with a silver U.S.N. centered across the anchor below three silver stars.

••

"Attention on deck, stand by."

"Good morning, Sir."

"Good morning.

"Please take your seats."

"Aye aye, Sir."

"Today marks the first day of your academic coursework. I will be your first instructor. The student guide you have in front of you is for Naval History. Your

terminal objective is to demonstrate knowledge of U.S. naval history and the role U.S. naval forces played in the development of national policies and military strategies of the United States. This course will meet nine times and includes one test period. The final exam will be given in session ten. The exam contains forty questions. The minimum passing grade for the exam is seventy-five percent. If you do not meet this bar, you will be sent to remediation. You will then be required to complete a makeup of the final exam within three working days of the initial exam. You do not want to fail the initial exam. Not this one. Believe me, it gets harder. I want that to get through, alright?"

"Yes, Sir."

"Ears."

"Open, Sir."

"To trace our naval history is to trace how we as Americans took to the sea in pursuit of our liberty and continued to use the sea to maintain that freedom for over two centuries. We will trace our history from its inception during our wars as Colonists and the American Revolution, through to the War of Eighteen-Twelve, World Wars One and Two, Korea, Vietnam and our current engagements in the Middle East. We will take a look at the strategies used in each of these conflicts, the types of warfare and our current policies. If you find yourself nodding off, Candidate Zombie style, go on and stand up in the back of the class. How does that sound?"

"Outstanding, Sir."

"Outstanding. Please turn to page two-decimal-one dash one. Your enabling objectives are the following. Foot stomp. I repeat. Foot stomp. At the end of this lesson topic you will be able to define strategy and tactics, describe the significance of the American Revolution to the development of the U.S. Navy, describe the events leading to the Navy Act of Seventeen-Ninety-Four, describe the major reasons for the U.S. involvement in the War of Eighteen-Twelve, state the impact of the War of Eighteen-Twelve on the development of the U.S. Navy, list significant technological developments affecting the U.S. Navy between the Revolutionary War and the Civil War, and describe the impact of the Mexican-American War on the development of the U.S. Navy. Foot stomp. Got all that? Alright, let's get going. Two-decimal-one dash two. When we talk strategy, we mean an overall plan for achieving an objective. For our purposes here, you will be held responsible, foot stomp, for knowing the definitions of three commonly employed strategies. The blockade. The quarantine. And commerce raiding. Officer Candidate Reston."

"Yes, Sir."

"Please give us the definition of blockade."

"Aye aye, Sir. A blockade is a naval restrictive measure used to obstruct the passage of commerce into or out of a country. The blockade is normally an act of war and is commonly pursued by the stronger navy."

"Thank you. By the stronger Navy. Foot stomp. Officer Candidate Masterson, please give us the definition of quarantine."

"Sir, the definition of quarantine is a naval restrictive measure used to prevent passage of selected contraband into or out of a country."

"Thank you. Officer Candidate Larson, the definition of commerce raiding, please."

"A predatory incursion and hit and run tactics by a warship against enemy merchant vessels that is normally pursued by the weaker navy, Sir."

"Commerce raiding. Weaker navy. Foot stomp. Clear enough?"

"Yes, Sir."

"Bearing strategy in mind, we start with the Seven Years War, Seventeen-Fifty-Six to Seventeen-Sixty-Three, a war between the British and the French over conflicting claims to the lands west of the Appalachians and Austria's efforts to take back Silesia from Prussia. All the major European powers were involved. Part of a World War fought by the great powers of the day all around the globe. Hostilities broke out on this side of the Atlantic when French forces defeated a certain Colonel George Washington at Fort Necessity in Western Pennsylvania. Notwithstanding some French victories, after seven years of effective stalemate, with casualties on both sides topping a million lives, the British prevailed. In the Seventeen-Sixty-Three Treaty of Paris, the French ended up conceding all claims to land in North America east of the Mississippi and Canada. Among the lessons learned were the benefits of simple naval ship tactics, careful planning, inter-service cooperation, boldness of leadership and perseverance in carrying out successful amphibious operations. The greatest lesson learned, however, was the pervasive and inexorable power of naval preponderance in a world war, exhausting the power house Royal navy, which suffered significant declines in strength and efficiency. The Seven Years War was the first of a kind. What kind was that? Fortunato."

"World War, Sir."

"Bravo Zulu. Who was fighting who on this side of the Atlantic?"

"The British fought the French, Sir."

"Always fighting. Who won?"

"The British, Sir."

"At what cost?"

"A weakened Navy, Sir."

"Weakened but still relatively strong at the time, some ten odd years later, of our very own American Revolution. However depleted, at the start of the war, Britain still had a powerful navy and held the overwhelming advantages of

mobility, flexibility, concentration of power and continuous support inherent in a strong navy of any age. Returning to the naval strategies we defined, as the stronger Navy, Officer Candidate Reston, what strategy do you think the British Navy choose to employ?"

"A blockade, Sir."

"Bravo Zulu, Shipmate. The British chose to blockade the Colonies. And how did the Colonies counter?"

"Commerce raiding, Sir."

"Bravo Zulu, Shipmate. By necessity. The Colonies had no navy at the start of the Revolution and were forced to rely primarily on merchant vessels as privateers. By the war's end, however, we would have no less than four. First came Washington's Navy, known as the Army Navy, formed in Seventeen-Seventy-Five by George Washington and recognized when the Colonial schooner Hannah captured the first British ship, a British sloop named the Unity. The Hannah, foot stomp, and the Unity. The Continental Congress established a second force later on that year with legislation for a Continental Navy. Although not the world's most feared naval force, it did establish the reputations of some of our revered forbearers, daring Captains by the names of Biddle, Wickes, Conyngham and John Paul Jones and served as the forerunner of the modern navy. Foot stomp. Next came the Marine Corp. Established November tenth, Seventeen-Seventy-Five, you'll note, foot stomp, who now carry bragging rights as the U.S. service branch with the longest continuous history. And last but certainly not least, you had the Privateers, widely considered the most significant contributors to the Revolutionary effort. At least Navy wise. The Continental Congress issued commissions to one thousand and ninety-seven vessels, mounting fourteen thousand eight hundred and seventy-two guns, manned by fifty-eight thousand four hundred men. By the war's end, the British had lost two thousand nine hundred and eighty vessels to Privateers during the war, excluding recaptures, at a significant cost to the Crown, a source of increasing pressure on King George to end the war. Double foot stomp. Officer Candidate Tronstein."

"Yes, Sir."

"What is the U.S. armed force with the longest continuous service?"

"The U.S. Marine Corp, Sir."

"Which Colonial navy made the most significant war effort? A, the Army Navy? B, the Continental Navy? C, the Marine Corp? Or D, Privateers?"

"The Privateers, Sir."

"And which Colonial schooner captured the first British ship."

"The Hannah, Sir."

"Foot stomp. You will be held accountable for three Revolutionary naval battles. The Battle of Lake Champlain, Battle of Flamborough Head and Battle of the Virginia Capes. Got it?"

"Yes, Sir."

"We'll start with the Battle of Lake Champlain. Seventeen-Seventy-Nine. For you geography buffs, you'll find it northeast of Lake Ontario up along the Canadian border near Plattsburg. In the lead up to the battle, bracing against an invading force of thirteen thousand five hundred Redcoats under Sir Guy Carlton, the Colonials assembled a small squadron on Lake Champlain in the defense of New York. The British force overran the squadron. However, hidden behind this tactical victory lay an important strategic defeat, delaying the offensive into winter and convincing Carlton to retire to Canada rather than pursue his campaign in the snow. A tactical victory for the British. A strategic victory for the home team. Foot stomp. Got it?"

"Yes, Sir."

"The Battle of Flamborough Head and the legend of Sir John Paul Jones. Also in Seventy-Nine. In command of the forty-two-gun Bonhomme Richard and a four-ship squadron and tasked with causing havoc on the other side of the Atlantic, John Paul Jones encountered the far superior fifty-gun British H.M.S. Serapis off the English coast at Flamborough Head. The battle raged into the evening, the Bonhomme Richard sinking beneath its Captain. Yet when Captain Pearson hailed for surrender, Jones gave an immortal reply. Officer Candidate Koch."

"Yes, Sir."

"What was that reply?"

"I have not yet begun to fight, Sir."

"Now with some respect for the ghost of Admiral Jones."

"I have not yet begun to fight!"

"That's better. John Paul Jones uttered these famous words and, after suffering three more devastating hours of cannon fire, came along side of the Serapis and lashed the Bonhomme Richard to her, fighting on to victory and making the captured Serapis his new flagship as the Bonhomme Richard sank into the North Sea. Foot stomp. Officer Candidate Kramer."

"Yes, Sir."

"Go on and stand at the back of the class."

"Aye aye, Sir."

"I'm seeing a lot of heavy eyelids out there. Everyone up. On your feet. Shake it loose. That's it. Better?"

"Yes, Sir."

"Alright, be seated."

"Aye aye, Sir."

"We'll load up on extra caffeine in a little bit. Now where were we?"

"John Paul Jones, Sir."

"Remind me, what was the name of the captured British vessel? Anyone?"

"The Serapis, Sir."

"Bravo Zulu. And now for the last of the three take-away battles, the Battle for the Virginia Capes, no doubt the most significant of the war. Double foot stomp. In Seventeen-Eighty-One, General Washington out maneuvered and surrounded the British General Cornwallis at Yorktown, who summoned rescue by his Fleet. Washington countered, requesting support from Lafayette and the French to stop the British ships from entering Yorktown. Officer Candidate Zurich."

"Yes, Sir."

"What kind of strategy does this reflect?"

"A blockade, Sir."

"Very good. Unable to escape with his men, Cornwallis was forced to surrender, effectively bringing an end to the conflict. Both a tactical and strategic victory for the Colonists. Foot stomp. Two years after Yorktown, the Americans and the British signed the Treaty of Paris, recognizing the independence of the United States, stretching from the Atlantic to the Mississippi and from the Great Lakes to Florida. The birth of our nation. Officer Candidate Hibbs, quick reaction. True or false? The Battle of Lake Champlain was a strategic victory for the British navy. Without your work book."

"True."

"Negative, Shipmate. Try again."

"False."

"A tactical victory but a strategic defeat. What famous phrase did John Paul Jones utter as his ship sunk beneath him?"

"I have not yet begun to fight!"

"Hooyah. And where did General Washington effectively bring an end to the Revolutionary War?"

"Yorktown, Sir."

"Thank your Shipmates. Go stand at the back of the class."

"Aye aye, Sir."

"With the end of the war came the end of the Continental Navy. Nine years would pass before Congress saw the need to provide and maintain a U.S. Navy as we know it today. Unwelcome in Britain, American merchants began to look to the Mediterranean and the Far East for commerce. Problem was, then as now, not everyone respects the Law of the Sea. In the Med, Barbary State pirates demanded tribute from passing ships. Absent a navy for protection and unable to pay the bribes, U.S. ships were often taken hostage. This led to some vigorous debate back home in CONUS. The Federalists, led by Alexander Hamilton and supported by commercial interests in the New England states, pushed for a national effort, a Navy Act to build a Fleet. On the other side of the aisle were the Jeffersonians, led by Jefferson, who believed that the Navy envisioned by the

Navy Act would be too expensive and too imperialistic for our traditions. A good old-fashioned policy brawl followed by a good old fashioned policy decision. Although Hamilton prevailed, only three were initially built. Two-decimal-one dash nine. Top of the page. Officer Candidate Smith, what were the names of those ships?"

"The Constitution, the Constellation and the United States, Sir."

"Constitution, Constellation and United States. Hamilton succeeded in setting the course, but more was needed to convince the Nation of the value of power projection. Enter the Quasi-War. In Seventeen-Ninety-Seven, John Adams succeeded George Washington as President. He inherited a country sharply divided over foreign policy, some in support of closer ties with the British and others in support of closer ties with the French. Our relationship with France in decline, President Adams dispatched a diplomatic mission to Paris. The mission was greeted by French agents who demanded bribes before any talk, threatening that, without payment, we would suffer at the hands of French seapower. Got to love the French, folks. Am I right?"

"Yes, Sir."

"The delegation returned home. Although a declaration of war was never made, skirmishes became the norm. And Congress saw the need to act. A new Navy Department was created reporting to a Secretary of the Navy, authorized to seize, take and bring to port armed French ships hovering off the Atlantic seaboard. In Seventeen-Ninety-Seven, Stephen Decatur in command of the Delaware came upon an American coastal trader that had been plundered by the twelve-gun French schooner Croyable. He caught up with the enemy privateer that very night, forced her to surrender and returned to Philadelphia with her as a prize, commissioned into the Navy as the Retaliation. These types of skirmishes continued for the next several years. The French, however, were guilty of overreach and had bigger worries. Based on negotiations with France's soon-to-be Emperor, Napoleon Bonaparte, the Senate approved the Treaty of Mortefontaine, bringing the conflict to an end in Eighteen-O-One. Quasi-War. Stephen Decatur. Croyable. Retaliation. Peace treaty with Napoleon. Foot stomp. Got it?"

"Yes, Sir."

"Meanwhile, skirmishes with the Barbary Pirates continued unabated. In Eighteen-O-Three, under the command of Commodore Edward Preble, the U.S.S. Philadelphia ran aground on an uncharted reef off of Tripoli Harbor while giving chase to a Tripolitan vessel, the ship overrun and her crew imprisoned. Preble ached for revenge. He got his chance three years later, ordering Lieutenant Decatur to take command of a task force and sail for Tripoli. Decatur stood off the coast for ten days. On the tenth night, he stole into the harbor under the cover of darkness, leading a team of sixty men who silently boarded the

Philadelphia and killed the Tripolitan crew. Decatur then set fire to the ship and escaped out to sea, returning home a hero. The argument for our modern Navy continued to gain steam. Lin. Go stand in the back. For the rest of you, lock it up or head on back. Better than remediation."

"Aye aye, Sir."

"Officer Candidate Driver."

"Yes, Sir."

"The War of Eighteen-Twelve. Page two-decimal-one dash eleven. Who fought who?"

"Us versus the British again, Sir."

"That is correct. Go stand in the back with your Shipmates."

"Aye aye, Sir."

"The once proud Royal Navy, operating with undermanned crews depleted by desertions, insisted on the right to search neutral vessels for British subjects, including those American flagged. Desperate for experienced seaman in the struggled to contain Napoleon, they began impressing American sailors into service. Almost nine hundred American ships and six thousand men were impressed into British service from Eighteen-O-Six to Eighteen-Twelve. Not insignificant. Policy War Hawks back in Washington also believed the national destiny required the seizure of Spanish Florida and British Canada with an eye towards westward expansion. This belief was known as Manifest Destiny. So if we were to sum up two reasons for the War of Eighteen-Twelve, what would those two reasons be?"

"Impressed sailors and Manifest Destiny, Sir?"

"Bravo Zulu. The British impressment of American sailors and Manifest Destiny. Foot stomp. And based on our newfound understanding of naval strategy, what were the dynamics of the conflict? Eyes up here, Candidate. You don't need the script."

"Aye aye, Sir. A blockage, Sir?"

"Blockade."

"Blockade, Sir."

"Whose blockage? Christ, now you have me doing it. Whose blockade?"

"A British blockade, Sir."

"And our counterstrategy?"

"Commerce raiding, Sir."

"As the weaker naval force. Very good. Although the war was fought mainly on land, control of the Great Lakes would again prove pivotal to the outcome of the war. September tenth, Eighteen-Thirteen. The Battle of Lake Erie where Commodore Perry, foot stomp, leading a squadron of nine ships against British Commander Robert Barclay's smaller force, forced the collapse and abandonment of the British positions, denying a key route for communication

and resupply. The battle would prove both a tactical and strategic defeat for British efforts to capture American territory in the Northeast. We're talking both tactical and strategic this time. Foot stomp. Tactical and strategic. Got it?"

"Yes, Sir."

"The Battle of Lake Champlain. Sound familiar? Round two. Who remembers who won the first? Anyone? All this talk about heroes, and no one wants to jump on a fifty-fifty? Yes. A hero. You in the back. Who do we have?"

"Officer Candidate Jackson, Sir."

"Well, Officer Candidate Jackson? Who won that Battle?"

"Although the British won a tactical victory, the battle was a victory for us strategically, Sir."

"Outstanding. The ghost of John Paul Jones salutes you. Ding. Ding. Ding. The Second Battle of Lake Champlain would prove just as significant. Perhaps even more so for your testing purposes. Foot stomp. In the summer of Eighteen-Fourteen, the Canadians, yes, our friendly neighbors to the North, launched an invasion of Maine, a strategy that depended on British control of the supply route over Lake Champlain. Royal Navy Captain Downie, against what was the better judgment, led his force of poorly trained men into an engagement against the experienced crew of U.S. Navy Commodore MacDonough. Two hours and twenty minutes of close fighting followed at a cost of two hundred American and three hundred British lives, discouraging the British and paving the way for a favorable peace treaty for us in the Treaty of Ghent. The British went home again and all territorial boundaries were restored. No mention was ever made of the impressed seamen. In any case, after Napoleon's defeat at the hands of the armies of the Seventh Coalition, the issue faded. But what had now become abundantly clear given the lessons learned from the Barbary Pirate and British convoy raids was that we needed a real navy. A Navy to meet the enemy at sea and forestall or break blockades and protect the flow American merchant trade. Congress increased the Navy budget to eight-point-five million dollars. Enough said. War of Eighteen-Twelve. Battle of Lake Erie. Battle of Lake Champlain. Treaty of Ghent. Got it?"

"Yes, Senior."

"Officer Candidate Lyman."

"Yes, Sir."

"Back of the class."

"Aye aye, Sir."

"Lock it up. We're in the final stretch."

"Aye aye, Sir."

"In Eighteen-Forty-Six, we went to war with Mexico over the annexation of Texas. Naval engagement was limited, that is, until the very end, when the powers that were decided to go for the jugular by capturing Mexico City. This was

accomplished by an amphibious landing at Vera Cruz, marking the first time that the U.S. Navy planned and executed a successful full-scale amphibious landing, delivering U.S. Marines to their first beach. Left with little choice, Mexico accepted the Treaty of Guadalupe Hidalgo, a treaty that included some decent terms. Well, at least for us. In exchange for fifteen million dollars, Mexico ceded California, Arizona, New Mexico, Colorado and parts of Utah and Wyoming. From the halls of Montezuma to the shores of Tripoli. Treaty of Guadalupe Hidalgo. Foot stomp. That is all. On your feet."

"Aye aye, Sir."

"We'll take a fifteen minute break. Take advantage of the coffee in the student lounge. You'll find the Head down at the end of the passageway. Break."

"Aye aye, Sir."

An O-One in the United States Marine Corp is a Second Lieutenant. His insignia is a one gold bar collar device.

An O-Two in the United States Marine Corp is a First Lieutenant. His insignia is a one silver bar collar device.

An O-Three in the United States Marine Corp is a Captain. His insignia is a two silver bar collar device.

An O-Four in the United States Marine Corp is a Major. His insignia is a one gold oak leaf collar device.

An O-Five in the United States Marine Corp is a Lieutenant Colonel. His insignia is a one silver oak leaf collar device.

An O-Six in the United States Marine Corp is a Colonel. His insignia is a one silver eagle collar device.

An O-Seven in the United States Marine Corp is a Brigadier General. His insignia is a one silver star collar device.

An O-Eight in the United States Marine Corp is a Major General. His insignia is a two silver stars collar device.

An O-Nine in the United States Marine Corp is a Lieutenant General. His insignia is a three silver stars collar device

An O-Ten in the United States Marine Corp is a General. His insignia is a four silver stars collar device.

••

"Guide! Post the guide-on!"

"Aye aye, Section Leader!"

"Class Zero-Four-Zero-Zero! Ground your canteens to the starboard side!"

"Aye aye, Section Leader!!"

"Class Zero-Four-Zero-Zero! Upon receiving the command of execution march! You will! Half-step up this ladderwell, perform an immediate column-left, and reform at the door!"

"Aye aye, Section Leader!!"

"Ready! March!"

"Aye aye, Section Leader!!"

"Your left-right! Left-right! Ready! Halt! Ready! Halt!"

"Aye aye, Section Leader!!"

"Ready! Adjust!"

"Aye aye, Section Leader!! Discipline!! D!! I!! S!! C!! I!! P!! L!! I!! N!! E!! Discipline!! Is!! The unconditional!! Obedience-to-orders!! Respect-for-authority!! And self-reliance!! Freeze-candidate-freeze!!"

"Doorbody off the rear!"

"Doorbody, aye aye, Section Leader!!"

"Doorbody reporting as ordered, Section Leader!"

"Doorbody post!"

"Aye aye, Section Leader!"

"Doorbody! Report status of chow hall deck!"

"Aye aye, Section Leader! Chow hall deck not clear, Section Leader!"

"Chow hall deck not clear, Section Leader!!"

"Very well! Doorbody! Gouge the class!"

"Aye aye, Section Leader! Class Zero-Four-Zero-Zero! The Naval Aviator insignia is! A gold embroidered or gold metal winged pin with a fouled anchor behind a shield in the center!"

"Aye aye, Gougebody!! The Naval Aviator insignia is!! A gold embroidered or gold metal winged pin with a fouled anchor behind a shield in the center!!"

"Class Zero-Four-Zero-Zero! The Naval Flight Officer insignia is! A gold embroidered or gold metal winged pin with a set of small, crossed, fouled anchors behind a shield in the center!"

"Aye aye, Gougebody!! The Naval Flight Officer insignia is!! A gold embroidered or gold metal winged pin with a set of small, crossed, fouled anchors behind a shield in the center!!"

"Class Zero-Four-Zero-Zero! The Surface Warfare insignia is! A gold embroidered or gold metal pin, with the bow and superstructure of a modern naval warship! Superimposed on two crossed swords, on a background of ocean swells!"

"Aye aye, Gougebody!! The Surface Warfare insignia is!! A gold embroidered or gold metal pin, with the bow and superstructure of a modern naval warship!! Superimposed on two crossed swords, on a background of ocean swells!!"

"Class Zero-Four-Zero-Zero! The Special Warfare insignia is! A gold metal pin with an eagle holding a trident and a handgun in front of an anchor!"

"Aye aye, Gougebody!! The Special Warfare insignia is!! A gold metal pin with an eagle holding a trident and a handgun in front of an anchor!!"

"Class Zero-Four-Zero-Zero! The Submarine Warfare insignia is! A gold embroidered or gold metal pin showing the bow view of a submarine! Proceeding on the surface with bow planes rigged for diving! Flanked by dolphins in horizontal position! Their heads resting on the upper edge of the bow planes!"

"Aye aye, Gougebody!! The Submarine Warfare insignia is!! A gold embroidered or gold metal pin showing the bow view of a submarine!! Proceeding on the surface with bow planes rigged for diving!! Flanked by dolphins in horizontal position!! Their heads resting on the upper edge of the bow planes!!"

"Class Zero-Four-Zero-Zero! The Naval Aviation Supply insignia is! A gold embroidered or gold metal winged pin with a supply corps oak leaf in the center!"

"Aye aye, Gougebody!! The Naval Aviation Supply insignia is!! A gold embroidered or gold metal winged pin with a supply corps oak leaf in the center!!"

"Class Zero-Four-Zero-Zero! The Submarine Supply insignia is! A gold embroidered or gold metal pin with two dolphins facing a supply corps oak leaf in the center!"

"Aye aye, Gougebody!! The Submarine Supply insignia is!! A gold embroidered or gold metal pin with two dolphins facing a supply corps oak leaf in the center!!"

"Class Zero-Four-Zero-Zero! The Surface Supply insignia is! A gold embroidered or gold metal pin with a supply corps oak leaf! Centered on the bow and superstructure of a modern naval warship! Superimposed on two crossed naval swords on a background of ocean swells!"

"Aye aye, Gougebody!! The Surface Supply insignia is!! A gold embroidered or gold metal pin with a supply corps oak leaf!! Centered on the bow and superstructure of a modern naval warship!! Superimposed on two crossed naval swords on a background of ocean swells!!"

"Class Zero-Four-Zero-Zero! The Diving Officer insignia is! A gold metal pin with two upright sea horses facing a diving helmet! And two tridents projecting upward and canted outward from the diving helmet's cover! A double carrick bend superimposed on the breast plate!"

"Aye aye, Gougebody!! The Diving Officer insignia is!! A gold metal pin with two upright sea horses facing a diving helmet!! And two tridents projecting upward and canted outward from the diving helmet's cover!! A double carrick bend superimposed on the breast plate!!"

"I don't think so, you freaking Pig Whisperers! Get in my grass! Now, damnit!"

"Aye aye, Sir!!"

"Twenty-nineteen-eighteen-seventeen-fourteen-twelve-eight-seven-four-two-one. Push! Aye aye, Sir!"

"Aye aye, Sir!!"

"Down-up!"

"Zero-one!!"

"Down-Up!"

"Zero-two!!"

"Down-up!"

"Zero-three!!"

"Down-up!"

"Zero-four!!"

"Down-up!"

"Zero-five!!"

"Down-up!"

"Zero-six!!

"Down-up!"

"Zero-seven!!"
"Down-up!"
"Zero-eight!!"
"Down-up!"
"Zero-niner!!"
"Down-up!"
"One-zero!!"
"Down-up!"
"One-one!!"
"Down-up!"
"One-two!!"
"Down-up!"
"One-three!!"
"Down-up!"
"One-four!!"
"Down-up!"
"One-five!!"
"Down-up!"
"One-six!!"
"Down-up!"
"One-seven!!"
"Down-up!"
"One-eight!!"
"Down-up!"
"One-niner!!"
"Down-up!"
"Two-zero!!"

"On your feet! Eight-count body builders! You will count the cadence! You will count the repetitions! Aye aye, Sir!"

"Aye aye, Sir!! One!! Two!! Three!! Four!! Five!! Six!! Seven!! Zero-one!! One!! Two!! Three!! Four!! Five!! Six!! Seven!! Zero-two!! One!! Two!! Three!! Four!! Five!! Six!! Seven!! Zero-three!! One!! Two!! Three!! Four!! Five!! Six!! Seven!! Zero-four!! One!! Two!! Three!! Four!! Five!! Six!! Seven!! Zero-five!! One!! Two!! Three!! Four!! Five!! Six!! Seven!! Zero-six!! One!! Two!! Three!! Four!! Five!! Six!! Seven!! Zero-seven!! One!! Two!! Three!! Four!! Five!! Six!! Seven!! Zero-eight!! One!! Two!! Three!! Four!! Five!! Six!! Seven!! Zero-niner!! One!! Two!! Three!! Four!! Five!! Six!! Seven!! One-zero!! One!! Two!! Three!! Four!! Five!! Six!! Seven!! One-one!! One!! Two!! Three!! Four!! Five!! Six!! Seven!! One-two!! One!! Two!! Three!! Four!! Five!! Six!! Seven!! One-three!! One!! Two!! Three!! Four!! Five!! Six!! Seven!! One-four!! One!! Two!! Three!! Four!! Five!! Six!! Seven!! One-five!! One!! Two!! Three!! Four!! Five!! Six!! Seven!! One-six!! One!! Two!! Three!! Four!!

Five!! Six!! Seven!! One-seven!! One!! Two!! Three!! Four!! Five!! Six!! Seven!! One-eight!! One!! Two!! Three!! Four!! Five!! Six!! Seven!! One-niner!! One!! Two!! Three!! Four!! Five!! Six!! Seven!! Two-zero!! One!! Two!! Three!! Four!! Five!! Six!! Seven!! Two-one!! One!! Two!! Three!! Four!! Five!! Six!! Seven!! Two-two!! One!! Two!! Three!! Four!! Five!! Six!! Seven!! Two-three!! One!! Two!! Three!! Four!! Five!! Six!! Seven!! Two-four!! One!! Two!! Three!! Four!! Five!! Six!! Seven!! Two-five!!"

"On your feet! Aye aye, Sir!"

"Aye aye, Sir!!"

"Side-straddle hops! Side-straddle hops! Side-straddle hops is a four-count exercise! I will count the cadence! You will count the repetitions! Exercise!"

"Aye aye, Sir!!"

"One-two-three!"

"Zero-one!!"

"One-two-three!"

"Zero-two!!"

"One-two-three!"

"Zero-three!!"

"One-two-three!"

"Zero-four!!"

"One-two-three!"

"Zero-five!!"

"One-two-three!"

"Zero-six!!"

"One-two-three!"

"Zero-seven!!"

"One-two-three!"

"Zero-eight!!"

"One-two-three!"

"Zero-niner!!"

"One-two-three!"

"One-zero!!"

"One-two-three!"

"One-one!!"

"One-two-three!"

"One-two!!"

"One-two-three!"

"One-three!!"

"One-two-three!"

"One-four!!"

"One-two-three!"

"One-five!!"

"On-your-backs! On-your-backs! Leg-lifts! Start counting!"

"Aye aye, Sir!!"

"One-two-three! One-two-three! Now! Aye aye, Sir!"

"Aye aye, Sir!! One-two-three!! Zero-one!! One-two-three!! Zero-two!! One-two-three!! Zero-three!! One-two-three!! Zero-four!! One-two-three!! Zero-five!! One-two-three!! Zero-six!! One-two-three!! Zero-seven!! One-two-three!! Zero-eight!! One-two-three!! Zero-niner!! One-two-three!! One-zero!! One-two-three!! One-one!! One-two-three!! One-two!! One-two-three!! One-three!! One-two-three!! One-four!! One-two-three!! One-five!! One-two-three!! One-six!! One-two-three!! One-seven!! One-two-three!! One-eight!! One-two-three!! One-niner!! One-two-three!! Two-zero!!"

"On your feet! Run-in-place!"

"Aye aye, Sir!!"

"Knees up, Pigs!"

"Aye aye, Sir!!"

"On your backs! Scissor-kicks!"

"Aye aye, Sir!!"

"On your faces! Push!"

"Aye aye, Sir!!"

"On your feet! Side-straddle hops!"

"Aye aye, Sir!!"

"On your faces!"

"Aye aye, Sir!!"

"On your feet!"

"Aye aye, Sir!!"

"On your backs! Scissor-kicks!"

"Aye aye, Sir!!"

"One-two-three!"

"Zero-one!!"

"One-two-three!"

"Zero-two!!"

"One-two-three!"

"Zero-three!!"

"One-two-three!"

"Zero-four!!"

"One-two-three!"

"Zero-five!!"

"One-two-three!"

"Zero-six!!"

"One-two-three!"

"Zero-seven!!"

"One-two-three!"

"Zero-eight!!"

"One-two-three!"

"Zero-niner!!"

"One-two-three!"

"One-zero!!"

"One-two-three!"

"One-one!!"

"One-two-three!"

"One-two!!"

"One-two-three!"

"One-three!!"

"One-two-three!"

"One-four!!"

"One-two-three!"

"One-five!!"

"Mountain-climbers!"

"Aye aye, Sir!!"

"One-two-three!"

"Zero-one!!"

"One-two-three!"

"Zero-two!!"

"One-two-three!"

"Zero-three!!"

"One-two-three!"

"Zero-four!!"

"One-two-three!"

"Zero-five!!"

"One-two-three!"

"Zero-six!!"

"One-two-three!"

"Zero-seven!!"

"On your feet!"

"Aye aye, Sir!!"

"Cherry-pickers! You will count the cadence! You will count the repetitions! I want to hear it! Aye aye, Sir!"

"Aye aye, Sir!!"

"What are you waiting for, Pigs? Start counting!"

"Aye aye, Sir!! One-two-three!! Huh!! Zero-one!! One-two-three!! Huh!! Zero-two!! One-two-three!! Huh!! Zero-three!! One-two-three!! Huh!! Zero-four!!

One-two-three!! Huh!! Zero-five!! One-two-three!! Huh!! Zero-six!! One-two-three!! Huh!! Zero-seven!! One-two-three!! Huh!! Zero-eight!! One-two-three!! Huh!! Zero-niner!! One-two-three!! Huh!! One-zero!! One-two-three!! Huh!! One-one!! One-two-three!! Huh!! One-two!! One-two-three!! Huh!! One-three!! One-two-three!! Huh!! One-four!!"

"Louder!"

"Aye aye, Sir!! One-two-three!! Huh!! One-five!! One-two-three!! Huh!! One-six!! One-two-three!! Huh!! One-seven!! One-two-three!! Huh!! One-eight!! One-two-three!! Huh!! One-niner!! One-two-three!! Huh!! Two-zero!! One-two-three!! Huh!! Two-one!! One-two-three!! Huh!! Two-two!! One-two-three!! Huh!! Two-three!! One-two-three!! Huh!! Two-four!! One-two-three!! Huh!! Two-five!! One-two-three!! Huh!! Two-six!! One-two-three!! Huh!! Two-seven!! One-two-three!! Huh!! Two-eight!! One-two-three!! Huh!! Two-niner!! One-two-three!! Huh!! Three-zero!!"

"Donkey-kicks!"

"Aye aye, Sir!!"

"Kick! Kick! Kick! Start counting!"

"Aye aye, Sir!! One-two-three!! Zero-one!! One-two-three!! Zero-two!! One-two-three!! Zero-three!! One-two-three!! Zero-four!! One-two-three!! Zero-five!! One-two-three!! Zero-six!! One-two-three!! Zero-seven!! One-two-three!! Zero-eight!! One-two-three!! Zero-niner!! One-two-three!! One-zero!! One-two-three!! One-one!! One-two-three!! One-two!! One-two-three!! One-three!! One-two-three!! One-four!! One-two-three!! One-five!!"

"On your feet now! Aye aye, Sir!"

"Aye aye, Sir!!"

"On your faces!"

"Aye aye, Sir!!"

"Faster! On your feet!"

"Aye aye, Sir!!"

"On your faces!"

"Aye aye, Sir!!"

"Faster! Faster! On your feet!"

"Aye aye, Sir!!"

"On your faces!"

"Aye aye, Sir!!"

"On your feet!"

"Aye aye, Sir!!"

"On your faces!"

"Aye aye, Sir!!"

"On your feet!"

"Aye aye, Sir!!"

"On your faces!"
"Aye aye, Sir!!"
"On your feet!"
"Aye aye, Sir!!"
"Run in place!"
"Aye aye, Sir!!"
"Get them up!"
"Aye aye, Sir!!"
"Lock!"
"Motivation is contagious!!"
"Louder!"
"Motivation is contagious!!"
"Scum. On your faces! Push!"
"Aye aye, Sir!!"
"Down-up!"
"Zero-one!!"
"Why do I see freaking asses? That's a freaking response!"
"No excuse, Sir!!"
"Down-up!"
"Zero-two!!"
"Down-up!"
"Zero-three!!"
"Down-up!"
"Zero-four!!"
"Down-up!"
"Zero-five!!"
"Down-Up!"
"Zero-six!!
"Backs straight!"
"Aye aye, Sir!!"
"Down-up!"
"Zero-seven!!"
"Down-up!"
"Zero-eight!!"
"Down-up!"
"Zero-niner!!"
"Down-up!"
"One-zero!!"
"On your feet! Fall-in!"
"Aye aye, Sir!!"
"Ten-eight-seven-six-five-four-three-two-one! Freeze!"

"Aye aye, Sir!!"

"Cover! One arm's length! Aye aye, Sir!"

"Aye aye, Sir!!"

"Back in my grass! Aye aye, Sir!"

"Aye aye, Sir!!"

"Ten-nine-eight-seven! Back in formation!"

"Aye aye, Sir!!"

"Ten-nine-eight-seven-six-five-four-three-two-one! Faster! Too slow! Back in my grass!"

"Aye aye, Sir!!"

"Ten-nine-eight-seven-six-five-four-three-two-one! Get back in formation! Back in formation!"

"Aye aye, Sir!!"

"Back in my grass!"

"Aye aye, Sir!!"

"Back in formation!"

"Aye aye, Sir!!"

"Back in my grass!"

"Aye aye, Sir!!"

"Ten-nine-eight-seven-six-five-four-three-two-one! Back in formation!"

"Aye aye, Sir!!"

"Ten-eight-six-five-four-three-two-one! Freeze!"

"Aye aye, Sir!!"

"Cover. Proceed, Freak. With your Big Pair on."

"Aye aye, Sir! Guide! Post the guidon!"

"Aye aye, Section Leader!!"

"Class Zero-Four-Zero-Zero! Upon receiving the command of execution march! You will! Half-step up this ladderwell! Perform an immediate column-left! And reform at the door!"

"Aye aye, Section Leader!!"

"Ready! March! Your left-right! Left-right! Ready! Halt!"

"Aye aye, Section Leader!!"

"Ready! Adjust!"

"Aye aye, Section Leader!! Discipline!! D!! I!! S!! C!! I!! P!! L!! I!! N!! E!! Discipline!! Is!! The unconditional!! Obedience-to-orders!! Respect-for-authority!! And self-reliance!! Freeze-Candidate-freeze!!"

"Doorbody off the rear!"

"Doorbody, aye aye, Section Leader!!"

"Doorbody reporting as ordered, Section Leader!"

"Doorbody post!"

"Aye aye, Section Leader!"

"Doorbody! Report status of chow hall deck!"

"Aye aye, Section Leader! Chow hall deck all clear, Section Leader!"

"Chow hall deck all clear, Section Leader!!"

"Doorbody, crack the door!"

"Aye aye, Section Leader!"

"Class Zero-Four-Zero-Zero, marching into chow!"

"Class Zero-Four-Zero-Zero, marching into chow!!"

"Column of files! From the right! Forward!"

"Stand fast."

"March!"

"Good morning, Sir!"

"Zero-two!"

"Zero-three!"

"Zero-four!"

"Zero-five!"

"Zero-six!"

"Zero-seven!"

"Zero-eight!"

"Zero-niner!"

"One-zero!"

"One-one!"

"One-two!"

"One-three!"

"One-four!"

"One-five!"

"One-six!"

"One-seven!"

"One-eight!"

"One-niner!"

"Two-zero!"

"Two-one!"

"Two-two!"

"Two-three!"

"Two-four!"

"Two-five!"

"Two-six!"

"Two-seven!"

"Two-eight!"

"Two-niner!"
"Three-zero!"
"Three-one!"
"Three-two!"
"Three-three!"
"Three-four!"
"Three-five!"
"Three-six!"
"Three-seven!"
"Three-eight!"
"Three-niner!"
"Four-zero!"
"Four-one!"
"Good morning, Sir!"
"Doorbody, close the door!"
"Aye aye, Section Leader!"
"Class Zero-Four-Zero-Zero, proceed!"
"Aye aye, Section Leader!"
"Forward march!"
"Step freeze!!"
"Stand fast."
"Forward march!"
"Step freeze!!"
"Stand fast."
"Forward march!"
"Step freeze!!"
"Stand fast."
"Forward march!"
"Step freeze!!"
"Stand fast."
"Forward march!"
"Step freeze!!"
"Stand fast."
"Forward march!"
"Step freeze!!"
"Stand fast."
"Forward march!"
"Step freeze!!"
"Stand fast."
"Forward march!"
"Step freeze!!"

"Stand fast."
"Forward march!"
"Step freeze!!"
"Stand fast."
"Forward march!"
"Stand fast."
"Forward march!"
"Step freeze!!"
"Stand fast."
"Turkey or the beef?"
"Turkey please, Ma'am."
"Sides?"
"Green beans please, Ma'am. And a roll."
"Here you are."
"Thank you, Ma'am."
"You're welcome, Darling."
Gougebooks extend at an angle of ninety degrees.
"Put it away, Class Zero-Four-Zero-Zero!"
"Aye aye, Section Leader!!"
"Class Zero-Four-Zero-Zero! These tables! Both sides! Ready! Seats!"
"Kill!!"
"Adjust!"
"Kill!!"
"Pray at will!"
"Ready! Eat!"
"Snap!!"
"Class Zero-Four-Zero-Zero, this is your two-zero minute warning!"
"Aye aye, Section Leader!!"

••

An E-One in the United States Marine Corp is a Private. He has no insignia.

An E-Two in the United States Marine Corp is a Private First Class. His insignia is one chevron.

An E-Three in the United States Marine Corp is a Lance Corporal. His insignia is one chevron over crossed rifles.

An E-Four in the United States Marine Corp is a Corporal. His insignia is two chevrons over crossed rifles.

An E-Five in the United States Marine Corp is a Sergeant. His insignia is three chevrons over crossed rifles.

An E-Six in the United States Marine Corp is a Staff Sergeant. His insignia is three chevrons over crossed rifles over one rocker.

An E-Seven in the United States Marine Corp is a Gunnery Sergeant. His insignia is three chevrons over crossed rifles over two rockers.

An E-Eight in the United States Marine Corp is a Master Sergeant. His insignia is three chevrons over crossed rifles over three rockers.

An E-Eight in the United States Marine Corp is a First Sergeant. His insignia is three chevrons over one diamond over three rockers.

An E-Niner in the United States Marine Corp is a Master Gunnery Sergeant. His insignia is three chevrons over a bursting bomb over four rockers.

An E-Ten in the United States Marine Corp is a Sergeant Major. His insignia is three chevrons over a one star over four rockers.

••

"Attention on deck, Stand-by."

"Good morning, Ma'am."

"Good morning. Senior Chief will do just fine."

"Aye aye, Senior Chief."

"Got you wrapped around that axel, don't they? I'm going to need you to take it down a notch in my classroom. If you have a question, don't hesitate jump right in. I understand that some of you are seeing this material for the first time. There are no stupid questions. For you Priors out there, I expect the same understanding. Be courteous to your Shipmates. This might all be old hat to an old Sea Dog, but we were all there once too. Do you copy?"

"Yes, Senior Chief."

"Thank you. You are all here to learn Navy P.A. Some of it has rhyme and reason. Some of it you just have to memorize. Alright?"

"Yes, Senior Chief."

"Rank and rate structure. Supporting elements. Classified information. Shipboard organization. Correspondence and directives, Three-M maintenance and material management, and Performance Evaluations and Fitness Reports. Seventy-five percent is passing. We will get you there. This is not the one you want to fail. Test day is Friday. M.T.T. is Monday. You want to be prepping gear, not prepping for remedial. Bear that in mind this week. Even for you Priors, now. Easy to look past Admin. My advice is to put in the hours. How does that sound?"

"Outstanding, Senior Chief."

"Oh for crying out loud. Alright, let's get down to work. Your terminal objective, partially supported by this lesson topic is to be able to perform the administrative and personnel management duties of a newly commissioned Officer. What we will learn today is the Navy rank and rate structure. Your enabling objectives for this lesson topic are to describe general apprenticeship,

rating, paygrade and rate, along with the proper title and abbreviation for each Navy Enlisted and Officer paygrade. You should be able to state the collar, sleeve and shoulder insignia for Navy and Marine Corp Enlisted ranks, including the associated paygrade for each. And finally, you should be able to state the collar, sleeve and shoulder insignia for all Officer ranks in the Army, Navy, Air Force and Marine Corp. Sound at all familiar?"

"Yes, Senior Chief."

"I sure hope so. We'll start with paygrades. In the service, you'll always hear folks talking about paygrades. About their step in paygrade. That this or that is above my paygrade. You have two paygrade scales. Officer and Enlisted. Os and Es. Now all you'll need to know, count them, is three simple rules. Rule number-one. Each paygrade is associated with a level of proficiency and experience. Well, and time in grade. We'll be taking a closer look at that process later on in the week. Seniority between paygrades is reflected in the scale. An E-Five is senior to an E-Four. An O-Three is senior to an O-Two. Os are always senior to Es. That's clear enough right?"

"Yes, Senior Chief."

"Rule number-two. Seniority within any paygrade is based on the length of service in that paygrade, delineated by lineal numbers comprised of a six-digit whole number and a two-digit subnumber. Put another way, an E-Five that has been an E-Five for two years is senior to an E-Five that has been an E-Five for one year. Or maybe better like this. You all are Class Zero-Four-Zero-Zero. Right? You will graduate in November. Or at least most of you. Depending on whether you pay attention. Now Class Zero-Five reported to Officer Candidate School right after you did. And they'll graduate right after you do. You'll all be O-Ones. Ensigns. But you'll be senior to all those Ensigns from Zero-Five. Heck, based on how you break out in your own class, you will be more or less senior to your graduating classmates, not that it really matters. Odds are it's just a number telling you when you came into the service. But I'd bet three monkeys and a candlestick that a career has been decided on less."

"Senior Chief."

"Question in the back."

"Senior Chief, do you have different lineal numbers within different designators?"

"That's a negative. But you will be competing within your designators for promotion. So I suppose it does come out to the same thing. Does that answer your question?"

"Yes, Senior Chief."

"Rule number-three. The seniority system extends Navy wide. Take the seniority system within Master Chiefs. It goes Master Chief, Command Master Chief, Force Master Chief, Fleet Master Chief and Master Chief Petty Officer of

the Navy. Namely, the Master Chief Petty Officer of the Navy is the senior Master Chief in the Navy. Who's the most senior Master Chief in the Navy?"

"The Master Chief Petty Office of the Navy."

"Good. You'll all meet him one day on A.F.N. He's that important. Everyone get my drift?"

"Yes, Senior Chief."

"I sure hope so. Now there's paygrades. And then there's what folks do in the Navy. Everyone has a paygrade. But not everyone in the same paygrade has the same job. In the Enlisted ranks, your job is called your rating. That's right, a rating is just another word for a Navy job, a field of work or an occupation that calls for certain special skills. Add up a rating and paygrade, you get your rate. Everyone still with me? Yes?"

"Sorry, Senior Chief. What's the difference between a rating and a rate?"

"Great question. Don't over think it. The rating is for a specialty or job. Like an Intelligence Specialist or a Machinist Mate. In the old days, we're talking real old days, it was Boatswain Mates, Quartermasters, Gunner's Mates, Masters-at-Arms, Cooks, Armorers and Coxswains. Nowadays, as you might imagine, Navy needs a lot more specialized jobs. Stands to reason we now have a lot more ratings. You with me so far?"

"Yes, Senior Chief."

"Then you have your paygrade. Let's go with E-Five as an example. Now an E-Five is a Petty Officer Second Class. A P.O.-Two, if you will. So when you add Intelligence Specialist to P.O.-Two, you get an Intelligence Specialist Two. An I.S.-Two. Follow?"

"Yes, Senior Chief."

"If you have another P.O.-Two, but this time one who's a Machinist Mate, doing a different job, you add them both together just the same and that's a Machinist Mate Two. M.M.-Two. That's their rates. Is that a blank look, Shipmate?"

"No, Senior Chief."

"Don't worry, we'll run through some drills at the end of the section. You'll get the hang of it with a little practice. But does that answer your question?"

"Thank you, Senior Chief."

"You sure? This is going to get a little more complicated. If you're lost here, this is going to be a long road. Alright then. If you're sure, you're sure. Anyone else? Good. Now before you even get to a rating or rate, generally speaking, you go through an apprenticeship. This is for paygrades E-One through E-Three, fresh into the Navy Enlisted ranks. Navy needs some folks with some basic skills. There are six general apprenticeships. I would write these down if I were you. Seamen, or S.Ns. Seaman are responsible for keeping compartments, lines, rigging and deck gear shipshape. They also act as lookouts, members of gun

crews, helmsmen, security and fire sentries. Firemen, or F.Ns. Firemen care for and operate boilers, operate pumps, motors, turbines and damage control equipment. They may also be called upon to record the readings of gauges, maintain engineering machinery and stand security or fireroom watches. Airmen, or A.Ns. A.Ns perform various duties for naval air activities ashore and afloat like assisting in moving aircraft, loading and stowing equipment or serving as members of plane-handling crews. Constructionmen, or C.Ns. C.Ns operate, service and check construction equipment, performing semiskilled duties in the construction battalion. We're talking Seabees. Hospitalmen, H.Ns. Who help the Docs by arranging dressing carriages and sterilizing instruments, dressings, bandages and medicines, and keeping everyone's medical records. Good Landlubber gig if you can get it, on the Enlisted side. And last but not least, Dentalmen. D.Ns. Who assist Dental Officers in the treatment of patients, take care of the dental equipment and maintain everyone's dental records. And that's the six. Say them with me. Seaman. Fireman. Airman. Constructionman. Hospitalman. Dentalman."

"Seaman. Fireman. Airman. Constructionman. Hospitalman. Dentalman."

"One more time."

"Seaman. Fireman. Airman. Constructionman. Hospitalman. Dentalman."

"Great job. I'm seeing some tired eyes out there. We're now on seven-decimal-one dash nine for those of you staring at the wrong page. In the Fleet, you'll identify all these rates by sleeve insignia. A non-rated E-One has no insignia. Non-rated E-Two and E-Three apprentices are identified by two and three diagonal stripes, respectively, worn on the left sleeve. Depending on seasonal dress, winter and summer uniforms, these stripes sometimes change colors, dark on summer whites and light on the winter blues. For a Seaman Apprentice the stripe or stripes are white and navy blue. For an Airman Apprentice the stripes are emerald green. I repeat, Airman stripes are emerald green. For a Firemen Apprentice the stripes are red. Fire. Red. Red. Fire. For a Constructionman, the stripes are light blue. For a Hospitalman, the stripes are white and navy blue. Same for a Dentalman. Sounds like a lot, but think about it this way. If you add it all up, Seaman, Hospitalmen and Dentalmen all wear white and navy blue stripes. So if you see a young E-Two coming your way on Christmas Day in her winter blues, what would her sleeve insignia likely be? Volunteers? Anyone? Yes."

"Two white stripes."

"Very good. And, say at random, if you see a young sailor walking down the street with three emerald green stripes, what type of sailor would he be?"

"An airman."

"At what paygrade?"

"E-Three."

"Very good. I want to hear everybody, though. Now that's for non-rated, right? After apprenticeship training, these sailors, at least Seamen, Airmen and Firemen, earn the right to wear an apprenticeship insignia before they get designated. A wheel, an anchor or wings are the only badges for non-designated sailors. Do not, I repeat, do not confuse the absence of one of these badges on working dungaree uniforms with Constructionmen, Hospitalmen or Dentalmen. You are expected to know all of them, but do yourselves a favor and highlight dungarees. No insignia is worn on the working dungaree uniform. I repeat, no insignia is worn on the working dungaree uniform. So if you get a question asking what insignia an Airman apprentice wears on his dungaree uniform, the answer is none of the above. It's all about the dungarees, folks. Take my word for it. Can I make myself any clearer?"

"No, Senior Chief."

"Good. That's for the paygrades E-Three and below. Does anyone have any questions as to stripes or specialty marks? Going once. Going twice. Alright. Moving on to E-Four through E-Six, Third Class Petty Officers to First Class Petty Officers. Petty Officers wear their sleeve insignias on the left sleeve, centered between the shoulder seam and the elbow, consisting of a perched eagle, specialty mark and one, two or three chevrons. This should sound familiar. If it doesn't, you might want to go back and read your gouge. At this point, we in the Enlisted ranks have started to accumulate stripes, diagonal on the left sleeve. Climbing the ranks. Enlisted folks with twelve years of continuous good conduct service are permitted to wear gold service stripes on dress blue and dinner dress uniforms. Impressive looking. Hard to earn, easy to lose. I have mine. Proud of it. Like our junior colleagues, our rating badges, eagles, specialty marks, chevrons and service stripes will vary in color depending on the uniform. Rating badge background is blue chambray. Eagles and chevrons are dark blue. Questions? Yes."

"Senior Chief, will we be held responsible for the abbreviations?"

"You will indeed."

"What exactly do the numbers mean?"

"You mean on the chart?"

"Yes, Senior Chief."

"Great question. Don't worry so much about the table. It's plain confusing. I've told them as much. The number sign is just standing-in for the two-letter abbreviation of the apprenticeship. A.N., S.N., C.N., F.N. and so forth. You still with me?"

"Yes, Senior Chief."

"So for the full abbreviation for, say, a sailor at the E-One paygrade, also known as a Recruit, big R, who happens to be an Airman, abbreviated A.N., you would put the two together, apprenticeship then paygrade and get?"

"A.N.R."

"Exactly."

"So you can have an Airman Recruit?"

"Absolutely. You generally think of Seaman Recruits, but you also have A.N.Rs and F.N.Rs. Less so C.Ns, H.Ns or D.Ns, unless they come in as recruited. But don't hold me to that. Bottom line is that you're going to see a lot of S.N.Rs and A.N.Rs. Does that answer your question?"

"I think so."

"You think or you know?'

"I think I know, Senior Chief."

"Fair enough. Anyone else with a question? Good. Almost there. Next and final group of Enlisted paygrades. E-Seven through E-Nine. The Chiefs. We wear our insignias on the left shoulder of our service dress blues, dinner dress blues and dinner dress whites. Our rating badge system brings in perched eagles, chevrons, rockers, specialty marks and even a star, at least for Senior Chief and above. Like Officers, we also wear collar insignia, not just on raincoats. These devices consist of a gold fouled anchor with silver block letters U.S.N. superimposed on the shank of the anchor and one, two or three stars attached to the stock for Senior, Master and Master Chief Petty Officer of the Navy, respectively. In dress, we add shoulder insignias, soft shoulder boards and metal grade insignia, same as the collar insignia. Got it?"

"Yes, Senior Chief."

"Well, that about wraps up the Enlisted paygrades, E-One through E-Nine. Seems like a lot right now, I know, but you'll get to know them as you live and breathe out in the Fleet. Might as well learn it cold now. You will be tested on it. Questions? Going once. Going twice? You. You look like you've seen a ghost."

"No, Senior Chief."

"Good. Watch out for John Paul Jones after taps, though. He likes to roam the P-ways Ether Bunny in tow. Break. Break. Now for the Officers. There are ten commissioned Officer paygrades you should already be familiar with, O-One through O-Ten, as well as the three commissioned Warrant Officer paygrades, W-Two through W-Four. Our rule number-one controls. Seniority between paygrades is based on the paygrade. In other words, an O-Five is senior to An O-Four who is senior to an O-Three and so on. Like with us Es, seniority within paygrade is based on the date of rank. An O-Three with a date of rank in March is junior to an O-Three with a date of rank in February. As an aside, simply for your edification, there is a paygrade above O-Ten not mentioned here, at least technically. In Nineteen-Forty-Four, Congress established the Five-star grade, O-Eleven, of Fleet Admiral. Admiral Nimitz, of Admiral Nimitz fame, was the last living Fleet Admiral for the United States Navy. God bless that man. You Priors out there know what I'm talking about."

"Amen."

"Amen indeed, Shipmate. Sleeve insignias. I imagine you all now are well acquainted with the gold stripe system for Officer dress. Gold stripes in widths of two inches, a half inch, and, when warranted, a quarter inch stripe as the indicator of rank. And for our friends the Warrants, a broken one one-half inch gold stripe. Your main take away, at least for testing purposes, is the distinction between Line and Staff Officers. Some of you will go Line. Some of you Restricted Line. And some of you Staff. All Line and Restricted Line wear a five-pointed star. Each Staff Officer wears a different device. These are the Dental Officers, the Medical Officers, Medical Service Officers, Nurses, Civil Engineers, Chaplains, Jag Officers and Supply Os. For example, out of a hat, Officers in the Medical Corp wear a gold oak leaf with a silver acorn. A gold oak leaf with a silver acorn. What device do Medical Corp Officers wear? Yes?"

"A gold oak leaf with a silver acorn."

"And which Staff Officers wear a gold oak leaf with a silver acorn?"

"Medical Corps Officers."

"That's right. Food for thought. You might even see that again sometime soon. Officer shoulder insignias consist of hard shoulder boards, soft should boards and metal grade insignia. The rule of thumb is soft on shirts, hard on coats. Soft on shirts, hard on coats. As for collar insignia, just like you Officer Candidates, they wear miniature sized metal grade insignia. Easy enough to remember. Line Officers wear two metal grade insignia, same on both sides. Staff Corps Officers wear metal grade insignia on the right collar and the specialty device on the left collar. Same goes for Warrants. Silver senior to gold. Questions? Good. With M.T.T. around the corner, I sure hope this all is review. Who wears a gold oak leaf with a silver acorn? Altogether."

"Medical Corp Officers."

"Bravo Zulu. That about wraps up the lesson topic. By the looks of it from up here, heads nodding there in the back, think you all may be ready for a coffee break. We'll break in five. First, I want to work through some drills, hopefully clear up those questions as to ratings and paygrades. If you could please turn to page seven-decimal-one dash two. You should recognize the paygrades, E-One through E-Nine, right? All the way from Recruit to Master Chief. The two letter acronyms are for different types of rating. E.W. is for Electronic Warfare Technician. M.S. is for Mess Management Specialist. Q.M. is for Quartermaster. M.M. is for Machinist Mate. D.K. is for Disbursement Clerk. I.S. is for Intelligence Specialist. And so on and so forth. Don't worry. You will not be tested on all these. What you are required to know is the system of reference. Once you get out to the Fleet, all you'll hear is rating and rate. Anyone, other than Priors, want to take a crack at it? E-Four plus E.W., what do you get? Anyone? Don't be shy. Yes."

"E.W.-Four, Senior?"

"Negative. Easy trap. Go ahead and flip back to seven-decimal-one dash seven. Take a look at the table. Remember that a E-Four you get to Third Class Petty Officer. E-Five is Second Class. And E-Six is First Class. So for a Petty Officer Third Class, a P.O.-Three, who happens to be an E.W., you just put the two together. So what would that be?"

"E.W.-Three?"

"That's absolutely right. So for the same rating but at an E-Six paygrade, you would then have?"

"E.W.-One."

"Bravo Zulu. Now you have it. Let's change the rating to M.S. What do you get? Anyone?"

"M.S.-One, Senior."

"Correct. E-Five plus S.T.S.?"

"S.T.S.-Two."

"What about a Master Chief with a M.M. rating? Anyone? Use the chart now. Watch out. See how it flips over after E-Seven? A little counterintuitive. Just have to memorize. Well?"

"M.M.C.M."

"Who said that?"

"Officer Candidate Estephan, Senior."

"You a Prior?"

"Yes, Senior Chief."

"Well then say it loud so as everyone can hear."

"M.M.C.M., Senior."

"That's right. Master Chief flips over to Chief Master. Same thing for Senior Chief. Chief Senior. Let's try some more. Everybody now, using your chart. E-Three plus Q.M.?"

"Q.M.N."

"Very good. Couple more. E-Five plus J.O."

"J.O.-Two."

"E-Two Fireman Apprentice plus M.M."

"M.M.F.A."

"Everyone follow? Good. Same vein. What about an E-Three Seaman plus H.R.?"

"H.R.S.N."

"Now reverse engineer the rating to grade. Say you have a B.M.S.N., what would be his paygrade?"

"E-Three."

"A B.M.-Three?"

"E-Four."

"An S.A., no more no less?"

"E-Two."

"Y.N.S.N.?"

"E-Three."

"I want everybody. M.R.F.R.?"

"E-One."

"U.T.-Two?"

"E-Five."

"A.T.C.S.?"

"E-Eight."

"Clear as mud? Don't get hung up on these ratings. Like I said, if you're having trouble with this, keep running through the problem set. You'll get the hang of it. And if all else fails, get with a Prior. Alright, that should about do it for this topic. Quick review. What are the six General Apprenticeships?"

"Airman."

"That's one."

"Seaman."

"That's two."

"Fireman."

"That's three."

"Hospitalman."

"That's four."

"Dentalman."

"That's five. Last one."

"Constructionman."

"Bravo Zulu. True or false? Chief Warrant Officers wear their insignia with the rank on the right and the rating insignia on the left. Come on folks, it's a fifty-fifty. Live a little."

"True."

"Yes, indeed. Rank insignias on the right. Rating insignias on the left. Same goes with the Staff Corps. What's the highest Enlisted paygrade? Yes."

"Master Chief Petty Officer of the Navy."

"Well done. Who wants to describe the sleeve insignia worn on the dress white uniform for an E-Two Fireman, graduate of apprenticeship training? Take your time. You can look it up. Yes."

"A Fireman Apprenticeship badge over two diagonal red stripes."

"Bravo Zulu. Like what I'm hearing. Alright, last one. Million dollar question. Who wants to describe for me the sleeve insignia worn on the working dungaree uniform for M.M.F.N. Jones? Anyone? Trick question. No sleeve insignia on dungarees. Foot stomp. That's a wrap. Let's see. Back in your seats at

ten till. We're just getting started. Next up, supporting elements of the navy and classified information.

••

A W-Two in the United States Navy is a Chief Warrant Officer Two. His insignia is a single-bar collar device with a blue background and two gold breaks, or a gold one-half inch stripe with three blue breaks on a black shoulder board or the service dress blue uniform sleeve.

A W-Three in the United States Navy is a Chief Warrant Officer Three. His insignia is a single-bar collar device with a blue background and one silver break, or a gold one-half inch stripe with two blue breaks on a black shoulder board or the service dress blue uniform sleeve.

A W-Four in the United States Navy is a Chief Warrant Officer Four. His insignia is a single-bar collar device with a blue background and two silver breaks, or a gold one-half inch stripe with one blue break on a black shoulder board or the service dress blue uniform sleeve.

••

"Fall in!"

"Aye aye, Sir!!"

The squad forms as four columns behind the white line. Left arms extend parallel to the deck down to the last man. Heads veer off in the opposite direction. Rifles stand in a vertical position along the right side of the body. Butts hang four inches off the deck.

"Raise them up. Zero-four inches, damnit! Square the hips. Head straight to the right. I see your nose, Brooks. Arms up! Chins up! Brooks, fix yourself."

"Aye aye, Sir!"

"Back-the-hell-up! Freaking Candidate. No fixing a Turd."

"No excuse, Sir!"

"You have three weeks, Freaks. You're slow. You're behind. You have no discipline. You need to work harder. Is that clear?"

"Yes, Sir!!"

"Cover. Arms up. Get them up."

"Aye aye, Sir!!"

"You! Who the hell are you?"

"Officer Candidate Rooney! Officer Candidate School! Officer Candidate Class Zero-Four-Zero-Zero! United States Navy! Sir!"

"Where did you come from, Freak?"

"G.T.X., Sir!"

"Get your arm up!"

"Aye aye, Sir!"

"Morris. Head aligned."

"Aye aye, Sir!!"

"Column report."

"Steady!"

"Morris, damnit. You're looking behind his freaking neck. I can see your nasty freaking face. Is there a reason for it?"

"No excuse, Sir!"

"Column report."

"Steady!"

"Column report."

"Steady!"

"Column report."

"Steady!"

"Column report."

"Steady!"

"Ready! Front! Cover! Why the hell are you dragging your weapon, Lin?"

"No excuse, Sir!"

"Four inches, damnit."

"Aye aye, Sir!"

"Right! Face! One of you is not like the others. Aye aye, Sir."

"Aye aye, Sir!!"

"About! Face! Freaking miracle. Inspection! Arms! Fortunado, you lack bearing and discipline. Don't you, Pig?"

"No, Sir!"

"No? Maybe you think I'm freaking blind. I'm watching you. Peters. Jackson. Lower your carriage."

"Aye aye, Sir!!"

"Port! Arms! Steady. Order! Arms! Wake up, Rooster. Cockle doodle do."

"Aye aye, Sir!"

"Right shoulder! Arms! You got to be kidding me, Koch. That's your best brace?"

"No, Sir!"

"Then why are you not giving your best brace?"

"No excuse, Sir!"

"Raise your carriage. Christ."

"Aye aye, Sir!"

"Rifle! Salute! Elbows, up."

"Aye aye, Sir!!"

"I see your palm, Harris."

"No excuse, Sir!"

"Ready! Two! Better. Left shoulder! Arms! Raise your carriage, G.T.X."

"Aye aye, Sir!"

"You too, Tronstein."

"Aye aye, Sir!"

"Port! Arms! As you were. Port! Arms! Up."

"Aye aye, Sir!!"

"G.T.X., damnit. No wonder."

"No excuse, Sir!"

"Shut your freaking face. Order! Arms! Altogether now. Aye aye, Sir!"

"Aye aye, Sir!!"

"Present! Arms! I see daylight. Brooks. Paulson. You too Enriquez. Correct yourselves."

"Aye aye, Sir!!"

"Order! Arms! Toe-to-alignment, Saunders."

"Aye aye, Sir!"

"Toe-to-alignment, Chu."

"Aye aye, Sir!"

"Toe-to-alignment, Zurich."

"Aye aye, Sir!"

"Parade rest! Weapon ain't touching, Johnson."

"Aye aye, Sir!"

"Bring your weapon inboard, Hobson."

"Aye aye, Sir!"

"Weapon ain't touching, Masterson."

"Aye aye, Sir!"

"Weapon's canted, You. That's a freaking response."

"Aye aye, Sir!"

"Platoon! Attenhut! Forty-five degrees. Fix yourself, Rooster."

"Aye aye, Sir!"

"Foreman. Driver. Bremer. If I see you fidgeting around like schoolgirls this time, you're all going in the grass. Is that clear?"

"Yes, Sir!!"

"Is that clear?"

"Yes, Sir!!"

"Inspection! Arms!"

A bolt slips in the third column.

"Officer Candidate, Brooks. The command is for inspection arms. Correct yourself."

"Aye aye, Sir!"

"Pull in the freaking bolt, Pig!"

"Aye aye, Sir!"

"Port! Arms! Lower the weapon with the left hand too, You."

"Aye aye, Sir!"

"Left shoulder! Arms! Launch your goddamn weapons. Aye aye, Sir!"

"Aye aye, Sir!!"

"You launch your weapon. You launch your weapon or someone dies. Is that perfectly clear?"

"Yes, Sir!!"

"Open ranks! March! Left-right! Left-right! Left-right! Left-right! Left-right! Left-right!"

"Ready! Front! Cover!"

"Port! Arms!"

"Right shoulder! Arms!"

"Left-shoulder! Arms!"

"Port! Arms!"

"Order! Arms!"

"Present! Arms!"

"Order! Arms!"

"Right! Face!"

"Left! Face!"

"About! Face!"

"About! Face!"

"Parade rest!"

"Platoon! Attenhut!"

"Close ranks! March! Left-right! Left-right! Left-right! Left-right! Left-right! Left-right! Left-right!"

"Extend! March! Left-right! Left-right! Left-right! Left-right! Left-right! Left-right! Left-right! Left-right!"

"Dress! Right! Dress!"

"Ready! Front!"

"Cover!"

"Right shoulder! Arms!"

"Rifle! Salute!"

"Ready! Two!"

"Port! Arms! Freaking Brooks. Goddamn astronauts can see you from space. You push."

"Aye aye, Sir!"

"You too, Fortunato."

"Aye aye, Sir!"

"Foreman."

"Aye aye, Sir!"

"Bremer."

"Aye aye, Sir!"

"Nasties, all of you."

"Aye aye, Sir!!"

"You're disgusting. All of you. Get in my grass. Aye aye, Sir!"

"Aye aye, Sir!!"

"Push!"

"Aye aye, Sir!!"

"Down!"

"Aye aye, Sir!!"

"Nasty. Pathetic. Lethargic. Up!"

"Zero-one!!"

"Down!"

"Aye aye, Sir!!"

"Despicable. Face touching. Air sucking. Panties wearing. Freaks. Up!"

"Zero-two!!"

"Three weeks to inspection and you Pigs are unable to execute even the most basic commands. Down!"

"Aye aye, Sir!!"

"Parade you Nasties in front of a Sergeant Major in the United States Marine Corp. Not freaking likely. Up!"

"Zero-three!!"

"Honor. Courage. Commitment. Discipline. Obedience to orders. Respect for authority. And self-reliance. Down!"

"Aye aye, Sir!!"

"The United States Navy demands more than what you just showed each other out there. Up!"

"Zero-four!!"

"You disrespect your uniform and your flag. Down!"

"Aye aye, Sir!!"

"One Numb Nuts is all it takes. Up!"

"Zero-five!!"

"Somebody dies. Down!"

"Aye aye, Sir!!"

"You hear that Brooks? Somebody dies."

"No excuse, Sir!"

"Up!"

"Zero-six!!"

"Is that clear?"

"Yes, Sir!!"

"Is that clear?"

"Yes, Sir!!"

"Down!"

"Aye aye, Sir!!"

"On your feet!"

"Aye aye, Sir!!"

"On your backs!"

"Aye aye, Sir!!"

"On your feet!"

"Aye aye, Sir!!"

"On your backs! Leg-lifts!"

"Aye aye, Sir!!"

"Now! Now! Weapons up! You don't want to drill? We can do this all day instead. Start counting!"

"Aye aye, Sir!! One-two-three!! Zero-one!! One-two-three!! Zero-two!! One-two-three!! Zero-three!! One-two-three!! Zero-four!! One-two-three!! Zero-five!! One-two-three!! Zero-six!! One-two-three!! Zero-seven!! One-two-three!! Zero-eight!! One-two-three!! Zero-niner!! One-two-three!! One-zero!! One-two-three!! One-one!! One-two-three!! One-two!! One-two-three!! One-three!! One-two-three!! One-four!! One-two-three!! One-five!! One-two-three!! One-six!! One-two-three!! One-seven!! One-two-three!! One-eight!! One-two-three!! One-niner!! One-two-three!! Two-zero!!"

"Mountain-climbers!"

"Aye aye, Sir!! One-two-three!! Zero-one!! One-two-three!! Zero-two!! One-two-three!! Zero-three!! One-two-three!! Zero-four!! One-two-three!! Zero-five!! One-two-three!! Zero-six!! One-two-three!! Zero-seven!! One-two-three!! Zero-eight!! One-two-three!! Zero-niner!! One-two-three!! One-zero!! One-two-three!! One-one!! One-two-three!! One-two!!"

"Louder!"

"Aye aye, Sir!! One-two-three!! One-three!! One-two-three!! One-four!! One-two-three!! One-five!! One-two-three!! One-six!! One-two-three!! One-seven!! One-two-three!! One-eight!! One-two-three!! One-niner!! One-two-three!! Two-zero!!"

"Side-straddle hops!"

Aye aye, Sir!! One-two-three!! Zero-one!! One-two-three!! Zero-two!! One-two-three!! Zero-three!! One-two-three!! Zero-four!! One-two-three!! Zero-five!! One-two-three!! Zero-six!! One-two-three!! Zero-seven!! One-two-three!! Zero-eight!! One-two-three!! Zero-niner!! One-two-three!! One-zero!! One-two-three!! One-one!! One-two-three!! One-two!! One-two-three!! One-three!! One-two-three!! One-four!! One-two-three!! One-five!! One-two-three!! One-six!! One-two-three!! One-seven!! One-two-three!! One-eight!! One-two-three!! One-niner!! One-two-three!! Two-zero!! One-two-three!! Two-one!! One-two-three!! Two-two!! One-two-three!! Two-three!! One-two-three!! Two-four!! One-two-three!!

Two-five!! One-two-three!! Two-six!! One-two-three!! Two-seven!! One-two-three!! Two-eight!! One-two-three!! Two-niner!! One-two-three!! Three-zero!!"

"Fall in!"

"Aye aye, Sir!!"

"Ten-eight-seven-five-three-two-one. Freeze!"

"Aye aye, Sir!!"

"Cover! Column report."

"Steady!"

"Column report."

"Steady!"

"Column report."

"Steady!"

"Column report."

"Steady!"

"Ready! Front! Cover!"

"Open ranks! March! Left-right! Left-right! Left-right! Left-right! Left-right! Left-right!"

"Ready! Front! Cover!"

"Port! Arms!"

"Right shoulder! Arms!"

"Left-shoulder! Arms!"

"Port! Arms!"

"Order! Arms!"

"Present! Arms!"

"Order! Arms!"

"Right! Face!"

"Left! Face!"

"About! Face!"

"About! Face!"

"Parade rest!"

"Platoon! Attenhut!"

"Close ranks! March! Left-right! Left-right! Left-right! Left-right! Left-right! Left-right! Left-right!"

"Extend! March! Left-right! Left-right! Left-right! Left-right! Left-right! Left-right! Left-right! Left-right!"

"Dress! Right! Dress!"

"Ready! Front!"

"Cover!"

"Right shoulder! Arms!"

"Rifle! Salute!"

"Ready! Two!"

"Port! Arms!"

"Order! Arms!"

"Present! Arms!"

"Order! Arms!"

"Right! Face!"

"Left! Face!"

"About! Face!"

"About! Face!"

"Parade rest!"

"Platoon! Attenhut!"

"Close ranks! March! Left-right! Left-right! Left-right! Left-right! Left-right! Left-right! Left-right!"

"Right! Face!"

"Rest!"

"Platoon! Attenhut!"

"Port! Arms!"

"Ready! March! Steady! Your left! Your left! Your left-right! By the left flank! March! Da-ra-o-oh-oh-oh-o-eh-oh! Da-ra-oh-oh-oh-oh-oh! Da-ra-oh-oh-oh-oh-oh-leh-oh! Da-ra-leh-ho-leh-ho-ho! Column left! March! Column left! March! Column left! March! Da-ra-o-oh-oh-oh-o-eh-oh! Da-ra-oh-oh-oh-oh-oh! Da-ra-oh-oh-oh-oh-oh-leh-oh! Da-ra-leh-ho-leh-ho-ho! Column left! March! Column right! March! By the right flank! March! Da-ra-o-oh-oh-oh-o-eh-oh! Da-ra-oh-oh-oh-oh-oh! Da-ra-oh-oh-oh-oh-oh-leh-oh! Da-ra-leh-ho-leh-ho-ho! By the left flank! March! Da-ra-o-oh-oh-oh-o-eh-oh! Da-ra-oh-oh-oh-oh-oh! Da-ra-oh-oh-oh-oh-oh-leh-oh! Da-ra-leh-ho-leh-ho-ho! Da-ra-o-oh-oh-oh-o-eh-oh! Da-ra-oh-oh-oh-oh-oh! Da-ra-oh-oh-oh-oh-oh-leh-oh! Da-ra-leh-ho-leh-ho-ho! To the rear! March! Da-ra-o-oh-oh-oh-o-eh-oh! Da-ra-oh-oh-oh-oh-oh! Da-ra-oh-oh-oh-oh-oh-leh-oh! Da-ra-leh-ho-leh-ho-ho! Column left! March! Da-ra-o-oh-oh-oh-o-eh-oh! Da-ra-oh-oh-oh-oh-oh! Da-ra-oh-oh-oh-oh-oh-leh-oh! Da-ra-leh-ho-leh-ho-ho! Column left! March! Da-ra-o-oh-oh-oh-o-eh-oh! Da-ra-oh-oh-oh-oh-oh! Da-ra-oh-oh-oh-oh-oh-leh-oh! Da-ra-leh-ho-leh-ho-ho! By the left flank! March! Da-ra-o-oh-oh-oh-o-eh-oh! Da-ra-oh-oh-oh-oh-oh! Da-ra-oh-oh-oh-oh-oh-leh-oh! Da-ra-leh-ho-leh-ho-ho! Da-ra-o-oh-oh-oh-o-eh-oh! Da-ra-oh-oh-oh-oh-oh! Da-ra-oh-oh-oh-oh-oh-leh-oh! Da-ra-leh-ho-leh-ho-ho! Column right! March! Da-ra-o-oh-oh-oh-o-eh-oh! Da-ra-oh-oh-oh-oh-oh! Da-ra-oh-oh-oh-oh-oh-leh-oh! Da-ra-leh-ho-leh-ho-ho! Column right! March! Da-ra-o-oh-oh-oh-o-eh-oh! Da-ra-oh-oh-oh-oh-oh! Da-ra-oh-oh-oh-oh-oh-leh-oh! Da-ra-leh-ho-leh-ho-ho! Left-oblique! March! Da-ra-o-oh-oh-oh-o-eh-oh! Da-ra-oh-oh-oh-oh-oh! Da-ra-oh-oh-oh-oh-oh-leh-oh! Da-ra-leh-ho-leh-ho-ho! Right shoulder! Arms! To the rear! March! To the rear! March! Da-ra-o-oh-oh-oh-o-eh-oh! Da-ra-oh-oh-oh-oh-oh! Da-ra-oh-oh-oh-oh-oh-leh-oh! Da-ra-leh-ho-leh-ho-ho! Column left!

March! Da-ra-o-oh-oh-oh-o-eh-oh! Da-ra-oh-oh-oh-oh-oh! Da-ra-oh-oh-oh-oh-oh-leh-oh! Da-ra-leh-ho-leh-ho-ho! Platoon! Halt! And step!"

"Order! Arms!"

"Left! Face!"

"Parade rest!"

"Inspection! Arms!"

"Port! Arms!"

"Order! Arms!"

"What? Rooney! What?"

"No excuse, Sir!"

"You! You! You Nasty Thing! Touching your Nasty Face! Get in my grass! All of you! Now! Now! Now! That's a freaking response!"

"Aye aye, Sir!!"

"On your faces, Freaks! Eight-count body builders! Start counting!"

"Aye aye, Sir!! One!! Two!! Three!! Four!! Five!! Six!! Seven!! Zero-one!! One!! Two!! Three!! Four!! Five!! Six!! Seven!! Zero-two!! One!! Two!! Three!! Four!! Five!! Six!! Seven!! Zero-three!! One!! Two!! Three!! Four!! Five!! Six!! Seven!! Zero-four!! One!! Two!! Three!! Four!! Five!! Six!! Seven!! Zero-five!! One!! Two!! Three!! Four!! Five!! Six!! Seven!! Zero-six!! One!! Two!! Three!! Four!! Five!! Six!! Seven!! Zero-seven!! One!! Two!! Three!! Four!! Five!! Six!! Seven!! Zero-eight!! One!! Two!! Three!! Four!! Five!! Six!! Seven!! Zero-niner!! One!! Two!! Three!! Four!! Five!! Six!! Seven!! One-zero!! One!! Two!! Three!! Four!! Five!! Six!! Seven!! One-one!! One!! Two!! Three!! Four!! Five!! Six!! Seven!! One-two!! One!! Two!! Three!! Four!! Five!! Six!! Seven!! One-three!! One!! Two!! Three!! Four!! Five!! Six!! Seven!! One-four!! One!! Two!! Three!! Four!! Five!! Six!! Seven!! One-five!! One!! Two!! Three!! Four!! Five!! Six!! Seven!! One-six!! One!! Two!! Three!! Four!! Five!! Six!! Seven!! One-seven!! One!! Two!! Three!! Four!! Five!! Six!! Seven!! One-eight!! One!! Two!! Three!! Four!! Five!! Six!! Seven!! One-niner!! One!! Two!! Three!! Four!! Five!! Six!! Seven!! Two-zero!! One!! Two!! Three!! Four!! Five!! Six!! Seven!! Two-one!! One!! Two!! Three!! Four!! Five!! Six!! Seven!! Two-two!! One!! Two!! Three!! Four!! Five!! Six!! Seven!! Two-three!! One!! Two!! Three!! Four!! Five!! Six!! Seven!! Two-four!! One!! Two!! Three!! Four!! Five!! Six!! Seven!! Two-five!! One!! Two!! Three!! Four!! Five!! Six!! Seven!! Two-six!! One!! Two!! Three!! Four!! Five!! Six!! Seven!! Two-seven!! One!! Two!! Three!! Four!! Five!! Six!! Seven!! Two-eight!! One!! Two!! Three!! Four!! Five!! Six!! Seven!! Two-niner!! One!! Two!! Three!! Four!! Five!! Six!! Seven!! Three-zero!!"

"Supermans!"

"Aye aye, Sir!"

"Start rocking!"

"Aye aye, Sir!!"

"Rifles up!"

"Aye aye, Sir!!"

"Get them up, Pigs!"

"Aye aye, Sir!!"

"Up, Pigs!"

"Aye aye, Sir!!"

"Legs up!"

"Aye aye, Sir!!"

"Legs up, Pigs!"

"Aye aye, Sir!!"

"Up!"

"Aye aye, Sir!!"

"One-two-three! One-two-three! One-two-three! Your turn! One-two-three! One-two-three!"

"One-two-three!! One-two-three!!"

"One-two-three! One-two-three!"

"One-two-three!! One-two-three!!"

"One-two-three! One-two-three!"

"One-two-three!! One-two-three!!"

"One-two-three! One-two-three!"

"One-two-three!! One-two-three!!"

"One-two-three! One-two-three!"

"One-two-three!! One-two-three!!"

"One-two-three! One-two-three!"

"One-two-three!! One-two-three!!"

"One-two-three! One-two-three!"

"One-two-three!! One-two-three!!"

"One-two-three! One-two-three!"

"One-two-three!! One-two-three!!"

"One-two-three! One-two-three!"

"One-two-three!! One-two-three!!"

"One-two-three! One-two-three!"

"One-two-three!! One-two-three!!"

"One-two-three! One-two-three!"

"One-two-three!! One-two-three!!"

"One-two-three! One-two-three!"

"One-two-three!! One-two-three!!"

"Rifles up, Pigs!"

"Aye aye, Sir!!"

"Up, Pigs!"

"Aye aye, Sir!!"

"Louder!"

"Aye aye, Sir!!"
"One-two-three! One-two-three!"
"One-two-three!! One-two-three!!"
"One-two-three! One-two-three!"
"One-two-three!! One-two-three!!"
"One-two-three! One-two-three!"
"One-two-three!! One-two-three!!"
"Fall in!"
"Aye aye, Sir!!"
"Ten-nine-seven-five-four-three-two-one! Freeze!"
"Aye aye, Sir!!"
"Cover! Column report."
"Steady!
"Column report."
"Steady!"
"Column report."
"Steady!"
"Column report."
"Steady!"
"Ready! Front! Cover!"

....

A W-One in the United States Marine Corp is a Chief Warrant Officer One. His insignia is a bar with a red background and one gold break.

A W-Two in the United States Marine Corp is a Chief Warrant Officer Two. His insignia is a bar with a red background and two gold breaks.

A W-Three in the United States Marine Corp is a Chief Warrant Officer Three. His insignia is a bar with a red background and one silver break.

A W-Four in the United States Marine Corp is a Chief Warrant Officer Four. His insignia is a bar with a red background and two silver breaks.

A W-Five in the United States Marine Corp is a Chief Warrant Officer Five. His insignia is a single silver bar with a thin red break in the center.

••

I tip a drop of ink onto the blotter.

"Hey Mike, you got any more of that Simple Green?"

"Sure. Give me one second."

"Gouge from Zero-One. Takes the rust right off."

"Rifle brasso. Impressive, Potts."

"That's right. Who's in? Mike?"

"Rifle parts? That's alright. Thanks."

"Jackson?"

"I'm good."

"Fortunato?"

"What are we talking?"

"A shine? That's fair."

"Let me get a look at them."

"Already got a good base. Just can't get it to pop. See?"

"Alright."

"You'll do them? Serious?"

"Sure thing. Catch. Going to need a warranty on that rifle, though."

"What do you mean?"

"Quality assurance. Who says I don't end up with your hosed-up rifle parts?"

"I won't hose it up."

"Famous last words, my man."

"I said sleep with your rifle, not screw it, Weirdo! That's a response, Freak!"

"Get in my grass, Pigs! Scissor-kicks! Scissor-kicks! Til your nuts fall off! Seriously, Potts, what's your plan? Separate buckets? One after the other? What?"

"Separate buckets. Don't sweat it."

"Separate buckets? That was your plan all along or that's your plan now?"

"Whatever. Separate buckets. Deal or no deal?"

"Deal."

Potts busies himself with disassembly. My stencil peels off clean.

"Allow me to introduce myself. First name Stencil. Last name Picasso. M.D. Pleasure to make your acquaintance. Take a look at this. Perfection."

"Oh, that's nice, Doctor."

"Doctor. Wait one. I got some drawers need a once over. Six-by-six."

"How do you figure?"

"I mean, the way I see it, it's my Simple Green's doing all the work. Only fair."

"Negative."

"I mean flat. Less time than a shine. Only I want to be able to slide those puppies under the door, understood? Envelope thin. Oh, and quality assurance. I don't want to end up with your nasty drawers."

"No dice, Picasso."

"Actually, I do need a favor. Anyone got an extra gold belt tip? Mine went to silver."

"How'd that happen?"

"Iodized brass and brasso. Go figure. It shines alright. Only it shines to silver."

"You brassoed your iodized brass? What for?"

"Attention to detail saves lives, Shipmate. Seemed like a good idea at the time."

"Brasso Picasso."

"I go by many names."

"Hold on, Mike. I should have one around here somewhere. Well, looks like it's a little bent."

"That'll work. You need anything, brother?"

"I'm square. Well, maybe a pancake. What do you think?"

"You mean the spot?"

"You can see it?"

"Right off."

"No hits for stains."

"Never know. Let me check the Picasso N.E.X. Here we go."

"Really?"

"Sure. All good."

"How's it going over there, Potts? My eyes are starting to water. How long's this supposed to take, exactly?"

"I don't know, maybe five more minutes?"

"We'll be asphyxiated in five. Can't you take that out in the p-way?"

"It's not that bad."

"Not that bad?"

"Not that bad."

"Not that bad? Go on and hang your head over it with a towel, Potts. Not that bad."

"Knock it off, Fortunato."

"Add some salt. Deep breaths. Momma? Is that you? Momma? I'm a coming home. Momma, is that you? You look different, Momma!"

"Lay off."

"Hey now, just fooling around, Potts. Alright? Are we cool?"

Another stencil peels off clean.

"It's almost not fair."

"Hey, Shipmate. We good?"

"Yes, we're good. We're fine."

"You sure, now? I didn't mean anything by it. Want to review some gouge? Come on, Potts. A little gouge?"

"Okay."

"Really?"

"Yes! Hit me."

"Careful what you wish for, Shipmate. Let's see. Okay, from the top. Enlisted records. What is the difference between the Enlisted service record and Enlisted service jacket?"

"They're basically the same, right? The jacket's like a summary."

"The service jacket is a micro fiche copy of some of the service record. Which side of the service record is used to file Enlisted Evaluations or Fitness Reports?"

"Right?"

"Left."

"The left. Got it."

"True or false? The Court Memorandum, page seven, reports any non-judicial punishment that affects pay."

"True?"

"True."

"I mean I don't know how or why we're supposed to remember that."

"True or false? The Enlisted qualifications history, page four, replaced the Enlisted classification record, page three."

"False?"

"True."

"Fine."

"The Enlisted performance record, page nine, records all periods of unauthorized absence less than twenty-four hours."

"True."

"False. An Enlisted personnel health record is updated at least annually."

"True."

"Bravo Zulu."

"Thanks."

"Mike, you're sure you don't want in?"

"Sure."

"Supporting elements of the Navy?"

"Shoot."

"Which commissioning program produces technical managers?"

"Limited Duty Officer."

"Correct. List the Officer categories."

"Limited Duty Officer. Unrestricted Line. Restricted line. Chief Warrant Officer."

"One more."

"Hold on. I know it. Staff."

"That's correct. Jackson?"

"Okay. I'm in."

"Name the three steps of the logistics process."

"Logistics plan. Procurement. Distribution."

"Disclosure of what type of classified information can result in exceptionally grave damage to national security?"

"Top Secret."

"What administrative and punitive actions can result from a security violation?"

"How many are there?"

"Five."

"Give me the first one."

"Denial or revocation of clearance."

"Denial or revocation of clearance. Non-judicial punishment. Courts martial. Regular courts."

"And. I'll give you a hint."

"Not necessary, Shipmate. Administrative sanctions."

"Bravo Zulu. Alright, Gents. My turn."

"I got it. What section?"

"Surprise me."

"Classified information?"

"Need to know, baby."

"Who grants interim clearances?"

"Commanding Officer."

"What are the two types of security violations?"

"Compromise and poor security practice."

"Which one results in a loss, compromise or possible compromise of classified material?"

"Compromise."

"Nice. What are the prerequisites for access to classified information?'

"Appropriate clearance. Need to know. And approval from the Commanding Officer."

"What device is used to transmit classified phone conversations?"

"STU-three."

"What are the components of classified markings?"

"Tell me."

"Anyone?"

"Identity of the original classification authority. Agency of origin. Classification. Declassification date. And instructions for downgrading."

"Thank you, Officer Candidate Einstein. When can Top Secret information be copied?"

"Never?"

"With the consent of the originating activity or higher authority."

"Alright. Shipboard organization. What are the two types of basic organizations?"

"Operational and administrative."

"Name the components of the command structure in the basic shipboard organization."

"No idea. Might as well be speaking Greek."

"Commanding Officer."

"Oh, now I remember. Commanding Officer, Executive Officer and Executive Assistants."

"Who is ultimately responsible for the safety, efficiency and well being of the command?"

"The Commanding Officer."

"What department is responsible for the operation, care, and maintenance of all propulsion and auxiliary machinery as well as damage control?"

"The Engineering Department."

"What department is responsible for the collection, evaluation and dissemination of combat and operational information?"

"Operations."

"Who is the enlisted advisor to the Commanding Officer on the formulation and implementation of policies pertinent to morale, welfare, job satisfaction, discipline, utilization and training of all enlisted personnel?"

"Command Master Chief."

"That's all she wrote. My turn."

"Define by direction authority."

"No idea. What section are you in?"

"Correspondence and directives."

"Still no idea. What is it?"

"Commanding Officers have signature authority over all correspondence within their command, but it can be delegated to subordinates. Delegated authority is signed as by direction."

"Whatever that means."

"What is the maximum time limit for a notice to remain in effect?"

"Don't remember. A month?"

"One year. What are the three types of directives?"

"I guess I need to review this section."

"Instructions, notices and change transmittals. What are the four levels of precedence for naval messages?"

"I know this one. Flash. Immediate. Priority. And routine."

"What time requirements are associated for each?"

"Flash is right away, right? Something like ten minutes."

"As soon as possible with an objective of less than ten."

"That's right. Immediate is like thirty minutes."

"Right."

"Priority is an hour?"

"Three hours."

"Three hours. And then routine was six."

"Bravo Zulu. What times do you never use in a date time group?"

"Twenty Four Hundred and Zero-Zero-Zero."

"My turn."

"True or false? Fitness Reports are for E-Six and below."

"False. Evals."

"Correct. Leadership is an option performance trait for E-One to E-Three."

"True."

"False. The objectives of the Navy's counseling system are to provide feedback and assist in future performance."

"Got to be true."

"True. The evaluation team for an Eval is comprised of the rater and senior rater."

"No, there's someone else, right?"

"True or false?"

"False."

"Who's the other guy?"

"Blank."

"Reporting senior."

"Right."

"The reporting senior is usually the Commanding Officer."

"True."

"A Chief Petty Officer or above may serve as the reporting senior for E-Four and below."

"False."

"True."

"Really?"

"Apparently. A Lieutenant or above may serve as the reporting senior for reports of E-Five through E-Nine."

"True."

"False. Lieutenant Commander and above."

"Damn."

"Hey, Potts. How those rifle parts looking? Got to start closing up shop."

"Almost there."

"How do they look?"

"Good."

"Let's have a look. Uh, what's the difference, my man?"

"Still a little wet, that's all."

"Wet? You're going to rust me out. Deal's off."

"You'll see the shine. Give it a little time."

"We have no time, Potts. Kick me my pieces, will you?"

We stash away our gear.

"Class Zero-Four-Zero-Zero! Fall in! Let's go, Zero-Four! Let's go!"

"Freaking Macpherson. That guy is so tight."

"Let's go, Zero-Four-Zero-Zero!"

"Motivation is contagious."

"Giddy up."

"Hold up. One second. I want to get this badboy back together."

"Roger."

"Alright, let's go."

The Class assembles in the passageway.

"Class Zero-Four-Zero-Zero! Upon receiving the command of execution count off! You will! Count off zero-one to four-two! Ready! Count off!"

"Aye aye, Sir!!"

"Zero-one!"

"Zero-two!"

"Zero-three!"

"Zero-four!"

"Zero-five!"

"Zero-six!"

"Zero-seven!"

"Zero-eight!"
"Zero-niner!"
"One-zero!"
"One-one!"
"One-two!"
"One-three!"
"One-four!"
"One-five!"
"One-six!"
"One-seven!"
"One-eight!"
"One-niner!"
"Two-zero!"
"Two-one!"
"Two-two!"
"Two-three!"
"Two-four!"
"Two-five!"
"Two-six!"
"Two-seven!"
"Two-eight!"
"Two-niner!"
"Three-zero!"
"Three-one!"
"Three-two!"
"Three-three!"
"Three-four!"
"Three-five!"
"Three-six!"
"Three-seven!"
"Three-eight!"
"Three-niner!"
"Four-zero!"
"Four-one!"
"Four-two!"
"Class Zero-Four-Zero-Zero all present and accounted for, Section Leader!"
"*Stand Navy out to sea,*
Fight our battle cry.
We'll never change our course
So vicious foes steer shy-y-y-y.
Roll out the T.N.T.,

Anchors Aweigh,
Sail on to victory and
Sink their bones to Davy Jones,
Hooray!
Anchors Aweigh my boys,
Anchors Aweigh.
Farewell to college joy,
We'll sail at break of day-ay-ay-ay.
Though our last night ashore
Drink to the foam.
Until we meet once more,
Here's wishing you a happy
Voyage home.
Blue of the Mighty Deep,
Gold of God's Sun,
Let these colors be
Till all of time by done, done, done.
On seven seas we learn navy's stern call.
Faith, courage, service true, with
Honor, over honor, over all."
"The Marine Corp Hymn!"
"From the Halls of Montezuma
To the shores of Tripoli
We fight our country's battles
In the air, on land and sea
First to fight for right and freedom
And to keep our honor clean,
We are proud to claim the title
Of United States Marine.
Our flag's unfurled to every breeze
From dawn to setting sun,
We have fought in every clime and place
Where we could take a gun.
In the snow of far-off Northern lands
And in sunny tropic scenes,
You will find us always on the job
The United States Marines.
Here's health to you and to our Corps
Which we are proud to serve,
In many a strife we've fought for life
And never lost our nerve.

If the Army and the Navy
Ever look on Heaven's scenes,
They will find the streets are guarded
By United States Marines."
"Class Zero-Four-Zero-Zero-zero! Prepare for Taps!"
"Aye aye, Section Leader!"

Jackson kneels at the side of his bed head bowed.
"This night I lay me down to sleep
I give the Lord my soul to keep
If I should die before I wake
I pray the lord my soul to take
Four corners of my bed
Four angels over head
Matthew, Mark, Luke and John
Bless this bed I lay upon
I lay my head on our lady's knee
Jesus come this night and save me
Heart of Joseph I adore Thee
Heart of Mary I implore Thee
Heart of Jesus pure and just
In those three hearts I place my trust.
Lord, watch over my mother, my father and brother.
Watch over Amber and her family. Amen."

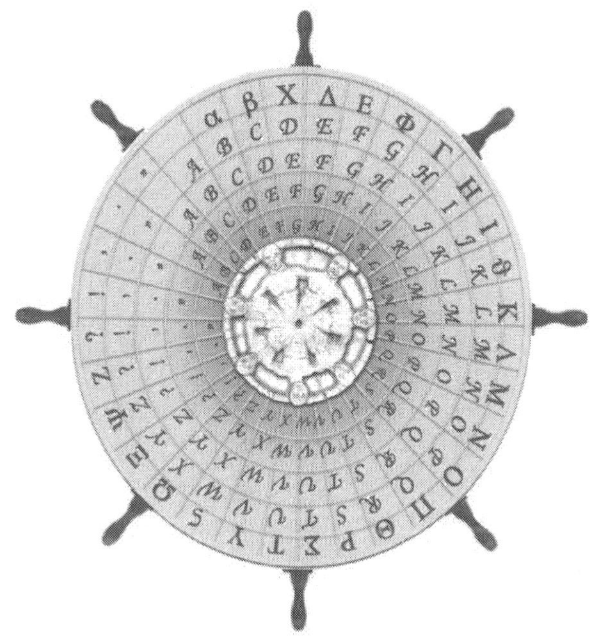

CHAPTER IV

WEEK 4

Fortunato grins at me from across the room. The diagonal catches Potts as he rocks from heel to toe. Jackson stands at ease in the peripheral. A crackle sounds over the one-M.C.

"Class Zero-Four-Zero-Zero, this is your zero-five minute warning."

"Class Zero-Four-Zero-Zero, this is your zero-one minute warning."

"Class Zero-Four-Zero-Zero, this is your immediate warning."

Steps deepen in the passageway.

"Attention on deck, stand-by."

"Good morning, Sir."

The Officers fan out into the room. A lieutenant squares up in front of me.

"Good morning, Sir."

"Good morning. Identification."

"Aye aye, Sir."

"Sir, this Officer Candidate's name is Officer Candidate Zurich, Officer Candidate School, Officer Candidate Class Zero-Four-Zero-Zero, United States Navy."

"Eagles flying?"

"Yes, Sir."

"Very well. Let's have a look at that cover."

"Aye aye, Sir."

The brim checks clean for fingerprints. Eagles fly at both ends of the gold band.

"Here you are."

"Aye aye, Sir."

"United States Navy personnel must set and maintain the highest standards of smartness in uniform appearance. Wouldn't you agree, Officer Candidate Zurich?"

"Yes, Sir."

"The public image of the Navy. Do you believe you have met those standards here today?"

"Yes, Sir."

"Confidence. I like that. Let's take some measurements, shall we?"

"Aye aye, Sir."

"Improper measurement on those anchors. Close but call it a hit."

"Aye aye, Sir."

"No noticeable I.Ps. Wait one. Eyeballs."

"Snap, Sir."

"Right hand pocket of the blouse. See?"

"Yes, Sir."

"I'll have to hit you for that as well. Second hit. Irish Pendant on blouse. Right breast pocket."

"Aye aye, Sir."

"Let's have a look at your brass."

"Aye aye, Sir."

I undo the clasp to my belt.

"Outside looks good. Real shine. But we can always do better, correct?"

"Yes, Sir."

"Hit."

"Aye aye, Sir."

"Very well. What is the fifth article of the Code of Conduct?"

"Sir, the fifth article of the Code of Conduct is when questioned, should I become a prisoner of war, I am required to give name, rank, service number and date of birth. I will evade answering further questions to the utmost of my ability. I will make no oral or written statements disloyal to my country and its allies or harmful to their cause."

"What is the sixth General Order of a Sentry?"

"Sir, the sixth General Order of a Sentry is to receive, obey, and pass on to the sentry who relieves me, all orders from the Commanding Officer, the Officer of the Day, and all Officers and Non-Commissioned Officers of the guard only."

"Are you sure?"

"Yes, Sir."

"Sure?"

"Yes, Sir."

"Which General Order requires giving an alarm?"

"Sir, the eighth General Order of a Sentry requires giving an alarm."

"Very good. So far. Let's graduate to something a bit more challenging. Eyeballs."

"Snap, Sir."

"Do you see this pin?"

"Yes, Sir."

"Describe it for me."

"Aye aye, Sir. Sir, the Surface Warfare insignia is a gold embroidered or gold metal pin, with the bow and superstructure of a modern naval warship on two crossed swords, on a background of ocean swells."

"What's your designator, Zurich?"

"Sir, this Officer Candidate's designator is one-six-three-five."

"Intel?"

"Yes, Sir."

"Spooks. What is the phonetic spelling of the word *intelligence*?"

"Sir, the phonetic spelling of the word intelligence is India, November, Tango, Echo, Lima, Lima, India, Golf, Echo, November, Charlie, Echo."

"What does that read backwards?"

"Echo, Charlie, November, Echo, Golf, Lima, Lima, Echo, Tango, November, India, Sir."

"Who is the eighth person in your Chain of Command?"

"Sir, the eighth person in this Officer Candidate's Chain of Command is Captain Richard Kimmer, Commanding Officer, Officer Training Command Pensacola."

"What is the mission of the Navy?"

"Sir, the mission of the Navy is to maintain, train, and equip combat ready

Naval forces capable of winning wars, deterring aggression, and maintain freedom of the seas."

"Describe an E-Six in the United States Marine Corp for me."

"Aye aye, Sir. An E-Six in the United States Marine Corp is a Staff Sergeant. His insignia is three chevrons over crossed rifles over one rocker."

"What about a W-Four in the Navy?"

"Aye aye, Sir. A W-Four in the United States Navy is a Chief Warrant Officer Four. His insignia is a single-bar collar device with a blue background and two silver breaks, or a gold one-half inch stripe with one blue break on a black shoulder board or the service dress blue uniform sleeve."

"All this come easy for you?"

"No, Sir."

"E-Seven in the Navy."

"Aye aye, Sir. An E-Seven in the United States Navy is a Chief Petty Officer. His insignia is three chevrons below one rocker below one eagle. In khaki uniform his insignia will be a gold fouled anchor collar device with a silver U.S.N. centered across the anchor."

"Confidence cuts both ways, Zurich. Careful with it."

"Aye aye, Sir."

"Two hits for appearance. One hit for bearing."

"Aye aye, Sir."

"At ease."

"Aye aye, Sir."

"Attention on deck, stand-by."

"Good morning, Sir."

The Officers depart in single file. Odor fills the room.

"What is that? Is that you, man?"

"Now is not the time."

"Lock it up. Here they come."

"Attention on deck, stand-by!"

"Good morning, Sir!!"

"Push! Push! Push! You disgusting! Pathetic! Lethargic! Candidates!"

"Aye aye, Sir!!"

"On your faces! Push!"

"Aye aye, Sir!!"

"Now! Now! Now!"

A drill instructor moves over me. He leans down close to my ear.

"That's a response! That's a freaking response!"

"Aye aye, Sir!"

"Eight-count body builders! Now! Now! Now!"

"Aye aye, Sir!"

"General Orders of a Sentry! Sound off!"

"Aye aye, Sir!"

"Now! Now! Now!"

"Aye aye, Sir! Sir! The first General Order of a Sentry is! To take charge of this post and all government property in view! Sir! The second General Order of a Sentry is! To walk my post in a military manner! Keeping always on the alert! And observing everything which takes place within sight or hearing! Sir! The third General Order of a Sentry is! To report all violations! Of orders! I am instructed to enforce! Sir! The fourth General Order of a Sentry is! To quit my post only when properly relieved!"

"Hit! Improper measurement! Freaking eyeballs!"

"Snap, Sir!"

"Does that look like six inches to you? Does that look like six inches to you?"

"No, Sir!"

"Who told you to stop building? Hop and pops! Hop and pops! Now! Now!"

"Aye, Aye, Sir!"

"Rank insignias for the Navy! Now! Now!"

"Aye aye, Sir! Sir! An E-One in the United States Navy is a Seaman Recruit! He has no insignia! Sir! An E-Two in the United States Navy is a Seaman Apprentice! His insignia is two parallel diagonal slashes! Sir! An E-Three in the United States Navy is a Seaman! His insignia is three parallel diagonal slashes!"

"Hit. Improper measurement. Sweatshirt. Pathetic."

"Aye aye, Sir! Sir! An E-Four in the United States Navy is a Petty Officer Third Class! His insignia is one chevron below one eagle! Sir! An E-Five in the United States Navy is a Petty Officer Second Class!"

"Hit. Freaking I.P."

"Aye aye, Sir! His insignia is two chevrons below one eagle! Sir! An E-Six in the United States Navy is a Petty Officer First Class! His insignia is three chevrons below one eagle! Sir! An E-Seven in the United States Navy is a Chief Petty Officer! His insignia is three chevrons below one rocker below one eagle! Sir! An E-Eight in the United States Navy is a Senior Chief Petty Officer!"

"Hit. Hit. Hit."

"Aye aye, Sir!"

"Side-straddle hops!"

"Aye aye, Sir! His insignia is three chevrons! Below one rocker! Below one eagle! Below one star! Centered about the eagle! Sir! An E-Niner in the United States Navy is a Master Chief Petty Officer! His insignia is three chevrons! Below one rocker! Below one eagle! Below two stars! Centered about the eagle! Sir! The Master Chief Petty Officer of the Navy is an E-Niner! His insignia is three

chevrons! Below one rocker! Below one eagle! Below three stars! Centered about the eagle!"

"Officer ranks, Pig!"

"Aye aye, Sir! Sir! An O-One in the United States Navy is an Ensign!"

"Sound off!"

"Aye aye, Sir! His insignia is a one gold bar collar device! Or one one-half inch gold stripe! Outboard of one gold five-pointed star on black shoulder boards! Or one one-half inch gold stripe! Below one gold five-pointed star! On service dress blue uniform sleeves! Sir! An O-Two in the United States Navy is a Lieutenant Junior Grade!"

"Hit."

"Aye aye, Sir! His insignia is a one silver bar collar device! Or one one-half inch gold stripe outboard of one one-quarter inch gold stripe! Outboard of one gold five-pointed star on black shoulder boards! Or one one-half inch gold stripe! Below one one-quarter inch gold stripe! Below one gold five-pointed star on service dress blue uniform sleeves! Sir! An O-Three in the United States Navy is a Lieutenant! His insignia is a two silver bar collar device!"

"Hit. Disgusting."

"Hit! You iron that with a freaking brick?"

"No excuse, Sir!"

"I asked you a question, Pinhead!"

"No, Sir!"

"Hit!"

"Aye aye, Sir!"

"Hit. Repulsive."

"Aye aye, Sir! Or two one-half inch gold stripes! Outboard of one gold five-pointed star on black shoulder boards! Or two one-half inch gold stripes below one gold five-pointed star on service dress blue uniform sleeves!"

"Hit!"

"Aye aye, Sir! Sir! An O-Four in the United States Navy is a Lieutenant Commander! His insignia is a one gold oak leaf collar device! Or one one-half inch gold stripe outboard of one one-quarter inch gold stripe! Outboard of one one-half inch gold stripe! Outboard of one gold five-pointed star on black shoulder boards! Or one one-half inch gold stripe! Below one one-quarter inch gold stripe! Below one one-half inch gold stripe!"

"Hit. Improper measurement."

"Aye aye, Sir! Below one gold five-pointed star on service dress blue uniform sleeves! Sir! An O-Five in the United States Navy is a Commander! His insignia is a one silver oak leaf collar device! Or three one-half inch gold stripes! Outboard of one gold five-pointed star on black shoulder boards! Or three one-half inch gold stripes!"

"Hit!"

"Aye aye, Sir! Below one gold five-pointed star on service dress blue uniform sleeves! Sir! An O-Six in the United States Navy is a Captain! His insignia is a one silver eagle collar device! Or four one-half inch gold stripes! Outboard of one gold five-pointed star on black shoulder boards! Or four one-half inch gold stripes! Below one gold five-pointed star on service dress blue uniform sleeves!"

"Hit. Dirt."

"Aye aye, Sir! Sir! An O-Seven in the United States Navy is a Rear Admiral Lower Half! His insignia is a one silver five-pointed star collar device! Or one silver five-pointed star! Outboard of one silver fouled anchor on black shoulder boards! Or one two-inch gold stripe! Below one gold five-pointed star on service dress blue uniform sleeves!"

"Marine Corp Officer ranks! Give them to me now!"

"Aye aye, Sir! Sir! Sir! An E-One in the United States Marine Corp is a Private! He has no insignia! Sir! An E-Two in the United States Marine Corp is a Private First Class! His insignia is one chevron! Sir! An E-Three in the United States Marine Corp is a Lance Corporal! His insignia is one chevron over crossed rifles! Sir! An E-Four in the United States Marine Corp is a Corporal! His insignia is two chevrons over crossed rifles! Sir! An E-Five in the United States Marine Corp is a Sergeant!"

"Hit! Spacing!"

"Aye aye, Sir! His insignia is three chevrons over crossed rifles! Sir! An E-Six in the United States Marine Corp is a Staff Sergeant! His insignia is three chevrons over crossed rifles over one rocker! Sir! An E-Seven in the United States Marine Corp is a Gunnery Sergeant! His insignia is three chevrons over crossed rifles over two rockers! Sir! An E-Eight in the United States Marine Corp is a --!"

"Stop! Stop! Stop! Freeze!"

"Aye aye, Sir!"

"That's all of you, Pigs! Attenhut!"

"Aye aye, Sir!!"

"I smell something funky. Napalm. Freaking Agent Orange. It's everywhere. Who is it? Who is it? Don't make me ask, you Nasty Thing You."

"Officer Candidate Potts! Officer Candidate School! Officer Candidate Class Zero-Four-Zero-Zero! United States Navy! Sir!"

"Oh you Nasty Thing. You Nasty Thing. I have never. Ever. Smelled anything so revolting. So disgusting. So despicable. In my entire life. You smell worse than a Bilge Turd, Pig. What does your mother call you?"

"Nastor, Sir!"

"Oh, I don't believe it. Nastor Potts?"

"Yes, Sir!"

"You hear that?"

"Impossible."

"It couldn't possibly be. God himself gave you that name, O' Nasty One. *Nasty Nastor. King of the Nastonians. Prince of the Nastylytes.* Say your name, you Nasty Freak."

"Sir! This Officer Candidate's name is Officer Candidate Potts! Officer Candidate School! Officer Candidate Class Zero-Four-Zero-Zero! United States Navy! Sir!"

"Improper response. That's a hit. Your Officer Candidate name is *Nasty Nastor, King of the Nastonians, Prince of the Nastylytes.* Well, what are you waiting on?"

"Sir! This Officer Candidate's name is Officer Candidate Nasty Nastor!"

"*King of the Nastonians.*"

"King of the Nastonians!"

"*Prince of the Nastylytes.*"

"Prince of the Nastylytes!"

"*The Nasty Potts.*"

"The Nasty Potts!"

"*The Stinky Potts.*"

"The Stinky Potts!"

"*The Smelly Potts.*"

"The Smelly Potts!"

"Stop whispering to me!"

"Aye aye, Sir! Sir! This Officer Candidate's name is Nasty Nastor! King of the Nastonians! Prince of the Nastylytes!"

"Don't you even know your own name, Pig Fart?"

"No excuse, Sir!"

"*The Nasty Potts.*"

"The Nasty Potts!"

"*The Stinky Potts.*"

"The Stinky Potts!"

"*The Smelly Potts.*"

"The Smelly Potts!"

"All together now, you Filthy Animal!"

"Sir! This Officer Candidate's name is Nasty Nastor! King of the Nastonians! Prince of the Nastylytes! The Nasty Potts! The Stinky Potts! The Smelly Potts!"

"Keep it going, Stinker!"

"Aye aye, Sir! Sir! This Officer Candidate's name is Nasty Nastor! King of the Nastonians! Prince of the Nastylytes! The Nasty Potts! The Stinky Potts! The Smelly Potts! Sir! This Officer Candidate's name is Nasty Nastor! King of the Nastonians! Prince of the Nastylytes! The Nasty Potts! The Stinky Potts! The

Smelly Potts! Sir! This Officer Candidate's name is Nasty Nastor! King of the Nastonians! Prince of the Nastylytes! The Nasty Potts! The Stinky Potts! The Smelly Potts!"

"Side-straddle hops! Exercise!"

"Who do you three think you're eyeballing? Is this a cocktail party? You want to buy me a drink?"

"That's a freaking response! That's a freaking response!"

"No, Sir!!"

"Doesn't smell like a cocktail party!"

"Sound off! You freaking sound off!"

"Aye aye, Sir!!"

"Side-straddle hops!"

"That's a freaking response! That's a freaking response!"

"Aye aye, Sir!!"

"Everybody's got the same name! Let's hear it, Pottsies!"

"Aye aye, Sir!! Sir! This Officer Candidate's name is Nasty Nastor!! King of the Nastonians!! Prince of the Nastylytes!! The Nasty Potts!! The Stinky Potts!! The Smelly Potts!! Sir!! This Officer Candidate's name is Nasty Nastor!! King of the Nastonians!! Prince of the Nastylytes!! The Nasty Potts!! The Stinky Potts!! The Smelly Potts!!"

"Hit! Bearing!"

"Aye aye, Sir!"

"Freaking sound off!"

"Aye aye, Sir!!"

"Stop whispering, Pukes! Stop freaking whispering!"

"Aye aye, Sir!! Sir!! This Officer Candidate's name is Nasty Nastor!! King of the Nastonians!! Prince of the Nastylytes!! The Nasty Potts!! The Stinky Potts!! The Smelly Potts!!"

"Hit! Improper measurement!"

"Aye aye, Sir!"

"Sir!! This Officer Candidate's name is Nasty Nastor!! King of the Nastonians!! Prince of the Nastylytes!! The Nasty Potts!! The Stinky Potts!! The Smelly Potts!!"

"Hit! Rifle arrangement! Hit!"

"Aye aye, Sir!"

"Sir!! This Officer Candidate's name is Nasty Nastor!! King of the Nastonians!! Prince of the Nastylytes!! The Nasty Potts!! The Stinky Potts!! The Smelly Potts!!"

"Hit! You-Nasty-Thing!"

"Aye aye, Sir!"

"Hit! Look at all these Nasty I.Ps! Hit! Hit! Hit! Six inches? I don't freaking

think so! Hit! Hit! Hit!"

"Outboard over inboard! Hit!"

"Hit!"

"Dust. Hit! Grime. Hit!"

"Aye aye, Sir!"

"Bearing! Hit. I can't hear you! Louder! Louder!"

"Sir!! This Officer Candidate's name is Nasty Nastor!! King of the Nastonians!! Prince of the Nastylytes!! The Nasty Potts!! The Stinky Potts!! The Smelly Potts!! Sir! This Officer Candidate's name is Nasty Nastor!! King of the Nastonians!! Prince of the Nastylytes!! The Nasty Potts!! The Stinky Potts!! The Smelly Potts!!"

"Hit! Hit! That's a hit!"

"Aye aye, Sir!"

"Sir!! This Officer Candidate's name is Nasty Nastor!! King of the Nastonians!! Prince of the Nastylytes!! The Nasty Potts!! The Stinky Potts!! The Smelly Potts!!"

"You catch this?"

"Disgusting. Hit!"

"More I.Ps. This is one Nasty Thing."

"Hit! Hit! Hit!"

"Sir!! This Officer Candidate's name is Nasty Nastor!! King of the Nastonians!! Prince of the Nastylytes!! The Nasty Potts!! The Stinky Potts!! The Smelly Potts!!"

"Check the drawer."

"Hit! Hit! Hit!"

"Aye aye, Sir!"

"Sir!! This Officer Candidate's name is Nasty Nastor!! King of the Nastonians!! Prince of the Nastylytes!! The Nasty Potts!! The Stinky Potts!! The Smelly Potts!!"

"As you were, Pigs!"

"Aye aye, Sir!!"

"You are nasty as all hell. What you need, Pig, is a fumigation. As you failed to properly apply your Navy provided antiperspirant, the antiperspirant will be applied for you."

"That's a freaking response! That's a response!"

"Aye aye, Sir!"

"You bet your Nasty Ass! Side-straddle hops, Pig!"

"Aye aye, Sir!"

"Grab your antiperspirants, Freaks. You're going to assist His Nastiness here. That's a freaking response! Move!"

"Aye aye, Sir!!"

"Upon receiving the command of execution *spray-at-will, Pigs*! You will freaking spray at will! *Aye aye, Sir*!"

"Aye aye, Sir!!"

"Steady! Ready! Hold! Hold! Spray at will, Pigs!"

"Aye aye, Sir!!"

"More! More!"

"Aye aye, Sir!!"

"I still see him! I still see him! And I don't want to see him no more!"

"Freaking *aye aye, Sir*! Freaking *aye aye, Sir*!"

"Aye aye, Sir!!"

"Oh, I can still smell you, you Nasty Thing You! I don't want to smell you no more! Hold positions!"

"Aye aye, Sir!!"

"Keep firing!"

"Aye aye, Sir!!"

"Make that Nasty Thing go away!"

"Aye aye, Sir!!"

"I don't want to see him no more!"

"Aye aye, Sir!!"

"Steady!"

"Aye aye, Sir!!"

"Louder!"

"Aye aye, Sir!!"

"Louder!"

"Aye aye, Sir!!"

"Louder!"

"Aye aye, Sir!!"

The space fills in haze.

"Evac."

"Attention on deck, stand-by!"

"Good morning, Sir!!"

Echoes reverberate between the bulkheads.

"We're clear."

"Damn."

"So that went well."

"Damn."

"Don't worry about it, brother. Let's just concentrate on getting this place back together."

"Man, looks like we got hurricaned."

"I just rolled."

"You don't know that."

"Did you not just hear them hitting me? G.T.X. for me."

"Say, Potts. Crack the window first, please."

"Not funny, Fortunato."

"I'm kidding. I got hit a lot too. They can't hit you for smell."

"They just did."

"Man, that was crazy as all hell."

"Let it be, brother. Let's just get the space squared away."

••

Dress Shoe

Plain toed, Oxford style black, brown, or white, low quarter, lace shoe, made of smooth leather or synthetic leather. The heel shall be an outside heel three-quarters and seven eighths inches high with a flat sole. Keep well shined and in good repair. Lace shoes from inside out through all eyelets and tie, outboard over inboard.

To shine. Add polish to duster or fine cotton T-shirt wrapped tightly over index finger. Apply with light pressure to leather in a circular pattern one-half inch in diameter. Add water to cloth. Resume circular motion, applying more liquid as polish begins to harden. Repeat while gradually reducing the amount of polish used on each layer. Continue process until surface is completely smooth. Buff away excess polish. Add a very light spot of polish to duster or fine cotton T-shirt. Apply with light pressure to leather in a tightened circular motion. Continue until the small swirls disappear into a smooth mirrored surface. Repeat as necessary. Buff lightly to bring out true shine. Estimated time for a good foundation is two hours per shoe.

••

"Today we pray. Repeat after me. *Aye aye, Sir.*"

"Aye aye, Sir!!"

"*This is my rifle!*"

"This is my rifle!!"

"*There are many like it! But this one is mine!*"

"There are many like it!! But this one is mine!!"

"*My rifle is my best friend!*"

"My rifle is my best friend!!"

"*It is my life!*"

"It is my life!!"

"*I must master it as I must master my life!*"

"I must master it as I must master my life!!"

"*My rifle, without me, is useless! Without my rifle, I am useless!*"

"My rifle, without me, is useless!! Without my rifle, I am useless!!"

"*I must fire my rifle true!*"

"I must fire my rifle true!!"

"*I must shoot straighter than my enemy who is trying to kill me!*"

"I must shoot straighter than my enemy who is trying to kill me!!"

"*I must shoot him before he shoots me!*"

"I must shoot him before he shoots me!!"

"*I will!*"

"I will!!"

"*My rifle and myself know that what counts in this war is not the rounds we fire! The noise of our burst! Nor the smoke we make!*"

"My rifle and myself know that what counts in this war is not the rounds we fire!! The noise of our burst!! Nor the smoke we make!!"

"*We know that it is the hits that count!*"

"We know that it is the hits that count!!"

"*We will hit!*"

"We will hit!!"

"*My rifle is human, even as I, because it is my life!*"

"My rifle is human, even as I, because it is my life!!"

"*Thus, I will learn it as a brother!*"

"Thus, I will learn it as a brother!!"

"*I will learn its weaknesses! Its strength! Its parts! Its accessories! Its sights and its barrel!*"

"I will learn its weaknesses!! Its strength!! Its parts!! Its accessories!! Its sights and its barrel!!"

"*I will ever guard it against the ravages of weather and damage!*"

"I will ever guard it against the ravages of weather and damage!!"

"*As I will ever guard my legs! My arms! My eyes! And my heart against damage!*"

"As I will ever guard my legs!! My arms!! My eyes!! And my heart against damage!!"

"I will keep my rifle clean! And ready! We will become part of each other!"

"I will keep my rifle clean!! And ready!! We will become part of each other!!"

"We will!"

"We will!!"

"Before God, I swear this creed!"

"Before God, I swear this creed!!"

"My rifle and myself are the defenders of my country! We are the masters of our enemy!"

"My rifle and myself are the defenders of my country!! We are the masters of our enemy!!"

"We are the saviors of my life! So be it, until victory is America's!"

"We are the saviors of my life!! So be it, until victory is America's!!"

"And there is no enemy! But peace!"

"And there is no enemy!! But peace!!"

"Again."

"Aye aye, Sir!!"

"This is my rifle!"

"This is my rifle!!"

"There are many like it! But this one is mine!"

"There are many like it!! But this one is mine!!"

"My rifle is my best friend!"

"My rifle is my best friend!!"

"It is my life!"

"It is my life!!"

"I must master it as I must master my life!"

"I must master it as I must master my life!!"

"My rifle, without me, is useless! Without my rifle, I am useless!"

"My rifle, without me, is useless!! Without my rifle, I am useless!!"

"I must fire my rifle true!"

"I must fire my rifle true!!"

"I must shoot straighter than my enemy who is trying to kill me!"

"I must shoot straighter than my enemy who is trying to kill me!!"

"I must shoot him before he shoots me!"

"I must shoot him before he shoots me!!"

"I will!"

"I will!!"

"My rifle and myself know that what counts in this war is not the rounds we fire! The noise of our burst! Nor the smoke we make!"

"My rifle and myself know that what counts in this war is not the rounds we fire!! The noise of our burst!! Nor the smoke we make!!"

"*We know that it is the hits that count!*"

"We know that it is the hits that count!!"

"*We will hit!*"

"We will hit!!"

"*My rifle is human, even as I, because it is my life!*"

"My rifle is human, even as I, because it is my life!!"

"*Thus, I will learn it as a brother!*"

"Thus, I will learn it as a brother!!"

"*I will learn its weaknesses! Its strength! Its parts! Its accessories! Its sights and its barrel!*"

"I will learn its weaknesses!! Its strength!! Its parts!! Its accessories!! Its sights and its barrel!!"

"*I will ever guard it against the ravages of weather and damage!*"

"I will ever guard it against the ravages of weather and damage!!"

"*As I will ever guard my legs! My arms! My eyes! And my heart against damage!*"

"As I will ever guard my legs!! My arms!! My eyes!! And my heart against damage!!"

"*I will keep my rifle clean! And ready! We will become part of each other!*"

"I will keep my rifle clean!! And ready!! We will become part of each other!!"

"*We will!*"

"We will!!"

"*Before God, I swear this creed!*"

"Before God, I swear this creed!!"

"*My rifle and myself are the defenders of my country! We are the masters of our enemy!*"

"My rifle and myself are the defenders of my country!! We are the masters of our enemy!!"

"*We are the saviors of my life! So be it, until victory is America's!*"

"We are the saviors of my life!! So be it, until victory is America's!!"

"*And there is no enemy! But peace!*"

"And there is no enemy!! But peace!!"

"Again."

"Aye aye, Sir!!"

"*This is my rifle!*"

"This is my rifle!!"

"*There are many like it! But this one is mine!*"

"There are many like it!! But this one is mine!!"

"*My rifle is my best friend!*"

"My rifle is my best friend!!"

"*It is my life!*"

"It is my life!!"

"*I must master it as I must master my life!*"

"I must master it as I must master my life!!"

"*My rifle, without me, is useless! Without my rifle, I am useless!*"

"My rifle, without me, is useless!! Without my rifle, I am useless!!"

"*I must fire my rifle true!*"

"I must fire my rifle true!!"

"*I must shoot straighter than my enemy who is trying to kill me!*"

"I must shoot straighter than my enemy who is trying to kill me!!"

"*I must shoot him before he shoots me!*"

"I must shoot him before he shoots me!!"

"*I will!*"

"I will!!"

"*My rifle and myself know that what counts in this war is not the rounds we fire! The noise of our burst! Nor the smoke we make!*"

"My rifle and myself know that what counts in this war is not the rounds we fire!! The noise of our burst!! Nor the smoke we make!!"

"*We know that it is the hits that count!*"

"We know that it is the hits that count!!"

"*We will hit!*"

"We will hit!!"

"*My rifle is human, even as I, because it is my life!*"

"My rifle is human, even as I, because it is my life!!"

"*Thus, I will learn it as a brother!*"

"Thus, I will learn it as a brother!!"

"*I will learn its weaknesses! Its strength! Its parts! Its accessories! Its sights and its barrel!*"

"I will learn its weaknesses!! Its strength!! Its parts!! Its accessories!! Its sights and its barrel!!"

"*I will ever guard it against the ravages of weather and damage!*"

"I will ever guard it against the ravages of weather and damage!!"

"*As I will ever guard my legs! My arms! My eyes! And my heart against damage!*"

"As I will ever guard my legs!! My arms!! My eyes!! And my heart against damage!!"

"*I will keep my rifle clean! And ready! We will become part of each other!*"

"I will keep my rifle clean!! And ready!! We will become part of each other!!"

"*We will!*"

"We will!!"

"*Before God, I swear this creed!*"

"Before God, I swear this creed!!"

"*My rifle and myself are the defenders of my country! We are the masters of our enemy!*"

"My rifle and myself are the defenders of my country!! We are the masters of our enemy!!"

"*We are the saviors of my life*! *So be it, until victory is America's*!"

"We are the saviors of my life!! So be it, until victory is America's!!"

"*And there is no enemy*! *But peace*!"

"And there is no enemy!! But peace!!"

"On your own. Pray at will."

"Aye aye, Sir!! This is my rifle!! There are many like it!! But this one is mine!! My rifle is my best friend!! It is my life!! I must master it as I must master my life!! My rifle, without me, is useless!! Without my rifle, I am useless!! I must fire my rifle true!! I must shoot straighter than my enemy who is trying to kill me!! I must shoot him before he shoots me!! I will!! My rifle and myself know that what counts in this war is not the rounds we fire!! The noise of our burst!! Nor the smoke we make!! We know that it is the hits that count!! We will hit!! My rifle is human, even as I, because it is my life!! Thus, I will learn it as a brother!! I will learn its weaknesses!! Its strength!! Its parts!! Its accessories!! Its sights and its barrel!! I will ever guard it against the ravages of weather and damage!! As I will ever guard my legs!! My arms!! My eyes!! And my heart against damage!! I will keep my rifle clean!! And ready!! We will become part of each other!! We will!! Before God, I swear this creed!! My rifle and myself are the defenders of my country!! We are the masters of our enemy!! We are the saviors of my life!! So be it, until victory is America's!! And there is no enemy!! But peace!!"

"Louder."

"Aye aye, Sir!! This is my rifle!! There are many like it!! But this one is mine!! My rifle is my best friend!! It is my life!! I must master it as I must master my life!! My rifle, without me, is useless!! Without my rifle, I am useless!! I must fire my rifle true!! I must shoot straighter than my enemy who is trying to kill me!! I must shoot him before he shoots me!! I will!! My rifle and myself know that what counts in this war is not the rounds we fire!! The noise of our burst!! Nor the smoke we make!! We know that it is the hits that count!! We will hit!! My rifle is human, even as I, because it is my life!! Thus, I will learn it as a brother!! I will learn its weaknesses!! Its strength!! Its parts!! Its accessories!! Its sights and its barrel!! I will ever guard it against the ravages of weather and damage!! As I will ever guard my legs!! My arms!! My eyes!! And my heart against damage!! I will keep my rifle clean!! And ready!! We will become part of each other!! We will!! Before God, I swear this creed!! My rifle and myself are the defenders of my country!! We are the masters of our enemy!! We are the saviors of my life!! So be it, until victory is America's!! And there is no enemy!! But peace!!"

"Louder!"

"Aye aye, Sir!!"

"Louder!"

"Aye aye, Sir!"

"This is my rifle!! There are many like it!! But this one is mine!! My rifle is my

best friend!! It is my life!! I must master it as I must master my life!! My rifle, without me, is useless!! Without my rifle, I am useless!! I must fire my rifle true!! I must shoot straighter than my enemy who is trying to kill me!! I must shoot him before he shoots me!! I will!! My rifle and myself know that what counts in this war is not the rounds we fire!! The noise of our burst!! Nor the smoke we make!! We know that it is the hits that count!! We will hit!! My rifle is human, even as I, because it is my life!! Thus, I will learn it as a brother!! I will learn its weaknesses!! Its strength!! Its parts!! Its accessories!! Its sights and its barrel!! I will ever guard it against the ravages of weather and damage!! As I will ever guard my legs!! My arms!! My eyes!! And my heart against damage!! I will keep my rifle clean!! And ready!! We will become part of each other!! We will!! Before God, I swear this creed!! My rifle and myself are the defenders of my country!! We are the masters of our enemy!! We are the saviors of my life!! So be it, until victory is America's!! And there is no enemy!! But peace!!"

"Get in my grass."

"Aye aye, Sir!!"

"Push. Starting position."

"Aye aye, Sir!!"

"I will count the cadence! I will count the repetitions! *Aye aye, Sir.*"

"Aye aye, Sir!!"

"You will pray at will. Pray at will."

"Aye aye, Sir!! This is my rifle!! There are many like it!! But this one is mine!!"

"Down."

"My rifle is my best friend!! It is my life!! I must master it as I must master my life!!"

"Up. Zero-one."

"My rifle, without me, is useless!! Without my rifle, I am useless!!"

"Down."

"I must fire my rifle true!! I must shoot straighter than my enemy who is trying to kill me!!"

"Up. Zero-two."

"I must shoot him before he shoots me!! I will!! My rifle and myself know that what counts in this war is not the rounds we fire!! The noise of our burst!! Nor the smoke we make!!"

"Down."

"We know that it is the hits that count!!"

"Up. Zero-three."

"We will hit!!"

"Down."

"My rifle is human, even as I, because it is my life!!"

"Up. Zero-four."

"Thus, I will learn it as a brother!!"

"Down."

"I will learn its weaknesses!!"

"Up. Zero-five."

"Its strength!!"

"Down."

"Its parts!! Its accessories!! Its sights and its barrel!!"

"Up. Zero-six. Down."

"I will ever guard it against the ravages of weather and damage!!"

"Up. Zero-seven."

"As I will ever guard my legs!! My arms!! My eyes!! And my heart against damage!! I will keep my rifle clean!! And ready!!"

"Down."

"We will become part of each other!! We will!! Before God, I swear this creed!!"

"Up. Zero-eight."

"My rifle and myself are the defenders of my country!!"

"Down."

"We are the masters of our enemy!!"

"Up. Zero-niner."

"We are the saviors of my life!!"

"Down."

"So be it, until victory is America's!!"

"Up. One-zero."

"And there is no enemy!! But peace!!"

"Fall in!"

"Aye aye, Sir!!"

"Ten-eight-seven-five-four-three-two-one. Freeze."

"Aye aye, Sir!!"

"Dress-right-dress! Report!"

"First squad! All present!"

"Second squad! All present!"

"Third squad! All present!"

"Fourth squad! All present!"

"Very well. Inspection! Arms!"

"Port! Arms!"

"Order! Arms!"

"Count! Off!"

"One!!"

"Two!!"

"Three!!"

"Four!!"

"Five!!"

"Six!!"

"Seven!!"

"Eight!!"

"Niner!!"

"One-zero!!"

"One-one!!"

"One-two!!"

"Open ranks! March! Left-right! Left-right! Left-right! Left-right! Left-right! Left-right!"

"Ready! Front! Cover!"

"Rooster! Port! Steady!"

"Ready! Front! Cover!"

"Port! Arms!"

"Right shoulder! Arms!"

"Left-shoulder! Arms!"

"Port! Arms!"

"Order! Arms!"

"Present! Arms!"

"Order! Arms!"

"Right! Face!"

"Left! Face!"

"About! Face!"

"About! Face!"

"Parade rest!"

"Platoon! Attenhut!"

"Close ranks! March! Left-right! Left-right! Left-right! Left-right! Left-right! Left-right! Left-right!"

"Extend! March! Left-right! Left-right! Left-right! Left-right! Left-right! Left-right! Left-right! Left-right!"

"Dress! Right! Dress!"

"Ready! Front!"

"Cover!"

"Right shoulder! Arms!"

"Rifle! Salute!"

"Ready! Two!"

"Port! Arms!"

"Order! Arms!"

"Present! Arms!"

"Order! Arms!"

"Right! Face!"

"Left! Face!"

"About! Face!"

"About! Face!"

"Parade rest!"

"Platoon! Attenhut!"

"Close ranks! March! Left-right! Left-right! Left-right! Left-right! Left-right! Left-right! Left-right!"

"Right! Face!"

"Rest!"

"Platoon! Attenhut!"

"Port! Arms!"

"Forward! March! Ho! Hai! Ho! Close! March! Da-ra-o-oh-oh-oh-o-eh-oh! Da-ra-o-oh-oh-oh-o-eh-oh! Da-ra-oh-oh-oh-oh-oh-leh-oh! Da-ra-leh-ho-leh-ho-ho! Da-ra-o-oh-oh-oh-o-eh-oh! Da-ra-o-oh-oh-oh-o-eh-oh! Da-ra-oh-oh-oh-oh-oh-leh-oh! Da-ra-leh-ho-leh-ho-ho! Da-ra-o-oh-oh-oh-o-eh-oh! Da-ra-o-oh-oh-oh-o-eh-oh! Da-ra-oh-oh-oh-oh-oh-leh-oh! Da-ra-leh-ho-leh-ho-ho! Da-ra-o-oh-oh-oh-o-eh-oh! Da-ra-o-oh-oh-oh-o-eh-oh! Da-ra-oh-oh-oh-oh-oh-leh-oh! Da-ra-leh-ho-leh-ho-ho! Da-ra-o-oh-oh-oh-o-eh-oh! Da-ra-o-oh-oh-oh-o-eh-oh! Da-ra-oh-oh-oh-oh-oh-leh-oh! Da-ra-leh-ho-leh-ho-ho! Da-ra-o-oh-oh-oh-o-eh-oh! Da-ra-o-oh-oh-oh-o-eh-oh! Da-ra-oh-oh-oh-oh-oh-leh-oh! Da-ra-leh-ho-leh-ho-ho! Left-right-lo! Left-right-lo! Left-right-lo! Left-right-lo! To the rear! March! Left-right-lo! Left-right-lo! Left-right-lo! Left-right-lo! Left-right-lo! Left-right-lo! Left-right-lo! To the rear! March! Left-right-lo! Left-right-lo! Left-right-lo! Left-right-lo! Column left! March! Left-right-lo! Left-right-lo! Left-right-lo! Left-right-lo! Left-right-lo! Left-right-lo! Column left! March! Left-right-lo! Left-right-lo! Left-right-lo! Left-right-lo! By the left flank! March! Da-ra-o-oh-oh-oh-o-eh-oh! Da-ra-o-oh-oh-oh-o-eh-oh! Da-ra-oh-oh-oh-oh-oh-leh-oh! Da-ra-leh-ho-leh-ho-ho! Left-right-lo! Left-right-lo! Left-right-lo! Left-right-lo! Column right! March! Left-right-lo! Left-right-lo! Left-right-lo! Left-right-lo! Platoon! Halt! Ready! March! Da-ra-oh-oh-oh-oh-oh-leh-oh! Da-ra-leh-ho-leh-ho-ho! Da-ra-o-oh-oh-oh-o-eh-oh! Da-ra-o-oh-oh-oh-o-eh-oh! Da-ra-oh-oh-oh-oh-oh-leh-oh! Da-ra-leh-ho-leh-ho-ho! Left-right-lo! Left-right-lo! Left-right-lo! Left-right-lo! Left oblique! March! Left-right-lo! Left-right-lo! Left-right-lo! Left-right-lo! Left-right-lo! Left-right-lo! Left-right-lo! Left-right-lo! Left-right-lo! Left-right-lo! Left-right-lo! Right oblique! March! Da-ra-o-oh-oh-oh-o-eh-oh! Da-ra-oh-oh-oh-oh-oh-leh-oh! Da-ra-leh-ho-leh-ho-ho! Da-ra-o-oh-oh-oh-o-eh-oh! Da-ra-oh-oh-oh-oh-oh-leh-oh! Da-ra-leh-ho-leh-ho-ho! Ready! Halt! Ready march!"

••••••••••••••••••••••••••••••••••••••

Collar Insignia – Open Collar

Shirt collar insignia consists of gold metal fouled anchors, right and left, five-eighths of an inch. On open collar shirts, the insignia is centered one inch from the front and lower edges of the collar and position it with the vertical axis of the insignia along an imaginary line bisecting the angle of the collar point.

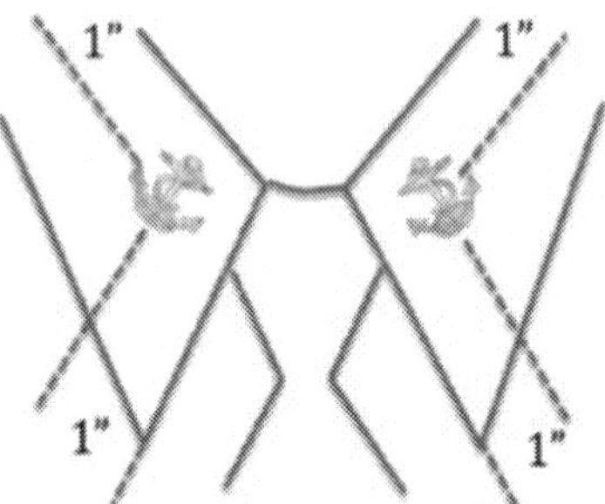

Collar Insignia – Closed Collar

On closed collar shirts, pin the anchor or eagle-anchor insignia to the collar in a vertical position with the center of the insignia approximately one inch from the front edge and one inch below the upper edge of the collar. The anchor's stock is parallel to the upper edge of the collar and the unfouled arm of the stock faces front.

••

"Where's my Section Leader?"
"Here, Sir."
"What's our head count?"

"All present, all accounted for, Sir."

"Right. If I could have your full attention directed up at the front. Let's get her started. I imagine you don't want to be late for chow. We were discussing the national command structure. The Chain of Command. The line of authority and responsibility along which most orders are passed. The line of authority and responsibly that leads to mission success, and, at times, failure. Admiral gets on the horn to the Captain, who schedules a Skippers' meeting, who readout the X.Os, who call in the Hinges to coral the Junior Officers, who rely on the Chiefs to rally the crew. The Captain. Skippers. X.Os. Officers. Chiefs. The rank and file. But even the Admiral gets his sailing orders from the same source as the rest of us. That's right, we all take our orders from the same person. And no, it's not your D.I., even if it might seem that way now. Anyone have the answer? This one's a gimme."

"The President, Sir."

"The President of the United States. The Commander-in-Chief of the Armed Forces. Leader of the Free World. The elected official who bears ultimate responsibility for the execution of national security policies and holds ultimate authority over those federal departments and agencies that affect security. *Ultimate responsibility and ultimate authority*. Let's hear it for the record."

"Ultimate responsibility and ultimate authority."

"But how? How exactly? How does the President reach out and touch you, touch all of us, as our Commander-in-Chief? That is the purpose of this lesson topic, to aid you in an understanding of the national defense structure and methodologies of Command and Control. Otherwise stated, your terminal objective is to develop a comprehensive understanding of the operational Chain of Command for the Navy from the National Command Authority to the individual unit Commanding Officer, as well as the fundamentals of Command and Control and joint organization. Any questions up to this point? Good. Officer Candidate Lin, start us off with the enabling objectives supported by this lesson topic. Nine-nine."

"Aye aye, Sir. Describe the principles of the Command and Control concept as it is utilized by the U.S. Navy."

"Nine one-zero."

"Describe the basic requirements of the Command and Control concept as it is utilized by the U.S. Navy."

"Nine one-one."

"Describe the operational Chain of Command from the National Command Authority to the Task Element Commander, including the major components of each level."

"Officer Candidate Andrews, nine one-two, please."

"State the purpose and originator of operation plans and operation orders."

"Nine one-three."

"State the purpose of the Naval Warfare Publications Library."

"Nine one-four."

"Describe the three basic rules which govern the conduct of hostilities."

"Nine one-five."

"State the Presidential authority to commit U.S. forces to hostilities contained in the War Powers Resolution Act of Nineteen-Seventy-Three."

"Officer Candidate Hobson. Look alive. Nine one-six."

"Aye aye, Sir. Describe the functions of the Unified Commands."

"Nine one-seven."

"Describe the current operational Chain of Command in the National Security Organization."

"Nine one-eight."

"Describe the mission and composition of the National Command Authority, National Security Council, and Joint Chiefs of Staff."

"Nine one-nine."

"Describe the mission of the Department of Defense."

"And nine two-zero."

"Describe the functions of the Joint Task Force Commander. Sir."

"Aftermath of World War Two. Europe decimated. Germany and Japan under occupation. Russia and China pretending that they still had fight. Millions upon millions dead. Laid to rest in the shadow of an atom. Ours. A unique window of opportunity to lay a new foundation for the long-term national security of the United States. A brave new world of American prestige, dominance, prosperity and leadership. And currency. Enter the National Security Act of Nineteen-Forty-Seven and modern era of the national security apparatus. We'll start with the Secretary of Defense. You will recall that the President as Commander-in-Chief bears?"

"Ultimate responsibility and ultimate authority."

"Ultimate responsibility and ultimate authority for the execution of national security policies. With just one caveat. Trust but verify. Under the Act and its amendments, the ultimate lawful source of military orders originates not solely from the President, but also a Secretary of Defense, a civilian appointed by the President. A Chain of Command vested with the Constitutional authority to direct the Armed Forces in the execution of war, but one with a dual-authority to concur, in essence, before the issuance of an order to launch a strategic nuclear strike against an enemy, foreign or domestic. You can trust the electorate with most everything. Just not nuclear weapons. The *National Command Authority*."

"National Command Authority."

"The N.C.A. Very important. The Act also created three Services. The Army. Our Navy, Marine Corp and Naval Aviation included. And, something

new. An Air Force to reflect modern warfare. All under the control a single Department, first referred to as the National Military Establishment, the N.M.E., then renamed the Department of Defense two years later when policymakers realized that Service Secretaries don't always work off the same page. So, were you to be asked whom is the sole source of lawful orders for the Chain of Command as part of the N.C.A., you would say?"

"The President."

"And?"

"The Secretary of Defense."

"Good. Now they do have some staff support in the decision-making process. The drafters of the Act also thought it wise to establish a council to consider national security issues requiring Presidential decision. The *National Security Council.*"

"National Security Council."

"The N.S.C. Chaired by the President and consisting of four, takeaway four, statutory members. A *Chairman of the Joint Chiefs of Staff.*"

"Chairman of the Joint Chiefs of Staff."

"His *Vice Chairman of the Joint Chiefs of Staff.*"

"Vice Chairman of the Joint Chiefs of Staff."

"A *Secretary of Defense.*"

"Secretary of Defense."

"Whom we already know. And a *Secretary of State.*"

"Secretary of State."

"Whom you should already know. *The Chairman of the Joint Chiefs of Staff, Vice Chairman, Secretary of Defense* and *Secretary of State.* Altogether now."

"The Chairman of the Joint Chiefs of Staff, Vice Chairman, Secretary of Defense and Secretary of State."

"As voting members of the council. Now there are also two statutory advisors. A *Director of Central Intelligence*, the head of a *Central Intelligence Agency*, that's right, serves as the statutory intelligence advisor to the Council and the aforementioned *Chairman of the Joint Chiefs of Staff* serves as the statutory military advisor. The pen and the sword. Let's hear it. The two statutory advisors are the?"

"Director of Central Intelligence."

"And?"

"Chairman of the Joint Chiefs of Staff."

"Very good. There's also a National Security Advisor, responsible for the day-to-day operation of the N.S.C. and interagency coordination. We're talking reach out. Folks like the Joint Chiefs. President's Chief of Staff. Counsel to the President. Assistant to the President for Economic Policy. Secretary of Commerce. The United States Trade Representative. Assistant to the President

for Economic Policy. Cabinet Secretaries, Deputy Secretaries and many more, as appropriate, to consider all aspects of national security policy as it affects the United States. Domestic, foreign, military, intelligence, and economic matters. National security policy. Picture an old executive building in Washington with wide corridors and a lot of little rooms where your big brothers live, grabbing the big pieces of chicken for the White House and splitting the scrambled-eggs between the Departments and Agencies. If the N.S.C. calls, you better darn well pull up trou and get on the horn. Even if it's just a Schedule-C on his first can of shaving cream with a Master's degree in *how very important I am* working on setting up a sub-I.P.C. for a P.P.D. on *where is Romania?* with input from Post. Never know what cc list it might put you on. That's Washington. For the purposes of your exam, I would focus on knowing the voting members and statutory advisors. Alright?"

"Yes, Sir?"

"In the real word, it's the Four-star to the Three-star to the Two-star to the One-star. Secretary to the Deputy Secretary to the Under Secretary to Assistant Secretary to Principal Deputy Assistant Secretary to the Deputy Assistant Secretary to the Director. Senior Advisor to the Senior Advisor to the Senior Advisor to the Senior Advisor. Supported by staff who have staff who have staff. All making sure the briefing materials were properly delivered and the PowerPoint was loaded for presentation. All still trying to make grade. Shifting alliances between senior policymakers who rise and fall upon the slightest hint of support or rebuttal from higher-ups or, as need be, the President. Public policy. Only the few survive. Quite often the weak. You will all go through D.C. at some point in your Navy careers. No way around it. Got it?"

"Yes, Sir."

"What we care about is the military. Over at the Pentagon cross the Potomac, the J.C.S. provides the highest level of operational planning and direction for the military. Comprised not only of the Chairman and Vice-Chairman, but an Army Chief of Staff, Air Force Chief of Staff, Chief of Naval Operations, and the Commandant of the United States Marine Corp. At the same time, and this is important, the J.C.S. have no authority, I repeat no authority, to command combatant forces. Instead, the Chairman of the Joint Chiefs of Staff functions within the Chain of Command by transmitting communications to the commanders of the combatant commands from the President and Secretary of Defense. More stars than the milky way, but advice and communications only. That's important. *No authority to command.*"

"No authority to command."

"Quick word about the other competing advisor, the Director of Central Intelligence, before getting into the weeds. Up until the Second World War and National Security Act, you didn't have a national intelligence apparatus for

peacetime operations. The wartime intelligence spyglass, the Office of Strategic Services was on the chopping block, surviving fragments bound for the War Department and State Department. Several dogs in this policy fight, this one in the Oval Office and the type of old fashioned brawl you get with a weak President. Should intelligence be the function of the military? Army and Navy thought so. Should it function as an element foreign relations, more of a *how may we help you, Sir or Ma'am* decentralized collection device? The State Department and Budget Bureau thought so. Or how about taking the G-men worldwide? Hoover was game, as always ahead of the curve, and tired of his dog-and-pony show in Latin America. In the end, when you can't find a compromise in Washington, you come up with something new. Not the military. Not our embassies. Not the F.B.I. A *Central Intelligence Agency*."

"Central Intelligence Agency."

"Led by a Director we now recall as?"

"Director of Central Intelligence."

"With what statutory role in the N.S.C.? I want everyone."

"Statutory Advisor."

"Good. Chief of everyone's favorite new spy movie C.I.A., an agency with over the horizon capability to prevent a surprise attack on our sovereign territory responsible for providing national intelligence to the President, the heads of departments and agencies of the executive branch, the Chairman of the Joint Chiefs of Staff and senior military commanders, and, where appropriate, to the Senate and House of Representatives and committees thereof. You can imagine how handing over the keys to some Ivy League consigliore, Russian studies major with a minor in Lit sat with the Brass. Enough said. Any questions? Alright. Let's take a look at the Unified Commands. You'll hear them also referred to as *Unified Combatant Commands*. Let's hear it."

"Unified Combatant Commands."

"That's important. Defined as a command with a broad continuing mission under a single commander composed of forces from two or more services. There are nine in total, organized either on a geographical or functional basis. Led by Four-stars called CINCs, Commanders-in-Chief. Awkward, to be sure. We'll start off with the Regionals. Five of them. *U.S. Pacific Command*."

"U.S. Pacific Command."

"*U.S. European Command*."

"U.S. European Command."

"*U.S. Southern Command*."

"U.S. Southern Command."

"*U.S. Atlantic Command*."

"U.S. Atlantic Command."

"And *U.S. Central Command*."

"U.S. Central Command."

"PACOM. CINCEUR. CINCSOUTH. CINCLANT. CINCENT. And four Functional Commands. *U.S. Special Operations Command.*"

"U.S. Special Operations Command."

"*U.S. Strategic Command.*"

"U.S. Strategic Command."

"*U.S. Space Command.*"

"U.S. Space Command."

"And *U.S. Transportation Command.*"

"U.S. Transportation Command."

"SPECOPS, STRATCOM, CINCSPACE, CINCTRANS. Unified Commands under Unified Commanders, all reporting to and under the direction of the N.C.A., tasked with the development and the ability to execute Operational Plans for possible conflict within respective *Areas of Responsibility.*"

"Areas of Responsibility."

"*A.O.Rs.* Functional or geographic. A.O.R specific and off-the-shelf. Activated only by the N.C.A. though an Executive Order given to the appropriate unified commander. For large-scale ops, you're usually talking a Joint Task Force with all the Services pitching in, more or less. But what about the Navy? Who do we work for? Other than the President. You'll be relieved to know that absent a designated Joint Task Force, the operational Chain of Command for the Navy remains in control of the Navy operating forces, organized as a *Component Command.*"

"Component Command."

"That's important. The Navy contributes to these Unified Commands as our contribution to Joint Warfare, but retains both operational and administrative control. Don't you forget it. Policy is fought over decades."

"Aye aye, Sir."

"*Operational and administrative control.*"

"Operational and administrative control."

"On the operational side, the component commanders report to the Unified Commander in the given region. Admin-wise, they report back to Washington and the C.N.O.'s office. Seven of them. *U.S. Pacific Fleet.*"

"U.S. Pacific Fleet."

"*U.S. Naval Forces Europe.*"

"U.S. Naval Forces Europe."

"*U.S. Atlantic Fleet.*"

"U.S. Atlantic Fleet."

"*U.S. Naval Forces Central Command.*"

"U.S. Naval Forces Central Command."

"*Naval Space Command.*"

"Naval Space Command."

"*Naval Special Warfare Command.*"

"Naval Special Warfare Command."

"*Military Sealift Command.*"

"Military Sealift Command."

"PACFLEET. NAVEUR. LANTFLEET. CENTFLEET. SPACECOM. SPECWARCOM. And M.S.C. Next are the Fleets. Yes, the world famous Fleet. Well, almost. The Fleet refers to the operational forces of the Navy. A numbered Fleet refers to the operational forces in a specific region. These are operational commands and report to the component commander for their area of operations. Second Fleet for the Atlantic. Third Fleet for the Eastern Pacific Ocean. Fifth Fleet for the Persian Gulf. Sixth Fleet for the Med. And Seventh Fleet for the Western Pacific and Indian Ocean. Each numbered Fleet is then divided by the Fleet Commander into a number of Task Forces, each with a specific operation or task, organized to meet real world commitments as required. Each is led by a Task Group Commander who divides the Task Force into a number of Task Groups and subsidiary Task Units, assigned specific responsibilities. The next organizational breakdown is at the Task Element level. Your individual detachment, ship, submarine or aircraft squadron. Your unit Commanding Officer. All this clear?"

"Yes, Sir."

"Good. I know this might sound complicated on paper. Not so much in the Fleet where you will live and breathe operations, from the time you wake up in the morning to the time you go to sleep in the morning and all this will be intuitive. Reflected in every Oplan. Every Navy message. You'll be able to spot the Chain of Command with one look at the message tag. Here, you just have to know it for the test. First number tells you the Fleet. Two. Three. Five. Six. Or seven. Followed by the Task Force number. Then the Group number sequentially starting with the number-one. Then the Task Unit number. And finally the Task Element number. Fleet. Task Force. Group. Task Unit. And Task Element. Is that clear?"

"Yes, Sir."

"So, was I to say Task Element twenty-four-decimal-one-decimal-two-decimal-three, what would be the Chain of Command? Koch."

"What was the number again, Sir?"

"Task Element twenty-four-decimal-one-decimal-two-decimal-three?"

"Second Fleet. Fourth Task Force. First Task Group."

"*Second Task Unit.*"

"Second Task Unit."

"*Third Task Element.*"

"Third Task Element. Sir."

"You're making me nervous, Koch. How about Task Unit seven two-decimal-five-decimal-two?"

"Seventh Fleet."

"Good."

"Second Task Force. Fifth Task Group. Second Task Unit."

"Well done. Is that clear to everyone now? Better yet. Is there anyone not clear on this yet? This will be part of your exam. Run through some of these drills on your own time. Believe me, with a little practice and memorization, this is not a heavy lift. You do not want to be staring blankly at this section come test time. Is there anyone not comfortable moving on? Hibbs."

"Yes, Sir."

"Go stand at the back of the classroom."

"Aye aye, Sir."

"You are responsible this material, Candidates. If you cannot stay awake when seated, you are required to stand."

"Aye aye, Sir."

"Moving on. You should now have an understanding of the operational Chain of Command of the Navy. We want to know how this structure is used to conduct operations, to exercise authority and direct assigned forces in the accomplishment of a mission. Our answer is Command and Control. Ultimately, you will operate within the framework of a decentralized Command and Control structure that, once armed with marching orders, is empowered to make good decisions. Officer Candidate Elkind."

"Yes, Sir."

"What are the two general requirements of Command and Control?"

"Information and action, Sir."

"Information and action. Information flow as forces encounter obstacles in the execution of a plan. And action as assigned forces carry out the instructions provided by higher commanders through the arrangement of personnel, communications equipment and procedures. Two important concepts. With two important caveats. Officer Candidate Zurich."

"Yes, Sir."

"Give me *Rules of Engagement*, R.O.E.?"

"Sir, Rules of Engagement are directives issued by a competent military authority which delineate the circumstances and limitations under which the U.S. Navy will initiate or continue combat operations with hostile forces."

"Thank you. And what about *Pre-Planned Responses*?"

"Sir, Pre-Planned Responses are initial actions to be carried out when faced with a specific situation concerning a specific threat to ensure a proper and rapid response to particular threat forces."

"The right to act or not act. Applying the ROE and Pre-Planned Responses

together, subordinates may act without seeking permission from superiors. That's right. You as a subordinate are perfectly capable of informing your superior or your Skipper of what action you are taking if you deviate from the Pre-Planned Response. If not countermanded, the Skipper will inform his superior of your action as part of the unit. If his superior disagrees with the actions being taken, that superior may negate your unit's decision by issuing an order that countermands your initial decision as a subordinate. Command by negation through trust in a system. A significant advance that separates us from the rest of the world militaries. The N.C.A. sees a need to act. A decision is made. The Joint Chiefs look at the board and communicate that decision, the order, to the necessary commanders of the combatant commands. An operational order is then generated by the component commanders in response to the Op-plan, detailing actions for assigned forces in an actual operation in the near future. Admiral gets on the horn to the Captain, who schedules a Skippers' meeting, who readout the X.Os, who call in the Hinges to coral the Junior Officers, who rely on the Chiefs to rally the crew. Back in your seats in five."

••

Working Khakis

Occasions for wear. Worn when other uniforms would be unsafe or become unduly soiled.

Shirt. Made of authorized fabric, with two breast pockets with button flaps. The short-sleeve shirt will have an open collar forming a V-neck. The long-sleeve will have a button closure at the neck. May be either long or short-sleeve as prescribed. Button all buttons except the collar button on the long-sleeve shirt when worn with working khaki uniform.

Trousers. Made of authorized fabric with fore and aft creases, belt loops, zippered fly front closure, and two side and back pockets. May be straight legged

or slightly flared. The shirt and trousers fabric must match. Poly/cotton may be worn only as part of working khakis.

Belt. Plain cloth or webbing, same color as uniform, one-quarter inch wide (men), one inch wide (women), and fitted with clip (gold for Officers/C.P.Os and silver for E-Six and below). A cotton or nylon web belt may be worn with all uniforms. If a cloth belt is worn, fabric shall match the uniform. The buckle is brass.

Correct wear. Button all buttons, close all fasteners, and wear a belt through all loops. Trousers shall hang approximately two inches from the floor at the back of the shoe. Trousers should be tailored to include a two inch hem to provide material for adjustments. Wear the belt buckle so that the belt clip end touches the left side of the buckle. Align the right side of the buckle with the opening of the shirt and opening of the fly, forming a straight line.

••

I march up the three steps of the ladderwell onto the veranda. A stiff about face brings me back around to the formation. Collar insignias catch the sun at angles.

"Guide! Post the guide-on!"

"Aye aye, Section Leader!"

"Class Zero-Four-Zero-Zero! Upon the command of execution *ground your canteens*! You will! Ground your canteens to the starboard side and return to formation!"

"Aye aye, Section Leader!!"

"Ground your canteens!"

"Aye aye, Section Leader!!"

"Class Zero-Four-Zero-Zero! Upon receiving the command of execution *march*! You will! Half-step up this ladderwell! Perform an immediate column-left! And reform at the door!"

"Aye aye, Section Leader!!"

"Ready! March!"

I proceed backwards down the length of the verandah with the platoon in tow.

"Your left-right! Left-right! Ready! Halt!"

"Aye aye, Section Leader!!"

"Ready! Adjust!"

"Aye aye, Section Leader!! Discipline!! D!! I!! S!! C!! I!! P!! L!! I!! N!! E!!

Discipline!! Is!! The unconditional!! Obedience-to-orders!! Respect-for-authority!! And self-reliance!! Freeze-candidate-freeze!!"

Willett appears of out nowhere.

"I don't freaking think so, Pigs! One of you is not like the others! What do you know about discipline, Fortunato?"

"This Officer Candidate does not know but will find out, Sir!"

"You think I don't see you, Fortunato?"

"No, Sir!"

"You think I don't see you?"

"No, Sir!"

"Arms dangling! Palms showing! Tongue wagging! Coking-and-joking with your Pig Buddy there? Get in my grass, Pigs. Now!"

"Aye aye, Sir!!"

"Not you, Piss Ant. Stand-by."

"Aye aye, Sir!"

"Move! Twenty-nineteen-eighteen-seventeen-fifteen-fourteen-twelve-ten-eight-seven-six-four-three-two-one. Freeze!"

"Aye aye, Sir!!"

"Back in formation!"

"Aye aye, Sir!!"

"Get in my grass!"

"Aye aye, Sir!!"

"Back in formation!"

"Aye aye, Sir!!"

"Get in my grass!!"

"Aye aye, Sir!!"

"Back in formation!"

"Aye aye, Sir!!"

"Twenty-Nineteen-Eighteen-Seventeen-Sixteen-Fifteen-Fourteen-Thirteen-Twelve-Eleven-Ten-Nine-Eight-Seven-Six-Five-Four-Three-Two-One. Back in my grass!"

"Aye aye, Sir!!"

"Ten-nine-eight-six-five-four-two-one. Freeze!"

"Aye aye, Sir!!"

"Well? What exercise do you want them to do, Fortunato? That's a freaking response."

"Side-straddle hops, Sir!"

"Try again."

"Cherry-pickers, Sir!"

"I don't think so, Worm. Well?"

"Push-ups, Sir!"

"What's that?"

"Push-ups, Sir!"

"You heard him, Pigs! He wants you to push!"

"Aye aye, Sir!!"

"You will count the cadence! They will count the repetitions!"

"Aye aye, Sir!"

"Tell them to push."

"Push!"

"That's an *aye aye, Friendly Fire.*"

"Aye aye, Friendly Fire!!"

"Louder!"

"Aye aye, Friendly Fire!!"

"Start counting."

"Aye aye, Sir! Down! Up!"

"Zero-one!!"

"Down! Up!"

"Zero-two!!"

"Down! Up!"

"Zero-three!!"

"Down! Up!"

"Zero-four!!"

"Down! Up!"

"Zero-five!!"

"Down! Up!"

"Zero-six!!"

"Down! Up!"

"Zero-seven!!"

"Down! Up!"

"Zero-eight!!"

"Slow it down, Pig."

"Aye aye, Sir! Down! Up!"

"Zero-niner!!"

"Down! Up!"

"One-zero!!"

"Down! Up!"

"One-one!!"

"Down! Up!"

"One-two!!"

"Down! Up!"

"One-three!!"

"Down! Up!"

"One-four!!"
"Down! Up!"
"One-five!!"
"Down! Up!"
"One-six!!"
"Down! Up!"
"One-seven!!"
"Slower."
"Aye aye, Sir! Down! Up!"
"One-eight!!"
"Down! Up!"
"One-niner!!"
"Down! Up!"
"Two-zero!!"
"Down! Up!"
"Two-one!"
"Down! Up!"
"Two-two!!"
"Down! Up!"
"Two-three!!"
"Down! Up!"
"Two-four!!"
"Down! Up!"
"Two-five!!"
"Down! Up!!"
"Two-six!!"
"Slower."
"Aye aye, Sir! Down! Up!"
"Two-seven!!"
"Down! Up!"
"Two-eight!!"
"Down! Up!"
"Two-niner!!
"Down! Up!"
"Three-zero!!"

"What do you think, Fortunato? Eight-count body builders or hop and pops?"

"This Officer Candidate does not know but will find out, Sir!"

"Well?"

"Hop and pops, Sir!"

"Very well. You will count the cadence. They will count the repetitions. You

heard him. That's a response."

"Aye aye, Friendly Fire!!"

"Louder."

"Aye aye, Friendly Fire!!"

"Start counting."

"Aye aye, Sir!!"

"One-two-three!"

"Zero-one!!"

"One-two-three!"

"Zero-two!!"

"Louder."

"Aye aye, Sir! One-two-three!"

"Zero-three!!"

"Louder."

"Aye aye, Sir! One-two-three!"

"Zero-four!!"

"Louder."

"Aye aye, Sir! One-two-three!"

"Zero-five!!"

"Louder."

"Aye aye, Sir! One-two-three!"

"Zero-six!!"

"In the ballistic!"

"Aye aye, Sir! One-two-three!"

"Zero-seven!!"

"One-two-three!"

"Zero-eight!!"

"One-two-three!"

"Zero-niner!!"

"One-two-three!"

"One-zero!!"

"One-two-three!"

"One-one!!"

"One-two-three!"

"One-two!!"

"One-two-three!"

"One-three!!"

"One-two-three!"

"One-four!!"

"One-two-three!"

"One-five!!"

"One-two-three!"
"One-six!!"
"One-two-three!"
"One-seven!!"
"One-two-three!"
"One-eight!!"
"One-two-three!"
"One-niner!!"
"One-two-three!"
"Two-zero!!"
"One-two-three!"
"Two-one!!"
"One-two-three!"
"Two-two!!"
"One-two-three!"
"Two-three!!"
"One-two-three!"
"Two-four!!"
"Louder."
"Aye aye, Sir! One-two-three!"
"Two-five!!"
"One-two-three!"
"Two-six!!"
"One-two-three!"
"Two-seven!!"
"One-two-three!"
"Two-eight!!"
"One-two-three!"
"Two-niner!!"
"One-two-three!"
"Three-zero!!"
"Tell them to push."
"Aye aye, Sir! Push!"
"Aye aye, Friendly Fire!!"
"He said *push*! You're pushing for him!"
"Aye aye, Sir!!"
"Louder!"
"Aye aye, Sir!!"
"Louder!"
"Aye aye, Sir!!"
"Do you want to rejoin your class, Fortunato?"

"Yes, Sir!"

"Give me *discipline.*"

"Aye aye, Sir! D!...I!...S!...C!...I!...P!...L!...I!...N!...E! Discipline! Is! The unconditional! Obedience-to-orders! Respect-for-authority! And self-reliance!"

"Louder."

"Aye aye, Sir! D!...I!...S!...C!...I!...P!...L!...I!...N!...E! Discipline! Is! The unconditional! Obedience-to-orders! respect-for-authority! And self-reliance!"

"Go."

"Aye aye, Sir!"

"Side-straddle hops!"

"Aye aye, Sir!!"

"You will count the cadence! You will count the repetitions!"

"Aye aye, Sir!! One-two-three!! Zero-one!! One-two-three!! Zero-two!! One-two-three!! Zero-three!! One-two-three!! Zero-four!! One-two-three!! Zero-five!! One-two-three!! Zero-six!! One-two-three!! Zero-seven!! One-two-three!! Zero-eight!! One-two-three!! Zero-niner!! One-two-three!! One-zero!! One-two-three!! One-one!! One-two-three!! One-two!! One-two-three!! One-three!! One-two-three!! One-four!! One-two-three!! One-five!! One-two-three!! One-six!! One-two-three!! One-seven!! One-two-three!! One-eight!! One-two-three!! One-niner!! One-two-three!! Two-zero!! One-two-three!! Two-one!! One-two-three!! Two-two!! One-two-three!! Two-three!! One-two-three!! Two-four!! One-two-three!! Two-five!!"

"Hop and pops!"

"Aye aye, Sir!! One-two-three!! Zero-one!! One-two-three!! Zero-two!! One-two-three!! Zero-three!! One-two-three!! Zero-four!! One-two-three!! Zero-five!! One-two-three!! Zero-six!! One-two-three!! Zero-seven!! One-two-three!! Zero-eight!! One-two-three!! Zero-niner!! One-two-three!! One-zero!! One-two-three!! One-one!! One-two-three!! One-two!! One-two-three!! One-three!! One-two-three!! One-four!! One-two-three!! One-five!! One-two-three!! One-six!! One-two-three!! One-seven!! One-two-three!! One-eight!! One-two-three!! One-niner!! One-two-three!! Two-zero!! One-two-three!! Two-one!! One-two-three!! Two-two!! One-two-three!! Two-three!! One-two-three!! Two-four!! One-two-three!! Two-five!! One-two-three!! Two-six!! One-two-three!! Two-seven!! One-two-three!! Two-eight!! One-two-three!! Two-niner!! One-two-three!! Three-zero!!"

"On your feet now!"

"Aye aye, Sir!!"

"Run-in-place!"

"Aye aye, Sir!!"

"Get them up!"

"Aye aye, Sir!!"

"On your faces!"

"Aye aye, Sir!!"
"On your backs!"
"Aye aye, Sir!!"
"On your faces!"
"Aye aye, Sir!!"
"On your backs!"
"Aye aye, Sir!!"
"On your feet!"
"On your faces!"
"Aye aye, Sir!!"
"On your backs!"
"Aye aye, Sir!!"
"On your feet!"
"Aye aye, Sir!!"
"Fall-in!"
"Aye aye, Sir!!"
"Ten-nine-eight-seven-six-three-two-one. Back in the grass."
"Aye aye, Sir!!"
"On your faces."
"Aye aye, Sir!!"
"Down-up."
"Zero-one!!"
"Down-up."
"Zero-two!!"
"Down-up."
"Zero-three!!"
"Down-up."
"Zero-four!!"
"Down-up."
"Zero-five!!"
"Down-up."
"Zero-six!!"
"Down-up."
"Zero-seven!!"
"Down-up."
"Zero-eight!!"
"Down-up."
"Zero-niner!!"
"Down-up."
"One-zero!!"
"Down-up."

"One-one!!"

"Down-up."

"One-two!!"

"Down-up."

"One-three!!"

"Down-up."

"One-four!!"

"Down-up"

"One-five!!"

"Fall in!"

"Aye aye, Sir!!"

"Ten-nine-eight-seven-five-two-one. Freeze!"

"Aye aye, Sir!!"

"Try it again, Pig. But this time as a Section Leader."

"Aye aye, Sir! Guide! Post the guide-on!"

"Aye aye, Section Leader!"

"Class Zero-Four-Zero-Zero! Upon receiving the command of execution *march*! You will! Half-step up this ladderwell! Perform an immediate column-left! And reform at the door!"

"Aye aye, Section Leader!!"

"Ready! March!"

"Aye aye, Section Leader!!"

"Your left-right! Left-right! Class Zero-Four-Zero-Zero! Ready! Halt!"

"Aye aye, Section Leader!!"

"Ready! Adjust!"

"Aye aye, Section Leader!! Discipline!! D!! I!! S!! C!! I!! P!! L!! I!! N!! E!! Discipline!! Is!! The unconditional!! Obedience-to-orders!! Respect-for-authority!! And self-reliance!! Freeze-candidate-freeze!!"

"Doorbody off the rear!"

"Doorbody, aye aye, Section Leader!!"

"Doorbody reporting as ordered, Section Leader!"

"Doorbody post!"

"Aye aye, Section Leader!"

"Doorbody! Report status of chow hall deck!"

"Aye aye, Section Leader! Chow hall deck not clear, Section Leader!"

"Chow hall deck not clear, Section Leader!!"

"Very well. Gougebody! Gouge the class!"

"Aye aye, Section Leader! Class Zero-Four-Zero-Zero! What is the mission of the Navy?"

"Gougebody!! The mission of the Navy is!! To maintain!! Train!! And equip!! Combat-ready naval forces capable of winning wars!! Deterring aggression!! And maintaining freedom of the seas!!"

"Class Zero-Four-Zero-Zero! What is the definition of undersea warfare?"

"Gougebody!! The definition of undersea warfare is!! Those actions taken to deny the enemy effective use of his submarines!! And the undersea environment!!"

"Class Zero-Four-Zero-Zero! What are the Navy's air-to-air missiles?"

"Gougebody!! The Navy's air-to-air missiles are!! The AMRAAM, the Advanced Medium Range Air-to-Air Missile!! The Sidewinder!! And the Sparrow!!"

"Class Zero-Four-Zero-Zero! What is the definition of littoral warfare?"

"Gougebody!! The definition of littoral warfare is!! Warfare in that portion of the world's land masses!! Adjacent to the oceans!! Within direct control of!! And vulnerable to!! The striking power of sea-based forces!!"

"Class Zero-Four-Zero-Zero! What is the naval tactical mission of electronic warfare?"

"Goubebody!! The naval tactical mission of electronic warfare is!! To deny the enemy effective use of the electromagnetic spectrum!!"

"Doorbody! Report status of chow hall deck!"

"Aye aye, Section Leader! Chow hall deck all clear, Section Leader!"

"Chow hall deck all clear, Section Leader!!"

"Doorbody, crack the door!"

"Aye aye, Section Leader!"

"Class Zero-Four-Zero-Zero, marching into chow!"

"Class Zero-Four-Zero-Zero, marching into chow!!"

"Column of files! From the right! Forward!"

"Stand fast."

"March!"

"Good morning, Sir!"

"Zero-two!"

"Zero-three!"

"Zero-four!"

"Zero-five!"

"Zero-six!"

"Zero-seven!"

"Zero-eight!"

"Zero-niner!"

"One-zero!"

"One-one!"

"One-two!"

"One-three!"

"One-four!"

"One-five!"

"One-six!"

"One-seven!"

"One-eight!"

"One-niner!"

"Two-zero!"

"Two-one!"

"Two-two!"

"Two-three!"

"Two-four!"

"Two-five!"

"Two-six!"

"Two-seven!"

"Two-eight!"

"Two-niner!"

"Three-zero!"

"Three-one!"

"Three-two!"

"Three-three!"

"Three-four!"

"Three-five!"

"Three-six!"

"Three-seven!"

"Three-eight!"

"Three-niner!"

"Four-zero!"

"Four-one!"

"Doorbody, close the door!"

"Aye aye, Section Leader!"

"Class Zero-Four-Zero-Zero, proceed!"

"Aye aye, Section Leader!!"

"Forward march!"

"Step freeze!!"

"Stand fast."

"Forward march!"
"Step freeze!!"
"Stand fast."
"Forward march!"
"Step freeze!!"
"Stand fast."
"Forward march!"
"Step freeze!!"
"Stand fast."
"Forward march!"
"Step freeze!!"
"Stand fast."
"Forward march!"
"Step freeze!!"
"Stand fast."
"Forward march!"
"Step freeze!!"
"Stand fast."
"Forward march!"
"Step freeze!!"
"Stand fast."
"Forward march!"
"Step freeze!!"
"Stand fast."
"Forward march!"
"Stand fast."
"Forward march!"
"Step freeze!!"
"Stand fast."
"Forward march!"
"Step freeze!!"
"Stand fast."
"Forward march!"
"Step freeze!!"
"Stand fast."
"Forward march!"
"Step freeze!!"
"Stand fast."
"Forward march!"
"Step freeze!!"
"Stand fast."

"Forward march!"

"Step freeze!!"

"Stand fast."

"Forward march!"

"Step freeze!!"

"Stand fast."

"Forward march!"

"Step freeze!!"

"Stand fast."

"Forward march!"

"Stand fast."

"Forward march!"

"Step freeze!!"

"Stand fast."

"Forward march!"

"Step freeze!!"

"Stand fast."

"Forward march!"

"Step freeze!!"

"Stand fast."

"Forward march!"

"Step freeze!!"

"Stand fast."

"Forward march!"

"Step freeze!!"

"Stand fast."

"Forward march!"

"Step freeze!!"

"Stand fast."

"Forward march!"

"Step freeze!!"

"Stand fast."

"Forward march!"

"Step freeze!!"

"Stand fast."

The last set of Candidates passes through the Chow line.

"Good afternoon, Ma'am."

"Good afternoon, Darling. What'll it be?"

"The roast beef please, Ma'am. Potatoes. And broccoli, please. And a roll please, Ma'am."

"Here you are. Enjoy."

"Thank you, Ma'am."

I square away my tray.

"Put it away, Class Zero-Four-Zero-Zero!"

"Aye aye, Section Leader!!"

"Class Zero-Four-Zero-Zero! These tables! Both sides! Ready! Seats!"

"Kill!!"

"Adjust!"

"Kill!!"

"Pray at will!"

"Ready! Eat!"

....

Service Khakis

Occasions for wear. Worn in summer or winter for office work, watchstanding, liberty or business as when prescribed as uniform of the day.

Shirt. Made of authorized fabric, with short-sleeves, two breast pockets with button flaps, and an open collar forming a V-neck. Shirts button to the right.

Trousers. Made of authorized fabric with fore and aft creases, belt loops, zippered fly front closure, and two side and back pockets. May be straight legged or slightly flared. The shirt and trousers fabric must match (i.e. poly/cotton with poly/cotton, C.N.T. with C.N.T. and poly/wool with poly/wool).

Correct wear. Button all buttons, close all fasteners, and wear a belt through all loops. Trousers shall hang approximately two inches from the floor at the back of the shoe. Trousers should be tailored to include a two inch hem to provide material for adjustments. Wear the belt buckle so that the belt clip end touches the left side of the buckle.

Align the right side of the buckle with the opening of the shirt and opening of the fly, forming a straight line.

Summer Whites

Occasions for wear. Worn in summer for office work, watchstanding, liberty, or business ashore when prescribed as the Uniform of the Day.

Shirt. Made of plain white authorized fabric, with short-sleeves, two breast pockets with button flaps, and an open collar forming a V-neck. Worn with hard shoulder board straps. Collar points measure no longer than three and one-quarter inches with a medium spread.

Trousers. Made of authorized white fabric with fore and aft creases, belt loops, zippered fly front closure, and two side and back pockets. May be straight legged or slightly flared. The trousers and shirt or service dress white coat fabric must match.

Correct wear. Button all buttons, close all fasteners, wear appropriate hard shoulder boards and put the belt through all loops. Trousers shall hang approximately two inches from the floor at the back of the shoe. Trousers should be tailored to include a two inch hem to provide material for adjustments. Wear the belt buckle so that the belt clip end touches the left side of the buckle. Align the right side of the buckle with the opening of the shirt and opening of the fly, forming a straight line.

••

"Everyone up on the bleachers. There you go. Good morning, folks."

"Good morning, Sir."

"Are we missing anybody? Got anyone med down today?"

"All present, all accounted for, Sir."

"Perfect. Are we ready, people?"

"Yes, Sir."

"Sure now?"

"Yes, Sir."

"Relax. We've trained for this. I want everyone to join me in a deep breath. One. Two. Three. Deep breath. One more. One. Two. Three. Deep breath. That's right. So where were we? Ah yes. The internationally known and locally respected Third Class Swim Test for the World's Greatest Navy designed to determine if you can stay afloat without the use of a personal flotation device in open water long enough to be rescued in a man-overboard situation. I sure hope that's just tired faces. If anyone has any questions, any questions or concerns at this point, now is the time to ask. Anything at all? There will be no surprises. This is not a rescue swimmer test. This is not Buds training. Each and everyone one of you is prepared to successfully complete this test. Remain calm. Remember the techniques. Don't forget to breathe."

"Aye aye, Sir."

"As always, your safety is our number-one priority. Hyperventilation to achieve underwater swimming endurance can result in shallow water blackout and is naturally strictly prohibited. This test will be carefully monitored by myself, as your Basic Swimming and Water Survival Instructor, and A.W.-Two Bowie, as your lifeguard. A.W.-Two Bowie is a qualified Navy Rescue Swimmer with eight SAR rescues to his name. I'm talking jumping out of helicopters into open ocean. Eight. The same A.W.-Two Bowie who will be in the water with you at all times this morning. Needless to say, you are in good hands. Do not confuse this test with the rest of your training. This is a swim test designed to make sure you have the necessary rudimentary swimming skills required for a worst case scenario out in the Fleet. We are not grading you. You will not fail this evolution. In the event that you do not pass this test, you will not roll directly to G.T.X. You will not be kicked out of O.C.S. because you can't swim. You will not have to join the Army. All it means it that you'll show up at the pool afterhours and do some remedial. We'll have you up to speed in no time. I've been here one and a half years. A Candidate rolling to the next class or facing an A.R.B. is extremely rare. Extremely rare. In other words, there is absolutely no need for desperation or heroics in an attempt to stay with your class this morning. Make sense?"

"Yes, Sir."

"Bottom line, folks. A.W.-Two Bowie or myself will step in and terminate individual participation in timed events and tests if we feel there is a question of safety or you need additional coaching. Anytime a student shows signs of panic, fear, extreme fatigue or lack of confidence, we have been trained and it is our responsibility to intervene. This is for your safety. Do not protest the decision. Do not argue the decision. That decision is an order. Is that clear?"

"Yes, Sir."

"Quick note on Training Time Outs or D.O.Rs. Swim Tests are voluntary. You have the option to individually request termination of testing. Any time you make a statement such as *I quit* or *D.O.R.* or words to that effect, you shall be

immediately removed from the testing environment. A T.T.O. may also be called by any student or instructor in any training situation where they are concerned for their own or another's safety, or they request clarification of procedures or requirements. T.T.O. is also an appropriate means to obtain relief if you experience pain, heat stress, or other serious physical discomfort. The purpose of the T.T.O. is to correct the situation of concern, provide clarifying information, or remove the test participant or tester from the possible hazardous environment. A T.T.O. may be signaled with the words *time out*, crossed hands in a *T*, or a *raised clenched fist*. Or, really, any sign of visible distress. We will attempt to relieve and remove you from the possible hazardous environment. If this is not practical, testing will be stopped until the situation is corrected. You will not be coerced or threatened to return to testing following removal, be it for a T.T.O. or D.O.R. Any questions? Any questions at all? Again, now is the time to ask. Good. Make sense?"

"Yes, Sir."

"Now for the substance. You will complete two modules this morning. Module one is composed of three separate events. A fifty yard swim using any stroke, a five minute prone float and a deep water jump. Module two consists of shirt and trouser or coverall inflation. You know the drill. Shirts and trousers. You will first be instructed to stay at the surface by inflating your shirt with our bubble of air. You will then be instructed to remove your trousers and create your very own personal flotation device. Again, we've trained for this. Easy manizzee. Down off of the bleachers. Let's stretch it out."

"Aye aye, Sir."

"Side to side. One. Two. Three. Four. Five. Six. Seven. Eight. Nine. Ten. Eleven. Twelve. Thirteen. Fourteen. Fifteen. Sixteen. Seventeen. Eighteen. Nineteen. Twenty. Triceps. Left side. One. Two. Three. Four. Five. Six. Seven. Eight. Nine. Ten. Eleven. Twelve. Thirteen. Fourteen. Fifteen. Sixteen. Seventeen. Eighteen. Nineteen. Twenty. Switch. One. Two. Three. Four. Five. Six. Seven. Eight. Nine. Ten. Eleven. Twelve. Thirteen. Fourteen. Fifteen. Sixteen. Seventeen. Eighteen. Nineteen. Twenty. Posterior shoulder. Left side. One. Two. Three. Four. Five. Six. Seven. Eight. Nine. Ten. Eleven. Twelve. Thirteen. Fourteen. Fifteen. Sixteen. Seventeen. Eighteen. Nineteen. Twenty. Switch over. One. Two. Three. Four. Five. Six. Seven. Eight. Nine. Ten. Eleven. Twelve. Thirteen. Fourteen. Fifteen. Sixteen. Seventeen. Eighteen. Nineteen. Twenty. Quadriceps. Left quad. One. Two. Three. Four. Five. Six. Seven. Eight. Nine. Ten. Eleven. Twelve. Thirteen. Fourteen. Fifteen. Sixteen. Seventeen. Eighteen. Nineteen. Twenty. Your right. One. Two. Three. Four. Five. Six. Seven. Eight. Nine. Ten. Eleven. Twelve. Thirteen. Fourteen. Fifteen. Sixteen. Seventeen. Eighteen. Nineteen. Twenty. Groin. To the left. One. Two. Three. Four. Five. Six. Seven. Eight. Nine. Ten. Eleven. Twelve. Thirteen. Fourteen.

Fifteen. Sixteen. Seventeen. Eighteen. Nineteen. Twenty. To the right. One. Two. Three. Four. Five. Six. Seven. Eight. Nine. Ten. Eleven. Twelve. Thirteen. Fourteen. Fifteen. Sixteen. Seventeen. Eighteen. Nineteen. Twenty. And center. One. Two. Three. Four. Five. Six. Seven. Eight. Nine. Ten. Eleven. Twelve. Thirteen. Fourteen. Fifteen. Sixteen. Seventeen. Eighteen. Nineteen. Twenty. Stretch your calves. Touch your toes. One. Two. Three. Four. Five. Six. Seven. Eight. Nine. Ten. Eleven. Twelve. Thirteen. Fourteen. Fifteen. Sixteen. Seventeen. Eighteen. Nineteen. Twenty.

Alright, let's do this. Make it happen. Everyone ready?"

"Yes, Sir."

"I mean it. Everyone ready?"

"Yes, Sir."

"Spirit, folks."

"Yes, Sir."

"That's what I like to hear. Everyone in the pool."

"Aye aye, Sir."

"This is your fifty yard swim. Fifty yards without stopping, standing or holding onto the sides of the pool. Breast stroke, side stroke, back stroke or the crawl. All are acceptable. A.W.-Two will demonstrate. Breast stroke. Start and glide position is facedown and streamlined with the waist straight, legs together and extended, and arms stretched in front of the head with palms approximately six to eight inches below the surface. Head is positioned with the ears between the upper-arms and the waterline near the hairline. Starting from the glide position, angle the hands slightly downward, turning the palms outward about forty-five degrees to the water's surface. With the arms straight, the palms are sculled out until the hands are positioned wider than the shoulders. From this position, bend the elbows and pull with the hands downward and outward until they pass under the elbows with forearms vertical, into your power phase. And recover. And glide. Don't forget to kick. Out of the glide, bring your heels up towards your rear. And kick like a frog back to the glide. Bottom line. What I'm looking for is your body face down. Any arm stroke acceptable as long as recovery and propulsion occurs underwater. Any kick is acceptable as long as recovery and propulsion occurs underwater and with the ability to lift the head up, get a breath, and return the face into the water with each arm stroke. Any coordination of arms, legs and breathing is acceptable. Any questions? Last call. How's everybody feeling?"

"Outstanding, Sir."

"Good. Side stroke. Can be on the left or right, whatever feels more natural. During the glide, the head, back and legs are straight with the legs fully extended and together with the toes pointed. Bottom arm is extended in front of the swimmer parallel to the surface with the palm down, in line with the body, a few

inches below the surface of the water. The top arm is fully extended aft with the hand above the thigh. The head lies with your face just high enough to clear the mouth and nose above the water. Recover the top arm by drawing the forearm along the body until the hand is approximately in front of the shoulder of the bottom arm. During the power phase, push the top hand downward slightly and then aft, close to the side of the body, as it returns to the glide position. The kick is called the scissors kick because the legs separate fore and aft, on one plane, well, like a pair of scissors. The recovery of both legs begins after the glide position by flexing slightly at the hips, bending the knees, and drawing the heels slowly towards the buttocks. Keep your knees close together. Don't let the feet pass each other and keep the toes pointed to streamline during the glide. Bottom line, for our purposes today, any arm stroke is acceptable as long as recovery and propulsion occurs underwater. Any kick is acceptable as long as recovery and propulsion occurs underwater. Any coordination between arms and legs is acceptable. Just make it happen. Won't nickel and dime you out there. Good stuff?"

"Yes, Sir."

"Alright. Now the backstroke. Body is face up in a near horizontal position with the back of the head resting in the water. Waist is straight, hips and thighs near the surface slightly lower than the head and shoulders, and the arms extended along the body with palms against the thighs. Legs are fully extended with the toes pointed. Beginning from the glide position with arms at sides, bend the elbows and draw both hands up towards the shoulders as if drawing a line along both sides of the torso with the thumbnails. Keep hands and arms just below the surface of the water. Continue to draw the hands along the sides of the body until they reach the armpits. From the armpits, point the fingers outward from the shoulders with palms facing back toward the feet. With fingers leading, extend the arms out sideward until the hands reach upward no farther than the top of the head. Palms and the inside of the arms push aft in a broad sweeping motion, elbows straight or slightly bent, returning arms to the glide position. And back into the power phase. For the legs, beginning from the glide position with legs together and extended, while keeping the waist straight, bend the knees and drop the heels downward. This forces the knees spread apart about as wide as the hips. The next motion is to rotate the knees inward, without spreading them wider, placing the heels to a point under and outside the knees. Flex the ankles and turn the feet outward to position for the catch. And kick. And kick. And kick. And kick. Bottom line, folks, is on your back. Any arm stroke is acceptable as long as recovery and propulsion occurs underwater. And any kick is acceptable. Everyone got it? Sure?"

"Yes, Sir."

"And finally, the Leroy Brown of strokes. The crawl. Body is prone, near

horizontal, and chest down. Depending on buoyancy, head should be positioned with the waterline between the eyebrows and hairline. Legs are extended aft, feet together, toes pointed, held just below the surface. Note the body roll. Rotation is at or around the midline extending along the whole body. Arms work alternately, but not completely opposite of each other, as the recovering arm starts to catch up with the stroking arm at the end of the recovery, generating most of the propulsion. Like an S, see? Hand enters into the water in front of the shoulder, index finger first, with the entire arm rotated in such that the thumb is turned down. The elbow should be kept higher than the rest of the arm and should enter the water last. But don't drag yourself through the water. Legs kick up and down in a flutter kick or with the heels just breaking the surface of the water and the legs rolling with the body. Bottom line for today. You must be face down. Any arm action where one arm pulls while the other arm recovers is acceptable. Any kick or no kick is acceptable. You must display continuous ability to lift your head up to get a good breath, face returning into the water. Any coordination among arms, legs and breathing is acceptable. How about a round of applause for A.W.-Two! Sweet stroke. Good stuff, right?"

"Yes, Sir."

"Fifty yards using one or all of these strokes. Got it? We're going to work this in groups of five. Ten meters between swimmers, twenty meters between groups. Follow the markers around the pool. You may pass the swimmer in front of you, but do not get tangled up. The quickest way out of the pool, even for you Olympians out there. You get tangled, out you come. Alright, line it up along the side. You know the drill."

"Aye aye, Sir."

"Ready. Begin."

The whistle sounds.

"Clear."

"Clear."

"Clear."

"Clear."

"Clear."

"Clear."

"Clear."

"Clear."

"Clear."

"Clear."

"Clear."

"Clear."

"Clear."

"Clear."

"Clear."

"Clear."

"Clear."

"Clear."

"Clear."

A steady crawl takes me around the pool. I pull out wide to avoid traffic. The class regroups in the shallows.

"You're good."

"You're good."

"You're good."

"You're good."

"You're good."

"You're good."

"You're good. You okay, there?"

"Yes, Sir."

"You're good."

"You're good."

"You're good."

"You're good."

"You're good."

"You're good."

"You're good."

"You're good."

"You're good."

"You're good."

"You're good."

"You're good."

"You're good. And we're good. Great job, everyone. Not necessarily pretty all round, but it'll get her done. Alright, let's keep this moving. Gather round. Ears."

"Open, Sir."

"Absolutely love that. Next up. Prone float. For review. A.W.-Two will demonstrate. The prone float is face down in the water, chin at chest, with the back of the head just breaking the surface. Upper back and shoulders are underwater, horizontal to the surface. Arms are at the surface with the elbows bent and hands separated slightly. Waist is bent with hips underwater, lower than the upper body, and the legs dangling beneath. Remember to keep that chin tucked but also to come up for air when you need it. That could be important. Pivot at the neck, lifting the chin off the chest until the mouth clears the surface. As the mouth clears the surface, exhale quickly and forcefully through the mouth and nose. If you're having trouble with buoyancy, use the modified frog kick,

getting back up to the surface. Once you have a good clean exchange of air, return to the resting position, chin on the chest, and back to the prone float. Thank you, A.W.-Two! Your mission is to maintain the prone float for five minutes, staying near or at the surface at all times. Safe. Calm. And relaxed. Any face down posture is acceptable. Any arm action or leg action is acceptable, as long as your position remains static. You must inhale from the mouth and exhale from the mouth and nose. Breathlessness, gasping, erratic breathing or swallowing water is unacceptable. You know what happens next. Questions? Alright. Over to the deep end. Space it out. Very good. Five minutes. Listen to my voice. Break at the whistle."

"Aye aye, Sir."

"Ready? Ready? Begin."

I bob on the surface in the dead man float.

"Four minutes!"

"Three minutes!"

"Two minutes remaining! Steady! Careful of forward or backward movement! No swimming, people!"

"One minute! Steady!"

"Thirty seconds!"

"Twenty!"

"Ten! Nine! Eight! Seven! Six! Five! Four! Three! Two! One! Everyone up! Up! Someone grab that guy, tell him drill's over. Make sure he's alive. Over to the side. Out of the pool, over to the bleachers. Good job everyone. Give yourselves a pat on the back. Almost through with Module One. I'll give you a minute to catch your breath. How's that?"

"Good, Sir."

"Is everyone feeling fine? Is there anyone who does not feel fine? Going once. Going twice. Alright. We're going to take a small detour now, saving our big jump for the end. Right now, I need you to grab a pair of dungarees and combat boots. Take your time."

I select a large pair of dungarees off of the rack. The extra large pair of workboots slides on with ease.

"Everyone set? Great. Back in the pool. You know the drill. A.W.-Two will demonstrate. You will unlace and remove your boots, one at a time. Once the boots are off, go to your survival float. Remove the trousers keeping the legs right side out. Tie the two legs together using a square or overhand knot. Do not forget to tie the knot as close to the end of the trouser legs as possible. More float for your buck. Start by tying the first half of the knot about halfway down the legs. Tie the second half near the end of the legs then place the cuffs between your teeth and cinch up the knot by pulling on the middle of the trouser legs. Anyone not with me? Alright. Once you have a good tight knot, it's time for

inflation. I don't care how you get there. You got the over the head method. Treading water, place trousers on the surface in back of you, fly open and facing down, waist open with the seat facing up. Got it? With one hand on the top of the waistband on each side of the fly, raise the trousers straight over the head by straightening the arms. Once the trousers are out of the water, quickly bring them down in front of you until the waistband is underwater. Quickly. But not like a crazy person. Remember the trick here is a good kick, getting the trousers high enough to force air into the waist on the way down. And control. Clear?"

"Yes, Sir."

"Or remember there's the splash technique. Treading water or in a side-stroke, place trousers on the surface of the water in front of you, fly facing down. Place one hand on the waistband and hold it about two inches underwater. Two inches. Just below the surface. Raise the other hand above the surface and with a sweeping motion splash air into the trousers. Oral inflation is fine too, but careful not to drink the Kool-Aid. Spread the trousers on the surface in front of you with the fly closed and facing down. Hold the waistband open using both hands. Take a breath and submerge, placing the waistband on the forehead. Blow into the trousers until full. Watch carefully. Here we go. Easy as it looks. Once we have our nice sack of air, carefully remove the belt and put it through the center loop in back of the trousers. Alright? With the fly facing towards you, careful with the cinch, put your head through the opening between the legs. Wrap the belt around your waist and secure it. And you're done. Lay back, relax and float the seconds away until rescue or landfall. Move at a deliberate pace. Breathe at a normal pace. The longer you tread, the greater the risk of exhaustion. Quicker you get those boots off, the quicker you can move on to the trousers. The quicker the trousers, the quicker you can move to inflation. Keep your head above water as much as possible. The longer you stay under, the greater the risk of C.O.-Two build up and oxygen depletion. Five minutes. Everyone ready?"

"Yes, Sir."

"To the deep end. On the count of three. Ready. One. Two. Three. Start the problem, start the clock!"

My boots sink to the bottom of the pool. The trousers inflate on the third try. Candidates splash around me. I lean back for buoyancy.

"Four minutes!"

"Three minutes!"

"Two minutes!"

"One minute!"

"Thirty seconds!"

"Ten seconds!"

"Five! Four! Three! Two! One! And you're clear! Out of the pool!"

"Aye aye, Sir."

"Good job, everyone. We are almost there. Hard part's over. Congratulations. Now, I know some of you may be experiencing some anxiety for this next part. Fear of heights is a normal thing. But rest assured, if you follow my instructions, this right here is the easiest part of your day. Heck, it'll be the easiest part of your week. How's that sound, folks? Good. Outstanding?"

"Yes, Sir."

"Say again?"

"Yes, Sir."

"That's more like it. You will be jumping off the ten meter platform. So easy, we save it for last. Follow procedure. Stand erect and look at the horizon. Using your right or left hand, pinch your nose with the thumb and forefinger and cup your chin in the palm with the little finger anchored under the chin. Tuck the right or left elbow close to the body. Reach across with the other hand over the top of the right or left arm and grab the biceps of the right or left arm or clothing near the shoulder. Tuck the elbow close to the body. Step off. Do not jump. Immediately after stepping off, cross the legs at the ankles. Keep the body vertical by continuing to look at the horizon. Do not attempt to slow the downward momentum by uncrossing arms or legs. Maintain this position after impact with the water and all downward motion stops. When downward momentum stops, orient yourself and immediately swim away from the impact area, exit the pool and head on back here. I'll be up on the platform. A.W.-Two will be monitoring the jumps down in pool. He will give the all clear for each jump. Trick is not to think about it, folks. Line it up."

"Aye aye, Sir."

"All clear!"

"Next!"

"All clear!"

"Next!"

"All clear!"

"Next!"

"All clear!"

"Next!"

"All clear!"

"Next!"

"All clear!"

"Next!"

"All clear!"

"Next!"

"All clear!"

"Next!"

"All clear!"

"Next!"

"All clear!"

"Next!"

"All clear!"

"Next!"

"All clear!"

"Next!"

"All clear!"

"Next!"

"All clear!"

"Next!"

"All clear!"

"Next!"

I climb up the metal ladder to the platform. Fortunato clears the landing area below.

"Ready?"

"Yes, Sir."

"Straight waist. Head up, eyes staring forward. Arms crossed. Nose pinched. Other armed wrapped across the chest. Legs straight and crossed at the ankles."

"Will do, Sir."

"All clear!"

"All clear. Off you go."

Space drops out from beneath me. Water rushes past my ears. I kick hard to the surface.

"All clear!"

Service Dress Blues

Occasions for wear. May be prescribed for wear year-round to all official functions when formal dress, dinner dress or full dress uniforms are not prescribed and civilian equivalent dress is coat and tie.

Coat. A double-breasted coat made of authorized navy blue fabric with three outside pockets, one on each hip and one on the left breast, and three thirty-five line Navy eagle gilt buttons down each forefront. Officer's coat has a sword slit over the left hip. Button all buttons.

Trousers. Made of plain, authorized blue fabric with fore and aft creases, belt loops, zippered fly front closure, and two side and back pockets. May be either straight legged or slightly flared. Fabric of trousers must match the uniform coat/shirt worn.

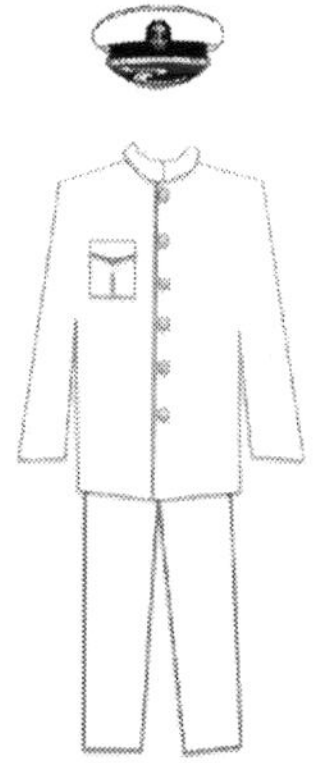

Service Dress Whites

Occasions for wear. May be prescribed for summer wear when formal dress, dinner dress, or full dress uniforms are not prescribed and civilian equivalent is coat and tie.

Coat. A single-breasted, standing collar coat made of authorized plain white, lightweight fabric, two breast patch pockets with pointed button down flaps fastened by detachable twenty-two one-half line Navy eagle gilt buttons, and five detachable thirty-five line Navy eagle gilt buttons on right front. Officer's coat has sword slit over left hip and loops for shoulder boards. Button all buttons and fasten the collar.

Trousers. Made of authorized white fabric with fore and aft creases, belt loops, zippered fly front closure, and two side and back pockets. May be straight legged or slightly flared. The trousers and shirt or service dress white coat fabric must match.

•••••••••••••••••••••••••••••••••••••••

"Attention on deck, stand-by."

"Good afternoon, Sir."

"As you were. Well? Where were we?"

"Basic ship handling, Chief."

"Thank you, Shipmate. Let's see. Four-decimal-two dash one. As a reminder, our terminal objective, partially supported by this lesson topic, is the ability to demonstrate knowledge of the duties of a newly commissioned Officer by identifying the basic tasks, procedures, roles and other related functions that allow for safe movement and operation of a ship on the high seas and in restricted waters. Everyone onboard?"

"Yes, Chief."

"Arriving. Now before we get started, some of you, especially you Mustangs, may be wondering where, as your Seamanship instructor, my pin ran off to. I did earn it. And I wore it on everything from Small Boys to carriers. I can assure you, when they took my pin away, it wasn't for no three balls. No, Sir. Sometimes in the Navy, and I want you to remember this when you put on your bars, you can find yourself in a pickle. Even the best of you. Some choose to pass the buck. Others eat the buck. I'll leave it at that. Does that work for you, Shipmates?"

"Yes, Chief."

"Good. Our enabling objectives for this lesson topic are the ability, one, to define course, speed, steerageway, pivot point, turning circle, advance, transfer, tactical diameter, final diameter, standard tactical diameter, and reduced tactical diameter. Two, list the controllable forces in ship handling. Three, state the two forces imparted to a ship by its fixed or controllable pitch propeller or propellers. Four, describe the relationship between the rotation of a ship's propeller or propellers and the production of thrust and side force for single and twin propeller ships. Five, state the four main factors contributing the effectiveness of a ship's rudder. Six, list the non-controllable forces in ship handling. And, seven, last but certainly not least, describe methods to overcome non-controllable forces in ship handling. Now not all of you will be ship handlers. Heck, some of you may never even get your sea legs. But all of you must pass this test. And some of you may not pass this test on the first try. So pay close attention, Shipmates. I will highlight what you need to know. Highlight. Everyone onboard?"

"Yes, Chief."

"Ready? Good. Now, the prerequisites to becoming a competent ship handler include an understanding of the forces that influence ship movement and the ability to use those forces to your advantage. Any ship handler must know the maneuvering characteristics of his ship, the effects of propellers and rudders and the effects of various sea and wind conditions. This comes with some basic terminology for seamanship. *Course*. The horizontal direction of travel through

water. Highlight. Course is expressed in angular units from a reference direction, either true or magnetic north, from zero degrees at the reference direction clockwise to three hundred and sixty degrees. Note that three-sixty and zero represent the same direction. North. However, highlight, due north is always, always expressed as zero degrees at the zero-zero-zero. Questions? No? Good. *Speed.* Speed, highlight, is the rate of travel of a ship through the water in knots. Not miles per hour, not kilometers per hour, not leagues per hour, but knots. One knot, highlight, is one nautical mile per hour. Do not confuse miles and nautical miles. One's got nothing to do with the other, other than each is a measurement unit for distance. When I'm talking nautical miles, I'm talking the unit of length corresponding approximately to one minute of arc of latitude along any meridian, eighteen hundred and fifty-two meters, six thousand and seventy-six feet. Don't think linear distance from A to B, think chart on a globe. Questions at this point? I know this is like drinking out of a fire house. Yes? In the back."

"Chief, what does that translate to in miles?"

"One nautical mile?"

"Yes, Chief."

"Now, like I said, careful not to get caught up in thinking regular old miles out at sea and trying to do the math. Understood?"

"Yes, Chief."

"One nautical mile we're talking one-point-one-five, give or take, thumb to the wind, good old Landlubber miles. But don't hold me to that. Better not to make the conversion. Put it out of your mind. Not the kind of math you want to be doing when the Skipper asks you to chart a course. Anyone else? Great. Next basic term for seamanship. *Steerageway.* Steerageway is the slowest speed at which a ship can proceed without losing directional control. In other words, if you're not moving, you're drifting. Steerageway varies naturally with wind, sea state and ship type. You'll get different steerageway for a Small Boy than you will for an aircraft carrier. Different animals. Different weights. Different hull structures. Same holds true for the *pivot point*, the point about which a ship turns, changes directions, pivots. The pivot point, highlight folks, is located approximately one-third of the length of the ship away from the bow. And where is the bow located, Shipmates? Forward or aft?"

"Forward."

"Just making sure. So the pivot point will be towards the fore of the ship, right? One-third of the way aft or two-thirds of the way forward. At any given point during your turn, you have a given pivot point. Add them all up and you get, highlight, a *turning circle*, defined as the path followed by the pivot point of a ship while making a turn of three hundred and sixty degrees or more. Pretty straightforward up to this point, right? Here's where it gets slightly more

interesting. No laughing at my artistic skills, alright? Alright?"

"Yes, Chief."

"This is our ship, the U.S.S. Man O' War. A real beauty. Looks like a cruiser to me. She's on a course of zero-nine-zero at a speed of let's say thirty knots. Just cruising along. The Captain orders a change course from zero-nine-zero to due north, a ninety degree turn. What's the course, Shipmates?"

"Zero-zero-zero."

"Bravo Zulu, Shipmates. Our U.S.S. Man O' War begins her pivot. Pivot. Pivot. Pivot. Growing into a turning circle. You'll note her *advance*, highlight, the distance gained in the direction of the original course while turning. Let's go ahead and plot out our original course, along the zero-nine-zero, her phantom path for what might have been. There we go. Beautiful. Alright. Back to the Man O' War, who continues on her turning circle. And pivot. Pivot. Pivot. You can see she is still gaining towards her original direction, only turning away. With our compass we can now trace out the turning circle to the zero-zero-zero. There we go. Pretty good if I do say so myself, Shipmates. Should be fairly intuitive. Everyone on the same page? Let me know. Don't be shy. I'm not the one taking this test. If I lose you now, next couple days are going to seem real long. For us all."

"Chief."

"Yes. Shipmate in the back."

"For the advance, Chief, how do you measure it? From what point?"

"Great question. Don't want to drift too far into Navigation, which we'll be tackling soon enough, but she's moving along, with minimum steerageway, remember? Controlling her own destiny. Captain has ordered a change of course to true north from the zero-nine-zero. Now we know that had she not changed course, she would have just continued down her original course, far as the eye can see, right? You with me so far? But now she starts turning, using her rudder. Takes a little while, but you can see her settle into her turning circle. See? All the way to true north. Right? Now imagine the Captain decides, for whatever reason not to straighten out that rudder, maintaining our turning circle. Drawing it out, she starts to turn away, following the circular course dictated by a steady rudder. Makes sense, right? What you would expect."

"Yes, Chief."

"Note the *maximum advance*, calculated as the distance gained in the direction of the original course while turning, or, better yet in plain English, the maximum way in the direction our Man O' War would have gone had the Captain not decided to change course. You can see that at every pivot point, she has a corresponding point of advance. By the time she gets to the turn, ninety degrees, you have your corresponding point of maximum advance. Any point past it, along the circle, you start coming back, right? And the advance starts shrinking.

We want the max. Does that answer your question?"

"Yes, Chief."

"Which brings us to *transfer*. Transfer is the distance gained at right angles to the original course when turning. What are we talking here? As the Man O' War advances, she also starts heading into her turning circle. See? The further into the turn, the greater the distance gained at the right angle. All the way to the ninety degree turn, the transfer for a ninety degree turn. Clear as mud? So, what happens if you stay in the turn? Running the compass all the way around, you start to see a circle. Right? Now it can't be perfect, at least from the Man O' War's original turning point, right? That's because of the time it takes to get into the turning circle. Called a *tactical diameter*. Highlight, folks. Otherwise known as the distance along the perpendicular between the original course of a ship and the opposite, reciprocal, course of the Man O' War after making a turn of a hundred and eighty degrees with a constant rudder angle. Here to here. See? Should she continue on, however, note that the turn will finish in a perfect circular path with a *final diameter*, highlight, defined as the diameter of a circle that would ultimately be carved by a ship turning through three hundred and sixty degrees with a constant rudder angle. She'll keep cutting that circle until she runs out of fuel. Got it, Shipmates? A perfect circle. See?"

"Yes, Chief."

"In the Fleet you'll work with a *standard tactical diameter* of fifteen degrees. Highlight. Highlight. Highlight. This is the turning distance prescribed for use by all ships in a formation so that all will turn together, avoiding the risk of collision or disarray in formation. The Captain may also call for a *reduced tactical diameter*, used for emergency turns obtained by going full rudder, roughly thirty degrees. Standard. Fifteen. Emergency. Thirty. Got it, folks?"

"Yes, Chief."

"Think fast. What is the definition of advance? Anyone. Officer Candidate Lin."

"The distance gained in the direction of the original course while turning, Chief."

"Now with the student guide closed."

"The distance gained in the direction of the original course while turning, Chief."

"So in our original example, what was the Man O' War's original course?"

"Zero-nine-zero, Chief."

"And at what point did she reach her maximum advance?"

"At zero-nine-zero, Chief."

"Bravo Zulu, Shipmate. Definition of transfer. Officer Candidate Macpherson."

"Distance gained at right angles to the original course when turning, Chief."

"Closed book. Now in English."

"It's the distance between the original course and the ship measured at a right angle."

"Very good. Everyone follow? True or false? The tactical diameter is larger than the final diameter. Mura."

"True."

"Very good. There you have it. We've highlighted course, speed, steerageway, pivot point, turning circle, advance, transfer, tactical diameter and final diameter. My advice. Be able to recognize these definitions and understand how these terms relate. Fair enough?"

"Yes, Chief."

"Good. Word to the wise. Seamanship is as much an art as it is a science. These are just your basic terms. You also will need to develop an understanding of speed, distance and time in ship handling. All forces that you can and will be expected to control. Ship's engines can be used to control *speed.* Ahead two-thirds. Ahead one-third. Back one-third. Back two-thirds. Back full. Back emergency. What have you. And so on and so forth, at least on the older ships. Some of the dials have changed. You'll get familiarized during your time on the Y.Ps. You also have your *rudder.* Your second controllable force, used to turn the ship as a result of the force imparted to the ship due to water pressure affecting the rudder surface. Seeing dazed looks. Let me try it this way. When a rudder is put over, a greater portion of its surface area hits the water flowing past it. This increased pressure against the rudder pushes the stern in one direction and the bow in the opposite direction about the pivot point, turning the ship. In one direction or the other. Reasonable enough, right?"

"Yes, Chief."

"Great. Now there are four main factors listed in your student manual that contribute to rudder effectiveness I should highlight. Rudder *location*, *angle*, and *size*, as well as the ship's *speed* through the water. Location. Angle. Size. Speed. I was taught to remember it by *LASS*. Over to you."

"Location. Angle. Size. Speed."

"*Location. Angle. Size. Speed.*"

"Location. Angle. Size. Speed."

"Bravo Zulu, Shipmates. The third controllable force in ship handling is with the propellers. Ships may have one, two or four propellers. Highlight. One, two or four. Not three. Not five. *One, two* or *four.*"

"One, two or four."

"They tend to develop a biting edge, which is dependent on their pitch, the distance a propeller travels through the water per one revolution. Make sense? Simple matter of physics, see? Up. Down. Up. Down. Well, at least with controllable reversible pitch. Note the angle of inclination of the blades from the

plane that lies perpendicular to the shaft that drives the propeller. What you're looking at is two forces, *thrust* and *side force.* Thrust, highlight, is the primary propeller force, coming from the force imparted to the ship as a result of the water flow created by the turning props moving the ship ahead or astern. This is just stepping on the gas, why we have props in the first place. Got it? Okay. Second type of force you get from props, highlight, is *side force.* Side force is the force imparted to a ship as a result of blade rotation, which tends to move the stern sideways. *Stern to starboard.* Highlight. Is that clear enough? We're moving quickly, I know, but I don't want to turn this into SWO school. I'm trusting you folks either know something about boats, or did your homework. If you don't, speak now or forever hold your peace."

"Chief."

"Officer Candidate Zurich. A Landlubber."

"Not quite clear on side force, Chief. Side-force is something you can actually control?"

"Yes and no. I see what you're saying, Shipmate. Think of it this way. Thrust is what you really control. That's your moneymaker. But it's not like a jet engine. As your prop starts turning, it tries to move the stern of the ship in the direction of its rotation, caused by the interaction of the propeller wash with the rudders and hull structure. See? Stands to reason your side force is practically negligible when a ship is moving at a steady speed. We're talking above bare steerageway. Gets drowned out. But you do have to keep it in mind when a ship has little or no way going, especially in traffic, when it really matters. If you're a skilled ship handler, you're using it to your advantage. Right? In or out of port. Least you don't want to forget about it. But, yes, side-force is really more of a secondary effect, like a wheel, see? Interaction of the propeller wash with the rudders and hull structure. Fair enough?"

"Thanks, Chief."

"Alright. Where were we? Are we onto mooring lines? Yes, indeed. *Mooring lines.* So we've talked about our main controllable forces, out there on the open ocean. Thing is, you're in the open ocean. Engines full speed ahead. That's the easy part. Like I said, hard part's coming into port, when you run into some traffic. Bread and butter of seamanship. Lines, knots and mooring in the seafaring tradition to pivot our Man O' War into her berth. Landlubbers associate all this with anchors, but they've got the wrong idea. Highlight. Anchor use is really only for emergencies, used to slow or stop the ship when proper handling has failed. You might see an old Sea Dog use an anchor in a tight berth every now and then, but not on my watch. When do we use anchors, Shipmates?"

"Emergencies."

"Only in emergencies. Absolutely right. Which brings us up to the forces that you cannot control but affect how you make use of the forces that you can

control. The first is *wind*, affecting the sail area, highlight, the areas of the hull and superstructure above the waterline. Wind is especially troublesome at low speeds when coming into port or mooring. Wouldn't necessarily think it, but you'd be surprised, especially on some of the Small Boys. There's also *currents*, highlight, the movement of water which tends to carry the ship in the direction of flow. We're talking ocean currents caused by prevailing winds, tidal currents caused by the rise and fall of the tides and river currents caused by river flow into the sea. We'll take a closer look at how to counter them during navigation. For now, just remember the three types of currents. All together now. *Ocean currents.*"

"Ocean currents."

"*Tidal currents.*"

"Tidal currents."

"*River currents.*"

"River currents."

"*Ocean currents. Tidal currents. River currents.*"

"Ocean currents. Tidal currents. River currents."

"Very good. Not to be confused with the effects of heavy seas, surface conditions which can make ship control a headache. Otherwise known as when you grow those old sea legs. You will need to remember three main effects associated with heavy seas. *Rolling.* The movement about ship's *longitudinal axis,* highlight, causing a ship to move from side to side. This occurs when the ship slides in aligned, parallel to the troughs of oncoming waves. *Pitching.* The movement about a ship's *athwartships axis*, highlight, causing the bow and stern to move up and down. This occurs when heading perpendicular to waves, pounding into the waves. I've seen it. Gets so strong at times that waves crash over the fantail when she runs with the seas. Called pooping, that's right. But don't worry about that for the test. And *yawing.* The movement about the ship's *vertical axis*, ship twisting and throwing the bow off course, first to one side, then the other. Got it? Rolling. That's in the trough, about what axis? Anyone?"

"Longitudinal axis."

"Pitching, heading into the waves, about what axis?"

"Athwartships axis."

"Good. And yawing, hitting the waves at an angle to the bow, along what axis?"

"Vertical axis."

"I see some blank stares, Shipmates. Know these differences. Got it?"

"Yes, Chief."

"Well, that should do it for basic ship handling. Let's review and then you can grab a cup of Jo, refill those canteens, splash some water on those sorry faces. Who can give me the definition of advance? Roberts."

"Just a second, Chief."

"What do you need your book for? It's right here on the white board."

"The distance --."

"*Gained.*"

"Gained."

"*In the direction.*"

"In the direction."

"Of?"

"The first course."

"This ain't a cooking class, Shipmate."

"Original course, Chef."

"Not bad, Roberts. Funny ha ha. And in what context?"

"When turning, Chief."

"There's helping Shipmates and then there's helping Shipmates. Test is on Thursday, folks. Word to the wise. This is one of those evolutions that can sneak up and bite you in the ass. Put you back in the drink. Do not get lulled into a false sense of security. Weekend liberty's all fine and good, but we see plenty of folks roll into G.T.X. with a one-two fail of Seamanship and Navigation. Especially those of you who are already riding the bubble. Give it to me again, Roberts."

"Distance gained in the direction of the original course when turning, Chief."

"Good. At least you're guaranteed of getting that one, right?"

"Yes, Chief."

"Someone give me the definition of transfer. Kramer."

"Distance gained at right angles to the original course when turning."

"Excellent. Tactical diameter. Zurich."

"Distance along the perpendicular between the original course of a ship and the reciprocal course of the same ship after making a turn of one-eight-zero degrees with a constant rudder angle."

"Now without reading."

"Distance along the perpendicular between the original course of a ship and the reciprocal course of the same ship after making a turn of one-eight-zero degrees with a constant rudder angle, Chief."

"Now in English."

"Distance you get from the point when you head into the turn and the point when you end up heading exactly opposite to the original course, Chief."

"Not too shabby. Factors that contribute to the effectiveness of a ship's rudder. All together now."

"Location. Angle. Size. Speed."

"All together."

"Location. Angle. Size. Speed."

"How do we remember that?"

"LASS."

"That's right. And what is the thrust for a single screw ship operating in the ahead direction?"

"Ahead."

"Or?"

"Astern."

"And side force. Stern to?"

"Starboard."

"Bow to?"

"Port."

"Bravo Zulu. When the Man O' War starts to pitch, it's on what axis?"

"Athwartships axis."

"Roll."

"Longitudinal axis."

"Yaw."

"Vertical axis."

"Well, that's it for now. Seems like a lot right now, but it's not so hard. If I can do it, folks, let me tell you that so can you. Bravo Zulu, Shipmates."

"Aye aye, Chief."

"Back in your seats in ten."

••

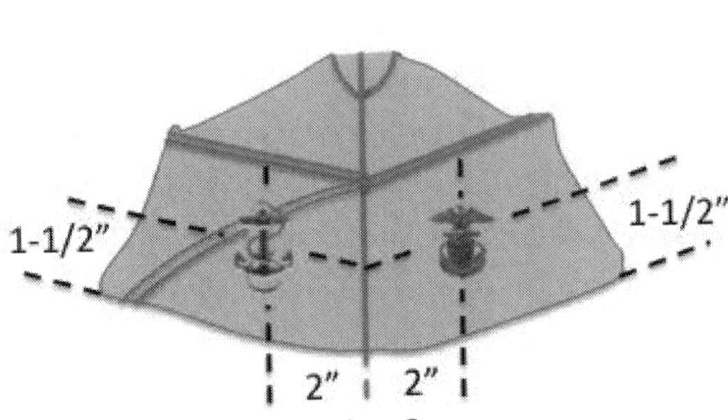

Garrison Cap

Fore and aft cap made of same fabric and color as uniform with which worn. Insignia on the garrison cap consist of metal collar size grade insignia and miniature cap device. The cap device consists of two gold crossed fouled anchors with burnished silver shield surmounted by a burnished silver spread eagle facing to wearer's right. It may be embroidered or made of metal (standard or high relief). The device is attached to the mount of the combination cap band.

Miniature cap devices have the same design but the overall size is reduced by one-half.

Correct wear. Wear squarely on the head, with fore and aft crease centered vertically between the eyebrows and the lowest point approximately one inch above the eyebrows. Outdoors, personnel remain covered at all times unless ordered to uncover, or during religious services not associated with a military ceremony. Personnel remain covered during invocations or other religious military ceremonies such as changes of command, ships' commissionings and launchings, and military burials, etc. The chaplain conducting the religious ceremony will guide participants following the customs of his church. Indoors, personnel shall remain uncovered at all times unless directed otherwise by higher authority for a special situation or event. Those Service Members in a duty status and wearing side arms or a pistol belt may only remove headgear indoors when entering dining, medical or FOD hazard areas or where religious services are being conducted. Tiaras may be left on indoors.

Combination Cover

A military style cap with black visor, rigid standing front, flaring circular rim and black cap band worn with detachable khaki, green or white cap cover, as required. Fabric match of cap cover and uniform is not required. For Officers of the rank of Lieutenant Commander and below the visor or hat band is plain. Consists of two gold crossed fouled anchors with burnished silver shield surmounted by a burnished silver spread eagle facing to wearer's right. It may be embroidered or made of metal (standard or high relief). The device is attached to the mount of the combination cap band. For all commissioned Officers and commissioned Warrant Officers, chin straps shall be a half inch wide, faced with gold lace, and shall be secured at each side of the cap by a Navy eagle, gilt button.

••••••••••••••••••••••••••••••••••••••

"Willett's outside."

"Mail call."

"Let's go."

"Stand-by."

"Lock check."

"Hold up. Alright. I'm good."

"Clear."

"Clear."

"Clear."

"Clear."

"Good evening, Sir!"

"Good evening, Sir!"

"Seventeen-sixteen-fifteen-fourteen-thirteen-twelve-eleven-ten-seven-five-three-two-one. Count off!"

"Aye aye, Sir!!"

"Zero-one!"

"Zero-two!"

"Zero-three!"

"Zero-four!"

"Zero-five!"

"Zero-six!"

"Zero-seven!"

"Zero-eight!"

"Zero-niner!"

"One-zero!"

"One-one!"

"One-two!"

"One-three!"

"One-four!"

"One-five!"

"One-six!"

"One-seven!"

"One-eight!"

"One-niner!"

"Two-zero!"

"Two-one!"

"Two-two!"

"Two-three!"

"Two-four!"

"Two-five!"

"Two-six!"

"Two-seven!"
"Two-eight!"
"Two-niner!"
"Three-zero!"
"Three-one!"
"Three-two!"
"Three-three!"
"Three-four!"
"Three-five!"
"Three-six!"
"Three-seven!"
"Three-eight!"
"Three-niner!"
"Four-zero!"
"Four-one!"
"Four-two! Class Zero-Four-Zero-Zero all present and accounted for, Sir!"
"Push."
"Aye aye, Sir!!"
"Down-Up."
"Zero-one!!"
"Down-up."
"Zero-two!!"
"Down-up."
"Zero-three!!"
"Down-up!!"
"Zero-four!!"
"Down-up."
"Zero-five!!"
"Down-up."
"Zero-six!!"
"Down-up."
"Zero-seven!!"
"Down-up."
"Zero-eight!!"
"Down-up."
"Zero-niner!!"
"Down-up."
"One-zero!!"
"On your feet."
"Aye aye, Sir!!"
"Mail call, Pigs."

"Aye aye, Sir!!"

"Brooks."

"Aye aye, Sir! Officer Candidate Brooks! Officer Candidate School! Officer Candidate Class Zero-Four-Zero-Zero! United States Navy! Reporting for mail call as ordered, Sir!"

"Fetch."

"Aye aye, Sir! Zero-two pieces of mail received, Sir!"

"Driscoll."

"Aye aye, Sir! Officer Candidate Driscoll! Officer Candidate School! Officer Candidate Class Zero-Four-Zero-Zero! United States Navy! Reporting for mail call as ordered, Sir!"

"Well, you waiting for me to read it for you?"

"No, Sir! Zero-one pieces of mail received, Sir!"

"Scram."

"Aye aye, Sir!"

"Erickson."

"Officer Candidate Erickson! Officer Candidate School! Officer Candidate Class Zero-Four-Zero-Zero! United States Navy! Reporting for mail call as ordered, Sir!"

"Side-straddle hops, Pig Nasty."

"Aye aye, Sir! One-two-three! Zero-one! One-two-three! Zero-two! One-two-three! Zero-three! One-two-three! Zero-four! One-two-three! Zero-five! One-two-three! Zero-six! One-two-three! Zero-seven! One-two-three! Zero-eight! One-two-three! Zero-niner! One-two-three! One-zero!"

"Fetch."

"Aye aye, Sir! Zero-two pieces of mail received, Sir!"

"Johnson."

"Officer Candidate Johnson! Officer Candidate School! Officer Candidate Class Zero-Four-Zero-Zero! United States Navy! Reporting for mail call as ordered, Sir!"

"Push."

"Aye aye, Sir! Zero-one! Zero-two! Zero-three! Zero-four! Zero-five! Zero-six! Zero-seven! Zero-eight! Zero-niner! One-zero!"

"On your feet."

"Aye, Aye, Sir! Zero-one pieces of mail received, Sir!"

"Harris."

"Officer Candidate Harris! Officer Candidate School! Officer Candidate Class Zero-Four-Zero-Zero! United States Navy! Reporting for mail call as ordered, Sir! Zero-one pieces of mail received, Sir!"

"Hobson."

"Officer Candidate Hobson! Officer Candidate School! Officer Candidate

Class Zero-Four-Zero-Zero! United States Navy! Reporting for mail call as ordered, Sir! Zero-one pieces of mail received, Sir!"

"Kramer."

"Officer Candidate Kramer! Officer Candidate School! Officer Candidate Class Zero-Four-Zero-Zero! United States Navy! Reporting for mail call as ordered, Sir! Zero-one pieces of mail received, Sir!"

"Lin."

"Officer Candidate Lin! Officer Candidate School! Officer Candidate Class Zero-Four-Zero-Zero! United States Navy! Reporting for mail call as ordered, Sir! Zero-one pieces of mail received, Sir!"

"Macpherson."

"Officer Candidate Macpherson! Officer Candidate School! Officer Candidate Class Zero-Four-Zero-Zero! United States Navy! Reporting for mail call as ordered, Sir! Zero-two pieces of mail received, Sir!"

"Rooster."

"Officer Candidate Rooster! Officer Candidate School! Officer Candidate Class Zero-Four-Zero-Zero! United States Navy! Reporting for mail call as ordered, Sir!"

"Reveille."

"Cockle-doodle-do! Sir!"

"Reveille."

"Cockle-doodle-do! Sir!"

"Fetch."

"Aye aye, Sir! Zero-two pieces of mail received, Sir!"

"Koch."

"Officer Candidate Koch! Officer Candidate School! Officer Candidate Class Zero-Four-Zero-Zero! United States Navy! Reporting for mail call as ordered, Sir!"

"Oh, wait. There's a note for me. *Dear Drill Instructor.* Sound off."

"Aye aye, Sir! Dear Drill Instructor!"

"*William enjoys long walks on the beach.*"

"William enjoys long walks on the beach! Sir!"

"*Playing with puppies.*"

"Playing with puppies! Sir!"

"*And dolphin-safe tuna.*"

"And dolphin-safe tuna! Sir!"

"Is that right, Koch?"

"No, Sir!"

"Push."

"Aye aye, Sir!"

"Down-up."

"Zero-one!"

"Down. *Long walks on the beach.* Up."

"Zero-two!"

"Down. *Puppies.* Up."

"Zero-three!"

"Down. *Dolphin-Safe tuna.* Up."

"Zero-four!"

"Down. *Long walks on the beach.* Up."

"Zero-five!"

"Down. *Puppies.* Up."

"Zero-six!"

"Down. *Dolphin safe tuna.* Up."

"Zero-seven!"

"Down. *Long walks on the beach.* Up."

"Zero-eight!"

"Down. *Puppies.* Up."

"Zero-niner!"

"Down. *Dolphin safe tuna.* Up."

"One-zero!"

"On your feet."

"Aye aye, Sir! Zero-one pieces of mail received, Sir!"

"Scram."

"Aye aye, Sir!"

"Postcard."

"Postcard, aye aye, Sir!!"

"*Dear Michael, just a quick note to say how much we miss you. Everyone is asking after you. I just booked our tickets for graduation. Aunt Barbara and Uncle Bill are driving up with --.*"

"Officer Candidate Lyman! Officer Candidate School! Officer Candidate Class Zero-Four-Zero-Zero! United States Navy! Reporting for mail call as ordered, Sir!"

"Talk of the town. Getting ahead of ourselves, aren't we, Pig?"

"Aye aye, Sir! Zero-one pieces of mail received, Sir!"

"Orton."

"Officer Candidate Orton! Officer Candidate School! Officer Candidate Class Zero-Four-Zero-Zero! United States Navy! Reporting for mail call as ordered, Sir!"

"What's this, Orton?"

"Drawings, Sir!"

"What kinds of drawings?"

"Hearts and butterflies, Sir!"

"Float like a butterfly, Freak."

"Aye aye, Sir!"

"Now sting like a bee."

"Aye aye, Sir!"

"Float like a butterfly."

"Aye aye, Sir!"

"Sting like a bee."

"Aye aye, Sir!"

"More flutter."

"Aye aye, Sir!"

"Go buzz about, Pig."

"Aye aye, Sir!"

"Siegel."

"Officer Candidate Shaffer! Officer Candidate School! Officer Candidate Class Zero-Four-Zero-Zero! United States Navy! Reporting for mail call as ordered, Sir! Zero-one pieces of mail received, Sir!"

"You're an airplane. Put your ears to use. Fly around. I want to hear them flapping."

"Aye aye, Sir!"

"Smith."

"Officer Candidate Smith! Officer Candidate School! Officer Candidate Class Zero-Four-Zero-Zero! United States Navy! Reporting for mail call as ordered, Sir! Zero-two pieces of mail received, Sir!"

"You're a police car. Join them. Sound your siren."

"Aye aye, Sir!"

"Sumarian."

"Officer Candidate Sumarian! Officer Candidate School! Officer Candidate Class Zero-Four-Zero-Zero! United States Navy! Reporting for mail call as ordered, Sir! Zero-one pieces of mail received, Sir!"

"Tronstein."

"Officer Candidate Tronstein! Officer Candidate School! Officer Candidate Class Zero-Four-Zero-Zero! United States Navy! Reporting for mail call as ordered, Sir!"

"Who the hell is writing you so much, Tronstein? You got pen pals?

"No, Sir!"

"Scram."

"Aye aye, Sir! Zero-five pieces of mail received, Sir!"

"Atten-hut!"

"Aye aye, Sir!!"

"Where's my Mailbody?"

"Officer Candidate Zurich! Officer Candidate School! Officer Candidate

Class Zero-Four-Zero-Zero Mailbody! United States Navy! Reporting as ordered, Sir!"

"The rest for distribution."

"Aye aye, Sir!"

"Atten-hut!"

"Aye aye, Sir!!"

"Gather round, Freaks."

"Aye aye, Sir!!"

"Go on and take a knee."

"Aye aye, Sir!!"

"Where's the guidon?"

"Guidon, aye aye, Sir!"

"You Maggots have heard a lot about leadership. You've heard it from Lieutenant Bryant. You've heard it from Chief Jones. And you've heard it from me. We've talked about *Justice*. Avoiding favoritism. Fairness and consistency at all times. Giving consideration to each side of a situation and giving rewards or punishment based solely on the merits. *Aye aye, Sir.*"

"Aye aye, Sir!!"

"*Judgment*. The ability to think about things clearly, calmly and in orderly fashion so as to make good decisions. Avoiding those rash decisions. Relying on a common sense attitude."

"Aye aye, Sir!!"

"*Dependability*. That your superiors and subordinates can rely upon you to perform your duties properly. The willing and voluntary support of the policies and orders of the Chain of Command. Putting forth your best effort in an attempt to achieve the highest standards of performance. The habits of being where you're supposed to be on time, by not making excuses and by carrying out every task to the best of your ability regardless of whether you like it or agree with it."

"Aye aye, Sir!!"

"*Initiative*. Taking action even though you haven't been given orders. Meeting new and unexpected situations with prompt action. Resourcefulness to get something done without the normal material or methods being available to you. Mental and physical alertness to the things that need to be done and then to do them without having to be told."

"Aye aye, Sir!!"

"*Decisiveness*. Making good decisions without delay. Assembling the facts and weighing them against each other. Announcing that decision in a clear, firm and professional manner."

"Aye aye, Sir!!"

"*Tact*. Dealing with people in a manner that will maintain good relations and

avoid problems. Polite, calm and firm. The Golden Rule. *Aye aye, Sir.*"

"Aye aye, Sir!!"

"*Integrity.* Honesty and truthfulness in what you say or do. Sense of duty and sound moral principles above all else. Standing up for what you believe to be right."

"Aye aye, Sir!!"

"*Enthusiasm.* A sincere interest and exuberance in the performance of your duties. Optimism. Cheerfulness. Willingness to accept challenges. Understanding and belief in mission. Jobs big and small."

"Aye aye, Sir!!"

"*Bearing.* The way you carry yourself, a reflection of alertness, competence, confidence and control. Holding yourself to the highest standards of personal conduct. Never settling for the minimum requirements."

"Aye aye, Sir!!"

"*Unselfishness.* Never making yourself comfortable at the expense of another. Never using your position or rank for personal gain, safety or pleasure. Giving credit where credit is due."

"Aye aye, Sir!!"

"*Courage.* What allows you to remain calm while recognizing fear. Having the inner strength to stand up for what is right and to accept blame when something is your fault. The ability to function effectively when there is physical danger present. Control at all times."

"Aye aye, Sir!"

"*Knowledge.* A broader understanding of the world around you. The sciences. The arts. Current events. Listening, observing and finding out about things you don't understand so as to better understand people."

"Aye aye, Sir!!"

"*Loyalty.* Unwavering devotion to your country, the Navy, seniors, peers and subordinates. Never speaking unfavorably of a senior in front of your subordinates. Once a decision is made and the order is given to execute it, carrying out that order willingly as if it were your own."

"Aye aye, Sir!!"

"*Endurance.* The mental and physical stamina that is measured by your ability to withstand pain, fatigue, stress and hardship. The ability to finish every task to the best of your ability by forcing yourself to continue when you are physically tired and your mind is sluggish."

"Aye aye, Sir!!"

"These leadership traits are there to guide you. *Aye aye, Sir.*"

"Aye aye, Sir!!"

"You are here to earn appointments as Naval Officers, solemnly swearing to support and defend the constitution of the United States, against all enemies,

foreign and domestic, bearing true faith and allegiance to the same, the obligation freely, without any mental reservation or purpose of evasion, to well and faithfully discharge the duties of a United States Naval Officer. You will walk out of that chapel and return your first two salutes. The first from Chief Jones. The second from myself. In that moment you will be vested with authority and responsibility in the Chain of Command. Significant authority. As Division Officers, you will be involved in every aspect of the lives of those subordinates who serve under you. You will be responsible their success. You will be responsible for their failures. You will be responsible for their lives. *Aye aye, Sir.*"

"Aye aye, Sir!!"

"There is no formula for how to lead. Some folks will talk to you about the ability to effectuate positive change in others, especially in the face of resistance. But that speaks to the goal and not the means of change. No amount of training can teach you leadership for the simple reason that indoctrination is no substitute for the practical wisdom you will learn through trial and by fire. I can't tell you what to do. Chief Jones can't tell you what to do. And Lieutenant Bryant, respectfully, can't tell you what to do. Leaders are made. Forged. Some of you will go by the book, choosing to abide by a strict reading of regulations as a guide to handle any and all indiscretion, real or imagined. Others will bend the rules until they break, willing to protect any allegiance. The remainder will no doubt fall someplace in-between, exercising practical wisdom learned over time. *Aye aye, Sir.*"

"Aye aye, Sir!!"

"You see these stripes?"

"Yes, Sir!!"

"One for every four years of duty. After twelve years, with good conduct, they turn to gold. One mistake they go back to red. Just like that. Now there are some bad apples out there. Bad apples with no business in a uniform. Rot that must be culled from the core without remorse or hesitation. But there's also that Sailor or Marine who makes a mistake, who came into the Service looking for a better way, who may have fallen back into old habits or just didn't know any better. A mistake that will cost them stripes. Mistakes worn in shame at every formal event and ceremony for the length of a career. You need to ask yourselves whether putting a man up in front of the Captain, taking away that man's stripes or changing the color of his uniform dress makes you a leader. You need to ask yourselves whether a personnel investigation opened with a pen will accomplish more than a well dug ditch. Because while he may hate you, curse your name, rank and authority as he digs, as his anger subsides and his temper cools, he will respect you for your decision and then follow you to the ends of the earth. As his leader. Am I clear?"

"Yes, Sir!!"

"Am I clear?"

"Yes, Sir!!"

"My Gunny told me you can trace the rise and fall of a civilization by its walls. *Aye aye, Sir.*"

"Aye aye, Sir!!"

"Continual readiness."

"Aye aye, Sir!!"

"Everlasting vigilance."

"Aye aye, Sir!!"

"And obedience to orders."

"Aye aye, Sir!!"

"Leadership."

"Aye aye, Sir!!"

"Am I clear?"

"Yes, Sir!!"

"Dismissed, Maggots."

"Aye aye, Sir!!"

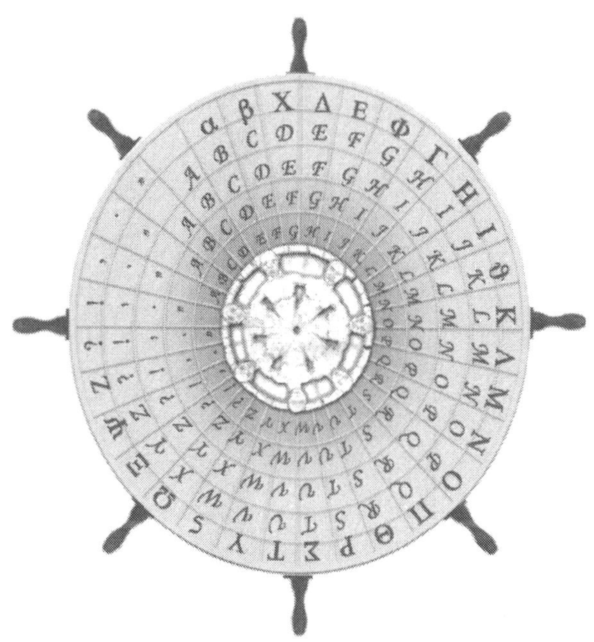

CHAPTER V

WEEKS 5-7

"Attenhut! Listen up, Nasty Candidates! This is the lighthouse run! I don't want to see no stinking! Pathetic! Lethargic! Disgusting! Revolting Candidates! Dropping out for my meat truck! You drop? You dead! You got that?"

"Yes, Sir!!"

"I'll be there to greet you at the morgue, fist full of chits! Am I freaking clear?"

"Yes, Sir!!"

"I can't freaking hear you, Maggots!"

"Yes, Sir!!"

"Upon receiving the command of execution *fall out*! You will fall out and regroup as four columns in the road, class-by-class, at close interval! Ready! Fall out!"

"Aye aye, Sir!!"

The ranks dissolve towards the road. Classes rejoin in a single formation.

"Ready! March!"

"Aye aye, Sir!!"

"Double time! March!"

"Aye aye, Sir!!"

"*Left*! *Left*! *Lefty-right-a-left-right*!"

"Left!! Left!! Lefty-right-a-left-right!!"

"*Lefty-right-a-lo*!"

"Lefty-right-a-lo!!"

"*Left-right*! *Left-right-left*!"

"Left-right!! Left-right-left!!"

"*Keep-it-in-step*!"

"Keep-it-in-step!!"

My eyes fade into the cadence.

"*C-One-Thirty rolling down the strip*!"

"C-One-Thirty rolling down the strip!!"

"*All aboard for a one-way trip*!"

"All aboard for a one-way trip!!"

"*Mission unspoken, destination unknown*!"

"Mission unspoken, destination unknown!!"

"*We don't know if we'll ever come home*!"

"We don't know if we'll ever come home!!"

"*Stand up, hook up, shuffle to the door*!"

"Stand up, hook up, shuffle to the door!!"

"*Jump right out and count to four*!"

"Jump right out and count to four!!"

"*If my main don't open wide*!"

"If my main don't open wide!!"

"*I got a reserve by my side*!"

"I got a reserve by my side!!"

"*If that one don't fail me too*!"

"If that one don't fail me too!!"

"*Look out ground, I'm a coming through*!"

"Look out ground, I'm a coming through!!"

"*Pin my medals upon my chest*!"

"Pin my medals upon my chest!!"

"*And bury me in the leaning rest*!"

"And bury me in the leaning rest!!"
"*P.T.!*"
"P.T.!!"
"*Good for you!*"
"Good for you!!"
"*Good for me!*"
"Good for me!!"
"*Left! Left! Lefty-right-a-left!*"
"Left!! Left!! Lefty-right-a-left!!"
"*Left! Left! Keep-it-in-step!*"
"Left!! Left!! Keep-it-in-step!!"
"*When I get to heaven Saint Peter's gonna say!*"
"When I get to heaven Saint Peter's gonna say!!"
"*How'd you earn your living? How'd you earn your pay?*"
"How'd you earn your living? How'd you earn your pay?"
"*And I'll reply with a whole lotta anger!*"
"And I'll reply with a whole lotta anger!!"
"*I earned my living as an Airborne Ranger!*"
"I earned my living as an Airborne Ranger!!"
"*Blood and guts!*"
"Blood and guts!!"
"*Sex and danger!*"
"Sex and danger!!"
"*That's the life of an Airborne Ranger!*"
"That's the life of an Airborne Ranger!!"
"*And when I get to Hell, the Devil's gonna say!*"
"And when I get to Hell, the Devil's gonna say!!"
"*How'd you earn your living? How'd you earn your pay?*"
"How'd you earn your living? How'd you earn your pay?"
"*And I'll reply as I clench my knife!*"
"And I'll reply as I clench my knife!!"
"*Get outta my way before I take your life!*"
"Get outta my way before I take your life!!"
"*Blood and guts!*"
"Blood and guts!!"
"*Sex and danger!*"
"Sex and danger!!"
"*That's the life of an Airborne Ranger!*"
"That's the life of an Airborne Ranger!!"
"*Left! Left! Lefty-right-a-left!*"
"Left!! Left!! Lefty-right-a-left!!"

"*Left! Left! Keep-it-in-step!*"
"Left!! Left!! Keep-it-in-step!!"
"*Staff Sergeant Willett come on out!*"
"Staff Sergeant Willett come on out!!"
"*We want to hear your motivational shout!*"
"We want to hear your motivational shout!!"
"*Take it on the left foot!*"
"Take it on the left foot!!"
"*The mighty-mighty left foot!*"
"The mighty-mighty left foot!!"
"*Take it!*"
"Take it!!"
"I got it!"
"He's got it!!"
"*Left-foot!*"
"Left-foot!!"
"*Left-foot!*"
"Left-foot!!"
"*Left! Left! Lefty-right-a-left!*"
"Left!! Left!! Lefty-right-a-left!!"
"*Left! Left! Keep-it-in-step!*"
"Left!! Left!! Keep-it-in-step!!"
"*My girl is a vegetable!*"
"My girl is a vegetable!!"
"*She lives in the hospital!*"
"She lives in the hospital!!"
"*But I'd do most anything!*"
"But I'd do most anything!!"
"*To keep that girl alive!*"
"To keep that girl alive!!"
"*She's got her own T.V.!*"
"She's got her own T.V.!!"
"*It's called an E.K.G.!*"
"It's called an E.K.G.!!"
"*But I'd do most anything!*"
"But I'd do most anything!!"
"*To keep that girl alive!*"
"To keep that girl alive!!"
"*My girl ain't got no eyes!*"
"My girl ain't got no eyes!!"
"*Just two holes and lots of flies!*"

"Just two holes and lots of flies!!"
"But I'd do most anything!"
"But I'd do most anything!!"
"To keep that girl alive!"
"To keep that girl alive!!"
"My girl ain't got no nose!"
"My girl ain't got no nose!!"
"Just a piece of rubber hose!"
"Just a piece of rubber hose!!"
"But I'd do most anything!"
"But I'd do most anything!!"
"To keep that girl alive!"
"To keep that girl alive!!"
"My girl ain't got no hands!"
"My girl ain't got no hands!!"
"Just a pair of Teflon pans!"
"Just a pair of Teflon pans!!"
"But I'd do most anything!"
"But I'd do most anything!!"
"To keep that girl alive!"
"To keep that girl alive!!"
"My girl ain't got no legs!"
"My girl ain't got no legs!!"
"All my friends they call her Pegs!"
"All my friends they call her Pegs!!"
"But I'd do most anything!"
"But I'd do most anything!!"
"To keep that girl alive!"
"To keep that girl alive!!"
"Left! Left! Lefty-right-a-left!"
"Left!! Left!! Lefty-right-a-left!!"
"Left! Left! Keep-it-in-step!"
"Left!! Left!! Keep-it-in-step!!"
"A whole lotta left!"
"A whole lotta left!!"
"Keep-it-in-step!"
"Keep-it-in-step!!"
"Left! Left! Lefty! Right! Layo!"
"Left!! Left!! Lefty!! Right!! Layo!!"
"Left! Left! Keep-it-in-step!"
"Left!! Left!! Keep-it-in-step!!"

"*Left! Left! Lefty-right-a-left-right!*"
"Left!! Left!! Lefty-right-a-left-right!!"
"*Lefty-right-left-right!*"
"Lefty-right-left-right!!"
"*Lefty-right-a-lo!*"
"Lefty-right-a-lo!!"
"*We love to double time!*"
"We love to double time!!"
"*Left! Left! Lefty! Right! Layo!*"
"Left!! Left!! Lefty!! Right!! Layo!!"
"*Left! Left! Keep-it-in-step!*"
"Left!! Left!! Keep-it-in-step!!"
"*Left! Left! Lefty-right-a-left-right!*"
"Left!! Left!! Lefty-right-a-left-right!!"
"*Left! Left! Lefty-right-a-left-right!*"
"Left!! Left!! Lefty-right-a-left-right!!"
"*Lefty-right-a-lo!*"
"Lefty-right-a-lo!!"
"*Left! Left! Lefty-right-a-left-right!*"
"Left!! Left!! Lefty-right-a-left-right!!"
"*Lefty-right-a-lo!*"
"Lefty-right-a-lo!!"
"*Ready on the left-foot!*"
"Ready on the left-foot!!"
"*Heavy on the left-foot!*"
"Heavy on the left-foot!!"
"*Motivated left-foot!*"
"Motivated left-foot!!"
"*Here we go!*"
"Here we go!!"
"*Feelin' good!*"
"Feelin' good!!"
"*Oh yeah!*"
"Oh yeah!!"
"*One mile!*"
"One mile!!"
"*No sweat!*"
"No sweat!!"
"*Two miles!*"
"Two miles!!"
"*Better yet!*"

"Better yet!!"

"*Three miles*!"

"Three miles!!"

"*Good run*!"

"Good run!!"

"*Four miles*!"

"Four miles!!"

"*Get me some*!"

"Get me some!!"

"*Kill*!"

"Kill!!"

"*The mighty-mighty left-foot*!"

"The mighty-mighty left-foot!!"

"*Get some*!"

"Get some!!"

"*P.T.*!"

"P.T.!!"

"*Good for you*!"

"Good for you!!"

"*Good for me*!"

"Good for me!!"

"*Gunnery Sergeant Burton come on out*!"

"Gunnery Sergeant Burton come on out!!"

"*We want to hear your motivational shout*!"

"We want to hear your motivational shout!!"

"*Take it on the left foot*!"

"Take it on the left foot!!"

"*The mighty-mighty left foot*!"

"The mighty-mighty left foot!!"

"*Take it*!"

"Take it!!"

"I got it!"

"He's got it!!"

"The *left-foot*!"

"Left-foot!!"

"*Left-foot*!"

"Left-foot!!"

"*Burn the village and kill the people*!"

"Burn the village and kill the people!!"

"*Drop some napalm on the square*!"

"Drop some napalm on the square!!"

"Do it on a Sunday morning!"
"Do it on a Sunday morning!!"
"While they're on their way to prayer!"
"While they're on their way to prayer!!"
"We love to double time!"
"We love to double time!!"

••••••••••••••••••••••••••••••••••••••

Commands and Command Voice

There are two types of commands. The first, the preparatory command such as forward indicates a movement is to be made. The second, the command of execution such as march causes the desired movement to be made. In some commands, such as fall in, at ease, and rest, the preparatory command and the command of execution are combined.

When giving commands, the commander faces the troops. For company formations or larger, when commanding marching troops from the head of a column or massed formations, the commander marches backward while giving commands. When commanding a unit which is part of a larger unit, the leader turns his head to give commands, but does not face about except when the unit is halted and the smaller units are in line. In this case, the leader faces about to give all commands except to repeat preparatory commands, for which he only turns his head.

Good posture, proper breathing, and the correct use of throat and mouth muscles help develop a commander's voice. If commands are properly given, they will carry to all Marines in the unit. If a commander tries too hard, his neck muscles might tighten. This will result in squeaky, jumbled, and indistinct commands, and will later be the cause of hoarseness and sore throat.

••••••••••••••••••••••••••••••••••••••

"Alright, Shipmates. Take your seats. Quick story to start us off. U.S.S. Enterprise, C.V.-Six, sailing off the Canadian coastline, Atlantic Fleet back in those days. Captain, ever vigilant, spots lights out in the distance, possible C.B.D.R. He initiates the call over comms. *Please divert your vessel course fifteen degrees north to avoid a collision.* Nothing. Couple of minutes pass. Up comes the response. *Recommend you divert your course fifteen degrees north to avoid collision.* The damndest, am I right?"

"Yes, Sir."

"Negative, Shipmates. I work for a living."

"Aye aye, Chief."

"That's more like it. Skipper, God bless him, has none of it. *I am the Captain of a U.S. Navy warship. I say again, divert your course.* Well, sure as heck, minute or two later. *No, I say again, you divert your course.* Captain now is blooming livid, you can imagine, some Hothead pissing in his cornflakes in front of his crew. *No. This is the aircraft carrier U.S.S. Enterprise, the second largest ship in the United States Atlantic Fleet. We are accompanied by three destroyers, three cruisers and numerous support vessels. I demand that you change your course fifteen degrees north, that's one-five degrees north, or counter-measures will be undertaken to ensure the safety of this ship.* Old school Navy, the Captain. Crackle comes back on the radio. *U.S. Navy warship. We are a lighthouse. Your call.* Badabing. Badaboom. Page three-decimal-eight dash six in your lesson plan. Macpherson, start us up."

"Aye aye, Chief. Forces such as wind, seas, ocean currents, gyro error, inaccurate engine calibrations, etcetera, are combined to cause a vessel to deviate from its dead reckoning track."

"*D.R.* track. Sorry, Shipmate. Go on."

"These forces are collectively called current, and current must always be assumed to some degree when safely navigating. How much current present depends upon the ship's situation. Accurately using current information calls for keen judgment and experience on the part of the Navigator and the Officer of the Deck. Set and drift are required to be calculated at each fix, unless the fix interval is less than three minutes. In the latter situation, set and drift is calculated every third fix."

"Thank you, Shipmate. Wind. Sea. Currents. Error. This is what you have got to be thinking at all times up on the Bridge. Every hazrep reads the same. *The Officer of the Deck failed to ensure the Quarter Master of the Watch was maintaining an accurate navigation plot, taking set and drift into consideration, to give him an accurate idea of ship's movement.* Well, most of the time. And guess who takes the fall? Right after the Chief and right before the Captain, that is. The Officer of the Deck. You might survive as an Ensign, but I guarantee you don't make Commander. No way, no how. Only takes a second. I've seen it. Now the Chief might lose his pin, but he's already a Chief. As an Officer, outside of a D.U.I. or cheating on your

wife, three balls is what you don't come back from. Adios, amigos. Am I getting through?"

"Yes, Chief."

"We'll start with *tide*. Someone want to give me the definition? Officer Candidate Elkind."

"Aye aye, Chief. Tide is the vertical rise and fall of a body of water."

"Want to guess where the tide comes from?"

"The moon, Chief."

"That's right. An educated bunch. Isn't that something? Always gets me. The daggone moon. Gravitation pull and the shallows. Low tide will leave you sitting up aground on a sandbar, standing by for administrative action. You'll need to be able to recognize four types of tide. *High tide*. The maximum height of the sea resulting from the rising tide. *Low tide*. You guessed it. The minimum height of the water resulting from the falling tide. *Semidiurnal tide*. The basic tidal pattern observed over most of the world. Two high and two low tides a day. And last. *Diurnal tide*. A pattern that has only one high and low tide a day. Only one I know is the Gulf of Mexico, but there's got to be more. Point is it's important. Any questions? Out of a hat. What tidal pattern has two high and two low tides a day?"

"Semidiurnal tide, Chief."

"Basic tidal pattern. Our second primary force is *current*. Current is, highlight, the horizontal movement of water, tidal or nontidal, meaning that tide can be a current. Actually, when we talk current, we're talking all factors causing a vessel to depart reckoning. A tidal current that flows towards shore as a result of a high tide is called a *flood current*. One that flows away from shore as a result of a low tide is called an *ebb current*. Makes sense, right? When in doubt, go with your gut. Now for your ocean currents. Most are known and charted, classified as major currents like the Atlantic Gulfstream. Everyone knows the Gulfstream. You can't miss it. So what does this mean for navigation? Anyone? Officer Candidate Hobson."

"Current affects navigation, Chief."

"That's a critical insight, Hobson. Can you be more specific?"

"You have to take current into consideration when setting course."

"Good. And why?"

"Current will take you off course."

"And what can happen when you are taken off course?"

"Accidents."

"And what happens to you if there's an accident?"

"It's a career killer, Chief."

"Game over, Shipmate. That's why when sailing in current, you need to determine the effect it has on your vessel, allowing for its effect when determining course and speed. Everyone onboard thus far?"

"Yes, Chief."

"Now current as we've just described has two components. *Set* and *drift*. Set is the true direction of current flow. Highlight. Highlight. Highlight. And drift, the current speed in knots. Time for another important equation. Better write it down. Drift equals the distance in nautical miles times sixty over the elapsed time in minutes. *Distance in nautical miles times sixty over the elapsed time in minutes.* That's an important equation. Know it cold. No time to think. Set and drift. Set and drift. Set and?"

"Drift."

"Equation?"

"Distance in nautical miles times sixty over the elapsed time in minutes."

"One more time."

"Distance in nautical miles times sixty over the elapsed time in minutes."

"That's your highlight. No matter the sea state, no matter your confidence in navigated waters, you can never, ever forget about the current. Never forget. Not on your exam. Please beware of the easy answer. And, more importantly, not in the Fleet. Got that?"

"Yes, Chief."

"So let's put current into practice. Every passage and every departure from and entry into port is planned in advance as an intended track. We're talking danger bearings, ranges, turn bearings and PIM times arrival at each track point. And that's just for planning purposes. Remember our six rules of D.R.? We plot at every change of course. At the time of every speed change. Every hour on the hour. At the time of obtaining a single line of position. At the time of obtaining a fix or running fix. For a new D.R. course line after each new fix or running fix. Don't try to game it. For some of you, this will be intuitive. For others, not as much. Don't worry. In two days all of you will be able to do this in your sleep. And if not, well, I wouldn't sleep. We're comfortable with dead reckoning, distance as a function of speed times time. Remember our triangle? Big D over Big S times Big T. Right? Cover the D and you have S times T. Cover the S and you have D over T. Cover the T and you have D over S. Simple. That's clear enough, right?"

"Yes, Chief."

"Anyone got any questions? Good. Then all you have to do is determine ordered course, ordered speed and the elapsed time between the last fix and the time of the desired D.R. position, solving for the distance the Man O' War has travelled. Semi-circle and corresponding time. I'm getting blank looks. Everybody with me, right? Anybody not with me, speak now or forever hold your peace.

Good. This is going to get a bit more complicated. Alright. Giddy-up. Grab your trusty compasses and radials from your kits. For our plotting procedure, we'll start at point A, fix at time Twelve Hundred, charting a course at the zero-nine-zero. Let's assume the Man O' War wants to sail sixty nautical miles by Eighteen Hundred. Go ahead and chart her intended course, zero-nine-zero for sixty nautical miles. We now have our position of intended movement, our PIM, which we always remember to indicate with a?"

"Gunsight, Chief."

"I want to hear everyone."

"Gunsight, Chief."

"Our trusty gunsight. Circle and cross, folks. Easy as pie. So what can we already tell from our PIM? Big triangle. We have *time*. Twelve Hundred to Eighteen Hundred. Six hours. And we have *distance*. Sixty nautical miles, right? So who wants to solve for *speed*? Officer Candidate Johnson."

"Ten nautical miles, Chief."

"Ten nautical miles per what?"

"Ten nautical miles per hour, Chief."

"That's right. Now we cover the Big S. That leaves D over T. Sixty nautical miles over six hours equals ten nautical miles per hour, the speed required for the Man O' War to arrive at Point B on schedule. As a minimum, each point should be labeled with a PIM time. Is that clear?"

"Yes, Chief."

"Real question is the tide and current we've been talking about. With navigation, you're looking at two scenarios. Once off-track, you have to come up with a course and speed that will counteract set and drift and allow the Man O' War to regain the intended track at a specified time and place. Or, from a position on your intended track, we have to come up with a course and speed that will counteract set and drift and allow the vessel to maintain the course and speed of her intended track. First is intuitive. Second not as much. Don't worry. Ready to try this out? Well, Shipmates?"

"Yes, Chief."

"That's the spirit. Let's start by plotting out some interim PIM times. Follow with me. Divide Twelve Hundred to Eighteen Hundred into equal time intervals. Right? Thirteen Hundred. Fourteen Hundred. Fifteen Hundred. Sixteen Hundred. Seventeen Hundred. Now assume we get a fix at Fourteen Hundred with set of zero-zero-zero degrees at four nautical miles based on two knots of drift. Trick now is to determine the position and time at which to regain our intended track. Let's say we want to regain our PIM by Sixteen Hundred. Captain's orders. First thing is to calculate the distance that the Man O' War will be pushed over the two hours. We know that she's been pushed out to four nautical miles at the zero-zero-zero at Fourteen Hundred. Assuming constant set

and drift, as least right now, stands to reason you would want to overshoot by an equivalent amount over the next two hours. Right? Our *aimpoint.* From PIM at Sixteen Hundred, measure in the reciprocal direction of set, your one-eight-zero, out to four nautical miles. We plot this as a dashed line. Do not, I repeat, do not label the aimpoint. You'll see why in a second. From our fix at Fourteen Hundred we can now plot a new D.R. course line to the aim point. Like so. Follow along folks. Connecting our two points for her new course, we now measure the distance between the fix and the aim point. Let's see. Twenty-one-and-a-little-over-a-half nautical miles. Right? Everyone follow? And we calculate the speed required to travel that distance in the two hours. Big S equals Big D over Big T. Anyone? Officer Candidate Zurich."

"Ten-point-eight knots, Chief."

"Course."

"One-one-two degrees, Chief."

"Very good. Use your radials. Big D of twenty-one-decimal-six nautical miles over Big T two hours equals ten-point-eight. Along with the course we have from our new charted course to our aimpoint. Fair enough? And where does she end up?"

"Back on course."

"Presto. Now let me be perfectly clear. In the problem here, the set just happened to be zero-zero-zero degrees coinciding with a course of zero-nine-zero. Folks seem to get confused come the exam when the ducks don't line up in a row. Set's not always perpendicular to the course. It gets trickier. And we're not done yet. Remember, there's not only course correction to regain the intended track but the course and speed to allow the Man O' War to maintain course and speed to our endpoint at Eighteen Hundred. Lucky for us, the process is just about the same. The difference is that you as Navigator can select an aimpoint for a convenient time interval, usually fifteen, thirty minutes. Word of caution as to what not to do on the exam. The resulting course and speed needed to maintain the track will be different than that to regain track, working against set drift, not with it. Seems like a no-brainer, right? Easy to forget under pressure come test time. Even easier on the Bridge. Big waste of time of time you just won't have. Got it?"

"Yes, Chief."

"Radials. Let's go with intervals of thirty minutes. Remember, we have got to first calculate the distance that our Man O' War will be pushed over the elapsed time. Given the same set and drift, we're talking another four nautical miles after another two hours. One nautical mile at Sixteen Thirty. Two nautical miles at an Seventeen Hundred. Four nautical miles at Eighteen Hundred. Easy as pie. But what about the Captain's new ordered course and speed? Try it on your own. Go

on and plot a new D.R. course to the aimpoint. Label the course. Now measure the distance between the fix and the aimpoint. Anyone?"

"Twenty-two nautical miles, Chief."

"Very good. Everyone follow? Now calculate the speed required to travel that distance in the designated time. Label the course line with the calculated speed. Think fast, folks. You know how to do this. Big D at twenty-two nautical miles. Time at two hours. Anyone?"

"Eleven, Chief."

"D over T. New ordered course?"

"One-zero-two, Chief."

"Bravo Zulu. Captain's new ordered course and speed is one-zero-two degrees at eleven knots. And label. We now have our completed plot. Show of hands. How many of you have accurate charts? Really? Fit for the Captain? I thought so. Going to take some practice, folks. On your own time. Alright, turn to three-decimal-eight dash thirteen. Two more definitions. *Course made good*, your C.M.G., and *speed made good*, your S.M.G. C.M.G. is the net course traveled by a ship between any two fix positions, taking into account steering inaccuracies, course change, and current. Simple addition. S.M.G. is your net speed traveled by a ship between any two fix positions, total distance traveled divided by the elapsed time between fixes. Clear as mud?"

"Yes, Chief."

"Alright, let's get to the problem sets. Lessons learned. Take it from me. Draw your lines heavy enough to see, but not so heavy you have to start over if you make a mistake. Avoid drawing unnecessary lines. Erase any lines used only for the purpose of measurement. Do not extend course lines beyond the point at which their direction is to be changed. Hold the pencil against the straight edge in a vertical position throughout the entire length of a line. Be neat and accurate in plotting work, using standard symbols, printing neatly, labeling each line and point immediately after the plot. And most importantly, Shipmates, measure and plot all directions and distances carefully. Oh, and remember the six Rules of Dead Reckoning. Copy, folks? Roger that?"

"Yes, Chief."

"Here we go, then. Sink or swim. You are the Navigator on board the U.S.S. Gladiator, M.C.M.-Eleven enroute Pensacola, Florida following PIM from a Point A to a Point C. Point A. Prepare to copy. Latitude thirty degrees, nine minutes north, longitude eighty-six degrees forty-eight minutes west. PIM time Zero-Nine Hundred. Point B. Latitude thirty degrees-decimal-five minutes north, longitude eighty-seven degrees sixteen-decimal-four minutes west. PIM time Fourteen Hundred. Point C. Latitude thirty degrees sixteen-decimal-two minutes north, longitude eighty-seven degrees seventeen-decimal-four minutes west. Time Fourteen Twenty-Five. Plot your track. At Zero-Nine Hundred you fix your

position at Point A. You depart Point A enroute to Point B on course two-eight-zero. Two questions from the Captain. What speed is required to arrive at Point B on time? On what reference plane are soundings based on the chart? Five minutes, folks. Start the problem start the clock."

I plot the course on my chart. The distance measures out to twenty-five nautical miles. Twenty-five divided by five gives five knots. I scan down to the reference plane on the title block.

"Time. Your recommended speed, Officer Candidate Rooney."

"Five knots, Chief."

"And how did you do it?"

"Speed equals distance over time, Chief. Measured it out, got twenty-five nautical miles and divided by five hours."

"Anyone disagree with Rooney? Very good. Required speed is five knots. Now what about the reference plane?"

"M.L.L.W., Chief."

"What does that stand for?"

"Mean Lower Low Water."

"And where did you find it, Shipmate?"

"Title block, Chief."

"Bravo Zulu. Everyone with me or do we just have ourselves a ringer? Stand-by for more comms. Ready? Zero-Nine-Thirty. G.P.S. fixes your position at latitude thirty degrees niner-decimal-two minutes north, longitude eighty-six degrees fifty-one-decimal-four minutes west. Plot your Zero-Nine-Thirty fix. First question. What has your set been since Zero-Nine Hundred? Second question. What has your drift been since Zero-Nine Hundred? And third. What is you C.M.G. and S.M.G? You have ten minutes. Start the problem. Start the clock."

I work out the problem on my chart.

"Time. Officer Candidate Koch, the set please."

"Two-three-eight, Chief."

"Going once? Going twice? Someone's got something different out there. Officer Candidate Larson. What did you come up with?"

"Two-four-three, Chief."

"Good on both of you. Each are ballpark. At the same time, be sure to measure and plot all directions and distances carefully. You may be able to triangulate on a multiple choice test. Not so in blue water out to a couple hundred nautical miles River City on the way to war. Officer Candidate Mura, what has your drift been since Zero-Nine-Hundred?"

"One-point-two knots, Chief."

"Everyone agree? How about C.M.G. and S.M.G.? Officer Candidate Reston."

"Still working on it, Chief."

"Net course travelled, Reston. Did you plot the Zero-Nine-Thirty G.P.S. fix?"

"Yes, Chief."

"And you have your Point A, right?"

"Yes, Chief."

"Measure the course from Point A to the Zero-Nine-Thirty fix."

"Aye aye, Chief."

"What do you get?"

"Two-seven-zero degrees, Chief."

"Measure it again. Take your time."

"Two-seven-three degrees, Chief."

"Your C.M.G is at the two-seven-three degrees. Now what about S.M.G? Apply the equation. Net speed traveled between our two fixes, total distance travelled divided by the elapsed time between Zero-Nine-Hundred and Zero-Nine-Thirty. Take your time."

"Five-decimal-eight, Chief."

"Five-decimal-eight what?"

"Five-decimal-eight knots, Chief.

"Close. Anyone else? Variation is the norm. Officer Candidate Lyman."

"Five-decimal-six knots, Chief."

"Captain takes your recommendation. Now plot your track to regain course at Ten Hundred. Captain wants a new course and speed. Five minutes. Start the problem, start the clock. Plot your aim point, reciprocal of set. Label the course."

"Officer Candidate Zurich."

"Three-zero-three degrees at three-decimal-five knots, Chief."

"Bravo Zulu. Captain takes your recommendation. At Ten Hundred, RADAR fixes your position at thirty degrees nine-decimal-niner minutes north, eighty-six degrees fifty-three-decimal-six minutes west. Thirty degrees nine-decimal-niner minutes north, eighty-six degrees fifty-three-decimal-six minutes west. You return to your PIM course and PIM speed of two-eight-zero degrees at five knots. At Ten-Thirty you sight an Aerostat vessel off your port bow making way at five nautical miles showing Ball Diamond Ball dayshapes. What is the status of the Aerostat vessel? Anyone?"

"RAM, Chief."

"Which is?"

"Restricted in the ability to move."

"Very good. Know your flags. Ball Diamond Ball. Highlight. And what maneuvering actions are required of your vessel by the Rules of the Road? I'll take that as a good sign. No action is in fact required, the Law of the Sea, although it might be a pretty good idea to slow down and alter course given

C.B.D.R. At Ten-Forty-Five you sight the following round of bearings. The R.A. Dome at thirty degrees twenty-three-decimal-one minutes north, eighty-six degrees fifty-decimal-three minutes west with a bearing of zero-three-zero. I repeat. Thirty degrees twenty-three-decimal-one minutes north, eighty-six degrees fifty-decimal-three minutes west bearing zero-three-zero. Next fix. The T.V. T.R. at thirty degrees twenty-four-decimal-two minutes north, eighty-six degrees fifty-nine-decimal-five minutes west bearing three-five-five degrees. Thirty degrees twenty-four-decimal-two minutes north, eighty-six degrees fifty-nine-decimal-five minutes west bearing three-five-five degrees. We're not done. Now the World Famous P-Cola Beach Tank at thirty minutes twenty-decimal-two minutes north, eighty-six degrees ninety-nine-decimal-five minutes west. Bearing three-one-five-decimal-five degrees. Thirty minutes twenty-decimal-two minutes north, eighty-six degrees ninety-nine-decimal-five minutes west. Bearing three-one-five-decimal-five degrees. Plot your Ten-Forty-Five fix. What are the coordinates of your Ten-Forty-Five fix? What is your set and drift? What is your C.M.G. and S.M.G? You have five minutes. You know how to do this. Label as you go. And keep it neat. Start the problem. Start the clock."

"Time. What do we got? Coordinates. Anyone? Officer Candidate Hibbs."

"Thirty degrees eleven-decimal-two minutes north, eighty-six degrees fifty-eight-decimal-two minutes west, Chief."

"Bullseye. Bravo Zulu. Attention to detail saves lives, Shipmates. Set and drift."

"Three-three-one degrees set. Zero-decimal-niner knots drift, Chief."

"C.M.G. and S.M.G."

"Two-eight-six degrees at five-decimal-six knots. Chief."

"Well done, Hibbs. This should be review at this point, Shipmates. Two-eight-six degrees at five-point-six knots. Now plot a course to regain PIM track at Twelve Hundred. What is your recommend course? What is your recommended speed? What are the coordinates of you aim point? Start the problem. Start the clock. Five minutes."

"Officer Candidate Larson. Your recommended course and speed."

"Two-six-six degrees at four-decimal-three knots."

"Aim point."

"Thirty degrees eleven minutes north, eighty-seven degrees four minutes west."

"On the dot?"

"On the dot, Chief."

"Close. Could be closer, but our Captain will take the recommendation nonetheless. Trusty G.P.S. fixes your Twelve Hundred position at thirty degrees eleven-decimal-seven minutes north, eighty-seven degrees five minutes west. Thirty degrees eleven-decimal-seven minutes north, eighty-seven degrees five

minutes west. Given set and drift two-four-zero degrees at point-five nautical miles from the PIM, plot a course to maintain PIM track and arrive at Point B on time. You have ten minutes. Start the problem. Start the clock."

"Time. Officer Candidate Estephan. What is your recommended course and speed?"

"Almost there, Chief. Two-eight-one at four-decimal-six knots."

"You sight a vessel off your port bow in a crossing situation. The vessel is displaying a Ball Diamond Ball configuration. What action do you take. A, maintain course and speed. B, stop engines. C, alter course and speed to avoid other vessel. D, increase speed to cross ahead of other vessel. Brooks."

"Alter course and speed, Chief."

"Captain takes your recommendation. At Thirteen Hundred you sight the following round of bearing and radar ranges. The World Famous P-Cola Beach Tank. Thirty minutes twenty-four-decimal-two minutes north, eighty-six degrees ninety-nine-decimal-five minutes west. Now at zero-one-five degrees. I say again. Thirty minutes twenty-four-decimal-two minutes north. Eighty-six degrees ninety-nine-decimal-five minutes west. At the zero-one-five. Fort Pickens Tower. Thirty degrees ninety-nine-decimal-three minutes north, eighty-seven degrees seventeen-decimal-one minutes west. At the three-two-zero. I repeat. Thirty degrees ninety-nine-decimal-three minutes north, eighty-seven degrees seventeen-decimal-one minutes west. At the three-two-zero. And, last but not least, Deer Point. Thirty degrees twenty-decimal-six minutes north, eighty-seven degrees eleven minutes west which radar places at eight nautical miles. Thirty degrees twenty-decimal-six minutes north, eighty-seven degrees eleven minutes west at eight nautical miles. Plot your Thirteen Hundred fix and continue your D.R. track. Assuming you arrive at Point B an hour later, what is your recommended course and speed to arrive at Point C right on time? You have ten minutes. Start the problem, start the clock."

••

Position of Attention to Parade Rest

The position of attention is the basic military position. It indicates you are alert and ready for instruction. In this position, stand with your heels together, feet forming an angle of forty-five degrees, head and body erect, hips and shoulders level, and chest lifted. Allow your arms to hang naturally -- thumbs along skirt or trouser seams and fingers joined and in their natural curl. Keep your legs straight, but not stiff at the knees. Direct your head and eyes to the front. Keep your mouth closed, and pull your chin in slightly. When called to attention, bring the heel of your left foot to the heel of your right foot.

The command for parade rest is given only when the formation is at attention. It is executed in one count. At the command rest, move your left foot smartly twelve inches to the left. Both legs should be straight so your weight rests equally on each foot. At the same time, join hands behind your back with your right hand inside your left, palms to the rear just below the belt. The right hand loosely holds the left thumb. Fingers are extended and joined. Do not move and do not talk. Hold your head and eyes in the same position as you would if at attention.

••

"*Left! Left! Lefty! Right! Layo!*"
"Left!! Left!! Lefty!! Right!! Layo!!"
"*Left! Left! Keep-it-in-step!*"
"Left!! Left!! Keep-it-in-step!!"
"*Left! Left! Lefty-right-a-left-right!*"
"Left!! Left!! Lefty-right-a-left-right!!"
"*Lefty-right-left-right!*"
"Lefty-right-left-right!!"
"*Lefty-right-a-lo!*"
"Lefty-right-a-lo!!"
"*Ready-on-the-left-foot!*"
"Ready-on-the-left-foot!!"
"*The mighty-mighty-left-foot!*"
"The mighty-mighty-left-foot!!"
"Right turn! March!"
"Aye aye, Section Leader!!"
"Your left! Your left! *I heard that in the Navy!*"
"I heard that in the Navy!!"
"*The Mighty-Mighty Navy!*"
"The Mighty-Mighty Navy!!"

"*The World's Greatest Navy*!"
"The World's Greatest Navy!!"
"*The chow is mighty fine*!"
"The chow is mighty fine!!"
"*Last night we had ten puppies*!"
"Last night we had ten puppies!!"
"*This morning only nine*!"
"This morning only nine!!"
"*Hoorah*!"
"Hoorah!!"
"*Hoorah*!"
"Hoorah!!"
"*The chow is mighty fine*!"
"The chow is mighty fine!!"
"*I heard that in the Navy*!"
"I heard that in the Navy!!"
"*The Mighty-Mighty Navy*!"
"The Mighty-Mighty Navy!!"
"*The World's Greatest Navy*!"
"The World's Greatest Navy!!"
"*The coffee's mighty fine*!"
"The coffee's mighty fine!!"
"*It looks like muddy water*!"
"It looks like muddy water!!"
"*It tastes like turpentine*!"
"It tastes like turpentine!!"
"*Hoorah*!"
"Hoorah!!"
"*Hoorah*!"
"Hoorah!!"
"*The coffee is mighty fine*!"
"The coffee is mighty fine!!"
"*I heard that in the Navy*!"
"I heard that in the Navy!!"
"*The Mighty-Mighty Navy*!"
"The Mighty-Mighty Navy!!"
"*The World's Greatest Navy*!"
"The World's Greatest Navy!!"
"*The toilets are mighty fine*!"
"The toilets are mighty fine!!"
"*You flush them down at seven*!"

"You flush them down at seven!!"
"*They come back up again at nine*!"
"They come back up again at nine!!"
"*Er*!"
"Er!!"
"*They come back up again at nine*!"
"They come back up again at nine!!"
"*Hoorah*!"
"Hoorah!!"
"*Hoorah*!"
"Hoorah!!"
"*The toilets are mighty fine*!"
"The toilets are mighty fine!!"
"*I heard that in the Navy*!"
"I heard that in the Navy!!"
"*The Mighty-Mighty Navy*!"
"The Mighty-Mighty Navy!!"
"*The World's Greatest Navy*!"
"The World's Greatest Navy!!"
"*The pay is mighty fine*!"
"The pay is mighty fine!!"
"*They give one hundred dollars*!"
"They give one hundred dollars!!"
"*And take back ninety-nine*!"
"And take back ninety-nine!!"
"*Ready-on-the-left-foot*!"
"Ready-on-the-left-foot!!"
"*The mighty-mighty-left-foot*!"
"The mighty-mighty-left-foot!!"
"Right turn! March!"
"Aye aye, Section Leader!!"
"Your left! Your left! Keep-it-in-step! *When my Granny was ninety-one*!"
"When my Granny was ninety-one!!"
"*She did P.T. just for fun*!"
"She did P.T. just for fun!!"
"*When my Granny was ninety-two*!"
"When my Granny was ninety-two!!"
"*She did P.T. better than you*!"
"She did P.T. better than you!!"
"*When my Granny was ninety-three*!"
"When my Granny was ninety-three!!"

"*She did P.T. better than me!*"
"She did P.T. better than me!!"
"*When my Granny was ninety-four!*"
"When my Granny was ninety-four!!"
"*She ran two miles and then ran ten more!*"
"She ran two miles and then ran ten more!!"
"*When my Granny was ninety-five!*"
"When my Granny was ninety-five!!"
"*She did P.T. to stay alive!*"
"She did P.T. to stay alive!!"
"*When my Granny was ninety-six!*"
"When my Granny was ninety-six!!"
"*She did P.T. just for kicks!*"
"She did P.T. just for kicks!!"
"*When my Granny was ninety-seven!*"
"When my Granny was ninety-seven!!"
"*She up and died and went to heaven!*"
"She up and died and went to heaven!!"
"*She met Saint Peter at the pearly gates!*"
"She met Saint Peter at the pearly gates!!"
"*Said hey, Saint Peter am I too late?*"
"Said hey, Saint Peter am I too late?"
"*Saint Peter looked at her with a big ole grin!*"
"Saint Peter looked at her with a big ole grin!!"
"*And said get down Granny and knock out ten!*"
"And said get down Granny and knock out ten!!"
"*Left! Left! Lefty! Right! Layo!*"
"Left!! Left!! Lefty!! Right!! Layo!!"
"*Left! Left! Keep-it-in-step!*"
"Left!! Left!! Keep-it-in-step!!"
"*Ready-on-the-left-foot!*"
"Ready-on-the-left-foot!!"
"*The mighty-mighty-left-foot!*"
"The mighty-mighty-left-foot!!"
"Ready! Halt!"
"Aye aye, Section Leader!!"
"Class Zero-Four-Zero-Zero! Right! Face!"
"Aye aye, Section Leader!!"
"Cover."
"Aye aye, Section Leader!!"
"Class Zero-Four-Zero-Zero! At ease!"

"Aye aye, Section Leader!!"

Sun beats down on the formation. I shift my weight from foot to foot with my legs bent slightly at the knees. Chief Jones leads the reviewing panel up Chambers Avenue.

"Prepare for inspection."

"Aye aye, Sir. Officer Candidate School Class Zero-Four-Zero-Zero! Attenhut!"

"Open ranks! March!"

"Ready. Front. Cover."

"Report!"

"First platoon. All present and accounted for, Sir."

"Very well."

"Second platoon. All present and accounted for, Sir."

"Very well."

"Third platoon. All present and accounted for, Sir."

"Very well."

"Fourth platoon. All present and accounted for, Sir."

"Very well."

"Class Zero-Four-Zero-Zero all present and accounted for, reporting for personnel inspection, Sir."

"Carry on."

"Aye aye, Sir. Class Zero-Four-Zero-Zero! Uncover! Two!"

"Cover! Two!"

"Atten-hut!"

"First platoon is standing by for your inspection, Sir."

"Very well."

"Second platoon is standing by for your inspection, Sir."

"Very well."

"Third platoon is standing by for your inspection, Sir."

"Very well."

"Fourth platoon is standing by for your inspection, Sir."

"Very well."

"Class Zero-Four-Zero-Zero! Close ranks! March!"

"Class Zero-Four-Zero-Zero! At ease!"

The Chiefs make their way down the line.

"Good afternoon."

"Good afternoon, Sir. Officer Candidate Orton, Officer Candidate School, Officer Candidate Class Zero-Four-Zero-Zero, United States Navy, ready for inspection."

"Revisit the nametag."

"Aye aye, Sir."

"Improper crease."

"Aye aye, Sir."

"Your identification, please."

"Aye aye, Sir."

"Thank you. What is today's date, Candidate?"

"Sir, today's date is the twenty-seventh of September Nineteen-Ninety-Nine, Sir."

"A fine Navy day."

"Aye aye, Sir."

"What is the third article of the Code of Conduct?"

"Sir, the third article of the Code of Conduct is if I am captured, I will continue to resist by all means available. I will make every effort to escape and aid others to escape. I will accept neither parole nor special favors from the enemy."

"Very well. At ease."

"Aye aye, Sir."

"Good afternoon."

"Good afternoon, Sir. Officer Candidate Fortunato, Officer Candidate School, Officer Candidate Class Zero-Four-Zero-Zero, United States Navy, ready for inspection."

"Improper gig line."

"Aye aye, Sir."

"Officer Candidate Fortunato, what is the definition of discipline?"

"Sir, the definition of discipline is the unconditional obedience-to-orders, respect-for-authority and self-reliance."

"Who is the tenth person in your Chain of Command?"

"Sir, the tenth person in this Officer Candidate's Chain of Command is the Chief of Naval Operations, Admiral Jay Johnson."

"And to whom does Admiral Johnson report?"

"Sir, the Chief of Naval Operations, Admiral Jay Johnson, reports to the Secretary of the Navy, the Honorable Richard J. Danzig."

"Very well. Let me see that cover."

"Aye aye, Sir."

"Fingerprints."

"Aye aye, Sir."

"Be more careful in the future."

"Aye aye, Sir."

"Good afternoon, Sir. Officer Candidate Zurich, Officer Candidate School, Officer Candidate Class Zero-Four-Zero-Zero, United States Navy, ready for inspection."

"Good afternoon. And how are we doing this afternoon?"

"Outstanding, Sir."

"A fine Navy day."

"Yes, Sir."

"Looks good on the outside. Eagles?"

"Flying, Sir."

"Trust but verify. Identification please."

"Aye aye, Sir."

"Very well. Officer Candidate Zurich, what is the first article of the Code of Conduct?"

"Sir, the first article of the Code of Conduct is I am an American, fighting in the forces which guard my country and our way of life. I am prepared to give my life in their defense."

"Is that true?"

"Sir?"

"Is that true?"

"Yes, Sir."

"Better to know."

"Aye aye, Sir."

"What is the sixth General Order of a Sentry?"

"Sir, the sixth General Order of a Sentry is to receive, obey and pass on to the sentry who relieves me, all orders from the Commanding Officer, Command Duty Officer, Officer of the Deck, and Officers and Petty Officers of the Watch only."

"Very well, Zurich. Carry on."

"Aye aye, Sir."

"Good afternoon, there, Candidate."

"Good afternoon, Sir. Officer Candidate Bremer, Officer Candidate School, Officer Candidate Class Zero-Four-Zero-Zero, United States Navy, ready for inspection, Sir."

"Identification, please."

"Sir."

"Were the eagles flying?"

"This Officer Candidate does not know but will find out, Sir."

"I'll have to dock you for that, Candidate."

"Aye aye, Sir."

"Very well. Who is the eleventh person in your Chain of Command?"

"Sir, the eleventh person in this Officer Candidate's Chain of Command is the Secretary of the Navy, the Honorable Richard J. Danzig."

"And to whom does he report?"

"Sir, the Honorable Richard J. Danzig reports to the Secretary of Defense, the Honorable William Cohen."

"Very well."

"Good afternoon, Sir. Officer Candidate Paterson, Officer Candidate School, Officer Candidate Class Zero-Four-Zero-Zero, United States Navy, ready for inspection, Sir."

"Oh my. Did you iron that uniform with a rock this morning, Paterson?"

"No excuse, Sir."

"What is today's date?"

"This Officer Candidate does not know but will find out, Sir."

"Careful, Paterson. This is not the evolution you want to fail. Today's date is the twenty-seventh of September Nineteen-Ninety-Nine."

"Aye aye, Sir."

"What is the Sailor's Creed?"

"Sir, the Sailor's Creed is I am a United States Sailor I will support and defend the Constitution of the United States of America and I will obey the orders of those appointed over me. I represent the fighting spirit of the Navy and those who have gone before me to defend freedom and democracy around the world. I proudly serve my country's Navy combat team with honor, courage and commitment. I am committed to excellence and the fair treatment of all."

"Ninth inning save. Very well. Carry on."

"Aye aye, Sir."

A candidate drops to a knee in the peripheral.

"T.T.O., Sir."

"What's that?"

"Training Time Out, Sir."

"Who is that? Mura? Everything okay, son?"

"Yes, Chief."

"You don't look fine to me. Officer Candidate Smith, please accompany Officer Candidate Mura directly to Medical."

"Aye aye, Sir."

The inspection fades as the Chiefs continue down the formation. Rivulets of sweat seep into my undershirt.

"Class Zero-Four-Zero-Zero! Attenhut! We have calculated your scores. Your sixth week Personnel Inspection average is, let me make absolutely sure, ninety-seven point two out of a total possible score of one hundred. Congratulations. Well done. Be advised that you remain secure at the discretion of the Naval Aviation Schools Command, privileges that may be revoked or suspended at any time due to lack of good order and discipline. Is that perfectly understood?"

"Yes, Sir!!"

"What's that?"

"Yes, Sir!!"

"Off you go. Section Leader, take charge of your platoon and carry out the Plan of the Day."

"Aye aye, Sir."

"Class Zero-Four-Zero-Zero! Assemble to the right! March!"

"Aye aye, Section Leader!!"

"Cover. Right! Face!"

"Aye aye, Section Leader!!"

"Forward! March!"

"Aye aye, Section Leader!!"

"Your left! Your left! Your left-right-left! Your left! Your left! Your left-right-left! Your left! Your left! Your left-right-left! Your left! Your left! Left! Left! Right! Left! Your left! Your left! Your left-right-left! Your left! Your left! Your left-right-left! Your left! Your left! Your left-right-left! Your left! Your left! Left! Left! Right! Left! Your left! Your left! Your left-right-left! Your left! Your left! Your left-right-left! Your left! Your left! Your left-right-left! Your left! Your left! Left! Left! Right! Left! When I say *sake*! You say bomb! *Sake*!"

"Bomb!!"

"*Sake*!"

"Bomb!!"

"*Hey, Hey Captain Jack*!"

"Hey, Hey Captain Jack!!"

"*Meet me down by the railroad track*!"

"Meet me down by the railroad track!!"

"*With a bottle in your hand*!"

"With a bottle in your hand!!"

"*Because I'm gonna be a drinking man*!"

"Because I'm gonna be a drinking man!!"

"*A drinking man*!"

"A drinking man!!"

"*Sake*!"

"Bomb!!"

"*Sake*!"

"Bomb!!"

"*Hey, Hey Captain Jack*!"

"Hey, Hey Captain Jack!!"

"*Meet me down by the railroad track*!"

"Meet me down by the railroad track!!"

"*With a K-bar in your hand*!"

"With a K-bar in your hand!!"

"*I'm gonna be a stabbing man*!"

"I'm gonna be a stabbing man!!"

"*A stabbing man*!"
"A stabbing man!!"
"*A drinking man*!"
"A drinking man!!"
"*Sake*!"
"Bomb!!"
"*Sake*!"
"Bomb!!"
"*Hey, hey Captain Jack*!"
"Hey, hey Captain Jack!!"
"*Meet me down by the railroad track*!"
"Meet me down by the railroad track!!"
"*With a bible in your hand*!"
"With a bible in your hand!!"
"*I'm gonna be a preaching man*!"
"I'm gonna be a preaching man!!"
"*A preaching man*!"
"A preaching man!!"
"*A stabbing man*!"
"A stabbing man!!"
"*A drinking man*!"
"A drinking man!!"
"*Sake*!"
"Bomb!!"
"*Sake*!"
"Bomb!!"
"*Hey, hey captain Jack*!"
"Hey, hey captain Jack!!"
"*Meet me down by the railroad track*!"
"Meet me down by the railroad track!!"
"*With a lady in your hand*!"
"With a lady in your hand!!"
"*I'm gonna be a loving man*!"
"I'm gonna be a loving man!!"
"*A loving man*!"
"A loving man!!"
"*A preaching man*!"
"A preaching man!!"
"*A stabbing man*!"
"A stabbing man!!"
"*A drinking man*!"

"A drinking man!!"
"*Sake*!"
"Bomb!!"
"*Sake*!"
"Bomb!!"
"*Hey, hey captain Jack*!"
"Hey, hey captain Jack!!"
"*Meet me down by the railroad track*!"
"Meet me down by the railroad track!!"
"*Because we are Navy*!"
"Because we are the Navy!!"
"*The mighty-mighty Navy*!"
"The mighty-mighty Navy!!"
"*Hey-ay*! *Navy*!"
"Hey-ay!! Navy!!"
"*World's finest Navy*!"
"World's finest Navy!!"
"*And we have our liberty*!"
"*And we have our liberty!!*"

••

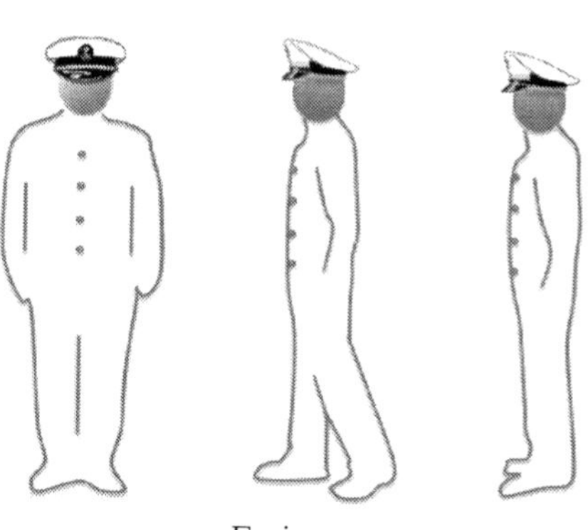

Facings

Facings are movements that can be made either to the right or left, with the exception of about face. While facing, your arms should remain at the position of attention. The following commands describe only the movement to the right. To perform a movement to the left, simply substitute left for right and right for left.

Right face. Right face is a two-count movement started on the commands right face. On the command face, raise your left heel and right toe slightly and

turn ninety degrees to the right. Keep your left leg straight but not stiff. Bring your left heel smartly alongside the right heel and stand at attention.

About face. About face is a two-count movement performed on the commands about face. On the command about, shift your weight to your left leg without noticeable movement. On the command face, place your right toe about six inches behind and slightly to the left of your left heel. On the ball of the right foot and the heel of the left foot, turn smartly to the right until you are facing the rear. Your feet will be in the position of attention when the turn is completed if you place your right toe properly behind your left heel.

••

"Class Zero-Four-Zero-Zero! Right face!"
"Aye aye, Section Leader!!"
"Forward march!"
"Aye aye, Section Leader!!"
"*Left! Left! Lefty! Right! Layo!*"
"Left!! Left!! Lefty!! Right!! Layo!!"
"*Left! Left! Keep-it-in-step!*"
"Left!! Left!! Keep-it-in-step!!"
"*Left! Left! Lefty-right-a-left-right!*"
"Left!! Left!! Lefty-right-a-left-right!!"
"*Lefty-right-left-right!*"
"Lefty-right-left-right!!"
"*Lefty-right-a-lo!*"
"Lefty-right-a-lo!!"
"*Everywhere we go-o!*"
"Everywhere we go-o!!"
"*People want to know-o!*"
"People want to know-o!!"
"*Who's the Zero-Four?*"
"Who's the Zero-Four?"
"*And so we tell them!*"
"And so we tell them!!"
"*We're not the Army!*"
"We're not the Army!!"
"*The backpacking Army!*"
"The backpacking Army!!"
"*We're not the Air Force!*"
"We're not the Air Force!!"
"*The low flying Air Force!*"

"The low flying Air Force!!"
"*We're not the Marines*!"
"We're not the Marines!!"
"*They're a little too mean*!"
"They're a little too mean!!"
"*We're not the Coast Guard*!"
"We're not the Coast Guard!!"
"*They don't even work hard*!"
"They don't even work hard!!"
"*We are the Navy*!"
"We are the Navy!!"
"*The world's greatest Navy*!"
"The world's greatest Navy!!"
"*The mighty-mighty Navy*!"
"The mighty-mighty Navy!!"
"*We are the Zero-Four*!"
"We are the Zero-Four!!"
"*Left! Left! Left! Right! Left!*"
"Left!! Left!! Left!! Right!! Left!!"
"*Left! Left! Left! Right! Lo*!"
"Left!! Left!! Left!! Right!! Lo!!"
"*Left! Left! Left! Right! Left!*"
"Left!! Left!! Left!! Right!! Left!!"
"*Left! Left! Left! Right! Lo*!"
"Left!! Left!! Left!! Right!! Lo!!"
"*Left! Left! Lefty*! *Right! Layo*!"
"Left!! Left!! Lefty!! Right!! Layo!!"
"*Left! Left! Keep-it-in-step*!"
"Left!! Left!! Keep-it-in-step!!"
"*Left! Left! Lefty-right-a-left-right!*"
"Left!! Left!! Lefty-right-a-left-right!!"
"*Lefty-right-left-right!*"
"Lefty-right-left-right!!"
"*Lefty-right-a-lo*!"
"Lefty-right-a-lo!!"
"*Around her hair she wore a yellow ribbon*!"
"Around her hair she wore a yellow ribbon!!"
"*She wore it in the spring-time, in the early month of May*!"
"She wore it in the spring-time, in the early month of May!!"
"*And if you asked her why the hell she wore it*?"
"And if you asked her why the hell she wore it?"

"*She'd say she wore it for her soldier who was far, far away!*"
"She'd say she wore it for her soldier who was far, far away!!"
"*Far away!*"
"Far away!!"
"*She wore it for her soldier who was far, far away!*"
"She wore it for her soldier who was far, far away!!"
"*Around the block she pushed a baby carriage!*"
"Around the block she pushed a baby carriage!!"
"*She pushed it in the spring time, in the early month of May!*"
"She pushed it in the spring time, in the early month of May!!"
"*And if you asked her why the hell she pushed it?*"
"And if you asked her why the hell she pushed it?"
"*She'd say she pushed it for her soldier who was far, far away!*"
"She'd say she pushed it for her soldier who was far, far away!!"
"*Far away!*"
"Far away!!"
"*She pushed it for her soldier who was far, far away!*"
"She pushed it for her soldier who was far, far away!!"
"*Behind the door, her father hid a shotgun!*"
"Behind the door, her father hid a shotgun!!"
"*She kept it in the spring time, in the early month of May!*"
"She kept it in the spring time, in the early month of May!!"
"*And if you asked her why the hell she kept it?*"
"And if you asked her why the hell she kept it?"
"*She'd say she kept it for her soldier who was far, far away!*"
"She'd say she kept it for her soldier who was far, far away!!"
"*Far away!*"
"Far away!!"
"*She kept it for her soldier who was far, far away!*"
"She kept it for her soldier who was far, far away!!"
"*Around his grave she laid the pretty flowers!*"
"Around his grave she laid the pretty flowers!!"
"*She laid them in the spring time, in the early month of May!*"
"She laid them in the spring time, in the early month of May!!"
"*And if you asked her why the hell she laid them?*"
"And if you asked her why the hell she laid them?"
"*She'd say she laid them for her soldier who was far, far away!*"
"She'd say she laid them for her soldier who was far, far away!!"
"*Far away!*"
"Far away!!"
"*She laid them for her soldier who was far, far away!*"

"She laid them for her soldier who was far, far away!!"

"*Left! Left! Lefty-right-a-left!*"

"Left!! Left!! Lefty-right-a-left!!"

"Left! Left! Keep-it-in-step! Ready! Right turn! March!"

"Aye aye, Section Leader!!"

"Your left! Your left! Your left-right-left! Your left! Your left! Keep-it-in-step! Ready! Halt!"

"Aye aye, Section Leader!!"

"Guide! Post the guide-on!"

"Aye aye, Section Leader!"

"Class Zero-Four-Zero-Zero! Ground your briefcases to the starboard side!"

"Aye aye, Section Leader!!"

"Upon receiving the command of execution *march*! You will! Half-step up this ladderwell, perform an immediate column-left, and reform at the door!"

"Aye aye, Section Leader!!"

"Ready! March!"

"Aye aye, Section Leader!!"

"Your left-right! Left-right! Ready! Halt! Ready! Halt!"

"Aye aye, Section Leader!!"

"Ready! Adjust!"

"Aye aye, Section Leader!! Discipline!! D!! I!! S!! C!! I!! P!! L!! I!! N!! E!! Discipline!! Is!! The unconditional!! Obedience-to-orders!! Respect-for-authority!! And self-reliance!! Freeze-candidate-freeze!!"

"Doorbody off the rear!"

"Doorbody, aye aye, Section Leader!!"

"Doorbody reporting as ordered, Section Leader!"

"Doorbody post!"

"Aye aye, Section Leader!"

"Doorbody! Report status of chow hall deck!"

"Aye aye, Section Leader! Chow hall deck not clear, Section Leader!"

"Chow hall deck not clear, Section Leader!!"

"Very well. Gougebody! Gouge the class!"

"Aye aye, Section Leader! Class Zero-Four-Zero-Zero! What is the definition of electronic warfare?"

"Aye aye, Gougebody!! The definition of electronic warfare is!! To deny the enemy effective use of the electromagnetic spectrum!!"

"Class Zero-Four-Zero-Zero! What are the Navy's fleet ballistic missiles?"

"Aye aye, Gougebody! The Navy's fleet ballistic missiles are!! The Trident One and Trident Two!!"

"Class Zero-Four-Zero-Zero! What are the Navy's air-to-ground missiles?"

"Aye aye, Gougebody!! The Navy's air-to-ground missiles are!! The HARM, the High Speed Anti-Radiation Missile!! And the Maverick!!"

"Class Zero-Four-Zero-Zero! What is the Aegis System?"

"Aye aye, Gougebody!! The Aegis System is!! The state-of-the-art surface-launched-weapon-system providing battle group area defense!!"

"Class Zero-Four-Zero-Zero! What is the definition of war-at-sea?"

"Aye aye, Gougebody!! The definition of war-at-sea is!! The application of decisive offensive force to achieve control of the sea!! Which is!! The first step in establishing our superiority in any region!!"

"Class Zero-Four-Zero-Zero! What is the definition of littoral warfare?"

"Aye aye, Gougebody!! The definition of littoral warfare is!! Warfare in that portion of the world's land masses!! Adjacent to the oceans!! Within direct control of!! And vulnerable to!! The striking power of sea-based forces!!"

"Doorbody! Report status of chow hall deck!"

"Aye aye, Section Leader! Chow hall deck all clear, Section Leader!"

"Chow hall deck all clear, Section Leader!!"

"Doorbody, crack the door!"

"Aye aye, Section Leader!"

"Class Zero-Four-Zero-Zero, marching into chow!"

"Class Zero-Four-Zero-Zero, marching into chow!!"

"Column of files! From the right! Forward!"

"Stand fast."

"March!"

"Good morning, Sir!"

"Zero-two!"

"Zero-three!"

"Zero-four!"

"Zero-five!"

"Zero-six!"

"Zero-seven!"

"Zero-eight!"

"Zero-niner!"

"One-zero!"

"One-one!"

"One-two!"

"One-three!"

"One-four!"

"One-five!"

"One-six!"
"One-seven!"
"One-eight!"
"One-niner!"
"Two-zero!"
"Two-one!"
"Two-two!"
"Two-three!"
"Two-four!"
"Two-five!"
"Two-six!"
"Two-seven!"
"Two-eight!"
"Two-niner!"
"Three-zero!"
"Three-one!"
"Three-two!"
"Three-three!"
"Three-four!"
"Three-five!"
"Three-six!"
"Three-seven!"
"Three-eight!"
"Three-niner!"
"Four-zero!"
"Four-one!"
"Doorbody, close the door!"
"Aye aye, Section Leader!"
"Class Zero-Four-Zero-Zero, proceed!"
"Aye aye, Section Leader!!"
"Forward march!"
"Step freeze!!"
"Stand fast."
"Forward march!"
"Step freeze!!"
"Stand fast."
"Forward march!"
"Step freeze!!"
"Stand fast."
"Forward march!"
"Step freeze!!"

"Stand fast."

"Forward march!"

"Step freeze!!"

"Stand fast."

"Forward march!"

"Step freeze!!"

"Stand fast."

"Forward march!"

"Step freeze!!"

"Stand fast."

"Forward march!"

"Step freeze!!"

"Stand fast."

"Forward march!"

"Step freeze!!"

"Stand fast."

"Forward march!"

"Step freeze!!"

"Stand fast."

"Forward march!"

"Step freeze!!"

"Stand fast."

"Forward march!"

"Step freeze!!"

"Stand fast."

"Forward march!"

"Step freeze!!"

"Stand fast."

"Forward march!"

"Step freeze!!"

"Stand fast."

"Forward march!"

"Step freeze!!"

"Stand fast."

"Forward march!"

"Step freeze!!"

"Stand fast."

"Good morning, Ma'am."

"Good morning, Darling. How are you doing today?"

"Outstanding, Ma'am. How are you?"

"I'm just fine, Sweetheart. What can I get you?"

"The chicken, please, Ma'am. Thank you. Green beans and mash potatoes."
"That good?"
"That's perfect, Ma'am."
"You sure, now?"
"Yes, Ma'am. Thank you."
"You're quite welcome. Enjoy."
"Yes, Ma'am."
"Put it away, Class Zero-Four-Zero-Zero!"
"Aye aye, Section Leader!!"
"Class Zero-Four-Zero-Zero! These tables! Both sides! Ready! Seats!"
"Kill!!"
"Adjust!"
"Kill!!"
"Pray at will!"
"Ready! Eat!"
"Snap!!"
"Class Zero-Four-Zero-Zero, this is your two-zero minute warning!"
"Aye aye, Section Leader!!"
"Class Zero-Four-Zero-Zero, this is your one-five minute warning!"
"Aye aye, Section Leader!!"
"Class Zero-Four-Zero-Zero, this is your one-zero minute warning!"
"Aye aye, Section Leader!!"
"Class Zero-Four-Zero-Zero, this is your zero-five minute warning!"
"Aye aye, Section Leader!!"
"Class Zero-Four-Zero-Zero, this is your immediate warning!"
"Aye aye, Section Leader!!"
"Class Zero-Four-Zero-Zero! Prepare to ground glasses on tray!"
"Aye aye, Section Leader!!"
"Ready! Move!"
"Aye aye, Section Leader!!"
"Class Zero-Four-Zero-Zero! Prepare to take your feet!"
"Aye aye, Section Leader!!"
"Ready! Move!"
"Aye aye, Section Leader!!"
"Class Zero-Four-Zero-Zero! Prepare to face the scullery!"
"Aye aye, Section Leader!!"
"Ready! Move!"
"Aye aye, Section Leader!!"
"Class Zero-Four-Zero-Zero! Prepare to recover trays!"
"Aye aye, Section Leader!!"
"Ready! Move!"

"Aye aye, Section Leader!!"
"Column of files! From the right!"
"Forward!"
"Stand fast."
"March!"
"Aye aye, Section Leader!!"
"Good afternoon, Sir!"
I dispose of my tray on the circular loop.
"Good afternoon, Sir!"
"Class Zero-Four-Zero-Zero! Left face!"
"Aye aye, Section Leader!!"
"Forward march!"
"Aye aye, Section Leader!!"
"*Left! Left! Left! Right! Left!*"
"Left!! Left!! Left!! Right!! Left!!"
"*Left! Left! Left! Right! Left!*"
"Left!! Left!! Left!! Right!! Left!!"
"*Left! Left! Left! Right! Left!*"
"Left!! Left!! Left!! Right!! Left!!"
"*Left! Left! Left! Right! Lo!*"
"Left!! Left!! Left!! Right!! Lo!!"
"*Left! Left! Left! Right! Left!*"
"Left!! Left!! Left!! Right!! Left!!"
"*Left! Left! Left! Right! Lo!*"
"Left!! Left!! Left!! Right!! Lo!!"
"*Everywhere we go-o!*"
"Everywhere we go-o!!"
"*People want to know-o!*"
"People want to know-o!!"
"*Who's the Zero-Four?*"
"Who's the Zero-Four!!"
"*And so we tell them!*"
"And so we tell them!!"
"*We're not the Army!*"
"We're not the Army!!"
"*The backpacking Army!*"
"The backpacking Army!!"
"*We're not the Air Force!*"
"We're not the Air Force!!"
"*The low flying Air Force!*"
"The low flying Air Force!!"

"*We're not the Marines*!"
"We're not the Marines!!"
"*They're a little too mean*!"
"They're a little too mean!!"
"*We're not the Coast Guard*!"
"We're not the Coast Guard!!"
"*They don't even work hard*!"
"They don't even work hard!!"
"*We are the Navy*!"
"We are the Navy!!"
"*The world's greatest Navy*!"
"The world's greatest Navy!!"
"*The mighty-mighty Navy*!"
"The mighty-mighty Navy!!"
"*We are the Zero-Four*!"
"We are the Zero-Four!!"
"*Left*! *Left*! *Lefty*! *Right*! *Layo*!"
"Left!! Left!! Lefty!! Right!! Layo!!"
"*Left*! *Left*! *Keep-it-in-step*!"
"Left!! Left!! Keep-it-in-step!!"
"*Left*! *Left*! *Lefty-right-a-left-right*!"
"Left!! Left!! Lefty-right-a-left-right!!"
"*Lefty-right-left-right*!"
"Lefty-right-left-right!!"
"Lefty-right-a-lo!"

....

Normal Interval

On the command fall in, the squad forms in line on the left of the right flank member (squad leader). Each member of the squad, except the left flank member, raises the left arm shoulder high in line with the body. Fingers are straight and touching each other palm down. Each member (except the right flank member) turns their head and looks to the right. To obtain a normal interval, move in line so that your right shoulder touches the fingertips of the person to the right. As soon as you are in line with the person to your right and the person on your left has obtained normal interval, return smartly and quickly to the position of attention.

Close Interval

Close interval is the horizontal distance between the shoulder and elbow when the left hand is placed on the left hip. The command at close interval requires the same movements as for normal interval. The only exception is that each member places the left hand on the beltline above the left hip with the elbow in line with the body. The heel of the hand rests on the hip with fingers straight, touching each other, and pointing down. The left flank member makes the adjustment without moving the arms.

••

Dance music pulses the room. Strobe lights wash across the surfaces.

"White tank top and jeans! Little black dress!"

"Where?"

"Nine o'clock!"

"Got it!"

"Well?"

"Wish me luck! I'll wave you down depending on how it goes! Long walk back in uniform! What?"

"Wait until the bartender goes over! Then you're just getting drinks! I mean, just in case! What's your plan?"

"*Hi, my name is Mike*!"

"Then what?"

"*Nice to meet you*!"

"Then what?"

"*Shots*!"

"God bless! Bottoms up!"

"Cheers."

"Drop the hammer!"

"It's time for action!"

I make my way down the length of the bar.

"What can I get you?"

"Two Heinekens!"

"You got it!"

I catch a glance.

"My name's Mike!"

"I'm Alison!"

"Alison?"

"Alison!"

"I'm Lisa!"

"Nice to meet you!"

"We like the uniform!"

"Thanks! I'm still getting used to it!"

"You're an Officer?"

"An Officer Candidate! We're in training to become Officers! Listen, I'm very shy!"

"You don't seem so shy!"

"Trust me! Here, give me your hand for a second!"

"My hand?"

"Your palm! Only for a second! See?"

"I can't decide whether that's charming or creepy!"

"Let's go with charming! See my friend over there?"

"Tough to miss! You guys glow something awful!"

"That's Francisco! We were hoping you might join us for a drink!"

"Is that how this goes? Don't you have to sing to us or something first?"

"Sing to you?"

"Sing to us! Don't you know?"

"No!"

"Oh, come on! How does it go again? *You don't love me anymore and it makes-me-sad*! Then it's like *Da Da-Da Da Da Da Da-Da*!"

"Sorry! Doesn't ring any bells!"

"You don't want to sing to us? I have to be honest, Mike! That's a little disappointing!"

"Very disappointing!"

"Later! I promise!"

The bartender returns with the drinks.

"Twelve dollars!"

"Oh, can I also get four shots of tequila?"

"What kind?"

"Patron if you got it!"

"You got it! Shots?"

"You might be trouble!"

"Trouble's not so bad! What about my friend Francisco?"

"Only if he sings too!"

I wave Francisco over. The Bartender returns with our shots.

"Alison and Lisa, this is Francisco! Francisco! Alison and Lisa! How does this go? I always forget!"

"Salt! Shot! Lime! Chaser!"

"What's this to?"

"Pensacola?"

"No, not Pensacola!"

"Why not?"

"You're not from here! How about *to all the guys I've ever known, you're some of them*?"

"I think I'm fine with that! Mike?"

"How about *to remembering this tomorrow*!"

"Yeah, I like that one!"

"Works for me!"

"Count of three, ready? Here we go!"

"One! Two! Three!"

"To remembering this tomorrow!!"

"Oh God! That's so brutal! Wow."

"Here, this will help!"

"Thanks."

"So, you're from here?"

"I think we're past that, Mike! You had me at *check out that guy at the end of the bar*! You don't have to sing, but you do have to dance! You are allowed to dance, aren't you?"

"Sure!"

"Well, come on then!"

She pulls me out onto the dancefloor. I step in close.

"*Remix my heart!*"
"*Remix my heart!*"
"*Remix my heart!*"

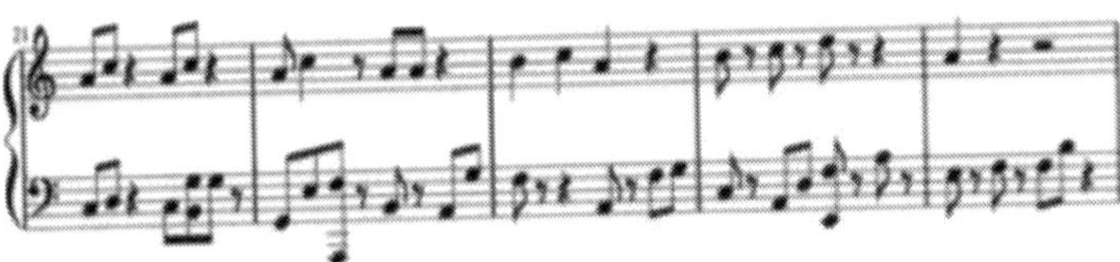

"*Remix my heart!*"
"*Remix my heart!*"
"*Remix my heart!*"

"*Remix my heart!*"
"*Remix my heart!*"
"*Remix my heart!*"

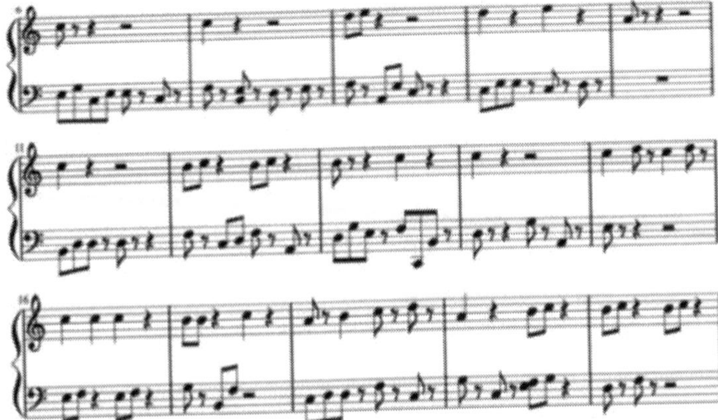

"*Remix my heart!*"
"*Remix my heart!*"
"*Remix my heart!*"

"*Remix my heart!*"
"*Remix my heart!*"
"*Remix my heart!*"

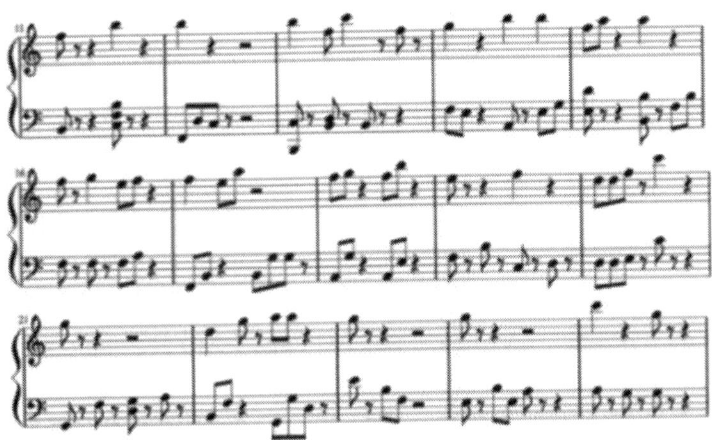

"Remix my heart!"
"Remix my heart!"
"Remix my heart!"

"Remix my heart!"
"Remix my heart!"
"Remix my heart!"

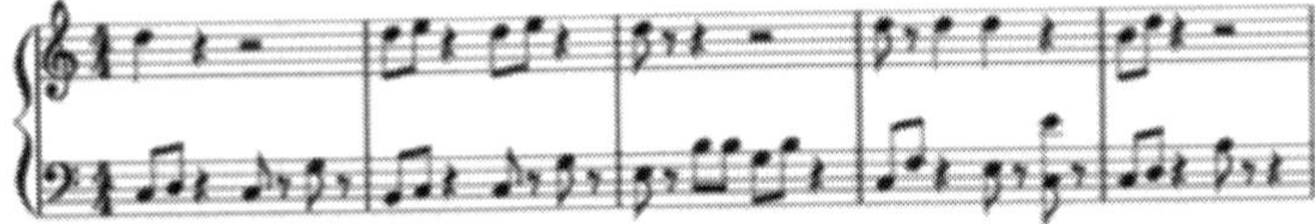

"Remix my heart!"
"Remix my heart!"
"Remix my heart!"

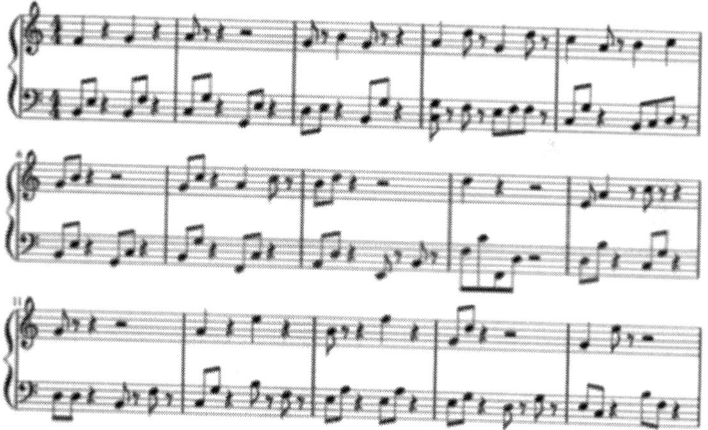

"Remix my heart!"
"Remix my heart!"
"Remix my heart!"

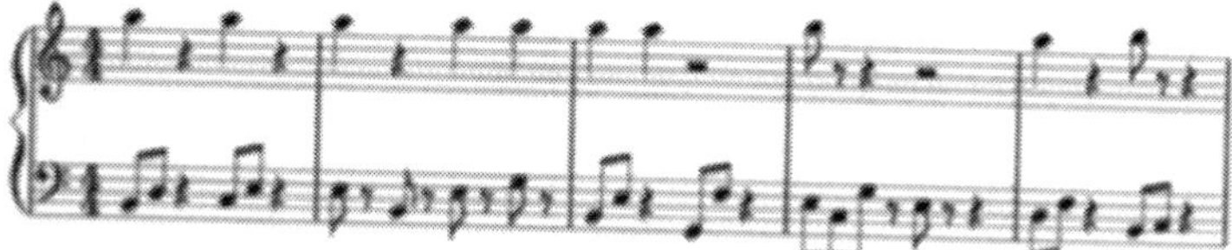

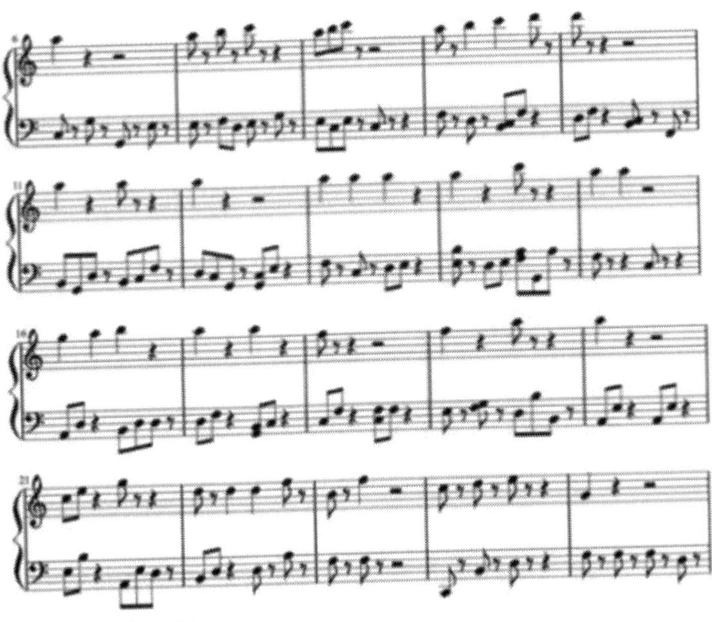

"Remix my heart!"
"Remix my heart!"
"Remix my heart!"

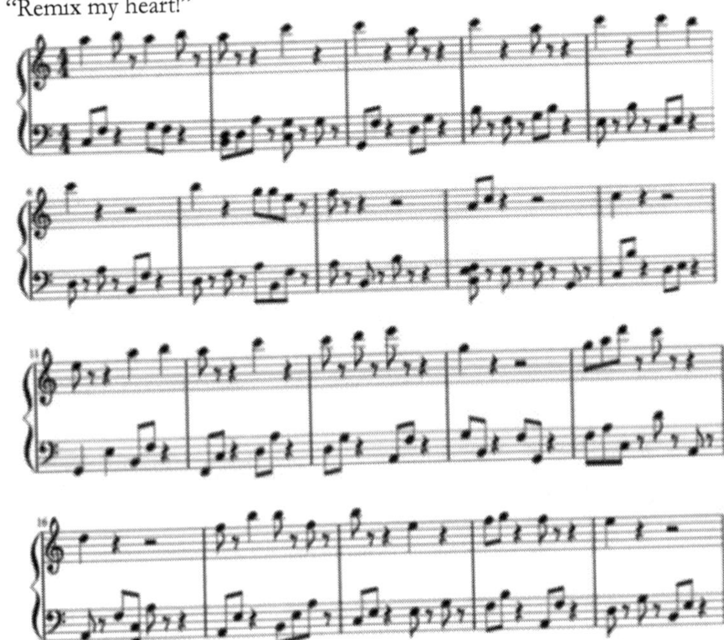

"Remix my heart."

••

Attention to Port Arms

Two methods are used for relieving armed sentries. One way (usually used ashore) is for the Petty Officer of the Watch (POOW) to fall in the reliefs and march them to their posts. Normally, each person in the relieving detail is armed with a rifle. At each post, the Petty Officer halts the ranks, and both the sentry being relieved and the reporting sentry come to port arms while the person being relieved passes any special orders or other information the relief should know.

In the other method (usually used aboard ship), each relieving sentry goes alone to the post. This sentry normally is unarmed and will relieve the sentry of the rifle or pistol as well as the post. The relief reports to the sentry that he is ready to relieve the sentry. The sentry executes inspection arms and port arms and repeats the orders. The relief then confirms that the sentry is properly relieved. The relieving procedure is completed when the sentry being relieved passes the rifle to the relief and stands relieved.

••

"*Everywhere we go-o*!"
"Everywhere we go-o!!"
"*People want to know-o*!"
"People want to know-o!!"
"*Who's the Zero-Four?*"
"Who's the Zero-Four?"
"*And so we tell them*!"
"And so we tell them!!"
"*We're not the Army*!"
"We're not the Army!!"
"*The backpacking Army*!"

"The backpacking Army!!"
"*We're not the Air Force*!"
"We're not the Air Force!!"
"*The low flying Air Force*!"
"The low flying Air Force!!"
"*We're not the Marines*!"
"We're not the Marines!!"
"*They're a little too mean*!"
"They're a little too mean!!"
"*We're not the Coast Guard*!"
"We're not the Coast Guard!!"
"*They don't even work hard*!"
"They don't even work hard!!"
"*We are the Navy*!"
"We are the Navy!!"
"*The world's greatest Navy*!"
"The world's greatest Navy!!"
"*The mighty-mighty Navy*!"
"The mighty-mighty Navy!!"
"*We are the Zero-Four*!"
"We are the Zero-Four!!"
"*Left*! *Left*! *Left-right-a-left*!"
"Left!! Left!! Left-right-a-left!!"
"*Left*! *Left*! *Keep-it-in-step*!"
"Left!! Left!! Keep-it-in-step!!"
"*Lo*! *Right-a-lo-right*!"
"Lo!! Right-a-lo-right!!"
"*Lo*! *Right-a-left-right*!"
"Lo!! Right-a-left-right!!"
"*Lefty-right-a-lo*!"
"Lefty-right-a-lo!!"
"*Left*! *Left*! *Lefty*! *Right*! *Layo*!"
"Left!! Left!! Lefty!! Right!! Layo!!"
"*Left*! *Left*! *Keep-it-in-step*!"
"Left!! Left!! Keep-it-in-step!!"
"*Left*! *Left*! *Lefty-right-a-left-right*!"
"Left!! Left!! Lefty-right-a-left-right!!"
"*Lefty-right-left-right*!"
"Lefty-right-left-right!!"
"*Lefty-right-a-lo*!"
"Lefty-right-a-lo!!"

"*On the left foot! A yel-low bird!*"
"A yel-low bird!!"
"*With a yel-low bill!*"
"With a yel-low bill!!"
"*He lan-ded on!*"
"He lan-ded on!!"
"*My win-dow sill!*"
"My win-dow sill!!"
"*Lo! Right-a-lo-right!*"
"Lo!! Right-a-lo-right!!"
"*Lo! Right-a-left-right!*"
"Lo!! Right-a-left-right!!"
"*Lefty-right-a-lo!*"
"Lefty-right-a-lo!!"
"On the left foot! *So I coaxed him in!*"
"So I coaxed him in!!"
"*With a piece of bread!*"
"With a piece of bread!!"
"*And then I smashed his!*"
"And then I smashed his!!"
Left feet stomp down hard on the pavement.
"Little head!!"
"*Lo-right-a-lo-right!*"
"Lo-right-a-lo-right!!"
"*Lo-right-a-left-right!*"
"Lo-right-a-left-right!!"
"*Lefty-right-a-lo!*"
"Lefty-right-a-lo!!"
"*Left! Left! Lefty! Right! Layo!*"
"Left!! Left!! Lefty!! Right!! Layo!!"
"*Left! Left! Keep-it-in-step!*"
"Left!! Left!! Keep-it-in-step!!"
"*Left! Left! Lefty-right-a-left-right!*"
"Left!! Left!! Lefty-right-a-left-right!!"
"*Lefty-right-left-right!*"
"Lefty-right-left-right!!"
"*Lefty-right-a-lo!*"
"Lefty-right-a-lo!!"
"*Well, I called the doctor!*"
"Well, I called the doctor!!"
"*And the doctor said!*"

"And the doctor said!!"
"*My dear good man*!"
"My dear good man!!"
"*This bird is dead*!"
"This bird is dead!!"
"*Lo*! *Right-a-lo-right*!"
"Lo!! Right-a-lo-right!!"
"*Lo*! *Right-a-left-right*!"
"Lo!! Right-a-left-right!!"
"*Lefty-right-a-lo*!"
"Lefty-right-a-lo!!"
"*Left*! *Left*! *Lefty*! *Right*! *Layo*!"
"Left!! Left!! Lefty!! Right!! Layo!!"
"*Left*! *Left*! *Keep-it-in-step*!"
"Left!! Left!! Keep-it-in-step!!"
"*Left*! *Left*! *Lefty-right-a-left-right*!"
"Left!! Left!! Lefty-right-a-left-right!!"
"*Lefty-right-left-right*!"
"Lefty-right-left-right!!"
"*Lefty-right-a-lo*!"
"Lefty-right-a-lo!!"
"On the left foot! *So the moral is*!"
"So the moral is!!"
"*My children dear*!"
"My children dear!!"
"*If you're a bird*!"
"If you're a bird!!"
"*Get the hell outa here*!"
"Get the hell outa here!!"
"Right turn! March!"
"Aye aye, Section Leader!!"
"*Left*! *Left*! *Left-right-a-left*!"
"Left!! Left!! Left-right-a-left!!"
"*Left*! *Left*! *Keep-it-in-step*!"
"Left!! Left!! Keep-it-in-step!!"
"*Left*! *Left*! *Lefty*! *Right*! *Layo*!"
"Left!! Left!! Lefty!! Right!! Layo!!"
"*Left*! *Left*! *Keep-it-in-step*!"
"Left!! Left!! Keep-it-in-step!!"
"*Left*! *Left*! *Lefty-right-a-left-right*!"
"Left!! Left!! Lefty-right-a-left-right!!"

"*Lefty-right-left-right*!"
"Lefty-right-left-right!!"
"*Lefty-right-a-lo*!"
"Lefty-right-a-lo!!"
"Ready! Left-turn! March!"
"Aye aye, Section Leader!!"
"*Lo! Right-a-lo-right*!"
"Lo!! Right-a-lo-right!!"
"*Lo! Right-a-left-right*!"
"Lo!! Right-a-left-right!!"
"*Lo! Right-a-lo-right*!"
"Lo!! Right-a-lo-right!!"
"*Lo! Right-a-left-right*!"
"Lo!! Right-a-left-right!!"
"*Lefty-right-a-lo*!"
"Lefty-right-a-lo!!"
"Left turn! March!"
"Aye aye, Section Leader!!"
"*Left! Left! Lefty-right-left*!"
"Left!! Left!! Lefty-right-left!!"
"*Left! Left! Keep-it-in-step*!"
"Left!! Left!! Keep-it-in-step!!"
"Platoon! Halt!"
"Aye aye, Section Leader!!"
"Right! Face!"
"Aye aye, Section Leader!!"

Staff Sergeant Willett stands at attention in full dress sword carried. An inspection team makes notations on clipboards off to the side.

"Class Zero-Four-Zero-Zero, reporting for duty as ordered, Sir!"

"Very well. At close interval! Fall in!"

"Aye aye, Sir!!"

"Pray-at-will!"

"Aye aye, Sir!! This is my rifle!! There are many like it!! But this one is mine!! My rifle is my best friend!! It is my life!! I must master it as I must master my life!! My rifle, without me, is useless!! Without my rifle, I am useless!! I must fire my rifle true!! I must shoot straighter than my enemy who is trying to kill me!! I must shoot him before he shoots me!! I will!! My rifle and myself know that what counts in this war is not the rounds we fire!! The noise of our burst!! Nor the smoke we make!! We know that it is the hits that count!! We will hit!! My rifle is human, even as I, because it is my life!! Thus, I will learn it as a brother!! I will learn its weaknesses!! Its strength!! Its parts!! Its accessories!! Its sights and its

barrel!! I will ever guard it against the ravages of weather and damage!! As I will ever guard my legs!! My arms!! My eyes!! And my heart against damage!! I will keep my rifle clean!! And ready!! We will become part of each other!! We will!! Before God, I swear this creed!! My rifle and myself are the defenders of my country!! We are the masters of our enemy!! We are the saviors of my life!! So be it, until victory is America's!! And there is no enemy!! But peace!!"

"Dress-right-dress! Report!"

"First squad! All present!"

"Second squad! All present!"

"Third squad! All present!"

"Fourth squad! All present!"

"Very well. Inspection! Arms!"

"Port! Arms!"

"Order! Arms!"

"Quarter Master Gunnery Sergeant, Class Zero-Four-Zero-Zero all present and accounted for, reporting for drill evaluation."

"Very well. Take your post."

"Aye aye, Master Sergeant."

"Count! Off!"

"One!!"

"Two!!"

"Three!!"

"Four!!"

"Five!!"

"Six!!"

"Seven!!"

"Eight!!"

"Niner!!"

"One-zero!!"

"One-one!!"

"One-two!!"

"Open ranks! March! Left-right! Left-right! Left-right! Left-right! Left-right! Left-right!"

"Ready! Front! Cover!"

"Rooster! Port! Steady!"

"Elkind! Port!"

"Ready! Front! Cover!"

"Port! Arms!"

"Right shoulder! Arms!"

"Left shoulder! Arms!"

"Port! Arms!"

"Order! Arms!"

"Present! Arms!"

"Order! Arms!"

"Right! Face!"

"Left! Face!"

"About! Face!"

"About! Face!"

"Parade rest!"

"Platoon! Attenhut!"

"Close ranks! March! Left-right! Left-right! Left-right! Left-right! Left-right! Left-right! Left-right!"

"Extend! March! Left-right! Left-right! Left-right! Left-right! Left-right! Left-right! Left-right! Left-right!"

"Dress! Right! Dress!"

"Ready! Front!"

"Cover!"

"Right shoulder! Arms!"

"Rifle! Salute!"

"Ready! Two!"

"Port! Arms!"

"Order! Arms!"

"Present! Arms!"

"Order! Arms!"

"Right! Face!"

"Left! Face!"

"About! Face!"

"About! Face!"

"Parade rest!"

"Platoon! Attenhut!"

"Close ranks! March! Left-right! Left-right! Left-right! Left-right! Left-right! Left-right! Left-right!"

"Right! Face!"

"Rest!"

"Platoon! Attenhut!"

"Port! Arms!"

"Forward! March! Ho! Hai! Ho! Close! March! Haight! Haight! Haight! Forward! March! Leh-haight-a-leh-oh! Lo-haight-lo! Leh-haight-a-leh-oh! Leh-haight-a-leh-oh! Extend! March! Left! Left! Left! Haight! Haight! Forward! March! Lo-right-lo! Lo-right-lo! Lo-right-a-leh-ho! Lo-right-a-leh-ah! Lo-right-lo! Lo-right-lo! Lo-right-leh-ho! Lo-right-lay-ho! Mark time! March! Da-ra-o-oh-oh-oh-

o-eh-oh! Da-ra-o-oh-oh-oh-o-eh-oh! Da-ra-oh-oh-oh-oh-oh-leh-oh! Da-ra-leh-ho-leh-ho-ho! Platoon! Halt!"

The Inspection Team combs the formation for irregularities clipboards in hand.

"Forward! March! Left-right-lo! Left-right-lo! Leh-haight-a-leh-oh! Lo-haight-lo! Leh-haight-a-leh-oh! Lo-haight-lo! By the right flank! March! Left-right-lo! Left-right-lo! Left-right-lo! Left-right-lo! By the left flank! March! Da-ra-o-oh-oh-oh-o-eh-oh! Da-ra-o-oh-oh-oh-o-eh-oh! Da-ra-oh-oh-oh-oh-oh-leh-oh! Da-ra-leh-ho-leh-ho-ho! Left-right-lo! Left-right-lo! Left-right-lo! Left-right-lo! To the rear! March! Left-right-lo! Left-right-lo! Left-right-lo! Left-right-lo! Left-right-lo! Left-right-lo! Left-right-lo! To the rear! March! Left-right-lo! Left-right-lo! Left-right-lo! Left-right-lo! Column left! March! Left-right-lo! Left-right-lo! Left-right-lo! Left-right-lo! Left-right-lo! Left-right-lo! Column left! March! Left-right-lo! Left-right-lo! Left-right-lo! Left-right-lo! By the left flank! March! Da-ra-o-oh-oh-oh-o-eh-oh! Da-ra-o-oh-oh-oh-o-eh-oh! Da-ra-oh-oh-oh-oh-oh-leh-oh! Da-ra-leh-ho-leh-ho-ho! Left-right-lo! Left-right-lo! Left-right-lo! Left-right-lo! Column right! March! Left-right-lo! Left-right-lo! Left-right-lo! Left-right-lo! Column right! March! Left-right-lo! Left-right-lo! Left-right-lo! Left-right-lo! Left-oblique! March! Left-right-lo! Left-right-lo! Left-right-lo! Left-right-lo! Platoon! Halt!"

Insects swarm overhead.

"Right shoulder! Arms! To the rear! March! To the rear! March! Da-ra-o-oh-oh-oh-o-eh-oh! Da-ra-o-oh-oh-oh-o-eh-oh! Da-ra-oh-oh-oh-oh-oh-leh-oh! Da-ra-leh-ho-leh-ho-ho! Column left! March! Da-ra-o-oh-oh-oh-o-eh-oh! Da-ra-o-oh-oh-oh-o-eh-oh! Da-ra-oh-oh-oh-oh-oh-leh-oh! Da-ra-leh-ho-leh-ho-ho! Da-ra-o-oh-oh-oh-o-eh-oh! Da-ra-o-oh-oh-oh-o-eh-oh! Da-ra-oh-oh-oh-oh-oh-leh-oh! Da-ra-leh-ho-leh-ho-ho! Platoon! Halt!"

"Order! Arms!"

"Left! Face!"

"Parade rest!"

The Drill Instructors gather around the Master Sergeant in deliberation.

"Platoon! Attenhut!"

"In my hand, I hold a banner. A banner earned by those dedicated few willing to invest themselves, to exercise the discipline required to master and perform the Drill Manual as a unit. Your performance reflects not only on yourselves, but also on your Drill Instructor, Staff Sergeant Willett, his dedication, his commitment to his Corp. I have every expectation he will stand in my shoes one day as a Master Sergeant of the Corp. Today, you needed a minimum of one hundred and one points to pass Drill Competition and earn this here banner. One hundred and one points to raise it to the top of your guidon.

Class Zero-Four-Zero-Zero, today you scored one hundred and six points. Congratulations."

"Hoorah!!"

"Guide. Front and center."

"Aye aye, Master Sergeant!"

"Raise it up. Get some."

"Hoorah!!"

"Staff Sergeant. They're all yours. Carry on."

"Aye aye, Master Sergeant. Lock!"

"Motivation is contagious!!"

"Freeze!"

"Motivation is contagious!!"

"Fall out! Gather round. Take a knee up front."

"Aye aye, Sir!!"

"You Maggots did good today. One-o-six is the top score in ten weeks. Don't let it go to your nasty little Pig Heads."

"Aye aye, Sir!!"

"Lose focus now and you will fail, together as a unit and as freaking individuals. Am I clear?"

"Yes, Sir!!"

"Am I clear?"

"Yes, Sir!!"

"Right now, you're three for three. That's a reason to be confident. Don't get cocky. Back it up."

"Aye aye, Sir!!"

"At all times."

"Aye aye, Sir!!"

"Sound off."

"Aye aye, Sir!!"

"Fall in!"

"Aye aye, Sir!!"

"Carry on!"

"Aye aye, Sir!!"

"Hoorah, Class Zero-Four-Zero-Zero!"

"Hoorah!!"

"Lock!"

"Motivation is contagious!!"

"Freeze!"

"Motivation is contagious!!"

"Class Zero-Four-Zero-Zero! Right! Face!"

"Aye aye, Section Leader!!"

"Platoon! Forward! March!"

"Aye aye, Section Leader!!"

"Your left! Your left! Your left-right-left! Your left! Your left! Keep-it-in-step! On the left foot! *Everywhere we go-o!*"

"Everywhere we go-o!!"

"*People want to know-o!*"

"People want to know-o!!"

"*Who's the Zero-Four?*"

"Who's the Zero-Four?"

"*And so we tell them!*"

"And so we tell them!!"

"*We're not the Army!*"

"We're not the Army!!"

"*The backpacking Army!*"

"The backpacking Army!!"

"*We're not the Air Force!*"

"We're not the Air Force!!"

"*The low flying Air Force!*"

"The low flying Air Force!!"

"*We're not the Ma-rines!*"

"We're not the Ma-rines!!"

"*They're a little too mean!*"

"They're a little too mean!!"

"*We're not the Coast Guard!*"

"We're not the Coast Guard!!"

"*They don't even work hard!*"

"They don't even work hard!!"

"*We are the Navy!*"

"We are the Navy!!"

"*The world's greatest Navy!*"

"The world's greatest Navy!!"

"*The mighty-mighty Navy!*"

"The mighty-mighty Navy!!"

"*We are the Zero-Four!*"

"We are the Zero-Four!!"

"*Left! Left! Left-right-a-left!*"

"Left!! Left!! Left-right-a-left!!"

"*Left! Left! Keep-it-in-step!*"

"Left!! Left!! Keep-it-in-step!!"

"One the left foot! *A ti-ny mousse! With ti-ny feet!*"

"A ti-ny mousse!! With ti-ny feet!!"

"*Was lying on*! *My toilet seat*!"
"Was lying on!! My toilet seat!!"
"*Well I pushed it in*!"
"Well I push it in!!"
"*And I flushed it down*!"
"And I flushed it down!!"
"*That little mouse*!"
"That little mouse!!"
"*Went round and round*!"
"Went round and round!!"
"*Left*! *Left*! *Left-right-a-left*!"
"Left!! Left!! Left-right-a-left!!"
"*Left*! *Left*! *Keep-it-in-step*!"
"Left!! Left!! Keep-it-in-step!!"
"*Well for that mouse*!"
"Well for that mouse!!"
"*The moral is*!"
"The moral is!!"
"*My children dear*!"
"My children dear!!"
"*If you're a mouse*!"
"If you're a mouse!!"
"*Get the hell outa here*!"
"Get the hell outa here!!"
"*Left*! *Left*! *Lefty*! *Right*! *Layo*!"
"Left!! Left!! Lefty!! Right!! Layo!!"
"*Left*! *Left*! *Keep-it-in-step*!"
"Left!! Left!! Keep-it-in-step!!"
"*Left*! *Left*! *Lefty-right-a-left-right*!"
"Left!! Left!! Lefty-right-a-left-right!!"
"*Lefty-right-left-right*!"
"Lefty-right-left-right!!"
"*Left*! *Left*! *Lefty-right-a-left-right*!"
"Left!! Left!! Lefty-right-a-left-right!!"
"*Lefty-right-left-right*!"
"Lefty-right-left-right!!"
"*Lefty-right-left-right*!"
"Lefty-right-left-right!!"
"*Lefty-right-a-lo*!"
"*Lefty-right-a-lo!!*"

••

Right Shoulder Arms

After the reviewing Officer has taken position back in the reviewing area and the troops are at attention, the commander to troops commands pass in review. The commander of the right battalion or independent company commands right shoulder arms and right turn march. The band steps off on the command of execution march with the right battalion or independent company. Succeeding battalions and independent companies are brought to right shoulder arms and execute a right turn in succession from right to left by their commanders so as to follow at the prescribed distances.

••

"There's a D.I. in there. Damn."
"What? How can you tell?"
"You can just tell."
"Come on."
"Dead quiet. It's a trap."
"Total paranoia."
"What time is it?"
"Fifteen till."
"You go on in first. No reason for both of us to take the hit."
"Relax."
"Go on. This is on me."
"No chance, brother. Could just as easily been my cover."
"Go."
"No dice, my man."
"I'm serious."

"Absolutely not."

"Christ."

"Ready? Worst case we get this over with, right?"

"Fine."

I proceed cautiously up the walkway palm on head. Silence greets us at the entranceway.

"Clear?"

"Negative."

I rap three times hard on the frame.

"Enter."

"Officer Candidate Zurich! Officer Candidate School! Officer Candidate Class Zero-Four-Zero-Zero! United States Navy! Reporting for duty as ordered, Sir!"

"You must be out of your damn mind. Is this serious?"

"Yes, Sir!"

"Am I on candid camera?"

"No, Sir!"

"Is this funny to you?"

"No, Sir!"

"Is this a story you want to tell your kids?"

"No, Sir!"

"You alone, Pig? I said, *are you alone*? That's a freaking response."

"No, Sir!"

"Where's your Pig Buddy, then? That's a freaking response."

"Outside, Sir!"

"Get your ass in here, Cowardly Pig!"

"Aye aye, Sir! Good morning, Sir! Officer Candidate Fortunato! Officer Candidate School! Officer Candidate Class Zero-Four-Zero-Zero! Reporting for duty as ordered, Sir!"

"Out all night, huh?"

"No, Sir!!"

"Likely freaking story. Where's the cover?"

"This Officer Candidate does not know but will find out, Sir!"

"You lost it?"

"No excuse, Sir!"

"You lost your cover?"

"Yes, Sir!"

"And you decided go uncovered? Just like that, Pig?"

"No, Sir!"

"No?"

"No excuse, Sir!"

"Figured you would sneak back in, Pig?"

"No, Sir!"

"Cover it up."

"No, Sir!"

"No one the wiser."

"No, Sir!"

"Scum. I'll tell you what happens now. You have zero-five minutes, zero-five minutes to return to your Pigsty, retrieve your rifles and secure two Class Alpha chits."

"Aye aye, Sir!!"

"Move!"

"Aye aye, Sir!!"

"Good morning, Sir!"

"Good morning, Sir!"

We double-time to the room in a flat-out sprint. Jackson looks up from his desk as we burst into the space.

"What's with you two?"

"Burton. Where can we get two Class Alphas?"

"Alphas?"

"No time."

"Let me check with Smith."

"Thanks, man."

I fumble with the combination lock. My rifle stares at me from the back of the locker. Jackson returns chits in hand.

"Alphas, huh? Need backup?"

"Won't argue. You'll need your rifle."

"That bad?"

"Worse."

"Best get it over with then."

"Ready?"

"Ready."

"Let's do this, baby."

We double time back down to The Pit. I take the pole position.

"Get in here, Pigs."

"Aye aye, Sir! Good morning, Sir!"

"Step!"

"Good morning, Sir!"

"Spare me."

"Aye aye, Sir!!"

"Who are you?"

"Officer Candidate Jackson! Officer Candidate School! Officer Candidate Class Zero-Four-Zero-Zero! United States Navy!"

"Like it matters. As you freaking wish. Where are my chits?"

"Here, Sir!"

"Shut your freaking holes. Brace."

"Aye aye, Sir!!"

"I said brace, Pigs!"

"Aye aye, Sir!!"

"When you leave this base, when you leave this command, you remain on active duty. You represent the United States Navy and the United States Marines who train you at all times. You remain under standing orders to present a proud and professional appearance that reflects positively on you as an individual, the United States Navy and the United States Marine Corp at all times. When you soil your uniform, when civilians see you in that soiled uniform, when the enemy sees you in that soiled uniform, you violate that privilege. You discredit the United States Navy and the Corp. You discredit the moral, pride and discipline of the armed services. You weaken us. You weaken this country. Am I clear?"

"Yes, Sir!!"

"You don't have weekends anymore. You don't have nights. What you have is liberty. Liberty is a privilege. Am I clear?"

"Yes, Sir!!"

"Your conduct merits a Class Alpha. A Class Alpha right here and now, explaining yourselves in front of the Captain. Is that perfectly clear?"

"Yes, Sir!!"

"On your faces. Push."

"Aye aye, Sir!!"

"Up. Give me the rifle creed. *Aye aye, Sir.*"

"Aye aye, Sir!!"

"Louder!"

"Aye aye, Sir!! Sir!! This is my rifle!! There are many like it!! But this one is mine!! My rifle is my best friend!! It is my life!! I must master it as I must master my life!! My rifle, without me, is useless!! Without my rifle, I am useless!! I must fire my rifle true!! I must shoot straighter than my enemy who is trying to kill me!! I must shoot him before he shoots me!!"

"Down. *Aye aye, Sir.*"

"Aye aye, Sir!! I will!! My rifle and myself know that what counts in this war is not the rounds we fire!! The noise of our burst!! Nor the smoke we make!! We know that it is the hits that count!! We will hit!! My rifle is human, even as I, because it is my life!! Thus, I will learn it as a brother!! I will learn its weaknesses!! Its strength!! Its parts!! Its accessories!! Its sights and its barrel!!"

"Up."

"Aye aye, Sir!! I will ever guard it against the ravages of weather and damage!! As I will ever guard my legs!! My arms!! My eyes!! And my heart against damage!! I will keep my rifle clean!! And ready!! We will become part of each other!! We will!! Before God, I swear this creed!!"

"Down."

"Aye aye, Sir!! My rifle and myself are the defenders of my country!! We are the masters of our enemy!! We are the saviors of my life!! So be it, until victory is America's!! And there is no enemy!! But peace!!"

"Up. Again."

"Aye aye, Sir!! Sir!! This is my rifle!! There are many like it!! But this one is mine!! My rifle is my best friend!! It is my life!! I must master it as I must master my life!! My rifle, without me, is useless!! Without my rifle, I am useless!! I must fire my rifle true!! I must shoot straighter than my enemy who is trying to kill me!! I must shoot him before he shoots me!!"

"Down."

"Aye aye, Sir!! I will!! My rifle and myself know that what counts in this war is not the rounds we fire!! The noise of our burst!! Nor the smoke we make!! We know that it is the hits that count!! We will hit!! My rifle is human, even as I, because it is my life!! Thus, I will learn it as a brother!! I will learn its weaknesses!! Its strength!! Its parts!! Its accessories!! Its sights and its barrel!!"

"Up."

"Aye aye, Sir!! I will ever guard it against the ravages of weather and damage!! As I will ever guard my legs!! My arms!! My eyes!! And my heart against damage!! I will keep my rifle clean!! And ready!! We will become part of each other!! We will!! Before God, I swear this creed!!"

"Down!"

"Aye aye, Sir!! My rifle and myself are the defenders of my country!! We are the masters of our enemy!! We are the saviors of my life!! So be it, until victory is America's!! And there is no enemy!! But peace!!"

"Up. Again."

"Aye aye, Sir!! Sir!! This is my rifle!! There are many like it!! But this one is mine!! My rifle is my best friend!! It is my life!! I must master it as I must master my life!! My rifle, without me, is useless!! Without my rifle, I am useless!! I must fire my rifle true!! I must shoot straighter than my enemy who is trying to kill me!! I must shoot him before he shoots me!!"

"Down."

"Aye aye, Sir!! I will!! My rifle and myself know that what counts in this war is not the rounds we fire!! The noise of our burst!! Nor the smoke we make!! We know that it is the hits that count!! We will hit!! My rifle is human, even as I, because it is my life!! Thus, I will learn it as a brother!! I will learn its weaknesses!! Its strength!! Its parts!! Its accessories!! Its sights and its barrel!!"

"Up."

"Aye aye, Sir!! I will ever guard it against the ravages of weather and damage!! As I will ever guard my legs!! My arms!! My eyes!! And my heart against damage!! I will keep my rifle clean!! And ready!! We will become part of each other!! We will!! Before God, I swear this creed!!"

"Down."

"Aye aye, Sir!! My rifle and myself are the defenders of my country!! We are the masters of our enemy!! We are the saviors of my life!! So be it, until victory is America's!! And there is no enemy!! But peace!!"

"Up. Again."

"Aye aye, Sir!! Sir!! This is my rifle!! There are many like it!! But this one is mine!! My rifle is my best friend!! It is my life!! I must master it as I must master my life!! My rifle, without me, is useless!! Without my rifle, I am useless!! I must fire my rifle true!! I must shoot straighter than my enemy who is trying to kill me!! I must shoot him before he shoots me!!"

"Down."

"Aye aye, Sir!! I will!! My rifle and myself know that what counts in this war is not the rounds we fire!! The noise of our burst!! Nor the smoke we make!! We know that it is the hits that count!! We will hit!! My rifle is human, even as I, because it is my life!! Thus, I will learn it as a brother!! I will learn its weaknesses!! Its strength!! Its parts!! Its accessories!! Its sights and its barrel!!"

"Up."

"Aye aye, Sir!! I will ever guard it against the ravages of weather and damage!! As I will ever guard my legs!! My arms!! My eyes!! And my heart against damage!! I will keep my rifle clean!! And ready!! We will become part of each other!! We will!! Before God, I swear this creed!!"

"Down."

"Aye aye, Sir!! My rifle and myself are the defenders of my country!! We are the masters of our enemy!! We are the saviors of my life!! So be it, until victory is America's!! And there is no enemy!! But peace!!"

"On your feet."

"Aye aye, Sir!!"

"Eight-count body builders."

"Aye aye, Sir!!"

"Start counting."

"Aye aye, Sir!! One!! Two!! Three!! Four!! Five!! Six!! Seven!! Zero-one!! One!! Two!! Three!! Four!! Five!! Six!! Seven!! Zero-two!! One!! Two!! Three!! Four!! Five!! Six!! Seven!! Zero-three!! One!! Two!! Three!! Four!! Five!! Six!! Seven!! Zero-four!! One!! Two!! Three!! Four!! Five!! Six!! Seven!! Zero-five!! One!! Two!! Three!! Four!! Five!! Six!! Seven!! Zero-six!! One!! Two!! Three!! Four!! Five!! Six!! Seven!! Zero-seven!! One!! Two!! Three!! Four!! Five!! Six!! Seven!! Zero-eight!!

One!! Two!! Three!! Four!! Five!! Six!! Seven!! Zero-niner!! One!! Two!! Three!! Four!! Five!! Six!! Seven!! One-zero!! One!! Two!! Three!! Four!! Five!! Six!! Seven!! One-one!! One!! Two!! Three!! Four!! Five!! Six!! Seven!! One-two!! One!! Two!! Three!! Four!! Five!! Six!! Seven!! One-three!! One!! Two!! Three!! Four!! Five!! Six!! Seven!! One-four!!"

"Louder."

"Aye aye, Sir!! One!! Two!! Three!! Four!! Five!! Six!! Seven!! One-five!! One!! Two!! Three!! Four!! Five!! Six!! Seven!! One-six!! One!! Two!! Three!! Four!! Five!! Six!! Seven!! One-seven!! One!! Two!! Three!! Four!! Five!! Six!! Seven!! One-eight!! One!! Two!! Three!! Four!! Five!! Six!! Seven!! One-niner!! One!! Two!! Three!! Four!! Five!! Six!! Seven!! Two-zero!! One!! Two!! Three!! Four!! Five!! Six!! Seven!! Two-one!! One!! Two!! Three!! Four!! Five!! Six!! Seven!! Two-two!! One!! Two!! Three!! Four!! Five!! Six!! Seven!! Two-three!! One!! Two!! Three!! Four!! Five!! Six!! Seven!! Two-four!!"

"Louder."

"Aye aye, Sir!! One!! Two!! Three!! Four!! Five!! Six!! Seven!! Two-five!! One!! Two!! Three!! Four!! Five!! Six!! Seven!! Two-six!! One!! Two!! Three!! Four!! Five!! Six!! Seven!! Two-seven!! One!! Two!! Three!! Four!! Five!! Six!! Seven!! Two-eight!! One!! Two!! Three!! Four!! Five!! Six!! Seven!! Two-niner!! One!! Two!! Three!! Four!! Five!! Six!! Seven!! Three-zero!! One!! Two!! Three!! Four!! Five!! Six!! Seven!! Three-one!! One!! Two!! Three!! Four!! Five!! Six!! Seven!! Three-two!! One!! Two!! Three!! Four!! Five!! Six!! Seven!! Three-three!! One!! Two!! Three!! Four!! Five!! Six!! Seven!! Three-four!! One!! Two!! Three!! Four!! Five!! Six!! Seven!! Three-five!! One!! Two!! Three!! Four!! Five!! Six!! Seven!! Three-six!!"

"Louder."

"Aye aye, Sir!! One!! Two!! Three!! Four!! Five!! Six!! Seven!! Three-seven!! One!! Two!! Three!! Four!! Five!! Six!! Seven!! Three-eight!! One!! Two!! Three!! Four!! Five!! Six!! Seven!! Three-niner!! One!! Two!! Three!! Four!! Five!! Six!! Seven!! Four-zero!! One!! Two!! Three!! Four!! Five!! Six!! Seven!! Four-one!!"

"Louder."

"Aye aye, Sir!! One!! Two!! Three!! Four!! Five!! Six!! Seven!! Four-two!! One!! Two!! Three!! Four!! Five!! Six!! Seven!! Four-three!! One!! Two!! Three!! Four!! Five!! Six!! Seven!! Four-four!! One!! Two!! Three!! Four!! Five!! Six!! Seven!! Four-five!! One!! Two!! Three!! Four!! Five!! Six!! Seven!! Four-six!! One!! Two!! Three!! Four!! Five!! Six!! Seven!! Four-seven!! One!! Two!! Three!! Four!! Five!! Six! Seven!! Eight!! Four-eight!! One!! Two!! Three!! Four!! Five!! Six!! Seven!! Four-niner!! One!! Two!! Three!! Four!! Five!! Six!! Seven!! Five-zero!! One!! Two!! Three!! Four!! Five!! Six!! Seven!! Five-one!! One!! Two!! Three!! Four!! Five!! Six!! Seven!! Five-two!! One!! Two!! Three!! Four!! Five!! Six!! Seven!! Five-three!!"

"Louder."

"Aye aye, Sir!! One!! Two!! Three!! Four!! Five!! Six!! Seven!! Five-four!! One!! Two!! Three!! Four!! Five!! Six!! Seven!! Five-five!! One!! Two!! Three!! Four!! Five!! Six!! Seven!! Five-six!! One!! Two!! Three!! Four!! Five!! Six!! Seven!! Five-seven!! One!! Two!! Three!! Four!! Five!! Six!! Seven!! Five-eight!! One!! Two!! Three!! Four!! Five!! Six!! Seven!! Five-niner!! One!! Two!! Three!! Four!! Five!! Six!! Seven!! Six-zero!! One!! Two!! Three!! Four!! Five!! Six!! Seven!! Six-one!! One!! Two!! Three!! Four!! Five!! Six!! Seven!! Six-two!! One!! Two!! Three!! Four!! Five!! Six!! Seven!! Six-three!! One!! Two!! Three!! Four!! Five!! Six!! Seven!! Six-four!!"

"Stop whispering to me!"

"Aye aye, Sir!! One!! Two!! Three!! Four!! Five!! Six!! Seven!! Six-five!! One!! Two!! Three!! Four!! Five!! Six!! Seven!! Six-six!! One!! Two!! Three!! Four!! Five!! Six!! Seven!! Six-seven!!"

"Leg-lifts. Start counting."

"Aye aye, Sir!! One-two-three!! Zero-one!! One-two-three!! Zero-two!! One-two-three!! Zero-three!! One-two-three!! Zero-four!! One-two-three!! Zero-five!! One-two-three!! Zero-six!! One-two-three!! Zero-seven!! One-two-three!! Zero-eight!! One-two-three!! Zero-niner!! One-two-three!! One-zero!! One-two-three!! One-one!! One-two-three!! One-two!!"

"Louder."

"Aye aye, Sir!! One-two-three!! One-three!! One-two-three!! One-four!!"

"Louder."

"Aye aye, Sir!! One-two-three!! One-five!! One-two-three!! One-six!! One-two-three!! One-seven!! One-two-three!! One-eight!! One-two-three! One-niner!! One-two-three!! Two-zero!! One-two-three!! Two-one!! One-two-three!! Two-two!! One-two-three!! Two-three!! One-two-three!! Two-four!! One-two-three!! Two-five!! One-two-three!! Two-six!!"

"Rifles up."

"Aye aye, Sir!! One-two-three!! Two-seven!! One-two-three!! Two-eight!! One-two-three!! Two-niner!! One-two-three!! Three-zero!!"

"Supermans."

"Aye aye, Sir!! One-two-three!! Zero-one!! One-two-three!! Zero-two!! One-two-three!! Zero-three!! One-two-three!! Zero-four!! One-two-three!! Zero-five!! One-two-three!! Zero-six!! One-two-three!! Zero-seven!! One-two-three!! Zero-eight!! One-two-three!! Zero-niner!!"

"Sound off."

"Aye aye, Sir!! One-two-three!! One-zero!! One-two-three!! One-one!! One-two-three!! One-two!! One-two-three!! One-three!! One-two-three!! One-four!! One-two-three!! One-five!! One-two-three!! One-six!! One-two-three!! One-seven!! One-two-three!! One-eight!! One-two-three! One-niner!! One-two-three!! Two-zero!!"

"Hello-Dollies."

"Aye aye, Sir!! One-two-three!! Zero-one!! One-two-three!! Zero-two!! One-two-three!! Zero-three!! One-two-three!! Zero-four!! One-two-three!! Zero-five!! One-two-three!! Zero-six!! One-two-three!! Zero-seven!! One-two-three!! Zero-eight!! One-two-three!! Zero-niner!! One-two-three!! One-zero!! One-two-three!! One-one!! One-two-three!! One-two!! One-two-three!! One-three!! One-two-three!! One-four!! One-two-three!! One-five!! One-two-three!! One-six!! One-two-three!! One-seven!! One-two-three!! One-eight!! One-two-three! One-niner!! One-two-three!! Two-zero!! One-two-three!! Two-one!! One-two-three!! Two-two!! One-two-three!! Two-three!! One-two-three!! Two-four!! One-two-three!! Two-five!! One-two-three!! Two-six!!"

"Rifles up."

"Aye aye, Sir!! One-two-three!! Two-seven!! One-two-three!! Two-eight!! One-two-three!! Two-niner!! One-two-three!! Three-zero!!"

"Push."

"Aye aye, Sir!!"

"Down-up. *Zero-one.*"

"Zero-one!!"

"Down. *Aye aye, Sir.*"

"Aye aye, Sir!!"

"I am an N.C.O. dedicated to training the new and influencing the old. Up."

"Zero-two!!"

"Down."

"Aye aye, Sir!!"

"I am forever conscious of each Officer Candidate under my charge, and by example will inspire them to the highest standards possible. Up."

"Zero-three!!"

"Down."

"Aye aye, Sir!!"

"I will strive to be patient, understanding, just and firm. Up."

"Zero-four!!"

"Down."

"Aye aye, Sir!!"

"I will commend the deserving and encourage the wayward. Up."

"Zero-five!!"

"Down."

"Aye aye, Sir!!"

"I will never forget that I am responsible to my Commanding Officer for the morale. Up."

"Zero-six!!"

"Down."

"Aye aye, Sir!!"
"Discipline. Up."
"Zero-seven!!"
"Down."
"Aye aye, Sir!!"
"And efficiency of those under my charge. Up."
"Zero-eight!!"
"Down."
"Aye aye, Sir!!"
"Their performance will reflect an image of me. Up."
"Zero-niner!!"
"Down."
"Aye aye, Sir!!"
"Am I clear?"
"Yes, Sir!!"
"Am I clear?"
"Yes, Sir!!"
"Am I clear?"
"Yes, Sir!!"
"Up."
"One-zero!!"
"On your feet."
"Aye aye, Sir!!"
"Brace!"
"Aye aye, Sir!!"
"Come find me next Saturday to collect your chits."
"Aye aye, Sir!!"
"Dismissed."
"Aye aye, Sir!!"

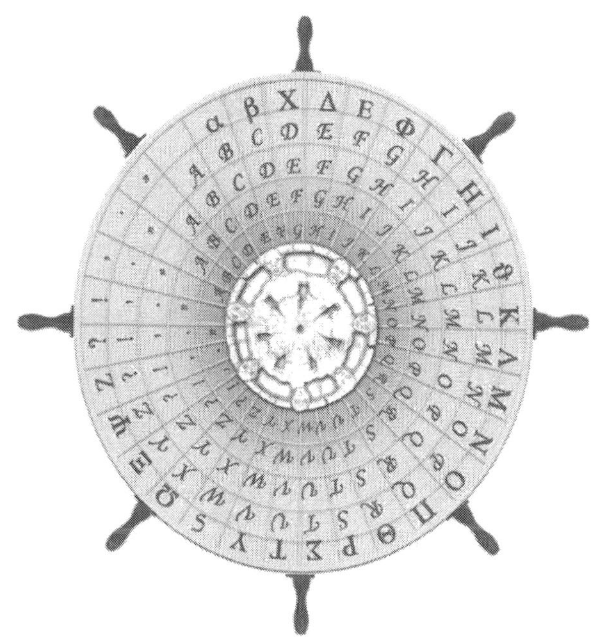

CHAPTER VI

WEEKS 8-11

"Class Zero-Four-Zero-Zero, this is your zero-five minute warning."

"Half-mast on the blinds."

"Good call."

"I got it."

"Over to the right. Keep it going. Keep it going. Alright. No. Now up six inches. Down an inch. You got it."

"What about the surfaces?"

"Clear."

"What else?"

"Desks?"

"Clear."

"Clear."

"Clear."

"What about you, Capitan?"

"Clear."

"What else?"

"Nothing. Lock it up. Positions."

"Class Zero-Four-Zero-Zero, this is your zero-one minute warning."

"Who's calling it?"

"I'll call it."

"Everyone got that? Mike's got the call."

"Roger."

"Fortunato?"

"What's that?"

"Be serious. And no sounding off on the Os."

"I think we're good, Jacko."

"No sounding off on the Os."

"We are good, Capitan."

"Class Zero-Four-Zero-Zero, this is your immediate warning."

"Attention on deck, stand-by."

"Good morning, Sir."

"Good morning. Identification please."

"Aye aye, Sir. Officer Candidate Zurich, Officer Candidate School, Officer Candidate Class Zero-Four-Zero-Zero, United States Navy."

"Officer Candidate Zurich, if I may, would you mind if I borrowed your ruler?"

"Aye aye, Sir."

"Where is the ruler located?"

"Sir, the ruler is located in the bottom drawer of the wall locker."

"Oh, there we are. Strikes me as a bit off, no? Remind me, Officer Candidate Zurich, where must the ruler be grounded in the wall locker?"

"Sir, the ruler must be grounded centered atop the shoebox in the bottom drawer of the wall locker."

"Centered? Is that right?"

"Yes, Sir."

"You're sure about that?"

"Yes, Sir."

"Would you bet your life on it?"

"Yes, Sir."

"Your life?"

"Yes, Sir."

"What about the lives of your Shipmates?"

"Yes, Sir."

"Really? Alright. Shall we look it up? Let's see. Military Training Test. Wall locker. Page eighty-six. Bottom drawer. Bottom drawer. Ah, here it is. The ruler. *A ruler shall be centered evenly on the drawer atop of the shoe box*."

"Aye aye, Sir."

"Centered on the drawer."

"Aye aye, Sir."

"Not the shoebox?"

"No excuse, Sir."

"Would you like to see for yourself?"

"No, Sir."

"Well that should be it for you, correct? I mean, if you were to live up to your bets."

"Aye aye, Sir."

"For you and your Shipmates."

"Aye aye, Sir."

"Two hits. For now."

"Aye aye, Sir."

"Officer Candidate Zurich, what is the breast insignia for a Submariner?"

"Sir, the Officer breast insignia for a Submariner is a gold embroidered or gold metal pin showing the bow view of a submarine proceeding on the surface with bow planes rigged for diving flanked by dolphins in horizontal position, their heads resting on the upper edge of the bow planes."

"Are you sure about that?"

"Yes, Sir."

"Really? Double or nothing?"

"Yes, Sir."

"Give me the fourteen leadership traits in the Navy."

"Aye aye, Sir. Sir, the fourteen leadership traits in the Navy are judgment, the ability to weigh facts and possible solutions on which to base sound decisions. Justice, giving reward and punishment according to merits of the case in question, the ability to administer a system of rewards and punishments impartially and consistently. Decisiveness, the ability to make decisions promptly and to announce them in clear, forceful manner. Initiative, taking action in the absence of orders. Dependability, the certainty of proper performance of duty. Tact, the ability to deal with others without creating offense. Integrity, uprightness of character and soundness of moral principles, including the qualities of truthfulness and honesty. Endurance, the mental and physical stamina measured

by the ability to withstand pain, fatigue, stress and hardship. Bearing, creating a favorable impression in carriage, appearance and personal conduct at all times. Unselfishness, avoidance of providing for one's own comfort and personal advancement at the expense of others. Courage, the mental quality that recognizes fear of danger or criticism, but enables a man to proceed in the face of it with calmness and firmness. Knowledge, understanding of a science or an art, the range of one's information, including professional knowledge and an understanding of your Sailors. Loyalty, the quality of faithfulness to country, the Navy, the unit, to one's seniors, subordinates and peers. Enthusiasm, the display of sincere interest and exuberance in the performance of duty."

"Is recklessness among those traits?"

"No, Sir."

"The Navy is responsible for your well being and the well being of your Shipmates. Your job is to obey lawful orders. That's another hit for bearing. Three hits."

"Aye aye, Sir."

"Would you like to place another bet?"

"No, Sir."

"Why not?"

"No excuse, Sir."

"Tough habit to break. Are you sure?"

"Yes, Sir."

"Will you gamble your life or the life of one your Shipmates in the Fleet?"

"No, Sir."

"Why should I believe you?"

"Sir, Officer Candidate Zurich, Officer Candidate School, Officer Candidate Class Zero-Four-Zero-Zero, United States Navy, will not bet his own life or the life of one of his Shipmates in the Fleet."

"Now, you mean?"

"Now or ever, Sir."

"Very well. Two I.Ps. Your gig line is off. Right anchor is askew. You have a nose hair. Plus the ruler and four hits for bearing. Total of nine. Count yourself lucky, Candidate."

"Aye aye, Sir."

"Attention on deck, stand-by."

"Good morning, Sir."

Sweat trickles from the inside band of my cover.

"Attention on deck stand-by!"

"Good morning, Sir!!"

"Hop and pops, Freak!"

"Aye aye, Sir!"

"Starting counting!"

"Aye aye, Sir!"

"One-two-three! Zero-one! One-two-three! Zero-two! One-two-three! Zero-three! One-two-three! Zero-four! One-two-three! Zero-five! One-two-three! Zero-six!"

"Hit! What does that look like to you?"

"Irish pennant, Sir!"

"Nasty. Keep counting."

"Aye aye, Sir! One-two-three! Zero-seven! One-two-three! Zero-eight! One-two-three! Zero-niner! One-two-three! One-zero! One-two-three! One-one! One-two-three! One-two! One-two-three! One-three! One-two-three! One-four! One-two-three! One-five! One-two-three! One-six! One-two-three! One-seven! One-two-three! One-eight! One-two-three! One-niner! One-two-three! Two-zero!"

"What the hell is this?"

"No excuse, Sir!"

"Why are you the only freaking Candidate to fold your T-Shirts like this?"

"No excuse, Sir!"

"On something of your own program are we, Freak?"

"No, Sir!"

"Three hits. For each freaking one."

"Aye aye, Sir! One-two-three! Two-one! One-two-three! Two-two! One-two-three! Two-three! One-two-three! Two-four! One-two-three! Two-five! One-two-three! Two-six! One-two-three! Two-seven! One-two-three! Two-eight! One-two-three! Two-niner! One-two-three! Three-zero! One-two-three! Three-one! One-two-three! Three-two!"

"Side-straddle hops!"

"Aye aye, Sir!"

"One-two-three! Zero-one!"

"I don't think so! Navy Enlisted rank structure! Starting with Master Chief! Now! Now!"

"Aye aye, Sir! Sir! The Master Chief Petty Officer of the Navy is an E-Niner! His insignia is three chevrons below one rocker below one eagle below three stars centered about the eagle! In khaki uniform his insignia will be a gold fouled anchor collar device with a silver U.S.N. centered across the anchor below three silver stars! Sir!"

"Hit!"

"Aye aye, Sir! An E-Eight in the United States Navy is a Senior Chief Petty Officer!"

"Hit!"

"Aye aye, Sir! His insignia is three chevrons! Below one rocker! Below one eagle! Below one star centered about the eagle! In khaki uniform!"

"Hit!"

"Aye aye, Sir! His insignia will be a gold fouled anchor collar device! With a silver U.S.N. centered across the anchor! Below one silver star!"

"Does this look like twelve inches to you?"

"No, Sir!"

"It's a freaking hit. On your face! Push!"

"Aye aye, Sir!"

"I don't think so! On your feet!"

"Aye aye, Sir!"

"Push!"

"Aye aye, Sir!"

"Who told you to stop sounding off?"

"No excuse, Sir!"

"Don't you talk to me on your freaking face!"

"Aye aye, Sir!"

"That's a freaking hit!"

"Aye aye, Sir!"

"Side-straddle hops!"

"Aye aye, Sir! Sir! An E-Seven in the United States! Navy is a Chief Petty Officer!"

"Officer ranks and insignia of the Marine Corp! Senior Officer on down!"

"Aye aye, Sir! Sir! An O-Ten in the United States Marine Corp is a General! His insignia is a four silver stars collar device! Sir! An O-Niner in the United States Marine Corp is a Lieutenant General! His insignia is a three silver stars collar device! Sir! An O-Eight in the United States Marine Corp is a Major General! His insignia is a two silver stars collar device!"

"Freaking I.P. Saint Paddy's Day. Disgusting! Revolting! Hit! Louder!"

"Aye aye, Sir! Sir! An O-Seven in the United States Marine Corp is a Brigadier General! His insignia is a one silver star collar device! An O-Six in the United States Marine Corp is a Colonel! His insignia is a one silver eagle collar device! Sir! An O-Five in the United States Marine Corp is a Lieutenant Colonel. His insignia is a one silver oak --."

"That's freaking dirt. Hit."

"Aye aye, Sir!"

"Eyeballs!"

"Snap, Sir!"

"Take a close look."

"Aye aye, Sir!"

"Closer."

"Aye aye, Sir!"

"Closer!"

"Aye aye, Sir!"

"What does that look like to you?"

"No excuse, Sir!"

"I asked you a freaking question. What does that look like?"

"An Irish pennant, Sir!"

"Hit! On your face! On your face! Code of Conduct, Pissant!"

"Aye aye, Sir! Sir! The first article of the Code of Conduct is! I am an American! Fighting in the forces which guard my country! And our way of life! I am prepared to give my life in their defense! Sir! The second article of the Code of Conduct is! I will never surrender of my own free will! If in command! I will never surrender the members of my command while they still have the means to resist!"

"Dirty go-fasters. Hit."

"Aye aye, Sir! Sir! The third article of the Code of Conduct is! If I am captured! I will continue to resist by all means available! I will make every effort to escape! And aid others to escape! I will accept neither parole nor special favors from the enemy! Sir! The fourth article of the Code of Conduct is! If I become a prisoner of war! I will keep faith with my fellow prisoners!"

"Louder!"

"Aye aye, Sir! I will give no information! Nor take part in any action which might be harmful to my comrades! If I am senior, I will take command! If not, I will obey the lawful orders of those appointed over me! And will back them up in every way! Sir! The fifth article of the Code of Conduct is! When questioned! Should I become a prisoner of war! I am required to give name, rank, service number and date of birth! I will evade answering further questions to the utmost of my ability! I will make no oral or written statements disloyal to my country and its allies! Or harmful to their cause!"

"Louder!"

"Aye aye, Sir! Sir! The sixth article of the Code of Conduct is! I will never forget that I am an American! Fighting for freedom! Responsible for my actions! And dedicated to the principles which made my country free! I will trust in my God! And in the United States of America!"

"What's the serial number of your rifle, Pig?

"The serial number of this Officer Candidate's rifle is! Six! Five! Three! Niner! Six! Three! Five! Sir!"

"Louder!"

"The serial number of this Officer Candidate's rifle is! Six! Five! Three! Niner! Six! Three! Five! Sir!"

"Louder!"

"The serial number of this Officer Candidate's rifle is! Six! Five! Three! Niner! Six! Three! Five! Sir!"

"Are you sure?"
"Yes, Sir!"
"Aye you freaking sure?"
"Yes, Sir!"
"Would you bet your life on it?"
"Yes, Sir!"
"What about his?"
"Yes, Sir!"
"What about his?"
"Yes, Sir!"
"What about his?"
"Yes, Sir!"
"Always be right."
"Aye aye, Sir!"
"Never be wrong."
"Aye aye, Sir!"
"Attention on deck! Stand by!"
"Good morning, Sir!!"

••

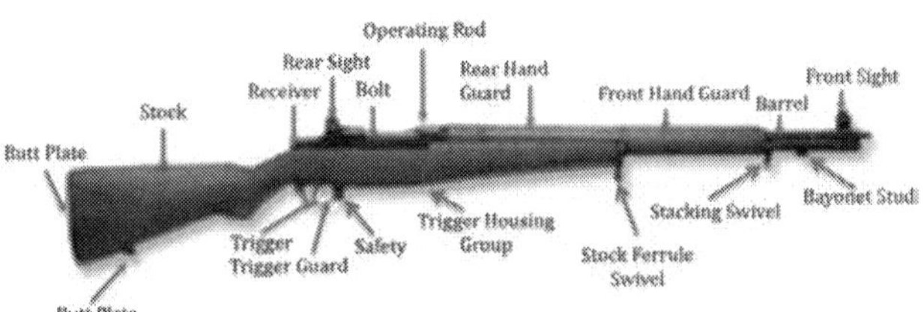

M-1 Garand military rifle

The three main groups are the trigger housing group, the barrel and receiver group and the stock group. To disassemble the rifle into the three main groups, first ensure that the weapon is clear and then allow the bolt to go forward by depressing the follower with the right thumb and allowing the bolt to ride forward over the follower assembly. Place the rifle butt against the left thigh, sights to the left. With the thumb and forefinger of the right hand, pull downward and outward on the rear of the trigger guard. Swing the trigger guard out as far as it will go and lift out the trigger housing group. To separate the barrel and receiver from the stock lay the weapon on a flat surface with the sights up, muzzle to the left. With the left hand, grasp the rear of the receiver and raise

the rifle. With the right hand, give a downward blow, grasping the small of the stock. This will separate the stock group from the barrel and receiver group.

••

"Alright. Let's get underway, Shipmates. Your enabling objectives are the following. State the elements of the fire triangle and the requirements for combustion. Define the terms fire, fire point, flash point and self ignition point. State examples of the four classes of fires and their primary extinguishing agents. Describe the basic characteristics of Halon, its principles of extinguishment and its method of employment. Describe the basic characteristics of Aqueous Film Forming Foam, its principles of extinguishment and its method of employment. Describe the components of the Single Agent A-Triple-F System. Describe the basic characteristics of potassium bicarbonate, its principles of extinguishment and its method of employment. Describe the basic characteristics of carbon dioxide, its principles of extinguishment and its method of employment. List the three combustion gasses produced by a fire. And state the significance of the following percentages of oxygen in a confined space. Twenty one percent, fifteen to seventeen percent, nine percent and seven percent. Got it?"

"Yes, Chief."

"I hope so. You don't play with fire. Aboard ship, fire is a constant potential hazard. All possible measures must be taken to prevent the occurrence of fire. You know if you've seen it. Unless fire is rapidly and effectively extinguished, it may cause more damage than the initial casualty and can result in the loss of the ship. Officer Candidate Sumarian."

"Yes, Chief."

"Please share with us the definition of *fire*."

"Aye aye, Chief. Fire is a rapid chemical reaction resulting in the release of energy in the form of light and heat."

"Fuel, temperature and oxygen are the elements of fire. You need a material that is combustible. Solid, liquid or gas. You need heat to break molecules away just above the surface of the fuel as a vapor to burn. And you need a sixteen percent minimum oxygen concentration for a fire to occur and sustain itself. This, everyone, is your *fire triangle*. A fire cannot exist if any side of the fire triangle is missing. A *combustible material*. A *sufficiently high temperature*. Or a *sufficient supply of oxygen*. Remove any one of these elements, any one, and the fire will go out. Officer Candidate Lyman. Please take us through ignition terminology. *Flash point*."

"The lower temperature at which a substance gives off vapors that will burn when a flame or spark is applied to those vapors. When the flame or spark is removed from the vapors, the burning stops."

"*Fire point.*"

"A few degrees higher than the flash point. The lowest temperature at which the fuel will continue to burn after it has been ignited and the flame or spark has been removed."

"*Self-ignition point.*"

"The lower temperature to which a substance must be heated to give off vapors that will burn without the application of a flame or spark. The temperature at which spontaneous combustion occurs."

"Thank you, Lyman. Flash point, fire point, and self-ignition point. Foot stomp. At the flash point, all you have to do is kill the light. After the flash point, fires that start very small can get big real quick. That makes firefighting the responsibility of all hands, not just the Fire Teams. Firefighting gear is all around aboard ship. Knowing how to recognize that gear and how to use that gear is on you, not only for this exam, but in the Fleet. Understand?"

"Yes, Chief."

"Now there's ignition and then there's classes of fires. We classify fires according to the nature of the combustible material involved. The classification is important, folks, because if you can't recognize the fire, you can't know what to use to put it out. Officer Candidate Siegel, talk to us about a *Class Alpha fire* and common associated materials."

"Aye aye, Chief. Common associated materials with Class Alpha fires are paper, wood, coal and cloth."

"Materials that leave *an ash*. And how do you typically recognize a Class Alpha?"

"White smoke, Chief."

"What agent do you reach for to extinguish a Class Alpha?"

"High velocity water fog, Chief."

"What common materials are associated with a *Class Bravo* fire?"

"Fuel, oil, paints and paint thinner."

"All *flammable liquids*. How do you typically recognize a Class Bravo?"

"Black smoke, Chief."

"And what agent do you reach for to extinguish a Class Bravo?"

"Halon and A.F.F.F.-P.K.P."

"*A-Triple-F and P.K.P.* Bravo Zulu, Shipmate. Not all ships are configured the same. What's in stock depends mostly on configuration. Some ships have Halon as the primary extinguishing agent. Others stock A-Triple-F or P.K.P. Use what you see. It's there for a reason. Officer Candidate Chu, talk to me about *Halon*."

"Halon extinguishes the fire by interrupting the chemical chain reaction in the combustion process, Chief."

"Through what's called, foot stomp, a *Fixed Flooding System*. Very effective. Generally speaking, you'll find Fixed Flood Systems in spaces with electrical or

electronic equipment, mostly engineering and machinery spaces. Great thing about a Fixed Flood is that it can be activated locally in the space or remotely from the outside. Comes in handy. You'll know it when the lever drops, an alarm blast giving you thirty or sixty seconds to get the heck out of Dodge and shut down ventilation. You want to give it at least fifteen minutes after the flood. This makes sure the space is cooled and avoids re-flash. And don't enter the compartment without an *O.B.A.* What's an O.B.A., people? Looking at you, Priors, or those who did their homework."

"Oxygen Breathing Apparatus, Chief."

"Bravo Zulu, Shipmate. A self-contained breathing unit designed to protect the respiratory system of the wearer. Foot stomp. Officer Candidate Estephan."

"Yes, Chief."

"Talk to me about A-Triple-F."

"Aqueous Film Forming Foam works to extinguish a fire by forming a vapor seal."

"Thank you, Estephan. With A-Triple-F you're talking both portable equipment and installed systems. You're not talking one hundred percent A-Triple-F liquid. The A-Triple-F is actually mixed in with saltwater or freshwater, ninety-four percent water and six percent A-Triple-F. Foot stomp. Forms a foam blanket when exposed to air, good all the way up to forty-eight hours. Good news for re-flash protection. We're talking a blanket of about a half an inch thick when properly applied. Footstomp. Forty-eight hours reflash protection. Half an inch thick. Got it?"

"Yes, Chief."

"Officer Candidate Driscoll."

"Yes, Chief."

"Talk to me about the *A-Triple-F Single Agent System.*"

"Aye aye, Chief. The A-Triple-F Single Agent System is a permanently installed foam system designed to deliver A-Triple-F to hoses installed in main engineering rooms, near flight decks and to auxiliary spaces."

"Go on."

"The system consists of a fifty gallon tank used to store the A-Triple-F concentrate and an F.P. One-eighty Foam Proportioner which mixes the A-Triple-F and hard rubber hoses with foam nozzles attached, stowed on hose reels."

"So, Shipmates. Were I to ask you, for example, what part of a Single Agent System mixes the A-Triple-F, what would you say?"

"An F.P. One-eighty Foam Proportioner, Chief."

"Bravo Zulu. Foot stomp. You also have the *High Capacity Foam System,* H.C.F.S. Officer Candidate Fortunato."

"Chief."

"Talk to me about H.C.F.S."

"A permanently installed foam system designed to deliver A-Triple-F to engineering spaces, flight deck and hangerbay sprinklers and hose reels."

"Go on."

"The system consists of a six hundred gallon tank used to store the A-Triple-F concentrate. An F.P. One-thousand Foam Proportioner then mixes the A-Triple-F and hard rubber hoses with foam nozzles attached, stowed on hose reels."

"And what would you say is the difference between a Single Agent System and a High Capacity Foam System?"

"This Officer Candidate does not know but will find out, Chief."

"That might work here, but you'll have to do better than that in the Fleet."

"The High Capacity Foam System is bigger, Chief?"

"Let's try it this way. What's the foam proportioner for a Single Agent System?"

"F.P. One-eighty, Chief."

"What's the foam proportioner for a High Capacity Foam System?"

"F.P. One-thousand, Chief."

"There you go. Foot stomp. A Single Agent System uses an *F.P. One-eighty*. The High Capacity Foam System uses an *F.P. One-thousand.* Thank you, Officer Candidate Fortunato. As long as we are having a good time, Officer Candidate Zurich."

"Yes, Chief."

"Take us through *P.K.P.*"

"Aye aye, Chief. Purple K Powder extinguishes a fire by interrupting the chemical reaction of the combustion process, a portable extinguishing agent designed primarily to put out small Class Bravo fires."

"Thank you, Officer Candidate Zurich. We're talking almost entirely of potassium bicarbonate crystals. Extremely corrosive and abrasive. For this reason P.K.P. should only be used on a Class Charlie fire and only as a last resort. Got it"

"Yes, Chief"

"You should also note that P.K.P. does not provide any re-flash protection, meaning the fire can immediately re-ignite. What it does well is to knock down or beat back larger flames as an effective heat shield for firefighter protection. You'll find eighteen pound portable P.K.P. extinguishers located throughout the ship, especially where flammable liquids are present. Effective range is nineteen feet. You also used to see twenty-seven pound portable extinguishers but I doubt they still exist. Go ahead and cross it on out in your workbooks, folks. Go on. Officer Candidate Hibbs."

"Yes, Chief."

"How do you apply P.K.P.?"

"To apply P.K.P., direct the discharge horn at the base of the fire and discharge in short bursts."

"Officer Candidate Andrews. *Class Charlie fires.*"

"Class Charlie fires. Ignited primarily from overheated electrical equipment. Examples of Charlie materials are motors, electrical controllers or wiring. Extinguished by securing the electrical power source. Removes the heat side of the pyramid. The primary agent for a class Charlie fire is carbon dioxide, used to extinguish any smoldering materials. If power cannot be quickly secured, it may be necessary to cool the electrical component with high velocity water fog to prevent spread. When using water, the spray pattern must be set to high velocity."

"At what distance?"

"Four feet, Chief."

"Double stomp. Go on."

"Class Charlie fires give off a blue-gray smoke. The carbon dioxide, C.O.-Two, extinguishes the fire by displacing the oxygen."

"Extinguishes the fire by *displacing the oxygen.* Stomp. Stomp. What about *fifteen-pounders*?"

"Fifteen pound portable extinguisher. Located throughout the ship. A Nonconductor of electricity. However, the frost that collects on the discharge horn may conduct electrical current."

"Careful around the wires. Range?"

"Maximum effective range is four to six feet from the end of the discharge horn."

"Duration?"

"Forty to forty-five seconds of continuous operation, Chief."

"Thank you, Officer Candidate Andrews. We're talking fire extinguishers. No more, no less and easily recognized. Know your spaces. Know where your fire extinguishers are located. Use your fire extinguishers if you see fire. Spray the horn at the base of the fire. You might be tempted to step back and set the discharge on blast. Not a good idea as you might just blind the fire with nothing to show in return. What you want is at the base. And only in short bursts. Officer Candidate Armstrong."

"Yes, Chief."

"Take us through the *Installed C.O.-Two Hose and Reel System.* A bit more mustard."

"Aye aye, Chief. Installed C.O.-Two Hose and Reel System. Installed in engineering spaces near large electrical components or switchboards. The system consists of the following equipment. Two or more fifty pound C.O.-Two cylinders and fifty feet of hard rubber hose stowed on a revolving hose reel. This

hose and reel system is applied to the fire in the same manner as the portable fifteen pound extinguisher with the same effective range. Each cylinder will last approximately forty-five seconds of continuous operation."

"How long?"

"Forty-five seconds, Chief."

"*Forty-five seconds of continuous operation.* Foot stomp. Thank you, Armstrong. Officer Candidate Jackson."

"Chief."

"*Installed C.O.-Two Fixed Flooding Systems*, please."

"Installed C.O.-Two Fixed Flooding Systems are located in flammable liquid storage rooms which are used to stow items such as paint, cleaning solvents and small containers of petroleum products. The system consists of the following equipment. Two or more fifty pound C.O.-Two cylinders, hard piped nozzles which are located throughout the space and a remote cable located outside and near the entrance of the space. Should a fire occur, take the following actions. Evacuate the space, set Zebra and pull the remote cable. When activated, the system automatically secures ventilation to the space and activates an audible and visual alarm. The C.O.-Two will discharge after a thirty second time delay."

"Class Charlie, folks. What's the maximum range of a fifteen-pounder, Jackson?"

"Four to six feet, Chief."

"How long will it last at full blast?"

"Forty to forty-five seconds."

"But you don't want to do that, do you?"

"No, chief."

"Where do you discharge the horn of an extinguisher?"

"Base of the fire, Chief."

"Discharged in?"

"Short bursts."

"How many cylinders in an installed hose and reel system?"

"Two."

"And how long does each cylinder last at full blast?"

"Forty-five seconds, Chief."

"You'll make a fine Mustang. Foot stomp. If you take away one thing, take away this. Never ever enter a compartment flooded with C.O.-Two unless wearing an O.B.A. Once flooded, stay out at least fifteen minutes. Allows the space to cool, prevents reflash. Let it sit. Even if it looks like nothing. Alright. Let's finish up with the *Class Delta.* Officer Candidate Rooney."

"Yes, Chief."

"Start us up."

"Aye aye, Chief."

"Combustible metals. Examples of Delta materials are magnesium, phosphorous and aluminum. The primary agent for a Class Delta fire is massive quantities of water."

"Thank you, Officer Candidate Rooney. Damned Deltas. Not always big, but almost always bad. So bad that other square-peg-round-hole fire materials like rocket or torpedo fuel and magnesium which just don't fit, well, we lump them in with Deltas. Faced with a Delta, you have three options. *Water.* We're talking high speed fog pattern to try and get rid of the heat. *Sand.* Drown it on out. Or *jettison.* Over the side, folks. Worse things can happen. Nobody will fire you for getting rid of a fire. Enough said. Everyone with me?"

"Yes, Chief."

"Alright. Now for the part you need to know for yourselves. What happens if there's a fire, smoke starts to fill the room? *Twenty percent* is the normal concentration of oxygen in the atmosphere. Below that, bad things start happening. At *fifteen to seventeen percent*, you start getting drowsy, develop headaches, become nauseous or dizzy. Buzzing in the ears or increase in heart rate. At *nine percent*, sustained exposure in a closed compartment results in unconsciousness. Damage to your central nervous system and brain damage. Unconsciousness. Foot stomp. At *seven percent or less*, death is likely to occur. Put that fire out. Got that?"

"Yes, Chief."

"Twenty-one percent, all good. Fifteen to seventeen drowsy. Nine percent unconsciousness and brain damage. Seven percent or less, well, that's all she wrote. Let's review. What are the elements of the fire triangle?"

"Fuel."

"Check."

"Oxygen."

"Check."

"Heat."

"Thank you, Shipmate. How long must a space flooded with C.O.-Two remain sealed before it can be entered?"

"Fifteen minutes, Chief."

"And what must be worn should you enter the space?"

"O.B.A., Chief."

"Very good. Everyone now, with what class of fire are flammable liquids most associated?"

"Class Bravo, Chief."

"I do need everyone. With what class of fire are flammable liquids most associated?"

"Class Bravo, Chief."

"What class of fire is best extinguished by securing the source of electrical power and displacing the oxygen with carbon dioxide?"

"Class Charlie, Chief."

"Bravo Zulu. What class of fire occurs with combustible metals such as magnesium?"

"Class Delta, Chief."

"And what class of fire leaves an ash."

"Class Alpha."

"Class Alpha. A-Triple-F is employed using a portable extinguisher called?"

"Eighteen pound portable extinguisher, Chief."

"With an effective range of?"

"Nineteen feet, Chief."

"And Fixed Foam Systems such as the?"

"Single Agent System, Chief."

"Or a?"

"High Capacity Foam System."

"Bravo Zulu. H.C.F.S. The normal concentration of oxygen in the air is?"

"Twenty-one percent, Chief."

"You will become drowsy when this percentage drops to?"

"Fifteen percent, Chief."

"Fifteen to seventeen, that's right. And at what point is death likely to occur?"

"Seven percent, Chief."

"Seven percent. A-Triple-F is mixed with what percentage of saltwater or freshwater?"

"Ninety-four percent, Chief."

"Halon, in an installed Fixed Flooding System, will be the primary agent for which class of fire?"

"Class Bravo, Chief."

"Bravo Zulu, folks, or at least some of you. Take ten. Come on back and we'll take a closer look at firefighting shipboard. Load up on the caffeine. We'll be throwing you in the fire locker this afternoon. You'll want to be locked in."

"Aye aye, Chief."

••

Nine Millimeter Beretta

The Nine Millimeter Beretta is eight and five-eighths inches in length and weighs three pounds fully loaded, with a maximum range of fifteen hundred yards and a maximum effective range of fifty yards.

In Nineteen-Eighty-Five, the armed forces selected a nine millimeter pistol to replace the forty-five caliber pistol. The pistol selected is a single or double action semiautomatic hand weapon. As soon as the pistol is fired, either a single or double action, the slide automatically comes back and cocks the hammer. To fire the pistol again, all you have to do is pull the trigger. The pistol has a large magazine capacity -- it can hold fifteen rounds in the magazine. Slots in the magazine help the user know the number of rounds that remain.

The pistol fires one round each time the trigger is pulled. The energy needed to operate the pistol comes from the recoil, which is created by the rearward force of expanding gases of a fired round. The double-action feature lets you fire a weapon when the hammer is in the forward position, the safety is in the fire position and the trigger is pulled. When the last cartridge from the magazine is fired, the slide remains locked to the rear.

••

"I am ready to relieve you, Sir!"

"I am ready to be relieved!"

"I relieve you, Sir!"

"I stand relieved! Attention on the bridge, Officer Candidate Zurich has the conn!"

"This is Officer Candidate Zurich! I have the conn!"

"Bring her up to speed, Zurich. Let's see what you got."

"Aye aye, Sir. All ahead standard!"

"All ahead standard, aye aye, Sir!"

"What's our position?"

"Navigation! This is the bridge! What's our position?"

"This is Navigation! Position, aye aye! Position is three-zero degrees niner-decimal-three minutes north! Eight-six degrees five-three-decimal-four minutes west! Over!"

"Copy three-zero degrees niner-decimal-three minutes north! Eight-six degrees five-three-decimal-four minutes west! Confirm!"

"Three-zero degrees niner-decimal-three minutes north! Eight-six degrees five-three-decimal-four minutes west! Aye aye, Sir!"

"How are we on PIM?"

"We are on PIM, Sir!"

"Navigation, this is the Bridge! What is our D.R. fix?"

"Bridge, this is Navigation! D.R. fix, aye aye, Sir! D.R. fix at two-niner-zero degrees set! One-decimal-two knots drift! Over!"

"Repeat!"

"D.R. fix at two-niner-zero degrees set! One-decimal-two knots drift! Over!"

"Two-niner-zero degrees set! One-decimal-two knots drift copy! Recommended course and speed!"

"Recommended course and speed, aye aye! Zero-one-zero degrees at eleven knots, Sir! Over!"

"Copy zero-one-zero degrees at eleven knots!"

"Clear!"

"Stand-by, Helm!"

"Helm standing-by, aye aye!"

"Right standard rudder, steady course zero-one-zero."

"Aye aye, Sir. Right standard rudder, steady course zero-one-zero."

"Mind your helm!"

"Mind my helm, aye aye, Sir!"

"Mark your head!"

"Three-five-zero, Sir!"

"Increase your rudder!"

"Increase my rudder, aye aye!"

"Steady on a course!"

"Steady on a course, aye aye!"

"Mark your head!"

"Zero-zero-two, Sir!"

"Ease your rudder!"

"Ease my rudder, aye aye, Sir!"

"Mark your head!"

"Zero-zero-seven, Sir!"
"Rudder amidships!"
"Rudder amidships, aye aye!"
"Mark your rudder!"
"Zero-one-zero, Sir!"
"Steady course zero-one-zero!"
"Zero-one-zero, aye aye!"
"Keep her so!"
"Aye aye, Sir!"
"Ready?"
"Ready, Sir!"
"Oscar away!"

"Man overboard! Man overboard! Starboard side! This is a drill! This is a drill! Man overboard! Man overboard! Starboard side! This is a drill! This is a drill! Man overboard! Man overboard! Starboard side! This is a drill!"

"Man overboard starboard side! Section Two man the rescue detail! Man overboard starboard side! Section Two man the rescue detail! This is a drill!"

"Section Two man the rescue detail, aye aye, Sir!"
"Throw flotation device!"
"Aye aye, Sir! Flotation device away! Flotation device in the water!"
"Lookout, this is the Bridge! Do we have visual?"
"Bridge, this is Lookout! Negative! No visual, Sir!"
"Launch Mark Six!"
"Launch Mark Six, aye aye, Sir!"
"Sound the whistle!"
"Sound the whistle, aye aye, Sir!"
"Break Oscar!"
"Break Oscar, aye aye, Sir!"
"Lookout, this is Bridge! Maintain lookout! Report sightings!"
"Bridge, this is Lookout! Maintain lookout, aye aye, Sir!"
"Stand-by, helm!"
"Standing by, aye aye, Sir!"
"What's your call, Zurich?"
"Foreman turn, Sir."
"Very well. Take her hard to port."
"Aye aye, Sir. Shift your rudder to left full rudder!"
"Left full rudder, aye aye, Sir!"
"Mark your head!"
"Zero-zero-seven, Sir!"
"Very well."
"Zero-zero-zero, Sir!"

"Very well."

"Three-five-zero, Sir!"

"Very well."

"Three-four-zero, Sir!"

"Very well."

"Three-three-zero, Sir."

"Very well."

"Three-two-five, Sir!"

"Mind your helm!"

"Mind my helm, aye aye, Sir!"

"Steady!"

"Steady, aye aye!"

"Stand-by for starboard turn."

"Standing by, aye aye!"

"Hard to starboard, Zurich. Now."

"Shift your rudder to right full rudder!"

"Right full rudder, aye aye, Sir!"

"Sir, my rudder is right full, no new course given!"

"Very well. Steady as you go!"

"Steady as she goes, aye aye!"

"Very well."

"Passing three-five-zero!"

"Very well."

"Very well. Belay your passing heads!"

"Belay my passing heads, aye aye!"

"Stand-by for port turn!"

"Stand-by for port turn, aye aye!"

"Do we still have visual?"

"Visual, aye aye!"

"Steady!"

"Swing her around. Go left full rudder."

"Left full rudder!"

"Left full rudder, aye aye, Sir!"

"Now all ahead full."

"All ahead full!"

"All ahead full, aye aye, Sir!"

"Very well."

"Sir, my rudder is left full, no new course given!"

"Very well. Steady as you go!"

"Steady as she goes, aye aye! Passing three-one-zero!"

"Very well."

"Passing three-two-zero!"
"Very well."
"Passing three-three-zero!"
"Very well."
"Passing three-four-zero!"
"Very well. Steady as you go!"
"Steady as she goes, aye aye! Passing three-five-zero!"
"Do we still have visual?"
"Visual, aye aye!"
"Very well."
"Passing zero-zero-zero!"
"Very well."
"Passing zero-one-zero!"
"Very well."
"Passing zero-two-zero!"
"Very well."
"Passing zero-three-zero!"
"Very well."
"Passing zero-four-zero!"
"Very well."
"Passing zero-five-zero!"
"Very well."
"Passing zero-six-zero!"
"Very well."
"Passing zero-seven-zero!"
"Very well."
"Passing zero-eight-zero!"
"Very well."
"Passing zero-niner-zero!"
"Very well."
"Passing one-one-zero!"
"Very well."
"Passing one-two-zero!"
"Very well."
"Passing one-three-zero!"
"Very well."
"Passing one-four-zero!"
"Very well."
"Passing one-five-zero!"
"Very well."
"Passing one-six-zero!"

"Very well."
"Passing one-seven-zero!"
"Very well. Belay your passing heads!"
"Belay my passing heads, aye aye!"
"Stand-by for helm ahead!"
"Stand-by for helm ahead, aye aye!"
"Rudder amidships!"
"Rudder amidships, aye aye, Sir!"
"Steady as you go!"
"Steady as she goes, aye aye!"
"Do we have visual?"
"No, Sir! Still no visual!"
"Very well!"
"Mark your head!"
"One-eight-zero, Sir!"
"Very well. Steady on one-eight-zero!"
"Steady on one-eight-zero, aye aye, Sir!"
"Sir, we have visual! Dead ahead!"
"Range?"
"Two hundred yards! Sir!"
"Very well!
"Slow her down."
"Engines back one-third!"
"Engines back one-third, aye aye, Sir!"
"Dead ahead, Sir! One hundred yards, closing!"
"All stop!"
"All stop, aye aye, Sir!"
"Mark your head!"
"One-seven-eight, Sir!"
"Range!"
"Fifty yards, Sir!"
"Visual?"
"Twenty-five yards, Sir!"
"Bearing?"
"Straight ahead!"
"Very well. Recovery team stand by!"
"Recovery team standing by, aye aye, Sir!"
"What's her speed?"
"Two knots, Sir!"
"Visual?"
"Man below! Port side!"

"Sound the whistle!"
"Sound the whistle, aye aye, Sir!"
"Go get him, Shipmates!"
"Getting him, aye aye!"
"We're right on top of him, Sir!"
"Port engine back one-third!"
"Port engine back one-third, aye aye, Sir!"
"How we looking, Lookout?"
"He's in range, Sir!"
"All stop!"
"All stop, aye aye, Sir!"
"Give us an update, Lookout!"
"Right below!"
"Throw a buoy!"
"Throwing a buoy, aye aye!"
"Give him the hook!"
"Giving him the hook, aye aye!"
"Steady!"
"I got him!"
"He's got him!"
"Stand-by!"
"Stand-by, aye aye!"
"We got him!"
"We got him, Sir!"
"Bravo Zulu, everyone. Bring him aboard."
"Bring him aboard!"
"Bringing him aboard, aye aye!"
"Steady!"
"Steady, aye aye!"
"Stand-by!"
"Over here!"
"There we go!"
"He's alive, Sir!"
"Oh, praise the Lord!"

"Alright, that's enough coking-and-joking. Everyone rotate positions. Set it up again."

"Aye aye, Sir!!"
"Who's up?"
"Officer Candidate Driver, Officer Class --!"
"Alright, Driver. Let's see you match Skipper Zurich, here."
"Aye aye, Sir."

"Places!"

"Aye aye, Sir!!"

"Start the problem, start the clock."

"I am ready to relieve you, Sir!"

"I am ready to be relieved!"

"I relieve you, Sir!"

"I stand relieved! Attention on the bridge, Officer Candidate Driver has the conn!"

"This is Officer Candidate Driver! I have the conn!"

•••••••••••••••••••••••••••••••••••••••

Lock and load

The Nine Millimeter service pistol incorporates single and double action modes of fire. With the safety in the fire position, in the double action mode, squeezing the trigger will automatically cock and fire the pistol. Always keep your finger away from the trigger unless you intend to fire. The safety should be in the down position (the red dot not visible), which indicates that the pistol is in a safe condition before loading. With the pistol pointing in a safe direction and the slide in its forward position, follow the steps listed below.

Insert a loaded magazine into the magazine well of the pistol until you hear a click. This ensures a proper catch engagement.

Grasp the serrated portion of the slide with the non-shooting hand.

Pull the slide all the way to the rear.

Release the slide. This will strip a cartridge from the magazine and chamber a round.

•••••••••••••••••••••••••••••••••••••••

"Guide! Post the guide-on!"

"Aye aye, Section Leader!"

"Class Zero-Four-Zero-Zero! Upon receiving the command of execution *ground your briefcases*! You will! Ground your briefcases to the port side, returning to platoon formation!"

"Aye aye, Section Leader!!"

"Ground your briefcases!"

"Aye aye, Section Leader!!"

"Class Zero-Four-Zero-Zero! Upon receiving the command of execution *march*! You will! Half-step up this ladderwell, perform an immediate column-left, and reform at the door!"

"Aye aye, Section Leader!!"

"Ready! March!"

"Aye aye, Section Leader!!"

"Ready! Adjust!"

"Aye aye, Section Leader!! Discipline!! D!! I!! S!! C!! I!! P!! L!! I!! N!! E!! Discipline!! Is!! The unconditional!! Obedience-to-orders!! Respect-for-authority!! And self-reliance!! Freeze-candidate-freeze!!"

"Doorbody off the rear!"

"Doorbody, aye aye, Section Leader!!"

"Doorbody reporting as ordered, Section Leader!"

"Doorbody post!"

"Aye aye, Section Leader!"

"Doorbody! Report status of chow hall deck!"

"Aye aye, Section Leader. Chow hall deck all clear, Section Leader!"

"Chow hall deck all clear, Section Leader!!"

"Doorbody, crack the door!"

"Aye aye, Section Leader!"

"Class Zero-Four-Zero-Zero, marching into chow!"

"Class Zero-Four-Zero-Zero, marching into chow!!"

"Column of files! From the right! Forward!"

"Stand fast."

"March!"

"Good evening, Sir!"

"Zero-two!"

"Zero-three!"

"Zero-four!"

"Zero-five!"

"Zero-six!"

"Zero-seven!"

"Zero-eight!"

"Zero-niner!"
"One-zero!"
"One-one!"
"One-two!"
"One-three!"
"One-four!"
"One-five!"
"One-six!"
"One-seven!"
"One-eight!"
"One-niner!"
"Two-zero!"
"Two-one!"
"Two-two!"
"Two-three!"
"Two-four!"
"Two-five!"
"Two-six!"
"Two-seven!"
"Two-eight!"
"Two-niner!"
"Three-zero!"
"Three-one!"
"Three-two!"
"Three-three!"
"Three-four!"
"Three-five!"
"Three-six!"
"Three-seven!"
"Three-eight!"
"Three-niner!"
"Four-zero!"
"Four-one!"
"Doorbody, close the door!"
"Aye aye, Section Leader!"
"Class Zero-Four-Zero-Zero, proceed!"
"Aye aye, Section Leader!"
"Forward march!"
"Step freeze!!"
"Stand fast."
"Forward march!"

"Step freeze!!"
"Stand fast."
"Forward march!"
"Step freeze!!"
"Stand fast."
"Forward march!"
"Step freeze!!"
"Stand fast."
"Forward march!"
"Step freeze!!"
"Stand fast."
"Forward march!"
"Step freeze!!"
"Stand fast."
"Forward march!"
"Step freeze!!"
"Stand fast."
"Forward march!"
"Step freeze!!"
"Stand fast."
"Forward march!"
"Step freeze!!"
"Stand fast."
"Forward march!"
"Stand fast."
"Forward march!"
"Step freeze!!"
"Stand fast."
"Forward march!"
"Step freeze!!"
"Stand fast."
"Forward march!"
"Step freeze!!"
"Stand fast."
"Forward march!"
"Step freeze!!"
"Stand fast."
"Forward march!"
"Step freeze!!"
"Stand fast."
"Forward march!"

"Step freeze!!"

"Stand fast."

"Forward march!"

"Step freeze!!"

"Stand fast."

"Forward march!"

"Step freeze!!"

"Stand fast."

"Forward march!"

"Stand fast."

"Forward march!"

"Step freeze!!"

"Stand fast."

"Forward march!"

"Step freeze!!"

"Stand fast."

"Forward march!"

"Step freeze!!"

"Stand fast."

"Forward march!"

"Step freeze!!"

"Stand fast."

"Forward march!"

"Step freeze!!"

"Stand fast."

"Forward march!"

"Step freeze!!"

"Stand fast."

"Forward march!"

"Step freeze!!"

"Stand fast."

"Forward march!"

"Good afternoon, Ma'am. Roast beef and potatoes, please. And a roll, please."

"Any greens?"

"No thank you, Ma'am."

"Greens are good for you."

"Yes, Ma'am."

"No greens."

"Not today, Ma'am."

"Suit yourself."

"Thank you, Ma'am."

I grab a seat.

"Class Zero-Four-Zero-Zero, this is your two-zero minute warning!"

"Aye aye, Section Leader!!"

"Why Emerson Moore. What a pleasant surprise. Been a little while. I was worried you might have rolled to G.T.X."

"Negative, Shipmate."

"Glad to hear it. Maria. How are you?"

"Good, Mike. Thanks for asking."

"Masterson."

"Zurich."

"Who's that to my right? I can't see. Vince, is that you, brother?"

"Ten-four, Shipmate."

"How's the beef?"

"Outstanding."

"Navspeak question for you Priors."

"Shoot, New Guy."

"Something I've been trying to figure out. Figure *Ricky* is short for recruit."

"That's right."

"And the Ricky stuff is whatever they make Rickies do."

"Detective."

"Detective."

"But who's the Rainmaker?"

"Why?"

"Overheard it the first week. Yet to solve for it."

"R.D.Cs. Same as D.Is, but Navy, licensed to grind."

"R.D.Cs?"

"You mean what it stands for? Beats me. Anyone remember?"

"Recruit Division Commanders."

"That's right. Navy Chief and above."

"Why *Rainmaker*?"

"On account of Great Lakes. Training's all inside, at least for the most part. Like a ship, savvy. Come winter, with the cold outside and warm inside, owing to P.T. and condensation, you can make it rain."

"Ever see it?"

"No, but we shipped in July."

"We got there once. R.D.C. Browne on the grind. Reveille. *Can you feel it coming? Can you feel the rain?* Only a couple of drops here and there, at first. But you feel that first drop, man, you start grinding. No early storm warning, but it rained alright. You could feel it. Felt good. Browne was so damned pleased with himself. Treated us different after that."

"Class Zero-Four-Zero-Zero, this is your one-five minute warning!"

"Aye aye, Section Leader!!"

"Didn't know you were a Prior, Vince."

"Who isn't? We're chalk full of Mustangs."

"So which is tougher, O.C.S. or Basic?"

"Depends. Apples and oranges, really. Better question might be whether you would rather be in Great Lakes trying to get to Seaman or here earning a Commission."

"Say the payout was the same. Measuring degree of difficulty or quality of life only."

"Wasn't a big fan of the Peanut Butter Shot."

"Forgot about the Peanut Butter Shot."

"How do you forget the Peanut Butter Shot? I think I can still feel that badboy."

"Forgot the name, is all."

"Or open berthing. That's not a lot of fun. Getting gassed kind of sucked too."

"I don't know. It wasn't so bad. Six weeks was over before you knew it. This here is starting to feel long."

"No runners here."

"No D.O.Rs at Great Mistakes. Imagine the attrition."

"True."

"Runners?"

"Guys who make a break for it, split for the fence."

"Sometimes they make it."

"Sometime they don't."

"Really?"

"We only had one. Didn't make it. Didn't even make it over the fence. Got stuck on the way up and they just peeled him off. Man he was crazy."

"We had a guy make it. He was crazy too. But good crazy, always talking about his great escape. How he was hoodwinked, snookered into it by The Man. Maravich. No one took him seriously. And then he made his break. Timed it just right, off the rear, full sprint, up over the fence, hit the tracks, down Buckley just as the train was pulling in to the station. Genius. Dead of winter too. R.C.P.O. tried to go after him, the little prick, but couldn't keep up in the snow."

"How far is the station?"

"Right across from Main Gate. Trick is to time your break with the Union Pacific. Otherwise, you're the guy in a Smurf suit waiting for a train. M.Ps will get you every time."

"Class Zero-Four-Zero-Zero, this is your one-zero minute warning!"

"Aye aye, Section Leader!!"

"D.Is are tougher for sure."

"That's true. The Chiefs look out for you. Some of these Leathernecks enjoy it a bit too much."

"You hear about the Seal in Zero-Eight?"

"No, what happened?"

"They were pushing him hard. Seal popped up and got in Froman's face."

"What did Froman do?"

"The other D.Is stepped in. Got to him before he threw a punch."

"Damn."

"He throws that punch, he's gone."

"Never happen at Basic."

"I don't know. That's a little different. I would say take care of you more here. Everybody knows we're walking out of here wearing butter bars. N.E.X. lady knows. Admin knows. Candios know. Candios can taste it. The Chiefs know. Hell, even the D.Is know."

"They take care of you in Basic."

"Basic is fine. It's what comes next. Most guys are headed off to be some kind of Dirty Deck Ape or Bilge Rat, playing dominos with some scary individuals in a sixty-four man and pining after the Boat Goat. Twelve on, twelve off. You show up at Moffett, the whole world's in front of you. Eight weeks later it's eat what you kill. Six years to finish your degree, working nights. Two to get picked up for O.C.S. and only if your Skipper agrees to put in your package."

"They messed with your app?"

"Didn't want to lose an able bodied E-Dawg. Put me through the week before his change of command. Then wanted a *thank you, Sir, I won't forget it.*"

"Class Zero-Four-Zero-Zero, this is your zero-five minute warning!"

"Aye aye, Section Leader!!"

"Don't get me wrong. I liked being a Sailor. I definitely like where I am now, least where I'm going. And I owe it to that. Only wish I'd known what I was buying. Or what they were selling. That's what tears you up out there. Zero-control. Butter Bars looking like Cadets reporting aboard. Maybe that's a bad attitude. The point is this. You got forty thousand kids who cycle through R.T.C. every year. Every year. It's a machine, just cranking out sailor after sailor. Here you have what, twenty-five, twenty-six classes?"

"Twenty-eight."

"Twenty-eight. Forty-odd Candidates a class. Some twelve hundred graduates per year. That's real intimate. All destined to do great things as Div-Os. All the bells and whistles. Officers' Mess. Single housing. Drinks at the O Club."

"Sunday brunch underway."

"Lord."

"And I don't mean slinging it."

"Don't forget steak and lobster night."

"All of it. You know they watched movies every night underway on the Admiral's staff? Movies. Every night. And you wouldn't believe the menus. So if you ask me which is tougher, O.C.S. or Basic, well, it's O.C.S. Probably hands down. But it's really the wrong question. Take a seventeen year old, put him through Basic, A-School, six months swabbing heads in First Lieutenant or slinging chow, followed by three years of open berthing working the Line or eight decks down IYAOYAS, all the while trying to get his pin, tacking on chevrons and working towards an Associates in whatever the hell is available online. That there is the tougher road. Initial success or total failure. All to start over as a Butter Bar."

"That's fair."

"Don't get me wrong. I'll be the better O for it. I just wish I could have a quick word with the me back then. Explain the choice. Probably would have done it anyway, all the same."

"Class Zero-Four-Zero-Zero, this is your immediate warning!"

"Aye aye, Section Leader!!"

"Always fun, gang. Thanks for the gouge. Appreciate it."

"You got it, Shipmate."

"Oh, and Masterson."

"Yeah?"

"I got a hug for you if you need it, okay?"

"Don't mess with me, Zurich."

"Ready! Move!"

"Aye aye, Section Leader!!"

"Class Zero-Four-Zero-Zero! Prepare to ground glasses on tray!"

"Aye aye, Section Leader!!"

"Ready! Move!"

"Aye aye, Section Leader!!"

"Class Zero-Four-Zero-Zero! Prepare to take your feet!"

"Aye aye, Section Leader!!"

"Ready! Move!"

"Aye aye, Section Leader!!"

"Class Zero-Four-Zero-Zero! Prepare to face the scullery!"

"Aye aye, Section Leader!!"

"Ready! Move!"

"Aye aye, Section Leader!!"

"Class Zero-Four-Zero-Zero! Prepare to recover trays!"

"Aye aye, Section Leader!!"

"Ready! Move!"

"Aye aye, Section Leader!!"

"Column of files! From the right!"
"Forward!"
"Stand fast."
"March!"
"Aye aye, Section Leader!!"
"Good afternoon, Sir!"

••

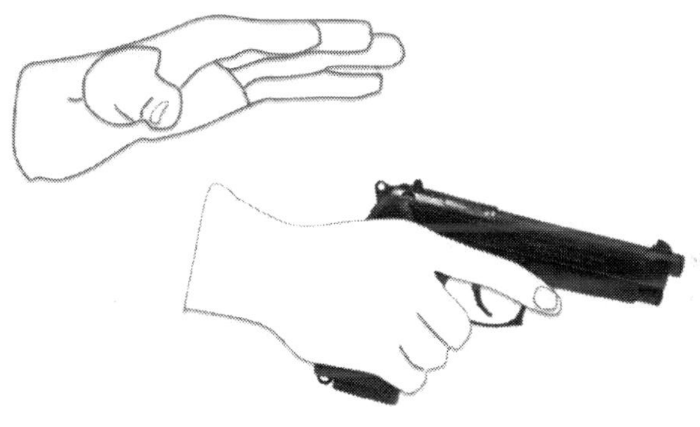

Safety first

When at the firing range, follow all safety precautions. Every firearm used by Navy personnel has some type of built-in safety device, and some have more than one. The safety device guards against accidental discharge of a firearm. In almost every case of accidental shooting, negligence or carelessness in the prime cause. A weapon is only as safe as the person using it. Learn to respect each firearm as a deadly weapon. You should observe the following general precautions when handling any type of firearm.

Treat every weapon with respect. Consider it loaded.

Never point a weapon at anything or anyone you do not intend to shoot.

Always make sure that the bore is clear and that all oil and grease have been removed from the barrel and chamber before firing.

Use only the proper size of ammunition.

Unload firearms before transporting them to and from a shooting area.

Always carry the firearm so as to control the direction of the muzzle. Keep the muzzle pointed in a safe direction until ready to fire.

Keep the safety on until you are ready to shoot.

Never shoot until you have positively identified the target.

Unload unattended weapons. At home, store firearms (with trigger locks installed) and ammunition out of the reach of children.

Do not climb trees or fences with a loaded firearm.

Do not pull a firearm toward you by the muzzle.

Avoid shooting a rifle over a hard, flat surface or body of water because of possible erratic and lengthy bullet ricochets.

Like oil and water, firearms and alcohol do not mix. Do not drink alcoholic beverages or partake of any narcotic or drug before or during shooting activities.

Know your weapon -- its shooting characteristics, its safeties, and its loading and unloading procedures.

Never indulge in horseplay when carrying a firearm.

••

"Let's get started, Zero-Four. Eleven-decimal-five dash one. Upon completion of this unit of instruction, you will able to demonstrate knowledge of the fundamentals of nuclear power plant and associated accessory systems. To achieve this terminal objective, your enabling objectives are the following. One. Describe the nuclear fission process to include mass defect and binding energy. Two. Define critical mass, critical reactor, sub-critical reactor, supercritical reactor, neutron thermalization, and thermal-neutron flux. Three. Define moderator and explain how the neutron thermal flux varies due to the moderator density. Four. Describe the functions of a reactor vessel, reactor core, pressurizer, steam generator, and reactor coolant pump. Five. State the purpose of the reactor control rods and control rod drive mechanism. And six. Define SCRAM as it applies to reactor plant operation. How do you feel about that?"

"Outstanding, Senior."

"Outstanding. We're here to talk about nuclear. And no, you don't have to be a nuclear physicist to understand this material. You all already know the steam cycle. With nuclear, only real difference is the source of energy to generate the steam. Atomic energy versus fuel oil. Nuclear power. At the same time, that there is an important difference. December second, Nineteen-Forty-Two. Three-thirty-six in the afternoon. When Enrico Fermi and his team of scientists created man's first controlled, self-sustaining nuclear reaction under the stands of Stagg Field. We, the Navy, leveraged this new technology with the commissioning of the Nautilus sub some short twelve years later. Three G Core Three. Admiral Rickover's baby. Legendary Turtle and, mind you, still the model for modern propulsion plants and propulsion for dang near all of Naval aircraft carriers and subs, except maybe the Kitty and Connie. Long life and unlimited power. You don't even need air. Twenty thousand leagues under the sea. And that's all thanks

to a little process called *fission*. That is the process we're going learn about today. You'll be Bubbleheads before you know it. Ready?"

"Yes, Senior."

"Alright, then. Prepare to copy. The energy in a nuclear powered vessel comes from the fission of an atom's nucleus, or, really, uranium atoms. Fission creates three products, you all might want to remember. Three products. *Neutrons, fission fragments* and *energy*. This is the process when uranium two-thirty-five, remember, combines with a neutron to form uranium two-thirty-six, a highly unstable isotope that splits to form two light nuclei, called fission fragments, F.F.-one and F.F.-two. And along with these fission fragments, also producing, on average, two-point-forty some extra neutrons. Basic fission. So what are our three fission products? Repeat after me. *Neutrons.*"

"Neutrons."

"*Fission fragments.*"

"Fission fragments."

"And *energy.*"

"Energy."

"Very good. Now let's talk about the theory. You may already be familiar with the equation. The law of conservation of energy states that the total energy of the universe is constant and that energy can be neither created nor destroyed. The key to understanding the source of nuclear energy is Einstein's theory, yes that Einstein, that mass and energy are equivalent and reciprocally convertible. *E equals M.C. squared.* Where E equals energy. M equals mass. And C equals the speed of light. To determine the energy produced by the fission process, you may want to remember this, you look to the difference in mass between the reactants and the products, known as the *mass defect.*"

"Mass defect."

"Since we know that the total energy of the universe must remain constant, given that mass is lost in the reaction, then we know that energy must be gained. Gained. This is what's called the *binding energy*, solved for in the equation as the energy gained from the loss of mass between the reactants and the products. Got it?"

"Yes, Senior."

"Good. Now for you math majors out there, the equation suggests that the rate of fission will increase exponentially, the reaction uncontrollable. Good thing for reactor techs is that the neutrons needed to react with the two-thirty-five must be at a substantially lower kinetic energy level than the neutrons produced by the fission. So to maintain the fission chain, fast neutrons must be converted into thermal neutrons, slow neutrons, by dissipating the kinetic energy. Ultimately, this is because a slow neutron is more likely to combine with the uranium two-thirty-five molecule than a fast, non-thermalized neutron. So what

are we really talking about? *Control.* Control of the reactor and control of the nuclear fission chain reaction. Without control, all you get is a nuclear disaster. And we don't want that, do we?"

"No, Senior."

"No indeed. So how do we do it? We build nuclear reactors assembled to maintain and control the fission chain reaction, creating a process where we can effectively thermalize those fast neutrons. Now there are three conditions, conditions you might want to remember, for thermalizing fast neutrons. *Critical,* where the process is just efficient enough to thermalize one fast neutron and cause a fission reaction. *Subcritical,* where the process fails to thermalize one neutron and cause a fission reaction, causing the chain reaction rate to decrease. And *supercritical,* where we have a very efficient process so that more than one of the fast neutrons produced by fission is thermalized, building on the chain reaction. And that's important. Let me be clear. When I say critical, subcritical and supercritical I am not, I repeat not, talking about the rate of fission. I'm talking about an increase or decrease to the rate of change of the fission process, of a particular condition. See in nuclear, it's not about how fast or slow you're going, it's about *how much faster or how much slower you're going.* Every class I talk myself blue in face making this distinction. And every time half the class misses this question on the test. Are you going to miss this question?"

"No, Senior."

"Are you sure, now?"

"Yes, Senior."

"Right. So how do we keep the genie in the bottle? Mostly water, as the moderator, thermalizing those fast neutrons before they leave the location of the uranium two-thirty-five in the light water reactor. Cheap. Effective. Easily replaceable. The way this works is pretty simple, actually. All that is necessary to control the effectiveness of water as a moderator is to control the temperature of the water. I'll repeat. All that is necessary to control the effectiveness of water as a moderator is to *control the temperature of the water.* Since cold water is more dense than hot water, it has more molecules per unit volume. Consequently, neutrons will collide with water molecules more frequently, lowering their energy levels and leading to an increase in thermalization. This causes the thermal-neutron flux of the reactor to rise, increasing the quantity of fission occurring. In other words, if the density of the water, as the moderator, is decreased, there will be fewer water molecules per unit volume for the neutrons to collide with, so that the neutrons will have to travel a greater distance, causing a greater number of fast neutrons to leave the reactor. This naturally results in a drop in the rate of fission. Got it? Not really? Just remember that all that is necessary to control the effectiveness of water as a moderator is to control the temperature of the water. Alright?"

"Yes, Senior."

"So that's the genie behind the curtain. But what we're really talking about is a heat source for high quality, non-radioactive, saturated steam. And that takes us right back to our conventional steam cycle. Well basically. Same basic idea, just a couple different components for reactor plants. Please turn to page eleven-decimal-five dash eight. Figure eleven. Your nuclear reactor steam cycle. The central region of the reactor, you might want to remember, is called the *reactor core.* This area contains the *fuel,* the *moderator* and part of the *reactor coolant,* the moderator and the reactor coolant being the same. Who wants to take a guess? Moderator and reactor coolant."

"Water, Senior."

"Pure water. Good to know I'm not talking to myself up here. Now, we have our uranium two-thirty-five as the fuel, enriched and in the form of uranium dioxide. But how do we package it, make sure the radioactivity is safely contained? Simpler than you might think, actually. We encase the uranium dioxide in a thin layer of metal called the cladding. *The cladding.*"

"The cladding."

"The cladding prevents the escape of fission products near the surface of the fuel element and also forms a corrosion-resistant layer to prevent the fuel element from being corroded by reactor coolant. A good idea if you don't want your nuke techs to glow something awful. We're talking zirconium, aluminum or stainless steel. What have you. Our moderator is then inserted between the core and the cladding. Our reactor coolant is used to remove the heat from the reactor core caused by fission in the fuel elements. But how do they relate as a system? We know fission also results in the energy given to the fission fragments. The slowing of these fragments by the atoms that make up the fuel elements results in the collisions that cause the fuel element to heat. This heat is then transferred to the reactor coolant as it circulates in the core. We're talking a range between five hundred and six hundred degrees Fahrenheit. White hot. Think fast. What do you call the thin layer of metal that encases the uranium dioxide?

"The cladding, Senior."

"Everyone."

"The cladding, Senior."

"Good. Our next systems component is the *reactor vessel,* along with its *closure head.* Cement and steel, folks. And lots of it. These provide the structural support not only to protect the core but also to direct the flow of reactor coolant. We're talking steel, five to eight inches thick, necessary to withstand the high pressure and temperature in the reactor. The top of the reactor vessel is closed by a removable cover called the closure head, easy enough to remember, which is bolted and welded to the reactor vessel to prevent any kind of leakage of the coolant. The closure head also houses the mechanism used to position the control rods in the reactor core. This means that any time you want to refuel, you

have to remove the closure head. Like a pickle jar, only tighter and bolted down like you would not believe. Got it?"

"Yes, Senior."

"Which brings us to the reactor's *control rods*. Control rods serve a dual purpose in the reactor, providing both the means of keeping the thermal-neutron flux at the desired level in a critical reactor core and as a means of rapidly shutting down the reactor by absorbing all of the neutrons, stopping the fission process. Repeat after me. *Controlling flux and shut down.*"

"Controlling flux and shut down."

"*Controlling flux and shut down.*"

"Controlling flux and shut down."

"These control rods are hung in the reactor core by lead screws, driven up and down by the *Control-Rod Drive Mechanisms*, C.R.D.Ms, attached to the closure head and allowing you to remote position the control rods into the reactor core. Up and down. Up and down. When the reactor is in a shutdown condition, the control rods are fully, fully, inserted into the reactor core. When you want to start her up, you partially, partially, withdraw the rods from the core until you get to critical. Now, over time, as they get depleted, you have to withdraw the rods further and further to obtain criticality. Please note that we are not, are not, talking about increasing or decreasing the reactor's power level. We are talking about reactor-coolant temperature. Once the reactor is critical, any movement of the control rods results in changing the reactor's operating temperature by varying the *thermal-neutron flux level.* Read that back to me."

"Thermal-neutron flux level."

"*Thermal-neutron flux level.*"

"Thermal-neutron flux level."

"Sounds important to me. That's the first purpose. The C.R.D.Ms are also designed so that, in the highly unlikely event of an emergency shutdown of the reactor, they will release the control rods, allowing gravity and a spring compressed on top of the control rod to insert them into the reactor core very rapidly. Shut her down. This type of shut down is known as a SCRAM, the *Super Critical Reactor Axe Man.* Let's hear it."

"Super Critical Reactor Axe Man."

"*Super Critical Reactor Axe Man.*"

"Super Critical Reactor Axe Man."

"The Axe Man, baby. Four seconds. Happens that quick, before she can get going. You also have some options involving what we call neutron poisons, but your basic shutdown is with the C.R.D.Ms. Questions? Getting some zombie stares. What's the purpose of control rods?"

"Controlling flux and shut down."

"Very good. That's what you need to remember. Next up the *pressurizer*. In a reactor that uses water as the reactor coolant, which we do, most designs require that the reactor coolant remain sub-cooled, we're talking liquid, at all times. This is because the heat produced by fission must be constantly removed from the fuel elements by the coolant to prevent them from melting, which you don't want. If the water is allowed to boil, the steam produced causes a meltdown of the reactor core. This happens because steam has a lower heat capacity than liquid and is not able to carry enough heat away from the fuel elements. If steam is allowed to enter the reactor coolant pump, it causes the pump to cavitate, stopping circulation and the water to boil. So as to prevent a boil, we keep the reactor coolant sub-cooled under high pressure. You might want to remember that. It's the reason why these reactors are often called Pressurized Water Reactors. *Pressurized Water Reactors.*"

"Pressurized water reactors."

"Good old P.W.Rs, once the future of American industry. Nuclear powered steel plants. Shame about Three Mile. The pressurizer, which keeps the reactor coolant under high pressure, is a cylindrical tank that operates at saturation conditions of about two thousand pounds per square inch, p.s.i.g, and six hundred and thirty-six degrees Fahrenheit, with liquid in the bottom of the tank and a steam blanket on top of the liquid. All done by electric heater. A pipe connected to the pressurizer below the liquid level transmits the pressure to the reactor coolant system. The entire reactor coolant system is pressurized, keeping the water sub-cooled. Important thing to remember is pressure. Pressurized Water Reactors. Got it?"

"Yes, Senior."

"There's also the *steam generator*. Basically talking a large heat exchanger. Since we can't have boiling water and meltdown in the core the steam needed for the turbines must be produced externally in the reactor. This is where we get into some advanced engineering where the heated high pressurized water coming from the reactor enters at the bottom, flows through the U-shaped tubes and then exits the steam generator. Can you spot them? Three of them. One. Two. And three. Now, the outside surfaces of these tubes are in contact with the feedwater from the main feed pump of the main steam-cycle. Heat is transferred from the hot reactor coolant inside the tubes to the main steam-cycle feedwater surrounding the tubes, causing the feedwater, which is at a lower pressure than the coolant, to boil, producing steam. The wet steam produced is then routed through moisture separators and exits the steam generator as high-quality saturated wet steam. Right here. This leaves us with two loops. The *reactor coolant system* as the primary system and the *non-radioactive steam plant system* as the secondary system or loop. Different daddies. So, at random, if I asked you to

identify the primary system for a pressurized water reactor system, you would name?"

"The reactor coolant system, Senior."

"Bravo Zulu. Our next component is the *reactor coolant pump*. The reactor coolant is circulated throughout the primary system by a pump, fittingly called the reactor-coolant pump. No need to reinvent the wheel. The reactor coolant pump is completely sealed, we're talking hermetically, for zero leakage of reactor coolant. This pump is then connected to a piping system known as the *main coolant loop*. Which piping system are we talking about now?"

"Main coolant loop."

"Bravo Zulu. And there you have it. The components for a system flow. The water enters the reactor vessel from the reactor-coolant pump at five hundred and eight degrees, directed into the coolant passages between the fuel elements in the core. See here? And as the coolant flows through the core, it acts as the moderator, picking up heat from the fuel elements. Makes more sense now, right? When the coolant exits the core it is now at five hundred and forty-two degrees Fahrenheit. The coolant then leaves the reactor and flows through the tubes of the steam generator. Heat is transferred to the secondary feed water on the outside of the tubes, producing our high-quality steam for propulsion. The reactor coolant flows out of the steam generator back down to five hundred and eight degrees, returned to the reactor by the reactor-coolant pump. See it? Meanwhile, the pressurizer maintains the entire reactor-coolant loop, like we said, at two thousand p.s.i.g. Coolant sub-cooled. Nuclear engineering. High-speed. Am I right?"

"Yes, Senior."

"The big takeaway is simply a basic understanding of the nuclear power generation cycle. Don't worry so much about the temperature and pressure. We're not talking actual operating parameters. But you need to know how to identify these components. What they do. Why they do it. And how they relate. Understood?"

"Yes, Senior."

"The time for questions is now. No questions? Alright. A quick note about safety. Nuclear reactors don't operate by themselves. You still need operators. These aren't tanning salons. We take special precaution to safeguard Techs from exposure to radiation with *shielding*, making sure those gamma rays and neutrons that result from the fission process stay within the closed system. This shielding, good to remember, of a nuclear reactor serves two purposes. First, it reduces the radiation level inside the reactor compartment so that it will not interfere with the operation of the instrumentation equipment. Second, it lowers the radiation level outside the reactor compartment to protect operating personnel. So how do we do it? We've found that the fast neutrons are best shielded by *elastic collisions* with

any material containing hydrogen. We're talking water, fuel oil, or even plastic as a suitable neutron shield. Gamma rays are different. Think X-rays. You need a dense material like *lead*. You'll be glad to know, the Navy does not skimp on its shielding. The shielding on a nuclear vessel is extensive, the greatest single contributor to the weight of the propulsion plant. You need not fear any way, shape or form of radiation. Typical radiation exposure per year to the crew is less than folks receive from the sun living at high altitude in Denver. Got it?"

"Yes, Senior."

"Don't worry, we're almost home. Last aspect is putting it all into practice. The whole point of the process is to generate the power required to get a vessel underway, aircraft carriers and subs. Initially at low speed and steady-state condition, heat in equivalent to the heat out. At time zero, the Officer of the Deck orders flank speed and the throttle man responds by opening the steam-supply valve to the propulsion turbines, allowing more steam to flow to the turbine and increasing ship speed. Right? Since we need more steam for more speed, the secondary water must remove more heat from the reactor coolant, more heat being taken out than is being put in, causing the average temperature of the coolant to drop. This drop results in an increase in the density of the moderator and an increase in the moderator's ability to thermalize neutrons. Everyone with me? The reactor then goes supercritical and reactor power starts to increase, reactor power increasing until the heat starts going into the coolant in the steam generator. At this point the heat imbalance is reversed and the temperature of the coolant is restored to normal. Naturally, as the coolant heats up to its normal temperature, the density of the moderator decreases, becoming sub-critical until there is no longer any heat imbalance. Mission accomplished. Reactor returns to critical and the vessel makes way at maximum power, flank speed. Our nuclear Navy. Any questions? Yes."

"Senior, just checking, how much of this will we have to know for the exam?"

"All of it. Next question. Only kidding. Listen, like I said, you have to know how to recognize the components. You have to know the terms. Or, how's this? The difference in mass between the reactant and fission products is known as?"

"Sorry, Senior."

"Anyone? The mass defect. And what is the associated energy called? Anyone?"

"Binding energy."

"*Binding energy*. Everyone."

"Binding energy."

"To maintain fission, fast neutrons must be slowed. This is referred to as?"

"Thermalization."

"To maintain a chain reaction, you must maintain a?"

"Critical mass."

"For chain reactions, an increasing rate is known as what kind of condition?"

"Supercritical, Senior."

"How about a decreasing rate?"

"Subcritical, Senior."

"Steady rate."

"Critical."

"Everyone, now. True or false? These conditions describe the rate of fission."

"False, Senior."

"Who said true? That's what I thought. Repeat after me. The reactor core contains three components. *Fuel, moderator* and *coolant*."

"Fuel, moderator and coolant."

"One more time."

"Fuel, moderator and coolant."

"What is the term for the material used to thermalize fast neutrons?

"The moderator, Senior."

"And what does the Navy use primarily as our moderator?"

"Water."

"I want everyone. If this is not getting through, I need to know. How do you control the effectiveness of water as a moderator?"

"Temperature."

"Very good. What do you use to shield gamma rays?"

"Lead."

"How does a SCRAM affect a reactor? Anyone?"

"Shuts her down, Senior."

"Spoken like a true E.T.N. That's the gouge you need to know. But word to wise. Don't just try and memorize the terms. If you don't understand the system, then you won't understand the questions. Everyone take ten. Stand-by for hydraulic systems theory."

••

Marksmanship

The most important single factor in marksmanship is trigger control. Everything about your position and aim may be perfect, but if you do not squeeze the trigger properly, your shot will not go where you aimed it. The key to trigger control is that the trigger must be squeezed smoothly, gradually, and evenly straight to the rear. Any sideward pressure, however slight, applied to the trigger during its rearward movement will likely result in a wide shot. Similarly, upward or downward pressure on the trigger will result in high or low shots.

When you fire from the standing position, coordinating the trigger squeeze and proper aim is critical. You must start and continue the squeeze only when the front sight is momentarily at rest or is slowly moving in the smallest area of the bullseye. Inexperienced shooters usually tend to snapshoot in this position, that is, they attempt to complete the trigger action instantly as the front sight moves across the aiming point. This invariably results in jerking the rifle.

And producing a wild shot.

With the trigger hand, grasp the stock or pistol grip firmly, but without strain, so the trigger finger has the proper support to overcome trigger weight. An unnatural, straining grasp causes excessive muscle tension in the hand, which results in a tremor that is transmitted to the weapon. With the trigger finger, make contact with the trigger where the contact produces a movement straight to the rear (usually between the first joint and the tip). Gradually increase the pressure until the hammer releases and the shot fires. If during this process, the sights drift off the target, interrupt the trigger squeeze but maintain the pressure. When the sight picture is correct, continue the squeeze until you fire the shot.

••

"What are these things?"

"Shirt stays."

"Shirt stays?"

"Keeps our uniforms from getting untucked. For a neater, smarter appearance."

"Mood killers is what they are. You must be enjoying this."

"What?

"Me. The girl. Fumbling around. The one tangled up."

"Works like a garter belt."

"What do I know about garter belts? I know some girl showed you how to unhook bra once upon a time."

"Sure. You want to grab it right at the top. Thumb and forefinger. See?"

"Okay."

"Stopper slides down."

"Got it."

"Press it out. Shirt goes free."

"Okay. Put it back."

"Put it back?"

"Yes. I want to try. I changed my mind. Who knew I had a thing. How many are there?"

"Two up front. Two in the back."

"Hold on. I want to try another. They go all the way down?"

"Clip to your socks."

"It's so strange."

"You get used to them."

"No, I mean all of it, really. Officer Candidates. Saltpeter. Poopies. I mean, Poopies? Are you serious? And shirt stays. Who would guess all you military guys are walking around with garter belts underneath your uniforms. No wonder you're all a little tense. Hey, is it true about the soap? Where they beat you up?"

"You mean in the pillowcases? I would imagine it still happens, occasionally, just as a function of the psychology, but I think that type of violence is more in the Enlisted ranks. Or with the Army. The Marines."

"Gotcha. Shirt goes free."

"Hang on. Give me one second."

"Here."

"I don't want to leave you with the wrong idea. The Navy, at least from what I can tell so far, isn't really all that violent. You might pull a guy aside who is getting the Class beat for one reason or another, but assault and battery isn't really part of the program. The illusion of violence, sure. But it's more folks talking amongst themselves."

"Like what?"

"Nice try."

"You said anything I wanted to know."

"I did. Most of it you wouldn't consider interesting."

"Try me."

"You want to move to the back?"

"No, I like it here better. So?"

"You mean the real story? Oh, I don't know. Let's see. If someone is not like the others, everyone just knows. Almost immediately now. Say another guy doesn't smell too good or is generally hosed-up, always behind. You get a couple of strikes, maybe more if you're trying. But eventually, you'll end up frozen out."

"That's not very nice."

"Not intentionally or unintentionally, really. You don't want to be associated, if only because other guys might think you're a hoser by association, start freezing you out too. Hard to get by on your own. If you get frozen out, you stop getting the gouge. If you stop getting the gouge, you're likely to fail a big-ticket item. If you fail a big-ticket item, you get put on the bubble. If you fail two big ticket items, you get sent to this remedial pool while you wait for the class behind you to catch up, along with all the other deadweight. You can imagine the morale. Then they drop you into that follow-on class, picking up at the point of failure. Only then you have to get in with a whole new crowd who all assume you're probably going to be a drag. So it's chilly going in. And so on. Downward spiral. Just had the son of a Navy Captain roll out a couple weeks ago. Got tripped up by Navigation. That seemed to mean something, especially to the Priors. Prior Enlisted."

"I wouldn't exactly call that the *real story.*"

"No?"

"There's got to be some real stuff. Like gossip."

"You want the stuff you have to promise not to tell anyone else."

"Yes."

"Well?"

"Who am I going to tell? I promise. You're so holding out. I bet you know everything, the way you're wired."

"Occasionally."

"Yes?"

"Occasionally, I do hear some tidbits."

"Tell me."

"Let's see. We had two hook up in the dumpster around back of barracks last weekend. One too many at the Old Crow's Nest."

"Two guys?"

"Guy and a girl."

"In the dumpster?"

"Apparently it was empty. Pretty safe all things considered. I imagine they were quiet about it."

"Who told you?"

"No dice."

"He talked, obviously. Are they boyfriend and girlfriend now?"

"No, at least I doubt it."

"What do people think?"

"Not that many people know."

"Does she know you know?"

"How do you know she wasn't the one to tell me?"

"Michael Zurich. What else? I know you have more."

"You want more gossip?"

"Yes. I want a lot more gossip. You're holding out on me."

"The Drill Instructors. Anything those guys do gets dissected like you wouldn't believe. Strict scrutiny. I know a couple of stories. That's the real gossip. Like anywhere, maybe. Well, maybe not."

"What happened?"

"Stories that would give you the wrong impression about the place, at least for right now. You'll have to use your imagination."

"What? Come on."

"Hey, that's relatively good for now. Gives you a taste of what's out there. With some give and take, you'll get where you want to go. To be continued. Lift up for just a second. What about you?"

"Me? You just gave me nothing. This is totally how you operate."

"I wouldn't say *nothing*."

"Fine. You are bad news, man. What do you want to know?"

"What do Pensacola natives think of Navy guys?"

"That's what you want to know?"

"Sure."

"I guess I would say boys don't like you all that much. At least the ones who aren't planning on joining up. Some girls really go for you Navy guys."

"I imagine."

"This is not that. You'll hear of a fight now and again. Nothing serious. I remember Becky Nix dated a Navy guy back in high school. Actually, I think she ended up marrying him."

"Becky Nix?"

"A friend of mine. Well, kinda."

"Kinda?"

"No, we were friends. Same home room and all. Plus she lived close."

"Where was that?"

"You mean the school or where we lived?"

"The school."

"Episcopal Day. At least, all the way up through Middle School. Pretty small. You get to know everyone real well over the years."

"Religious school?"

"Chapel and bible studies. Sure. It's just the best school."

"So you were friends but more from home room."

"No, we were real friends. She would come over to my house some days after school. Both of her parents worked late, so my mom kind of adopted her for awhile."

"So what happened?"

"Oh, I don't know. Nothing really. Pensacola High happened. We drifted. Just apart. I started hanging out with a different crowd. I didn't ditch her, if that's what you mean. You never went to high school?"

"Sure."

"This is in New York?"

"No. We can talk about that later. What happened to her? You ditched her for the cool kids and she ended up with a Navy guy. What was his story?"

"Navy Stan. Drove around this tricked out Mustang. Always super clean. I mean very shiny. He would pick her up after school. Back gate. Hair gelled. Collar popped. This big silver chain around his neck. Her boyfriend, boy, he sure wanted to kick Navy Stan's ass."

"Boyfriend?"

"Well, more like ex-boyfriend. They had already broken up."

"What was his name?"

"Chip Carmichael. They broke up and then like a month later Becky started dating Navy Stan. Disappeared after that. I think I heard she got her G.E.D and was out in Japan or something. She doesn't come back."

"What about Chip?"

"Chip? Oh, he ended dating some other girl. I heard he's married now too."

"Same girl?"

"Christin Hill."

"Christin Hill."

"Why do you want to know about Becky Nix and all these people so bad?"

"You learn a lot about someone by how they tell a story."

"What did you find out about me?"

"That you made prom queen?"

"I wish. Nominated. What's wrong with Prom Queen?"

"Who won?"

"Sarah Collins."

"Sarah Collins."

"And why do you keep saying all their names like that?"

"Sarah Collins."

"Don't say it at all. You wouldn't have liked Sarah Collins, anyway. Not your type."

"What about Christin Hill?"

"You would have hated Christin. Becky you might have liked. Be quiet a minute. Or, if you want to say any name, say mine."

I press my face into her damp skin lips parted.

••

Rifle display

A clean, properly lubricated and maintained rifle that is loaded with clean ammunition will fire when needed. To keep the rifle in good condition, you need to take care of it and clean it. Under bad weather conditions, some key parts may need care and cleaning several times a day. The cleaning material used for the care of the rifle is carried in the rifle stock. Special attention must be given to the barrel bore and chamber, bolt carrier group, upper receiver group, lower receiver group and the ammunition magazines.

Barrel bore and chamber. One. Dip a bore brush in the bore cleaner, then brush from the chamber to the muzzle, using straight-through strokes. Don't reverse the brush while it is in the bore as it may jam. A jammed brush is hard to remove, and removing the brush might damage the bore. Two. Clean the chamber with the bore brush. Three. Replace the bore brush with a slotted cleaning patch tip and push the dry patches through the bore and chamber until they come out clean. Four. After you clean the bore, lightly lubricate the bore and chamber to prevent corrosion and pitting. Use the recommended lubricant on a patch. Lightly lubricate the lugs in the barrel extension.

Disassembly. The three main groups are the trigger housing group, the barrel and receiver group, and the stock group. To disassemble the rifle into the three main groups, first ensure that the weapon is clear and then allow the bolt to go forward by depressing the follower with the right thumb and allowing the bolt to ride forward over the follower assembly. Place the rifle butt against the left thigh, sights to the left. With the thumb and forefinger of the right hand, pull

downward and outward on the rear of the trigger guard. Swing the trigger guard out as far as it will go and lift out the trigger guard. Swing the trigger guard out as far as it will go and lift out the trigger housing group. To separate the barrel and receiver from the stock lay the weapon on a flat surface with the sights up, muzzle to the left. With the left hand, grasp the rear of the receiver and raise the rifle. With the right hand, give a down ward blow, grasping the small of the stock. This will separate the stock group from the barrel and receiver group.

••

"Sweepers, Sweepers, man your brooms! Give the Battalion a clean sweep down both fore and aft! Sweep down all lower decks, ladderwells and passageways! Dump all garbage clear of the fantail! Now sweepers!"

The Sweeper Team assembles in front of the First Lieutenant locker.

"Okay, folks. Thanks for the good turnout. Understand everyone is real busy right now with prep and all, but I'm asking you, please, not to start cutting corners."

"Sailors will drown."

"That's right. At the same time, let's get her done. I'm in the same boat as everyone else. Who wants The Pit? Going once."

"Promise?"

"Sold."

"What?"

"Nice to have a volunteer. Look, it's already buffed. All she needs is a once over and a surface check. Piece of cake. It's all clear. You can take a spin in the chairs. One more."

"Who's on duty?"

"Burlton."

"All clear my ass."

"Sold to the American hero in the back."

"Christ."

"God bless. Now who wants the Head? No D.Is. Think about it. We've got gloves and bleach. It's dirty but it's quick."

"I'm in."

"Tally one."

"Me too."

"Tally two. One more."

"Roger."

"Perfect. That leaves the p-way. Who's left?"

"Me and Mike. I think we're short a bucket, though."

"That's the great thing about sharing. This is not supersweepers, folks. Field day, that's all she needs. Get her done. Break."

The team disperses. I stir the cleaner into the flow. Rainbow colored bubbles build on the surface of the water.

"Start at the end? Work back?"

"Makes sense."

"You take the left side. I'll take the right."

"Works for me."

"Lord! *Swing low, sweet chariot.*"

"Coming for to carry me home."

"*Swing low, sweet chariot.*"

"Coming for to carry me home."

"*I looked over Jordan, and what did I see?*"

"Coming for to carry me home."

"*A band of angels coming after me.*"

"Coming for to carry me home."

"Watch is going to be screaming tomorrow morning. Imagine having to wake up Burton? Better yet. Imagine having him as your D.I.?"

"You would almost want to roll. Tough bead."

"You talk to the guys in Zero-Seven, they all hate his guts."

"It's still early. I remember hating Willett too."

"Maybe, but I doubt it. Did you ever think of bailing? The first couple of weeks?"

"No, not really."

"What about that night you put your civvies back on?"

"No. I was sick from the crud. Regiment was freezing. Should of gone to sick call, only I was worried they wouldn't let me come back to the class."

"That's when Hobson wouldn't kick you some meds? Pretty weak."

"I thought so too at the time, but he might have been more right than wrong."

"Negative."

"Man, I was in bad shape. Getting mashed in the heat, and then blasted by that A.C. vent at chow. The Candios noticed, almost pulled me the day before Outpost. Who knows had I rolled. The concept of G.T.X. and showing up in another class right off would have been tough. Time to think."

"So no regrets?"

"Regrets? No. No regrets. I may have slightly underestimated exactly what I was getting into, though."

"Almost there, Brother."

"I'm not so sure."

"How do you figure?"

"Well I guess I figured I could show up, run the gauntlet, and come on through to the other side, same as I arrived."

"Sure."

"Only there is no other side. That's why everyone here is always talking about the Fleet. So we're about halfway through getting mashed the other day, hop and pop three-zero, and I got to thinking. There's a reason for everything."

"You know, I'm not so sure."

"Well, if there is a reason most everything, this is only the very beginning. The minute we take that oath, I'll never find the door I came in. Indoc training is just that. Stand-by for the real thing."

"That's pretty deep, my man."

"You asked. I'm fine with it. Just thinking out loud."

"Why did you decide to come in?"

"I think we've talked about it."

"Not sure if I ever got a proper response."

"Improper response!"

"Improper response!"

"Not sure if I have one for you. Come Spring semester, everyone was dropping resumes for investment banking and consulting jobs. All dressed up in suits shoving cream-colored resumes into these little slots."

"Sounds like good Career Services to me."

"That part was okay. A little dystopian, but fine. Then it was either you got a phone call or you didn't get a phone call. *Congratulations, Michael, you have been granted a round-one interview.* Walk in, shake hands, few minutes of small talk and get hit with a question. *So Michael, there are two candles. Each will burn for one hour. You must burn both candles in an hour and a half, only you're not allowed to cut the candles in half. What do you do? You have a wolf, a goat and a cabbage and you need to get them across the river. Your boat is only big enough to take one at a time. If you take the wolf, the goat eats the cabbage. If you take the cabbage, the wolf eats the goat.* Start the problem, start the clock. Then round-two, if you're lucky. *How does he eat? How does he order? Did he salt before tasting?* Something about the whole thing."

"So you up and joined the Navy?"

"In a sense. I had looked up the local recruiter in the Yellow Pages, fooling around at work."

"Enlisted?"

"Enlisted. I had no idea about Officer and Enlisted at the time. I did have this vague notion about the Services. Army and Marines seemed too violent. Air Force was a maybe, but I never got much further than the thought. Walked in off the street and introduced myself, signed up to take the ASVAB."

"What's that?"

"Aptitude test they give Enlisted recruits."

"Must have scored fairly well."

"Target audience is high school students. Not exactly the LSATs. Ninety-ninth percentile. Recruiter first tried to sell me on sub-nuke. Ten thousand dollar signing bonus. Credit for college. I went along for the ride. Already feels like a different world. We set up for MEPS on a Friday morning, early wake up call, right before Spring break. Up all night drinking and playing cards with my college buddies the night before. Didn't say a word. Rolled out like I was going to bed. Recruiter picked me up out front around five in the morning, drove me downtown. Talking to me about responsibility. How he had told his superiors about me and everyone was really excited and counting on me."

"He knew that you were in school, though?"

"He knew. Decent guy, just under a lot of pressure. Talked about the number of calls he had to make every week. Markers to meet. Performance goals. Convincing mom and dad. Categories of enlistment. How close he was to E-Six. So we get downtown. Still dark. Street lights on. Walk in and it's hustle and bustle. Florescent lights. Lines. They take me down to this room in the basement with all these rough house Philly kids to fill out all the forms. Talking real tough about the Marine Corp, different types of guns, how they can't wait to get out there and be a Marine."

"Semper Fi."

"I'm out to lunch the whole time, hitting the coffee as they do the block by block. The battery of tests. Guy next to me wouldn't stop mumbling. *Welcome to the Navy. Hurry up and wait. Hurry up and wait.* Over and over. Had to be some kind of Prior. At the end, they took us into this empty room to get weighed. There was this masking tape on the floor. Blue line. They had line us, drop trough, grab our ankles."

"Really? Why?"

"Hemorrhoid check. Philly kids grumbling because they thought the guys were gay. I think they were, too. I mean, whatever. Totally parallel universe. Last stop was with this military doctor. Old guy. I mean old. The Marine Corp kid I was talking to went in before me. Turned out he had a metal plate in his head. Immediate disqualification. Poor kid couldn't believe it. In absolute shock. Gone. So I go in, introduce myself. Very civil conversation. Said he had been screening kids for forty-five years. Forty-five years. Screened just about every Navy and Marine Corp recruit coming out of Philadelphia since the Sixties. And he asked me the same question. *Why.*"

"Well? What did you say?"

"Not sure, really. I was fairly out of it at that point. Probably told him honestly that I didn't quite know if I was joining up at that point. It was all notional."

"So how did you get here?"

"Well, after I got through all the tests, the recruiter shows back up and takes me up to this small room on the upper floor. Three of his buddies in there waiting me with a contract for Intelligence Specialist. Came at me with a sort of good cop, bad cop routine. They tell me, fingers crossed, they just pulled some strings and can get me in as an E-Three, maybe even E-Four with my college credit coming out of Basic. That I'd be crazy to pass up the opportunity. Said they would set me up in this hotel for the night, put me on a bus to Great Lakes the next morning. And, who knows, maybe get picked up for O.C.S. once I got to Basic. Quickest way, they told me."

"You didn't sign."

"I wasn't pulling any trigger, not before graduation. I mean, definitely not that morning. Flew down to Miami in the afternoon. We hit the beach. Washington Avenue. Didn't give it a second thought. That might very well have been the end of it. But lo and behold, when I get back to my apartment, there's a message on my answering machine from a Senior Chief Marick. I call him up and he fills me in on Officer recruiting, apologizes for the confusion and invites me to come down to the station to take the O.C.S. Test. No clue what the aviation section was all about, probably should have studied, harder than the ASVAB, but I did fine. Intel eligible, whatever that meant. Interviewed with the Lieutenant, passed the P.R.T., filled out my dream sheet. Totally different environment. Clear they were interested, but just as interested, if not more interested, in a strong Officer corp. Something worthwhile waiting at the end of the tunnel."

"I thought you came down from New York."

"Hadn't heard anything by graduation and I wasn't even sure if I was serious, so I picked up a job in the City in an investment banking shop. Excel spreadsheets. Data entry. Not a bad gig. Had my friends. Nice paycheck. And a cubicle life."

"I got you."

"So it's mid-August and I'm sitting there doing something or other and the phone rings. Wouldn't you know, it's Senior Chief. *Good news, you've been accepted as a Sixteen-Thirty-Five in the World's Greatest Navy. Your start date is Monday. Can you be ready?* I said yes. Walked straight into my boss' office, Joe T, told him it was my last day and I was joining the Navy. Snap decision. I couldn't believe it. He couldn't believe it. No one could believe it. Met you three days later. You know the rest. I guess I ended up just following the river."

"Fair enough."

"What about you?"

"Oh, man. This goes all the way back. I was that kid with all the models. A-Four Skyhawks. F-Four Phantoms. Hornets. Tomcats. You name it. If it had wings, I put it together."

"This is in West Virginia?"

"Charlestown, baby. And I know I probably won't get jets. I'm fine with that."

"Really?"

"Long as it's helos out of San Diego."

"Two girls."

"Beautiful girls. Just waiting."

"I'm still unclear on these two girls."

"What's not to understand?"

"It's you and two girls? Or you and the two girls?"

"We shall see, my man. We shall see. Little house down near the beach. Seventy-five degrees year-round. Happy days. Little late to D.O.R. anyway. Downhill run from here on out. One Great Pumpkin Race, two butter bars and three silver dollars. Home by the holidays."

"You would be okay with helos?"

"As long as it's helos out of San Diego. Now, if you ask me if I would rather get jets, I mean sure. Who dreams of helos? But take a guy like Meister. Guy has like two hundred flight hours. I have fifteen. Who gets jets?"

"You know he D.O.R.'ed his first week?"

"Meister?"

"Meister."

"That guy's a future Fleet Admiral."

"For sure. Apparently he really didn't appreciate Indoc. All the yelling and screaming."

"I remember him from day one."

"More like day zero-two or zero-three. Captain convinced him to give it another go during out-processing. They rolled him back in, none the wiser."

"Miester?

"Miester, man. Surprised me too. You know he put the base coat on these puppies? Saw me getting nowhere, walked over and shined them right up. Not something that he had to do. So you're saying no regrets?"

"Regrets? No. Heck, I've only had two regrets my whole life."

"Is that right?"

"Tennessee-Kentucky last year. Battle for the Barrel. I had half a bottle of Crown Royal left over after the tailgate. We're talking a full half bottle of Royal. Only we can't take it into the stadium. Only way is to smuggle it in and there's zero chance through security. Wouldn't you know, we meet these two girls on the way in and they, bless their souls, volunteer to help us sneak it in. Nobody ever checks girls."

"The two girls?"

"Hell no. These are a very different two girls. So everything was fine and dandy. Mission accomplished, Scott free, all laughing, *here's to ole Tennessee.* Then they beg off to the restroom. *Be right back, fellas!*"

"And there went a full half bottle of Crown Royal."

"About ruined a classic."

"The other?"

"True regret? Selling my cable descrambler. Damn hard to come by. I had like every channel. Every channel."

"So no regrets."

"Another day, another A."

We work down the rest of the passageway in silence.

"Mike."

"Yeah."

"Maybe I can tell you something. This here's a hard one. Personal. I'm serious now."

"Sure."

"It's about my Dad. He passed this year."

"I'm sorry."

"I've been meaning to tell you for awhile now, only I'm still not sure how to bring it up ever. Thing is, I still want to talk about him. Hard to get around the fact that he's gone."

"You want to talk about him now?"

"No, not really. I just want to be able to talk about him when he comes to mind. The tense is still a little tough if you don't already know. That's all."

"Sure."

"He was a great Dad. Great guy period. Real special like. That's not his son talking. That's everyone who ever knew him."

"Social like you?"

"Me? No, way more social. Way more social. Type of guy who fills up a room. I mean like a magic trick. *How you all enjoying the evening? Is there anything I can get you? Jimmy, how's the leg? Harry, how are the girls? This round's on me.* Really hard to describe. Take my game and double it. Or whatever. Maybe then you have my Dad. Still doesn't seem somehow real."

"How are you guys holding up?"

"It's hard. We'll get through. You'll get to meet them, you know. My mom and my sisters."

"Angela and Maria."

"I told them about you."

"What did you say?"

"That I met a good guy on my way in, how you helped me out for M.T.T. How you were from all over and crazy as all hell. That we got to become friends, you know."

"You helped me as much as I helped you, brother."

"Think we'll keep in touch?"

"Only so many people who are around at the end of the night."

"Amen. Lord! *Swing low, sweet chariot.*"

"Coming for to carry me home."

"*I looked over Jordan, and what did I see?*"

"Coming for to carry me home."

"*A band of angels coming after me.*"

"Coming for to carry me home."

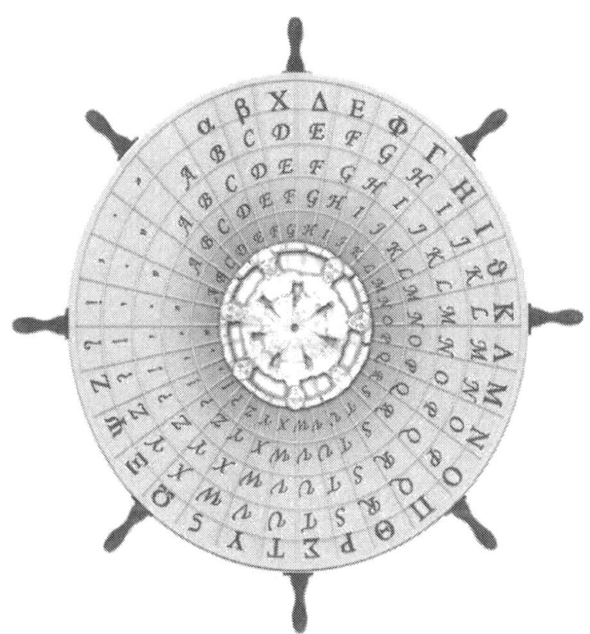

CHAPTER VII

WEEKS 12-13

The Color Guard proceeds up the center aisle.

"We gather here today to honor our Lord and Savior, Jesus Christ, he who gives us the strength and the courage we need in our moments of weakness. Welcome to worship. I invite you to take out your worship bulletin and follow

along in our call to worship. The Lord is near to all who call upon Him, to all who call upon Him in truth. He will fulfill the desire of those who are in awe of Him."

"He will hear their cry, and save them."

"Lord, you have been our dwelling place in all generations. Before the mountains were brought forth, or ever You had formed the earth and the world, even from everlasting to everlasting. You are God."

"Glory be to the Father."

"Sitting or kneeling let us confess our sins before almighty God. Join with me in our prayer of confession. Almighty and most merciful Father, we have erred and strayed from Thy ways, like lost sheep. We have followed too much the devices and desires of our own hearts. We have offended against Thy holy laws. We have left undone those things which we ought to have done and we have done those things which we ought not to have done. But Thou, oh Lord, have mercy upon us. Spare Thou those who confess their faults. Restore Thou those who are penitent according to Thy promises declared unto mankind in Christ Jesus our Lord. And grant, oh most merciful Father, for his sake, that we may hereafter live a godly, righteous and sober life to the glory of Thy holy name. Amen."

"Amen."

"Let us say together the Lord's Prayer, as Jesus taught his disciples. Our Father who art in heaven, hallowed will be Thy name, Thy kingdom come, Thy will be done, on earth as it is in heaven. Give us this day our daily bread and forgive us our trespasses, as we forgive those who trespass against us, and lead us not into temptation, but deliver us from evil, for Thine is the kingdom and the power, and the glory for ever and ever. Amen."

"Amen."

"The scripture tells us that the Lord is merciful and gracious, slow to anger and abounding in steadfast love. He does not deal with us according to our sins, nor repay us according to our inequities, for as high as the heavens are above the earth, so far does He remove our transgressions from us. As far as the East is from the West, so far does He remove our transgressions. Brothers and sisters the Lord has heard our prayer and forgiven your sins. Amen."

"Amen."

"The first reading is written in the second chapter of Colossians, in the first verse, page three-forty-six of your pew Bibles. Officer Candidate Jennings."

"The Word of our Lord. For I would that ye knew what great conflict I have for you, and for them at Laodicea, and for as many as have not seen my face in the flesh. That their hearts might be comforted, being knit together in love, and unto all riches of the full assurance of understanding, to the acknowledgement of the mystery of God, and of the Father, and of Christ. In whom are hid all the

treasures of wisdom and knowledge. And this I say, lest any man should beguile you with enticing words. For though I be absent in the flesh, yet am I with you in the spirit, joyous and beholding your order, and the steadfastness of your faith in Christ. As ye have therefore received Christ Jesus the Lord, so walk ye in him, rooted and built up in him, and established in the faith, as ye have been taught, abounding therein with thanksgiving. Beware lest any man spoil you through philosophy and vain deceit, after the tradition of men, after the rudiments of the world, and not after Christ. For in him dwelleth all the fullness of the Godhead bodily. And ye are complete in him, which is the head of all principality and power. In whom also ye are circumcised with the circumcision made without hands, in putting off the body of the sins of the flesh by the circumcision of Christ, buried with him in baptism, wherein also ye are risen with him through the faith of the operation of God, who hath raised him from the dead. And you, being dead in your sins and the un-circumcision of your flesh, hath he quickened together with him, having forgiven you all trespasses, blotting out the handwriting of ordinances that was against us, which was contrary to us, and took it out of the way, nailing it to his cross. And having spoiled principalities and powers, he made a shew of them openly, triumphing over them in it. Let no man therefore judge you in meat, or in drink, or in respect of a holyday, or of the new moon, or of the Sabbath days, which are a shadow of things to come, but the body is of Christ. Let no man beguile you of your reward in a voluntary humility and worshipping of angels, intruding into those things which he hath not seen, vainly puffed up by his fleshly mind, and not holding the Head, from which all the body by joints and bands having nourishment ministered, and knit together, increaseth with the increase of God. Wherefore if ye be dead with Christ from the rudiments of the world, why, as though living in the world, are ye subject to ordinances. Touch not, taste not, handle not. Which all are to perish with the using, after the commandments and doctrines of men. Which things have indeed a shew of wisdom in will worship, and humility, and neglecting of the body, not in any honor to the satisfying of the flesh. The word of our God. O Lord, open our lips."

"A mighty fortress is our God, a bulwark never failing. Our helper he amid the flood of mortal ills prevailing. For still our ancient foe doth seek to work us woe. His craft and power are great, and armed with cruel hate, on earth is not his equal. Did we in our own strength confide, our striving would be losing, were not the right man on our side, the man of God's own choosing? Dost ask who that may be? Christ Jesus, it is he. Lord Sabbath, his name, from age to age the same, and he must win the battle. And though this world, with devils filled, should threaten to undo us, we will not fear, for God hath willed his truth to triumph through us. The Prince of Darkness, we tremble not for him. His rage we can endure, for lo, his doom is sure. One little word shall fell him. That word above

all earthly powers, thanks to them, abideth the Spirit and the gifts are ours, thru him who with us sideth. Let goods and kindred go, this mortal life also. The body they may kill. God's truth abideth still. His kingdom is forever."

"The second reading is written in the first chapter of Book of Job, in the first verse, page two-thirty-four of your pew Bibles. The Word of our Lord. Officer Candidate Hanson."

"There was a man in the land of Uz, whose name was Job, and that man was perfect and upright, and one that feared God, and eschewed evil. And there were born unto him seven sons And three daughters. His substance also was seven thousand sheep, and three thousand camels, and five hundred yoke of oxen, and five hundred she asses, and a very great household, so that this man was the greatest of all the men of the East. And his sons went and feasted in their houses, everyone his day, and sent and called for their three sisters to eat and to drink with them. And it was so, when the days of their feasting were gone about, that Job sent and sanctified them, and rose up early in the morning, and offered burnt offerings according to the number of them all. For Job said, *It may be that my sons have sinned, and cursed God in their hearts.* Thus did Job continually. Now there was a day when the sons of God came to present themselves before the Lord, and Satan came also among them. And the Lord said unto Satan, *Whence comest thou?* Then Satan answered the Lord, and said, *From going to and fro in the earth, and from walking up and down in it.* And the Lord said unto Satan, *Hast thou considered my servant Job, that there is none like him in the earth, a perfect and an upright man, one that feareth God, and escheweth evil?* Then Satan answered the Lord, and said, *Doth Job fear God for nought? Hast not Thou made an hedge about him, and about his house, and about all that he hath on every side? Thou hast blessed the work of his hands, and his substance is increased in the land. But put forth Thine hand now, and touch all that he hath, and he will curse Thee to Thy face.* And the Lord said unto Satan, *Behold, all that he hath is in thy power. Only upon himself put not forth Thine hand.* So Satan went forth from the presence of the Lord. And there was a day when his sons and his daughters were eating and drinking wine in their eldest brother's house. And there came a messenger unto Job, and said *The oxen were plowing, and the asses feeding beside them. And the Sabeans fell upon them, and took them away. They have slain the servants with the edge of the sword. I only am escaped alone to tell thee.* While he was yet speaking, there came also another, and said, *The fire of God is fallen from heaven, and hath burned up the sheep, and the servants, and consumed them. I only am escaped alone to tell thee.* While he was yet speaking, there came also another, and said *The Chaldeans made out three bands, and fell upon the camels, and have carried them away, yea, and slain the servants with the edge of the sword. I only am escaped alone to tell thee.* While he was yet speaking, there came also another, and said, *Thy sons and thy daughters were eating and drinking wine in their eldest brother's house. And, behold, there came a great wind from the wilderness, and smote the four corners of the house, and it fell upon the young men, and they are dead. I only am*

escaped alone to tell thee. Then Job arose, and rent his mantle, and shaved his head, and fell down upon the ground, and worshipped. And he said, *Naked came I out of my mother's womb, and naked shall I return thither. The Lord gave, and the Lord hath taken away. Blessed be the name of the Lord.* In all this Job sinned not, nor charged God foolishly."

"In response to hearing the word of God, please join me as we stand together and we say together the Apostle's Creed."

"I believe in God, the Father almighty, creator of heaven and earth. I believe in Jesus Christ, God's only Son, our Lord, who was conceived by the Holy Spirit, born of the Virgin Mary, suffered under Pontius Pilate, was crucified, died, and was buried, he descended to the dead. On the third day he rose again, he ascended into heaven, he is seated at the right hand of the Father, and he will come again to judge the living and the dead. I believe in the Holy Spirit, the holy Christian church, the communion of saints, the forgiveness of sins, the resurrection of the body, and the life everlasting. Amen."

"Amen."

"The Lord be with you."

"And also with you."

"Sitting or kneeling, let us pray."

"Almighty Father, whose way is in the sea, whose paths are in the great waters, whose command is over all and whose love never faileth. Let me be aware of Thy presence and obedient to Thy will. Keep me true to my best self, guarding me against dishonesty in purpose and in deed, and helping me so to live that I can stand unashamed and unafraid before my Shipmates, my loved ones, and Thee. Protect those in whose love I live. Give me the will to do my best and to accept my share of responsibilities with a strong heart and a cheerful mind. Make me considerate of those entrusted to my leadership and faithful to the duties my country has entrusted in me. Let my uniform remind me daily of the traditions of the Service of which I am a part. If I am inclined to doubt, steady my faith. If I am tempted, make me strong to resist. If I should miss the mark, give me courage to try again. Guide me with the light of truth and keep before me the life of Him by whose example and help I trust to obtain the answer to my prayer, Jesus Christ our Lord. Amen."

"Amen."

"*Oh, Shenandoah,*
I long to see you,
Away you rolling river.
Oh Shenandoah,
I long to see you,Away, I'm bound away,
Across the wide Missouri.
Oh Shenandoah,

I love your daughter,
Away, you rolling river.
For her I'd cross,
Your roaming waters,
Away, I'm bound away,
Across the wide Missouri.
Tis seven years,
since last I've seen you,
And hear your rolling river.
Tis seven years,
since last I've seen you,
Away, we're bound away,
Across the wide Missouri.
Oh Shenandoah,
I long to see you,
And hear your rolling river.
Oh Shenandoah,
I long to see you,
Away, we're bound away,
Across the wide Missouri."
"Glory be to the Father, the Son and the Holy Ghost."
"*With proud thanksgiving, a mother for her children,*
England mourns for her dead across the sea.
Flesh of her flesh they were, spirit of her spirit,
Fallen in the cause of the free.
Solemn the drums thrill; Death august and royal
Sings sorrow up into immortal spheres,
There is music in the midst of desolation
And a glory that shines upon our tears.
They went with songs to the battle, they were young,
Straight of limb, true of eye, steady and aglow.
They were staunch to the end against odds uncounted;
They fell with their faces to the foe.
They shall grow not old, as we that are left grow old:
Age shall not weary them, nor the years condemn.
At the going down of the sun and in the morning
We will remember them.
They mingle not with their laughing comrades again;
They sit no more at familiar tables of home;
They have no lot in our labour of the day-time;
They sleep beyond England's foam.

But where our desires are and our hopes profound,
Felt as a well-spring that is hidden from sight,
To the innermost heart of their own land they are known."
"Praise thee the Lord."
"*Eternal Father, strong to save,*
Whose arm hath bound the restless wave,
Who bid'st the mighty ocean deep
Its own appointed limits keep.
O hear us when we cry to Thee,
for those in peril on the sea.
O Christ! Whose voice the waters heard
And hushed their raging at Thy word,
Who walked'st on the foaming deep,
and calm amidst its rage didst sleep.
Oh hear us when we cry to Thee
For those in peril on the sea!
Most Holy spirit! Who didst brood
Upon the chaos dark and rude,
And bid its angry tumult cease,
And give, for wild confusion, peace.
Oh, hear us when we cry to Thee
For those in peril on the sea!
Lord, guard and guide the men who fly,
Through the great spaces of the sky.
Be with them traversing the air,
In darkening storms or sunshine fair.
O God, protect the men who fly,
Through lonely ways beneath the sky
O Trinity of love and power!
Our brethren shield in danger's hour.
From rock and tempest, fire and foe,
Protect them wheresoe'er they go.
Thus evermore shall rise to Thee,
Glad hymns of praise from land and sea."
"Recession of colors."

"Almighty God, we remember this morning the souls of Thy servants who paid the highest price to be called an American. We remember their sacrifice so that we are free to kneel before you in prayer. We pray for each soul who left a family with one last embrace, and then one more, promising to write, to call at the first chance, to return. We pray for those souls who spent the last lingering moments in pain, knowing that the return home would not now come. We pray

for their families, wives and husbands, daughters and sons, mothers and fathers who suffer at the news. We pray in honor of their memory, in honor of their courage, in honor of their sacrifice. Amen."

"Amen."

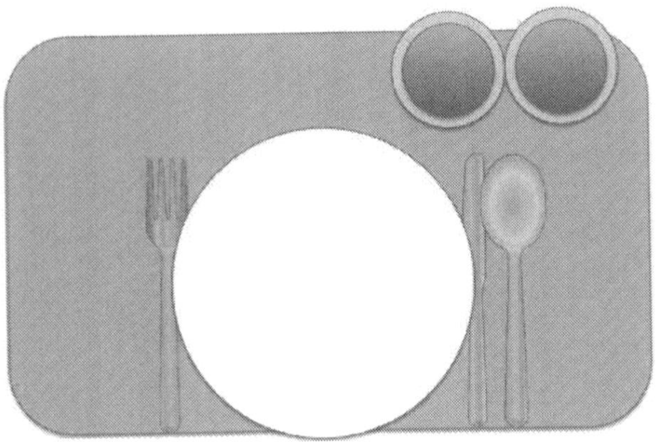

Chow

Hold tray with elbows tucked into sides, wrists and forearms straight and parallel to deck. Place tray on the table. Pull out chair. Arrange glasses and silverware. Enter place on starboard side of and then stand in front of their chair. Drape parkas, all weather coats or Eisenhower jackets over back of chair. Take out gougebook. Hold arm extended and parallel to the deck.

••

"Zero-four inches from the bulkhead! Position of attention!"
"That's a response! That's a response!"
"Aye aye, Sir!!"
"Heels touching."
"Aye aye, Sir!!"
"Chests out. Guts in."
"Aye aye, Sir!!"
"Louder!"
"Aye aye, Sir!!"
"Fingers extended and joined!"
"That's a response!"

"Aye aye, Sir!!"

"Tightly curled! Thumbs locked!"

"Aye aye, Sir!!"

"Find your seams!"

"Aye aye, Sir!!"

"Louder!"

"Aye aye, Sir!!"

"Stop whispering! In the ballistic! That's a response!"

"Aye aye, Sir!!"

"Hey you. You eyeballing me, Poopie?"

"That's a response, Poopie! That's a response!"

"No excuse, Sir!"

"Are we girlfriends?"

"No, Sir!"

"Am I the Thelma to your Louise?"

"No, Sir!"

"Do you want me to join your book club?"

"No, Sir!"

"Is this dinner and a movie?"

"No, Sir!"

"Do you want me to surprise you with something unexpected?"

"No, Sir!"

"Do you miss me when I'm gone?"

"No, Sir!"

"Do you want to take random pictures of each other and add funny captions?"

"No Sir!"

"Then quit eyeballing me, Poopie."

"That's an order! That's a response!"

"Aye aye, Sir!"

"Louder!"

"Aye aye, Sir!"

"Louder!"

"Aye aye, Sir!"

"Unbelievable. Poopie problems. Just never quits."

"Thousand yard stare at all times, Poopie! Got that?"

"Yes, Sir!"

"At all times!"

"Aye aye, Sir!"

"I don't believe it. He just did it again."

"Thousand yard stare at all times!"

"Aye aye, Sir!"

"Are you gonna be my problem child, Poopie?"

"No, Sir!"

"Do you have to be reprogrammed?"

"No, Sir!"

"What?"

"No, Sir!"

"Louder!"

"No, Sir!"

"Louder!"

"No, Sir!"

"Louder!"

"No, Sir!"

"I think a Three-bar just stepped on deck! I think he's entitled to his greeting of the day! Where is his greeting of the day?"

"Good morning, Sir!"

"Louder!"

"Good morning, Sir!"

"Louder!"

"Good morning, Sir!"

"Gentlemen, I received intel that we may have ourselves a problem child on our hands?"

"Intel checks out, Indoctrination Commander. We've identified a grade-A eyeballer."

"One in every batch, I'm afraid. Thousand yard stare at all times, Indoctrination Candidate."

"Aye aye, Sir!"

"Louder!"

"Aye aye, Sir!"

"Louder!"

"Aye aye, Sir!"

"What's your designator?"

"One! One! Three! Five! Sir!"

"Special Ops?"

"Yes, Sir!"

"I'll say. My God, what's that on his face?"

"We believe it's a booger."

"Disgusting. This might be a new Indoctrination Candidate low. How on earth did it get all the way over there?"

"That's a response! That's a response, Poopie!"

"This Indoctrination Candidate does not know but will find out, Sir!"

"Do something about it."

"Aye aye, Sir!"

"Why you touching your face? Why you touching your face?"

"No excuse, Sir!"

"Louder!"

"No excuse, Sir!"

"Follow me."

"Aye aye, Sir!"

"*Left-right-left-right!*"

"Left-right! Left-right! Left-right! Left-right! Left-right! Left-right! Left-right! Left-right! Left-right! Left-right! Left-right! Left-right! Left-right! Left-right! Left-right! Left-right!"

"Cutting the deck! Cutting the deck!"

"That's a response! That's a response!"

"No excuse, Sir!"

"Halt!"

"Aye aye, Sir!"

"You cut corners, Indoctrination Candidate and people die."

"Ships sink! Sailors drown!"

"That's a response!"

"No excuse, Sir!"

"Up against the bulkhead. Position of attention."

"Aye aye, Sir!"

"Zero-four inches, Indoctrination Candidate."

"Aye aye, Sir!"

"Zero-four inches!"

"Aye aye, Sir!"

"Off you go."

"You heard him, Poopie. Move!"

"Aye aye, Sir!"

"Louder!"

"Aye aye, Sir!"

"Wrong way, Poopie! One way only!"

"Aye aye, Sir!"

"Off you go."

"Aye aye, Sir!"

"Find another way! Find another way!"

"That's a response!"

"Aye aye, Sir!"

"*Left-right-left-right!* Sound off!"

"Aye aye, Sir! Left-right! Left-right! Left-right! Left-right! Left-right! Left-right! Left-right! Left-right! Left-right! Left-right!"

"Zero-four inches from the bulkhead!"

"Aye aye, Sir! Left-right! Left-right! Left-right! Left-right! Left-right! Left-right! Left-right! Left-right! Left-right!"

"We can't hear you! Louder!"

"Aye aye, Sir! Left-right!"

"Zero-four inches!"

"Aye aye, Sir! Left-right! Left-right! Left-right! Left-right! Left-right! Left-right! Left-right! Left-right! Left-right! Left-right! Left-right! Good morning, Sir! Left-right! Left-right! Left-right! Left-right! Left-right! Left-right! Left-right! Left-right! Left-right! Left-right! Left-right!"

"Louder!"

"Aye aye, Sir! Left-right! Left-right! Left-right! Left-right! Left-right! Left-right! Left-right! Left-right! Left-right! Left-right! Good morning, Sir! Left-right! Left-right! Left-right! Left-right! Left-right! Left-right! Left-right! Good morning, Sir! Left-right! Left-right! Left-right! Left-right! Left-right! Left-right! Left-right! Left-right! Left-right! Left-right! Left-right! Left-right! Left-right! Left-right! Left-right! Left-right! Left-right! Good morning, Sir!"

"Good morning, Poopie."

"Left-right! Left-right! Left-right! Left-right! Left-right! Left-right! Left-right! Left-right! Left-right! Left-right! Left-right! Good morning, Sir! Left-right!"

"Louder!"

"Aye aye, Sir! Left-right!!"

"Get in there!"

"Aye aye, Sir! Good morning, Sir!"

"Find water."

"Aye aye, Sir!"

"Not there."

"That's an *aye aye, Sir*!"

"Aye aye, Sir!"

"Not there."

"Aye aye, Sir!"

"Thousand yard stare at all times, Indoctrination Candidate."

"Aye aye, Sir!"

"Right here. In you go."

"Aye aye, Sir!"

"Attenhut."

"That's a response!"

"Aye aye, Sir!"

"Attention to detail saves lives, Indoctrination Candidate. Is that clear?"

"Yes, Sir!"

"Ships sink. Sailors drown."

"Ships sink! Sailors drown!"

"That's a response!"

"Aye aye, Sir!"

"Take your finger and rescue Colonel Booger there."

"Aye aye, Sir!"

"No. A little to the left."

"Aye aye, Sir!"

"Little bit up. Warmer."

"Aye aye, Sir!"

"Little to the right. You're burning up. Okay stop."

"Aye aye, Sir!"

"Now scoop him up."

"Aye aye, Sir!"

"The Colonel is secure. Burial at sea, Poopie."

"Aye aye, Sir!"

"Louder!"

"Aye aye, Sir!"

"Louder!"

"Aye aye, Sir!"

"As you were."

"Aye aye, Sir!"

"Please tell me you're weren't just about to flick Colonel Booger out to sea?"

"No excuse, Sir!"

"Not one to stand on ceremony, are you? How would you feel if someone tried to flick you out to sea?"

"That's a response! That's a response!"

"No excuse, Sir!"

"The Colonel deserves a proper send off. An honest burial for a job well done. Grab some T.P."

"Aye aye, Sir!"

"Easy now. Careful with the remains."

"Aye aye, Sir!"

"Gently."

"Aye aye, Sir!"

"Thousand yard stare at all times! Thousand yard stare at all times!"

"No excuse, Sir!"

"Steady."

"Aye aye, Sir!"

"Go on. Lightly. I do believe he's earned it."

"Aye aye, Sir!"

"All hands bury the dead. Atten-hut! Now send him out to sea."

"Aye aye, Sir!"

"A moment of silence please."

"That's a response!"

"Aye aye, Sir!"

"Louder!"

"Aye aye, Sir!"

"Louder!"

"Aye aye, Sir!"

"Quiet."

"That's a response! That's a response!"

"Aye aye, Sir!"

"Firing party, present arms."

"Flush him down, Indoctrination Candidate."

"That's a response!"

"Aye aye, Sir!"

"R.I.P., Colonel. Fair winds and following seas. What's wrong with this picture, Indoctrination Candidate?"

"That's a response! That's a response!"

"This Indoctrination Candidate does not know but will find out, Sir!"
"Think."
"Aye aye, Sir!"
"Louder!"
"Aye aye, Sir!"
"Louder!"
"Aye aye, Sir!"
"Well?"
"This Indoctrination Candidate does not know but will find out, Sir!"
"Louder!"
"This Indoctrination Candidate does not know but will find out, Sir!"
"Louder!"
"This Indoctrination Candidate does not know but will find out, Sir!"
"Think."
"Aye aye, Sir!"
"Louder!"
"Aye aye, Sir!"
"Louder!"
"Aye aye, Sir!"
"Here's a hint. Starts with a T and ends with a P. Fix it."
"This Indoctrination Candidate does not know but will find out, Sir!"
"I thought we had covered this."
"This Indoctrination Candidate does not know but will find out, Sir!"
"Very well. Eyeballs. *Snap, Sir.*"
"Snap, Sir!"
"Louder!"
"Snap, Sir!"
"Not at me, Poopie."
"No excuse, Sir!"
"Let's try this again. Eyeballs."
"Snap, Sir!"

"T.P. must be chevroned at all times. At a four-five degree angle. Razor's edge, meeting in a middle point. Got it?"

"Yes, Sir!"
"Your turn."
"Aye aye, Sir!"
"Good. Repeat after me."
"That's a response!"
"Aye aye, Sir!"
"*T.P. must be chevroned at all times.*"
"T.P. must be chevroned at all times!"

"*At a four-five degree angle.*"

"At a four-five degree angle!"

"*Razor's edge.*"

"Razor's edge!"

"*Meeting in a middle point.*"

"Meeting in a middle point!"

"All together now. *Aye aye, Sir.*"

"Aye aye, Sir! T.P. must be chevroned at all times! At a four-five degree angle! Razor's edge! Meeting in a middle point!"

"Excellent. Go inform your Shipmates. Spread the gouge."

"Aye aye, Sir!"

"*Left-right-left-right!*"

"Left-right! Left-right! Left-right! Left-right! Left-right! Left-right! Left-right! Left-right! Left-right! Left-right! Left-right! Left-right! Left-right! Left-right! Left-right! Left-right! Left-right! Good morning, Sir! Left-right! Left-right! Left-right! Left-right! Left-right! Left-right! Left-right! Left-right!"

"Halt. And face."

"Aye aye, Sir!"

"Give them the news."

"Aye aye, Sir! T.P. must be chevroned at all times! At a four-five degree angle! Razor's edge! Meeting in a middle point!"

"Proceed."

"Aye aye, Sir! Left-right! Left-right! Left-right! Left-right! Left-right! Left-right! Left-right! Left-right!"

"Halt. And face."

"Aye aye, Sir!"

"Well?"

"T.P. must be chevroned at all times! At a four-five degree angle! Razor's edge! Meeting in a middle point!"

"Proceed."

"Aye aye, Sir! Left-right! Left-right! Left-right! Left-right! Left-right! Left-right! Left-right! Left-right! Left-right! Left-right! Left-right! Left-right! Left-right! Left-right!"

"Halt. And face."

"Aye aye, Sir! T.P. must be chevroned at all times! At a four-five degree angle! Razor's edge! Meeting in a middle point!"

"Proceed."

"Aye aye, Sir! Left-right! Left-right! Left-right! Left-right! Left-right! Left-right! Left-right! Left-right! Left-right! Left-right! Left-right! Left-right! Left-right! Left-right!"

"Halt. And face."

"Aye aye, Sir! T.P. must be chevroned at all times! At a four-five degree angle! Razor's edge! Meeting in a middle point!"

"Again but louder!"

"Aye aye, Sir! T.P. must be chevroned at all times! At a four-five degree angle! Razor's edge! Meeting in a middle point!"

"Proceed. You know the drill. On your own. Begin."

"Aye aye, Sir! Left-right! Left-right! Left-right! Left-right! Left-right! Left-right! Left-right! Left-right! Left-right! Left-right! Left-right! Left-right! Left-right! Left-right! T.P. must be chevroned at all times! At a four-five degree angle! Razor's edge! Meeting in a middle point! Left-right! Left-right! Left-right! Left-right! Left-right! Left-right! Left-right! Left-right! Left-right! Left-right! Left-right! Left-right! Left-right! Left-right! Good morning, Sir! Left-right! Left-right! Left-right! Left-right! Left-right! Left-right! Left-right! Left-right! Left-right! Left-right! Left-right! Left-right! Left-right! Left-right! T.P. must be chevroned at all times! At a four-five degree angle! Razor's edge! Meeting in a middle point! Left-right! Left-right! Left-right! Left-right! Left-right! Left-right! Left-right! Left-right! Left-right! Left-right! Left-right! Left-right! Left-right! Left-right! T.P. must be chevroned at all times! At a four-five degree angle! Razor's edge! Meeting in a middle point! Left-right! Left-right! Left-right! Left-right! Left-right! Left-right! Left-right! Left-right! Left-right! Left-right! Left-right! Left-right! Left-right! Left-right! T.P. must be chevroned at all times! At a four-five degree angle! Razor's edge! Meeting in a middle point!"

"Very well. As you were.Return to your hole."

"Aye aye, Sir!"

••

Dining

From the left. Meat fork, salad fork, seafood cocktail in place plate, salad knife (if needed), meat knife, soup soon (when needed), seafood fork. The water

goblet stays throughout the dinner, but wine glasses are removed with their accompanying courses with the exception of the dessert wine glass, which remains throughout the serving of demitasse. Only two wines, sherry and champagne may be served. For a very formal table, fish forks and knives would be in place, and extra wine glasses for the courses they accompany. Individual salts and peppers are placed above the place plate, or one set may be a little below and to the right of the outer glass so that two guests may share one set.

Use utensils from outside to inside. Never put used utensils back on the tablecloth since they may soil it. Don't wipe the utensils with your napkin. If you drop a utensil, don't pick it up. Ask the waitress or the hostess for another one. When not in use, don't prop your knife and fork against the plate with the handles resting on the table. They belong on the plate, with the knife across the top of the plate, blade turned toward you, and the fork on the bottom of the plate. Some foods require large serving spoons or forks to transfer the food from the serving platter to your plate. Place the spoon under the food and use the fork to ensure that the food stays on the spoon, by holding the fork tines down on top of the food.

When pausing during a meal, place your fork in the lower quadrant of the plate and the knife in the upper right quadrant with edge in. When you've finished with the main course, place knife across dinner plate in upper right quadrant with cutting edge in, and place the fork below the knife. Don't place knife and fork half-on and half-off the plate.

••

"One-little-two-little-three-little-Alisons. Four-little-five-little-six-little-Alisons. Seven-little-eight-little-niner-little-Alisons. Ten-little-Alison toes. Oh my."

"Do it again."

"One-little-two-little-three-little-Alisons. Four-little-five-little-six-little-Alisons. Seven-little-eight-little-niner-little-Alisons. Ten-little-Alison-toes."

"*Oh my.*"

"Oh my."

"Again."

"One-little-two-little-three-little-Alisons. Four-little-five-little-six-little-Alisons. Seven-little-eight-little-niner-little-Alisons. Ten-little-Alison-toes. Oh my."

"That's nice. I don't know why."

"Makes them happy."

"Happy?"

"Sure. Just waking up. New day. A little attention."

"They do seem a little happier."

"Only a little? Hold on. Let me get a good look at them."

"What? Don't you make fun of my feet! I have lovely feet."

"You do. It's the toes I'm a little worried about."

"Worried?"

"The sad part."

"I said they were happier."

"A little happier. Hold on. *What's that? Come again? I see. Good idea. I will.*"

"What'd they say?"

"Seems they weren't big fans of the heels last night, but they're otherwise fine. The lot of them."

"What's the good idea?"

"They want to make you breakfast."

"That's awful sweet of them."

"Got any eggs? They're recommending the *over easy.*"

"Oh, I'm sure they are."

"*Daggers on the over easy, Gentlemen. Mademoiselle is not inclined.*"

"No, I'm not opposed to an over easy. What does it come with, garçon?"

"The blinis and caviar come recommended to start."

"As long as it tastes good."

"Beluga sturgeon from the Caspian. Bottle of Eighty-Eight Dom. Some fresh fruit on the side. Florida Oranges."

"Not the season. What else?"

"Georgia peaches?"

"Alabama blackberries."

"Alabama blackberries. Then the over easy."

"Okay."

My dog tags dangle from my neck in chime. The ceiling fan cycles overhead. A teddy bear stares at me from off to the side.

"Something sweet for dessert. Quiet."

I drop back into the pillows.

"So breakfast? I'm starving. We could also go out for brunch. There's got to be some good Southern places."

"Navy guys. You couldn't let it last. Absolutely not. I believe I was promised breakfast."

"Certainly."

"Do you have to go?"

"I thought we were spending the day together." "I didn't know for sure."

"Someone will cover for me. Least for a couple of hours. Where to?"

"Really? I was thinking beach. We could play volleyball. I'm pretty good, you know?"

"Love the beach. I'm out a suit, though."

"There's tons of places on the boardwalk. Plus I can show you where I want to open the shop."

"*Makeover Madness*?"

"I don't see how you remember everything. Sometimes I can't even tell if you're even listening."

"It's a good business idea."

"You can't tell anyone. You promised."

"Not a soul. I might lose the *Madness*, though. I was also thinking about a clothes section or some kind of retail. That way you could go complete makeover. Hot date? Try the Saturday Night Special. *Meet him again for the first time.*"

"Proms. Weddings. Sweet Sixteens. Girls night. I really like that idea."

"*Be the hot one tonight.*"

"Stop it."

"*At Makeover.*"

"But I wouldn't want it to be second-hand."

"New or like new. Option to buy. Girls love to share."

"Some things. I could do makeup."

"Sure."

"I get so excited about this. You have no idea. You really think it will work?"

"It's a good business idea."

"But you don't think I'll actually do it."

"I think you're serious."

"I'm very serious. You're not the only one with big plans, you know? Wait! Don't get up. Not yet. Please? It's nice for a minute."

"Can I just check on my uniform real quick? I just want to get some idea."

"Sorry. Of course. Nevermind."

"Hey. No rush. Uniform isn't going anywhere. All the time in the world."

"No. Go on."

"Hold on now. The temperature just changed."

"Temperature's the same, Mike."

"You sure?"

"Just got a little sad for a split second, that's all. Me being me again. It's normal. It's over. Let it go. Puppies and rainbows."

"*Puppies and rainbows*?"

"What's wrong with puppies and rainbows?"

"Nothing. *Storm clouds and the horizon* is a little different. Got to get inside."

"It's nothing. How's the uniform? I would have hung it up for you, you know?"

"Looks like it held up. I was a little worried."

"Now you're going to get all quiet?"

"No. I'm good. We still hitting the beach?"

"Mike!"

"What?"

"Yes, I still want to go to the beach. God. Alright. Let me see if I can explain it away. I just need two minutes. Two minutes, okay? No questions. No interruptions. Okay?"

"Sure."

"We used to play this game back in elementary school."

"So far so good."

"Nevermind."

"My mistake. Really. Go on. I'm serious."

"No, it was stupid anyway."

"Not at all. Come here. I'm very sorry for interrupting. No excuse. Two minutes. I promise. If only because I'll feel terrible."

"We used to play this game back in elementary school. Not every day, because the little boys, they couldn't spare the time. But every now and then. There was this open part of the playground where we, the little girls, would carve out this maze through the gravel. All these twisting paths leading to these big hearts. If we caught one of the little boys, those adorable little boys, he had to go stand in the middle of your heart. No escape. These crazy little girls waiting for you at every turn, ready to pounce. So there was this one little boy that I really, really liked. Thought about him all the time. These little daydreams. All day long. Every time we played, there I was, bearing down on him, mad as hell when those other little girls got too close."

"Sure."

"That little boy. My little boy. He was too quick for the other little girls."

"Too quick."

"But not for me."

"I don't imagine."

"I would catch him and put him in a heart. And then I would let him go. Every time. And the process would start all over again. I loved it. Looked forward to it. Everything was fine. I was so happy. Then came this one day when they took us to the movie theatre. I guess it was a class trip. He was next to me. It was all dark. It was like this silent Zorro movie, or something. But that can't be right. I took his hand and did the whole linked fingers thing. You know."

"Sure."

"Like this. We stayed that way the whole movie. I never caught him again."

"I see."

"You do?"

"I think so."

"Great. Whatever this is, it's not that. Everything's fine. Don't worry about the temperature. The temperature is great."

"You mean I'm not the little boy?"

"Actually, you might be the little boy. Only it doesn't matter. I'm allowed. I don't need to feel bad about it, either way."

"Eggs?"

"These better be good. Can you throw me that T-shirt, please?"

"Reluctantly."

"I'll let you take one of your mental pictures, if you want."

"I can have a mental picture?"

"You may. Real quick. Don't be creepy."

"Got it. Hey, you keep this place pretty ship shape. Are these alphabetical? That's pretty committed."

"Put them back. Stop. I'm serious."

"Are these your folks?"

"Yes."

"Who's this bunch?"

"Those are my cousins."

"This must be your brother."

"Yes."

"Daniel. Looks like a nice guy. Young. When was this taken?"

"He's the baby."

A island separates the kitchen from the living room. She takes a seat on a high stool.

"May I?"

"Make yourself at home. Honestly, I'm not sure what I have in there. I know I have eggs. Tomorrow's grocery day. I don't want you to think I'm some kind of wreck. There shouldn't be any science experiments, but keep an eye on the expiration dates. Things have been pretty crazy lately. Especially the milk. That's been in there for awhile. Eggs are in the door. Should be ham and cheese too. In the drawer."

"This is perfect. So, you're sure you don't want to talk about it?"

"You will not stop, will you? Always after my goat. Relentless. Trying to get at him. Like a goat hunter."

"Capture and release."

"I don't know. You kinda stole my thunder somehow. After my big speech."

"Oh, I doubt that's possible."

"Sure, I want to talk about it. Only you'll get freaked out and you won't let on. Then the day will be super awkward."

"What if I don't listen?"

"You mean I can say any number of awful things, only you won't be listening and can't get mad?"

"Maybe I'll do omelets instead."

"You really are the worst. Life is so totally easy for you. Your swing forever untangled. Never a knot in your rope. Must be nice."

"Bowls?"

"Second shelf."

"You know a fresh egg in water lies down nice and flat? You'll know a bad egg if it floats."

"Wish I could put you in a bowl of water."

"Skillets?"

"Skillet. Under the stove."

"Perfect."

"See, I wasn't expecting to think about you so much. It was a lot this week. I mean, you really came out of nowhere man. One minute it's *check out the cute Navy guy*. Next minute you're talking to my toes."

"Forks?"

"Side drawer."

"Bowls?"

"Cabinet. Upper Left."

"So, if you're going make an omelet, you got to break some eggs."

"Wondering. Is he going to call? And then you do and it's like *Oh, hi there, Mike*. You know that, don't you? You do. Whatever. I can see you now. Girl in every port. They will absolutely love you."

"You want to make sure the whites and the yolks are completely combined. I use a fork. Quick whisk. Not so much they foam. Salt, pepper. And you're done for kitchen prep."

"All this, by the way, is totally allowed. Or I think it should be. You're probably thinking how to get out of here right now. Small steps. No sudden movements."

"Butter. Butter's important. Both as a non-stick and as an ingredient. Traditional way is over medium to high heat, shaking those eggs and stirring like crazy with your fork, breaking up the curds as they form. I do it a different way. Slow cooked on a very low flame. Add in the eggs. Lightly swirl in the extra butter and you're good for a while. Gives you time to make the toast, set the table, stuff like that."

"You didn't need throw this much game at me, you know? That was my blind spot. The whole Officer and a Gentlemen thing would have done just fine. You know what I mean? You show up in the uniform. I let my hair down. No spilt milk. No one gets burned."

"See how it starts to harden on the bottom? That's when you know you're getting close. You want to err on the side of undercooked."

"I think you want me to fall hard and that's not the nicest thing to do. Because that can really hurt."

"Sprinkle in the cheese. Right at the end. And roll. This is the tricky part. Gotcha. Flash of heat. And plate. Ready?"

"They do look beautiful. Where did you learn how to do that?"

"Growing up. Taste it. Go on. Before they get cold."

"Where's yours?"

"Mine are coming right up."

"We could go halvsies?"

"Sure. Halvsies."

"You have to make sure we're even."

"How does that look?"

"I think you got more."

"Salt and pepper. Go on, try them before they get cold."

"Wow. These are yum."

"Really?"

"Best eggs I've ever had."

"You're only saying that."

"An angel gets its wings."

"Thanks."

"Just try not to leave me all tangled me up in your wake. You won't just disappear, will you? Goodbye forever. That's all I really care about. I wouldn't like that."

"No."

"Promise?"

"I promise."

"I don't know. That kind of sounded like someone who is going to disappear forever. Guess what? It doesn't matter. You know something?"

"What?"

"If this is a port. And I am your girl. I am your girl, right?"

"Yes."

"No matter what. We're talking worst case."

"Worst case."

"I'm your first. The first girl in the first port."

"Are you really sure about that?"

"What? Stop it! You are really the worst. Anyway, I'm done now. You can start listening."

"You're beautiful. You know that."

"Whatever. Where's my other halvsie?"

"Coming right up."

••

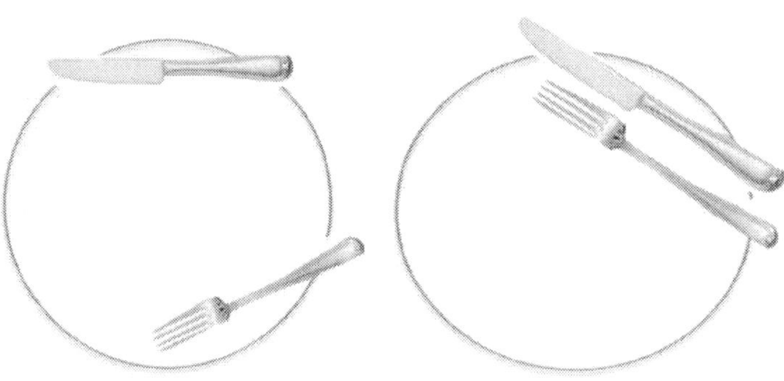

Manners

Use utensils from outside of setting to inside. Never put used utensils back on the tablecloth since they may soil it. Don't wipe utensils with your napkin. If you drop a utensil, don't pick it up. Ask the waitress or the hostess for another One. When not in use, don't prop your knife and fork against the plate with the handles resting on the table. They belong on the plate, with the knife across the top of the plate, blade turned toward you, and the fork on the bottom of the plate. Some foods require large serving spoons and or forks to transfer the food from the serving platter to the plate. Place the spoon under the food and use the fork to ensure that the food stays on the spoon, by holding the fork tines down on the food. When pausing during a meal, place your fork in the lower quadrant of the plate and the knife in the upper right quadrant with edge in. When you've finished with the main course, place knife across dinner plate in upper right quadrant with cutting edge in, and place the fork below the knife.

••

"Good morning, everyone."

"Good morning, Sir."

"Please give a warm O.C.S. welcome to P.S.C. Marin who will take you all through some useful information for your follow-on duty stations as newly Commissioned Officers."

"Thank you, Lieutenant. How you all doing this morning?"

"Outstanding, Chief."

"Outstanding. So, just like the Lieutenant said, I'm here to talk to you about what happens next. Re-entry into the real world, for when you leave this base as United States Naval Officers. In the packets in front of you, you will find some useful information for newly commissioned Officers. Now if you'll all be good enough to open your packets, you will also find five copies of your orders, issued by the Chief of Naval personnel. I think pretty much all of you will be heading back home for a spell on O-HARP duty while you wait on training dates and permanent duty stations. Just to be sure, you'll want to follow-up with us at P.S.D. before you head out after graduation. Flights, personal status, expected date of arrival, family stuff, what have you. At the very least, we'll make sure to put you in touch with a P.O.C. at your next command, making your transition as seamless as possible. Let's take a look at these bad boys, shall we? See what's important. That sound like a plan?"

"Yes, Chief."

"You'll see your home address. One twenty three Main Street, Anywhere U.S.A. Next you'll see your intermediate activity. The main thing you want to register is your *report date.* Navy tries to give some flexibility between duty stations. *Proceed time* is a period of time not chargeable as leave, delay or allowed travel time not to exceed four days. We're talking about commencing travel status, not an entitlement to proceed time. Just know it's out there. If you feel like taking a couple of well-deserved days, you will have *travel time* and *leave.* If your orders require travel, they will specify the number of days authorized for travel. This is in addition to any proceed time or *delay time.* Any delay authorized in permanent change of station orders in excess of allowed proceed time or travel time is chargeable as leave. Leave, proceed time and travel time will be charged in that order following your day of detachment. If you report to your new duty station before your required reporting date, you will only be charged leave for the number of days between your detachment date and your reporting date. That is, less any authorized proceed or travel time. This unused leave is then credited to your leave account. Clear as mud? Let me give you an example. You all are scheduled to graduate on the nineteenth, correct?"

"Yes, Chief."

"Assume you are ordered report to your new command not later than the first of December. Say your orders authorize four days proceed time, three days travel. You graduate on the nineteenth and detach the twentieth. Simple math taking the detachment date and report date. If you report on the first, how many days of leave will you be charged?"

"Three days, Chief."

"Former P.N.?"

"Yes, Chief."

"Everyone got it? Yes, in the back."

"Are we required to take that leave?"

"Great question. The answer is no. If you report to your next command within the maximum time allowed, you will save the corresponding number of days of leave. You can save leave and carry it forward with you, year to year. Up to sixty days max. Only thing proceed time means is that you can either report directly or take a couple days of leave, if you got it. Remember you're now active duty military. No such thing as a weekend. If you leave on Saturday, that counts as your first travel day. If you're traveling by P.O.V., you may get a couple of days. If you're going commercial air, that's your day. After that, you're on the clock. Every day you do not report, past your estimated day of arrival, and get that stamp on your orders, that's a day of leave. Got to get that stamp to kill the clock. Authorized number of days leave has no effect on the effective date of your orders. You must report on or before, but not later than, the effective reporting date specified in your orders. If you report early, it's just the day you report. No leave charged. Everyone got it?"

"Yes, Chief."

"Anyone not got it? Great. Travel expenses. On a permanent change of station involving travel within the continental United States, the Navy will reimburse you in one of the following two ways. First off, if you furnish or choose your own method of transportation by privately owned conveyance, your P.O.V., you will receive a mileage allowance for the number of travel days authorized or used, whichever is less, to cover your entire travel expense, varying on your number of dependents and travel arrangements. Second option. If the Navy furnishes transportation, read commercial air or bus, you will receive a per diem allowance for the day of departure or the day of arrival at your permanent station if you are in a travel status and, importantly, if government quarters are not available. This includes certain miscellaneous expenses such as taxi fares and baggage handling tips. Navy isn't cheap. You shouldn't be either. Not to say you should be a big spender. Remember to keep all receipts, especially lodging and anything over twenty-five dollars. Best to keep them all, though, just in case. How does that sit with you?"

"Outstanding, Chief."

"Now I want you all to pay attention to this next bit, especially you Mustangs out there. D.L.A. Dislocation allowance. When changing permanent duty stations, be sure to ask your P.S.D. about D.L.A. to partially reimburse Service Members, with or without dependents, for expenses incurred in the relocation of a household. This is in addition to all other authorized allowances. For you non-Priors, be sure to remember this when you get to the Fleet. For the Priors, I strongly encourage you to swing by and put in the paperwork. Nice chunk of change."

"Chief."

"Question?"

"What if my wife wants to go on ahead early, find a place for us before I report?"

"Good question. It depends. Spouses can go anywhere they want. No such thing as an A-WOL spouse, at least in Navy admin terms. Only the Navy won't provide compensation for travel outside official travel associated with your orders. That said, you are eligible to receive a travel advance up to ten days before detaching from your permanent duty station, computed based on the anticipated mode of transportation and the official distance between duty stations. Now if you receive a travel advance and do not follow through with your plans, just know you might have to repay amounts because of your change in travel modes. Careful on your report date folks. If you're authorized five days travel and you burn the midnight oil to report two days later, you have to pay back that extra three days travel money. Just be aware. And that's only after your receive the orders. Travel performed in advance of receipt of orders or official notification that orders are forthcoming will not be paid for. Everyone got it? Don't worry, this stuff is going to be second nature to you in no time. If you're still scratching your heads, just drop by and see us at P.S.D. We'll sort you out, make sure you know your entitlements. Well, that does it for my portion. Any questions?"

"Chief, what's the Uniform of the Day for traveling?"

"Yes, indeed. We get that question a lot. Navy life's a lot different than what you've seen so far around here. Civilian attire is authorized. But don't make the mistake of reporting aboard in civvies. Go with the Uniform of the day for that area, usually khakis, or, if you want to be safe, your S.D.Bs."

"Thanks for your time, Chief. Everyone, how about a round of applause for Chief Marin?"

"Don't be strangers. Building six-thirty-three. Can't miss us."

"Alright, people. That's how to get there. Next up is Y.N.C. Browne to go over the important job of maintaining your records over the course your career. Important from day one. Please give him your full attention. Might not seem that important sitting here right now. But in ten, fifteen years, when you're wondering why you were passed over by the selection board, don't say we didn't warn you. Chief Browne, the floor is yours."

"Thank you, Lieutenant. Good morning, everyone."

"Good morning, Chief."

"How you all doing today?"

"Outstanding, Chief."

"A fine Navy day. Just like the Lieutenant says, your record is very important. The Bureau of Naval Personnel, some of you might already know it as BUPERS, maintains a microfiche record of each and every one of you. Big brother. This record contains any document that bears or reflects on the

character, performance, professional qualifications and fitness of an Officer. Anything you accomplish professionally, or, Lord forbid, missteps in your personal life is recorded in those microfiches. It's on the Navy to maintain these records. It's on you to make sure they stay up to date. Fiche number-one tracks your fitness for duty, past and present. Your assignment Officer code. Your latest photograph. Fitness Reports and medals, awards, citations. You will getting your official photos taken later on this morning. That's all fine and dandy. You all look great, don't get me wrong. But when you're up for promotion to O-Four, staring back at the panel at a hundred and fifty pounds looking like a Boy Scout, not exactly the image you want them thinking about when they decide on the next step of your career. When it comes time for promotion, you want them looking at a senior Lieutenant, not a junior Ensign fresh on the boat. A senior Lieutenant, no less, who didn't think it important to maintain his, or her, own service record. It's on you to have the wherewithal to send in that updated portrait. Enough said. Good to go on portraits? Yes?"

"Yes, Chief."

"Fiche number-two. Professional history. This includes your education data, qualifications, classifications, designation date, appointments, promotions, commission, reserve status, separation, and the like. Fiche number-three. Your personal data. Includes everything from your security investigations, clearance and personal history statement to your Record of Emergency Data and physical. Fiche number-four. All your orders. Fiche number-five. Privileged information. What you want to avoid. Any adverse information to your military record. Statement of the Officer, you, in reply to adverse information. Extracts from the findings and recommendations of courts and boards concerning you as an Officer. Big takeaway here is that you must be notified should your Commanding Officer decide to add adverse information to your record and be given the opportunity to respond, oh by the way, which I highly encourage you to make sure you do. And finally, fiche number-six, Enlisted records for you Mustangs here who have served more than two years in the Navy. Taken together, this information represents your Navy record. It's incumbent on you to protect it and keep it up to date. Once a document is rightfully placed in that official record, it becomes the property of the United States Navy and is not subject to change or removal except by authorization of the Secretary himself. I don't need to tell you how often that happens. Twenty years of service, I've only seen it twice. Mistake in wartime and a wrongful conviction. Basically folks, once it's in, it's in. Exceptions are extremely rare. Everyone still with me?"

"Yes, Chief."

"Now for your performance. You will be evaluated at least annually, on detachment and upon the detachment of your reporting senior. Special, concurrent and operational commander reports may be issued under special

conditions. Get them if you can. Always looks good. You'll find NAVPERS form sixteen-eleven in your packets. All reports for Captain and below are done on this form. Together, these FITREPS will end up as the running record of your performance throughout your career, the primary tool used in both the promotion and assignment process. The better you perform, the better your assignment, the further your promotion. Continuity matters. A gap means you might not care enough about that next level. At least not enough to check and make sure your FITREPS are in order. Or, better yet, if that's how much you care about yourself, what does it say about how much you care about the records of your troops? Enough said. You don't know what will be the difference. Maybe they looked at your portrait and it was you smiling back at them from O.C.S. Maybe your first Fitrep at sea, Admin forgot to send it in and you didn't make sure to double check. Take it from me, it's the difference between Commander and Captain. All adds up in the end. Defend your record. You all still with me?"

"Yes, Chief."

"Alright. Moving on. Touching briefly on your health records. Also important. Most of the time, these will take care of themselves in Medical. Between commands, however, you will carry your health record in your possession. You are responsible for the record. Take care of it. You wouldn't want to take your immunizations shots over again, would you? Also make sure to document any medical conditions over time. Come retirement, it's your health history they review to determine any and all entitlements to disability allowance. You get a bad back in the last year of service, it's going to raise some red flags. You have a bad back for twenty years, properly documented and described, you're going to rate disability. Careful, though, it's a real fine line between a disability and early retirement as an N.P.Q. Especially for you pilots. Any questions? Great. Now what about pay? Thought I'd see heads pick up. We all like our paydays, don't we?"

"Yes, Chief."

"You will be receiving Ensign pay. O-One for all you non-Priors. O-One E for the Priors stepped based on the number of years you already have in. Pay charts are in your packets. Last time I checked, I believe the base pay comes in around nineteen K a year. Not to worry. That's just your basic pay. The Navy also has a responsibility to house you and your dependents. Most common way is payment of basic allowance for quarters, your B.A.Q., and variable housing allowance, your V.H.A. Those of you without dependents, no need to run out and get hitched. You still qualify if you maintain a residence. You will also receive a basic allowance for subsistence. All Officers, regardless of status, qualify. Place to sleep and three square meals a day. Before taxes. You'll see it as a deduction on your L.E.S. The good news for some of you is that you won't have to pay State taxes. When you get to your follow-on stations, be sure to inquire about a waiver

with your disbursing Officer. Neither here nor there, but I encourage you ask around for the gouge on this. Got that, everyone?"

"Yes, Chief."

"Which brings us to actual payday. Lock up your guns. Hide the children. Payday takes place twice each month as decided by the C.O., usually the first and the fifteenth by direct deposit. Pay and allotments is something you want to have squared away. Things are different in the Fleet. Aboard ship you might go River City. Get those dependents squared away. Just because they can get on base doesn't mean you can rest easy underway. Whatever you had coming in, I encourage you to take a look at Navy Federal. Testament to the availability of credit a low rates as part of a community with guaranteed pay. Alright?"

"Yes, Chief."

"Same goes for life insurance. You are entering a high-risk profession, especially you pilots out there. The Navy's a family. Worst thing in the world to evict some of your own from base housing with no place to go and no S.G.L.I check coming and your death gratuity already eaten up. And you want to set a good example for your troops. Make sense?"

"Roger?"

"Roger."

"Couple of stories for you. May hit close to home. At least, I hope. An Ensign, recent O.C.S. grad no less, educated at considerable sacrifice on the part of his family, marries a woman from the next State over. After twins are born, he makes his insurance payable in one lump sum to his wife, if living, and otherwise to his children in monthly installments. Sometime later, tragically, an auto accident occurs. The Ensign dies first, then his children and then his wife. His insurance goes to his wife's estate and then to his wife's relatives. His own family, who had worked so hard to give him a chance in life, gets nothing. Poor planning. Understand?"

"Yes, Chief?"

"Or take the seasoned Lieutenant who has a life insurance policy payable to his wife in installments covering a twenty year period. Our Lieutenant, tragically, dies. After receiving about a quarter of the installments, his wife dies too. Their only child, a son, is not named in the policy and the Lieutenant failed to change the beneficiary clause. The remaining proceeds, therefore, go to his wife's estate. Since his wife had no will, an administrator is appointed, which costs money. Even worse, the wife remarried after the Lieutenant's death. Therefore, that second husband is entitled to a share of the estate. So the Lieutenant's son receives a greatly reduced share of the insurance proceeds. Fortunately for the son, no other children are involved. Moral of the story. Do not forget your insurance policies. Fill them out carefully. Today. And examine them once a year from here on out. Update any change of status. Talk them over with the

insurance and benefits Officer aboard your ship or station. Talk them over with your wife. Your family. Make sure you include complete commercial insurance information in your Record of Emergency Data. Include any additional insurance policies. Navy will do its due diligence. Legal is handcuffed if you don't do yours. I know it's a lot of information. You'll find Admin a good place to find answers to any question. Swing by any time. We mean it. That's all I got."

"Let's give our thanks to the Chief for that excellent presentation. Thank you, Chief. Good gouge."

"Yes, Sir."

"Listen. Before the break, I want to add a quick point. Like the Chief said, there's only one time to make a first impression. In ten days, you'll be walking out these doors not only as Ensigns, but O.C.S. grads. If you show up to your next duty station in jeans, we all show up in jeans. Carry yourselves accordingly. The first impression you make will be important. Make it ready for inspection. And for those heading home to OHARP, don't fall back into old habits. That ship won't sail out in the Fleet. Got it?"

"Yes, Sir."

"Okay, break time. Hit the head. Grab some coffee. Come on back for health care and death benefits."

"Aye aye, Sir."

••

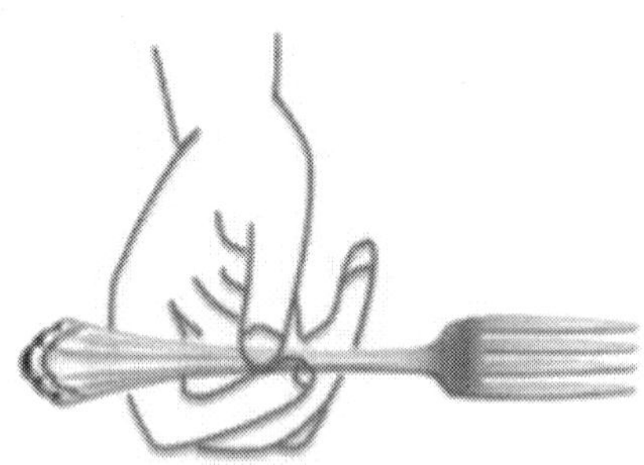

When eating

Hold the fork or spoon face up, resting the handle on the middle finger of the right hand and hold it with index finger and thumb. When cutting food, keep your elbows in, extending the index finger along handles of knife and fork. Keep knife and fork as close to horizontal as possible. Arms, hands, and silver should form a smooth, graceful line. After cutting, if food is carried to the mouth with

the fork held in left hand, continue to keep the tines down the index finger extended. Never grasp a fork or spoon handle from above, as if it were a small trowel. Never hold the knife and fork vertically when cutting. Humps formed by bent wrists look very awkward and unattractive. Never turn a fork right side up when holding it in the left hand to convey meat to the mouth. Never cut food without extending index fingers to provide proper leverage.

••

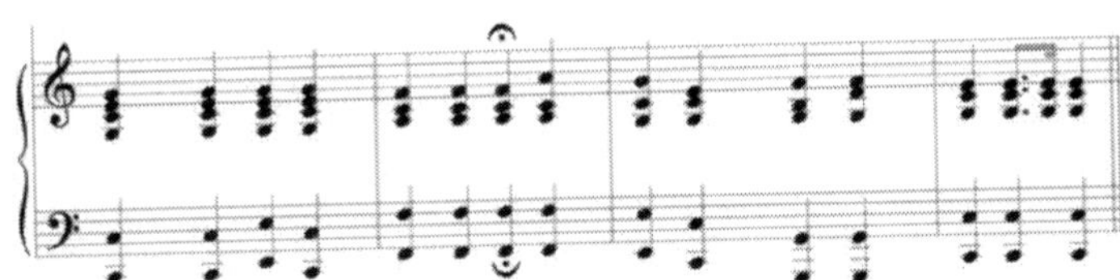

"Mister President, all Officers and their guests are present."

"The Mess will come to order. Mess President, Captain Richard Kimmer, Commanding Officer, Officer Training Command Pensacola."

"Devotion to the U.S. Navy and its traditions begets equal earnestness and devotion from all. Welcome to the Navy Officer Candidate School Dining-in. Tonight we honor custom and tradition as a means of remembering our past. Ladies and Gentlemen, the Official Party. We welcome our distinguished guest of honor Vice Admiral Hertzog, Commander Caleb Pedroia, Lieutenant Commander James Wallace, Lieutenant Mark McDonald, Lieutenant Sandra Day, Lieutenant Michael Pimbrooke, Lieutenant Junior Grade Jody Bucknell, and Lieutenant Junior Grade Joseph Billingsley. Lieutenant Jonathan Higgens, as Mister Vice. Regimental Commander, Candidate Officer Kern. And last, but not least, our Officer Candidates. Welcome."

"Welcome."

Spoons rap on the linen cloth.

"Parade the colors."

"Carry colors."

"Ready, cut."

"Right turn, march."

"Forward, march."

"Colors, halt."

"Present, colors."

"Ready, cut."

"Carry, colors."

"Countermarch, march."

"Forward, march."

"Left, turn."

"Colors, march."

"Colors, halt."

"Order, colors"

"Present, arms."

"Order, arms."

"Center, face."

"Forward, march."

"Colors, halt."

"Shoulder, arms."

"Forward, march."

"Ladies and Gentlemen, the grace."

"Father, we thank you for the blessings you have given us today and throughout our lives. We are especially thankful for the privilege of gathering here in this mess tonight, honoring the traditions and esprit so deeply rooted within our Navy. We invoke your blessing on this assembly, the meal we are about to enjoy, and the fellowship that will follow. For what we are about to receive, may the Lord make us truly thankful. Amen."

"Amen."

"Please be seated."

"Mister Vice."

"Yes, Mister President."

"The Mess hungers."

"Yes, Mister President. I will inquire as to the meal. Yes, indeed. Mister President, the mess is now open!"

"Where's the beef?"

"Aye aye, Mrster President. Chief steward, bring forth the beef for inspection."

"Aye aye, Mister Vice. Parade the beef!"

"You can't possibly be serious. Give it to Vice."

"Aye aye, Mister President."

"The meat is grossly unfit for human consumption. Mister President, this chef must be shot."

"So be it."

"Aye aye, Mister President."

"Bring forth another beef."

"Aye aye, Sir. Chief steward, bring forth another beef for inspection."

"Aye aye, Mister Vice."

"Better. The beef is fit for human consumption."

"Very well, Mister President."

"Is the wine fit for human consumption?"

"Mister President, if all be true that I do think, there are five reasons we should drink. Good wine, a friend, or being dry. Or lest we should be, by and by, or any other reason why. The wine is quite fit for consumption, Sir."

"Outstanding, Mister Vice, are the wine glasses charged?"

"The wine glasses are charged, Mister President."

"Dinner will now be served!"

"Dinner is served!"

The wait staff passes through with the table service.

"Which fork is the salad fork?"

"Start from the outside."

"Negative. Go with the smaller fork, Shipmate."

"I thought it was from the outside."

"Salad's the small fork."

"Looks pretty good."

"Hey Brooks, pass the wine please."

"Passing the wine, aye aye."

"Gentlemen?"

"Sure. Top me off. Thanks, Mike."

"Here. Might as well."

"Let's keep them charged, Gentlemen. To *the New York Yankees*!"

"Negative."

"I was waiting for that."

"It's almost not fair."

"Don't start, Mike."

"Sweepers. Sweepers. Man your brooms."

"Would have been close."

"Knoblauch! Wish I could have seen it."

"Luck."

"Luck? You mean Derek Jeter, Paul O'Neill, El Duque, Clemens, Pettitte? Or you mean dynasty?"

"God, I hate the Yankees."

"I could win every year with that payroll."

"So do we."

"I think Steinbremer hired Cashman just for his name."

"So where were you, Mike? Inquisitive minds want to know."

"Not at liberty to say."

"Not at liberty is right."

"Pass the rolls, would you? Nothing shady. Had to take care of something. Let it go. You guys catch Bloomfield's bulldog yet?"

"The Colonel. You bet. Gave him his greeting of the day, too."

"Seriously?"

"In the ballistic. New requirement."

"That's hilarious."

"Only he's not a Colonel anymore."

"How so?"

"Apparently he took a crap on the parade deck in front of the Admiral last graduation ceremony. Bloomfield busted him down to Private. Supposedly, he's working his way back through the ranks."

Enlisted staff pass through with the table service.

"May I, Sir?"

"Cutlery, Brooks."

"Oh, that's right. Thank you."

"Well that was good. I could re-attack right now."

"Beats the chow hall. That's for damn sure."

"Infraction."

"Come off of it."

"I'm reporting it."

"You're not."

"I am. What? That's part of this. That's what we're supposed to be doing."

"A man's got to do what a man's got to do, brother."

"Lock it up folks."

"Why? What's up?"

"Missing Man."

"The wine is ready to pass, Mister President."

"Mister Vice will acknowledge Regimental Commander Smith."

"Regimental Commander Kern with the Missing Man Honors."

"As you entered the dining room this evening, you may have noticed a small table in the place of honor near Mister Vice. This table is reserved in honor of comrades who have fallen in battle and for those still missing in action, commonly called P.O.Ws and M.I.As. Those who have served with them and depended upon their strength shall always remember, as we shall remember, these great Americans who have not forsaken us. Until we have a full accounting, they remain with us in spirit. This table is set for one. I shall explain the meaning of this table and each item. The table is smaller than the others, symbolizing the frailty of one prisoner alone against their oppressors. The white tablecloth represents the purity of their response to our country's call to arms. The empty chair depicts an unknown face, representing no specific Soldier, Sailor, Marine or Airman, but all who are not here with us. The table is round to show that our concern for them is never ending. The Bible represents faith in a higher power and the pledge to our country, founded as one nation under God. The black napkin stands for the emptiness these warriors have left in the hearts of their families and friends. The single red rose reminds us of their families and loved ones, the red ribbon representing the love of our country, which inspired them to answer the Nation's call. The yellow candle and its yellow ribbon symbolize the everlasting hope for a joyous reunion with those yet unaccounted for. The slices of lemon on the bread plate remind us of their bitter fate. The salt upon the bread plate represents the tears of their families. The wine glass turned upside down reminds us that our distinguished comrades cannot be with us to drink a toast or join in the festivities this evening. All of us who served with them and called them comrades, who depended on their aid, who relied on them, surely they have not forsaken us, all of us who will soon join these ranks, remember. Let us now raise our water glasses in a toast to honor American's P.O.Ws and M.I.As and to the success of our efforts to account for them."

"Please be seated."

"Ladies and Gentlemen, during the early days of trans-Atlantic sailing, the shipping insurance company Lloyd's of London would mark the loss of a ship and her crew by ringing a bell outside the insurance office. The sound of that lonely bell echoed along the waterfront, tolling the loss of fellow Shipmates. That tradition continues today in the bell ceremony. Each strike of the bell reminds us of the reverence we owe to our departed Shipmates and to those now guarding the honor of our country, upon the sea, under the sea, in the air and upon foreign soil."

The bell tolls twice.

"Let us who gather here tonight never forget our obligation and in silence, breathe a prayer for our absent Shipmates."

The bell tolls twice more.

"Each in his own words, and each in his own way, bow your head and let us pray, offering a silent prayer for our departed Shipmates who now serve on the staff of the Supreme Commander."

The bell tolls once more.

"Mister Vice, a toast to our fallen comrades and those missing in action."

"A toast to our fallen comrades and those missing in action."

"To our fallen comrades and those missing in action."

"Fellow Officers and Candidates, please stand for the toasting ceremony."

"Fellow Officers and Candidates, I propose a toast to Her Majesty The Queen."

"Fellow Officers and Candidates, *to Her Majesty The Queen*!"

"To her Majesty The Queen!!"

"Fellow Officers and Candidates, I propose a toast to our Commander-in-Chief, the President of the United States."

"Fellow Officers and Candidates, *to our Commander-in-chief, the President of the United States*!"

"To our Commander-in-Chief, the President of the United States!!"

"Fellow Officers and Candidates, I propose a toast to our spouses and sweethearts."

"Fellow Officers and Candidates, *to our spouses and sweethearts*!"

"To our spouses and sweethearts!!"

"Mister Vice will acknowledge Officer Candidate Demarco."

"Officer Candidate Demarco with a toast."

"Officers and fellow Candidates, I propose a toast to the United States Marine Corp."

"Fellow Officers and Candidates, *to the United States Marine Corp*!"

"To the United States Marine Corp!!"

"Mister Vice will acknowledge Officer Candidate Wong."

"Officer Candidate Wong with a toast."

"Officers and fellow Candidates, I propose a toast to the Chief of Naval Aviation."

"Fellow Officers and Candidates, *to the Chief of Naval Aviation*!"

"To the Chief of Naval Aviation!!"

"Mister Vice will acknowledge Officer Candidate Mitchell."

"Officer Candidate Mitchell with a toast."

"Officers and fellow Candidates, I propose a toast to our honored guests."

"Fellow Officers and Candidates, *to our honored guests*!"

"To our honored guests!"

"Here, here!"

"Please rise for the final toast."

"*Long live the United States and success to the Navy*!"

"Long live the United States and success to the Navy!!"

"There's Vice. Here we go. This should be fun. You ready, Masterson?"

"Mister Vice, open the floor for challenges."

"Mister President, fellow Officers and Candidates. The floor is now open for challenges."

"The Officer Candidate will be recognized."

"Mister Vice President. Officer Candidate Masterson, Class Zero-Four-Zero-Zero, requests permission to entertain the mess with this here guitar."

"Mister President, Officer Candidate Masterson requests permission to entertain the mess with song."

"The floor is yours, Officer Candidate."

"*I have a story that pains my heart*
It's about a girl, you know that part
Her hair so soft, her face so fair
A girl I'd follow most anywhere.
I bought her a rock and dropped a knee
Darling will you marry me.
She said I want to marry a Navy sailor
Two sea bags sitting by the door
See my man off to sea
Go now if you want to marry me.
So I called the recruiter for her sake
And he put me on a bus to Great Lakes
Made me a Ricky and shaved my hair
Made it rain but I didn't care
Sailor cap and a shoe shine
Asked her again if she would be mine.
She said I want to marry a Petty Officer
Two sea bags sitting by the door
See my man off to sea
Go now if you want to marry me.
So I worked real hard to advance
Swabbed the decks every chance
Got my SWO pin, got my wings

Had my Div-O pull some strings
Tacked an eagle on my arm
Told my girl I'd keep her warm.
She said I want to marry a Navy chief
Two sea bags sitting by the door
See my man off to sea
Go now if you want to marry me.
So I tucked my head and began the climb
Made my rank in record time
My nights were short, my days long
Sea legs mighty-mighty strong
Left directly from the board
To present her with my cutlass sword.
She said I want to marry a Naval Officer
Two sea bags sitting by the door
See my man off to sea
Go now if you want to marry me.
So off I went to O.C.S.
Thirteen weeks without rest
Soon an Officer of the Fleet
Her promise now a rapid beat
Back I went for her hand
Three silver dollars and a wedding band.
She said Look at you now as a Naval Officer
Two sea bags sitting by the door
I just don't know how to tell you
I've gone off and married your drill instructor."

"Thank you, Gentlemen. A valuable lesson indeed. The Officer Candidate is recognized."

"Mister Vice President, Officer Candidate Ross, Class Zero-Six-Zero-Zero, requests permission to report a violation."

"Mister President, Officer Candidate Ross requests permission to report a violation."

"Proceed."

"Officer Candidate Carlson, Class Zero-Six-Zero-Zero, is guilty of unduly loud and obstructive remarks."

"The mess recognizes Officer Candidate Carlson. What say you in your own defense?"

"It's no secret that our D.I. is a humdinger.
He puts us through the freaking wringer
So when it comes time to give salute

For all the fun spent under his boot
We returned the favor with just one --."

"As you were!!"

"I said *defense*, Candidate. I do believe you just earned yourself a trip up to the grog bowl. Let's put it to a vote by the mess."

Spoons rap on the tables.

"The mess has spoken. Come on up."

"Aye aye, Sir."

"For grog is our starboard, our larboard. Our main mast, our mizzen, our log. At sea or ashore, or when harbored, the mariners' compass is grog."

"Thank you, Mister President."

"Prudent seamen husband the ship's store during long voyages. Off you go."

"Aye aye, Sir."

"Yes?"

"Mister President, Officer Candidate Shafer, Class Zero-Six-Zero-Zero, requests permission to report a violation."

"Proceed."

"Officer Candidate McKesson, Class Zero-Five-Zero-Zero is guilty of a uniform violation."

"What is the specific charge?"

"Oh, nothing in particular, Sir. Zero-Five presents an odorous appearance in general."

"Well, now. The mess recognizes Officer Candidate McKesson. What say you in your own defense?"

"Mister Vice President, Officer Candidate McKesson, Officer Candidate Class Zero-Five-Zero-Zero, requests permission to entertain the mess with a limerick."

"Mister President, Officer Candidate McKesson, Officer Candidate Class Zero-Six-Zero-Zero, United States Navy, requests permission to entertain the mess with a limerick."

"Proceed."

"How to respond to Zero-Six? I could say they have no class. Or Burlson feeds them too much grass. But that would unbefit an *Honor Class*."

"I would remind Candidates that rising to applaud witticisms as such are in violation of mess rules and will be recorded as such."

"Thank you, Vice. All in good fun, Gentlemen, I'm sure. Come and calm your tempers with some fine grog."

"Aye aye, Sir."

"For grog is our starboard, our larboard. Our main mast, our mizzen, our log. At sea or ashore, or when harbored, the mariners' compass is grog."

"Thank you, Mister President."

"Prudent seamen husband the ship's store during long voyages. How about a good natured handshake, Gentlemen. On your way."

"Aye aye, Sir."

"Let us now shed a tear for Lord Nelson."

••

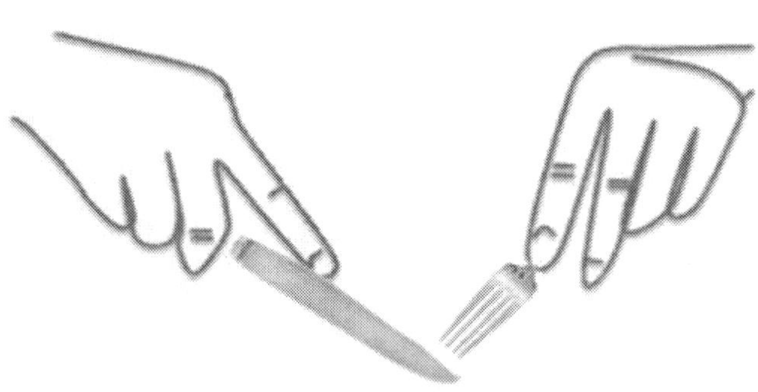

Bon Appétit

Main course. Meat should be placed closest to you for better leverage in cutting. Cut meat carefully, one piece at a time. Keep elbows in and cut firmly, don't use a sawing movement. To start with, the knife and the fork are both held at the usual position for cutting meat. The fork remains in the left hand with tines facing down and then lifted to the mouth. During this second step, the knife may be held in the right hand in cutting position close to the plate or laid on the plate, depending on convenience. It is impolite to pack the back of the fork with an assortment of food.

••

We disembark the bus in character. I follow George Washington up to the second floor of the school house. The children eye us warily as we file into the classroom.

"Children. Boys and girls. Tyler! If I can have your attention please. Thank you. We have special guests with us today. These nice young men and women are Navy Cadets. They are here to perform a flag ceremony for us as a community service. A *community service.*"

"Community service."

"Let's give them a big West Welcome."

"We welcome you to West! We feel so very blessed!"

"Mister Smith, the stage is yours."

"Thank you, Miss Downs. Hello, everybody. Thank you so much for that warm welcome. How does it go again?"

"We welcome you to West! We feel so very blessed!"

"That's great, guys. Thank you very much. So hello everyone! My name is Candidate Officer Smith. I am the Class President for Naval Officer Candidate School, Officer Candidate Class Zero-Four-Zero-Zero and these folks in the kind of funny historical outfits are my classmates. We are all studying to become Junior Officers in the United States Navy. That's right, we have homework and need to study hard just like you do for Miss Downs. One of the things we study is the history of the American flag. We are taught to care for the flag as the symbol of this country's freedom. A freedom to live as we wish, enshrined in our Constitution, the written shield for our basic rights in life, liberty and the pursuit of happiness. Today you're going to meet some of the people who have gone before us, to whom we all owe a big debt of gratitude. So are you guys ready to learn about our national flag?"

"Yes."

"What's that? I'm afraid I couldn't hear you. I thought you guys were in the first grade?"

"Yes!"

"That's more like it. Miss Downs, are we all set?"

"All I have to is press play?"

"That's it. Thank you. Miss Downs, if you could, please."

"Ladies and Gentlemen, the Naval Aviation Schools Command takes great pleasure in asking you to join us in paying tribute to our national flag. The performers are all from Officer Candidate School, Naval Air Station, Pensacola, Florida. Flags are as old as civilization, yet they still maintain their ancient power. Throughout history men and women have realized that they could express their feelings for their country and its people, their loyalty and sense of patriotic duty by showing respect for their emblem, their national flag. And by understanding something of its meaning, its history."

"Lower flags."

"Raise flags."

"The year Fourteen-Ninety-Five. Flying the Portuguese flag, Amerigo Vespucci, following the trail blazed by Columbus, proclaimed the discovery of a new world. European mapmakers gave the new country Vespucci's name, Amerigo or America."

"Lower flags."

"Raise flags."

"In Fifteen-Thirteen, Ponce Deleon, under the Castilian colors, landed in Florida and claimed that land for Ferdinand the Fifth of Spain."

"Lower flags."

"Raise flags."

"In Fifteen-Thirty-four, the French made their first explorations to the New World. Flying the ancient Fleure de Lis banner, sturdy Jacques Cartier of France sailed into the Gulf of Saint Lawrence and claimed half the North American continent for Francis the First."

"Lower flags."

"Raise flags."

"In the next century, Spain and France solidified and strengthened their claims in the new world as English settlers raised their flags over Colonies founded in Jamestown in Sixteen-O-Seven."

"Lower flags."

"Raise flags."

"In Sixteen-O-Nine, Henry Hudson sailed into what is now New York Harbor with a red, white and blue banner of the Netherlands flying from the main mast."

"Lower flags."

"Raise Flags."

"In Sixteen-Twenty-Eight, Peter Medwin organized the New School Company and ten years later founded a Swedish settlement on the Delaware River within the present limits of Wilmington. Medwin's historic banner of a gold cross on a blue field still remains the national colors of Sweden. The flags of many nations form a part of our collective history but, of all of them, the British Ensign was to play the most important role in the early evolution of our national flag, a flag of honor, truth and virtue. The design of the Union Jack was based on the red cross of Saint George on a white field and a white cross of Saint Andrew on a blue field. From this, to our present flag of fifty stars and thirteen stripes of red and white, the flags that have represented the United States of America throughout our history have all played an important part in the tradition, the honor, and prestige which are America's tradition."

"Lower flags."

"Raise flags."

"The year Seventeen-Seventy-Five. In Seventeen-Seventy-Five, the Bunker Hill flag was one of the first to include the pine tree emblem. It was carried by the American Colonial troops who opposed the British regulars at the Battle of Bunker Hill, June seventeenth, Seventeen-Seventy-Five. Later, a white flag with a green pine tree and the inscription *An appeal to heaven* became familiar on the seas as the Navy Ensign on cruisers commissioned by George Washington."

"Lower flags."

"Raise flags."

"The year Seventeen-Seventy-Six. As the day of America's revolution drew near, there appeared flags of defiance, cause and purpose, determination and appeal. For instance, our rattle snake flag *Don't tread on me.* It proclaimed to the world that young America would fight for its freedom. On July fourth, Seventeen-Seventy-Six, General Washington adopted our grand Union Flag bearing thirteen stripes of our thirteen states and the British Union Jack to show the origin of our land. Under this flag, a group of American patriots led by Thomas Jefferson presented to an infant nation a Declaration of Independence that to this day is known as one of the great compositions in history. In the words of Jefferson, *This document could never have been written without the helping hand of God.*"

"Lower flags"

"Raise flags."

"June fourteenth, Seventeen-Seventy-Seven, the birthday of our modern flag. On this day we broke tradition with our British forbearers and abandoned the crosses of Saint George and Saint Andrew. Now a new flag, the Stars and Stripes, was presented to the young nation and its proud citizens. To many of those who saw this flag for the first time, it was a combination of red, white and blue. But to George Washington and those patriots who had brought our country through its fight for freedom, it meant much more. The thirteen stripes of red and white represented the thirteen Colonies which were the genesis of our nation's struggle and the cause of liberty. First, the stripes of red indicating honor and valor and the blood of that had been spilled in order to gain the victory. The stripes of white, the symbol of purity and purpose. And the field of blue, a heavenly panorama for thirteen stars to show a new constellation in the nations of the world. This is why June fourteenth, Seventeen-Seventy-Seven, the birthday of our Stars and Stripes is a treasured American heritage. About the time General George Washington sent his flag along, America's first Fleet rode in anchorage in the Delaware. As Commodore S.S Hopkins came aboard the flagship Alfred, an ambitious unknown named John Paul Jones hoisted this flag of America to the roar of guns and the cheers of spectators. Later, on the Bonham Richard, Captain Jones afforded a rich heritage to our great Navy through his immortal words *I have not yet begun to fight.*"

"Lower flags."

"Raise flags."

"The year Eighteen-Twelve. In Eighteen-Twelve, Freedom of the seas was our cry for equality among nations. Then, *through the rockets' red glare and the bombs bursting in air*, an American patriot, inspired by pride in his native land, stood as the country's flag, now bearing fifteen stripes and fifteen stars was hoisted swiftly

to the top of the mast by brave defenders of Fort McHenry, inspiring Francis Scott Key to write the words of our National Anthem."

"Lower flags."

"Raise flags."

"Now let us remind ourselves that it is only because of the sacrifice of brave Americans who have gone on before us that the Star Spangled Banner still waves from the Land of the Free and the Home of the Brave."

"Lower flags."

"Raise flags."

"The year Eighteen-Forty-Six. During the war with Mexico, events of American ideals and principles, still another American flag was unfurled. For almost a quarter century which our flag wore fifteen stars and fifteen stripes, the leaders of our nation came to realize that there would be many more states. So they decreed by law that a star would be added for each new state. And so it was that during the Mexican War, our banner wore twenty-six stars and thirteen stripes."

"Lower flags."

"Raise flags."

"The year Eighteen-Sixty-One. In Eighteen-Sixty-One a shadow crossed our Nation. The smoke of battle disclosed under the flag. The unity of our country was at stake, American fought American, brother against brother. But, in the end, a tall, lean, God-respecting man named Abraham Lincoln reunited our nation under the Stars and Stripes, a stronger United States of America destined, in Lincoln's words, *not to perish in history*."

"Lower flags."

"Raise flags."

"The year Eighteen-Ninety-Eight. This was a year when westward progress was on the march. A great moment of freedom loving pioneers answered the call of the West. New states came rapidly on the scene and more stars were added to the blue field of our flag. In the Spanish-American War, a handful of dedicated Americans in defense of the Monroe Doctrine unfurled an American flag now bearing forty-five stars."

"Lower flags."

"Raise flags."

"The year Nineteen-Seventeen. For the first time, America was recognized as a world power. And, for the first time, in a war that encompassed the world, a new red, white, and blue flag now bearing forty-eight stars was carried over the battlefield of the world by defenders of liberty, freedom, and justice. To soldiers, there is one moment above all others during which the flag assumes a supreme meaning. It is when the last volley is stilled and the flag is gently removed and

carried to where the mourners stand. A Service Member has given their best for their country, and she in turn gives back her best acknowledgment, her colors."

"Lower flags."

"Raise flags."

"Sunday, December seventh, Nineteen-Forty-One. A day of infamy. A day that will live in the hearts of Americans for generations to come. A day when millions of our citizens rallied around the flag to renew their vows of loyalty. They proclaimed, as the patriots of Seventeen-Seventy-Six and as they would in future years and areas of conflict, *Woe be on those who seeks to destroy our freedom*. In recent years, two territories have won their right to statehood. July fourth, Nineteen-Fifty-Nine the forty-ninth star for Alaska made obsolete the flag of forty-eight stars flown since Nineteen-Twelve. For the first time in history, the Union was extended to a state outside our continental boundaries."

"Lower flags."

"Raise flags."

"July fourth, Nineteen-Sixty. Hawaii added the fiftieth star. This addition created the twenty-seventh national flag in our history. The ideals that the flag stands for were fostered by the experiences of a great people. Everything it stands for was written by their lives. Their flag is the embodiment of this history, representing the experiences of men and women who live under the flag. Pioneers of the day are much the same as our forefathers who through their patriotism, courage, and love of country founded and developed this great nation. Our new pioneers have succeeded in achieving unthought-of goals and will continue under our democratic way of life."

"Lower flags."

"Raise flags."

"The day today. The hour now. As Americans today, we must be vigilant and ready to defend the cause of freedom. This is nothing new. We have lived in troubled times before. In Korea, Vietnam, and Desert Storm many great men and women served in armed conflict to protect, uphold, and preserve the freedom of others. Their bravery and heroism will not be forgotten. Perhaps in the course of our past history, we may find the answers to our problems today. So, let us turn back the pages of history to a cold day a Valley Forge when our young nation faced a moment of severe trial. A group of patriots approached General Washington and told him the situation was desperate and that a strong British attack was expected at anytime. They asked him what could be done to save our nation and our cause? And, with tears in his eyes, not tears of fear or failure, but rather tears of pride, pride for his fellow comrades in arms, and admiration for a struggling nation, Washington gave his military patriots a simple command. *Put none but Americans on guard tonight*. What General Washington meant was simply this. That the salvation of our great cause required truly dedicated men and

women, willing to stand guard in the face of great odds. Who love this flag, liberty, and freedom more than life. And are willing to prove it. His words are just as true now as they were in Seventeen-Seventy-Six."

"Lower flags."

"Raise flags."

"May the God we trust as a nation throw the light of his peace and grace on a flag with its striped untarnished and every star in place."

"Miss Downs, would it be alright if I lead in a recitation of the Pledge of Allegiance?"

"Of course."

"Ladies and Gentlemen, please rise for the pledge of allegiance. Thank you. *I pledge allegiance to the flag.*"

"I pledge allegiance to the flag."

"*Of the United States of America.*"

"Of the United States of America."

"*And to the republic for which its stands.*"

"And to the republic for which its stands."

"*One nation, under God, indivisible, with liberty and justice for all.*"

"One nation, under God, indivisible, with liberty and justice for all."

"And salute."

"Ready, two."

"Thank you, Gentlemen. That was absolutely wonderful. Wasn't that great everyone? Let's give them a well-deserved round of applause."

"Thank you. That's much appreciated. Thank you."

"Gentlemen, without further ado, the class wanted to give you something to take back with you as a small token of our appreciation for your service and coming out to see us today. Betsy was nominated to go first. We thought that was appropriate. Come on up Betsy."

"I'm supposed to read you my letter, Mister Officer."

"A letter? Why that's a perfect present for a Serviceman. We love getting letters."

"Officer Ma-Mas --."

"*Masterson.*"

"Masterson.

"Lee, come on over and meet your new pen pal."

"Hi there, Betsy. My name is Lee. It's nice to meet you."

"I'm supposed to read you my letter."

"I can't wait to hear it."

"Dear Officer Masterson. My name is Betsy. I am in first grade. I have five people in my family. I have a dog. His name is Rufus. You are great. Are you cozy? Thank you for serving our country. Sincerely, Betsy."

"That was very nice, Betsy. Thank you. That means a lot."

"You're welcome."

"Betsy, you did a very good job. You can return to your seat now. Let's give Betsy a big round of applause. Off you go. Would anyone else like to read their letter out loud in front of the class? Josh. Do you want to read your letter?"

"Yes, Miss Downs."

"Come on up."

"Hi, my name is Josh."

"Hi, my name is Candidate Officer Smith."

"Nice to meet you, Officer Smith."

"It's nice to meet you too, Josh."

"Do you live on a boat?"

"Not yet. Who did you write to?"

"Mister Logan."

"Dressed up for you today as a soldier from Vietnam."

"Hi Josh. Nice to meet you."

"Hi."

"You wrote me a letter?"

"Yes."

"Want to read it to me?"

"Yes. Dear Officer Logan. My name is Josh. I am in first grade. I have four people in my family. I have a turtle. His name is Stu. Thank you for serving our country. Sincerely, Josh."

"Thank you, Josh. That is a very nice letter."

"Off you go, Josh."

"Yes, Miss Downs."

"Would anyone else like to read their letter out loud in front of the class? Peter. Is that you volunteering?"

"No, Miss Downs."

"Come on up with your letter."

"Yes, Miss Downs."

"Hi, Peter. Who did you write to?"

"Officer Lyman."

"That's me. Hi, Peter. How's it going?"

"Hi. Dear Officer Lyman. My name is Peter. I am in first grade. I have five people in my family. I have a dog. His name is Marco Polo. I like pizza. Thank you for serving our country. Sincerely, Peter."

"*Marco.*"

"Polo."

"*Marco.*"

"Polo."

"Settle down, everyone."

"Thanks, Peter."

"You're welcome."

"Off you go. Any more volunteers? How about another girl? Suzy? Don't be shy. Come on up."

"Hi, Suzy."

"Hi."

"And who did you write to?"

"Officer Foreman."

"Steve-o. Where are you?"

"Right here."

"Suzy, meet Candidate Officer Foreman, our resident Doughboy."

"Hi there, Suzy. It's nice to meet you."

"Hi."

"Do you want to read me your letter?"

"Dear Officer Foreman. My name is Suzy. I am in first grade. I have three people in my family. I want a puppy. His name is Gruff. Thank you for serving our country. Sincerely, Suzy."

"Thank you, Suzy."

"Good job, Suzy. Off you go. The rest of you, please pass your letters up to Mister Smith. In an orderly fashion. Nice and easy."

"Don't worry, guys. Mike, our Mailbody, or Thomas Jefferson here, will make sure the letters get to all the right people. We also have a class gift for you guys. Your very own American flag."

"Did you hear that, everyone? These Gentlemen brought us a present. A true blue American flag. Red, white and blue."

"We thought we might show the kids how to fold it."

"Of course. That would be very nice. Thank you."

"We need two volunteers. Who wants to be a Flagbody? Two Flagbodies? Don't be shy. It's a piece of cake. Trust me. Do I see two heroes in the back?"

"Kevin. And Jeremy. I want you to pay close attention now."

"Yes, Miss Downs."

"We'll demonstrate first. Morris, how about a hand?"

"Roger."

"Don't worry guys, we'll take it slow. Ready?"

"Yes."

"So you start out lengthwise, two people on each side. You fold the lower striped section over the blue field. Okay?"

"Okay."

"Then you take the folded edge and fold it again so it meets the open edge. See? Next you start a triangle fold by bringing the striped corner of the folded

side over to the open edge. Like this. And you're off. You take the outer point inward, bringing the stripped corner of the folded edge to the open edge. Okay?"

"Okay."

"Don't worry. That there's the hard part. Now you just keep on folding triangles until you get to the end. Easy as pie. Tuck the remaining into the open fold. And there you have your triangle. Your turn, Gentlemen. Unfold it the same way. Spread it out. Perfect. Now shake it out, it won't break, that there's an American flag. Good. So step one. Fold the lower half over the field of stars, holding the bottom and top edges securely. That's right. You got it. Step two. Fold it again keeping the blue field on the outside. Other way, guys. There you go. Keep it tight now. That looks pretty good. Step three. Make the triangle fold, bring the stripped edge here to meet the open edge up top. This side to this side. Perfect. You guys are naturals. Best Flagbodies I have ever met. Step Four. Now you bring it over for your second triangle. And you're off. Keep it going guys. Nice and tight. There you go. Keep it going, keep it going. And you're ready to tuck. There. See? A perfect triangle. Let's hear it for Kevin and Jeremy. Great job, guys."

"What do we say when someone gives us a present?"

"Thank you."

"Well, I know you Gentlemen must get back. On behalf of our class, I want to thank you so much for coming by and sharing this with us today. That was absolutely wonderful. Please feel free to drop-by anytime. Anytime at all."

"Absolutely, Miss Downs. It was great for us too. Thanks for inviting us to come to your class today, guys. And thank you for all the letters."

••

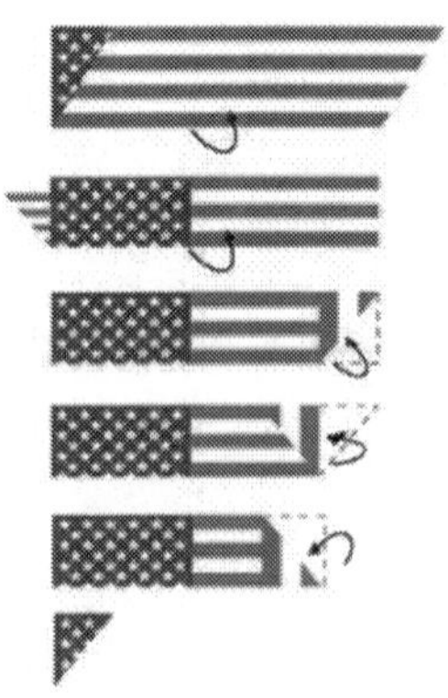

To properly fold a flag

Begin by holding it waist-high with another person so that its surface is parallel to the ground. Fold the lower half of the striped section lengthwise over the field of stars, holding the bottom and top edges securely. Fold the flag again lengthwise with the blue field on the outside. Make a rectangular fold then a triangular fold by bringing the striped corner of the folded edge to meet the open top edge of the flag, starting the fold from the left side over to the right. Turn the outer end point inward, parallel to the open edge, to form a second triangle. The triangular folding is continued until the entire length of the flag is folded in this manner (usually thirteen triangular folds, as shown at right). On the final fold, any remnant that does not neatly fold into a triangle (or in the case of exactly even folds, the last triangle) is tucked into the previous fold. When the flag is completely folded, only a triangular blue field of stars should be visible.

••

"First platoon! Ready!"

"Second platoon! Ready!"

"Third platoon! Ready!"

"Fourth platoon! Ready!"

"Ready! March!"

"Left-right-lo-right! Left-right-left! Left-right-lo-right! Lefty-right-lo! Left-right-lo-right! Left-right-left! Left-right-lo-right! Lefty-right-lo! Left-right-lo-right! Left-right-left! Left-right-lo-right! Lefty-right-lo! Left-right-lo-right! Left-right-left! Left-right-lo-right! Lefty-right-lo! Left-right-lo-right! Left-right-left! Left-right-lo-right! Lefty-right-lo! Left-right-lo-right! Left-right-left! Left-right-lo-right! Lefty-right-lo! Left-right-lo-right! Left-right-left! Lefty-right-lo!"

A snare drum carries the cadence.

"Column-left! March!"

"Column-left! March!"

"Column-left! March!"

"Column-left! March!"

"First platoon! Ready! Halt!"

"Second platoon! Ready! Halt!"

"Third platoon! Ready! Halt!"

"Fourth platoon! Ready! Halt!"

"Please be seated."

"First platoon! Order! Arms!"

"Second platoon! Order! Arms!"

"Third platoon! Order! Arms!"

"Fourth platoon! Order! Arms!"

"First platoon! Left face!"

"Second platoon! Left face!"
"Third platoon! Left face!"
"Fourth platoon! Left face!"
"Dress-right-dress!"
"First platoon! Dress-right-dress!"
"Second platoon! Dress-right-dress!"
"Third platoon! Dress-right-dress!"
"Fourth platoon! Dress-right-dress!"
"First platoon! Ready, front, cover!"
"Second platoon! Ready, front, cover!"
"Third platoon! Ready, front, cover!"
"Fourth platoon! Ready, front, cover!"

"On behalf of the Commanding Officer, Naval Aviation School's Command, welcome to the graduation parade of Class Zero-Four-Zero-Zero, consisting of forty-two Candidates. Located in front of the reviewing stand is the regimental staff for today's parade. It is comprised of the senior ranked Candidate Officers of the graduating class. Additionally, these Candidate Officers have earned distinguished graduate status by graduating in the top ten percent of their class. They are the Commander of Troops, Regimental Commander, Candidate Commander Smith. Regimental Sub-Commander, Candidate Lieutenant Commander Foreman. Battalion Commander, Candidate Lieutenant Commander Jackson. Indoctrination Commander, Candidate Lieutenant Commander Harper. Regimental Adjutant, Candidate Lieutenant Commander Erickson. The platoon on the left is comprised of the graduating class, Class Zero-Four-Zero-Zero and platoon staff consisting of Platoon Commander, Candidate Lieutenant Lin, Platoon Sub-Commander, Candidate Lieutenant Junior Grade Johnson, and Platoon Guide, Candidate Lieutenant Junior Grade Larson. As represented by the streamers on their Gideon, Class Zero-Four-Zero-Zero has distinguished itself by achieving standards of excellence in Drill, Physical Fitness, Military Training Test, and Inspection. The second platoon, a rifle platoon, is comprised of Candidates in their Ninth week of training. This platoon staff consists of Platoon Commander, Candidate Lieutenant Mura, Platoon Sub-Commander, Candidate Lieutenant Junior Grade Reston and Platoon Guide, Candidate Lieutenant Junior Grade Paterson. The third platoon, also a rifle platoon, is comprised of Candidates in their seventh week of training. The platoon staff consists of Platoon Commander, Candidate Lieutenant Masterson, Platoon Sub-Commander, Candidate Lieutenant Junior Grade Moore and Platoon Guide, Candidate Ensign Logan. The fourth platoon is comprised of Candidates in their fifth week of training. The Platoon Staff consists of Platoon Commander, Candidate Lieutenant Siegel, Platoon Sub-Commander, Candidate Lieutenant Junior Grade Macpherson and Platoon Guide, Candidate Ensign Fortunato. The

Band Commander is Candidate Lieutenant Tronstein. The Band is composed of Officer Candidates from all classes. Guests are encouraged to take photographs during the ceremony, except during the singing of the National Anthem. At this time, guests are invited to proceed out onto the parade field to take photographs."

"Present arms!"

"First platoon! Ready! Hand salute!"

"Second platoon! Present arms!"

"Third platoon! Present arms!"

"Fourth platoon! Hand salute!"

"Staff! Post!"

"Staff! Present swords!"

"Please remain standing for the arrival of the distinguished parties and the playing of the National Anthem."

"Patrol and Reconnaissance for Atlantic arriving."

"Side Boys! Ready! Two!"

"Side Boys! Ready! Post!"

"Staff! Carry! Swords!"

"Staff! Hut-Hut! March!"

"Staff! Present! Swords!"

"O! say can you see by the dawn's early light
What so proudly we hailed at the twilight's last gleaming?
Whose broad stripes and bright stars
Through the perilous fight,
O'er the ramparts we watched were so gallantly streaming?
And the rockets' red glare, the bombs bursting in air,
Gave proof through the night that our flag was still there.
O! Say does that Star-Spangled Banner yet wave
O'er the land of the free and the home of the brave?
On the shore, dimly seen through the mists of the deep,
Where the foe's haughty host in dread silence reposes,
What is that which the breeze, o'er the towering steep,
As it fitfully blows, half conceals, half discloses?
Now it catches the gleam of the morning's first beam,
In full glory reflected now shines in the stream
'Tis the Star-Spangled Banner! Oh long may it wave
O'er the land of the free and the home of the brave.
And where is that band who so vauntingly swore
That the havoc of war and the battle's confusion,
A home and a country should leave us no more!
Their blood has washed out their foul footsteps' pollution.

No refuge could save the hireling and slave
From the terror of flight, or the gloom of the grave
And the Star-Spangled Banner in triumph doth wave
O'er the land of the free and the home of the brave.
O! thus be it ever, when freemen shall stand
Between their loved home and the war's desolation!
Blest with victory and peace, may the heav'n rescued land
Praise the Power that hath made and preserved us a nation.
Then conquer we must, when our cause it is just,
And this be our motto *In God is our trust.*"
The rifle volley sounds thirteen times. Smoke drifts across the parade field.
"Ladies and Gentlemen, please be seated."
"First platoon! Ready! Two!"
"Second platoon! Ready! Two!"
"Third platoon! Ready! Two!"
"Fourth platoon! Ready! Two!"
"Staff! Present swords!"
"Sir, the parade is formed."
"Very well. Exercise the Candidates."
"Aye aye, Sir."
"Staff! Carry, swords!"
"Staff! Hut-Hut! March!"
"Exercise the Candidates!"
"First platoon! Parade rest!"
"Fourth platoon! Parade rest!"
"Second platoon! Inspection! Arms!"
"Third platoon! Inspection! Arms!"
"Second platoon! Port! Arms!"
"Third platoon! Port! Arms!"
"Second platoon! Right shoulder! Arms!"
"Third platoon! Right shoulder! Arms!"
"Second platoon! Left shoulder! Arms!"
"Third platoon! Left shoulder! Arms!"
"Second platoon! Port! Arms!"
"Third platoon! Port! Arms!"
"Second platoon! Order! Arms!"
"Third platoon! Order! Arms!"
"Second platoon! Parade rest!"
"Third platoon! Parade rest!"
"Regiment! Attention!"
"First platoon! Attention!"

"Fourth platoon! Attention!"

"Make the report!"

"Aye aye, Sir!"

"Report!"

"First platoon! All present or accounted for, Sir!"

"Very well!"

"Second platoon! All present or accounted for, Sir!"

"Very well!"

"Third platoon! All present or accounted for, Sir!"

"Very well!"

"Fourth platoon! All present or accounted for, Sir!"

"Very well!"

"All present and accounted for, Sir!"

"Very well. Publish the orders."

"Aye aye, Sir!"

"Attention to orders! Headquarters, Naval Aviation Schools command, Naval Air Station, Pen-sa-coooooo-la, Florida! The orders of the day are to! Graduate Class Zero-Four-Zero-Zero!"

"Hoorah!!"

"Prior to! Continuing the training schedule and carrying out the Plan of the Day! By the order of! R.! J.! Kimmer! Captain! United States Navy! Commanding!"

"Officers! Post!"

"Officers! Halt!"

"Officers! Cover!"

"Officers! Carry! Swords!"

"Staff! Return!"

"Swords! Ready! Two!"

"Sir, the Candidates are ready for inspection."

"Very well."

"Hand salute."

"Very well. Take them to parade rest."

"Aye aye, Sir."

"First platoon! Parade rest!"

"Second platoon! Parade rest!"

"Third platoon! Parade rest!"

"Fourth platoon! Parade rest!"

"The Reviewing Officer for today's parade is Rear Admiral John W. Sanders. His decorations include the Defense Superior Service Medal, Legion of Merit, Bronze Star with Combat V, Meritorious Service Medal with two gold stars, Air

Medal, twenty-five strike devices, Navy Commendation Medal with two gold stars and numerous service ribbons."

"Staff! Post!"

"Return! Swords!"

"The graduates assembled in front of the reviewing stand are to be honored for their outstanding achievement while undergoing training here at Naval Aviation Schools Command. Candidate Commander Smith is from Dayton, Tennessee. Candidate Commander Smith is a distinguished graduate who served as the Regimental Commander. Candidate Lieutenant Commander Foreman is from Colchester, Vermont. Candidate Lieutenant Commander Foreman is a distinguished graduate who served as the Regimental Sub-Commander. Candidate Lieutenant Commander Jackson from Casper, Wyoming. Candidate Lieutenant Commander Jackson is a distinguished graduate who served as the Battalion Commander. Candidate Lieutenant Commander Harper is from Boca Raton, Florida. Candidate Lieutenant Commander Harper is a distinguished graduate who served as Indoctrination Commander. Candidate Lieutenant Commander Erickson is from Durham, North Carolina. Candidate Lieutenant Commander Erickson is a distinguished graduate who served as Regimental Adjutant."

"Carry! Swords!"

"Staff! Present! Swords!"

"I await your orders, Sir!"

"Very well."

"Pass in review."

"Aye aye, Sir!"

"Staff! Carry! Swords!"

"Staff! Hut-Hut! March!"

"Regiment-to-Order!"

"First platoon! Attention!"

"Second platoon! Attention!"

"Third platoon! Attention!"

"Fourth platoon! Attention!"

"Pass-in-Review!"

"First platoon! Right face!"

"Staff! Post!

"Second platoon! Right face!"

"Staff! Post!"

"Third platoon! Right face!"

"Staff! Post!"

"Fourth platoon! Right face!"

"Staff! Post!"

"Second platoon! Right shoulder! Arms!"

"Third platoon! Right shoulder! Arms!"
"Pass! In! Review!"
"Regiment! Forward!"
"First platoon! Forward!"
"Second platoon! Forward!"
"Third platoon! Forward!"
"Fourth platoon! Forward!"
"Forward! March!"
"First platoon! Left turn! March!"
"Second platoon! Left turn! March!"
"Third platoon! Left turn! March!"
"Fourth platoon! Left turn! March!"
"First platoon! Left turn! March!"
"Second platoon! Left turn! March!"
"Third platoon! Left turn! March!"
"Fourth platoon! Left turn! March!"
"First platoon! Eyes! Right!"
"Second platoon! Eyes! Right!"
"Third platoon! Eyes! Right!"
"Fourth platoon! Eyes! Right!"
"Ready! Two!"
"First platoon! Left turn! March!"
"Second platoon! Left turn! March!"
"Third platoon! Left turn! March!"
"Fourth platoon! Left turn! March!"
"First platoon! Left turn! March!"
"Second platoon! Left turn! March!"
"Third platoon! Left turn! March!"
"Fourth platoon! Left turn! March!"
"Regiment! Ready! Halt!"
"Second platoon! Port! Arms!"
"Third platoon! Port! Arms!"
"Second platoon! Order! Arms!"
"Third platoon! Order! Arms!"
"First platoon! Left! Face!"
"Second platoon! Left! Face!"
"Third platoon! Left! Face!"
"Fourth platoon! Left! Face!"

"Ladies and Gentlemen, please rise for the passing of the colors. The graduating class will momentarily be walking to the center of the reviewing stand for their final dismissal"

"Officers! Forward march!"
"Column-left! March!"
"Column-left! March!"
"Column-left! March!"
"Officers! Halt!"
"Officers! Right face!"
"Cover!"
"Military guests. Anchors Aweigh and The Marine Corp Hymn."
"*Stand Navy out to sea,*
Fight our battle cry.
We'll never change our course
So vicious foes steer shy-y-y-y.
Roll out the T.N.T.,
Anchors Aweigh,
Sail on to victory and
Sink their bones to Davy Jones,
Hooray!
Anchors Aweigh my boys,
Anchors Aweigh.
Farewell to college joy,
We'll sail at break of day-ay-ay-ay.
Though our last night ashore
Drink to the foam.
Until we meet once more,
Here's wishing you a happy
Voyage home.
Blue of the Mighty Deep,
Gold of God's Sun,
Let these colors be
Till all of time by done, done, done.
On seven seas we learn navy's stern call.
Faith, courage, service true, with
Honor, over honor, over all."
"Ladies and gentlemen, The Marine Corp Hymn!"
"*From the Halls of Mon-te-zu-ma,*
To the shores of Tri-po-liii
We will fight our country's ba-a-ttles,
In the air, on land, and sea.
Fight to fight for right and freedom,
And to keep our honor cleeean
We are proud to claim the ti-i-tle

Of United States Marines.
Our flags unfurled to every breeze
From dawn to setting sun
We have fought in every clime and place
Where we could take a gun.
In the snow of far-off Northern lands
And in sunny tropic scenes
You will find us always on the job
The United States Marines."
"Guide! Present the guide-on!"
"Aye aye, Sir!"
"Class Zero-Four-Zero-Zero! Dismissed!"
"Aye aye, Sir!!"
A wave of white combination covers reaches the sky.

••

Wall locker

Wall lockers will be locked at all times except when the candidate is present. Each candidate's gear will be displayed in accordance with the Officer Candidate Regulations. The candidate's name will be stenciled in one-half inch letters on a six inch strip of white adhesive tape sixteen inches from the top of the wall locker and centered on the wall locker door.

••

"Attention on deck."

"Good morning. I invite all family members and guests to stand for the invocation as we begin today's graduation ceremony. Chaplain Perry."

"Let us pray. Almighty and gracious God, we have gathered this morning to celebrate a tremendous accomplishment in the lives of these young men and women. Over the past thirteen weeks, your hand of protection, wisdom and grace has been upon these Officer Candidates of Officer Candidate Class Zero-Four-Zero-Zero. We have come to honor them, for demonstrating their honor, their courage and their commitment in every challenge they have faced in order to stand before us today to be commissioned as Naval Officers. A new journey is about to begin for them as they assume the mantle of leadership. It is a journey steeped in tradition. A journey full of pride. And a journey that could not be possible without the gifts and abilities you have given to each of these new Officers. But without a fine leadership team, this class would have been without a rudder. We thank you for Lieutenant Bryant, for Chief Machinist Mate Jones, for Staff Sergeant Willett. With their combined experience and wisdom they have helped to shape and mold these men and women into the young leaders you see in front of you. We also thank you for the parents that began the training process over these many years. As these Officers prepare to leave this chapel today, may they leave with the confidence of knowing that you will be with them and protecting them as their new journey begins. It is in his name that I pray this morning. Amen."

"Good morning Ladies and Gentlemen, family and friends. Please be seated. Rear Admiral Sanders, welcome to Class Zero-Four-Zero-Zero's commissioning ceremony. I am Commander Caleb Pedroia, the Commanding Officer here at Officer Candidate School and it is my honor to oversee this Officer ascension program on a daily basis. Congratulations to Class Zero-Four-Zero-Zero for the successful completion of this arduous program which included intense academic, military and physical training. Thank you Chaplain Perry for your invocation. The Chaplain provides counseling for many students at Aviation Schools Command, including our Officer Candidates. I would like to now acknowledge those key staff members who were closest to these Candidates and instrumental in their training. Their Class Officer, and primary role model, Lieutenant Bryant. Conduct of training and leadership development was in his capable hands. He was assisted by Chief Jones. The Chief Petty Officers at Officer Candidate School are the Navy's finest and hand selected to educate Officer Candidates regarding the roles of our Senior Enlisted. Their superb leadership skills and technical expertise are used to develop these Junior Officers. As these new Ensigns enter the Fleet, *ask the Chief* has become their standard phrase. Military indoctrination is the primary responsibility of our Marine Corp Drill Instructor. Staff Sergeant Willett is the Corp's finest and was Class Zero-Four-Zero-Zero's drill instructor. The superb military bearing, discipline, physical conditioning and high motivation begins with this Class Team and the soon to be Naval Officers that you see here today were molded primarily by this team. Please join me in congratulating them."

"And now, ladies and gentlemen, it is my distinct privilege to introduce our guest speaker for today's ceremony, Rear Admiral John W. Sanders, a native of Pensacola. Admiral Sanders began his military career as an Army Warrant Officer, flying more than six hundred combat missions in helicopter gunships during the Vietnam conflict. Upon completion of his Army Tour, he earned a bachelor's degree from Florida State University and entered Naval Aviation through the Aviation Officer Candidate School program in September Nineteen-Seventy-Two. Receiving his Wings in May Nineteen-Seventy-Three, his follow-on assignments with patrol squadrons include V.P.-Fifty-Two, V.P.-Two, V.P.-Thirty-Three and command of V.P.-Fifty in Moffett Field California. He attended Naval Test Pilot School and was assigned as a fixed wing and rotary wing test pilot. His other assignments include the Defense Systems Management College, the Naval Air Systems Command and Chief of Naval Operations Staff. In December Nineteen-Ninety-Four, Admiral Sanders reported to Kamiseya, Japan as Commander of Patrol Wing One, Commander Patrol and Reconnaissance Seventh Fleet and Commander Patrol and Reconnaissance Fifth Fleet. He assumed duties as Command Iceland Defense Force and Island Commander, Iceland in August of Nineteen-Ninety-Six. He reported to his present assignment as Commander of Reconnaissance Force Atlantic in May Nineteen-Ninety-Eight. He has earned Master's degrees in both Aeronautical Engineering and National Resource Management and is rated as a Navy jet, helicopter, and prop aviator with seven thousand five hundred flight hours in over sixty different aircraft. His decorations include the Defense Superior Service Medal, Legion of Merit, Bronze Star with Combat V, Meritorious Service Medal with two gold stars, Air Medal, twenty-five strike devices, Navy Commendation Medal with two gold stars and numerous service ribbons. Ladies and gentlemen, please welcome a warrior and a truly great Naval Officer, Rear Admiral John Sanders."

"Thank you very much for that introduction, Commander. That always just reminds me how old I'm getting. It's a two-edged sword when you have a bio quite that long. But thank you very much. Captain Johnson, Avery and Brooks, X.O. Wilson who couldn't join us today. He was my old Ops O up in Iceland. Ladies and gentlemen, family and friends, and most importantly Commissionees. Good morning. It is an honor to be with you here and share this special day. It's wonderful to be here in my hometown and the cradle of Naval Aviation. This particular chapel holds many memories for me. I was actually married here twenty-seven years ago. I was commissioned on that parade field just adjacent to this chapel. Most recently here in March my daughter was married in this chapel. On all these occasions I was joined by my mother and father in law, Carla and Bill Warner, a thirty-year plus Navy veteran in his own right. Veteran of World War Two, Korea, and Vietnam. And just as importantly, Carla Warner, a thirty year veteran Navy wife. And I thank you again for joining us today.

Today's truly a day for celebration. We are celebrating our Commissionees. We are celebrating the infusion of new talent into our Navy. Talent that will be the foundation for tomorrow's leadership. I hope you are exited as I am for the wonderful challenges and opportunities that await you on the far side of this first step of your journey in this noblest of endeavors. Serving as a Commissioned Officer in the Navy is an awesome responsibility. But that responsibility also carries with it exciting challenges and the opportunity to really make a difference. Ceremonies such as this are common. And though they are common, they carry with them a great deal of meaning. You are about to assume the mantle of selfless dedication and responsibility for the safety and defense of this nation, its people, and its ideals. This is your oath. This is your personal commitment. As a result, you are special. A breed separate and distinct from all others. A key national resource to be cherished by your countrymen. You represent everything that is good about this great nation of ours.

And what an honor it is to return to this place where I started my naval career. It seems like just yesterday my wife Brigit dropped then Candidate Sanders in front of Poopieville. She dropped me off at the front steps and I was politely shown to my room by several caring and sensitive senior Candidates. The class here will appreciate that I'm sure more than some of you will. It seems like only yesterday I had my first one-on-one with my Marine Drill Instructor. You know, many things have changed here at Officer Candidate School but many things remain the same. And they should. I still fondly remember my Poopie suit. And chrome dome. Matter of fact, I saw some chrome domes out there by the galley last night. Dubbed as the Company Smile Body when I first arrived, I can vividly remember my personal counseling sessions conducted by my Drill Instructor as he pointed out the finer points of discipline and exercise. As the weeks progressed, I quickly learned the seriousness of what I was about to enter into. I've always maintained a great admiration and respect for the dedication and military bearing that is fundamental to the Marine Corp for the influence it had upon me in those formative days.

So here I stand before you almost twenty-seven years later. A graduate of Class Zero-Four-Seven-Three. The Smile Body returns. It really does seem like just a few years ago that I was standing out there in the ranks and this much I can guarantee you. The qualities that you have demonstrated here during the past thirteen weeks -- self-discipline, teamwork, determination, physical stamina, level headedness -- together with the technical knowledge that you've obtained and the confidence to perform any task under extremely difficult conditions will serve you well and are critical to your success in the future. Trust me. One or more of you in this audience will be speaking to a group like this in twenty or thirty years. And you, like me, will be trying to figure out how to turn back the clock and start all over again. Before I go any further, I would also like to recognize the parents,

grandparents and families of the Commissionees. I thank you for laying the foundation for these men and women. Choosing a military career is an admirably unselfish decision, the kind made by men and women raised in environments where responsibility, loyalty and service matter. Military service demands these qualities and we have you, parents and family, to thank for showing our new Commissionees the way. In return, we will take good care of your sons and daughters as they make a difference for our Navy and our country.

Since we're commissioning Navy Officers, I thought I would give a brief rundown of the kinds of things that your Navy is doing today. Three hundred and seventy-one thousand men and women are on active duty in the Navy today. As I speak, forty-five percent are away from their homes deployed around the world in places many of us have never heard of in Kosovo, Saudi Arabia, the Arabian Gulf and Korea. Currently, the aircraft carriers Kennedy and Constellation are on duty in the Arabian Gulf. The Lincoln, Kitty Hawk and Stennis are in the Pacific. Over thirty-percent of the submarine force is underway and thirty-three percent of our ships are deployed to include the U.S.S. Grapple and other Naval and Coast Guard units involved in recovery efforts related to the Egypt Air tragedy. In the Caribbean, the Navy is patrolling the skies and the seas in an effort to stem the flow of illegal drugs into this country. And in the Pacific, Naval Forces are forward deployed to reassure our friends and allies that America continues to have enduring interest in that region.

What I've described isn't out of the ordinary. It's what our Navy does every day of the year. The combat power of the United States Navy underwrites peace and stability around the world, the kind of peace and stability that is in the interest of all nations. And when crisis erupts, it is that military force that enables Democracy to work. We saw it in Iraq and we saw it in Kosovo this year. Now that I've told you about what the Navy that you are about to join is doing today, let me talk a bit about what is expected of you when you first report to your command. Your commission today asks one very important service of you. That service is leadership. Leadership is the fuel on which the Navy runs. It is what transforms inexperienced recruits into the world's finest Sailors and Marines. From this day forward, you will be senior to one-point-two million Enlisted men and women in the active duty military. They expect and deserve quality leadership. And it's going to be your responsibility to provide it. This task, as you may suspect, is easier said than done. But nothing that you do in uniform will be more important. Remember, respect means more than pinning on that rank and insignia today. It's earned by respecting others and caring for them and proving that you are worthy of their respect. It's the only respect worth having.

As I prepared for today's ceremony and gathered my thoughts on leadership, I sought to identify those elements of character that are common to leadership and successful Officers that I've admired. I thought long and hard about it only

to arrive at the simple notion, not simplistic but simple, that effective leaders define and embrace a set of unshakeable principles to guide them and the way they lead. These firmly grounded beliefs manifest themselves every day in the way leaders make decisions and interact with those they lead. I offer you today three such principles. *Honor*, *Courage* and *Commitment*. For those of you about to be commissioned these principles are familiar, or they should be. They are the Navy's core values.

Honor is your word, your bond. Do you honor the dignity of those you work with irrespective or personal differences. Do you do what is right even when no one is looking? Thomas Jefferson once said *No one can acquire honor by doing the wrong thing.*

Courage. Moral courage. We often read about great acts of physical courage. Sailors can and will risk their lives in order to save others at sea and at home. What isn't as common is moral courage. The kind of courage that will enable you to tell a friend or Shipmate that what they are doing is wrong. The kind of courage that will enable you to tell the truth in spite of the consequences. The kind of courage that enables you to look your boss in the eye and respectfully say there is a better way of doing things.

And finally commitment. Are you committed to making your unit the very best it can be? Are you committed to the people who look to you for leadership? This is important because leadership is not a nine-to-five job. Are you committed to being the very best Pilot, Submariner, Surface Warrior, Staff Officer, you name it, that you can possibly be? Are you committed to being the best Officer that you can possibly be?

Honor. Courage. Commitment. These are principles worth holding onto. These are values worth putting into action. You must set the example on and off duty. You are a commissioned Officer in the United States Navy and everything you do from this point will reflect directly on all of those in uniform and all of those who have gone before you. We are counting on you to turn the challenges you face in the future into opportunities, to make the best Navy in the world even better in the Twenty-First century. Your service, dedication and sacrifice will help make these goals reality.

After almost three decades of service, I am still excited about putting on my uniform every morning. There is no profession that provides better career satisfaction and a sense of mission. I wish I was joining you today as you begin your great journey. Your duty, your noble calling is vital to the future.

In closing, I would like to direct my comments once again to the family and friends of today's Commissionees. Using the words of Herman Wouk, *Our duty is to reassure our men and women in uniform that their hard, long training is needed. That love of county is noble, that sacrifice is rewarding, and that to be ready to fight for freedom fills one with a sense of worth like nothing else. For if America is still the great beacon against gloom, the*

promise to hundreds of millions that liberty exists, that it is the shining future, that they can throw off their tyrants and learn freedom and cease learning war, then we still need heroes to stand guard in the night.

I look forward to serving with these heroes. I look forward to the new infusion of energy and dedication to our Navy. And most of all I look forward to your leadership. Best of luck to all of you in Class Zero-Four-Zero-Zero. And may God continue to bless our Navy and this great nation. Thank you very much."

"Admiral, thank you very much for your kind words, certainly an inspiration for our soon to be Ensigns. And it is a pleasure for me to present the Schools' Command Flag to you, Sir. John W. Sanders, Guest Speaker, Class Zero-Four-Zero-Zero graduation, nineteen November Nineteen-Ninety-Nine."

"Class Zero-Four-Zero-Zero, please rise for the Oath of Office. Raise your right hand. *I*, say your full name."

"I, Michael Zurich."

"*Having been appointed an Ensign in the United States Navy.*"

"Having been appointed an Ensign in the United States Navy."

"*Do accept such appointment.*"

"Do accept such appointment."

"*And do solemnly swear.*"

"And do solemnly swear."

"*That I will support and defend.*"

"That I will support and defend".

"*The constitution of the United States.*"

"The constitution of the United States."

"*Against all enemies, foreign and domestic.*"

"Against all enemies, foreign and domestic."

"*That I will bear true faith and allegiance to the same.*"

"That I will bear true faith and allegiance to the same."

"*That I take this obligation freely.*"

"That I take this obligation freely."

"*Without any mental reservation or purpose of evasion.*"

"Without any mental reservation or purpose of evasion."

"*And that I will well and faithfully discharge.*"

"And that I will well and faithfully discharge."

"*The duties of the office of which I am about to enter.*"

"The duties of the office of which I am about to enter."

"*So help me God.*"

"So help me God."

"The guests may be seated. Those persons desiring to take photographs may do so at this time."

"Class Zero-Four-Zero-Zero, ready two. The graduating class will now come forward to receive their certificates."

"Margaret Andrews. Ensign Andrews will be assigned to Surface Warfare Officer School, Newport, Rhode Island where she will commence training as a Surface Warfare Officer."

"Brian Armstrong. Ensign Armstrong will be assigned to Naval Air Station, Pensacola, Florida where he will commence training as a Naval Aviator."

"Eric Bremer. Ensign Bremer will be assigned to Navy Nuclear Power School, Charleston, South Carolina, where he will commence training as a Submarine Warfare Officer.

"Jeremy Brooks. Ensign Brooks will be assigned to Navy Nuclear Power School, Charleston, South Carolina, where he will commence training as a Submarine Warfare Officer."

"Shannon Chu. Ensign Chu will be assigned to Surface Warfare Officer School, Newport, Rhode Island where he will commence training as a Surface Warfare Officer."

"Shauna Driver. Ensign Driver with be assigned to Naval Supply School, Athens, Georgia where she will commence training as a Supply Corp Officer."

"LeAnne Driscoll. Ensign Driscoll will be assigned to Navy and Marine Corp Intelligence Training Center, Damneck, Virginia where she will commence training as a Naval Intelligence Officer."

"Christopher Elkind. Ensign Elkind will be assigned to Naval Air Station, Pensacola, Florida where he will commence training as a Naval Aviator."

"Laura Estephan. Ensign Estephan will be assigned to Surface Warfare Officer School, Newport, Rhode Island where she will commence training as a Surface Warfare Officer."

"Vincent Erickson. Ensign Erickson will be assigned to Naval Air Station, Pensacola, Florida where he will commence training as a Naval Aviator."

"Steven Foreman. Ensign Foreman will be assigned to Surface Warfare Officer School, Newport, Rhode Island where he will commence training as a Surface Warfare Officer."

"Francisco Fortunato. Ensign Fortunato will be assigned to Naval Air Station, Pensacola, Florida where he will commence training as a Naval Aviator."

"Christopher Harper. Ensign Harper will be assigned to Navy Nuclear Power School, Charleston, South Carolina, where he will commence training as a Submarine Warfare Officer."

"Laura Harris. Ensign Harris will be assigned to Naval Air Station, Pensacola, Florida where she will commence training as a Naval Aviator."

"Michael Hibbs. Ensign Hibbs will be assigned to Navy and Marine Corp Intelligence Training Center, Damneck, Virginia where he will commence training as a Naval Intelligence Officer."

"Harry Hobson. Ensign Hobson will be assigned to Surface Warfare Officer School, Newport, Rhode Island where he will commence training as a Surface Warfare Officer."

"Brad Johnson. Ensign Johnson will be assigned to Surface Warfare Officer School, Newport, Rhode Island where he will commence training as a Surface Warfare Officer."

"James Kramer. Ensign Kramer will be assigned to Navy and Marine Corp Intelligence Training Center, Damneck, Virginia where he will commence training as a Naval Intelligence Officer."

"William Koch. Ensign Koch will be will be assigned to Naval Air Station, Pensacola, Florida where he will commence training as a Naval Flight Officer."

"Brett Larson. Ensign Larson will be assigned to Naval Air Station, Pensacola, Florida where he will commence training as a Naval Flight Officer."

"Daniel Lin. Ensign Lin will be assigned to Surface Warfare Officer School, Newport, Rhode Island where he will commence training as a Surface Warfare Officer."

"Robert Logan. Ensign Logan will be assigned to Civil Engineer Corp Officer School, Port Hueneme, California when he will commence training as a Civil Engineer Corp Officer."

"Michael Lyman. Ensign Lyman will be assigned to Navy and Marine Corp Intelligence Training Center, Damneck, Virginia where he will commence training as a Naval Intelligence Officer."

"Michael Macpherson. Ensign Macpherson will be assigned to Naval Air Station, Pensacola, Florida where he will commence training as a Naval Aviator."

"Lee Masterson. Ensign Masterson will be assigned to Naval Air Station, Pensacola, Florida where he will commence training as a Naval Aviator."

"Emerson Moore. Ensign Moore will be assigned to Surface Warfare Officer School, Newport, Rhode Island where he will commence training as a Surface Warfare Officer."

"Davis Morris. Ensign Morris will be assigned to Naval Air Station, Pensacola, Florida where he will commence training as a Naval Flight Officer."

"Maria Mura. Ensign Mura will be assigned to Naval Supply School, Athens, Georgia where she will commence training as a Supply Corp Officer."

"Shawn Meister. Ensign Meister will be assigned to Naval Air Station, Pensacola, Florida where he will commence training as a Naval Aviator."

"William Orton. Ensign Orton will be assigned to Surface Warfare Officer School, Newport, Rhode Island where he will commence training as a Surface Warfare Officer."

"Scott Paterson. Ensign Paterson will be assigned to Naval Air Station, Pensacola, Florida where he will commence training as a Naval Aviator."

"Robert Reston. Ensign Reston will be assigned to Surface Warfare Officer School, Newport, Rhode Island where he will commence training as a Surface Warfare Officer."

"David Roberts. Ensign Roberts will be assigned to Naval Air Station, Pensacola, Florida where he will commence training as a Naval Aviator."

"Harold Rooney. Ensign Rooney will be assigned to Civil Engineer Corp Officer School, Port Hueneme, California when he will commence training as a Civil Engineer Corp Officer."

"Paul Rooster. Ensign Rooster will be assigned to Naval Air Station, Pensacola, Florida where he will commence training as a Naval Aviator."

"Kevin Shaffer. Ensign Shaffer will be assigned to Surface Warfare Officer School, Newport, Rhode Island where he will commence training as a Surface Warfare Officer."

"John Siegel. Ensign Siegel will be assigned to Naval Air Station, Pensacola, Florida where he will commence training as a Naval Aviator."

"Willard Smith. Ensign Smith will be assigned to Navy Nuclear Power School, Charleston, South Carolina, where he will commence training as a Submarine Warfare Officer."

"Sarkis Sumarian. Ensign Sumarian will be assigned to Navy and Marine Corp Intelligence Training Center, Damneck, Virginia where he will commence training as a Naval Intelligence Officer."

"Peter Tronstein. Ensign Tronstein will be assigned to Naval Air Station, Pensacola, Florida where he will commence training as a Naval Flight Officer."

"Michael Zurich. Ensign Zurich will be assigned to Navy and Marine Corp Intelligence Training Center, Damneck, Virginia where he will commence training as a Naval Intelligence Officer."

EPILOGUE

"To all who shall see these present greetings. Know ye that, reposing special trust and confidence in the patriotism, valor, fidelity, and abilities of Michael Zurich, I do appoint him an Ensign, special duty (intelligence), in the United States Navy, to rank as such from the 19th day of November, 1999. This Officer will therefore carefully and diligently discharge the duties of the office to which appointed by doing and performing all manner of things thereunto belonging.

And I do strictly charge and require those Officers and other personnel of lesser rank to render such obedience as is due an Officer of this grade and position. And this Officer is to observe and follow such orders and directions, from time to time, as may be given by the President of the United States of America or other superior Officers, acting in accordance with the laws of the United States of America.

This commission is to continue in force during the pleasure of the President of the United States of America, under the provisions of those public laws relating to Officers of the Armed Forces of the United States of America and the component thereof in which this appointment is made.

Done at the City of Washington, this 18th day of October, in the year of our Lord, 1999, and of the Independence of the United States of America, the 223rd. By the President."

Made in the USA
Middletown, DE
14 February 2018